SOUL DREAMS

WOFFORD LEE JONES

This book is dedicated to:

CHAD McGLOTHLIN

A guy who knows a good story when he reads one.
(hopefully this one ranks up there among your top ten)

PROLOGUE: LAST REQUEST

*Be careful of what you wish for; it could very well become
a reality.*

-Helen Roquemore

*Loosing a grip on reality, slipping deeper into the abyss,
where darkness swallows all and you can't resist,
the intense welcome of voids that pull you to a closeness,
of a more bizarre but embraceable madness.*

*Innocence of one's mind scream out for release,
Inner silence turning over time into a diabolical beast,
When escaped from its finite space its power will never cease,
Once unleashed from its bondage on revenge will it feast.*

-Excerpt from *Macabre Dreams* by Wofford Lee Jones

PROLOGUE — EIGHTEEN YEARS AGO

IN A FLEETING glimpse, Edward McDaniel looked Death in the face. Death was smiling at him, not in a bemused way but with contempt of who Edward was. Then Death disappeared behind a dismal curtain of lake water. Edward knew Death wasn't gone for good but was just lurking in the shadowy depths waiting for him to breathe his last breath.

Edward understood he was going to die; that was inevitable, but he continued to fight against the pressure to surrender that was quickly overpowering him. For a split second, he thought about how ironic this day had been. Just minutes before, he had wondered at how perfect the day was and how his life was full of limitless possibilities, but now they were quickly fading away.

What he remembered rolled again through his mind in perfect clarity. He had been sitting on a beach towel by himself and was looking out at the sun-dappled wakes on the shimmering lake. He sat with his elbows perched on his knees as his toes clenched the stubby grass beneath his bare feet. He swiped his reddish-brown hair out of his eyes as a gust of wind blew off the lake. He took a long, deep breath and relished the scent in the warm summer air. As he sat there, his left hand unconsciously stroked a silver-dollar-sized medallion that hung around his neck on a leather strand.

Edward looked up at the sun hovering high above the lake. It levitated in a realm of its own and radiated warmth upon the world below. The rich, deep, blue sky was blended with sporadic white clouds that drifted in on a gentle summer breeze. Birds circled in the air, cried out and chased each other as they dove and soared between altitudes. Some landed on the shore, hopped over the grass and scavenged the picnic areas for bits of dropped food. Jagged mountains towered high above the tall spruce, pine, and oak trees that stretched toward the rays of the bright sun. Boats floated on the lake currents and drifted into the vast horizon.

Edward glanced over to where his classmates were playing a game of volleyball and longed for the day—if it would ever come—when he would be able to associate with them and not be looked upon as the oddball of his senior class. He wanted nothing more than to fit in and to be part of the popular crowd.

One of his many downfalls that denied him that privilege was his physical appearance. In his own opinion, he didn't think he was an ugly boy, but he knew he had features that were different from theirs. His face was adorned with numerous unwanted freckles. His ears stuck out instead of sloping back, which gave him a slight cartoonish look. He had a small pug nose, and his eyes were a plain, dark brown. When he smiled, his crooked teeth peeped out from behind a lopsided grin. He was lean, scanty, and his self-esteem had been worn down over the years from countless jokes and pranks that had been played on him. He was tired and weary of being a loner, an outcast, but Edward always suppressed these feelings deep within himself and never let them show.

Edward was also uncoordinated when he played sports. He rarely volunteered to be a part of any game played in high school, unless it was a mandatory part of his gym class. He chose to sit on the sidelines and observe the others play rather than get involved and make a fool of himself.

Another reason for his classmates' dislike, and probably the worst, was that he had skipped two years of high school. Compared to the other kids, he exceeded all of them in the subjects of their classes. The work had been too easy for him. It was sometimes hard for him to believe, that he was going to be a senior in the coming school year. His life was spent studying and reading books; besides, what else can an individual do when excluded by his peers?

At fifteen years of age, being in the senior class was quite an accomplishment in some cases, but not for him. He didn't care about the recognition and was tired of the compliments between his grandparents and teachers. All this praise put up a wall between him and his classmates. Edward could imagine what was said about him as the students whispered among themselves when he walked by, but he just bowed his head, ignored the ridicule, and kept to himself.

Edward built a world of his own in daydreams, but he could never enjoy the thoughts about an average life of fun, friends, and laughter. Whenever he did make wishes, the words that his grandmother, Helen Roquemore, always said whispered softly to him from the back of his mind, "Be careful, Edward," she warned. "Be careful of what you wish for; it could very well become a reality."

Edward always shot back, "Good. That would really be great. I hope so, because that's what I want. Want it above all else; more than anything. I wish earnestly for that and long for it. You always make it sound like that would be a bad thing. I just want to be normal."

"But Edward, you are normal. Don't you see? Let people see you for who you are."

"I try grandmomma; I really do but it's no use."

"You're special in your own way."

"That's your opinion. There are plenty of kids at school who see me differently than you and granddad do and, well, their opinion is what really matters right now."

Edward would always run out of the house in the middle of conversations like that. It was no use discussing it with them. They didn't understand the situation or him and his feelings, and they never would.

A cry from a crow perched in a nearby pine tree snapped him out of his daydream. The black bird eyed him curiously and angled its head to look at him in a different perspective. The crow bobbed its head, flapped its wings, and disappeared through the foliage.

Beads of sweat dotted his forehead. He put his hands to his sweaty face and wiped away the residue, then shook his head to revive himself even more. He slowly rolled over to his side and pushed himself up onto one knee. It took him close to a minute to move into a standing position.

It was the first day he was forcing himself not to use his crutches. Once he was on his feet, he took a long, relaxing stretch.

The stretch hurt more than it did to relax him, especially around his waist. His pelvis still ached from the accident. The pain made his mind drift again to that memory but only for a few brief seconds. He forced the memory to the back recesses of his mind. He wasn't going to think about it again. He shook his head at how bad the word "accident" summed up that moment in time. He doubted he would ever be physically and mentally the same again.

He brushed off the seat of his shorts and walked—more like limped—toward the pier that extended into the lake. The fallen pine needles and grass tickled his feet as he neared the dock. He slowly and painfully stooped to gathered four stones before continuing the length of the old wharf.

There were seven quays built around this part of the lake, each jutting out from the property into the water. Some piers still had boats attached to them. He carefully walked out on the dock, not wanting to receive a bad case of splinters. The boards were still sturdy but had aged from the combined amount of traffic and weather. He slid his hand along the dry, cracked railing—using it for much needed support—as he watched the classmates of his high school.

When he reached the end of the wharf, he pitched one of the rocks into the air, leaned against the chipped green banister, and watched the rock vanish beneath the surface with a resounding splash.

What are you afraid of? His inner voice asked himself. *It's evident that you want to be over there with them. So go.* Edward answered himself, *I can't go over there. Bruce and Kelly, Travis, Alex and Suzanne are over there. That's what I'm afraid of. After what they did to me. No, I'm not going over there.*

Edward had visited the lake numerous times before the summer season and loved the atmosphere that the lake provided. He shifted his eyes from the volleyball game again and leaned further over the balustrade to view his own reflection on the mirrored surface. He peered deep into the eyes that stared back. The ripples in the water started to hypnotize him. It held his gaze as his own eyes searched his soul. One of the rocks he held slipped from his grasp and hit the surface. It dissolved his reflection. When the undulation calmed down to a flat even plane, he once again stared at his reflection.

He continued to stroke the medallion while he stared at the serene water. It had been worn down over the past years from nervous tension at first and then later by habit.

The medallion had been a gift from his grandfather who had died two years earlier. Edward's grandfather, Jonas Cyrus Roquemore, had been in the military, a number of wars, and had spent most of his earlier life overseas. Jonas had been a collector of rare antiques, relics, and curios from the many mysterious lands he had lived in and visited.

"You know, Edward," his grandfather had said as they sat on the screened in front porch of the house where they lived. "Although I don't remember where this amulet came from, it has very special and mystical powers, or that's what the person said when they sold it to me." Jonas used exaggerated enunciation of his words and dramatic theatrical tones to enhance his speech. "I guess you could say it's my good luck charm. I call it my 'good luck Mojo'. It has protected me through the wars. I believe I have a few more good years left on this planet, but I won't be here much longer, so I want to pass it on to you now. I want you to go ahead and get some of the benefits while I'm still alive. Now I'm bequeathing it to you. I also pass on the peace and the good luck that it brings. Don't ever take it off or the magic and the good luck won't work. Take good care of it, Edward, and it will take good care of you."

When his grandfather placed the amulet around Edward's neck, a peace unlike anything he had ever known coated his body. His body shuddered as if a brief wind had blown under the porch eaves and chilled him. He wondered if it was his imagination, but when he looked out beyond the porch, the limbs of the nearby trees were motionless. Edward sat stunned and mesmerized as he stared at the medallion in his hand. The sunlight lovingly caressed the mother-of-pearl surface—the surface like that of an Abalone shell.

That was all Jonas had said about it. There were no special stories of protection in wars, no bizarre coincidences in his travels. Nothing.

Edward never actually believed his grandfather; he thought Jonas was bullshitting him or trying to spook him as all grandfathers did to their grandsons from time to time. But ever since his grandfather had given it to him, Edward had worn the talisman as a good luck charm and as a memoir with which to remember his grandfather. The odd thing about it was exactly seven days after his grandfather had given him the charm, Jonas had died of a severe heart attack. Edward had often wondered how much longer Jonas might have lived if he hadn't given him the amulet. It was as if his grandfather's good luck had finally run its course.

As he strolled through his memories with his grandfather, a soft voice called out to him.

"Edward?"

He didn't budge, but the interruption slowly brought him out of his reverie.

"Edward!" the voice called out again, slightly louder than before.

Edward felt a hand on his shoulder. It nudged him cautiously.

His body jerked as he snapped out of his trance. "Huh?"

"Oh, I'm sorry. I didn't mean to startle you," she apologized.

"What?" he said, a little annoyed. He was shocked that someone was actually speaking to him. "Oh, no-no, you didn't startle me," he said, immediately feeling stupid that he had just lied to her.

Panic immediately engulfed him, his mouth went dry, and he became instantly nervous from being confronted by her.

It was Adrian Connell—the pretty girl from his Algebra class—who stood in front of him. Her brown shoulder length hair curled around the sides of her prominent cheekbones and curved down above her big, brown eyes that stared intently on Edward. Her thin nose, beautiful white teeth, full, pink lips, and an evenly tanned body that was well on its way to womanhood, all combined to make his hands start to sweat, heart leap, and stomach tighten with nervous tension.

On the boring days, when Edward wasn't paying attention to the teacher—which was most days—he had sat at his desk and dreamed of what it would be like to have a relationship with some of the girls in his class. Adrian was one of the girls that had always been at the top of his list.

"Edward, close your mouth, you're catching flies," she teased.

Edward obeyed. His mouth slapped shut but the dumbfound look remained.

She eyed him curiously. "Not jumpy, huh? Then why did your body go into a conniption when I called your name? You have a guilty conscience or something?"

Edward was surprised to hear himself agree with her. "Ha, yeah," he said. "Guilty conscience, that's me." He shrugged his shoulders and looked down at their reflections in the water, unsure of what else to say. He wished she would change the subject or just leave. He dropped another rock from his hands and watched as their images melded together and then separated.

"What were you thinking about?" she asked.

"M-my grandfather," he stammered as his eyes dropped once more to the water below. "I-It's something I do when I-I'm by myself."

"There's nothing wrong in that. It's good to reminisce about family now and then." She paused and then went on. "Anyway, we were just wondering, I mean, *I* was wondering, if maybe you wanted to come over and join us." She pointed in the direction of her friends. "You've been over here by yourself for quite a while now, and I thought you might like to help start another game. Britney had to leave and we need another player to keep even teams so I thought you might want to be that extra guy."

His inner voice thought, *So in other words, you're just using me, right? It's always the same story. It never fails. If you had even teams you wouldn't have even bothered to ask me. You only need me when it's convenient for you.* He wished he could scream it out at someone, anyone, who would listen. He just needed to let them know how he felt.

Instead he said guiltily, "I, I'm r-really not that good of a player."

How could I have been so stupid to give her an answer like that? Why doesn't talking to girls come natural for me? Why do I get so nervous? Why is she really here? What does she really want of me? Ideas ricocheted off the boundaries in his head. *Is this one of the other kid's tricks? Did they put her up to it to come over here to sucker me in to go with her to be made fun of yet again?* Although he asked himself these questions, he knew he was going to go no matter what kind of dirty trick waited for him. He had to take a chance. He was starved for attention.

Then Edward remembered and added out loud, "Besides, I'm literally in no condition to play. You know, since the accident I am a lot slower than I use to be."

"Oh, right," she said, smacking her forehead. "I am so sorry. I totally forgot. I really feel like a dumbass for asking now."

"No, please, don't worry about it. I am getting faster though. A little bit more each day. Maybe next year I'll be fast enough to play with you guys."

The look of embarrassment on Adrian's face became worse.

"Adrian," Edward said. "You can laugh at that. That was my weak attempt at humor."

"Oh," Adrian said and began to smile. "Well, you could at least watch us play. You could at least laugh at us while we attempt to play."

"I don't know…" Edward said looking in the direction of where the others stood.

"They're not going to mind. C'mon."

Yeah, but you don't know what I know, Edward thought. *You don't know what they did to me. Or maybe you do.* Even though he thought that, he gave in and reluctantly agreed to watch. *OK, whatever happens to you, you take it like a man. Show these people that you can have a good time, no matter what. If this is a set up, take it, then walk away and deal with your emotions later. Don't let them know you're hurt, it would just please them all the more. You can do this. Take a gamble for once in your life and for God's sake, talk to this girl.*

As they slowly walked side by side down the pier, Edward heard the familiar sound of Adrian's ex-boyfriend's '75 Chevy. The truck rumbled over the gravel in the parking area and kicked up plumes of dust clouds that engulfed it as it skidded to a stop.

Edward noticed a change in Adrian's whole demeanor. Upon seeing and hearing Jeremy's truck, she instantly went rigid with fear.

"Son of a bitch. What the fuck is he doing here?" Adrian said, more to herself than to Edward.

Edward looked up to see a tall, dark haired figure emerge from the pickup. It was Jeremy Taylor. He was dressed in work boots, jeans, and an unbuttoned long sleeve shirt that was rolled up to his elbows. It seemed like the most inappropriate attire for a hot day like today.

Great! Edward thought. *The one day I get to associate with one of the most beautiful and popular girls in school, fate or luck would have it for Jeremy to show up. Good morning, Edward. May the sun shine upon you today. Oh, and by the way, may it shit upon you as well.*

"What's Jeremy doing here? I was under the impression you two broke up. Didn't know you were back together again." Edward couldn't believe he had just blurted the information out.

"We *did* break up. We're *not* back together," she said defiantly. "How did you know that?"

"You think I live here around the lake, roaming about, standing on the piers and reminiscing about my grandfather all day? I have a personal life too, you know. I know all the juicy gossip on all the students at school."

She laughed, sounding slightly amused, but then diverted her attention back to the fact that Jeremy was here. Panic tainting her voice and through gritted teeth Adrian said, "I've told him a dozen times it's over between us, but he won't listen."

Adrian looked angry. She looked as though she wanted to kill Jeremy.

"It's none of my business," Edward said, taking a chance on comforting her. "But why don't you leave him? I mean, why do you let him dominate you?"

"I've tried, but he won't take the hint."

"Well, I've seen the way he treats you at school and I don't like it, but *look* at me," he gave a little laugh, "What can I do about it? You know if you don't stand up to him sometime, he'll keep coming back and lord over you until you're his forever."

Jeremy stood at the edge of the parking area, leaning on the hood of the pickup smoking a cigarette, drinking from a bottle, and viewing the people that had gathered at the lake, obviously looking for Adrian.

Jeremy's gaze swiveled from the volleyball game to the pier. When he spied Adrian, he started to walk toward the pier.

Ok, the S-H-I-T just hit the F-A-N.

The closer Jeremy approached, the further away Edward wished he could be. He knew about Jeremy's problems of jealousy. Jeremy became insane to the tenth power when he saw other boys even talk to Adrian.

I hope Jeremy doesn't get mad at me and become crazy, just because I'm talking to her. Why should he? There's nothing I can even remotely do to attract her to me. It's just my luck that Adrian is a beautiful girl with a maniac boyfriend.

He knew he couldn't stand up to Jeremy, because Jeremy was taller and stronger than he was. He also knew he couldn't turn away from Adrian, lean against the pier, and pretend he hadn't been talking to her. It would disappoint her if he did. It would also look like an admission of guilt to Jeremy. He simply had to accept the consequences that were obviously coming his way.

Jeremy stood six feet tall and weighed around two hundred thirty pounds. His boots thumped hollowly as he walked down the pier. He took one last drag on his cigarette and flipped it over the pier.

"Adrian, what in the hell do you think you're doing?" he asked with an exhalation of smoke.

"Nothing that would be any of your business," she countered and started to stand her ground. "You smell like stale beer and I so *hate* beer. Go sober up; we'll talk later."

"Wrong answer," he said, and slapped her without any warning.

Damn, this guy doesn't waste any time. Edward thought.

Edward's heart went out to Adrian, and in that moment, he wanted nothing more than to kill Jeremy.

Adrian paused, looking away at the pier railing. Finally, she turned back to face Jeremy; her face was cold and her eyes were filled with hate.

Edward could tell it was a hard slap; her cheek began to turn pink and a single tear ran down her face from the corner of her eye. Edward didn't know if it was the first time Jeremy had slapped Adrian, but he doubted it was.

"Now listen to me," Jeremy continued, grabbing her arm to emphasize his statement. "I'm not going to take that bit about 'we'll talk later.' You've already put me off long enough; besides, you were supposed to meet me down at Rudy's last night at ten. You chose to bail on me then so we're going to take a little drive and talk about it right now."

Edward hobbled forward and stepped between Adrian and Jeremy. "Come on, Jeremy. Take it easy. Can't you see she doesn't want to have anything to do with you?" He was shocked to hear himself speak, but his voice and emotions had taken over. He had to try and stand up to Jeremy; he couldn't allow him to push Adrian around.

"Correct me if I'm in the wrong here, shithead, but I don't think I was talking to you. Was I?" He let go of Adrian's arm and focused in on Edward. He took a long drink from the bottle he was holding and pitched it over the handrail not caring that he had just littered.

Edward started to step back as Jeremy closed in. He wondered how he was going to get out of this predicament. Everything was happening too fast, and he didn't know what to do. He felt like a caged lab animal. His eyes darted back and forth and looked for a place to escape, but there was none.

"Wait, come on. Let's talk about this," Edward pleaded.

"Oh, so now *you* want to talk?" Jeremy asked as he placed a hand on Edward's chest and pushed him backwards.

Edward lost his balance and fell on his butt. His pelvis exploded in pain from his awkward landing. The rough boards scratched his elbows and hands as he tried to catch his balance. He lay sprawled on the pier writhing to get up.

Jeremy towered over Edward and said, "I didn't come here to waste my time talking to a little shitsplat like you. This is none of your concern."

Jeremy turned his attention back toward Adrian, forgetting about Edward. "Why did you stand me up? Why didn't you meet me—?"

"I never agreed to meet you there," she said cutting him off in mid sentence. "That's all in your head!"

On the shore, heads started to turn; some of Adrian's friends noticed the commotion and began to run toward the pier.

Edward began to get up. His legs still didn't work properly from his accident, and his pelvis had started to hurt again. He was still dazed and wondered what he should do.

"Get this in your head once and for all, Jeremy. I'm not yours. I never really was. But after you did what you did to me, there is no ounce of forgiveness in me to give you. I could kill you right now and feel totally justified." Adrian held up her hands to calm herself and change the subject. She continued and simply said, "You're not going to own me anymore so just leave." Adrian put her hands on his chest and tried to push him backward.

"What the hell are you talking about?"

"You know the reason." Adrian paused and looked directly in Jeremy's eyes. "You don't remember, do you?"

"Are we actually talking about this again? I apologized about that. I said I was sorry. What more do you want me to do or say?"

"You can't just apologize for that, Jeremy. There is not, nor will there ever be, any forgiveness from me. Do you understand?" Adrian didn't wait for a reply or acknowledgement. "Look, I'm not going to talk about it anymore." She abruptly turned to leave.

Jeremy countered her movement and grabbed her arm. "If I leave, you leave, which is what we are going to do right now, understand? Now get your shit and let's go," he said, trying to escort her to the truck.

"Jeremy!" Edward yelled. "Can't you see she doesn't want to go with you? Why don't you just leave her alone?" He didn't think it was the best idea to confront Jeremy, but when he noticed the look of appreciation in Adrian's eyes and the weak smile that formed around her lips, he felt he was doing the right thing.

"I don't think you got the point did you, buddy boy?" he asked as he reeled around and backtracked toward Edward. "I guess I'll just have to explain it in a way you can understand."

Jeremy's fist caught him right below the sternum, which caused his feet to slip out from under him, and he dropped to the dock with all his weight on his elbows and knees. Pain shot through his arms, legs, and pelvis from his awkward landing. He doubled over, trying to retrieve the air that had been knocked out of him. Edward got up awkwardly and slowly hobbled backward toward the end of the pier, clutching his chest and gasping for air. His midsection was on fire. He didn't know how much more of this he could take.

Adrian ran toward Jeremy, hit him in the back, and yelled at him to stop punching Edward. Jeremy turned around, grabbed her by the side of the face and shoved her against the railing. Adrian collapsed on the deck.

Jeremy advanced on Edward again; his knuckles connected with Edward's jaw and split his lip. A fire storm of pain engulfed Edward's head. Another fist landed in his stomach. Edward felt like he was going to throw up but fought to keep his composure. He didn't want to be known as the little wimp who threw up all over the lakeside pier.

Jeremy knelt down beside Edward and listened to him gasp for air. He softly said with stale cigarette breath, "Did you learn anything in our class today, Little Romeo, because if you didn't, we can continue this session we have going here. I think today's lesson should be called," he paused to think how he wanted to say it, and then shouted, "DON'T FUCKING MESS WITH MY GIRLFRIEND EVER AGAIN!" He dropped back to a soft whisper, "You got that, you little shit?" Jeremy then slapped him in the side of the head for emphasis.

Edward's ears rang. He refused to say anything, scared whatever he said would be a wrong answer and he would be humiliated in front of Adrian even more.

To prove his point further, Jeremy held Edward close and whispered in his ear, "I notice that you're walking again. That's good, that's really good, but if you continue on the path you're on, it's going to end up in a far worse beat down. Now, I don't mean just any beat down, I'm talking about one that you'll never get up from again or walk away from after it's over. Do we fucking understand each other?"

Edward didn't even register the last question Jeremy had asked, but he slowly turned his head toward Jeremy. Their eyes locked on each other. He was already seething with hatred from the threat. Jeremy was talking about the accident, the accident that had almost crippled him for life. The hatred for Jeremy and his friends came back in an unbridled fury.

"One day, I am going to fucking kill you in the worst possible way. I promise you that."

Edward thought the threat-promise had come from Jeremy's mouth. He hadn't realized he himself had said anything until it was actually out of his mouth. It was as though his anger possessed him and he was speaking without realizing it.

Without any conscious thought, his body did the only thing he would never do when threatened. He lashed out; or rather his subconscious lashed out. Edward's hand had already turned into a fist by the time Jeremy had asked his last question.

The sucker punch came without warning and on the tail end of his threat to Jeremy. Edward's body was blocking the swing from Jeremy's perspective and Edward's fist came up and over and into the middle of Jeremy's face. There was a crunch underneath Edward's fist. It was a good satisfying crunch of shifting bones. For Edward, the punch was liberating. Months of pent up aggression was released in that instance. But it wasn't enough; he wanted more, needed more.

"You son of a bitch! You broke my fucking nose!"

Jeremy's exclamation brought Edward back to reality. He was still stunned that he had delivered the punch that he barely had time to register the fury of jackhammer blows that rained down on him from every direction. Everything became a painful blur. All Edward knew to do was to roll into a ball for protection.

That's when the kicks came. Brutal blows to his ribs and back. He prayed that a boot to his pelvic region wouldn't stray below his belt line. A boot to his lower waist would've surely crippled him for life.

But as soon as the attack had started; it stopped. Edward slowly looked up through his locked arms and fingers that were protecting his face and head and saw Travis Sheridan and two other boys pulling Jeremy back and away from him. He began to stand again.

"That's enough, Jeremy," Travis was saying. "Jesus Christ, what the hell are you doing?"

"Schooling that little punk ass bitch kid. Did you see what he did to me?"

"Yeah, it's called fighting back. It's the same thing I would've done if you'd started anything with me. You're out of control, dude. Back the fuck off. We've treated him like shit long enough."

"Yeah, okay, sure, you're right. I'll back the fuck off." He jerked his arms free of the three boys and charged Edward again. "I'll back off as soon as I finish what I started."

Edward's body almost locked down. He began to do a pitiful hobble back step, but the limp he'd received from the accident wouldn't allow his legs to move fast enough. Jeremy was on him in a heartbeat, delivering more heavy blows.

As they neared the end of the pier, Jeremy surprised Edward by switching from punches to a front forward mule kick to the center of his chest. The kick was sudden, abrupt, and powerful. It sent him pinwheeling backward, his arms flailing for balance. The banister cracked as his lower back connected with it. The dry wood gave way under the momentum of his body. Edward was through the railing and falling head over heels as he sailed through the air, landing headfirst in Silver Ridge Lake. He was still gasping for air when he hit the water, which caused him to suck fluid into his nose and mouth. He quickly surfaced, grabbed the side of the pier, dragged himself up the side, rolled over, and coughed up stale water.

By this time, Jeremy had diverted his attention back to Adrian but Travis was continuing to play referee.

"What the fuck is your problem!" Travis yelled, as he broke Jeremy's grip on Adrian and stepped between them. "Lay off of her, Jeremy. I don't know why she would even want to talk to *him*," an accusatory glance was shot in Edward's direction. "But what Adrian does on her time is her business. You're my friend, but I don't think now is the right time. Go sober up or something."

They stood there, eyes locked on one another, both standing their ground.

"What? Do I have to spell it out for you, Jeremy?" Travis repeated. "TAKE OFF!"

Jeremy finally broke eye contact with Travis and shifted his attention to Adrian. "We'll talk, Adrian! This isn't over! Believe me, we'll talk again! That goes for you too, you little shit!" Jeremy stumbled through the group of people, pushing them out of the way as he went.

Jeremy stepped into his truck and slammed the door. He turned the ignition; the wheels spun, caught the dirt, and shot out of the gravel parking area at a reckless speed.

When Edward stood and looked up, he saw he had an audience. The main ones were Travis Sheridan, Kelly Morgan, Jessica Anderson, Alex

Riley, Bruce Saliers, and Suzanne Baldwin. They all stared at him with looks of disdain.

If only I had my backpack, Edward thought. *I would take care of all of you right now.*

Then he saw Adrian and the look on her face. The only one that held compassion for him. That's when he knew he wasn't going to do anything to anybody.

He knew he must have looked like a half-drowned rat with his matted hair, soaked tank top and shorts. He could tell by the looks that they gave him and their whispered comments that he had fucked up again. Clutching his chest and stomach, he awkwardly stood, and mumbled a pitiful apology as he limped and pushed his way through the crowd. Adrian tried to stop him, but he jerked his arm away as he passed. He was too embarrassed and ashamed to even look at her. He'd just had his ass gift wrapped and handed to him on a silver platter in front of everybody.

Edward walked back to where he had been before the incident had taken place. He sat down as carefully as he could and watched as the people left from the area. Edward noticed that Adrian had started to walk his way but was stopped by Kelly and Suzanne, who had probably talked her out of it. Adrian looked his way and smiled but then began to walk toward the volleyball sandlot with the others.

He watched them closely as they drifted further away. The rage was coming back. Without taking his eyes off them, he blindly reached and found his backpack that was leaning against an Aspen. He grabbed and placed it in front of him and unzipped the top. He reached inside where his hand found the butt of his grandfather's pistol that he had been carrying around for weeks. It felt natural in his hand. He had held it on many occasions, although this is the first time where he withdrew it from his backpack. Most of the time, he just needed the comfort in knowing how close it was to solving all his problems or ending them completely.

How many times had he sat in class with his hand inside his backpack imagining what it would be like to shoot that one shithead-of-a-classmate in the back of the head? *Unmasking them, so to speak,* Edward thought. *Because we all know it's not the entry wound that causes all the mess; it's the exit wound.* Sometimes he walked down the school hallway pretending he was trying to find an item deep within his backpack only to really be holding tightly to the handle of the pistol imagining what the person would do if he jerked the gun out of his backpack, shove the barrel into the person's mouth, and pull the trigger. Not giving them time to react since they never gave him time to react.

Eye for an eye, my grandmother always said, he thought. *There's just nothing like a little Picasso painting to brighten the school hallways. Talk about your splatter effect to liven up a mural.*

Only when he withdrew it from his bag did his eyes leave the classmates he loathed. He admired the smooth, grey metal and ran his free hand over its polished contours. How easy would it be to walk down to the volleyball court and take them unaware; to just go ballistic and pop them off in quick succession? He had plenty of bullets with him. He could easily reload and pop some more into them just for good measure. That would really show them. Maybe if Jeremy were still here; maybe he would open up his fury on him as well as the others.

But no, Adrian was here. He couldn't do something as maniacal as that in front of her.

He sat there again with his arms on his knees and the gun leaning against his forehead. He slowly let the gun rotate until the end of the barrel was the only thing resting against the center of his forehead. He lowered it further until it dropped off the end of his nose and found his lips. He opened his mouth and let the barrel slide in. His finger looped inside the trigger guard and tightened. He began to cry.

Just end it all. Right here, right now. Don't hesitate. Just drop myself like a bad habit. That would change their way of thinking. If I off myself they would feel differently about me then.

The cry from a crow pierced the silence. His body tensed and he thought it was all over. He jerked the gun from his mouth and guiltily shoved it back inside his backpack. He looked over to where the crow stood and shook his head. "That damn bird again," Edward muttered. He picked up his shoe and pitched it in the direction of the crow. The bird snatched something in the grass and flew away just as the shoe bounced into the area where it was standing.

Edward's heart was pounding like a running jack rabbit. "Whoa. I thought for sure I had already shot myself. That was fucking scary."

He lay back on the grass breathing deeply and stared into the treetops. The leaves and limbs were turning in a counterclockwise direction that dizzied him. He closed his eyes and swallowed hard to stop the nauseous feeling that welled up inside him. Eventually the spinning stopped.

A voice called out to him, and he felt a hand on his chest that shook him softly.

When he opened his eyes and looked up, a flash of blinding light painted dots in front of his eyes.

"Gotcha," Adrian said laughing, as she lowered the camera. "Now that's a Kodak moment, if I've ever seen one; definitely a picture worth keeping."

"Damn it," Edward muttered. "Thanks. Yeah, you got me. You got me good." He winced at the pain as he sat upright. Through clinched teeth he asked, "Ah, um, why-why one of me?"

"Are you kidding me? You were awesome back there. Son of a bitch thinks he's untouchable. Well, you showed him."

"And he showed me real quick that if you stick your nose into somebody else's business, it gets cut off."

"But don't you see? You stood up to him. You at least made him think that he can be stood up to. That was amazing."

Edward wanted to interject and bring up the fact that *she* needed to continue standing up to him, but he stayed silent. Adrian continued. "You helped me out there today. You gave me confidence and I appreciate that. That's why I took your picture. I had to get a pic of my hero."

Edward noticed the sun had moved to a different area of the sky. It wasn't late, but his clothes were now dry. He'd fallen asleep and hadn't realized it.

"Hero, huh? How long have I been asleep?"

"I don't know; beats me. How long have you been over here?"

"Since I got the shit kicked out of me."

"Then that would be about three hours." Her eyebrows furrowed with concern. She touched his arm. "Sorry about that. I wish it could have been different."

He blinked and looked over into Adrian's brown eyes. "It's okay. Anything for you. I'd die for you."

"Aww, Edward. That the sweetest thing anyone has ever said to me." She leaned over and pressed her lips to his cheek. She held it there for a long moment then pulled away. "You want to go swimming with me? I came over here after everyone else went home. I thought we could take the boat out. Want to come along?"

Edward hesitated; he was still trying to figure out how to react from Adrian's kiss.

"Oh come on. Come with me," she teased.

Edward still hesitated.

"I'll make a deal with you. I have a secret that no one else knows about, but I'll tell you if you go with me, but you have to promise not to tell anyone else."

Edward was still not convinced. "Is Jeremy coming back?" he asked sarcastically. "Because if he is, I'll hope you'll understand why I will have to decline. I'm not in the mood for getting my teeth kicked in." He rubbed his jaw. "If he isn't coming back, then sure, I'll go, but I'm not going to swim. It may sound stupid, but I don't know how." Then he added, "And not to keep using this as an excuse but, you know, my condition. I can't use my legs as well as I would like right now. You know…since the accident."

The embarrassed look crossed her face again. She nodded, "Sure. Of course. I understand."

He zipped up his book bag and leaned it back against the Aspen again. Then they began to walk toward the dock again. He was hesitant about leaving his backpack behind. *What if someone came across it while he was gone?* Better to take the chance of that than for Adrian to open it in the boat. He really didn't want to explain its contents to her. He just hoped no one found it while they were gone. He would retrieve it when they came back.

"I don't want to take a chance on my camera falling out of the boat and getting ruined. "Can I leave my stuff here with yours? You mind?"

Edward hesitated again, thinking only of the gun in his backpack; then finally nodded his head.

"One question I would like to ask," Edward said as he retrieved his shoe he'd thrown at the crow.

"Sure, anything."

"Why would you want me to go with you? I failed you today and embarrassed myself in front of everybody, as I always do."

She asked without hesitation, "Does there have to be a reason? I don't know. You're different than other boys around here."

"Different. Yeah, that's something I've never heard before."

"Stop beating yourself up; you're a great guy."

"I wish more people felt that way. But thanks." He paused then added, "So, what's this secret?"

"Oh no, I'm not telling you yet. We're not even in the water. Just be patient."

When they reached the end of the pier, they worked together to untie the ropes that held the boat in its place and pushed off of the dock. They were quiet for a long time as he rowed. Everything was peaceful and serene. No noise emanated from the lake, except for the rhythmic sound of the paddles, the occasional cry from a bird as it flew by, or the splash from a fish that flipped out of the water to snatch an insect that hovered above its surface.

When they reached deeper waters, Adrian stood up and stripped off her tee shirt and shorts, which left her two-piece bathing suit and golden tanned body for Edward to admire. He looked up at her and then away quickly as his face turned a slight pink from embarrassment.

She stood with her hands on her hips. "Last chance; you coming in or not?"

"I'm still debating, but we're in the water now. I just might come in if you tell me your secret."

Her hands self-consciously slid from her hips to the slope of her belly between her naval and her bikini bottoms. She looked down at her hands as they caressed her lower stomach.

Edward cocked his head. It seemed to him that she was trying to convey something to him but was hesitant to say anything at that particular moment.

She seemed troubled. Her eyebrows furrowed. Her face was

unreadable, but there was a lot going on behind Adrian's eyes. Then her eyes welled with tears then fell down her face. She quickly looked away for a moment as she wiped absently at her face. When she looked back, a broad smile had illuminated her face once more. She took one last look at Edward then, still smiling, dove over the side of the boat.

Edward was bewildered; he didn't know what to think. There was so much emotion going on in that moment.

When she resurfaced, she said, "Come on, Edward. The water feels great."

"No, no. You go ahead. I-I'm going to stay here in the boat. I'm n-not a swimmer."

"OK, I guess I'll just have to enjoy this all of this by myself," she said mockingly.

Edward smiled as she dove under the water again. Her feet appeared out of the surface for a moment before projecting herself into the deep abyss.

As she dove under the water, the sound of an outboard motor became eminent. Edward looked around to see which way the sound was coming from. From around an outcropping that jutted into the lake, a utility boat propelled itself toward the small rowboat Edward was in. It was coming at a fast speed, but there was plenty of room for the boat to go around. Edward didn't sense any danger, so he ignored it and turned his attention back to the area Adrian had disappeared and waited for her to surface.

An irregular force suddenly jerked the boat. Startled, Edward grabbed the crossbars to steady his himself.

From behind, he heard laughing. When he turned, he saw Adrian hanging on the side of the boat. She had swum underneath, come up behind him and had given the boat a sudden jolt to spook him.

"Cut it out, Adrian," Edward commanded, still trying to steady the boat.

"Oh come on, Edward. I'm just having a little fun. Lighten up."

She ducked underneath the water again before he could say anything.

"Yeah. Lighten up," he muttered to himself. He glanced back at the other boat and realized it was much closer than he expected and now realized it was intentionally headed for his boat.

Adrian's head broke the surface of the water right in the path of the oncoming boat. She had swum back under the boat and was unaware of the approaching danger.

"Get down, Adrian! The boat, behind you! Get out of the way!" he screamed. He pointed franticly with one hand for her to look behind her, as he grabbed under the seats to brace himself for the impact with the other. Edward saw that Jeremy was the one who operated the other boat and his heart sunk with fear as the boat closed in.

Adrian turned and saw the boat practically on top of her. Instinct took over her body, and she used her arms and legs at the same time to quickly submerge herself underwater again.

Jeremy heard Edward's shouts and then realized that Adrian was between the two boats. When he saw Adrian, he immediately tried to maneuver the boat to miss her but not enough for the boats not to have a rigid impact.

Frozen in horror, Edward stared wide eyed as he saw the hull of the oncoming boat strike Adrian's head as she went below the surface.

Edward's attention was diverted back to reality when the boats collided and tilted up. The angle was too severe to retain his grip on the boat; he lost his balance and fell backward, causing the boat to capsize over top of him. As he had searched for a better placement to give him balance, his foot unknowingly became entangled in the rope that was attached to the boat's anchor.

As soon as he was under water, he fought to get back to the lake's surface. Right before he broke its surface he felt something attached to his ankle. When he realized what had happened, he flailed his arms wildly and tried frantically to unravel the strands from around his foot, but it was to no avail. The anchor descended, slowly pulling him with it into the depths of the lake. He looked up and saw the boats slowly become smaller and smaller until tendrils of the dismal waters gradually closed out the light. Darkness, along with the chill of the deeper waters, quickly closed around him like the loving arms of a mother protecting her child.

Edward snapped back to reality. Yes, he knew he was going to die, and with that realization, fear crept over him in a paralyzing embrace. There was no way out now. His mind was starting to get hazy. His lungs ached for air. He held on until he could no longer suppress his breath. His natural breathing response took over, and water filled his nose, mouth, and lungs in a watery possession. The water burned his nose and throat. His hands went to his throat as he choked on the putrid lake water. He was too weak to reach his neck, but his hands found the medallion instead. His fingers closed around it.

Edward remembered the iridescent glimmer that always flickered off of the medallion's surface when the light hit it at a certain angle. The same way the light cascaded off an Abalone seashell lined with mother-of-pearl. He remembered the relaxing feeling he felt the day his grandfather had given it to him; the feeling of peace like he had now as he began to rub it.

His thoughts rewound to happy memories of times with his grandfather and grandmother. They were the only ones that had cared about him in his sorry life.

Though his body was weak, his hand gripped the medallion slightly tighter.

Soothing colors reflected through his mind's eye.

He thought about practical jokes that had been made at his expense.

His grasp tightened.

The rainbow-like colors glittered across his mind again.

He remembered the students that made fun of him for no reason at all. The memory fueled that hate from those thoughts until it overwhelmed him.

His grasp tightened even more.

Again, the iridescent mother-of pearl glimmer flickered in his mind.

The peace that he felt the day his grandfather gave him the Mojo. He heard his grandfather's voice say once again from the deep recesses of his mind, *"Be good to it, and it will be good to you."*

This is just a bad dream. Edward thought, and he willed himself to wake up, but his nightmare continued.

All I ask is to have one more chance. I don't want to die. I have too much to live for. Edward screamed inside his mind. *I wish I had just one more chance to live.*

All at once, he felt a strong force pull against his body, as if two huge hands dug deep inside his flesh and tore him into two separate entities. His mind shifted along with his core. It wasn't painful, but was strangely uncanny. Even though it was dark, through the new eyes of his soul, he saw his soul detach itself from his body. He was now floating outside his torso, looking back at his hollow frame.

Edward McDaniel was now dead.

His mind, essence and being felt complete, like a duplicate of himself had been made. In another strange sense, he could still feel what his body was like. Like a shell an insect has crawled out of and disregarded—utterly void of life.

The force on Edward's soul was still growing, and he now saw where that energy originated. The object that had hung around his neck for the past two years and that was still in the tight fist embrace of his carcass. Through some greater discernment and insight, Edward's soul realized that this wasn't normal in the after-life. He now knew it was evil, and he fought against its magnetizing power. Incapable of escape, it pulled Edward's spirit down through his knotted fingers inside the center of the amulet.

By the time the anchor reached the muddy bottom, Edward McDaniel's body was still. It wanted to emerge naturally from the liquid limbo and the ropes that held him submerged underwater. Though his body was relaxed, his left hand was paralyzed in a death grip and in that handclasp, deep within the confines of the Mojo; Edward McDaniel's soul screamed a silent scream.

PART ONE: THE SOURCE OF FEAR

The light of the body is the eye:
if therefore thine eye be single,
thy whole body shall be full of light.

But if thine eye be evil,
thy whole body shall be full of darkness.
If therefore the light that is in thee be darkness,
how great is that darkness!

St. Matthew 6:22-23

CHAPTER 1 — PRESENT DAY

TYLER CURTIS WAS afraid as he ran through the woods, trying to escape the creature that was pursuing him. The ground was damp and frosty. His feet were numb from the cold and bleeding from sharp rocks that protruded from the ground. His muscles ached and his legs were scratched from the briars and bramble in his rush to find refuge. The timberland smelled of mildew and discarded rotting matter. Even though it was dismal, the shadows weren't dark enough to conceal him. Bits of fog drifted in on the wind, appearing like small wraiths, as if they were ushering in something immense and evil. As the thing approached, Tyler could hear its heavy breathing and was compelled to find a better hiding place.

He crossed a creek and scrambled up a sloped grade. At the top of the rocky incline, it leveled off for a few yards and then angled up to a higher elevation, but here it was much steeper. Even though his body ached and his lungs burned from the frigid air, Tyler forced himself to ascend the precipice. Footfalls echoed hollowly throughout the undergrowth as the thing's stride quickened.

At the top of the grade, he dropped and slithered beneath a fallen log and pressed himself as far back into the darkness as possible. All at once, the footfalls, the grunting, and the sounds of all the forest creatures stopped. Tyler quietly peered out of the entrance way trying to find a hint of where the beast was. Time seemed to pass too slowly. Tyler held his breath and closed his eyes, praying that he would escape the beast that was tracking him.

Suddenly, the earth around Tyler reverberated as if a great weight had dropped upon it or as if something beneath it was trying to emerge. Tyler's eyes opened in shock, and he saw part of the creature's leg from his hiding place. Its mutated mixture of scales and fur was splattered with mud. That was all Tyler needed to conjure up images of the immense and grotesque creature.

The fallen timber he was hiding beneath was suddenly ripped from the ground. Clots and grains of dirt dropped and sifted down upon him. The beast raised the tree like a club over its head, arched its back and let out a guttural howl of victory that echoed throughout the forest valley.

Tyler rolled out of the way as the tree arched down and obliterated the spot where he had been. He stood and ran across the clearing, looking back every few steps to see how much distance he was putting between himself and the creature. As he ran through a thicket, he looked forward again just as the ground gave way beneath his feet—not so much gave way as disappeared from under him altogether.

He looked down as he started to fall. He was headed directly toward churning water and canyon rocks below. He then realized that running in fear from the beast, he had been careless and had ran headlong off the side of a cliff. The wind whistled by his ears as he descended toward the tumult below.

He turned in time to see the beast reach the edge of the cliff. It let out a cry of abject frustration, angry that it had lost the hunt. Then as the howl subsided, the beast started to fade away. Its fur began to turn into a gray-yellow smoke. Its body vaporized and disappeared into the muggy air; blown away by a sudden gust of wind.

Tyler concluded the creature was only his imagination, but he knew this fall wasn't. He turned his attention back in the direction he was falling. The ground below came toward him at break neck speed. The rocks looked as if they were open hands beckoning him to them and rushed up with tremendous speed to welcome him. As his body disintegrated on the jagged rocks below—

Tyler Curtis awoke from his nightmare with a convulsion and a scream that stuck in his throat. He involuntarily sat up and slammed his head between the back of the couch and the wall it was leaning against

"Ohh, what the hell?" he said.

His arms were outstretched—as far as they could go in the cramped space—in self defense toward the imaginary boulders that would have surely destroyed him had this been a real-life situation. His heart was thumping rapidly. Breathing heavily as confusion painted his forehead, he lay back down. A sense of claustrophobia and disorientation overcame him as a fine dew of perspiration collected on his forehead. The reason for his bewilderment was because he awoke in the oddest place and because it was his first night sleeping in a new house.

As he crawled out of the tight space that was confining him, Tyler found himself face to face with Raven, the family's black Labrador. Raven was sitting on her haunches with her ears pricked and head turned on edge, obviously confused at why her master was being birthed out from behind a couch.

"I know, I know. Don't ask. I look silly, don't I?"

Raven simply whined and licked her master's face then padded off leaving the ridiculousness of the whole situation for Tyler to figure out.

When Tyler finally stood, he found he had emerged from behind the couch in their new game room upstairs.

Thinking Raven was still there, Tyler said, "Huh, I guess I was going through the motions of my dream for real. When I crawled up that slope in my dream, I guess I superimposed the slope onto the stairs. When I crawled under that log in my dream, I guess I figured the couch was the old fallen tree. Jeez, that's fucking weird, isn't it girl? Raven?" Noticing Raven wasn't there, he looked back at the couch and scratched his head. "That was so damn weird. Talk about living out your nightmares."

He walked back downstairs to his room and slid back into his wrinkled comforter as he dwelt on the nightmare that clung to the edges of his mind. Soon after his head hit the pillow, he was asleep again.

Tyler jumped when the alarm clock on his night stand started buzzing. He punched the snooze button on top without hesitating but then concluded he was just taking his frustration of being startled out on his clock. For a brief moment, his dream had come back to haunt him and he actually thought he had exploded again on those welcoming rocks from his earlier dream.

"Shit. I'll never get used to my dreams."

Taking a couple of deep breaths, Tyler leaned back in the comfort of his mattress forgetting about the dream and thinking about the new life he was about to begin in a new school and new town.

Every two or three years, Tyler and his parents had to pack up and move to a new place, because his dad's work required him to relocate. Tyler had been programmed to accept these moves since childhood. Each new area brought new experiences and different challenges for him, and he welcomed these ventures without malice.

After a cool shower, he dressed in jeans, a T-shirt of one of his favorite bands: FUEL underneath a long-sleeved blue shirt, and new tennis shoes.

Tyler was athletic. His tanned, muscular physic came from the many hours he spent outdoors and his workouts in the gym. Working out wasn't his favorite pastime; he mainly did it because the sports he played demanded it. Personally, he would rather do anything than lift weights. He had won many trophies because of his ability to lead his teams to the championships. Tyler had been captain of the track, wrestling, basketball, and football teams at different times in various schools.

Connecting to people was easy for him no matter where he went, but as far as being a class president or holding any of the other class offices, he had no interest in it at all.

Tyler brushed his thick, black hair into place and double checked his appearance in the mirror then headed downstairs for breakfast.

He heard the familiar clicking of toenails on the hardwood floor as Raven greeted him at the bottom of the stairs.

"How ya doing, girl?" Tyler asked, kneeling down to scratch her behind the ears. "Did I scare you this morning?"

Raven sneezed in reply.

"No? Well, I scared the living shit out of myself. You should've been there on the mountain with me. You could've taken that thing. No creature is a match for you. You aren't tired from the move? Huh? Shit, if I were you I'd still be snoozing, but unfortunately, I have school today."

Raven whined softly at each comment as if she understood and tried to answer. She placed her paw on Tyler's knee and then licked him in the mouth as a gesture of affection.

Tyler pulled away spluttering, "Ahh, you got me. No french kisses. I love you girl, but I have no interest in making out with you. C'mon, let's get some breakfast."

Raven's toenails clicked softly as she delicately padded across the floor to her food bowl. She chuffed impatiently. And to argue her point even more, she picked up her bowl in her mouth and carried it over to Tyler and placed it at his feet.

"Alright, alright. I got it, I got it. You've made your point."

Raven waved her paw and tapped her bowl in answer to his statement.

Tyler retrieved the bag of dog food from the pantry and poured a helping in Raven's bowl. Upon seeing Raven urging Tyler to get her food, one might think that she would simply devour the helping, but Raven didn't gulp or consume the food hastily but ate it gingerly as if tasting a fine, expensive cuisine.

As Raven ate, Tyler rummaged through the boxes on the kitchen table for the cereal bowls. Finding them in the last box—it was always that way—he grabbed the cereal from the cabinet and the milk from the refrigerator and started to eat.

Raven glanced up every now and then to keep tabs on her master to make sure she would be able to faithfully trot after him in case Tyler suddenly left.

"Is it good, girl?" Tyler said through a mouthful of Cheerios.

Raven's ears pricked as she cocked her head. She licked her chops, lowered her head, and continued to eat her breakfast.

Tyler felt two arms encircle him. One slid around his waist and the other slid down over the opposite shoulder and across his chest.

"Good morning, precious. How's the love of my life?"

"I don't know, Mom. I haven't talked to Dad this morning," Tyler said, smiling.

Gwen Curtis kissed him on the check, "Oooh, good one."

"Thank you, I do my best. I didn't hear you come downstairs. You been up long?"

"I actually never got to bed. I crashed on the sofa downstairs and didn't wake up till I heard you in here." She yawned and tried to talk at the same time, "Ish way touu eer-ry to be up."

"Say again," Tyler said. "I don't understand yawn."

She gave him a look and made sure she enunciated clearly for him this time. "I said, it's way too early to be up."

They shared a smile.

Even though she had been up late last night unpacking and was sleep deprived, Gwen was beautiful this early in the morning. He took a moment to admire his mother.

She had an oval face with light green eyes. Her naturally curly strawberry blonde hair complimented her fair skin. She had freckles that were sprinkled across the bridge of her nose and dotted her cheeks. She usually wore her hair down but this morning it was pulled back as best as she could manage with some sort of hair clip.

"Sorry I woke you."

"Don't be. I needed to get up. Lots to do today. Did you sleep well?"

"I don't rightly know. I'm still trying to figure that out."

"Figure what out?"

"I think I did a little sleepwalking last night."

"Sleepwalking?"

"Uh-huh."

"Well, where did you go?" Gwen asked as a hint of a smile crept in at the corners of her mouth.

"Upstairs. I woke up behind the couch in the game room."

"What?"

"Tell me about it. I was as surprised as you are now."

"Sleepwalking?"

"Well, now that I think about it, it was more like sleep running."

"Sleep running? Oooh, even better. I've never heard of that. Why were you running?"

"A monster was chasing me."

Gwen started laughing.

Tyler looked up from his bowl of Cheerios confused at why she was laughing at him. He gave her a hurt, pitiful look.

"I'm sorry, honey. You sounded so much like a little kid just then.

I don't mean to make light of the situation, but you have to admit it is kind of humorous. You're a senior in high school, practically an adult and just the mention of monsters chasing you sounds so—," she paused grasping for the right word. "Childish."

Tyler gave her a fake laugh through mouthfuls of Cheerios. "You wouldn't be laughing if that damn thing was chasing you. He was a big son of a..."

"Ah, ah, ah," his mother warned.

"Gun, mom. Son of a gun. What, you thought I was going to say 'bitch', didn't you? Mom, what have I told you about language?"

She shot him an evil eye look as well as an amused smile to go along with it.

He tilted his head up toward hers and grinned broadly showing as many pearly whites as possible. Gwen couldn't be upset with him when he gave her those adorable looks.

"I have some boxes of stuff we're not going to need right now. They are ready to be stored in the attic. Do you think you can take them up there for me before you head out to school?"

"Anything for you, doll face." Tyler said. "I'll do it because I love you."

"Thank you, hon. I love you more."

Raven had long since finished eating and had lain down by her food bowl to watch Tyler and Gwen's conversation.

Tyler stood, went to the sink, washed his bowl, and set it in the strainer then headed back toward his room. Before he was out of the kitchen, Raven was at his side. Loyalty ran in the dog's blood.

Tyler found the boxes his mother had talked about by the stairway that led to the second floor. He picked up the boxes and walked upstairs to another door that led to the attic. He opened the door, flipped on the light to the attic, and started to the third floor.

As he ascended the attic stairs, they squeaked slightly from his weight and old age. The house was old but had been solidly built. The usual pungent attic smells of aged wood and insulation tickled his nose. Filigreed dust danced in the rays of the early morning sunshine that streamed through the paned windows as if it had been kicked up by a back draft upon opening the downstairs attic door.

When he switched on the light, shadows that blanketed most of the attic scurried for deeper and darker corners. Tyler recognized most of the boxes as miscellaneous odd and ends from the move; various rickrack that should have been thrown out long ago but kept in the event it may be needed. There were a couple of different pieces of small furniture, boxes, and crates that weren't theirs as far as he could remember. Why they were still here, he had no idea. Most of the attic's contents were scattered throughout the attic floor and were blanketed with off-white sheets. He glanced briefly over all the junk looking for the best place to set his boxes. Not taking the time to investigate any of the other junk that littered the attic floor, he placed his boxes on top of a miniature dust covered table. Completing his mother request, he wiped his hands, descended the stairs, and turned off the light.

Back on the first floor again, he stopped back by his room and grabbed his backpack and jacket.

"You have anything else for me to do before I go to school?" Tyler asked as he stepped back into the kitchen.

"You put those boxes in the attic?"

"Yup."

"Then that's it for now. I'll have more for you to do tonight."

Tyler leaned over and kissed his mom on the forehead, "Love you. Tell dad the same for me."

"Love you too. And I will."

"Don't work too hard today. Save some for me?"

"Nope. Going to do it all myself."

"It's your party."

Tyler petted Raven one last time and stepped out onto the spacious front porch.

Tyler wondered what accomplishments, goals, and possible dreams were waiting for him in this new city. As he thought about his second day in a new county and his first day in a new school, he walked toward his late model, black Mustang GT. He saw red-throated robins searching for worms in the dew-glistened grass and heard more birds chirping in the trees. He breathed the fresh scent of honeysuckle and lilac that floated on the morning air. It was a smell he had missed while living in the congested smog-encased heart of Chicago.

He started his Mustang and pulled to the end of the driveway. As he pulled onto the neighborhood street, he cranked up the song that was coming out of the speakers and headed toward Silver Ridge High School.

ଔ

When Tyler arrived at the school, he passed the main entrance sign that stated: SILVER RIDGE HIGH SCHOOL. HOME OF THE SIDEWINDERS.

Tyler's first notion of the school was that it looked like a prison lacking the lookout towers, fences with barbed wire, attack dogs, and night patrol watchmen armed with machine guns. The school was rectangular with the longest portion facing the highway. At each end of the building there were octagon-shaped parapets connected to each corner of the building. These corners—stairs that led to each floor and to the roof—jutted out and rose higher than the building itself, which gave Tyler the impression of a fortress or a state penitentiary.

Tyler parked his Mustang in the student parking lot, stepped out, grabbed his book bag, and started toward the main entrance.

He noticed the structure was made of a light colored brick with huge front lobby doors that rose eight to ten feet high. In the lobby were huge paintings of principals, deans, and different administrative personnel that had been remembered throughout the lifetime of the school. The halls branched off to either side, leading to the different classrooms. From visiting the school earlier that week, Tyler remembered that the door ahead led to an outside enclosed area where school pep rallies took place. It was where students passed the time by throwing Frisbee or football and where Romeos and Juliets sat hand-in-hand between classes talking about wishes, dreams, and the future, or just simply making out, not caring who was watching them.

In his first class, before the class bell rung and before many of the students had arrived, Tyler walked up to a short, blond haired student who was looking over his class schedule.

"Anyone sitting here?" Tyler asked.

"No," the boy said shaking his head.

"You mind?" Tyler asked, motioning to the chair behind the boy.

"No, help yourself."

As Tyler sat down the boy asked, "You're new here aren't you?"

"Is it that noticeable?"

"No, not really. You just don't look familiar to me, that's all. If you'd gone to this school as long as I have, you know a new student when they start. A lot of students have been going here since we were kids."

"I'm Tyler Curtis," he said, holding his fist out.

"Cass. Cass Cambell," he said, and bumped his knuckles.

"It's my second day in this area but my first official day at Silver Ridge High."

"I've lived in this area my whole life. You'll like it here. Where in Silver Ridge did you move?"

"Desdemona Heights. The subdivision has been there for a while."

"I know the neighborhood."

"My parents are into antiques," Tyler said. "They've been collecting for a number of years. They bought that house because it's more than five decades old. They say an older modeled house such as it brings out the beauty of the antiques. I think it was just an excuse to buy it. It's nice, so I can't complain about that."

"You play sports?" Cass said changing the subject, obviously uninterested in the subject of antiques.

"Sure, I played a little. I was a quarterback and captain for the football team at my other school, and I dabbled around for a little while on the wrestling team as well."

"No shit, really? You planning on playing for the Sidewinders? Tryouts are Monday, you know. Four o'clock. We could definitely use you. We got our asses handed to us last year."

"I was already planning on it."

"Cool. I won't."

"Why not?"

"Look at me," Cass said. "I'm too short to. I've tried out two years in a row but never made the cut. There were too many other players who are taller—or stockier than me."

"So. That was last year," Tyler said. "Don't you want to play?"

"You fucking kidding me? It's the Sidewinders. Of course I do. I've always wanted to play."

"Well. Don't let your height stop you. Is the same coach going to be coaching this year too?"

"Yeah, he's always been the coach at this school."

"And he knows you? He'll remember you from last year, right?"

"Sure," Cass said not seeing Tyler's point.

"Then you show this coach what you're made of. Go out there and show him that you are worth putting on the team. Don't take no for an answer this year."

"Okay, I'll do it. I'll try at least one more year."

"Good. You'll be glad you did."

More students filed into the room, and the chatter steadily grew louder. Tyler noticed an auburn haired girl enter with her friend and a spark of interest hit him. He felt like asking Cass who she was but decided against it. He would figure out who she was on his own time and in his own way.

Cass kept talking, but Tyler had stopped paying attention to him since she came on the scene. He watched her walk down the aisle toward the front. As she sat down by her friend, she glanced in Tyler's direction. For a split second, their eyes locked. Tyler smiled, nodded his head, and gave her a quick wave. She returned the smile and slowly turned around in her chair but then turned back to take a second look. The look lingered a little longer than he was expecting.

Cass had stopped talking and was waiting for Tyler's attention again. He raised his voice to get Tyler's attention again. "Hey, Romeo?"

Tyler's head whipped back in Cass's direction. "Huh?"

"That's Savannah Matthews, in case you were wondering."

"Who? What are you talking about?"

"Who? Yeah right, like you're not interested, lover boy. You know exactly what and who I'm talking about."

Tyler just smiled and glanced back over at Savannah.

Before Cass could go into more detail about her, a tall, muscular boy with a crew cut and glasses came up behind Cass and thumped him hard in his ear. "What's up, ass-face?"

Cass turned around with a start, "Owhh Jeez, cut it out." He rubbed his ear, "Oh, it's just you," he said, realizing it was Derrick.

Derrick mimicked Cass's phrase in a guttural cartoon voice and exaggerated facial expressions.

Cass said, "This is Tyler. Tyler, meet dickhead—I mean, Derrick."

Derrick nodded. They bumped knuckles as Derrick leaned against the desk to the left of Cass. They got better acquainted while more classmates filled the room and took their seats. To Tyler, Derrick's personality seemed fake. He tried to act a little too cool. A trait that wasn't working for him.

"Hey, Tyler, you have anything going on tomorrow?" Derrick asked.

"Just helping my dad and mom with some more unpacking. Why?"

"Well, if you can get away for a few hours, you want to come down to Silver Ridge Lake with us?"

"Hey yeah, great idea," Cass said interrupting. "Everybody that's anybody's going to be there." Then he added as he punched Tyler's arm, "Savannah's gonna be there."

"Well then I'm definitely interested. What time are you going?"

"Three o'clock high, so don't be late kid," Derrick said.

"All right, I'll be there."

"If you're not, we'll track you down," Derrick added.

"Yeah, I know where you live now," Cass said.

"Don't worry about me. After the trip and unpacking, I'll need a little R&R."

"R and R? What the hell's that?" Derrick asked.

"Rest and relaxation, dumbass," Cass said slapping him in the crotch. "That was for thumping me in my ear earlier."

"Damn, dude, don't do that. People will start to think you're gay. Besides, I'm going to need those later in life. Maybe later on this weekend if I'm lucky. Know what I'm talking about."

Cass countered, "You gonna need a lot of fucking luck, lover boy."

"Damn, that hurt. That hurt big time." Derrick cupped himself and sat down in the desk he was leaning on. To Cass he said, "You know I'm going to get you back for that. Paybacks are a real bitch, you know."

"Yeah, yeah," Cass said. "Promises, promises."

The school bell rang and a man Tyler could only assume was their teacher walked to the front of the classroom.

As the last few students hurriedly took their seats, Tyler thought about how his new life was turning out. In less than ten minutes, he had just made two new friends that seemed genuine enough to hang out with. He had been invited to try out for the school football team and had caught the eye of one of the many goddesses of this school. Tyler felt his life was slipping into place. This school year was off to a great start.

CHAPTER 2

THE GLORIA WILLMINGTON Memorial Library sat cater-corner to Silver Ridge High School in a level landscaped area. The library seemed like a smaller version of the school but lacked the lookout towers at the four corners that the school possessed.

When the engineering plans were being drawn up for the high school, they knew ahead of time that the school would also need a library. Since the community was in need of a new, bigger public library, they combined the two in hopes to save on overall building expenses.

The library was named after Gloria Willmington—an influential teacher at the high school—because of her driving force on education. Literacy was her main focus, and she pushed hard to get reading and education programs started within the schools and surrounding communities. She had also helped with the resurrection of the high school and library before she had passed.

Tyler stood in front of Gloria Willmington's memorial picture that hung in the main lobby of the library. He read the plaque that was placed below her name: "Dedicated in loving memory to a true hero. Thank you for making Silver Ridge what it is today."

He stepped back and took a quick mental snapshot of her and walked further inside.

Tyler saw that the library was indeed spacious. Bookshelves lined most of the four sides of the first floor walls. A children's reading area was located on the south wall, and the checkout area was on the right near the entrance. Walking further inside there were eight steps descending into the ground floor or a number of other steps that led to the second floor. Tyler descended into the adult reading and study area where couples and groups of friends were sporadically seated. In passing, Tyler glanced up into the second floor stairway. He was sure there was plenty of space and books on the second floor but only saw a banistered opening at the top. A separate entrance and stairway for the public was located directly opposite from where he entered. The walls inside were painted a vibrant blue with a light purple accent, which was easy on the eyes. There were potted plants and small trees planted in various areas. Both the plants and paintings combined to give a spark of life that promoted a spirit of imagination and learning.

The air smelled of potpourri with an underlying scent of lemon furniture polish.

Even though it was crowded, it was quiet for a library, just a low hum of whispering between students and friends.

Tyler headed straight for the study area to get started on the assigned homework. When he approached the study area, he stopped short. Savannah Matthews, the girl from his first period class, was sitting at a table near the corner by herself. Locks of auburn hair fell over her face as she moved her pencil across the page.

Huh. What are the odds? he thought.

He chose a table directly in front of her. As he sat down, he half expected her to look in his direction. When she didn't, he opened his book and started on his assignments. In time, he felt she would notice him. Whether or not conversation would come out of it he didn't know; all he could do was hope. He wasn't going to press the issue, at least not right away.

Tyler thought, *The connection—ahem, make that, the 'supposed' connection earlier this morning—could've just been a fluke.*

Tyler barely started reading before he heard the sound.

"Pssst."

He looked up to see Savannah staring at him.

And then again, maybe not.

She made a hand motion for him to come over to her table.

Smiling, he left his books and sat down in a chair directly across from her.

"Hey," she said.

"Hey, yourself."

"You're in my English class. First period right?"

"Yeah, you're Savannah Matthews, aren't you?"

A curios look crossed her face as if to say how do you know my name? As the curious look changed into a smile she said, "Yes, as a matter of fact I am. You're the new kid in town, aren't you?"

"I get that a lot. Is it that obvious?"

"It's not a bad thing," she assured him. She paused for a moment, thinking.

"What is it?" Tyler asked.

"I'm almost embarrassed to say."

Tyler tilted his head to urge her into telling him what she was thinking about.

"You'll have to forgive me, because I'm not at all as observant as you. I know it sounds bad of me, but I don't even know your name."

Tyler laughter and said, "It's Tyler. Tyler Curtis."

He stuck out his hand, which as an after thought felt stupid and ridiculous, but it had happened before he realized it. Savannah—still laughing—went with it and accepted his hand.

"Well it is really nice to meet you, Tyler."

"Believe me, the pleasure is all mine."

Changing the subject, he tapped her Algebra book and said, "They really pour it on thick at this school, don't they?"

"I've been going to this school my whole life and it seems like every year the homework loads becomes bigger and harder."

"So you're used to this amount of homework?"

Savannah said, "I don't think anyone could ever get used to the amount of homework they give you here."

"I guess they want you to be everything you should be once you've finished school and are ready for the real world."

"I believe I'll be ready," she said with a hint of sarcasm. "I'll probably be able to run for the Presidency once I've finished Silver Ridge High."

"You sound very determined."

She dropped the sarcasm and became serious, "I am determined. I have to be. The teachers here make you determined. You can't help but be that way with the teachers always on your back about homework. But just listen to me carrying on; you don't want to hear about all this. You're already experiencing the side effect of this school, aren't you? All the homework the bestow on us."

"Yeah, that Creative Writing assignment has me worried," he said, knowing exactly what she was talking about.

"Me too. But you got it."

"He's a great teacher; my favorite so far. I'm going to enjoy his class. I've got to figure out what I'm going to write on though. You know what you're doing yet?"

"Been brainstorming all day," she said, "But can't think of anything. I want it to be different. I want to write on something that hasn't been explored in detail before."

"I have to do better than I've done in the past. I've had a rough time with my grades at other schools."

"What's wrong with your grades?"

"Nothing yet, that's why I'm here getting a head start. If I don't start out this semester right, then I can kiss being a member of any football team goodbye. Tryouts are on Monday from what I hear; that's why I'm going to get started on these projects early and get my work finished ahead of time. Back at the other schools, I was almost kicked off the sport's teams because of my low grades. Playing sports took up a lot of my time back home, but I've already made a goal to myself that I'm not going to let that happen again."

"I don't blame you for that. It's good to have a goal to strive for. I wish you the best of luck come Monday."

"Speaking of luck, would you mind coming to tryouts and being my good luck charm? That is, if you're not studying then. I don't want to take you away from that. But if you're not, it would be good to have at least somebody I know there, a friend, in my corner cheering me on."

Obviously blindsided by the question, she said, "You're asking me out?"

"Yes. I guess I am."

The look of shock was quickly wiped away and replaced by a wide smile. "Well then, I don't foresee anything standing in my way at this point in time, but I don't think I would be good luck for you. I think you would make the team because of your ability, not because I'm there. But if you think it would help. Sure. I'll be there for you."

"That would be awesome. Tryouts start at four o'clock sharp."

"Then I'll be there at three-fifty."

There was a small passage of time where neither of them said anything.

Tyler panicked; something that never happened to him when talking to girls. Savannah was obviously unnerving him. He was rattled and felt very uncool in her presence. Rather than stay there and come up with an uninteresting or dumb subject, he baled on the perfect setup.

"Well Einstein, I guess I should let you get back to your Algebra. I don't want to hinder you from your homework."

"Hinder me, please. I'm tired of this shit. You don't have to go if you don't want to." She spoke shyly, not wanting to come across as being too forward. "I needed to rest my brain from these math problems anyway. It's been a good break so far."

"I guess I could get my stuff and we could share this table, if you don't mind."

"I'm already sharing it with you. Of course, I don't mind."

Tyler quickly retrieved his books from the other table and sat down again in a seat across from Savannah. From out of nowhere, he asked, "Are you hungry?"

"Starving," she said almost cutting him off.

"Because I haven't eaten anything since lunch and I was wondering if you would like to grab a bite to eat with me. I know you barely know me, and it may seem strange for me to even be asking you out. Again. But we could drive separate cars and meet at a restaurant. We could go dutch if that would be less pressuring to you, but I'm all prepared to pay, that's not an issue." He took a deep breath, relieved that the question had been asked.

Without hesitation she answered, "I thought you would never ask. The answer to your first question, yes, I'm hungry. Your second question, no I wouldn't mind grabbing a bite to eat with you. Third, meeting at a restaurant would be fine. That's normally where people eat. And fourth, I don't have a problem paying for my own meal."

"Wow, you summed that up really well." He was surprised that she had remembered each question he had asked. "Since I'm new in the area, I have no idea where the good places to eat are so you'll have to suggest a restaurant."

Without missing a beat she said, "Darryl's. It's the best place to eat around here. A little pricey, but the food is amazing."

"Darryl's it is then."

∞

As they strolled inside Darryl's, they were assaulted mostly by a mixture of seafood aromas but there was a host of other scents of garlic, vegetables, steak, chicken, herbs, and spices as well.

Darryl's was built in the fashion of being below deck of an old, gigantic, wooded ship but with regular windows instead of port holes. Lots of unpainted wood. Very rustic. The walls were adorned with all manner of fishing industry trade from sunset paintings to long harpoons. Some fish—mainly Marlin—were mounted on the walls. A few small wooden boats and colorful flags hung from the ceiling's cross beams.

Two long fish tanks ran the length of the restaurant. Inside the tanks were sharks that were two to three feet in length. The sharks swam in a constant circle from one end of the restaurant to the other. There were a few small stingray and some other various colored fish that darted out of the way whenever the sharks cruised by.

The restaurant was lit by wooden chandeliers that held fake candles that gave off a dim overcast. Tables were covered with light blue tablecloths and had red candle holders with burning votives. Ferns hung on arched wall-mounted hangers and gave the restaurant a bit of color, liveliness, and vigor.

Silverware clink-clanked against the dishes as patrons ate. Customers were talking and laughing while relaxing after a hard day's work.

A friendly Asian waitress showed them to their table, seated them, told them about the evening specials, and took their drink and appetizer orders. Tyler, a coke; Savannah, an unsweet tea; appetizer, bottomless nachos with salsa.

"So, tell me about yourself," Tyler said. "I know nothing about you."

"There's really not much to tell. Kind of boring, really. Born and lived here in Silver Ridge my whole life."

"Do you ever get tired of it here?"

"Not really. I do travel from time to time, just to get out and see what else is out there in the world. Even though I travel, my path in life always brings me back here. Silver Ridge is my home. I don't think I'll ever leave.

"What about *you*? Tell me about *you*," he said more to the point.

"Well for starters, my biggest claim to fame was being Queen of Silver Ridge Elementary School when I was in third grade. The elementary school is all the way across town. Don't know why they didn't put those two together when they built the new school, but that is beside the point. It's not what you're thinking, really. It wasn't a beauty or talent pageant or anything like that. I was crowned queen because I raised the most money in a contest they were having at the time. Can't remember what the money went for, but I was the big winner. See, pretty lame."

"Your life has been that bad?"

"No, not bad; it's just nothing major happens in this area that is remotely interesting at all. Only interesting thing that has happened lately is you showed up in class this morning."

"Wow, I'll take that as a compliment," Tyler said a little shocked at her comment. "I'm glad I could bring a little excitement to your life."

"Me too."

"Surely you're dating somebody around here. Someone in school."

"Me? Date? Ha. No, not dating anyone."

"That's hard to believe."

"How so?"

"In a word, you're beautiful."

She smiled and blushed, "Thank you. But that's two words."

Tyler smiled. She had him on that one.

Savannah continued, "I needed to hear that. It's been a long time since someone has told me that. It's nice to hear." There was a slight pause, neither one of them knowing what to say. Savannah continued, "So, just because I'm beautiful, I should be dating someone?"

"No of course not, I just find it hard to believe no one has asked you out. I would jumped on the chance to go out with you."

"I believe you just did. And that's why we're here."

"Yes—yes, I did. But there are so many more reasons that I've just noticed since we've talked at the library."

"Like what, for instance?"

"Oh, wow, that spotlight is really hot. Any way you could turn it down a bit?" he joked.

She was amused and smiled but was still waiting for an answer.

"Well for starters, you're intelligent or at least appear to be."

"Thank you. I try not to look stupid as often as I can."

"And there is an example of why you're so funny. Very quick-witted. I like that. But yeah, studying Algebra and who knows what else tells me you're crazy intelligent. That's just a few. I don't want to overwhelm you with too many compliments right off the bat. I have to keep some in the reserve for later."

"I'll try not to let it go to my head." Changing the subject back to dating issue, she said, "When you have been going to the same school for as long as I have, you get to know everybody better from year to year. I have been going to school with some of the students since I was in kindergarten. I have dated some guys over the years, but it feels more like I'm dating a brother my parents never had, and that's just way too weird for me. I saw you talking to Cass this morning. We used to date for awhile."

"Cass? Really? Cass didn't mention anything about that this morning when we saw you."

Savannah slapped the table and said, "Ha, I knew it. I knew you guys were talking about me." She pointed at him, "Ah-ha, you just gave yourself away."

Tyler was stunned. "You set me up."

"I sure did and you fell for it," There was a long pause between them; a slight embarrassment from Tyler at being caught and a gloating

Savannah at busting Tyler. "So. You were talking about me with Cass. Interesting. What were you talking about?"

"I can't say. I don't know you well enough to talk about Savannah with you."

"Touché."

"Yeah. It would be rude."

"That's very cute." She paused and then chuckled to herself. "Cass? No, no, no. We never dated. Not Cass. He *really is* more like a brother to me. Besides, he's not my type."

"What exactly is your type?"

"Oh wow, you're right. That spotlight really is kind of warm." She bowed her head, thought for a moment then raised her head again. Her right eyebrow rose slightly, giving her a cute, inquisitive look. "Hang around long enough and it could be you."

The waitress came back with their drinks, not giving Tyler a chance to reply. They both knew it was a great moment that could've turned out to be a more interesting, but it had been ruined by the waitress's timing. Savannah gave Tyler a wink and a wry smile. Tyler returned the gesture.

As the waitress set the glasses down, both Tyler and Savannah realized they hadn't chosen an entrée and hurriedly picked something from the dinner selections. Tyler ordered the angel hair pasta with meat sauce; Savannah, the quesadillas.

Tyler said, "Funny thing about this restaurant."

"What's that?"

"This is mainly a seafood restaurant and we ended up ordering something that couldn't be further from a seafood dish."

"I'm just in a Mexican mood, I guess." Savannah said. "Must be because I'm eating all these chips."

"Good nachos."

As they talked, they nibbled on tortilla chips and salsa. Conversation started out again discussing favorite music styles, movies, hobbies, different interests, school, and friends. During their conversation, their meals came.

After they had finished eating their meals, they continued talking about family, goals accomplished, and relationships. Tyler ordered cheesecake with vanilla ice cream that he and Savannah both shared. After dessert they each paid for their meal; Tyler left the tip and they ventured outside.

The sun was slowly losing its grip on the silver ridges in the distance. Purple cloaks of twilight had just started to spread themselves across the horizon. Stars were beginning to peak out from behind dusk's gloomy cloak. As nightfall approached, insects began their evening mating ritual calls.

"Wow, look at that."

Savannah noticed Tyler was looking up into the twilight sky. She followed his gaze. "What?"

"The stars."

Tyler sounded absolutely amazed.

"Yeah?" Savannah didn't understand.

"Sorry, it's just been a really long time since I've seen a night sky as clear as this. Back in Chicago you hardly ever see the stars. All the smog mixed with the bright city lights. It's just great to finally see a clear view like this again."

Savannah took turns between looking at the starry sky and the amazement on Tyler's face. He was like a little kid; in total awe of something as simple as a night sky. It was really adorable and she couldn't help but smile. She let him have his moment.

Almost abruptly, he turned to her and said, "I really enjoyed tonight, and I want to thank you for coming out to eat with me. I had an amazing time."

She paused to take in what he had just said, "You really are, aren't you?"

"Really what?"

"You really appreciate my coming out with you?"

"Of course. It's true. I don't want you to think that I'm taking you for granted."

"That's very sweet. Nobody has ever said that to me before."

"I'm glad I could be the first, but I'm not just saying it. I really mean it. Someone as intensely beautiful as you could've went out with anyone, but I was lucky enough to be that guy, even if it was only for tonight."

"Don't sell yourself short, Tyler. You're pretty awesome yourself."

He blushed and turned away. "Thanks," he said.

What is it with me? I've never blushed in my lifetime. Something about this girl is carrying me away. What is it about her?

He paused, took a deep breath and continued. "I hope I'm not overstepping my bounds here, because we've just met, but I know Cass Campbell and Derrick Mitchell—well, we both know now that you know Cass, you dated him for heaven's sake." They both laughed reliving the earlier memory at dinner.

"Yeah, I know Cass really well," she teased in a breathy whisper making the earlier joke that much funnier. "We all grew up together."

"They invited me to go to Silver Ridge Lake tomorrow to do some swimming and, well, whatever else they do down there. I was wondering if you're not busy tomorrow around two-thirty or three o'clock, if you would like to go with me and sort of be my guide? I don't really know too many people here except you three. I don't want to force the issue and I don't want you to feel obligated or pressured because we just ate dinner together tonight, but Cass told me that everybody who is anybody is going to be there."

"Of course, I'd love to go," Savannah said quickly. "I was already planning on being there but I forgot all about it. I would've invited you if I hadn't forgot about it. My three best friends, Amber, Erica, and Iris are going to be there. Amber was who I was with in class this morning."

"Great. I can pick you up if you would like. But I will need your address so I can put it in my phone so I can find where you live tomorrow to pick you up."

"I've got a better idea. If you're not in a hurry to get home, why don't you come by my house and meet my parents, that way you could find out how to get there. And by the way, my parents are cool, they meet all my friends, boys and girls. I'm not suggesting this to scare you away."

"Oh, no, I understand. I could come by for awhile, but I will have to get home to help my parents with some of the unpacking. Our house is still like a war zone from the move. Utter chaos.

"OK," she said, getting into her car. "Follow me and try and keep up."

"I'll do my best."

❃

Bright front porch lights were already on when Savannah and Tyler pulled in front of a huge two story house sitting at the end of a cul-de-sac. It reminded Tyler of the house they had just moved into. Tyler could tell from the backwash of porch light that the house had been painted pale yellow with white trim. A front porch that connected to two side porches had a white cast iron table and chairs near the front door. Opposite that was a front porch swing. Flower gardens filled with daisies, petunias, and snapdragons flanked the front and side porches. Walkways led from the road to the porches and around into the backyard. Two immense oak trees sat on opposite sides of the house, framing it between their huge limbs that fanned out and shaded the front and side yards. The smell of fresh cut grass, along with the sweet scent from the flower beds, hung in the lazy night air.

When Tyler and Savannah strolled up the walkway, a white cat with black paws jumped down from its perch on the porch banister and stretched. The cat sauntered between their legs, rubbed around their ankles, making it difficult to walk.

"Hey there, Curiosity. How's my baby doing? Savannah said, scooping the cat up in one fluid motion and snuggling it to her neck.

"Curiosity?" Tyler asked.

"That's right. The best damn cat in the whole wide world," she said holding it out in front of her. "Isn't that right, girl?"

She brought the cat back to her face and gave Curiosity an Eskimo kiss with her nose.

"That's very cute."

"Suits her, doesn't it? We named her Curiosity because she's always getting into everything. Way too much energy."

Savannah gave the cat another scratch behind the ears then placed her on the ground. Curiosity sat down in the grass and started licking her paw, forgetting about Tyler and Savannah all together.

Tyler followed Savannah up the front porch stairs and inside.

In the living room, they were greeted by a man who was dressed in

51

golf attire; long black pants, black belt and a cream colored golf shirt and a camouflaged hunting hat. The camouflaged hat gave his outfit a skewed look. If he wore that hat with that outfit to a country club, he would be laughed off the golf course. The situation was almost humorous, except for the fact that the man stood by a gun cabinet and held a shotgun in the crook of his arm.

The man spoke to Tyler, "I would like to know exactly what you are doing with my daughter."

"Dad, not now please," Savannah pleaded. "Don't do this to me now."

Tyler stopped short, "I, um."

Ignoring his daughter's request, he said, "I haven't got all night, son. Just what in the hell do you think you're doing with my daughter?"

Tyler held out his hands to explain. "I, ah, I, *we* just had dinner together."

"Dinner? Oh, is that right?"

"Yes, sir. We were at the library studying. We got hungry then decided to get dinner. I didn't think there was any harm in that."

"No harm in it? Is that what you thought?"

"Dad. You're not funny. Stop it."

"Oh I'm not trying to be funny. I'm the furthest thing from being funny."

Tyler continued to try and explain, "Wasn't a date or anything, if that's what you're worried about, sir. We just went out as friends."

"Oh really? Is that a fact?"

"Yes, sir."

"You saying you're too good to date my daughter?"

"No, sir."

Savannah yelled into the kitchen. "Mom, would you come put a muzzle and harness on Dad and drag him into the back room? He's embarrassing me again."

"We paid separately if that means anything, but on second thought, maybe I should've paid for your daughter's meal. Maybe that would've been the respectful thing to do."

"Uh-huh. No, I think paying for her meal would've made it a date. Then you and I would have a real problem."

Tyler's eyebrows crinkled in confusion.

Savannah's mom quickly came around the corner and swatted him with a dishtowel. "Lawrence, put that gun away. You're scaring the kids."

Lawrence didn't move. He and Tyler stared at each other not saying anything.

The woman threw her hands up in frustration, shook her head, and turned toward Tyler. "Ignore him," the woman said. "Don't let him fool you. It's all just a big tough guy act. He thinks he's funny. He's been watching too many Dirty Harry movies, if you ask me." She came at Tyler with outstretched arms. "Hi, I'm Julia Matthews, and I am so glad to meet you."

Tyler hugged her back. "I'm Tyler, and the feeling is mutual. Is it okay that I'm hugging you?"

Julia laughed, "Yes, it's fine."

"I'll be the judge of that," Lawrence countered.

"You just caught Lawrence in his hunting mode. He's going on one of his hunting trips tomorrow and he's just getting his stuff ready."

Tyler held back the urge to comment about his golf attire. He thought he just might take it personally. Instead, he asked, "Did I do something wrong, sir?"

"Yeah," Lawrence said. "I'm just wondering why you didn't call Julia and myself and invite us to dinner. We haven't eaten yet."

Lawrence's joke didn't register with Tyler because of the man's demeanor. Lawrence rotated the gun one hundred eighty degrees from the floor to where it was propped up on his left shoulder.

"I didn't have your phone number, sir?" Tyler said, unsure of himself.

"Oh, we have someone here who likes to throw out wise cracks," Lawrence said.

Tyler barely heard him. He was still trying to figure Lawrence out. "Could I make a suggestion, sir?"

Everyone glanced in Tyler's direction curious of what he might say. Savannah and Julia looked a little scared at what Tyler was going to say.

"I don't suppose there would be any harm in it," Lawrence said.

"If you're going to shoot me, is there any way you could do it with that Winchester 30-30 as opposed to that 12 gauge you're holding now?

The Winchester, in my opinion, is a much better gun and probably wouldn't leave too much of a mess for you to clean up."

Lawrence glanced back at his gun cabinet and nodded. His bluff had been called. He dropped the act and smiled back at Tyler. "Oh, you're good." He started to laugh as he leaned the gun against the cabinet then walked forward with his hand out. "I like you. You're good. I'm Lawrence Matthews."

Tyler tentatively accepted his hand and they shook. "Tyler Curtis."

Savannah slapped her dad playfully on the shoulder. "Why do you always do that when I bring friends home?"

"Because it's funny, and it gets on your nerves." He moved to hug his daughter. "How's my baby doing?"

She hugged him back and kissed him on the cheek. "Fine. I guess. I'm just glad you didn't draw it out as long as you usually do."

"You know I love you and I have to tease you every now and then."

"There's no 'every now and then'. It's every time I bring somebody home."

Lawrence laughed and glanced back to Tyler. "So, you know guns, huh?"

"Oh yeah. My dad and I try to go hunting a couple of times a year. I've bagged a buck or two in my day, but I'm more of a bowhunter myself."

"Oh, a bowhunter?" Lawrence was nodding. "Nice." Tyler had his approval.

Julia butted into their conversation, "Oh no, you don't. You're not going to talk about guns or hunting right now. You can do that some other time. You can take him over to The Warehouse and show him all your trophies sometime if he's interested."

"Warehouse?" Tyler asked.

"She calls it 'The Warehouse' but it's actually my office. It's a four roomed building where I keep most of my mounted trophies; the ones that are too big to put in this house."

"The ones *Mom* won't let you put in here," Savannah countered.

"Just how big are you talking about?"

"Let's just say I'm a big game hunter. All my real guns are over there."

"Oh really? I would be interested in seeing that sometime, sir."

Julia chimed in, "As I was saying, you can talk about all that until you're blue in the face, but you can do it later."

Tyler asked, "You weren't thinking of adding me to your collection were you?"

Lawrence laughed. "No, of course not. I was just playing to get on my daughter's nerves."

"That's good to know." Tyler paused for a moment then added. "You had me going there for a few minutes."

Julia said, "Sit down Tyler. I want to know about you. Tell us about yourself."

Tyler did so. It was mostly a carbon copy conversation of what he and Savannah had discussed over dinner, but he didn't mind.

Tyler was able to find out a little about her parents as well. Lawrence liked golf and hunting equally, and whenever he planned a hunting trip, he made sure there was a golf course within a decent driving distance and vice versa. Julia had a green thumb. Her hobby and main drive in life were flowers. Whether it was at home or at work, she was always working with flora in some way, shape, or fashion. Tyler remembered how the yard looked when they had arrived. He saw and smelled the neatly cut grass and an over abundance of flowers all around the yard. As far as work went, Julia owned a prodigious florist shop and did most of the arrangements that went out to the businesses and residents in and around Silver Ridge.

Tyler's nervousness from the earlier confrontation with Lawrence was wearing off. He was really enjoying his time here talking with them. Even though they asked him questions about his future and what he wanted to do with his life, he didn't feel scrutinized by them. He felt they were genuinely interested in who he was and what his interests were. Tyler didn't feel uneasy sitting here talking with them but felt genuinely comfortable around them. He spent enough time with them that when it was time for him to leave it didn't seem like he was rushing off. He thanked them for their hospitality, the scare and excused himself.

As they walked back down the front porch stairs Savannah said, "Sorry about all that."

"About what?"

"My parents."

Tyler laughed. "What, are you kidding? Your parents are perfect. Your dad, I have to say, is a very intense guy, and your mom, well, she's just a sweetheart."

Savannah smiled. "Thanks. I hope my dad's antics didn't scare you off."

"What? No way. Besides, it takes a lot to scare me away."

"But I was also talking about the whole third degree questionnaire they gave you, about what you are going to do with your life, what you want to become, and everything else. They tend to go overboard sometimes."

"That's parents for you. Always watching out for their children, but I didn't see it as that. They were just interested, and I really enjoyed talking with them. They didn't make me feel nervous if that's what you're worried about. They're just concerned about who you keep company with that's all. Hopefully I have passed their test."

"I hope so too."

There was a slight awkward silence. Tyler looked up into the night sky again.

Finally Tyler turned and said, "What time should I pick you up tomorrow?"

"Everyone is supposed to be meeting at three o'clock, but some of them will start arriving earlier than that. It's really up to you because I can be ready to go at a moment's notice. I know you have to do some of your unpacking tomorrow morning and I don't want to interfere with those plans. I don't mind getting there later if you need more time in the afternoon.

"I could be here around two thirty."

"Perfect. I'll be here in the front porch swing waiting."

"Great, I'll see you then."

Tyler stepped toward Savannah with his arms outstretched. He didn't want to rush anything between them but wanted to show how much he appreciated her and their time together. She stepped forward and hugged him with the same gentleness that he was showing her. As they broke their embrace, their cheeks slowly brushed together. There was a slight pause between them as they stood cheek to cheek; then their heads slowly shifted until their lips touched. The kiss was soft and lingered for a long moment.

"That was really nice," Savannah whispered, obviously stunned by the kiss received.

"Yes, very nice," he said softly. "Wow, this has never happened to me, as far as moving to a new town, meeting a new girl and it turn out like this."

"I'm glad I could be the first. It's really been an unbelievable night for me as well."

"That was so good I wish I could do it again."

"What's stopping you?"

"The fear that I might be overstepping my boundaries."

She gave a cute little laugh. "Trust me. You wouldn't be. No boundaries with me."

Their lips met again. Savannah's lips were soft and the kiss was passionate. Tyler pulled her into him and she followed suit by wrapping her arms around him tightly. The kiss grew heated and their tongues lightly caressed each other's. She held on, not wanting the moment to end. When the kiss finally ended it was in the same way it had started; no one making the first move but both pulling apart simultaneously.

Both were slightly breathless at the end of the kiss and paused with their foreheads softly touching. Nothing needed to be said; the kiss itself spoke volumes and that was enough for both of them.

Tyler saw something drop from her cheek. He pulled his head back and asked, "Hey, what is this? You're crying."

Embarrassed at being caught crying, she hurriedly wiped the tears from her cheek and smiled. "Not crying. Eyes are just watering."

"No really, what's wrong?"

"Nothing," she assured him. "Trust me. It's all good. Perfect, really."

Still puzzled and concerned, Tyler waited for a better answer.

"If you really need to know, they are happy tears. Sometimes I cry when I'm really happy. That's all I can say at the moment."

You're sure?"

"Yeah."

"Okay then. I'll let it go. Come here." He pulled her back into him and hugged her tightly for a long time. She hugged him back intensely, almost clinging to him.

Tyler was the first to break the silence. "I could stand here and hold you all night but I'm afraid your dad would come out here with his guns ablazing."

Savannah laughed out loud. It was one of those beautiful, slightly guttural, Julia Roberts-type laughs. A laugh that is honest and deep from the soul. Tyler was glad to see her laughing now instead of crying even though she was gorgeous either way.

"Tomorrow comes soon though. See you at two thirty?"

"Can't wait."

"Me either."

"Should I bring anything?"

"Just you will be enough."

He smiled, leaned in, and kissed her again on the cheek. "See you soon." Then he got in his car and drove away.

Tyler wished he had a picture of the image in his rearview mirror.

Savannah had just scooped up Curiosity again and was snuggling the cat to her chest as she waved. She was caught in the light of the street lamps and he thought it was a perfect moment in time.

Simply beautiful.

CHAPTER 3

IT WAS AROUND nine o'clock on Saturday morning when the bright sun passed through the slats of the Venetian blinds and woke Tyler. He lay there for a long while basking in the warmth that began to flood his room. He tried to go back to sleep but his mind was reeling with the memories from yesterday.

Don't get your hopes up too high, dude. Something this good just might be too good to be true. He shook his head. *No. Yesterday was perfect. Just take it one moment at a time.*

He glanced at his nightstand clock and realized he had to pick Savannah up in less than five hours. He pulled himself out of bed and headed for the bathroom. A quick shower would wash away the last of his laziness and he would be ready for another rendition of another exhausting day.

After the cool shower, he dressed in a gray T-shirt printed with another band: Amaranthe, a pair of blue stripped swimming shorts, and gray Nike running shoes with blue accents.

He gathered an extra set of clothes—shorts, tee shirts, jeans, sandals; he had no idea what to expect, but wanted to be prepared for anything— and stuffed them into a sports duffel bag and headed downstairs.

The house was especially quiet for a Saturday. Many people slept in on Saturday because it was the only day they had to do so. Tyler's parents usually awoke around dawn. As he passed his parent's room, he looked in and saw they were sound asleep. The unpacking must have been too much for them. He closed their bedroom door, not wanting Raven to come in and wake them before they had a chance to get their rest. They had worked hard during the move and letting them sleep was the least he could do.

As he passed through the living room, he noticed Raven passed out and dead to the world in front of the couch. He quietly set his duffle bag in a recliner and passed through to the kitchen. Surprisingly enough, Raven didn't stir as expected.

He turned on the kitchen's boob tube as he gathered materials for breakfast.

The Power Rangers were fighting some demented alien from another world.

"That show is still airing? I thought it blew out of here ages ago," he said, quickly changing the channel. "There can't be that many aliens for them to fight."

The news was on the next channel.

Definitely better than the Power Rangers, he thought.

He watched it for a while as he started eating a bowl of Shredded Wheat.

An Oriental anchor woman was spilling off the main issues that were just hot off the presses. Most of the material offered was the same as it always had been, the bad always outweighed the good. There was another wildfire in Yosemite National Park out West, more flooding in the South, and another hurricane in the East. The North didn't have any Mother Nature tragedies, but was still filled with murder, drug related offenses, police raids, gang riots, and rape. You name it, bad news was pretty much everywhere.

Tiring of the news he said, "Same shit, different day," and changed channels to one hosting Saturday morning cartoons.

"I heard that," his mother said as she shuffled quietly into the kitchen and dropped the newspaper on the counter.

"Mom, you're like a ninja," he said as he shoved the last spoonful of cereal into his mouth. "I never hear you. I wish the floors squeaked liked they did back at the old house. It would at least warn me when you're coming around."

"Just keeping you on your toes, Dear."

She retrieved a bagel from the bread bin and cream cheese from the refrigerator.

"So long as you don't ask me to do ballet. People will think I'm gay."

"I would never ask you to do anything you didn't want to do," she said, pouring a cup of coffee. "Are you ready for your date with Savannah?"

"You remembered her name."

"Of course I did. You don't think I would forget something that important do you?"

"No. I'm just surprised, that's all."

"Well, the way you talked about her last night when you came in, I knew she was something special."

"I wouldn't go that— "

Gwen held up a hand even though she was still looking over the newspaper and said, "I didn't say she was a lot special or a little special but I could tell you have a huge interest in her."

Folding in their conversation poker game he said, "Yes ma'am, there is a big interest."

"Told ya so."

"You know me best," he said and started to down a glass of milk.

Changing the subject she said, "I've got some more shit for you to carry upstairs to the attic before you leave."

Tyler about choked on a mouthful of milk.

Gwen looked at him innocently and said, "What? What did I say?"

"Mom, you said *shit*."

"You say that like you think it's my first time." She winked at him.

He chuckled and winked back. "You're cool, Mom."

"I know."

"Never change."

"Don't worry. I hadn't planned on it."

He took his dishes and placed them inside the dishwasher, washed and dried his hands then kissed his mother on the top of her head. He didn't say anything, he didn't need to. They didn't always say the 'I love you' line. They didn't want to run it into the ground, but they always felt it.

As he left the kitchen, his mother caught his attention, "Oh, Tyler."

"Yes, ma'am," he said and turned back toward her.

She grabbed a loose banana from the fruit bowl in the center of the table and pitched it over her shoulder. It was a good throw even if it was blind. Tyler only had to take a step forward to catch it.

"You need your potassium."

"Right again, Mom. Thanks."

He found the boxes in the same place as yesterday, only this time there were more. He was going to have to make two trips this time.

He opened the attic door, turned on the light, and grabbed the first load and started up the stairs. He found another cleared out area to the left at the top of the stairs and placed them in that space then bounded back down the stairs for the second load. He set the second batch in front of the first but pushed both stacks further back out of the way. As he stood, he looked slowly around the attic, taking everything in this time. He had a lot of time before he had to pick up Savannah. He could take a little time to investigate.

As he surveyed the attic in a circular sweep, his eyes caught sight of an old, wooden chest Tyler had never seen before. The box looked to be approximately three feet wide by one and a half feet in depth by two feet high. It also had a slightly convex lid. Metal enforcers were attached at each corner for durability. The top was covered with dust from being tucked away and forgotten for countless years. He knew it wasn't part of their furniture because he had personally moved in every piece of furniture with his father and hadn't noticed it during their move. It sat just within reach of fingered shadows, not completely shrouded from the dull light. The chest struck his curiosity but he approached it with trepidation.

He half expected something monstrous to spring out at him from within—perhaps the creature from his dream two nights ago or at least a smaller, more evil version of it—if that was at all possible.

Approaching the chest reminded him of a story he'd heard when camping as a kid with some friends and their parents. Most of the story was hazy, but he would never forget the ending. The story went that a certain pirate owned a treasure chest and had put a curse on it when he had buried it. Years later, a man in search of the legendary treasure chest had been warned by a fortune teller that if he ever found this certain chest, he should never, ever be greedy. The gypsy's warning being that he could take the gold from the chest one handful at a time, but never under any circumstances should both hands be used to retrieve the riches. After years of searching and finally finding the treasure chest and seeing the gold, the gypsy's warning was instantly forgotten and the man hurriedly jammed both hands deep within the gold coins. Before he could withdraw the golden trinkets to view them up close, the lid slammed shut on its own accord, severing his forearms in half, just shy of his elbows.

Now kneeling in front of this wooded chest himself, he wondered what he would find, what secrets had been sealed inside, and if he would be foolish enough and use both hands to view its contents.

The chest was unlocked and nothing lurked inside waiting to spring out at him. No gold or expensive jewels either, just ordinary memorabilia. There were ribbons stating first, second, and third prize in various sporting events—mainly swimming and gymnastics. Some of the ribbons had metals attached to them.

Tyler realized that the natural reaction was to use both hands. He was relieved when the lid didn't slam shut on its own and sever his hands.

He withdrew other keepsakes: diaries, stamps and coins from other countries, books of classic poetry, a small box of ceramics, a few packages of mixed jewelry, three watches, an Indian dream chaser, and numerous photo albums. Whoever's chest this was really had a thing for pictures.

Tyler opened one of the wooden boxes of jewelry, curious at what it contained, but nothing spectacular hit his eye. There were some interesting designs but nothing he could wear; not that he was expecting to find anything. He didn't wear any jewelry because it was too cumbersome for him. He grabbed another box that was as deep as the first but slightly longer and much heavier. A huge amount of rickrack was nonchalantly strewn inside the box. Gold and silver chains were intertwined around all the other miscellaneous jewelry. Tyler used his forefinger to shuffle through the junk. On the third swipe, the light from the attic's bare bulb reflected off a smooth surface and painted a rainbow of colors across his face.

Tyler angled his head and peered in at it a little closer, then glanced around the attic cautiously—almost guiltily—then hesitantly grabbed the smooth, flat stone and pulled it out of the box. The charm had a leather strap attached to it, and he had to gently shake loose the other looping chains that were intertwined around it. He flipped the charm over and over in the palm of his hand, studying each surface as though he could pull the meaning of life from the ancient hieroglyphics. A variety of markings were carved around the outer edges of both sides of the charm. In its center, there was a symbol that was bigger than the rest. Both sides were slightly worn.

"Wonder what these markings mean?" he said to himself.

The surface shimmered again with a silky, surrealistic haze. He flipped it again in his hand. The other side glistened with the same shiny mother-of-pearl intensity.

Almost simultaneously, a chill uncoiled itself from the base of his spine, slithered up his spinal column, and reattached itself around his neck, making his hair stand on end. The feeling, as well as the iciness that had accompanied it, had been preternatural; it was like a warning as well as a promise. A thought that the talisman was evil filtered through his mind, but it was only short lived. It was mesmerizing and had captured his full attention.

It's just a small, insignificant little charm, he thought. *What harm could it do?*

He slowly slid the leather strap over his head and let it rest on his chest. As he did so, a soothing peace unlike anything he had ever experienced coated his body and made him shudder. Even though it was peaceful, it wasn't expected, and the shock of it made him instantly stand and sway on his feet.

"Whoa, holy shit. What the hell was that?"

He paused for a moment and closed his eyes. The peaceful feeling rolled over him again like a tidal wave and washed away any threat of it being evil from his mind. He reveled in the moment. If the earth itself fell away from beneath his feet or were totally obliterated from around him, Tyler felt he could dwell in this peace and be perfectly content for the rest of his life.

Without thinking, he started gently massaging the surface of the medallion. The texture of the ornament was utterly smooth, except for the grooves of the carvings.

Tyler glanced over each item in the chest. He then grabbed one of the photo albums and was about to settle down on the attic floor to brief through it when his mother's voice drifted up from downstairs.

"Tyler!" she called.

"Yeah!"

"I need your help with some more stuff down here when you finish whatever you're doing upstairs."

"Uh, okay, Mom!" he shouted again. "Be there in a minute!"

"Take your time! No rush. Just hurry up!"

Tyler almost took her up on her request of taking his time but decided against it for now; he could play detective later. He put everything that he had taken out of the chest back in again. He closed the lid and pushed it back over to where he had retrieved it. He even took the precaution of throwing one of the off-white sheets over it to conceal it even more then descended the stairs and turned off the light.

Ω

After he helped his mother hang some pictures that could have waited until later in the weekend, Tyler picked up his sports bag and slung it over his shoulder.

He stooped to pet Raven, who hadn't been too excited with the idea of his hanging pictures. The hammering hadn't allowed her to continue with her "cat nap."

Henry Curtis, Tyler's father, came through the living room door. "You know, with all that noise you were making down here earlier, it was enough to wake the dead."

"Talk to Mom about it. She's the one who wanted it done now."

"But you're the culprit," Henry said, nodding his head toward Tyler's hand. "You're the one holding the hammer."

"Yeah, but its guilt by association. I'm her accomplice."

Ignoring them, Gwen asked, "Looks great doesn't it?"

"Beautiful, Dear," Henry said. "You've got a magic touch. You should change careers. You've really got a knack for interior decorating."

"That's because every time we move, I decorate each room with the same materials. It's not too hard to put old stuff in a new place."

"You know what I mean, Dear." He leaned down and kissed her a little longer than Tyler wanted to witness.

Henry Curtis was a tall, athletic man. He had a balding widow's peak, but he always kept his dark red hair buzzed close to his head. Tyler liked the short, close-cropped look, it seemed to work for his dad. Like Gwen, Henry also had fair skin with freckles. But where Gwen's freckled her face, Henry's dotted his arms and legs.

"Get a room you two, or else break it up completely," Tyler said.

Rising, Henry said smiling, "Not when I can make you uncomfortable." He laughed, then asked, "So you're off to the lake today, huh?"

"Yes, sir. Can't wait."

"Why don't you take Raven along with you? I'm sure she would enjoy it just as well."

"I'll be on a date, Dad. Savannah wouldn't want a dog in the back seat slobbering all over her."

"Tyler, I'm shocked. Why would you make Savannah ride in the back seat with Raven?"

Understanding his dad's joke, Tyler smiled and said, "Ha, funny, Dad. Real funny. But no, Savannah will be sitting up front right next to me where she belongs."

"That's why I think Raven should go along with you. You need a chauffeur. Raven will keep you on your toes. You start showing Savannah too much attention, Raven will break that love connection up in a hurry. Besides, that's one of the best ways to get a girl to fall in love with you. Have the dog do all the work for you. If I remember right, that's the way it happened between your mother and I."

"Aww, Redwing," Gwen said, remembering Henry's Irish Setter from when they were dating. "I really miss that dog. Redwing was perfect."

"We've already had dinner. It's not like we haven't been out on a date yet or haven't even met."

"Touchy, touchy. You were right, babe. He is hooked."

Gwen and Henry laughed, then Henry said, "Just giving you a hard time about it, son. Do what you want, but I'm sure Raven would love a day at the lake."

Tyler looked into Raven's eyes and asked, "Hey, girl, you wanna go for a ride?"

Raven's ears shot up and she cocked her head sideways as though asking, "Could you repeat that please? I thought I heard you say, 'go for a ride.' Did you say 'ride?' I thought you said 'ride.'

Tyler repeated it as if he understood her confusion. "That's right, girl. You wanna go for a ride to the lake?"

Raven barked twice, padded over to the front door, and barked twice more. She looked around as though impatient.

Tyler looked over at his dad and mom with a look that said *she's spoiled rotten*. "I guess that answers that question. I don't know if I'm taming her or she's taming me."

"I believe she's taming you," Henry said. "Have fun today and be careful."

"I'm always careful, you know me."

Even though it was early August, the summer seemed like it had swelled hotter than ever. It had possessed the city and lay over it in a dry heat.

At the end of the driveway, Tyler took a deep breath and slid on his pair of sunglasses.

"Today is the first day of the rest of your life," he said aloud. He cocked his head in Raven's direction. "You ready to live the rest of yours?"

Raven answered by sticking her head over the seat and giving three ear-splitting barks into Tyler's ear.

"Okay, okay. I guess you are. I'm going, I'm going."

Raven leaned over the seat and licked Tyler's ear as though in apology.

As he pulled into the neighborhood street, he added in the voice of a carnival ride announcer, "While the ride is in motion, we would ask the passengers to keep their arms, legs, head, tail, and tongue inside the vehicle at all times."

Tyler stuck in a CD—*Skillet*—into the player and exceeded the speed limit as he accelerated through the neighborhood. The tunes blasted through the speakers as he hung a right onto Highcourt Drive, completely avoiding the stop sign. He whizzed by house after house as he cut across the town to Savannah's house.

The miles of blacktop meandered through the lush acres the houses were built upon. Immense hickory and oak trees flourished through the yards, their limbs fanning out over the properties and shading each home from the late summer sun. The sun filtered through the clusters of leaves in the trees, creating strobes of bright sunbursts across his vision. Many of the homes had colonnaded porches and shutters on either side of the symmetrical windows. Most of the neighboring houses had huge fresh cut lawns of rich green grass and trimmed hedges. To enhance the looks of each property, most houses had a sun deck for summertime community cookouts. It was a perfect suburb, the kind of neighborhood where everybody trusted everybody.

&

When Tyler pulled up in front of Savannah's house, she was sitting in the front porch swing—as promised—with a set of ear buds in her ears. Her eyes were closed while she listened to the music coming from something in her lap—most likely her I-pod or phone.

Tyler noticed that she didn't move when he pulled in front of the house. Her eyes were lulled shut from the harmony that filtered through her headphones. Not wanting to alert her by a slammed car door, he slid from the car and softly shut it behind him then jogged to the side of the front porch that was facing away from her.

Her long slender legs flexed as she gently rocked back and forth to the rhythm of the music. She was dressed in a loose-fitting sleeveless half shirt, white shorts, and sandals. Savannah looked beautiful with her long, curly reddish-brown hair flipped over the back of the swing.

Tyler crept upon the porch and cautiously stepped toward the swing. When she pushed back, Tyler quickly wrapped his arms around her and tried to kiss her on the cheek at the same time.

Savannah jumped in alarm and instead of either one of them receiving a good morning kiss—as Tyler had anticipated—their heads connected with a loud crack.

They both moved in opposite directions. Savannah threw his arms off her, jumped out of the swing and grabbed her head. He countered away from her to soothe the dull pain in his head. Her I-pod jerked free from her headphones when she bailed out of the swing. It hit the porch and bounced to the side, clattering to a stop near one of the porch columns. Realizing who it was, she yelled, "Damn it, Tyler! Don't do that. You scared me to death." She pulled her headphones from her ears and stuffed them into the pocket of her shorts.

"I scared you? I think it's the other way around. You scared the shit out of me. Damn, you've got a hard head," he said as he tried to rub the pain away. "I mean, I had to do something because I've been sitting in my car blowing the horn for the past twenty minutes."

She laughed and bent down to retrieve her I-pod. "Bet you've never been known to lie either, right?"

"I would never lie to you," he said sincerely. "But believe me, if I had known we would have cracked heads like that I would've chosen a different tactic to scare you with like, let's say," He thought for a second. "Maybe soaking you with the garden hose."

"Oh, that would've been a big mistake," she said laughing. "I would've really had to kick your ass then."

He walked toward her sliding his arms around her tanned waist and said, "I'm still sorry."

"Forgiven." She wrapped her arms around his neck. "Maybe you learned your lesson. Hopefully, you won't try that again." She pulled his head closer to hers and kissed him. "Is that what you were trying to go for?"

"Yes, as a matter of fact it was. May I have another please?" They kissed again, even deeper this time. "And if I receive a kiss like that every time I try to scare you, I'm going to be doing that more often."

"Oh, you are, are you?"

"You can count on it. By the way, may I add that you look amazing today," he said, stepping back to view her completely.

In reply, she simply said, "Thank you. Someone just got brownie points."

He slung her backpack over his shoulder and guided her toward the steps.

"Is this all you're carrying?"

"It's got all I need. Clothes, some towels, a little make-up, and some music."

"You ready?"

"You know it."

"Then we're off."

As they neared the car, Raven anxiously stood and wagged her tail as if to say, "Pet me, pet me. I won't bite you. See my nice shiny black coat? You can touch it, I don't mind."

"Oh, wow. You didn't tell me you had a dog. What's his name?"

"*Her* name is Raven," Tyler corrected.

He opened the door for Savannah, dropped her bag in the floorboard, and closed the door behind her. Savannah immediately started loving on Raven, and Raven tried to bestow her appreciation by licking her lavishly.

As he rounded the car, he added, "Hope you don't mind that I brought another girl with me. It's just that I didn't know how it was going to work out between us, so I'm covering all my bases."

Savannah smiled. "That's very clever, but I think it's working out fine between us." As an added thought, she said, "This is the only other type of girl that it's okay to see when I'm not around."

"Duly noted," Tyler said and cranked the car again.

He pulled away from the front of her house and cut onto the highway that led to the outskirts of the town toward Silver Ridge Lake. For all three of them, it was turning out to be one of the better days they each have had in a long time.

CHAPTER 4

AFTER STOPPING FOR drinks at a nearby gas station, Tyler and Savannah soon turned into the lake's parking area that was already packed with cars. Some of the early arrivals were still hanging out in the parking lot listening to music, smoking, drinking, and waiting for everyone else to arrive. Tyler quickly pulled into a parking space. They hopped out and grabbed their duffle bags. Raven scrambled out and immediately began sniffing the other cars and people who were standing around. They stepped to the back of the Mustang just as a muddy, dented Jeep weaved around a few teens, rumbled in beside them, and rocked to a stop.

Savannah shouted over the blaring music, "Where the hell did you get your driver's license, Jay? It sure as hell wasn't from the highway department!"

"Hey, everyone around here knows how I drive, girl!" Jay shouted back as he killed the engine.

Jay, Cass, and Derrick jumped out of the doorless Jeep and grabbed their backpacks.

Jay Becknell, the tallest of the three, had a husky frame for a body, short black hair, long sideburns, and a goatee that ended in a point. He was wearing an old Troy Aikeman football jersey, dark blue shorts, and tennis shoes with no socks. He took one last drag on his cigarette and flipped it over into the gravel.

"Someday you're going to wind up killing someone drinking and driving like the psycho you are."

"They should know to get the hell out of the way when I'm coming through. Besides, I haven't been drinking," He paused for effect and then added, "Yet. Key word. Ha."

Savannah introduced Tyler to Jay and pleasantries were exchanged.

Cass grabbed a cooler out of the back of the Jeep. He placed the cooler—filled more with beers than with soft drinks—on the ground and flipped the lid. He grabbed a Mountain Dew from within, popped the top, and closed it again. He sat on the lid and flipped a towel over his head. Because of his size, he looked like Yoda from Star Wars but with light, tanned skin instead of green.

Raven walked over to Cass and nudged his arm. Cass, like all the other people when confronted with Raven's bright eyes and excited personality, consented to pet him.

Derrick leaned back against the Jeep. He lit the cigarette hanging from his lips. He wore a towel around his neck, dark yellow shorts, socks, and tennis shoes.

Raven was torn between Cass, Derrick, and the Jeep, excited about all this new territory to explore. Derrick just looked down at Raven as he puffed on his cigarette. Raven didn't waste time on Derrick's lack of attention and started inspecting the Jeep again.

"Want a beer?" Jay asked, pitching Tyler one out of a smaller personal cooler.

Tyler caught it and pitched it back. "Can't do it, man. I'm getting ready for the football tryouts. Gotta be at my best."

"Come on man, one beer won't hurt you."

"Maybe later."

"Okay. I'm going to hold you to that."

Tyler, Savannah and Jay followed Derrick and Cass as they carried the bigger cooler down the path toward the lake.

"Cass and Derrick told me you're trying out for the team. We had some good games last year, but didn't walk away with a championship."

"Let's see what we can do to change that for this year," Tyler said.

"That sounds like a plan. I can just taste that championship."

Raven had run ahead of them and was inspecting a picnic table when they came into the spacious clearing.

Jay said, "I talked to Jim, a friend of mine, last night and he said he would be down here with his Jet Skis later today. Man, I can't wait to wind it out across the water."

"You sure it's going to still float after you get on it?" He jumped in front of him and fake punched him in his beefy stomach then turned and ran toward the lake.

"Hey, I'm not fat," Jay said. "This is tempered-steel, baby!" He slapped his stomach then charged down the path after Tyler.

Tyler ran by a boy and a girl who were sitting on a beach towel. He snatched up the football near the boy's feet. "You mind if I borrow this for a minute?" he asked but didn't wait for a reply. "I swear I'll give it right back."

"Um, yeah. Sure, no sweat," the boy answered.

Ignoring the boy's comment, Tyler had already turned around right as Jay reached him.

Tyler pretended the football had just been hiked and he did a faked hand-off to Jay. "Go deep. That is, if you're up to it."

"Hell yes, I'm up for it," Jay said but was already off and running.

Jay was a big guy but he was also built for speed. Immediately switching to football mode, he charged toward the lake. He vaulted over a few picnickers and maneuvered around a few students who were just milling about.

Jay took Tyler at his word and really went deep. He was already running down the pier yelling for teens to get out of his way. A few teens jumped back and toppled over the pier railing.

Tyler made a careful judgment of where Jay was headed and the distance he was covering. He took a few steps forward and hurled the football in a perfect arching spiral.

Jay turned to find the ball just out of reach but close enough to catch. It was going to be close. At the last possible moment, Jay dove over the bannister and snatched the ball in his fingertips and pulled it in to his Troy Aikman numbers just as he splashed down in the lake.

Everyone who was watching the scene lost it. Cheers went up as if it were a real Hail-Mary pass in a real football game and the Sidewinders just scored the winning touchdown pass.

Tyler jogged back over to Savannah.

"That was pretty damn awesome," she said and grabbed the back of his head and pulled him to her. She kissed him deeply.

"What was that for?"

"Maybe it was because you just won the game with that long-bomb you just threw, or maybe I just felt like doing it."

"No complaint from me. Feel free to do that anytime."

"Holy shit, man," Jay said, jogging back to them. His comment broke up their moment. "What the hell do you have in that arm? You on steroids or something?" Jay was still surprised at how hard Tyler had thrown the ball.

"Yes. Yes I am," Tyler lied.

"Can you do that again?"

"I've been known to duplicate it a time or two."

"I know for a fact that the coach could use you on the team this year."

"That's what I'm hoping for," Tyler assured him.

"Oh shit, I can't wait till the season starts. We are going to kick some major ass this year."

They walked to where Amber Lewis, Iris Jackson, and Erica Weaver were already sunning themselves; their firm bodies were already glistening with light sweat and suntan oil. They had picked a spot close to a backdrop of huge boulders. Introductions were made again as Savannah and Tyler spread their towels out and sat down to take advantage of the sun's rays.

"Yo, Tyler! Savannah!" Cass yelled. "We're starting a volleyball game! Get your asses over here."

"Not right now! We'll be over there later!" she yelled. She was already rubbing suntan lotion on her partially exposed chest. "I know you want to go. So go."

"I'd rather stay here and watch you."

When Savannah saw what he was looking at, she playfully slapped his arm. "Get out of here."

Tyler laughed but remained seated beside her.

"Seriously, you don't have to stay here with me and keep me company. All I'm going to be doing is soaking up some sun. I'll be here when you get back."

"Promise."

"On my word of honor; besides you're driving. Can't go anywhere without you."

"Okay. I'll take your word for it," he said, as he pulled off his T-shirt.

The charm Tyler had found but had forgotten about thumped against his chest. Tyler leaned over and kissed Savannah on the cheek. As he did so the charm landed on the right side of her upper chest. It was cool on her skin and startled her when it touched her.

"Oh wow, that's nice," she said, as she sat up and grabbed the medallion. "Where did that come from?"

"Huh, I'd forgotten about that. You like it?"

"It's beautiful."

"Believe it or not, I found it in my attic this morning."

"Really? Very nice."

"It's okay I guess," Tyler said.

"I like it."

"See you soon."

"You promise," she asked.

"On my word of honor," he said repeating her line she'd used on him.

As she watched him run across the grass, she noticed the muscles in his back, shoulders, and calves. Tyler had great definition in his toned muscles.

Savannah had liked Tyler from the moment she had noticed him in English class and was drawn to him. She didn't think it was love at first sight, but a spark of interest had been ignited and was steadily growing. Tyler was different from the other boys she had dated in high school. He had a great sense of humor, personality, and seemed to fit right in and get along with everybody else. She considered herself lucky to have met him and felt equally fortunate that he liked and wanted her as well.

Savannah leaned back on her elbows to view the area. Silver Ridge Lake was humming with a great deal of lake activity.

Jim, who had arrived earlier than anticipated, was already skimming across the water on his Jet Ski at high velocities. Trey Dobbins was in another one right behind Jim. Trey timed hitting the wakes from Jim's Jet Ski and became airborne. Each time he hit another wave, he tried for a higher jump or a farther distance. Trey even worked in a flip or two as he showed off for all the onlookers.

A few couples were throwing a Frisbee. Another group of teens were tossing a football. Teams had been already been divided and the volleyball was already being pounded back and forth over the net. Most of the females were just relaxing and lying out. Music from numerous stereo systems mingled together in the humid August air.

The famous tire swing everybody enjoyed was in nonstop motion. It had been hung from a huge Ash tree that grew close to the water's edge. There was a height of about twelve to fourteen feet on the up-swing of the arc. The depth of the water was about the same as the swing's height. Teen after teen took turns flipping off once they were out over the water. Each person tried to outdo the maneuvers of the person before; each flip becoming more and more charismatic. Some succeeded in doing so, but others only resulted in plunging awkwardly into the lake.

One kid everyone had been watching belly flopped into the lake with a loud smack.

"Oh snap, I can't believe he tried that!" one boy exclaimed, as he threw a hand to his mouth.

Everyone burst into laughter as the kid came up choking on lake water and clutching his chest.

"Damn, that's going to leave a mark," the boy continued. "Son of a bitch is going to feel that in the morning."

Raven was getting plenty of attention and ran from student to student for any kind of affection. She sniffed and investigated everything from teens to towels and from bottles of suntan oil to empty drink cans.

Someone made the mistake of throwing a tennis ball they had with them. It was an even worse mistake when they threw it into the lake. Raven obediently charged after it and immediately brought it back in hopes it would be thrown again. When one person stopped throwing the ball, Raven would approach someone else. Everyone accepted Raven and took turns playing with her.

After numerous volleyball games, Tyler and Savannah took to the high seas on one of the Jet Skis. They had been on the Jet Ski for what seemed like an hour and had just come back in as the sun was beginning to set.

Time really does fly when you're having this much fun, Savannah thought as they arrived back at the docks.

There were still some time left in the day, but daylight was quickly fading. Part of the dimming effect was caused by storm clouds beginning to crawl down from the higher peaks in the North that crept slowly across the dimming sky. The wind blew chilly breaths of air off the water's cooling surface.

The air had grown cold quicker than expected and some classmates were now wrapped up in towels or blankets they had brought with them. Tyler and Savannah found their friends huddled around a roaring bonfire talking, eating, and drinking beer. Gray-white smoke sifted up through the burning wood and thinned out in the air.

Jay was scratching behind Raven's ears. Iris and Erica were roasting hot dogs on the end of bent coat hangers; Amber had opted for marshmallows. Derrick was standing outside the circle drinking a beer. Cass was eating chips and drinking a Vanilla Coke.

Savannah joined the girls while Tyler strolled over to Jay and Raven.

"That's an awesome dog you have there," Jay said as Tyler approached. "I wish I had a dog that was this obedient. You sure have trained her well."

"Thanks, man. It's hard work but well worth it. She's been a good dog to train. You just have to invest the time with them. It's time I wouldn't trade for anything."

Raven panted heavily and smiled broadly as though she knew they were talking about her. She looked at the Frisbee lying at Jay's feet then back at them as if to say, "Ah come on, please. Just one more throw."

"You want to fetch it again, girl?" Tyler asked.

Raven actually nodded, she licked her chops in anticipation and whined.

Tyler gave the Frisbee to Jay and said, "Go ahead but this time throw it toward the water."

"Why?"

"You'll see."

"Okay, you asked for it," Jay said. He hurled the disk as hard as he could.

The disk sailed far and spun out over the water. Raven was no more than a few feet behind it but gained on it quickly. As she reached the water she bounded out over the surface. She actually looked like she was running on the water's surface. At the last second before gravity took her under, Raven snagged the frisbee out of thin air as Jay had done catching the football.

Cheers from various onlookers went up again as they applauded Raven's awesomeness.

Breaking the surface, she turned and headed back to the shore. Upon bringing it back to Jay, Raven trotted through the campfire group and stopped long enough to shake off the excess of water. The campfire sizzled, everyone groaned and leaned their bodies and faces away to avoid the incoming splatter of water.

"Ahhh, Raven!" Amber shouted. "Stop it. That's gross."

"Get her the hell away from me," Erica chimed in.

"Of all the places you could've shaken your mangy ass," Derrick crooned. "You had to do it right here?"

Tyler turned to Jay and said, "That's why."

They high-fived and everyone laughed. The damage was done.

Raven trotted over and dropped the Frisbee in front of Jay again. She looked up at him and smiled as she panted.

As Jay stooped, he said, "You did that on purpose didn't you, girl?"

Raven barked twice and shook herself again.

"That's her way of saying yes."

"You should have her come try out on Monday. She would definitely make the team."

Eventually everyone settled down around the fire. They had done everything that was possible to do at the lake and were exhausted from the day's events. Relaxation was the only thing anyone wanted to do now.

Tyler and Savannah sat in front of a log sharing a blanket to knock off the growing chill. Cass sat on a cooler behind Amber giving her a friendly back massage to relieve her tension from the nothing she had done that day. Derrick was still standing on the outskirts of the campfire.

Iris and Erica had finished eating their food and were leaning against another log. Iris pulled a cigarette from her pack and lit up while Jay needled the fire with a stick. Everyone was chit-chatting about what went on that day when Jay raised the major question for the night.

"Anyone up for a good ghost story?" He asked in a spooky theatrical tone. His deep set eyes and pointy goatee, combined with the dancing reflections of the firelight gave him the eerie semblance of a troll contemplating his next evil deed.

"No, I really don't want to be scared tonight," Amber whined.

"Yeah, me too," Iris chimed in. "I'll have bad dreams."

Everyone looked at them with disbelieving faces.

Iris continued, "No, I'm serious, you guys. It's happened before. That's the reason I don't watch horror movies."

"What? I can't believe you," Cass said chuckling. "You're missing half of your life. Horror movies are the best."

"Come on ladies, humor me," Jay pleaded.

"Come here, babe. I'll protect you." Derrick said as he slid in beside Iris. He threw his arm around her. "You can grab onto me when you get scared. Feel free to grab me anywhere you want."

Iris playfully slapped him before she leaned back and placed her head in the crook of his arm.

"Pervert," Amber said.

"Yes ma'am, I am. Guilty as charged," Derrick replied, widening his eyes and smiling with a goofy smile.

Bringing them back to the question at hand, Cass said, "That story is going to be bullshit. It's all going to be made up. He's done it before and he'll do it again."

"Cass, would it be possible, for once, for you to shut the fuck up? Please."

Cass held his hands up in a surrendering pose. "Alright. Sorry, Jay. Don't get your panties all in a bunch. The floor is yours, big guy."

"Why don't we let Tyler decide?" Erica asked. She was looking at Tyler and smiled, then winked.

Savannah didn't say anything and pretended not to notice. *I can't believe Erica is flirting with Tyler right in front of me. Doesn't she know we are kind of seeing each other? Thought she was my friend. Talk about your sluts.*

Tyler grinned then looked away into the growing twilight.

The surface of the lake looked solid, like a flat plane of blackened steel, dark as abandoned coal mine tunnels. Menacing.

Tendrils of storm clouds were still stretching toward Silver Ridge. The approaching clouds looked swollen and ready to burst. In the far distance some clouds had been ripped open and slanted sheets of rain were already blanketing the peaks. The wind had kicked up a couple of notches but wasn't unbearable. It was cool and refreshing but ominous.

Tyler said, "It looks like the perfect weather for the telling of a ghost story."

Tyler had felt Savannah stiffen at Erica's slight advance. *Wish there was a way I could convey she has nothing to worry about.*

At this particular time, they weren't holding hands. Tyler didn't know why that was the case. It could be that they had just started seeing each other and she didn't want to be shoving their "relationship"—if he could be so bold—in everybody's face. Everyone might think they were moving too fast. Whatever the case may be, Tyler slid his hand from his lap onto her knee. He patted the inside of her knee twice then gave it a gentle, reassuring squeeze.

"Tyler hasn't heard any of the stories from around here," Amber added, not knowing what had just happened.

"How about it, Tyler-boy? What's it going to be?" Jay asked. "Yeah or nay?"

He looked at Iris and Erica and said, "Sorry ladies, but I'm always in the mood for a good ghost story whether it's made up or not. Please forgive me, but I'm going to have to give Jay the green light on this one."

Being in tune only with Tyler's non-spoken comment, Savannah slid her hand on top of his and squeezed tight. She held on to him like that for a long time.

Out of the corner of his eye, Tyler could see that Savannah was smiling and knew the message he had sent through touch had been received. It made him start smiling as well.

How awesome is it to sit beside someone else and know exactly what they were thinking. To my knowledge, this is the first time that this has happened to me.

"I hope you brought your waders," Cass said, as he slid his hands down to work on Amber's lower back. "Because it's going to be a incredible line of bullshit that he'll be shoveling."

Jay opened the ice chest and racked through the ice until he found two beers. He tossed one over in Tyler's direction. Tyler's snagged the beer from out of the air.

"Sorry, man," Jay said. "I should've warned you I was passing it to you."

"No problem," Tyler said. "If it's in my aura, I'll catch it."

"That's the beer I saved for you from earlier."

Tyler popped its top and then raised it toward Jay and said, "To new friends, great times, and to future championships. Cheers."

Jay nodded back, "Hell yeah! I'll drink to that."

"Are you going to tell the ghost tale or not?" Amber asked.

"Patience, my dear. For me to scare you, it happens best when you don't know it's coming."

Jay took a long chug on his beer then began his story. His voice had dropped an octave lower. It was hollow, guttural, and very soothing.

"Years ago before Silver Ridge became the city it is today, the town of Juniper Grove barely existed."

He looked around the campfire at the vacant faces slowly became concerned. They stared back in anticipation.

"Juniper Grove used to be sitting right out there where Silver Ridge Lake is today. At one point in time, most of the people that were living here moved away to other towns and outlying cities, leaving Juniper Grove to waste away into nothing. A ghost town, if you will. But there were a few hard-headed families that stayed because they had lived here their whole life and their family roots had grown too deep to take any chance of living elsewhere. No matter what their reason, they were all killed just the same."

Eyebrows were raised in interest and a few gasps of surprise escaped open mouths as the group became more intrigued.

Cass saw the looks on everyone's faces and shook his head in disgust.

He mimicked Jay's tall tale voice as he walked his fingers up Amber's back as though they were two giant five-legged spiders. "No matter what the reason, they were all killed just the same." He ended the sentence by enclosing his fingers around Amber's neck in a light choke hold. He shook her as though he were a psychopathic killer strangling the life out of an unsuspecting victim. Amber played along to a certain extent by rolling her eyes in the back of her head and sticking her tongue out in a grimace of fake pain. Then she turned and punched him hard in the thigh for creeping her out as she said, "Shut up Cass, I'm trying to listen."

"Ohhh damn, girl. Ease up. Jeez." To Jay he said, "When did you write this bullshit script? Last night? Sounds like a story out of a real bad B movie."

Jay gave one harsh look at Cass and in his regular voice said, "One more outburst from you and I will clear this court room." He turned toward the others and whispered, "I've always wanted to say that."

Cass gave him a "who, me" look and continued massaging Amber's back.

"Yes you, ya dumb mook. If I hear your voice again, I'll wipe the lakeside with your ass."

Jay paused making sure he had their attention again giving their brains time to come back to the story at hand then dropped his voice for effect and continued. "Now I know what you are thinking. You're thinking that one of the loners that didn't move away, went insane, ended up slaying everyone in his own sick way, and then disappeared into the dusk, never to be seen or heard of again. Right?" he hesitated, chuckling to himself.

He was enjoying this storytelling time. He had most of the teens looking over their shoulders into the forest behind them or out at the water.

"Well, you're all wrong. This is the real story. A few months after most of the people left, there was one old woman that most of the people had seen a few times in their lives. Her name was Sarah Gilgould. Now Sarah was known as one of the crazy folks. She was loco en la cabeza, man. She thought she was a witch and maybe she was, I don't know for sure, but she had this crazy notion that Armageddon was approaching.

She warned the people that the end of the world was coming, that the wrath of God was upon the town, and pleaded with the people to pack up and leave. Well of course, the townsfolk thought she was a raving lunatic. They didn't leave when the others left. Why should they leave at this particular time? Right?" Jay asked, getting them more engrossed in the story.

The teens all nodded simultaneously.

"Needless to say, they all died that night. I heard the town of Juniper Grove was totally destroyed by an asteroid or some damn thing like that."

There were signs of obvious disbelief from their facial reactions.

"A fuckin' asteroid?" Derrick mused. "You've got to be shitting me."

"Told you," Cass said.

The others agreed.

"Should've stuck with the psycopathic killer, man," Tyler said then added. "You would've had us with that angle of the story for sure."

"Seriously, that's the way the story goes," Jay retorted, trying to win back their belief and attention. "There was no sign of survivors, just bits and pieces of the town scattered over a five mile radius and you know what?" he continued not giving them time to disapprove. "We are sitting close to where that meteor hit. That lake behind you," he paused, as the listeners turned around. "That lake is the crater that the meteor made when it impacted and destroyed what was left of Juniper Grove."

"Really?" Iris asked. She had been looking out at the lake but turned to face Jay again.

"Oh hell yeah," Jay replied nodding.

"Don't believe him. He's yanking your chain," Cass said, leaning back against a log.

"Can *I* tell this story please?" Jay asked, obviously perturbed. "Can you please stop interrupting me?"

"Sorry, bitch! I forgot! I outbursted again! My bad. Go ahead and tell your retarded story, but you know what?" Cass asked.

"What?"

In the accent of an old wise Chinese man, Cass relaying his words of wisdom, "De more you stir shit de worse it stink."

"Ignore him please," Jay commanded to the others disregarding

Cass's comment. "Look out at the lake. Have you noticed how round it seems to be? Granted, there are some inlets, coves, and outcroppings, but you can see that it is mainly—for the most part—circular in shape."

"But how did it become a lake? I mean, where did the water come from?" Iris asked, as she inhaled the last bit of nicotine then flipped her cigarette into the fire.

"You know Harper River that's on the west side of town? It feeds Silver Ridge Lake. See, when the meteor hit, the crater ended up close to the river; over time the river and the crater merged. The water flowed into the crater, which created what we now know is Silver Ridge Lake."

"All right, when does the ghost story come into the picture?" Erica asked impatiently. "I'm tired of hearing a made up story about the history of this city,"

"Yeah!" Amber said emphatically. "If you're going to scare us then scare us. Get it over with."

In a deep, throaty voice that portrayed a horror storyteller, Jay said, "Patience my dear. Daddy will scare. Daddy will please. I had to give Tyler here a brief synopsis of how this city came to be what it is today." He put his fist to his mouth and cleared his throat then adjusted himself on the rough log he was sitting on and said. "Now, you've heard the story about Wisherman's Abyss, haven't you?" Jay asked everybody. "You know the deepest part of Silver Ridge Lake?"

Body language varying from shakes, nods, and shrugs was offered.

"At the center of the crater there is another impression. Don't ask me how it got there because I don't know, but legend says that if you make a wish by throwing a coin or a personal item you treasure into the lake and if it sifts down through the currents and lands inside that Wisherman's Abyss, then supposedly your wish will come true." Meandering off the main story onto a tangent, Jay continued, "I remember three summers ago, Aaron Roslow and I went snorkeling to try to scavenge Wisherman's Abyss for peoples wishing items but we didn't get anything out there because the undercurrents were too great and we weren't going to chance swimming all the way to the bottom."

"I don't blame you," Tyler said, sitting forward beginning to hang on every word that Jay was saying. "Did you have snorkeling or diving gear?

"Just snorkeling gear. If we had've had diving gear we could've done some real damage. Who knows what kind of shit is down there. Depending on how seriously people take it, you could come up with a lot of loot. Who knows."

Tyler asked, "And that's right out in the middle of the lake?"

"Yeah. We couldn't hold our breath that long. It's pretty damn deep out there, but that was three summers ago. I haven't tried to do anything like that in a long time. I would be surprised if I could hold my breath a good thirty seconds."

"You might think about going on a diet," Cass teased.

Jay ignored Cass and guzzled the last half of his beer then continued, "Anyway, the last part of this story." He looked in Tyler's direction. "The main part these hoodlums have been hounding me about. It's the story my parents have said they experienced first hand when they were in school years ago. See, there was a boy that was always treated badly, you know, the one who always received the blunt end of the deal; the one who was always the center of everyone's aggression. His name was uh," Jay scratched his head and tried to remember. "Eddie McDoggal, Edwin Davidson or something like that, I can't remember."

"Edward McDaniel." Savannah corrected.

"Yeah, him. A lot of the kids picked on him and called him names, shit like that. There were some bullies in the school that took it a little too far and they played a practical joke that turned into a tragedy." He hitched his thumb toward the lake behind him. "Out there at the deepest part is where Edward drowned." He nodded his head slowly for emphasis for the unbelievers. Jay stared blankly into the fire. "Whether it was accidentally or on purpose nobody knows. The small rescue team they had back then dragged the lake for his body and found him after a grueling three to four hour search. The story goes that his grandmother lost it when she heard the news; had a nervous breakdown or some damn thing like that. His grandfather had already past away. She stayed boarded up in that dilapidated old house on the south side of the lake and was never heard from again." He broke his unwavering gaze and started making eye contact while he told the rest of the tale. "Some people have said that she buried Edward's body somewhere around the lake in an unmarked grave. Others have said that his body was cremated and his grandmother scattered his ashes out over the lake. Some people have even said that the old women wrapped him in some old, thick burlap and weighted his body down with stones and actually buried him in the lake where he drowned. They say she was hoping he would land in Wisherman's Abyss and that her prayers and wishes would bring him back to her. Some say that it actually happened because some of those people fishing the lake late at night claimed to have seen him—or his ghost—standing by the banks. Just standing there staring out over the water. There has been some claiming that they have even seen his spirit walking across the surface of the water."

Breaking the eerie mood of the story, Iris asked, "Who is this Edward guy, God or something?"

"Shhh! Don't disrespect Edward's ghost. What's the matter with you, Iris? Don't you see, his spirit still walks the shores of Silver Ridge Lake even today and could be anywhere right now, listening to you?" He dropped his voice and continued in a soft whisper. "You'd better be careful what you say about Edward McDaniel. They say he's still holding grudges even today. The storytellers say that someday he's going to pay back all the individuals that made his life a living hell while he was here on earth and there is no telling what Edward will do to you if he gets hold of you."

He paused long enough to pick up a stick from the fire and adjusted the logs so they would burn better. Crackles and pops escaped the intense heat and red hot cinders spiraled like fireflies into the stormy night sky. Jay stared around the bonfire at the illuminated faces. Some of their mouths hung open in awe from the freaky story they obviously had missed as a child.

"Now listen up, everybody. The last thing I've got to say about this is that if you ever find yourself down here late at night for any reason, whether it be walking or fishing on the shores and you sense someone watching you, or you're even unlucky enough to feel a strong presence behind you, like a cold breath at the base of your neck, don't ever turn to confront it. Just RRRRRUUUUUNNNNN!"

Jay yelled the last word of the sentence with all his might. He stood and lunged toward all his friends with outstretched arms. The word stabbed through the cool night air and echoed across the lake. Startled birds in the nearby trees squawked into the night.

For a split second everyone thought he was a fiery demon hurling itself out of the fire at them. The whole group dispersed in opposite directions as though the ground was electrically charged and had shocked them into motion.

"Shit and two is eight!" Derrick yelled as he shoved Iris away from him and dove behind the log he was leaning against.

Iris couldn't get any words out but she had the loudest scream of the group. She didn't jump or dive out of the way as Derrick did; she ran. Erica did likewise.

"Fuck me!" Amber shouted. She tried to escape through a combined pin-wheeling of her arms and a backward crab-walk. She bumped into Cass and almost took him down also.

"Christ Almighty!" Cass exclaimed. He tried to hurdle the log that he and Amber were leaning against but tripped backward over it and slammed in to the cooler that was sitting right behind it. The cooler tipped over and the lid popped loose; watered down ice and drinks spilled all over the ground.

Savannah screamed and Tyler yelled but they couldn't get away fast enough. They were wrapped in a blanket and couldn't go anywhere but under it. They jumped at the same time and pulled the blanket over their heads to hide from the hulking monstrosity that came at them.

Startled by the whole ordeal, Raven jumped back and started barking then ran around to different sides of the bonfire. She continued to bark at the confusion of the situation.

"You suck!" Iris yelled from the banks of the lake. She hadn't stop running until she had reached the water's edge.

Derrick popped his head up from behind the log to see if the coast was clear. "Oh, you *bastard!*" he said, as he stood and dusted the sand off his body.

"I knew it!" Tyler said sticking his head out of the blanket again. "I knew you were going to do that. I just didn't know when."

"What are you doing yelling like that for, man?" Derrick asked, already hugging Iris to his chest. "Are you trying to give us heart failure?"

Jay tried to contain his laughter but it soon became too much to bear. His laugh was infectious and contagious and soon everyone was laughing uncontrollably.

"Hey, you wanted a ghost story. I gave you a ghost story." Jay said. "It worked, didn't it? You were scared, weren't you?"

"No. We all have this disease where we always jump simultaneously like that for no fucking reason whatsoever," Amber said in a flat, sarcastic tone.

"Dude, that was righteous," Cass applauded as they exchanged their special handshake of bumping knuckles and slapping palms. "It doesn't matter how much I tell them that it's going to be a bullshit story, you can always change their opinion. You just suck them in and then spit them out." Cass turned and pointed accusingly at the group. "I told you guys not to believe him but you wouldn't listen."

"You mean to tell me that you were in on it the whole time?" Amber asked.

"From the very beginning," Cass answered.

"I could kill you for pulling a stunt like that," Iris said. She breathed deeply; her nerves were still obviously shaken, and much worse than the others.

"You should have seen the look on your faces. You all are just a bunch of gullible pansie-asses," Jay said. "I'm sorry but I just couldn't help it."

"Dammit, Jay," Amber said. "I think I peed my pants a little."

A round of laughter encircled the fire again at Amber's expense.

When the laughter died, the nerves were settled and heart rates were slowed once again, Tyler asked. "Is any of that story really true?"

"Shit, man, I don't know. The only part that I know is true is the part about the Edward boy. According to my dad, he did get drowned as a teenager but they don't know what happened to his body. All that other shit, I just made it up as I went along.

മ

The thunderheads soon became too threatening to stay any longer at the lake. As the group met back at their cars, God's bowling ball of thunder rumbled across the sky's alleyway and crashed into a set of electrified pins on the opposite side of the darkened heavens. Upon impact, jagged streaks of lightning cascaded out of the blackness and jolted the earth in the distance.

God must've gotten a strike on that one, Tyler thought as he put their belongings in the back floorboard of his car.

There was a smaller settling rumble as though another set of pins were being set, then the rumbling subsided.

The group said their goodbyes then quickly dispersed. Who knew how long it would be before the rain hit, but it felt like it was coming sooner rather than later.

Raven was already in the back seat in the process of falling asleep. She was the only one who truly had a workout.

As they pulled out of the parking lot, Savannah turned to Tyler and asked, "Do you like Erica?"

Caught off guard by her question, he paused long enough to give her a truthful answer, "Not as much as I like you."

As soon as he answered her he knew it sounded dumb but couldn't help picturing himself with his fists raised over his head in a victory pose yelling, *Brownie points for me. Oh yeah, nothing but big brownie points for me. Nothing like the perfect answer to win the prom queen's heart.* It was a spur of the moment thought but it made him smile.

Continuing, he said, "I'm sorry, that was really bad. I know that sounds coy but it's the truth. Why do you ask?

He couldn't tell if she liked or disliked the answer or not.

"Well, she seemed really interested in you today; at least she did when we were around the campfire."

"I was so caught up in paying attention to you that I didn't even notice."

Okay Tyler, that's two, he thought. *One more dumbass comment like that from you and I will throw you out of this car myself.*

"That's sweet, Casanova," Savannah said, thinking he made the statement as a way to avoid this conversation all together.

"No, I'm serious. I didn't even notice her," Tyler said, glancing in her direction. "All right, yeah, I like her, but not in the sense you're talking about. I like all your friends. They're a great group of guys and gals." Tyler added, "You're smiling again. What did I do now?"

"Nothing. You're just really cute."

Slightly relieved, he said, "You really side swiped me with that question."

"Got to keep you on your toes. Sorry. I was just curious, that's all."

"Just for argument's sake, even though we're not having an argument, say I was interested in her. What then?"

"I don't want you to think I'm jealous or anything like that. I was just wondering. I don't want you to think I'm crazy for saying this and I know it's going to sound worse than it is, but we don't owe each other anything, you know? You have a right to go out with whoever you want."

"I know. That's why I'm here with you."

That comment made Savannah smile but she continued. "If you did like Erica you wouldn't have to apologize for it. I would understand. You're new in this area and probably want to see what all Silver Ridge has to offer."

"You say that like I'm on the prowl to get into any and every girl's pants I come in contact with."

Realizing he knew what she meant, she went on, "You may not have wanted anything remotely resembling a relationship even with me this soon after you've moved here. I don't know. It's just that I don't want to smother you, but I would like to know what your intentions are, that's all."

Tyler grabbed her hand and kissed it.

"I know we've only known each other close to twenty four hours, but to tell you the truth. All I want is you." He told her this softly but emphatically. "You ever have certain moments in your life or even days that are emphasized above all others in your mind?"

"Yeah," she said giving him a hesitant nod. "I guess so." She thought she knew where he was going with this line of questioning.

"I call them perfect moments in time."

She agreed with him again.

"I don't know about you, but the past twenty four hours have been some of the most perfect moments of my life. They couldn't have been any better."

Savannah smiled and surrendered. "I get it." She wished she had never even brought the subject up but was happy her mind was eased. "That's the best compliment I have ever been given."

"Surely not."

"I'm afraid so."

They drove along in silence for a long time not knowing which way to go with the conversation. Neither one wanted to press the issue further and end up ruining the moment.

Not being able to control herself, Savannah leaned over and gave his arm a tight hug. She was careful not to impede his driving. She kissed him on the cheek and said, "Thank you for caring about me," then whispered, "I hope you know that the feeling is mutual."

When she whispered the words, her lips softly grazed his ear. The combination of the light caress and huskiness of her spoken words made his body explode in chills.

Tyler swung his arm around her and pulled her close. She nuzzled up into his neck and closed her eyes. They rode the rest of the way to her house in silence. They didn't need to speak. They were communicating through touch again, both realizing they each needed the other equally.

When they pulled into her driveway, Savannah reluctantly leaned back into her seat, disappointed to be home.

Tyler asked, "You believe any of the stories Jay told us tonight about that Edward character?"

"I've heard so many different versions over the years. I guess you could say I believe in some of it. But I'm sure the truth has been stretched way out of proportion over the years for dramatic effect. That's the way legends get started."

"As well as rumors."

Savannah opened her door, got out, and slammed the door behind her. Tyler did likewise. He grabbed her backpack, slid it over his shoulder, then met her on the other side of the car. He slid his arm around her waist and they moved toward the front porch.

Curiosity the cat, evidently not curious at this particular time, was nowhere to be seen.

"Rumors are the same thing as legends, just smaller tales," Savannah agreed. "I've heard Edward's story many times growing up, but there's still mystery in it."

"What's that?"

"Nobody knows what really happened to all the people involved. It's just an old ghost story. Why, what's wrong? Jay didn't scare you, did he?"

"Yes. Well, the ending of the story scared me. He weaves a spooky tale. He scared everyone, but the story intrigued me more. It's interesting."

"Really?"

"Yeah. Know what?"

"What's that?"

"I think I've just found the subject I'm going to write about for my English paper."

"You have got to be joking."

"No, really. Our teacher asked for creativity. He's going to get creativity. It would be interesting to find out exactly what happened to Edward."

"Good luck."

Taking on Jay's crazy theatrical voice, Tyler said, "I might even discover where his crazy ass grandmother buried his body."

"You mean you would dig up his remains if you found the location?"

"Oh, I don't know about that. Probably not, but ask me that question when and if I get that far in my research."

"Okay." She pointed a finger at him, "You better keep me informed. I would love to hear all the juicy details."

"Deal."

When they reached the top of the stairs, Savannah turned in front of him and slid her other arm around his body. Tyler, surprised at her actions, returned the favor.

"Something bothering you?" Tyler asked.

"No, I'm just happy and it's all your fault," she said with as much humor as she did seriousness.

"I'll take that as a compliment," Tyler assured her.

"You better or I'll hold a grudge," she commanded.

"Well, I wouldn't want to get on your bad side. Somehow I don't think I would like it."

"Just kidding. I'm not one to hold a grudge." Now it was her time to be theatrical and she dropped her voice into a deeper register. "Edward is the one you have to worry about."

"Ohh, don't start that again. One heart attack is enough for one night."

Their heads moved closer and their lips joined once again. The kiss was longer this time. It was filled with the same equal amount of trust and passion as the kiss given and received the night before. Their tongues gently caressed the other and their arms followed suit; both of them were caught up in the moment.

They soon said their good byes and Tyler, feeling light headed and ecstatic about another great day in Silver Ridge, was once again on his way home.

Other than the onslaught of a summer storm, it seemed that nothing could break the spell that his new life was under.

CHAPTER 5

BILLOWY STORM CLOUDS gathered in dark veils across the bruised sky like robed monks worshipping in a mysterious ceremony; ominous, foreboding, and threatening. Sheets of lightning lit up the dismal horizon in luminous pulses. Wind whipped through the nearby trees, stripping loose foliage from their branches and scattering them in flurries across the road. Thunder rumbled across the heavens as if it were an apocalyptic transport carrying the souls of the damned.

Tyler's mind was a million miles away from the oncoming storm. He was ecstatic about Savannah and felt he needed to vent his euphoria or he would simply explode with enthusiasm. He smiled as he remembered the way Savannah's amber hair was always pulled back over her right ear. He loved the way her eyes narrowed and the slight sneer of her mouth as it turned into a warm smile when he said something amusing. She had a great sense of humor herself and a perfect laugh to match—so infectious. Without paying attention to the rising speedometer, he was soon traveling well beyond the normal speed limit, lost in the thoughts of Savannah.

Negative thoughts also joined the others and tried to hamper his emotional high.

This is a too good to be true situation. How did you get so lucky? You'll never have a long lasting relationship with her; she's too good for you. It's only going to turn out a friendship in the end. She can't be that serious about you.

He pushed those thoughts aside and continued to dwell on the positive. Everything was going so well since he set foot in Silver Ridge.

Granted, he wasn't thrilled about the move at first, but now things were looking up and he was beginning to change his opinion about the matter.

Tyler passed individual fast food chains, main restaurants, and night clubs that were still open for business. Each sign standing in front of the establishments looked like beacons in the gloom, and each building looked like impervious shelters in the onslaught of the coming storm.

A cataclysmic boom, like the detonation of a doomsday weapon, rocked the twilight.

Raven, shaken from her sleep, sat up quickly in the back seat and looked frantically out at the oncoming tumult beyond the windows and whined.

"It's okay, girl. We're safe," Tyler said in a soothing voice. "It's just a little thunder. Loud, but it's just thunder. Nothing to be scared of."

Tyler's gentle voice wasn't enough to calm Raven's nerves and she continued to pace back and forth in the backseat and worriedly peered out each window.

Another thunderclap, sudden and unexpected, shook the first fat raindrops from the swollen clouds. The rain started to spickle-spackle on the windshield but then grew into a steady drumming, sounding like they were surrounded by raging steeds. It was a flash flood, instantaneous and precipitated.

Tyler turned on his windshield wipers as he swung off the main highway onto a two-lane road that lead to his neighborhood.

The silver gray downfall looked like strands of mercury in the glare of the headlights. Like native drum beats wafting across African plains, the steady rain pounded hollowly on the Mustang's roof.

The avenue rose slightly then sloped into a long straight-away. There was a small bridge at the end of the straight away before the road crested a small rise again in the distance. It was a lonely stretch of road that connected to other neighborhoods and into deepening shadows. Trees lined each side of the highway; their limbs connected overhead, creating small canopies.

"I don't need this teeny-bopper bullshit," Tyler muttered as he glanced down to switch the radio station. "I want something that rocks the house."

Tyler sped through water that was rushing from one side of the high shouldered road to shallow drainage banks on the other. The water crested in silvery wings on either side of the car. Tyler felt the car hydroplane slightly on the thick water. Even though the car lurched, it wasn't enough to make him let up on the gas. He was still caught up in the memory of the day's events.

A dark streak suddenly shot out in front of his car, just within the headlights' reach. It hunched down in Tyler's lane, either paralyzed by fear or blinded by the intense beams. It was a black cat. Its fur was slick and shiny as oil; dark as the night itself. Its back was arched and its eyes reflecting green, luminous contempt.

Raven saw the cat the same time as Tyler and started barking.

Whether it was by instinct or by shock, Tyler slammed on his brakes. The wheels locked and the car hydroplaned on the layer of water standing on the highway.

Realizing it had enough time to escape death's snare, the cat darted off, continuing on its way, vanishing within the obscure depths of the storm. As quickly as Tyler had noticed it, the form was gone—so quick Tyler wondered if it had been real or part of his imagination.

The front of the Mustang veered into the opposite lane as the tail end started to swing around to the front. Tyler fought against this rotation, turning the steering wheel back into the spin. The wheels finally grabbed pavement, but the angle of rotation was too severe, which caused the back end to fishtail and then whip around in front the opposite way.

Raven continued to bark in protest.

From memory, Tyler remembered there hadn't been any other automobiles approaching head-on or from the rear.

Tyler whipped his head around to look through the rear window to see which way they were headed. Raven's barking head was in Tyler's view and he yelled at her to get down so he could see. She quickly obeyed but never stopped barking. He fought to keep the car in the road. He tried to make an assumption about which direction he needed to go but had become addled. The Mustang now seemed to be spinning in all directions, and Tyler fought to control the revolutions.

Rain continued to fall. The headlights' glare glinted off the surfaces of the raindrops making them look like thousands of falling needles.

Tyler felt the car leave the road, the tires still screeching as they left the pavement. He heard the sound of buckling metal as the Mustang collided and plowed through a decrepit guard rail.

The equal and opposite reaction of the abrupt impact caused Tyler's head to whip sideways and strike something—he didn't know what. Tendrils of pain surged throughout his head. Spots of bright light spiraled behind his eyes. Blood instantaneously gushed from the jagged cut gained from his head injury. It streamed into his left eye and down the side of his face.

Small trees and shrubs scraped the undercarriage and sides of the car. It sounded strangely like scrabbling claws on imprisoning metal. Except for the rain, there was a moment of silence when the Mustang hovered in mid air before the front passenger's side headlight collided with a spruce tree that grew just beyond the embankment.

Through blood-stained eyes, Tyler saw the tree rushing toward him and he feebly grasped the steering wheel to brace himself. His preparation was too late and as the car met the tree, his sternum connected with the steering column. He turned his head away from the blow he knew he would receive. He felt and heard ribs crack and splinter under the force of the impact. His breath was driven out of him as he was lifted up and over the steering wheel only to be stopped when the right side of his forehead connected with the front windshield. The glass spider-webbed, and more blood began to flow freely. Intense pain flared inside his body. It felt as though his whole body were on fire.

Tyler heard Raven yelp in agony and assumed it was the end of the road for her but hoped she would be spared.

The car spun away as it dropped into the darkness below. The final jolt that tossed their bodies came as the tail end of the Mustang splashed into a flooding creek that was surging underneath the small bridge that held up the two-lane road. The front end followed suit and slammed down on the edge of the creek's bank, landing near the base of the tree.

Tyler was thrown back into his seat gasping for air. The violence of the storm as well as the darkness swarmed in around him once more.

In the aftermath of the wreck, Tyler gradually opened his eyes but quickly closed them again from the blood that had pooled around his left eyelid. He lifted a weak hand and feebly wiped the blood away as best he could. Eventually, he blinked his eyes open again. He sat teetering on the brink of unconsciousness, his body racked with pyrotechnic spasms from the wreck.

"I should've just hit that fucking cat," Tyler murmured through tortured gasps of air.

That was the last thing he thought before his eyelids turned into lead blinds and he was submerged in the realm of unconsciousness. He tried to swim out of the blackness but it was too powerful, and he finally submitted to its persuasion.

ଔ

Raven sensed danger the moment the explosion rocked the sky.

She quickly stood in the backseat and peered out into the darkening night and whined.

She heard her master say something to her. She ignored him and looked out the windows again.

She heard something fall on the roof of the car. She looked up as her body hunched and became on guard. There it was again. There was another one. Now there were a lot of them. She looked out the window again. A lot were falling out there. Bunches. Hundreds. Thousands. She remembered what that was. Falling wetness. Wetness falling all around. She liked playing in the wetness. She liked it especially when there was a lot of it so she could swim around in it like she did earlier today in the giant puddle.

Something ran out into the middle of the road. She saw the black thing crouch the same moment as Tyler.

She knew what that was. She knew about them. Some mean. Some nice. This one looked mean though.

She barked at it.

She saw it scamper off into the woods. Maybe she scared it. Raven smiled and barked again.

Raven's smile was wiped clean when she felt the car surge. Not a good time to smile. The car swerved. She fought to get a firm foothold. She saw her owner man-handling the steering wheel. Raven was scared but was powerless to do anything to help. Maybe barking would help. She had scared the cat away.

She barked again.

Her barking didn't seem to help.

Now things were out of control. Her world was thrown in circles.

Her master was yelling at her.

She crouched in the floorboards for protection if anything happened and continued to bark.

She felt a jarring; some harsh bumps and a mild impact.

A big collision followed the smaller jolt that tossed her around the back seat as if she were a rag doll.

She thrust her feet out to brace against anything but felt a sharp pain in her leg instead. She yelped in agony.

She heard an explosion of glass and then everything was quiet except for the relentless drumming of that falling wetness.

Dazed, Raven slowly sat up in the back seat and shook her head fiercely to arouse herself. Her ears pitter-pattered against her head. It felt good. Dizzying spirals looped around and behind her eyes, threatening to make her black out. She steadied herself and blinked the dizziness away and whined. When she felt she could move again, she wriggled and kicked herself over the arm rest between the two front seats until she could sit up in the passenger seat. It was a chore, since her right front leg had been injured.

Her master was asleep, or so Raven thought. Raven leaned over and licked his face and nose. Her master wouldn't move.

Raven tilted her head in bewilderment, not understanding. That wasn't right. Usually her master pulls away from this affection, but he is always smiling when he does so. Even in the early mornings when he's sleeping too late, a few licks to his face and he is wide awake and smiling.

She chuffed softly and whined in her master's ear.

She nudged Tyler under the chin to try to awaken him.

She licked her master again and whined.

She tasted blood. It was bitter but she licked him again.

She pulled her head back in confusion.

Nothing. That was not a good sign.

Her master kept sleeping.

Raven was baffled.

She had to do something, and quick.

Get help.

The window on her master's side was gone. She carefully maneuvered over Tyler's body, planted her feet on the window sill, and judged the distance.

A short drop to the ground. Too high to land on both feet. One foot really hurting now.

Raven carefully measured the distance again and then cautiously jumped free from the car. She tried not to use her injured foot, but changed her mind in mid-air.

Her legs buckled and her chest and head abruptly stopped her fall.

She yelped in pain as she landed.

Leg hurt even more now.

She rolled over in the sticky leaves, tested her footing, slowly stood, and shook her head. She took a moment to get her bearings.

Help. She had to get help.

She slowly hobbled up the steep slope to the road they had just left.

၈

In a choking gasp, Tyler managed to swim out of suffocating blackness and awoke into pain and fear.

"*Where am I?!*" his mind screamed.

He was hoping to hear an answer but none came. Being in this vastness, he felt he would die from shock if someone actually *did* answer him.

He didn't know how long he had been knocked out. Time seemed to be jumbled; seconds had turned into minutes, minutes into hours and hours—if he had been out that long—into eternities.

Tyler had never felt so forsaken and alone in all his life. He tried to take a deep breath to calm his nerves, but couldn't make anything but short shallow breaths. He felt as if his heart and lungs had been surgically removed from his chest and nothing remained but a desolate void. He realized he was sitting down and was clutching an object in his uninjured hand. He gently began to stroke the medallion he had found that morning. A tide of reality washed over him as he remembered what happened in quick memory bursts.

A day at the lake, Savannah, a ghost story, the storm, a black cat, brakes, hydroplaning, an instantaneous crash, then darkness.

The forlorn feelings came in waves, as if he were sitting in the surf at a beach. He took a deep breath of relief as the recognition and feel of his own Mustang washed over him.

Darkness, once again, began to press in at the periphery of his vision. Tyler's eyes fluttered, struggling to keep them open from their threat of closing forever.

Tyler still gasped for air but oxygen never came in satisfying breaths.

The darkness retreated as a spiral of bright light shot down through the windshield. Mixtures of purple rays and tongues of blue caressed his face. Tyler instantly knew what this was: the end of his life. This wasn't the way he remembered hearing it from books and documentaries.

When people die they see, or they are supposed to see, a pure white light. A tunnel. This isn't right. This isn't death. It can't be.

But even as those thoughts sifted down through Tyler's mind, he knew it was.

Why ask questions about it, Tyler? Just accept it. NO! I don't want to die! Tyler yelled from inside his mind. *I want to see my family again, see my new friends, see Savannah. Oh, if only I had one more chance. Just one more chance to live. I wish I had one more moment, if even that, to see Savannah again. It would be worth it all. I WANT TO LIVE!*

Radiant colors of the rainbow rippled across his memory and then blurred.

A mind rip.

A disconnection of his body and soul.

For one brief moment, Tyler saw his soul leave his body, and ascend slowly into the violet light.

He was mystified and stared in awe as his own outer body experience took place. On one level it was amazing, truly amazing, but on another it was seriously horrifying. He knew now it was over. It was useless to fight anymore, because he was now going to a better place. In that moment, he gave up fighting for his life. He knew there was no way to stop the inevitable.

As he slowly drifted up through the rain-streaked night and into the bright blue and purple haze, he stared at his body slumped rigidly in the driver's seat. His eyes were wide with fear and wonder. There was a small amount of dread that Tyler felt flow through his soul as he watched his body become smaller. He turned his head and moved faster into the unbelievable soothing light, forgetting about his earthly body, concentrating on the afterlife and where he was headed.

CB

When Raven passed through the space where the guardrail was missing, a bad feeling came over her, a sense that all animals seem to have when danger is nearby. Her sixth sense had kicked in and now instinct took over.

Something different was in the air around her.

Raven looked in all directions of the stormy night. She lowered her head and scrutinized the darkness for strange movement.

Something bad was lurking in the night around her and she didn't like it.

Her fur was drenched from the cold rain, but the hair on the back of her neck stood on end. Her ears pricked in attention from any tale-tell noises of mischief. Her nose flared wildly as she tried to pick up a scent. Her lips quivered with nervous tension. A growl rumbled in the back of her throat.

Something bad was loose in the night. She could sense it. She could feel it, but she just couldn't see it.

She thought again of her master and looked back in his direction. He didn't look like himself. He looked scared.

Help. She needed to get help. That was the most important thing right now.

She started shuffling her weight in one direction on the slick pavement, still wary of the bad thing that was just out of reach from her. Maybe she was just within its reach.

That bad thing was out there in the night.

Raven didn't get far before two bright beacons crested the hill in the distance.

Raven barked as the lights approached her. It had to be someone who could help.

The lights slowed and then stopped in front of her.

CHAPTER 6

AS AN EXPLOSION in the sky blew shrapnel of rain from the clouds, Bruce Saliers leaned forward and glanced up out of the front windshield to judge the severity of the coming storm.

"Great," he said between clenched teeth. "Another flash flood. But who am I to complain?" He turned his windshield wipers to their highest setting. "One thing about it, we do need the rain. Boy, it's coming down like a son of a bitch."

He spoke as though another person were actually listening to him. Sometimes he pretended he had a partner sitting next to him, or that's what he told people anyway. It was just an easy explanation to cover up the bad habit of talking to himself.

Bruce Saliers had dark red hair that was always cut close to his scalp during the summer months. He felt he looked more military—more intimidating—when it came to serious police matters. His freckled, ruddy complexion and stocky build added to his charisma. He did his best to keep in shape by going to the gym a few times each week, but between eating fast food on his long work hours and gym visits—well, let's just say that the gym visits were winning the battle, but the fast food was winning the war. Bruce was somewhat fit, but a few extra unneeded pounds were still wrapped around his belly.

He loved being a State Trooper. He enjoyed keeping the highways safe from the speed demons that possessed the roadways and other miscellaneous madness that went along with his job. Sometimes the day-to-day routine of bequeathing speeding tickets to law breakers got old. It got old really quick, because it had never really been *his* dream to become a cop.

Since his childhood, he had never really known what he had wanted to do or be when he grew up. He had just followed in his father's footsteps, subconsciously playing copycat with his dad's occupation. But Bruce had never forgotten the look of pride on his father's face when he had graduated from the Academy, and since then it had always felt right; at least it did to a certain extent.

This year though, he had already put in the paperwork to be transferred to the investigations division. He wanted to get out of the monotony his current job was giving him and to add a lot more spice and excitement to get him through the remainder of his career.

His long shift that day was finally over and he was heading home. He had pulled double duty and he couldn't wait to put his head on a pillow and sleep until his eyes popped opened late the next morning.

As he crested a small ridge and descended into a straight away, he noticed something in the middle of the road.

"What the hell do we have here?"

It was a black dog, rain soaked and abandoned.

As he drew closer, the dog started to bark at him. One foot was lifted and it hobbled weakly toward his car.

"Get out of the way, dog," he said, as if the dog could hear him through the windshield and over the drumming rain.

The dog stood firm, still barking.

It quickly hobbled to the side of the road and barked at nothing, then trotted back toward him just as fast and barked again.

Bruce honked the horn, but the dog was unwavering. It just continued to bark and look toward the opposite side of the road.

He could easily go around the dog, speed away, and be gone but this was too peculiar and interesting.

The dog repeated its ritual as before.

Bruce laughed and muttered to himself, "Dumbass dog."

He let his eyes follow the dog and noticed through the illumination of his headlights, that part of the guard rail was missing. A bad feeling immediately started to creep over Bruce's body. He quickly switched on the mounted searchlight and rotated it in that direction to see that area with better clarity. It looked as though part of the railing had been ripped away. Even the wooden piers that had held the guard rail together were broken off close to the ground. He looked beyond the railing and saw fresh major abrasions that had scarred a tree beyond the embankment. Some of the tree limbs had been broken and were sagging vertically to the ground.

The thought hit him like a Mac truck.

"Holy shit," he exclaimed and turned on the cruiser's rooftop lights. He grabbed his hat as he jumped out of the car. The rain was cold and he was instantly drenched. "That damn dog was trying to tell me something and if it's what I'm thinking, this isn't going to be pretty."

Ignoring the barking dog, he ran to the broken railing and saw what he had imagined. It was a car wreck, plain and simple, and it looked to be a bad one.

The dog copied the man's action and put his good front paw upon a wobbly, wooden guardrail post and peered into the ravine below and whined.

From the bright intensity of the search light and the red and blue police beacons, he saw that there was at least one person in the driver's seat.

"Who's the dumbass now?" Bruce said, mentally kicking himself that he didn't understand the dog's actions sooner.

All his senses of caution left him. His only priority now was to help, if the figure in the car could be helped at all. As he descended the ravine he stumbled, fell forward, threw his arms out in front of himself and stopped his fall. He stood, braced himself, and continued to the car, wiping his muddy hands on his uniform as he went.

When he reached the car, he immediately stuck his hand through the missing window and felt the boy's neck for a pulse. The boy looked as though he was barely hanging on. Bruce had to reposition his fingers a few times because he couldn't find any pulse at first, but then finally, he felt a slow, irregular rhythm underneath the boy's jaw line. It was weak; almost too weak. The boy's chest wasn't moving, and Bruce assumed he wasn't breathing.

He cursed himself again for being so slow to realize what the dog was trying to communicate.

Through the radio mic hooked to his shoulder, he called headquarters and requested emergency medical assistance. He gave them details on the location of the accident as well as the injuries that he could see that needed to be treated. Then he returned focus on the boy to do as much as he could until the paramedics arrived.

"Shit. Damned if I do, damned if I don't. I have to try and do what I can for the boy."

Bruce knew he had to move as fast as possible. The kid's life depended on it.

He opened the car door and gently pulled the boy by his clothes toward himself. Bruce kept the boy's head and spine in place by resting the kid's head on his chest. He worked his arms under his shoulders until his elbows were in the boy's armpits.

"Please forgive me if I'm wrong," he said as he drug the boy away from the car.

He knew from CPR classes that unknown injuries could be made worse—even paralysis—by moving an individual from an accident without the knowledge of what their injuries were. The boy wasn't breathing. He had to keep the boy alive even if he made unknown injuries worse by doing so. Those injuries could be treated and would heal in time, but that would only happen if he kept the boy alive.

The night was still alive and the storm reigned supreme. Thunder rumbled, lightning crackled, and rain fell in torrential sheets.

Bruce placed the boy on a level plane. The boy's head flopped back due to the lack of consciousness. Bruce caught the back of his head and gently placed it on a cushion of wet leaves. The boy's complexion was ashen and his lips were a dark purple. Bruce lifted the boy's eyelids and saw only the white conjunctiva staring blankly into a rainy, starless night. The boy looked like a blind man staring at nothing in particular. Bruce continued feeling the boy's wrist and neck, but the pulse had faded. If a rhythm was there, it was too weak for him to find.

I have to save this kid's life. I have to get this kid's blood flowing back to his heart.

He immediately began CPR, pushing fast and hard.

The situation was frustrating for Bruce. His body was becoming unstrung and he was shaking nervously with apprehension.

On more than one occasion, the boy coughed. Bruce stopped CPR, turned him over on his side to prevent asphyxiation, but each time he did so, the boy stopped breathing again. When that happened, he immediately began CPR again.

"Fuck. It's like taking three steps forward and two steps back," Bruce said, amazed at the difficulty of trying to bring him back. "Come on, damn you. Don't die on me. LIVE! You want to live don't you?"

He yelled at him and slapped him repeatedly in the face hoping that would bring him around. He wanted to beat on his chest with his fists and punch him in the face from frustration, but he knew that would only add to the boy's injuries.

All of a sudden, the boy shuddered awake with a deep, raspy breath.

Startled and cursing as he staggered backward in shock, Bruce let go of the boy as though he had been dead but was now animated with demonic energy.

The boy's back arched as he inhaled a single, huge breathe. His eyes were filled with fright. Their eyes locked on each other. The moment held between then. Bruce didn't know what to say. He was about the say something encouraging, but the boy turned his head to look more directly at Bruce. Bruce had this uncanny feeling that the boy knew him although Bruce had never seen this kid before in his life.

Then the boy spoke seven words in an abraded voice "Help me! Please don't let me die!" After that, the boy's eyes rolled into the back of his head as his eyelids closed. His body went limp, dropped back to the wet leaves, and lay still again.

"What the fuck was that all about?" he asked his invisible partner. Bruce knew it wasn't his imagination. He had distinctly heard what the boy had said. A locomotive of trepidation traveled up the tracks of his spine and derailed at the base of his neck, sending his whole body into a giant shudder.

"Hang in there, kid. Help is on its way," Bruce replied. "Hold my hand and don't let go. I'm here with you." To himself or his non-existent partner he said, "I wanted more excitement on the job, but this is ridiculous. It is definitely a far cry from traffic duty." He silently wished he was better prepared for this situation.

The dog hadn't stopped barking since Bruce had left the roadway, but now his barks were fiercer. It seemed to Bruce that its intentions now seemed aimed at the boy instead of the sky.

"You're a smart dog, but you're really fucking strange."

Bruce kept coaxing and begging the boy not to die. Each time the boy began to breathe shined another ray of hope that he might actually be able to save this kid. It was difficult for him to look at this boy that was probably going to die anyway and his heart crumbled with sorrow, but nevertheless he was relentless in continuing CPR until the paramedics arrived.

❧

As gravity's hold on Tyler was lifted and he floated further into the amethyst beyond, he sensed something menacing emanating from below. It seemed to be coming from within the confines of the car. Tyler felt that if he didn't move faster into the soothing light, he would never make it to whatever new place where he was supposed to arrive, and that was almost too much for his soul to bear.

Tyler turned and looked below and a sense of wonder overcame him. It was truly amazing. He had traveled much farther than he had imagined. He saw the ruined Mustang far below. It looked like the size of a crumpled Hot Wheels toy at this distance. He could see every detail clearly with his new eyes. The brightness of his new body was strong where he was, and he illuminated the night sky.

Lightning flashed nearby. It seemed as though time slowed down when he glanced over at it. He saw how crisp and clean the lightning bolt was and saw it plot out its direction of descent as it arched toward the ground. It was amazing to see its white, hot power and to feel the heat of it burn the air around him and evaporate the raindrops without even touching some of them.

Tyler noticed the brightness of his lifeline grew dimmer the further away from his body that he went. It was as though he were still tethered to his earthly body by a strand of illuminated thread. He felt as though his body was playing kite with his soul. It was as if his body was still hanging on and not wanting to give up and let go of this world.

It was time though, he knew that now. He had held on long enough. Where he was and what he was experiencing now was far better than what was going on in his life. With some trepidation and regret, he grabbed the life line that connected his soul to his body far below and gave it a gentle tug. It didn't take much to pull free.

With one last look at the tableau far below, Tyler took it all in. Blue and red lights from the police cruiser twinkled as if sending out lighted Morse code. He saw now that he wasn't in his car anymore. Between the time of his first look back and the amazing moments he had experienced, his body had been moved. He was now lying in a clearing near his car; apparently moved there by a man who was stooped over him frantically pumping his chest to revive him. Amused, Tyler's soul smiled. "There's really no use in continuing that. It's over."

Turning from the scene for the last time, he looked toward the heavens. Expecting to move faster now that nothing was holding him back, Tyler was shocked to feel his soul violently jerked back toward the ground.

He turned again and in horror saw something he would've never imagined. Of all the nightmares he had over the years, this, by far, was the worst.

A dark ink—darker than the night itself— seemed to be pouring out of his chest and pooling around his body. He was bleeding black. A tendril of that darkness was sticking up out of his chest and was wrapped tightly around the tail end of his soul's lifeline. It had obviously been snagged after he had pulled it free earlier and stopped before he could travel into the vast beyond. It was slowly pulling him back toward the earth. It started slow at first, then became more violent. As it reeled his lifeline back in, it disappeared back inside his body. He wanted nothing more than to escape and to be away from this earth.

When he was close enough, the dark liquid shadow came together. It surged around Tyler's frail body, shuddered, folded in on itself, and then sprang toward Tyler's soul, like a dark wave cresting on a rocky shore.

It grasped Tyler's ankle in a vice-like grip. He stared down the length of his soul in horror at the dark silhouette that had seized him, but he couldn't make out what it was. It was just a dark void that kept changing positions to keep him from journeying beyond this realm.

Either the dark void crawled over the top of Tyler's soul or it gave him one hell of a jerk, but the end result was the same. The shadow moved up his body in one quick movement to where they were face to face. It felt as though he were dropped into a skin tight glove. Within what Tyler assumed was "Its" face, a menacing grin formed, and through telekinesis it communicated it's thoughts to Tyler's soul. The voice Tyler heard was harsh and scratchy. Nothing but pure evil.

And just where do you think you're going?

Tyler's soul was trying to process what was happening but was too scared to answer.

I'll tell you where. Nowhere. Because I want you. I need your body. The shadow continued speaking as it engulfed Tyler in an icy grip.

No, I can't go back, Tyler thought. *I'm dead now; once you're dead, that's it. Sianara. You're history pal. End of story.*

The thing laughed. *This subject of death is new to you, I know. It was hard for me to accept, too. You're not finished in this life yet. You can't go on, just as I haven't been able to leave this realm for a long, long time. You know, we could be friends. I don't have any friends. You want to be friends? It'll be fun.*

Tyler's soul struggled within the confines of the diabolical black form, trying to break its hold and escape.

Quit squirming! It yelled. *You'll just make it worse. Let it happen. Don't fight it. I didn't when I was in your shoes. You made your wish, your one last dying wish not to die. To live on. Just like me. That was just enough to bring me back. You saved my soul and now I'm going to save your life. I'm your angel of mercy, buddy boy. I'm your genie in a bottle, so to speak. I'm granting your wish. My grandmother always told me to be careful what you wish for, because someday it just might happen. Well, today is your lucky day.*

Tyler saw the face of the thing that pulled him close to itself in a tight embrace. An eerie rictus broke through on its ominous countenance. The face of a young boy with a lopsided grin appeared from within the shadows of the void.

111

In a more soothing voice, the boy said, *Hey, relax. You don't have to be afraid of me.*

After the sentences were spoken and not waiting for a reply, the apparition overpowered Tyler's soul and pulled it down out of the blue and purple haze toward Tyler's already cooling carcass.

With Edward leading, soul against soul, they swirled around in a dancer's tango and then permeated through every pore and opening in Tyler's skin and settled deep within the core of his body again.

Déjà vu, Edward whispered to himself within his new mind. *Déjà vu from an eternity ago.*

The feeling of the entity entering his body chilled the marrow deep within Tyler's bones. He revived instantly after the souls repossessed his body once again. His back arched in spasms from the force of receiving both souls. System overload. His lungs inhaled one deep breath as he sat halfway up. Pain seared the inside of his chest as his lungs expanded and pressed against his broken ribcage. The pain was so intense that his eyes widened and released rivers of flowing tears.

In opening his eyes, Tyler saw a man he had never seen before kneeling over him.

Am I dreaming again? If it's not a dream, then this man is real. He's got to help me.

A split second after he locked eyes with the man, another feeling of de ja vu came over him. Recognition flickered in his mind but it wasn't a feeling that *he* knew this man. The recognition came from the entity that had just possessed him. The entity knew him and the entity didn't like him. Confusion wrinkled his forehead. Tyler angled his head in an attempt to recognize him and satisfy his unbelief.

Tyler felt hatred boiling up inside him but he didn't know why. He didn't know this man, so why he should hate him. The feeling was brief and then it was gone.

Then Tyler felt his mouth open and he heard himself say, "Help me! Please don't let me die!" Then darkness began to cloud his mind.

Another version of what the specter had said echoed inside Tyler's head. The last thing Tyler thought he heard within his mind before slipping into unconsciousness were the words: *Will you be my friend? I would like to be yours. My name is Edward.*

As the dark, cold shroud of unconsciousness overlaid his eyes and embraced his body, inside his mind Tyler screamed a silent scream.

଼ଷ

The wailing cry that came out of the darkness was soft at first but then grew steadily louder. When Bruce first heard the sirens, his heart was electrified with relief.

"Oh thank God! It's about damn time," he muttered through exhausted breaths. "Thank you, God."

He was fatigued and didn't know how much longer he could continue. He was pleased with himself he had held up as long as he had but thankful now that someone was here to take over.

"If you die now," Bruce whispered. "It won't be because of what I have or haven't done. Once they get down here, you will be in their hands."

The swirling lights from the ambulance took turns with the blue and red beams from the police cruiser and painted psychedelic colors on the nearby trees.

Bruce heard doors slam and then voices as they hurried down the ravine. One of the men carried a backboard and the other carried cases of medical instruments.

"All right, we'll take it from here," the lead paramedic said already pushing Bruce out of the way. He wasted no time taking over the situation.

Bruce stepped back as the two paramedics swarmed over the body. They were like two bees tending to the queen in the hive. Bruce put his arm to his forehead and wiped his brow. It was still raining hard and he hadn't even realized he had been sweating.

One paramedic began intubating the boy with an endotracheal tube for easier airway access.

"What happened?" The second paramedic asked.

Bruce explained everything that he knew about the situation in the fullest detail, careful not to leave anything out. It was nothing but a simple but fatal car wreck that warranted those injuries.

"Any idea how long he's been out?" Number One asked.

"No, I don't. He was unconscious and wasn't breathing when I got to him. I revived him a few times but he only came to for a few brief moments."

"Any response from the CPR?" Number Two asked.

"Yeah. I can't recall how many times, but he would take two or three breaths on his own but would stop after a few seconds later. Then I began the procedure again."

"What's the dog's problem? Doesn't he know when to shut the hell up?"

"I don't know. I can't figure her out, but if it hadn't been for her blocking the road, I would've never known this boy was down here."

"Did you move him at any time?" Number Two asked.

"Yes, of course. From the drivers seat to where you see him now. He wasn't thrown from the vehicle if that's what you were wondering. If that overflowing stream had pulled the backend of the car away from the bank it could've dropped the driver's side into the water. Then we would've had a drowned kid on our hands. I wouldn't have moved him if there had been anyway around it. I would've tried to do CPR while he was still sitting up in the car, but the rain is still coming down thick and it was just a matter of time."

"Any idea who he is?" Number One asked.

"No, I haven't searched him yet. I was too caught up in the moment of trying to save the kid's life to find out. I'm sure he has a wallet. If it's not on him, it's hopefully in his car somewhere."

"Can't you silence that damn dog?" Number One stated.

"Don't worry about the dog," Bruce suggested. "In my opinion, she's the one that saved the boy's life in the first place. Let her bark if she wants to."

Bruce noticed the dog had directed her attention away from the night sky where she had been barking earlier. It seemed that the dog was focused toward the boy now. *Why? Maybe she's just trying to wake him up.*

The combined CPR efforts between the two men caused the boy to come around. The boy wanted to cough but couldn't with the endotracheal tube down his throat.

"And he's back," Number One said.

"That's a good sign, but he's not out of the woods yet." his partner agreed.

Tyler grunted hard and tried to cough the tube up; he even grabbed at it and tried to pull it free. Before Tyler could do so, Number One grabbed his hands and pulled them back down to his sides.

"Vent him!" Number One said.

"Check," Number Two said and put the bag over his mouth and pumped the bag mask.

Tears began to stream out of Tyler's eyes.

"I have waterworks. This kid's in a tremendous amount of pain. I'm going to give him a high dosage of Versed. That'll calm him down and help against the pain."

The two paramedics discussed and confirmed the correct dosage, then it was prepared and applied.

"I think he's got some busted ribs; possibly a punctured lung," Number One said.

"Pneumothorax," Number Two agreed.

"How do you know?" Bruce asked.

"This kid's having a very hard time breathing," Number Two said to Bruce. "He's messed up real bad. I wouldn't doubt that he has multiple traumas."

"His pulse is still weak," Number One stated.

"He still can't breath well on his own. He needs to be on a ventilator," Number Two said.

"We need to load him up and get him to the ER ASAP," Number One said.

"Let's do it."

Number Two hooked Tyler up to a portable ventilator so it could continue giving him quality breaths of air while they made it up the steep incline. Number One moved the backboard into place after Number Two finished hooking up the ventilator. They both loaded the boy on the backboard so they could get him up the ravine. They quickly attached ropes to the backboard and then secured the ropes to themselves. They moved quickly and in perfect unison like a well-oiled machine. It was a hurried procedure, but they were careful not to take a wrong step, lose their footing, and drop the kid—or themselves—back down the ravine.

As they loaded the boy into the ambulance, another patrol car, blue and red lights flashing, came speeding over the hill. The cop guided his car to the shoulder of the highway and turned the motor off.

The paramedics piled into the ambulance and sped away with the lights flashing and the siren screaming into the night.

Bruce Saliers crossed his fingers and prayed a small prayer for the boy as the ambulance disappeared over the hill. Bruce wondered who the boy was, who his parents were, and how they would react to the situation if the boy died.

Keeping the lights flashing, the new cop jumped out as he threw on his raincoat and hat and met Bruce near where the ambulance had been.

"Kennedy! Man, am I glad to see you. We have a bad one."

"Is he alright?" Bill asked, watching the ambulance dwindle into the night.

"I don't know. He's barely hanging on. I wouldn't be surprised if he dies on the way to the hospital."

"That bad, huh?"

"Yeah. Maybe."

"What's with the dog?" Kennedy asked.

"I have no idea, but she's been that way since I got here. I can't figure her out."

"I tried to calm her down, but she's full of nervous tension or something. Barking at the sky, then barking at that car, then running around to nowhere in particular. She's weird."

"Yeah, odd dog. What can I do to help?"

"Now we find out who that kid really is."

"You don't know?"

"Well, I certainly didn't have the time to ask him while trying to revive him."

"True. Copy that."

"No ID on him and I haven't been able to search his car. Could you start a traffic report for me while I go search his car? Who knows, I might get lucky."

"Of course. Anything to help."

"Thanks, I appreciate it."

Kennedy didn't hesitate but went directly to his car to retrieve the proper papers to process the scene.

As Kennedy moved away, Bruce made his way to the bottom of the ravine again.

At the Mustang again, Bruce leaned in and sat in the driver's seat. After a quick view of the contents, Bruce saw there were no stray papers on the front or the back seats that would give the mystery boy's name away. The glove compartment was open, and CDs had spilled out onto the floor. He found the boy's wallet in the floor board almost under the seat. Bruce briefed through and finally dug out the license and read the name.

"Tyler Curtis. Well, apparently that mystery is solved."

The picture was of the same black haired, handsome kid that had just been carried away.

"Well, it's good to finally meet you, Mr. Curtis. I hope I can personally meet you again under better circumstances."

Bruce left everything else as it was and made his way back up the steep hillside.

Kennedy had avoided the weather by staying in his patrol car to work up the traffic report.

Bruce took a second look at the license and noticed that the address was wrong.

"You're a long way from home, Mr. Curtis; that is, if you still live in Chicago."

At his own car, he called headquarters and asked them to look up the license plate number and to find out if a Silver Ridge address is attached to the name. Dispatch told him to wait as they tried to locate the information.

In a matter of minutes, headquarters radioed back with no luck. They suggested that he probably hadn't taken the time to take care of that information before the move.

I guess I'm just going to have to find that information out another way, Bruce thought.

He looked over at the dog. Her barks had subsided somewhat since the ambulance had left, but she still seemed worried about something.

Bruce walked over to the dog and stooped near her. He lifted a palm raised hand toward the dog and asked, "What is it, girl?"

Raven whined softly at the man, shook herself dry only to be drenched again by the rain, then turned her head back and bayed into the moonless night.

Bruce looked up into the sky, puzzled, "I know, I hate the rain, too."

The dog stopped barking when he spoke and turned to him.

He looked back at the dog and clicked his tongue on the roof of his mouth. "It's okay, girl. Everything is all right now. Tyler's going to be just fine, I hope." He stood and cautiously edged himself toward the dog until his hand was underneath her nose. Raven sniffed his hand and then granted her permission to be stroked. She stiffened at first then relaxed.

"Whatcha barking at, girl? What's up there that's got you so riled up? Huh?" Directing his next comments as much to the dog or his invisible partner as to himself, he said, "My dad always told me that storms like this are the result of battles fought on a spiritual level."

The dog sat down to listen and whined again.

"Yeah, it's true. Spiritual warfare. The thunder is the sounds of their swords. The lightning is produced by the clash of their weapons. The blood of demons, the sweat of angels, and the tears of all the ones lost in that combat all combine to make the rain. My dad always told me they were and are fighting our conflicts. I've often wondered what it would be like to view one of those fights if the veil that divides our dimension from theirs could somehow be lifted then—," He paused, letting his imagination take a course of its own then he said, "That would be an awesome sight, wouldn't it? Scary but awesome."

Unbeknownst to Bruce, ethereal rivalry had been engaged tonight, and if that veil could have been ripped open, he would have seen two souls enraged on a rain-soaked battlefield. No weapons, but each possessing the sheer will to live on. Both entities had won, survived, but contention still seethed within the body of Tyler Curtis.

"Tell me something. What are we doing getting rain soaked on a night like this anyway? We need to get out of this damn storm."

As Bruce stroked and soothed Raven, he noticed the dog tag attached to her collar. He looked closely and saw the dog's name as the rotating blue and red lights from his police cruiser reflected off its surface.

"Raven?" Bruce stated as he read the tag. "Raven, huh?" Bruce laughed, assuming the name had something to do with how black the dog's hair was. "Is that your name, girl?"

Raven whined, answering him.

He read the address that followed beneath the name. A Silver Ridge address to be exact.

Bruce's eyebrows lifted in surprise. "Now we're getting somewhere."

Bruce couldn't figure out why the dog had a new address on her dog tag but Tyler's records hadn't been updated on his license. He figured that Tyler's driving records would be more important, but so many times people procrastinated with the more important things in life.

"You are a lifesaver, you know that? On two accounts." Bruce said, shaking Raven's coat vigorously. "You saved Tyler's life by stopping me, and you saved me a lot of time and effort. I could kiss you right now for that, but I'm not going to."

As if she had understood, Raven sneezed, barked two times, and licked Bruce's face.

"Quit it." he commanded as he stood, then, "I don't know where your tongue has been. Get your mangy butt in the car. C'mon. Let's see if we can get you home and dried off."

Raven hobbled over and scampered up into the enclosed backseat. Bruce knew her foot was injured because she hadn't put any weight on that paw since he had arrived.

Bruce slammed the door and jogged over to Kennedy's patrol car and rapped on his window.

"Hey, Bill!"

Kennedy cracked his window enough to talk.

"I think we're in luck. The dog's collar has a Silver Ridge address on it. I'm going to check it out. Can you cover this for me?

"It's all taken care of. Consider it done. Already called the towing service to pull that bad boy up." He paused and glanced out his from window. "And speaking of, how's that for service?" Kennedy continued, pointing behind Bruce.

The bright beams and the yellow lights of the tow truck rounded the bend and slowed to a stop.

"That's great," Bruce replied. "Thanks. I'll get with you soon to fill in the details of the report."

"Sounds good. Now get out of here and find that kid's parents."

As he left the scene, he was thrilled that everything had happened the way it had. Of course, he hated that Tyler had ever been in the wreck in the first place. But, he had saved a boy's life today with the help of his new found friend; but that wasn't what was important. He would now have to inform the parents of their son's condition. They were most likely at home relaxing thinking that everything was just fine in their son's life. He dreaded this chore, but it came with the job, so he was obligated to follow through. No votes had been cast, but he was automatically nominated the bearer of bad news.

CHAPTER 7

WHEN HENRY CURTIS opened the front door and saw a policeman in a dirty, rain-soaked uniform, he instantly knew something was wrong. His face went slack, losing its usual cheerful eagerness and was replaced with worried attention.

Henry knew from countless watched movies and from sheer common sense that when a cop comes knocking at your door, he usually isn't there as part of a Publisher Clearing House event. He's more like the Grim Reaper—complete with his billowing black shroud and giant, gleaming scythe—with no news of an extension of life. For all Henry knew, the man that stood on the front porch could very well be the Grim Reaper; he was just bringing the grave news dressed in a different outfit. Henry never thought a scene he had watched so many times on the silver screen would suddenly become a reality in his life as it was now.

Henry immediately thought of his son. They haven't even been in this town a full three days and already something had happened to Tyler. He could be dead for all he knew; his life snuffed out before they were able to start over in this area.

As Henry opened the iron and glass door to talk to the gentleman, Raven hobbled between the cop's legs and through the half open door, anxious to get inside and out of the storm.

"Raven!" Henry exclaimed.

"I take it I'm at the right address," Bruce suggested. "Is that your dog, Mr. Curtis?"

"Yes. Well, it's actually my son's. It's Tyler's dog. Is there a problem, officer?" Henry asked. He immediately felt stupid. *Of course there was a problem; why else would he be here?*

"Yes, sir." Bruce said, "Is this 194 Summerset Lane?"

"Yes it is, Officer…," he paused, trying to read his badge name.

"Saliers," he said, finishing Henry's sentence for him, "Bruce Saliers."

"This is about Tyler, isn't it?"

"I'm afraid so. May I come in, please?" Bruce asked, wanting to get out of the blowing wind, if only for a couple of minutes.

"Yes, of course. Sorry, officer," Henry said as he opened the outside door. "You'll have to excuse my behavior. I'm in somewhat of a shock right now."

"Who is it, Henry?" Gwen called out as she stuck her head around the doorway of the kitchen to the living room to see who it was. As she looked, her confusion changed to understanding dread as she saw the officer step up into the living room.

"It's an Officer Saliers," Henry called over his shoulder. He looked back again at Bruce and said, "What exactly is this all about, officer?"

"Sorry about the run around and all the questions, but I had to make sure I was at the right residence."

"I understand, sir," Henry said quickly, trying to rush the conversation along.

Gwen came out of the kitchen wiping her hand on a dishtowel. Worry had already spread across her face.

"Mr. and Mrs. Curtis, I'm sorry to have to tell you this, but your son, Tyler, was in a severe car accident earlier tonight."

"Oh my God," Gwen whispered as her legs went limp. She eased down onto the couch and placed her head in the clutched dish towel. She braced herself for the worst news of her life and half expected to hear the officer add that Tyler was dead, but those words never came.

Henry sat down beside his wife and placed a strong comforting arm around her shoulders and pulled her close.

Bruce saw the shock of the news and how hard it had hit them. He held out his hands and tried to calm them before they thought the worst. "Now I want to assure you, Tyler is still alive; at least he was when the ambulance took him from the scene. I don't want to give you any false hope, and I don't want take any hope away from you either, but he is in pretty bad shape. I don't know the extent of his internal or external injuries because the paramedics that arrived on the scene didn't have time to discuss that information with me. They stabilized Tyler and then rushed him to Silver Ridge Memorial." He glanced at his watch and continued, "It's going on about twenty-five minutes now. I would say he's already there and I'm sure he is in good hands with the doctors on call. I am prepared to escort you to the hospital as I'm sure you would like to check in on your son."

"What happened?" Gwen asked looking up. Her voice had taken on a shaky quality and her eyes were brimming with tears.

"As far as I can tell, ma'am, with the weather as it is, it appears his car simply hydroplaned on slick pavement. I don't believe any other cars were involved. It's an accident that could have happened to anyone. His car seemed to have slid through a guard rail that bordered a small ravine and dropped down the embankment." Bruce turned his attention toward Raven, who was lying near the fireplace licking her hurt leg, "To tell you the truth, your dog, I mean Tyler's dog, was the one that really saved your son. If she hadn't stopped me by blocking the road, I never would have seen your son's car."

Bruce thought the Curtis's were taking the situation well, so he plodded on with the news. As Gwen listened to the story unfold, Bruce noticed she was nervously washing her hands in her lap with invisible water. Henry Curtis, on the other hand, had grown silent, but now tears slowly trickled down his face in parallel lines.

"Now Mrs. Curtis, I pulled your son out of the wreckage…," he stopped to revise his sentence, thinking his words were to dramatic at this time, "ah…out of his car and…"

"That's OK, officer," Gwen said cutting him off. "If something does happen to my son, I want to know the full details. You don't have to sugar coat anything on my account. I'm a big girl. I can take it. I guess it's better to hear the worst accounts of it now so it will be easier to take later on if anything negative happens. Don't leave anything out."

Bruce glanced over at Henry again. He was deep in thought. Tears continued to run down his face.

"All right then. I took Tyler from the wreckage and performed CPR until the paramedics arrived. They took over and rushed him to the ER. I can escort both of you to the hospital. We can leave right now."

Gwen took the dishcloth and rolled it around in her hands to relieve the full blast of bad news that had dropped her to the couch. There was a moment of silence, each having their own individual thoughts. Eventually, Gwen stood and steadied herself from the risk of surrendering to the couch again. "I'll just be a minute."

Henry finally came out of his meditation. "I can't believe he's in the hospital. Hydroplaning in weather like this? He's such a great driver. I taught him myself."

Even the best students fail sometimes, Bruce thought. Thinking of something more encouraging, he said, "It *is* a bad storm out there tonight." If he thought about the way it really sounded it made it seem like the accident was inevitable.

"Yeah. Terrible. Bad."

Bruce felt Henry's pain. It wasn't on the same level as Henry's, but he felt it nonetheless. Bruce wasn't married, didn't have any kids but had lost his mother to cancer four years earlier. It had been a hard road to travel at first, but he had learned to cope with the pain, and each day it was less severe. If Tyler did die, then Henry would have to surrender to cope with the loss and the memories of Tyler.

"That's a hell of a dog you have there," Bruce complemented, trying to change the subject. "Did you train her to be that smart?"

"What? Oh, no. No-no, that was all Tyler's doings. When Tyler isn't studying, when he's not in school or dating; it seems like all the rest of his free time is put in with Raven here."

"Well, however much time was spent with her was well worth it. You need to give that dog some extra dog biscuits in the near future. She deserves them."

At the mention of the word 'biscuits', Raven's ears pricked and she whined.

Bruce smiled. "I think she knows we're talking about her,"

Henry finally looked up and smiled, "Oh, she does." Henry then turned his attention to the carpeted floor again.

"I didn't know if I was going to find you tonight. I ran a search on your son's license plate number to see if the DMV had a record of your new address, but I came up with nothing. Your boy Tyler put a new tag on your dog's collar that had this address on it. I guess he did that before you moved. I think your son should be commended also for thinking ahead like that."

"Yeah, that's Tyler for you," Henry said laughing. "He's always thinking of the important things."

Gwen came through the doors again. Her eyes were red and slightly puffy. She had been crying.

Even though Gwen's crying was a sign of mother concern and love, Bruce supposed she didn't want anyone staring at her. He turned to look at the dog to avoid eye contact.

"We'd better be going now," Gwen said. "I want to see Tyler. I'll drive."

"Are you sure you're up to driving after hearing this news?"

"Oh yes, officer. This is my son we're talking about. I may be a bit emotional but I can drive to the hospital for my son, don't you think?"

"Yes ma'am. I guess so."

 og

As the hospital doors slid open, the clean smell of antiseptic wafted over them. Once inside, they went directly to the administration desk.

Henry immediately took charge. "Good evening, we're looking for Tyler Curtis. He was brought here within the last hour. Teenage boy. Injuries stemmed from a car accident."

"Yes, I know who you're talking about," the lady at the desk answered. "But we have him on record as a John Doe. The medical team didn't have or couldn't find any identification on him."

"I can vouch for them," Bruce said, getting her attention. "I was the officer who found Tyler at the accident site and called it in. I was the one who performed CPR on him as well until they arrived. Once the paramedics took him, I located his parents."

"Congratulations," the nurse said. "The doctor mentioned you briefly tonight when she was checking…Tyler, did you say?"

Bruce nodded.

"When she was checking Tyler's vital signs." She turned to Henry and Gwen. "The doctor said if it wasn't for the person who performed CPR on him, Tyler would have most likely been dead before the ambulance even arrived on the scene. I guess you're looking at Tyler's real guardian angel."

Gwen thought it was odd at how this lady talked about medical cases so nonchalantly. It seemed that she would have the same enthusiasm and voice inflection for an ICU patient as she would a child with cold symptoms.

"When can we see him?" Henry asked.

"I don't believe you can. At least not right away. I don't think they are out of surgery yet."

"Surgery?" Gwen asked.

"That's right Mrs.—?" she left the sentence hanging in the air.

"Curtis. Gwen Curtis. I'm Tyler's mother."

"Yes, Mrs. Curtis. It was a life or death situation. I'm sure you would approve."

"Of course," Henry said. "Do whatever you and the hospital need to do to save our son's life."

"What exactly can you tell us, Mrs. Young?" Henry asked glancing at her identification tag.

"All I know is that he has some broken ribs, but there could be some other extremities that were damaged. He also has a head injury. Don't know how severe it is. If you will just wait patiently, the doctor will be able to give you a more accurate account of everything when surgery is over. In the meantime, could one or both of you come with me? I need some information to get Tyler registered in the system."

Gwen was the one who knew all the registration information, but Henry went along with his wife mainly for support reasons. He knew she would appreciate it later. Bruce, on the other hand, retreated to the waiting room, grabbed a few magazines and began to flip through the pages. For him, it was already turning out to be a long, crazy night.

CZ

After the relentless onslaught of admission papers, continued signatures, and countless cups of coffee, Henry, Gwen, and Bruce still weren't able to calm down. Administration had asked everything from hospital records to what medicines Tyler was allergic to. After the paperwork was completed, they were released to the boredom of the waiting room. They would frequently talk to various nurses to see if new information had come available. When they weren't told any news of his condition, each of them took turns pacing the floor in worry.

Henry stepped over to Bruce as he was pushing the vending machine button for a Snickers bar.

After Bruce stooped to retrieve his snack, Henry patted him lightly on the shoulder, "Bruce, I want you to know that you don't have to stay here the whole time. We don't expect that of you. You know that, don't you?"

Bruce ripped open the wrapper. He was starving and was eager to get anything in his stomach. "Of course. I just don't feel like leaving right now," he said.

"You've done enough already and we appreciate everything. We know you must be exhausted."

"I can get all the rest I need when I'm dead," Bruce said, quoting one of his dad's numerous bad one-liners. After the words were out of his mouth, Bruce's heart felt like it dropped to the bottom of his stomach. He hoped Henry wouldn't take it the wrong way with what could happen to his son.

Henry didn't seem to make any connection and continued, "Gwen and I just thought you ought to know that we don't expect anything else from you. You saved our son tonight, and we can't thank you enough. We'll never be able to repay you."

"Wait, just stop right there," Bruce said swallowing a big bite of his Snickers. "Don't even think that. I was just doing my job out there. I am beyond thrilled that I was able to help your son. It really made my day. You would've done the same thing, so let's not talk about a payback. No payback is needed. Let's just get through this thing together. Deal?"

"Deal," Henry said nodding.

Henry looked over at Gwen who was nervously pacing again. He smiled at her but she was deep in thought and didn't see him staring. He went to her, put his arms around her and gave her a reassuring squeeze.

Henry tried to be encouraging. "Let's sit down, okay hun? I know this is bad, but let's try to take it easy."

"We've been taking it easy ever since we arrived. I don't want to take it easy anymore. I want to see my son."

"I know, and we will soon enough."

Her eyes were puffy from the tears she had cried, and new ones puddled on the rim of her eyelids. She buried her head in his chest as he hugged her tighter.

"That feels good. Just hold me for a little while longer," Gwen begged.

And so Henry did. He held Gwen securely for a long time as they stood in the center of the waiting room.

Bruce saw Henry and Gwen in a tight embrace. Bruce felt uncomfortable while they were sharing a moment, so he walked back down the hallway to give them some time alone.

Bruce saw one of the paramedics from the scene come down the hallway and stop at the nurse's station. Bruce recognized him as the lead paramedic that worked on Tyler.

The other paramedic, Number Two, stood nearby writing something in a folder. Bruce made his way toward the front desk where they stood studying their paperwork.

"Excuse me," Bruce said, distracting Number Two's attention. "Remember me?"

Number Two's expression changed from a baffled expression of chart contemplation to a comical air of recognition.

"Shitchyeah, man," he said as he shook Bruce's hand. "How are you doing?"

"Tired but good. Better now that I'm out of that weather. I'm just worried about Tyler. How's our boy doing?"

"Oh, his name is Tyler?"

"Yeah, Tyler Curtis."

"Good to know. Good to know. But to answer your question, I

really don't know. That was one of the strangest calls I've ever been on. I thought for sure we were going to lose him. You know, that boy did the same thing to us as he did for you. He flat lined twice on the way here."

"Hey, not too loud," Bruce warned. He nodded and pointed over his shoulder toward the couple standing in the middle of the waiting room. "That's the kid's parents. I tracked them down after you brought Tyler here. Don't say anything too harsh. They're getting weary from the wait."

"Oh yeah, thanks for the head's up."

"Anything else you can tell me about Tyler?"

The paramedic shook his head and answered, "Nothing 'cept that he will probably have to breathe by a ventilator until he's able to do it on his own. Broken ribs and a punctured lung that's an affirmative. But doc seems to think something else was wrong. That's why they are in surgery."

The answer wasn't the one Bruce was looking for and his heart sank. He wanted to hear good news and he took a deep, frustrated breath.

A mechanical voice came from the speakers overhead, "Dr. Wright, please report to room 373, STAT."

"Now I don't know how long they will keep him on the ventilator. That it will depend on Tyler. They are going to run some CAT scans and MRIs later on if they haven't done so already to see if there was any brain damage."

"That's too bad."

"Now I wouldn't tell his parents about that. It would be better coming from the doctor that's performing his surgery, if you know where I'm coming from."

Bruce nodded in agreement, "Oh yeah, I understand totally, besides I've already been the bearer of bad news once tonight. Time for somebody else to do it for a change."

Down the hallway, the elevators doors dinged and opened. A woman in her mid-thirties dressed in green doctors' scrubs walked out and headed in their direction.

Number Two pointed and nodded toward her, "There's the woman you need to talk to right there. Dr. Baldwin. There's your surgeon. She can give you the low down on his condition right now."

Bruce smiled when he saw her. "Suzanne."

"What? You know her?"

"Yeah, we go way back. Went to the same high school together."

"No shit. Really?"

"No joke. Graduated together."

"She looks great, doesn't she?" Number Two said.

"She's always looks incredible. Hey, thanks for everything you did today. You did a great thing tonight, you know that, don't you?" Bruce asked, as he stepped backwards and turned on his heels.

"It's all part of the job, man. Hey, don't forget to thank yourself, too. You're the real hero Saliers," Number Two praised. "It's all you."

Hero? Bruce thought. *How odd.* The last sentence stunned Bruce and he laughed at how ridiculous it sounded. He never thought he would ever hear that word attached to his name in the same sentence.

ɔʗ

Just as the sun and moon hang in their prospective realms in the universe, Tyler's mind, body, and soul hung as one in the balance between life and death. Tyler hung in limbo; suspended over a chasm of pure madness and complete insanity. His soul was now traveling the thin line where dreams became nightmares; where nightmares evolved into grim realities; a place where they all merge into one grotesque netherworld.

The netherworld was the space in Tyler's head. Although his head was of average size as other boys his age, his mind was vast; so vast in fact that he would probably lose himself in its enormity.

Edward McDaniel's mind was reeling; it had been since the abrupt transfer from the charm to where he was now. He had been disoriented and thoughts bounced around the inside of this new mind.

Where have I been? Or should I say, where has the charm *been? I thought I was going to be stuck in that damn thing on the bottom of Silver Ridge Lake forever. How long has it been? How fucking long have I been trapped inside that charm Jonas gave me,* Edward thought. *And where is my body now? Where have I been all this time? As big as this world is and as long as I have been inside the charm, I could possibly be anywhere in the world. What am I in now? Or rather,* who *am I in* now?

He was having trouble focusing. He shook himself within his new host then froze. Edward half expected Tyler's body to jerk uncontrollably because of his actions but Tyler remained still in the physical world.

Edward had to be careful in this new body. He wasn't used to it yet; wasn't sure of its capabilities. If he had a stray thought, it might command Tyler's body to perform a certain action unconsciously. He was going to have to sit tight until Tyler's body recuperated, then he could experiment all he wanted with his new possession to figure out its strengths and weaknesses. Edward could tell right away that Tyler's body had more of the former than the latter. Even though it was racked with pain and laden with injuries now, Edward knew it was a strong body by reminiscing through Tyler's memories. All those numerous sports he had played over the years and trips to the weight room.

Oh yeah, Edward thought. *This body I was lucky enough to be blessed with now is definitely strong. It's a far cry from the puny one God cursed me with when I was alive.*

When Edward became trapped inside the charm, he had been constricted in the most uncomfortable position. For the longest time, he'd wanted nothing more than to stretch and move himself. He relished the feeling at how cozy and comfortable this new dwelling place felt.

Edward began to stretch his soul out inside his new body. It opened and unraveled down through this new entity until it had expanded to the dimensions of Tyler's body. Edward nestled deep inside his new shell.

How amazing is this? Edward thought. *My soul fits this new body like a glove. Such a perfect feeling. So comforting to know I have a new body and a new chance at life.*

Tyler tried to oppose the invasion upon his inner being, but insubordination proved to be futile.

Upon granting Tyler's wish and entering his body, Edward knew Tyler was scared almost to the point of death. Edward surged through Tyler's body and went straight to his brain and zeroed in on the area that had inhabited Tyler's mind and body with fear. Edward used the numerous chemicals in his new brain to subdue the fear. Once he found the right combination, it was just like turning off the flow of water from a faucet. Edward had found that it was particularly easy to control

Tyler's actions, and Tyler had submitted without a fight. Now all Edward needed was time. Time for this new body to heal.

Memories that Tyler had never seen, remembered, or experienced flashed like a movie behind his eyelids; horrifying images of abuse, neglect, mistreatment, isolation, and betrayal. The three dimensional images accelerated through his detached mind with horrifying clarity. Others slowed to torturous crawls to relay the colossal effect they had on Edward's life. Sometimes the memories stretched into oblong shapes until they ripped themselves apart and then melded back together into a totally different memory, and then the process repeated itself.

Edward had fed upon these memories for years while confined inside his small sanctuary. As the memories played again in his mind, they fueled his anger as he continued to set up reign. He had complete control over Tyler with minimal resistance. One of the main reasons there was not a lot of fight coming from Tyler was because his body was so weak from the trauma he had sustained from the wreck and that couldn't have been more perfect for Edward.

Edward was anxious to start living again but forced himself to remain patient. *Time is of the essence,* he told himself. *I've waited a long time to escape. What's a little more time going to hurt? I can't do what I want without a healthy body, right? I've got to give this kid a little time to mend. I only have one shot at this. I don't want it to end before it's even started. Like my other life.*

A new thought zinged through Edward's mind. *What year is it? How long have I been trapped inside it that amulet? I can figure this out,* he told himself. *What do I know right now from what I've seen and witnessed since being released from my fucking prison?*

Edward's thoughts replayed everything very quickly: The sudden release once the power of the charm opened up. *Like being sucked out by a huge vaccum.* The disoriented feeling after being release into the storm. Seeing Tyler's lifeline retracting away from his body. *Holy shit, that was so close. I really had to think quick to grab onto it. If I hadn't caught it when I did, who knows where I would be now.* The repossession of Tyler. Then, abruptly coming awake and being face to face with that guy.

Edward's thoughts went to the man who was leaning over Tyler and yelling at him to live. Rain cascaded all around the face that was peering down at him. He had recognized that man and knew him immediately.

Bruce Saliers, Edward thought. *One of those shithead bullies from my high school days. But how? Why? What are the odds? This guy was older. But not by much. Maybe fifteen or twenty years.*

Edward made a few quick calculations in his new mind of the last year he remembered that he had been alive.

That would mean Bruce is in his early to mid-thirties now. That would also mean that all the others would be close the same age.

Edward's mind started working overtime. He saw the six people in his new mind now and he remembered what each of them did to him. His life had been taken away almost before it had really started; before he even had a chance to really live and make something of himself.

They got to live their lives from then till now, Edward thought. *It isn't fair. They're the ones who always drew the short stick for me. Well, that's not going to happen anymore. There is no fucking way they are going to get away with what they did to me. Not while I'm still around.*

Edward started to smile but thought better of it. He didn't want anyone to see this new body doing anything out of the ordinary. Celebration could come later when no one was around.

CHAPTER 8

AS BRUCE WAITED for Suzanne to make her way down the hallway toward him, he admired her as he always did during his days in high school.

Suzanne was in green scrubs and her hands were stuffed deep into the pockets of her white lab coat. Her hair was pulled back into a pony tail but a few sweaty strands had pulled free and fallen around her face during the night's long procedures. Her face was set in a grim, exhausted expression.

Bruce couldn't tell if she brought good or bad news. He smiled and waved once she was close enough for her to recognize him.

"Suzanne."

Suzanne brightened, "Hey Bruce. It's been a while, hasn't it?"

"Too long. Still beautiful as always, I see."

"Ha, I don't feel like it. You were always too kind to me."

They hugged for a long moment. A really good hug between old friends that had become distant over the years. It was nice to reconnect with her after all this time even it it was under these circumstances.

"I didn't know you were the surgeon in charge. If I had known, I would've told Tyler's parents they had nothing to worry about."

"That's sweet," she said. "You look like me; like you've been through the ringer." She touched a place on his shirt.

Bruce looked down at his muddy shirt and wiped absently at a dried patch of mud. "I feel better than I look."

"That's not saying much," she teased.

They shared a laugh.

Henry and Gwen had noticed Bruce talking with someone who looked in charge. They were already walking toward them, preparing themselves for whatever news this lady might be able to give them.

Bruce introduced them. "Suzanne. This is Henry and Gwen Curtis, Tyler's parents, the boy that was in the MVA. This is Doctor Baldwin."

As they exchanged handshakes, Suzanne said, "I'm so glad to know our John Doe finally has a name."

"I went to school with Suzanne at Silver Ridge High," Bruce bragged.

Ignoring the history lesson, Henry asked, "How's Tyler doing, doctor? Is he alright?"

Suzanne shoved her hand back into her lab coat pocket again, "Yes, that's the good news. Tyler is still alive," Suzanne began. "The bad news is that he's not out of the woods yet. He has a long way to go. He's in critical condition at the moment. We've done all we can do right now. The rest is up to him. The emergency surgery was a success. It was a tough one, but there were no major complications during the procedures, but he is currently breathing by a ventilator."

Henry and Gwen's hearts dropped again with disappointment.

Suzanne continued, "The reason we had to perform emergency surgery was because a part of Tyler's sternum was fractured. I would assume it was caused from the impact with the steering wheel. Most likely, Tyler wasn't wearing his seat belt. That sort of blunt force trauma is the only thing I can think of that can cause enough power to cause these injuries to him. The part of the ribs closest to his sternum were broken, and his left lung was punctured. In addition to the broken ribs and punctured lung, and because of the hard, sudden blow to his chest, Tyler suffered from cardiac contusion and tamponade. This causes blood to accumulate around the heart. This was one of the most severe of all the injuries we had to treat. There was no way around the emergency surgery. While were were inside, we found the area where he was bleeding internally. We stopped that fairly quickly. Also, his liver had two severe lacerations. We fixed those as well. With the help from the ventilator, he's getting sufficient oxygen. We will be taking him down for tests as soon as it's safe to move him. We need to assess the extent of his brain damage, if there is any at all. There is no indication of any brain swelling at this time so that is a huge positive."

"Thank you, doctor," Henry said.

"Right now, the only other thing I can tell you is that he's currently unconscious." Suzanne saw the looks of horror on their faces. She pressed on. "The good news about that is his mind is active. Very active. More active than I would expect coming from someone who had been through that sort of trauma. I don't understand why. That is very rare in a case like this. I don't want to say too much until I can get the proper tests completed on his brain. The good thing about this is that your son should be dead, but yet, he's alive and he's hanging on. To tell you the truth, I don't know how he is doing it, but he's fighting hard."

A monotone voice scratched over the hospital intercom, "Doctor Baldwin! You are needed in ICU six! Doctor Baldwin! ICU number six! STAT!"

Suzanne didn't pause to say goodbye, she just moved toward the door, but not before Henry and Gwen saw the look of recognition and fear cross her face.

"Doctor Baldwin? Henry asked as she exited into the hallway. He yelled again, "Is that my son? Is that Tyler's room?"

Suzanne had no time to answer. She had a life to save if it was possible.

Henry, Gwen, and Bruce rushed from the waiting room and followed Suzanne into the ICU.

As Suzanne entered Tyler's room, she threw a thumb over her shoulder and shouted to a short Puerto Rican nurse, "Keep those people out of here." Suzanne knew Tyler's parents had followed her. She'd heard their footsteps behind her as she ran up the hallway, not to mention their barrage of questions as they were in route.

Not missing a beat, the nurse caught Henry's chest with both hands and pushed him back, along with Gwen and Bruce despite their wishes to enter.

"Please wait out here," she commanded. "Thank you."

Suzanne, as well as this nurse, knew what a hindrance it was for hysterical family members to be in the same room as the hospital staff. It was just added pressure that they didn't need.

After Henry, Gwen, and Bruce were pushed into the hallway, the door was closed and a beige curtain was quickly drawn, but not before they caught an individual glimpse of Tyler. All three stood frozen staring at the door. Through the iron-mesh and glass window they saw Tyler on a bed. His eyes were closed and his skin was pale. He had too many tubes and wires coming out of his mouth, nose, and body.

Henry and Gwen hugged each other fiercely.

He looks like my dad when he came out of heart surgery, Gwen thought, remembering what her father looked like after his triple bypass last year. She covered her mouth and blinked away tears that were standing in her eyes.

Henry, Gwen, and Bruce also saw an IV of clear fluid attached to Tyler's right arm and an IV of red liquid attached to his left. Tyler's upper torso had been wrapped or placed in a cast. At a brief glance, it looked like a futuristic bulletproof vest.

Probably for taping his ribs and to keep them in place, Henry thought.

Six suction pads had been placed on his forehead and areas of his exposed chest.

For monitoring purposes, Bruce thought.

Each of them continued hoping and praying the doctors and nurses would perform the right procedures on Tyler. They were putting their son's life in the doctor's hands—a doctor they had just met and didn't know at all—and to a certain extent that scared them more than anything.

After a couple of minutes when the worst of the devastation was over, Bruce put an arm around each of them.

"C'mon," he said. "Let's let the doctors do their job."

Bruce then escorted them back to the waiting room.

⁊

It was close to three in the morning when Doctor Baldwin came to them again. Her features were expressionless even though she tried to look as cheerful as possible.

Henry knew she was weary from working on Tyler most of the night. She looked like she could go to sleep where she landed if she fell to the floor.

Henry nudged Gwen. "You asleep?"

Responding to his question the way her mother always answered her, Gwen said, "No, just checking my eyes for cracks. Why?"

He nodded in the direction of Suzanne and said, "We're up. It's our turn again."

They knew something else was wrong from the troubled look Suzanne wore on her face. As she approached, they stood expecting to hear the worst news they had ever heard in their lives.

"Is Tyler still with us?" Gwen asked frantically.

Suzanne guided them to the far side of the waiting room.

Before Suzanne could even begin, Gwen asked, "What's wrong with him, doctor?"

"Sit down, please," Suzanne urged.

"I don't want to sit down, damn it; I've been sitting all night. I want to know what is wrong with my Tyler."

Realizing she may have been too abrupt, Gwen sat down in spite of her frustration.

Henry waited, knowing whatever news Suzanne was going to tell them would come out soon enough, but his patience was also wearing thin. He placed his hand on the crown of Gwen's head and pulled her to his chest then slid his hands down the back of her head and began slowly rubbing her neck and shoulders. "Doctor, please. We've all been through a great deal tonight. Just tell us what's going on."

Suzanne took a deep breath, "Yes, your son is still with us. But, I'm afraid at this time he has now lapsed into a coma."

"What? A coma?" Henry asked disbelieving. The word "coma" felt weird coming out of his mouth.

Suzanne nodded, "I'm afraid so."

Gwen bowed her face into her cupped hands. She had been strong throughout the night. Now her grief was too overwhelming, and the tears she had held back for so long broke through their barrier and started to flow.

Not knowing what to say, Henry resorted to protest, "I thought you said he was stable."

Calling his bluff, Suzanne said almost before Henry had finished speaking, "No, Mr. Curtis. I never said your son was *stable*. I do remember saying he was in *critical condition*. There's a big difference. Hopefully with some luck, some prayers, and the hospital's care, he'll be *stable* eventually, but that will take time and probably a lot of it. If everything goes as planned, and *when* he comes out of the coma, he'll eventually be up and about, but let's not jump to any conclusions right now.

"Do you know we have only seen a glimpse of him, and that was before your sidekick nurse forced us out of the room? Does anyone here actually know what the hell they're doing?"

Suzanne was taken aback. She didn't interrupt him but let him vent. She didn't like the blame being put on her shoulders when she was innocent in every way, but she didn't take it personally. There were upset parents before Henry and Gwen, and there would be some of the same after them. She knew it was pent up frustration because of paperwork and the long wait during surgery. Even though she knew this, she never rushed in an emergency situation unless it was mandatory. She certainly wasn't going to rush through surgery and do a half-assed job just so the family and friends wouldn't be inconvenienced with a long wait.

When Henry was finished with his point of view, Suzanne gave him hers. She leaned forward and placed her hands on the small table between them and said, "Yes sir, actually, we do know what the hell we are doing."

Henry realized he had jumped the gun and looked to his wife for solace. Gwen shrugged her shoulders and shook her head as if to say, "You got yourself into this, you can get your own ass out."

Suzanne continued, "I'm certainly doing the best I can for the needs of your son. Not to toot my horn, but I can say without a shadow of a doubt that I saved your son's life today. Twice. Now I say that without taking any credit away from what Bruce Saliers did. He should be commended for everything he did. As well as the paramedics. But once Tyler arrived under my care, I did everything by the medical book. Look, sometimes we don't know what the human body is going to do. There was no indication that this was going to happen. But now, on second thought, I'm thinking that is probably a good thing. It is the body's way of shutting down so it can heal faster. I have been with your son all night to make sure he's not going to die. Medical procedures take a lot of time. I'll say that again. Medical procedures take a lot of time. I've been doing my part, all I ask of you two is that you try and be patient with us. We're doing the best we can."

"I'm sorry," Henry said. "I got caught up in the moment. It won't happen again."

"That's understandable. Under the circumstances, I would be upset as well. Just don't take it out on the doctors and nurses at this hospital. Take your aggression out on someone else, or better yet take it out on *something* else. Take up some sport like boxing. You can even pretend I'm the actual punching bag if you wish."

On that note, everyone smiled. Henry even gave a bemused laugh.

"Look, I'm not going to say I know how you feel because I don't. I've never been married and I don't have any children, but I have the hopes— high hopes—of that blessing one day. I would hope I would react in the same way as you if a situation like this ever happened to me. By your reaction, I can tell you're concerned and that you love Tyler very much. I wouldn't expect anything less from you. I assure you we have done everything possible for now."

"Thank you, doctor," Gwen said sniffling.

"It's my pleasure," Suzanne replied. She shoved her hands into her lab coat pockets. "Oh, I almost forgot," she said withdrawing a plastic bag. "When Tyler was brought in, I found this in is hand. I thought you might want to hang on to it for him for when he wakes up?"

Suzanne handed the bag to Henry and Gwen. They opened the bag, retrieved the object inside and examined it together.

It was a silver-dollar-sized medallion that was attached to a worn and broken strap. The surface radiated a rainbow-colored glimmer off its surface. Both surfaces were smooth underneath, except for the places where slashed markings had been engraved into it.

Their brows were creased. They looked perplexed.

"Are you sure this is Tyler's?" Gwen asked. She said it as much to Suzanne as she did to Henry.

"Yes, very sure. I took it from his hand myself when he first came in tonight, but the leather strap was already broken when I found it."

I haven't seen Tyler wear any type of jewelry or charms like this, have you Henry?"

"Never." Henry took the charm from his wife. "What kind of markings are these?"

"Anyway, I thought you should have it since it's Tyler's." She made sure not to use the past tense word—"was"—but kept everything in the present tense. She didn't want to add any doubt to their already unsettled feelings. "It took awhile to pry it loose from his hands. You've got a strong boy. He's hanging on. It may take some time, but I think eventually he'll pull through. You just have to be strong with him."

"Yes," Henry and Gwen said at once. "Thank you, doctor."

"Don't thank me yet. Tyler has a long road ahead of him. Now, if you'll follow me, I'll take you to see him. Visiting hours have long since been over but I'm going to make an exception tonight since I'll be with you. I'll let you stay as long as possible."

PART TWO: FACADE

A double-minded man is unstable in all his ways.

James 1:8

CHAPTER 9 — THREE MONTHS LATER

ENVELOPED IN A chrysalis of white sheets, unconscious to his surroundings, Tyler heard voices that seemed distant and hollowed out. The murmuring sounded as though it was echoing down a long corridor, and he couldn't quite understand the words.

On the other hand, Edward was very much on guard. He lay just beneath Tyler's skin, alert and attentive to every detail around him.

Tyler was no longer in the intensive care ward; he had been moved to a different area of the hospital. He no longer had the endotracheal tube down his throat and was no longer breathing by a ventilator; he was now able to breathe on his own. He was stable and had been for quite some time now. All that equipment had been detached and removed from him early in his recoupment process.

Occasionally, a doctor or nurse would come in and make adjustments to the remaining medical equipment he was attached to.

There isn't anything you can do to revive Tyler, Edward thought. *I'm the only one who can and will bring him out of this coma, and I'll do that when I'm good and ready.*

"I tend to think it's hopeless every day I see the boy like this," a familiar voice said. "I hope he comes out of his coma soon, because I'm running out of encouragement for his parents. They have been devastated by this tragedy."

"You're right, doctor," another voice said in return. "It seems that all we can do is make him comfortable."

"I agree. The rest is left up to him."

"Yes, doctor."

"Michael, I've told you before that you can call me Suzanne."

The man's voice took on a flirty air, "Well, Miss Suzanne Baldwin, now that we are on first name basis, how about I take you to dinner tonight? I know the cafeteria is a far cry from candlelight and wine, but until I can take you out later in the week for a real meal and a great time on the town, it will have to suffice."

Tyler's mind froze; he didn't listen to her answer.

Suzanne Baldwin? The spoken name stabbed like a knife into his brain. *Surely not. It can't be the same person.* Edward rolled the two words over in his mind. Edward had heard those words before, but that had been a long time ago. Edward knew that name, remembered who she was but more importantly what she had done to him.

Edward's thoughts sent Tyler's mind reeling, and his heart beat began to race.

The electrocardiogram's silent blip increased but wasn't noticed. The switch for the sound on all the medical instruments—the cardiac monitor and the pulse oximeter attached to his index finger—had been turned off a long time ago. It was most likely turned off by request of the parents, visitors, or because the doctors didn't see fit to have the redundant blip constantly bombarding the ears of a comatose patient. All the other machines were also silent, unable to call attention to Tyler's— make that Edward's—arousal.

Wouldn't want to make the monitors go off the rails, now would we? Edward asked himself. *No, no, that wouldn't be the best timing in the world.*

Controlling Tyler's vital signs, careful not to make the monitors surge, Edward slowly opened Tyler's eyes. The temptation was too great. He had to look at her just to make sure it was the same person he knew.

The figures were blurry at first. They became focused, then blurred out again. When his eyes came into a final focus, the figures were too busy talking to notice Tyler was alert, awake, and staring at them.

The woman was definitely the Suzanne Baldwin he knew from high school ages ago. He had a snapshot view of her as she moved back around the bed to the male nurse named Michael. She had matured even more from the high school days, if that was possible. She was still graced with the drop-dead gorgeous looks of a model and could have easily been seen on the covers of numerous magazines such as *Cosmopolitan, Elle,* and *Vanity Fair* if she had pursued that line of work.

The male nurse flirting with her was handsome—certainly good-looking enough for her to invest a few minutes of innocent flirtation. Suzanne hadn't changed a bit from their high school days—that was apparent.

Suzanne was leaning against the stainless steel rail that restricted patients from rolling on to the floor when unattended. Suzanne's back was to Tyler, but Edward could see her hips were cocked to one side in a seductive stance. Her shoulders were erect to emphasis her chest, which stretched her uniform tight across her breasts as an enticement as well as an invitation.

"So you're not asking for a bite to sample, you're wanting the whole meal?" Suzanne teased in a husky voice.

Michael played coy and ran a hand through his locks of black curly hair and smiled to the sexual suggestion, "Yes ma'am, as a matter of fact I am."

"In that case, I accept *both* invitations."

You're still the same tease you were back then; no wonder you never got married. You never could settle down, could you? Still playing the field. You may still be a looker, but you will always be the same slut you were in high school.

Edward hated her. But it hadn't always been like that. There was a time when he wanted her just as much as all the other testosterone-laden guys.

I think I still want you Suzanne, Edward thought. *But this time, I think I want you more dead than alive.*

He remembered the suggestive clothing she used to wear and the way she would flaunt her body that would turn the head of any guy.

Both heads, Edward thought figuratively.

It was her way of getting a man. Too bad for Suzanne that her beauty is only skin deep. The talk around school was that Suzanne had been used and abused. She had been passed around from one guy to the other. Maybe she liked that lifestyle—if you can honestly call it a lifestyle—or maybe it was her that was using each guy for whatever reason. In either case, and in Edward's book, she was still a whore, plain and simple.

An old one-liner Tyler and his friends used when they talked trash about loose women drifted into Edward's thoughts. *Her legs are just like the doors of Wal-Mart, they are always open. Twenty-four seven.* Edward began to laugh inside. *You're just like a doorknob, Suzanne. Everyone gets a turn with you.* He was still laughing inside when another thought joined the last. *Me included.*

He didn't conjure those images up in his head at that moment. He didn't want to relive that moment again right now. Instead, he began to think about what he would do if he had another moment alone with her.

That was then, this is now, nothing's changed, Edward thought. *So why the medical field, Suzanne? How did you go from your wild, crazy lifestyle in high school to being a nurse? Or doctor? Surgeon? Whatever it is you do here? I guess time will tell.*

"How about we meet at six o'clock in the cafeteria?" Michael asked.

"Sounds like a date."

"Alright. I'll see you then," Michael said.

As Michael turned to leave, he glanced down at Tyler one last time. There was a split second that their eyes locked on each other. Edward closed his eyes right as Michael took a double take to make sure of what he had just seen.

Michael had taken a startled backward shuffle step upon first sight of the boy staring up at them. His body erupted in goosebumps and he cried out. "Doctor?"

Shit, Edward cursed inside. *He saw me. He fucking saw me staring at them.* Edward had been so lost in the hated memories of Suzanne that Michael had caught him off guard.

"Yes," she answered.

"Ah, this may sound strange but, um, I don't think Tyler is asleep anymore, I mean, in his coma. That's not possible is it?"

Suzanne looked at the monitors around the bed. "I seriously doubt it. Everything looks normal. The sound on the monitors have all been turned off, but if there was any brain activity or movement they would've notified us from the station out front."

"Um, his eyes were open," Michael said. "He was looking right at me. I-I swear to God he was."

Suzanne double-checked the monitors. "There doesn't seem to be any new activity."

"I swear on a stack of Bibles. His eyes. They were open. And he was staring at us."

"Michael," she scoffed. Suzanne thought he was playing a trick on her. "You need a vacation, but I can only grant you a break. Come on, I'll buy you a drink. Wish it could be a beer, but a Coke will have to do for now."

Michael continued to stared at the body in disbelief.

Suzanne had to grab Michael's shoulder and twist him in the direction of the door. "Trust me," she said. "The monitors don't lie. The machines would've let us know."

That's right, stupid. The monitors don't lie. I'm half-dead. Can't you tell, Edward said chuckling to himself.

"I guess you're right," Michael said. "Doctors know best. But I know what I saw. Apparently, I've been working too long. I'm seeing things."

"Yeah, you're seeing things. Come on, let's go. You've been working the graveyard shift far too long. A break will do you some good."

The fading squeak of their shoes on the linoleum floor told Edward he was alone in his quiet room. He opened Tyler's eyes again and peered out and around. Inside Tyler, Edward began to grin. That grin was matched on the outer surface when a smirk spread across Tyler's face as well.

Oh yeah, Edward thought. *This is going to be so much better than I expected. This is going to be a lot of fun.*

Eventually the smile loosened from his lips, and an expressionless look came back to Tyler's face. Soon Edward and Tyler lapsed back into a boundless sleep.

ɕ

From deep within Tyler's mind, a voice whispered his name. *Tyyllleeeerrrrr.* A mental coaxing; a vocal nudging.

Tyler opened his eyes. The movement wasn't of his own accord; it was involuntary, as though someone or something other than himself did the task for him. The voice came again. *Tyyllleeeerrrrr.*

He thought he had heard someone call his name, but the room was quiet and dark. He knew it was a room, because the only thing he saw above him was a recessed tiled ceiling. He could just make out the squared sections in the darkened gloom. He also saw what he thought was a metal track that encircled the bed. Out of the corner of his eye, he saw that the attached curtain was pulled back completely.

His brow furrowed. *Where am I? Hospital? Has to be.*

Even though the thoughts crossed his mind, it seemed different to him like they really weren't *his* thoughts but thoughts someone else was feeding his mind. He felt out of his element; out of touch with himself. It was almost as though his inner being wasn't there at all. If it was, it felt like it had been replaced by and with something else.

Tyler slowly sat up in bed determined to puzzle this out. His chest hurt for the moment, but the pain wasn't completely unbearable. The bed creaked softly under his weight.

He finally noticed the smell of flowers. It had been there all along, but just then an overabundance of floral scents assaulted his nostrils.

Tyler looked around the room. By the window in the far corner was a table that held a few bouquets of flowers. There were more on the shelf to his right.

In searching the room he saw there was another bed to his right, but it was unoccupied. He was all alone in the room. But somehow, he didn't feel alone.

Yeah. Definitely a hospital.

He didn't know why all of a sudden he had the urge to sit up. One thing was for sure, though; he knew he couldn't lie there anymore. He had to get up and move around. His body was aching because of the length of time he had been bedridden. It felt like he'd lain here for months.

How long had it been, and why was it here?

He slowly stretched as far as he could and in all directions. He found he couldn't raise his arms above his shoulders; his chest and ribs hurt. His joints and the vertebrae in his spine took turns cracking. The sudden stretch and release, albeit a small one, helped him relax.

Tyler didn't feel like his old self. He felt as though he were a marionette figure that was being guided by invisible strings that were attached to each of his joints. He knew it was a stupid thought, but he actually looked toward the ceiling to see if there was some trace of an unseen puppet master that was guiding his movements. Tyler's inner being seemed so far away but close enough to be just out of reach from himself. Something odd felt different about him. Something *was* different about him. Something *was* wrong.

He looked down at his hands and arms as if seeing them for the first time. He couldn't remember how or why these wires were protruding from his body. He removed the pulse oximeter that covered his left index finger and pulled the IV needle out of his right arm. A small shoot of blood squirted out at its removal. He grabbed a Kleenex that was on the tray table and tucked it into the crook of his arm and bent it to hold it in place. Tyler grabbed the electrodes that were stuck to his chest and jerked them loose.

Free, he thought, but it didn't feel like it was his thought.

Tyler also found something wrapped around his neck that didn't pull free. He held it up and realized it was his good luck charm he'd found the morning he went to the lake with friends. He kissed it and dropped it back onto his chest.

Tyler vigorously wiped his face with his hands. As soon as he started rubbing his face, he stopped and pulled his hands away. He was immensely puzzled by the scruff—almost full beard—that had grown nearly overnight or at least within the last few days. He tentatively put his hands back to his face, thinking the beard was his imagination.

Jesus, how long have I been asleep? he mused.

His beard was soft and his skin felt pleasant as if it had been ages since he had last touched it. He scratched his head and stroked his oily hair in a ten-fingered comb.

He looked around again.

"Why the fuck am I here? What the hell happened to me?" he asked himself.

No one answered back at first then the voice whispered again.

Tyylllleeeerrrrr.

151

A cold wash of fear splashed through Tyler at the sound of the voice. All of a sudden, he had a strange sense of de ja vu but with this feeling he couldn't put his finger on what the relived thoughts were exactly. He felt like it had something with all the new thoughts and awful memories or was it crazy dreams he'd been reliving. But now those thoughts and dreams seemed as though he'd only imagined them. He felt he'd been out of it for a long time.

Tyyllleeeerrrrr.

Tyler was looking at the light that was coming from underneath the door but wheeled around to face the person who was speaking. At first, it sounded as though someone to his left had spoken his name out loud. He thought maybe he had overlooked someone who was actually in the room with him, but no one was there. He then realized that the voice was coming from inside his own head.

"I thought I was alone," he mused as he scratched the back of his head.

You are and you aren't, the voice said again.

"This isn't funny. Who's there?" Tyler asked, his voice beginning to take on a nervous edge.

No answer.

Tyler didn't want to ask the next question because he was afraid of the answer that he might receive, but he asked anyway. "Where are you?"

The answer that he didn't want to hear came back to him, *Inside you.*

Tyler instantly became scared. A cold serpent of fear slithered up his spine, causing chills to multiply over his body. He shuddered.

Don't get excited, the voice said. *In time, I'll explain everything.*

Tyler shook his head and dug his index finger in each ear to unclog them. He felt as though he had been asleep for a long, long time. His mind could be playing tricks on him. The voice could be an after effect of the long doze or maybe medications he was on.

He looked over at the IV bag again to see if he could read on it what was being put into his body.

The voice spoke once again, *I knew you wouldn't remember. I guess that's best for now.*

"Who are you?" Tyler snapped.

Ignoring the question, the voice continued, *Damn Tyler, I owe you big time for what you did. If our paths hadn't crossed when they did, you would be worm food right now, and I would still be where I was. You should be as indebted to me as I am to you.*

"How come?"

Because I saved your life, that's why. I saved your life and you saved mine, so to speak.

Tyler's hand flew up, and his fingers snapped in a jester of remembrance. He was about to speak aloud when the voice interrupted him again.

Oh by the way, if I were you, I would start thinking your questions instead of asking them out loud.

Taking the voice's advice, Tyler dropped his hand back down to the bed sheets.

The voice continued, *If people hear you talking to yourself, they're liable to think you're crazy. Talking to yourself isn't normal. It's a first class ticket to the nut house. As far as hearing voices in your head, get used to it, because you're going to hear mine for a very long time to come.*

Why? Why are you doing this?

It's actually the only way to do it. C'mon, let's get out of here.

We can't just leave, Tyler thought. *Do you have any idea how long we've been here?*

I have an idea. Don't worry about that now. C'mon, let's get out of here. I know you don't want to be here any more than I do.

Yeah, but you just can't walk out of a hospital in the middle of the night.

Even as Tyler was thinking that, his feet swung off of the bed.

Watch me, Edward replied mentally.

Hey, wait a minute. What are you doing?

Getting out of here, and there's nothing you or anyone else can do to stop me. Just enjoy the ride. I'll take you places you've never been before, kiddo.

Tyler's feet eased to the cold tiled floor.

Edward slowly stood and tested his new legs.

Tyler's body was moving involuntarily. It was the strangest feeling he had ever felt. He was moving, although he wasn't telling himself to do so.

Tyler made the choice to fight back. He mentally willed himself against Edward's forward movement. Tyler latched on to the metal guardrail attached to the bed. Guided by Edward, Tyler's head swiveled back to look at his own hand.

That's very uncool, Tyler. Don't fight me. Every time you do, I'm going to do this.

Edward mentally forced Tyler's hand to release the bed's guardrail. It took a few tries, but his hand finally relaxed and opened. His hand opened and jerked closed in a short-circuited-robot fashion. His hand involuntarily swung away so it couldn't latch on to the bed again. Edward turned to take a step toward the door, but his legs locked up because Tyler mentally forced them to stay put. In doing this, Tyler lost his balance and crumpled to the floor.

Great, now look what you did. Quit fighting me, Tyler. This would go so much smoother if you would just let me navigate.

Tyler felt as though the sinister puppet master was playing a sick joke on him by cutting the puppeteer strings. In a way, that was the case, but instead of being an outside guider, this one was on the inside.

Edward grabbed the bed railing this time and pulled himself up. He flexed his feet and legs then tried again. When he moved away from the bed this time, he was ready for Tyler's resistance and mentally overrode any command Tyler gave his body. This compensation caused his body to move with a lurch; it was a strange, jerky motion.

Tyler felt as though he was a cross between Frankenstein's monster and a re-animated zombie.

He stumbled to the door but managed to grab the door handle and pulled himself up before he crumpled to the floor again. He opened the door and cautiously emerged into the corridor.

The hallway was half lit, spooky, and reminded him of the old Halloween movies.

Tyler leaned against the wall of the hallway. After a quick rest, he slowly made his way toward the lighted nurses' station in the center of the corridor. He used the wall to steady himself as he went. His walk became easier and not as constricted.

When Tyler reached the unit desk, it was empty. He stood there for a few moments stupefied at why he had gone to the trouble of coming all the way up here when he could barely walk. Edward was looking around in bewilderment trying to figure out which way the exit was.

Down the hall, a door opened and the tale-tell sound of nurse's shoes squeaked on the linoleum floor.

Someone's coming, Tyler thought.

Yeah, no shit, Edward thought back.

Overcome by the fear of being caught, Tyler half crawled—half baboon scuffled down the hallway in the direction he had come. He dropped behind a gurney into concealing shadows as a nurse stepped into the light. Unable to move his right leg because of exhausted muscles, Tyler grabbed his leg above the knee and pulled it out of the bleak light into the shadows with him. In the process of doing so, he bumped the wheeled stretcher. This movement pushed it down the corridor about six inches. It was just enough for one un-oiled gurney wheel to squeak back a response to the nurses shoes.

Tyler heard the scuffle of her shoes stop abruptly as the woman came into view. There was a pause, then, the nurse asked hesitantly, "Hello. Is anyone there?"

Tyler peered over the gurney from within his hiding place and noticed it wasn't a nurse, but Suzanne Baldwin.

Hello yourself, Suzanne, Edward whispered. *Yeah, someone is definitely here.*

Suzanne looked rigid; a little spooked.

Why the hell is she still here? It's very unlike her to be working the night shift. Thought you would be off at some strip club making every man's dream come true. Maybe we won't leave so quickly after all.

What's that supposed to mean? Tyler asked.

Never mind. It doesn't concern you.

Yes it does. This is my body you're tampering with.

And there isn't anything you can do about it, so shut up. I need to concentrate.

Suzanne shrugged her shoulders and shook her head. As she walked into the nurses' station, Tyler heard her say to herself, "Get a grip on yourself, Suzanne. This job is screwing with your mind. It's going to make you crazy. People are going to start thinking you're whacko; then you'll have to get an appointment with a shrink. And nobody is a better personal shrink than Kelly."

Kelly? Which Kelly? Kelly Morgan? It can't be the same one. Can it be that they are still good friends after all these years? They were practically inseparable in school.

Tyler soon heard her typing on a keyboard.

Eventually, Tyler emerged from behind the gurney; he came out of the hallway shadows and moved cautiously up to the counter again. Suzanne's back was to him with headphones in her ears.

Each room was hooked up by biotelemetry devices. The monitors in this command station beeped and blinked in accordance to the patient's vital signs. All the screens, except one. One screen showed a continuous horizontal flat line. The numbers for the heart beat, pulse and blood pressure each showed a blinking zero or a dash in their space. Edward figured that was the screen that was registering Tyler's vital signs.

You never paid attention to detail did you, Suzanne? Edward thought. *I could have died in there and you wouldn't have even noticed.*

Tyler's right leg buckled from the weight, and his knee slammed against the wall of the counter.

Suzanne stopped typing and cocked her head; contemplating if her imagination was still running wild or if she had indeed heard a dull thud behind her. She pulled the earphones from her ears and turned around a moment after Tyler dropped behind the counter.

Edward was careful not to make any other sound as he crouched out of sight.

"Hello. Is anybody there?" Suzanne asked, swallowing hard and listening to nothing. "Michael, if that's you playing a trick on me, I swear to God I'm going to kick your ass if you try anything." She paused to wipe some hair strands out of her eyes then said to herself, "I really hate working this late at night."

Edward grinned beneath his new skin, which caused Tyler's mouth to form his contemptible smile. *I've scared Suzanne two times now. This is going to be so much fun.*

When the click of the keyboard began again, Edward stood. He was about to slip into the nurses' station, but before he could, he heard a door open down the corridor off to his right. Edward immediately left the counter for his gurney hideout again.

As Edward crossed back across the hallway, he turned to get a look at who was coming. It was blind luck he didn't get caught. The man's head was down, making sure the coffees he was carrying didn't spill. Edward thought it was that nurse guy, Michael, again.

From his hideout, Edward saw Michael stop short near the nurses' station. He watched as Michael notice Suzanne's back was to him. He placed the coffees on the counter, then he crept to the nurse's station entrance and slipped inside. He quietly moved around behind Suzanne and crept up behind her.

That is exactly what I was going to do, Edward thought.

If Suzanne had looked deep within the reflection on her computer screen cast by the fluorescent lights overhead, she would have seen the slight movement of a distorted image coming up behind her.

Michael's hands and arms quickly encircled her body.

Suzanne let out a blood-curdling scream as she stood to defend herself. She backed up into another desk so hard she almost knocked herself into the floor. Her eyes were wide. Her hands were shaking. Her nerves were stunned as though shocked by an electrical charge. Files, reports, and a desk lamp were scattered and shattered on the floor as she fought to stabilize herself. It was like a murderous tango.

"Damn it, Michael!" Suzanne said, as she spun to see who had attacked her. "What the hell are you doing here? You scared the shit out of me."

Michael couldn't speak or pick himself up off the floor; he was too busy laughing at her.

Suzanne was feisty though; she kept slapping, punching, and unleashing her aggression out on him.

"All right, all right; I give, I give." Michael said. "Ease up, damn. I bruise easily. That probably wasn't the best idea I've ever had. I'm sorry."

"You're damn right it wasn't."

"At least you're awake. Here, not that you need it now, but I brought you some coffee." He grabbed one of the coffees he had set on the counter. "Maybe it can be my peace offering."

"Don't count on it. You're going to have to do a lot to make up for what you just did."

"Great, I always like to make up with you. Not to mention, making *out* with you."

She smiled. She was no longer upset, but she punched him in the chest for good measure.

Tyler's head shook in disgust although it was Edward who was thinking, *Young love; so beautiful it makes me want to puke. If you were going to do it right, Michael, like I was going to do, you would've just went ahead and snapped her neck like a stalk of celery.*

The thought that Edward thought scared Tyler and his body when cold with fear but he didn't have time to question Edward on it.

Michael had already glanced over to the bay of monitors and said, "Hey, did the coma patient in room three-forty-two finally awake or did he pass on?"

Not looking at what he saw on the monitor, she said, "No, why?"

Tyler thought, *Coma?* That word scared him worse than the thought Edward had just let drift through their mind.

"Because he's either awake or he's dead."

Tyler looked over the gurney again.

He saw Suzanne glance at the monitors and say, "What do you mean?"

"It appears he's flat lined. There are no vital signs whatsoever." He started punching buttons on the monitors. The sound of a patient flat lining finally became evident. Just the monotone sound of a flat line. "No pulse or anything."

"Holy shit. This isn't good. Come with me. I may need your help."

Time to go, Edward thought.

Not fighting against each other now, Tyler and Edward bolted toward their room and closed the door as silently as possible. They moved toward the bed and noticed the electrodes that had been attached to his head, his IV, and other connections were displaced haphazardly. There was no time to reattach anything the way it had been, especially the IVs. He felt trapped. He had no idea what to do.

Edward made the final decision for them both. For him, it would be easier if he was in control. To render Tyler helpless in this situation, Edward pulled the plug on Tyler and shut him down.

All of a sudden, Tyler's world went black. One second he was looking around the room trying to decide what to do, the next second his whole world was engulfed in darkness. His eyes were still open, but he could see nothing whatsoever. He blinked in surprise. He had no time to become scared; he only had enough time to think, *Did I just go blind?* That thought followed him as he felt himself go slack and fall to the floor.

After he landed, Suzanne and Michael stormed into the room. They found a sprawled body and assumed Tyler had awakened then attempted to leave.

They immediately began searching for signs of life.

Suzanne shined a pen light into his vacant eyes to see how alert he was.

The light was bright and blinded Edward. He screamed out, and the scream would've been voiced aloud through Tyler's mouth if Tyler had been awake.

Suzanne saw that Tyler was alert. What used to be dazed eyes had a spark of life in them.

"He's asleep now." Suzanne said aloud.

"That's not normal, is it?" Michael said.

"Far from normal; it's very abnormal."

"What do we do?"

"Nothing, except wait for him to wake up. Something tells me he'll be awake sooner than we expected."

"Are you going to contact his parents?"

"Yes. I think a call to them is in order. It may help the Curtis's emotional condition if they hear some good news about their son."

"You sure that's a good idea, seeing as how he's not completely awake?"

"Not completely, but he's far from where he was."

"What if he lapses back into a coma during the night? What then?"

"I'll cross that bridge if and when it happens. I just think they need to hear some good news for a change. Come on, let's get him back in bed and make him comfortable. Tomorrow is going to be a big day for everyone."

CHAPTER 10

IT WAS CLOSE to lunch time the next morning when Tyler's index finger twitched on the top of the sheets. A few minutes later, his eyelids fluttered and then slowly opened. The overhead lights, combined with the sun streaming through the windows, weren't favorable to a waking person, and he squinted against their glare. He blinked a couple of times and then opened his eyes wider. His vision blurred slightly at first. He took turns opening and closing his eyes; each time he kept them open longer, allowing them time to adjust to the brightness. When everything came into focus, he noticed the white ceiling, the white walls, and the light blue curtain dividers.

Hospital, he thought, but couldn't remember the reasons that put him here.

His head ached with a dull throb at the base of his skull and seemed to increase the more he tried to force remembrance.

He breathed deeply, taking the air in slowly. The air expanded his achy chest. He gritted his teeth against the pain.

He felt congested, but what little he could smell was like bitter anesthetics along with an overpowering scent of fresh flowers. It was a mixed floral scent that was almost too sweet. Then he remembered all the flowers he saw the night before.

His mouth felt clammy, like tasteless, stagnant glue had been poured into his mouth and then forced shut.

He wanted to move around, but his body was limp and racked with bed-ridden anxiety.

Movement in the hallway caught his attention, and he rolled his head to the side to see what the distraction was. He saw a doctor and a nurse pass in front of his dad and mom. They were talking to someone whose back was to him. It was a girl with long, auburn hair. When he saw the hair, his heart skipped a beat and his smile grew even bigger realizing it was Savannah.

Tyler was thrilled to see her but couldn't help but wonder why. They weren't dating, or were they? The details were foggy. Maybe they were farther along in a relationship than he realized. The déjà vu feeling from a few days ago replayed again; the feeling he had now was the same as when he saw her walking down the aisle in his first period class.

As Savannah talked with Tyler's parents, Gwen glanced away from her and noticed Tyler was staring at them. She exclaimed, "You're awake!" then broke into a run and entered his room.

Startled by the outburst, the others turned in the direction Gwen was headed. When they realized what she was doing, they instantly followed and fanned out around the bed to welcome Tyler back to the land of the living.

"Yeah, yeah, I'm awake alright. I'm just trying to figure out what's going on."

"It's about time," his dad joked.

"What do you mean?"

"How do you feel?" Gwen asked propping herself upon the bed to get near Tyler.

"Like shit, to tell you the truth. Sorry, Mom."

"Hey, Tyler," Savannah said and grabbed his hand. "It's really great to have you back."

He grasped her hand as tightly as he could. "It's good to be back, although I have no idea where I have been or how long I've been there." When they didn't answer he asked again, "How long *have* I been out?"

They all saw the expectant look on Tyler's face. Tears started to flow down sleep weary cheeks as they grabbed his hands, each wanting to ensure this moment wasn't a hallucination.

"Are you going to answer me, or am I going to have to guess as to what the hell is going on?"

No one said anything. They were still in a disbelieving mode.

Savannah was the first to break the silence. "Why don't you just take it easy for a little while? Don't worry so much about that now. It will all come back to you in time."

Henry said, "I couldn't agree with her more."

Trying to help move to a different subject, Gwen said, "Yes, we'll talk about all that soon enough."

Tyler asked, "You think you've got enough flowers in here?"

Gwen laughed in agreement, "Yes, baby, you've got lots of flowers; sent by all your friends and family members too."

"Can we get you anything, son?" Henry asked. "Are you hungry or thirsty?"

"Yeah. Don't ask me why, but I'm really in the mood for some ice tea. My mouth feels really nasty."

"You're in luck, because I brought a glass of iced tea from home." Henry said. "You can have the rest of it if you like."

"That would be great."

"Hope you don't mind the lemon."

"Not in the least. Anything, I don't care what it is. I just need something."

Tyler took a sip and sloshed it around in his mouth then swallowed. He did this a number of times then took a few more drinks. "Oh wow, that did the trick. Much better now."

"How are you doing, son?" Gwen asked. "How do you feel?"

Tyler laughed softly and shifted his weight, "Stiff. Really stiff," he muttered. "I feel like I haven't moved in months."

Everyone exchanged knowing glances, but Tyler didn't see their faces; he was too busy trying to sit up in bed.

If he only knew, Savannah thought.

"Ohh man, I feel like I've been hit by a Mac truck. What happened?" he asked as he rubbed his head. "Why am I in the hospital?"

When Tyler opened his eyes again, he noticed the tears on his mom's face and he knew something was wrong.

"What's the matter with everyone? Why are you crying?"

He searched their blank faces for answers.

Henry, Gwen, and Savannah exchanged glances again; mentally asking the other how much they thought Tyler remembered from the accident, wondering if they should tell him what had happened since then or if they should wait for the doctor to relay the information.

"Well, is anyone going to say anything, or are you just going to stand there with those stale looks on your faces?"

They didn't answer, but he beseeched their faces for a tale-tell sign that would give the answer away.

Trying to solve the mystery for Tyler, Henry said, "It's really good to have you back. At times we didn't think you were going to pull through." Henry's words dropped off at the end of his sentence. He realized he said the wrong thing.

Savannah bowed her head. She knew his words weren't the best ones to use with someone that had just emerged from a coma, but she didn't say anything. She felt it wasn't her place; at least, not right now. It was a family moment and she didn't think she needed to interrupt it. She just sat there and squeezed Tyler's hand tight to let him know she was there for him.

"What do you mean, 'didn't think I was going to pull through'?" Tyler asked. He switched looks from each person. His voice was starting to take on an edge of frustration. "What—what are you talking about?"

"Okay Tyler, just calm down," Henry said, as he rubbed his son's shoulder. "Now, I probably didn't use the best words just then; we really don't know what to say. We're still in shock about the whole situation, but just give us time to tell you what happened, all right?"

Tyler leaned back in the comfort of the hospital bed, folded his arms and muttered, "All right."

"Do you remember anything before this morning?" Gwen asked.

"Well—I remember going to the lake with Savannah yesterday. I picked her up—um, we had a great time with some of her friends—I even made some new friends myself. They were pretty cool. I, um," he cleared his throat more as a way to give himself time to think about yesterday's events. "Well, after that, I took her home and dropped her off at her house. Then I, I left her house and then, um, well, from there on it's become a little hazy for me. I don't know. I guess something happened that brought me here, right?"

"Yes. You're at Silver Ridge Memorial," Gwen added.

"Why? What happened?"

"Before we tell you that, can you tell us anything else that you remember?" Henry asked.

"Why can't you just tell me?"

"That's too easy, as your doctor says. She mentioned that it would be in your best interest if you figure as much of it out on your own," Henry said. Suzanne had never said anything of the like, but Henry wanted him to start using his mind again. "So let's have it. What do you remember?"

"I, ah; I was, huh," he was trying out different scenarios but they didn't seem to work. "I really don't know."

Henry was about to coax him a little more, but then Tyler began again.

Tyler began with somewhat of a bemused smile on his face, as though he really didn't actually believe what he was about to say. "I do know this. It was really weird. I did have a really strange dream last night; so bizarre." He turned to Savannah and said, "I had a dream that after I left your house, I totaled my car. Can you believe that? I ran off an embankment on a two lane highway because this damn black cat ran out in front of my car. It wasn't the black cat himself that scared me. I knew what it was as soon as I saw it. It was more the reflection of his eyes in the glare of my headlights that spooked me. Scared me so bad I hit the brakes a little too hard and hydroplaned off the road. Man it was crazy; really freaking scary, too." He only used "freaking" because his parents were in the room.

Savannah gave him a half-hearted smile. She hoped he didn't notice her smile wasn't genuine.

Tyler nudged her hand and smiled. "It's good to wake up and see you here, though."

Savannah smiled back and whispered. "I'm glad. It's great to see you, too." She winked again then looked down to their enclosed hands.

"Tyler, you don't remember anything else, anything at all?" Henry asked.

Tyler looked back at his parents. "No, I can't think of anything else right now, but you all seem so enthused about all this. What did happen, exactly?"

Nobody said anything at first.

"Come on, sometime this century. Enough with the secrecy."

Gwen began by grabbing his other hand to soften the coming blow. "Tyler, I don't know how to tell you this or how you might take it, so I'm just going to come out and say it. The dream you just explained really did happen. It really wasn't a dream at all. That's why you're here. The accident actually happened," she paused, not wanting to tell him the disturbing part, but she continued anyway, "the accident happened a little more than three months ago. You have been in a coma for about three months now."

At first Tyler thought she was joking and was almost ready to break into laughter but saw their faces were unwavering and nodding agreement.

Tyler's smile quickly faded. His mouth dropped open as though he were about to say something but nothing came out. All of a sudden, his world started spinning out of control as his mind dealt with the news.

He blinked his eyes and closed them for a second as he leaned further back into the bed, put his hands to his head, and pressed against his temples as though he were trying to block that reality from his mind. A vein popped out on his forehead as he tried to reason his mother's words, but it was useless to try and make sense of them.

Impossible, Tyler thought.

His chest seemed constricted as though his heart and lungs were clamped in steel bands and were slowly tightening. His breathing became laborious. He breathed deeply to try and ease the anxiety.

He thought about the loss of time he could have spent cultivating the relationship between himself and Savannah. What about the development of new friends he had made at school and the lake? How many games would he have helped win already if he had made it to those Monday tryouts and the team? Where would he be today if he had those past days and months back again? It was all too bizarre for his mind to comprehend.

"Tyler?" Savannah asked.

He was startled back to reality.

"Yeah."

"You okay?"

"Yeah. Just got lost in my thoughts. Three months? You've—you've got to be kidding me. It seems like just yesterday we were at the lake together and I drove you home."

"It's true, son," Henry added. "You awoke out of your coma last night around two in the morning."

Savannah added, "You've just got to realize that those past months are not what matters now. What matters now is that you are still among us. Still alive and kicking. You got a second chance at life. Don't worry about the time you've lost. Look at all the life you've gained."

"She's absolutely right, Tyler," Gwen agreed. "I know it doesn't make sense right now but don't worry about that. Just be glad it was three months and not three years or even worse. Be glad you're still alive."

"You do remember that stormy night, don't you? The car wreck?" Henry questioned.

"The car wreck was true? I really did total my Mustang?"

"Yeah, the Mustang was a total loss. Sorry."

"Ohh man," he said punching the mattress with his free hand. "I loved that car. Raven loved riding in it, too. Raven!" The thought of Raven hit him hard and he sat bolt upright in the bed. He winced in pain from the quick movement and grabbed his chest. "What about Raven? She was with me at the lake. Please, tell me she didn't die in the wreck." Tears were already starting to bead up in his eyes.

"No, no, son. Calm down," Henry said. "Raven's all right. She's a trooper. She's at home waiting for you. From what I hear, Raven actually saved your life."

"What? Really? How so?"

Henry and Gwen told Tyler the story Bruce Saliers told them. During the story, a dark hatred began to fester deep within Tyler's mind. Tyler couldn't understand why he began to have an ill will toward a man who had recently saved his life.

"Tyler?" Henry asked.

Tyler was pulled from his thoughts and looked up at his dad. "Yeah, Dad."

"You still with us, son? You seemed like you drifted off to Never Never Land there for a few seconds."

"Oh yeah. Still here," Tyler said but looked away and seemed to go into the trance again. He wasn't able to get fully focused because another voice grabbed his attention.

"Well, well, well, Mr. Curtis. You're finally awake," Suzanne Baldwin said from the doorway. "It's about time, don't you think?" She was standing just inside the room with a hand on one hip and an obnoxious but comical look on her face.

"That's what my dad said."

"And rightly so. Your next mission, should you choose to accept it, is to be up and about within the hour. Physical therapy time. Think you can handle that?"

"You've got no argument from me. I've been here three months too long already."

"So you've heard the news. That's good. How did you take it, and how are you coping with it?"

"I think he had a rough time dealing with it at first," Henry said. "It probably hasn't totally sank in yet, but Savannah put things in perspective for him."

Tyler broke in, "Everyone reminded me that I have the rest of my life ahead of me and that's better than the alternative."

"That's even better advice than I can give," Suzanne said.

Henry and Gwen moved back from the bed as Suzanne checked Tyler over.

"I'll have the physical therapy nurse come get you in a few minutes. Nothing major, just a light workout to get you focused and on your feet."

"The sooner I can get out of this bed, the better."

"That's what I like to hear."

Henry chimed in. "He knows all the news and about why he's here. He's told us everything he knew, but his memory is still somewhat hazy."

"That's typical. You probably have what we call collective amnesia," Suzanne said. "Depending on the situation, a person will purposely forget a part or all the details surrounding a certain situation. Don't be alarmed. You seem to be taking it well, but I'm sure some of it hasn't caught up with you yet. Your mind is probably in shock from an overload of information given to you today. Everything will come back to you. Just take it easy and let it happen of its own accord."

"If I take it any easier, you might as well have me stuffed," Tyler said.

Suzanne laughed as she typed some notes into the small handheld tablet she was carrying. "You sound like you're coming around to being your old self again. I still have my rounds to do, but I'll be back to check on you later to see how the therapy session went. I know you want to catch up on what has happened in the last few months so I'll leave you with your family. Don't over exert yourself; you're still recovering, understand?"

"Not a problem."

"Thank you, doctor," Gwen replied and propped herself back upon the bed again.

After Suzanne left, they sat around and talked about the horror everyone had went through. The thought that the Saturday with Savannah three months ago could have been his last filled Tyler with mild apprehension. He was still shocked at how close he had come to Death's edge but not topple into It's abyss. During the silent moments between everyone's comments, he prayed a special prayer and gave reverence to God for sparing his life and giving him another chance to make it worth something.

Eventually, Tyler became worn down from all the questions. He was still weak. He felt tired but didn't want to go back to sleep. He was afraid another three months would go by before he woke up again.

"You look exhausted, Tyler," Henry said. "We were just about to go grab a bite to eat when Gwen saw that you were awake. Since your physical therapy session is in a few minutes, we're going to leave you now."

"What?" Gwen questioned.

"Sure, no, you guys go ahead," Tyler said.

Henry continued, "We'll be back by the time you've finished. We can catch up then."

"I don't care to eat right now when my baby boy has just woken up. I want to talk with him now."

"Gwen," Henry said firmly. "So do I, but right now, I think Tyler needs some alone time to process the news. That is a pretty heavy blow of news to receive." He grabbed Gwen's arm and pulled her off the bed. "C'mon. Let's grab a bite and we'll be back in no time."

"But—" Gwen protested again.

"I do have a lot to think about. Process time would be good for me."

"Savannah, would you like to join us?" Henry asked.

"Thanks for the offer, but I'll have to pass this time. I have to be somewhere soon. I was just going to stay for a minute or two longer if that's okay and then I have to go."

"It's okay by us," Henry said. "What about you, Tyler?"

"Are you crazy? Of course she can stay. I'd be disappointed if she didn't."

Savannah blushed.

"We're glad you're back with us." Gwen said then leaned over and kissed his forehead.

"We'll see you in a little while," Henry said. "Oh, and Savannah?"

She turned toward Henry.

"Thanks for all you did for us and Tyler these past few months."

"Oh—don't mention it. It was nothing, really. I was happy to help all of you out."

"Well, we really appreciate it," Gwen added.

Henry and Gwen exited as Savannah propped herself more comfortably on the bed. They sat in silence staring at each other for a long while saying nothing.

Eventually Tyler reached for her hand again and she took it without hesitation.

"What did they mean when they said 'thanks for all you've done these past few months'?"

"I'm not the kind of person that brags on what I've done. It wasn't a big deal."

"My parents thought it was. So?"

Savannah bowed her head; she seemed embarrassed and continued to be quiet.

"You might as well tell me, because I'm going to ask them when they get back."

"Well if you must know, I've pretty much came by here everyday to check on you to make sure you were okay."

"What? Really? You did that for me?"

She nodded, "Don't make a big deal about it. It was nothing."

"Don't make a big deal about it? That's amazing. "*You're* amazing," he emphasized.

"You don't remember do you?"

He shook his head. "That doesn't mean I don't appreciate it. I do. That's actually the best thing anyone has ever done for me." They were quiet for a moment then Tyler said, "On a different level, you coming to check on me probably helped me out more than you think. Who knows how long I would've been asleep had you not done that, so from the bottom of my heart, thank you."

"You're welcome. You've been to hell and back haven't you?"

"You don't know the half of it. Three months down the drain. It's so hard to believe."

"I know what you mean, and yet I don't," Savannah said.

"No. Not unless you've been through it."

"I guess you could say I went through it with you, in a way; not on the same level as you, but in a different way."

"Yeah, I guess you're right." Tyler paused for a moment and then asked, "Why did you stay with me that long? You don't really know me at all."

"For exactly that reason. I don't know you, but those first two days we spent together were enough for me to know that I care enough about you to stick around for awhile. I hope you didn't mind."

"Mind? In my wildest dreams, I couldn't have wished for anything better."

"Really?"

"Yes, really."

At the risk of sounding cliché, Savannah added, "That's good to know, because it's going to take more than a three month coma to get rid of me." She quickly leaned down and kissed him deeply. She was almost afraid the moment would get away from her again if she didn't. Tyler pulled her to him and held her tight. They held the embrace for a long time, enjoying the moment.

"You need a shave," she said rubbing his face.

"What, you don't like my beard?"

"It's okay, I guess. I like you better without one. You're way too good looking to hide it under facial hair. You woke up a few hours before your weekly shave."

"You shaved me while I was, um," he paused. The words were hard for even him to say. "While I was, ah, under. I mean, asleep?"

"Every week, just like clock work. It was the least I could do."

"Wow, you really did take care of me, didn't you?"

"The best care in the world."

"I would've done the same for you if the tables were turned."

"I would hope so."

"I'm not just saying that; I would."

"I know."

Tyler scratched absently at an itch on his neck. His fingers found the rawhide strand that was looped through his amulet. He picked it up from his chest again, stared at for a second, then placed it on his chest again.

Noticing Tyler's actions, Savannah said, "I see you found your good luck charm."

"Yeah, why am I still wearing it?" he asked.

"You weren't. I think the doctor gave it to your parents after you came out of surgery. I think they put it in this drawer by your bed. I found it a few days after I started to come take care of you. The strand it was on was okay, but not the strongest. I brought a brand new length of rawhide from home."

"Why?"

"I don't know. I guess it was just the way I remember you that day at the lake. You seemed to like the charm, and I thought it was cool. It seemed important to you, so I fixed it up nice for you."

"Thank you," he said, and pulled her back into him and kissed her again. When they broke away, Savannah looked him dead in the eyes and said, "It's really great to have someone kiss me back for a change."

"You kissed me when you came to see me?"

"No, not at first, but after the first week or so I started sneaking a quick goodbye kiss every time I would leave. Hope you don't think that's weird."

"Of course not. I would've kissed you back if I had known."

"I know."

"It was hard sometimes, but I understood the circumstances."

"All right you two, break it up," a voice said from the doorway behind them.

They turned to find a beautiful black woman with a wheel chair standing in the doorway smiling at them.

The woman continued, "I would say get a room, but it appears you've already done that." She laughed at her own joke, and Tyler and Savannah joined in. "Tyler, my name is Krystal and I'll be your physical therapist today. Sorry Miss Savannah, I need to kidnap your man for a little while."

"Hey, Krystal. Not a problem," Savannah said. "I have to go anyway." She turned again to Tyler and asked, "I'll come back a little later to check on you?"

"Please do. I need the company; I mean I need you."

Savannah smiled, "Then I'll be here."

"Can't wait. See you soon."

"Take good care of him, Krystal," she said as she left the room.

Over her shoulder Krystal said, "You know it girl, the best care in the world. I'll take care of your man."

cg

For the next few weeks, Tyler underwent intense daily physical therapy, and it proved to be very worthwhile. Tyler's strength came back to him quicker than the doctors were expecting.

The hospital staff was amazed how far Tyler had come since the automobile accident three months earlier. The only thing anyone could say was that he was a lucky son of a bitch.

One middle aged nurse who adored Tyler said, "Tyler's guardian angels were working overtime on the night of the crash."

Another nurse said, "That was pure luck; after that, he probably doesn't have any more lucky stars to count."

Another elderly doctor said, "It was a miracle, plain and simple. We see those from time to time. They are, most of the time, unexplainable. You just have to take them on faith."

Henry and Gwen thanked the doctors and nurses for everything they had done to get him back to his old self again. They said more than once that they couldn't see a difference in him since he woke up.

Tyler, on the other hand, knew something had happened to him. Something bad. He knew exactly what was wrong with him but was unable to voice that fact. Every time he tried to speak out about what was inside him, his new inner being held him in checkmate. From the haunted thoughts and dreams Tyler had since the accident to the strange feeling beneath his skin that seemed to have settled deep within his bones, Tyler didn't quite feel himself; and he, along with the other citizens of Silver Ridge, had yet to experience what the true sense of the word "fear" really meant.

CHAPTER 11

AN IMMENSE FLOCK of black birds whipped back and forth in a frantic figure-eight pattern that polka-dotted the azure sky. Brisk mid-November winds ruffled the orange and red tree-lined boulevard and blew through the windows of the Curtis family's Yukon. Like the weather, traffic was moderate.

The whole world looked so different than three months prior to the accident. Tyler had only a two day glimpse of the city when they first moved here, but it looked so much more unfamiliar to him now. He felt so lost.

Looking through brand new eyes, Edward was astounded at how huge Silver Ridge had become. It was now a bustling metropolis compared to what it used to be when he was alive. Huge buildings—that were taller than the typical two to three stories—had been erected since he had been around eighteen years prior. Those monstrosities could still be seen in his rear-view mirror that reflected the city area they had just left. But it wasn't just the city area that had grown; all along the highway, more privately owned businesses and neighborhoods had sprouted up. Another mall, a movie Cineplex, and more grocery stores had been constructed as well. Even a couple of Wal-mart superstores had been completed; one on either side of Silver Ridge.

"Tyler, you look like a tourist. I swear it looks like you've never seen a big city before."

"This place is huge," Tyler said without thinking. But it wasn't his thoughts he was voicing. Edward was so taken aback by how Silver Ridge had grown that his thoughts were being spoken instead of Tyler's. "I've never seen buildings this big before," Edward continued.

Gwen's eyes narrowed suspiciously and she glanced over at him. "Really? Then I suppose you've forgotten all about the big city of Chicago, right? You know, the Chicago where we *used* to live?"

"Chicago?" Edward questioned and then quickly briefed through Tyler's recent Chicago memories.

"Yeah. Chicago," Gwen said. "We only lived there for the past two years."

"Oh yeah, Chicago. Ah, the windy city," Edward said quickly. He thought even quicker, "I guess I must still be in that selective amnesia phase the doctor was talking about. I just forgot all that for a second, that's all."

Gwen's gaze lingered on him a little longer than it should have since she was driving.

From the corner of his eye, Edward noticed her scrutiny of him. *Don't push it,* Edward told himself. *Better to shut up and not say anything than to totally give myself away. I'll just sit here and be a good little boy.*

Eventually, Gwen turned her attention back toward the road.

Time passed, and for awhile nothing was said. Edward forced himself not to make a big deal of seeing how Silver Ridge had changed. He could do that later when he was on his own. He just stared out at the circling cluster of birds in the distance.

After a time, Gwen said, "I didn't mean for you to get embarrassed and clam up on me. If you're going to ride in my car, you just can't sit there in silence. You're going to have to talk to me. What's on your mind?"

Edward released his hold on Tyler slightly, allowing him to speak freely but still guarded his every word. He didn't want Tyler to all of a sudden shout out that he was possessed by some crazy teenage boy. That wouldn't go over so well. Things were complicated enough right now as they were.

"It's weird, you know," Tyler replied.

"And why is that?"

"It seems like we arrived here in Silver Ridge only two or three days ago and sometimes it feels like it's been a whole year. I've lost so much time. I still can't believe this has happened to me."

Gwen glanced over at her son again. His head was cocked at the jittering cloud of birds. "I'm sure it will take a while to get used to," she said.

"Yeah, I guess you're right."

"A mother knows everything." She grabbed hold of his knee and shook him. "Come on, Tyler, snap out of it. You've got the rest of your life ahead of you. You should be thankful for that."

"I am."

"You don't sound like you are. Cheer up. You're out of the hospital, aren't you?"

"Yeah."

"Well, that in itself should put a smile on your face," Gwen said.

"You're right, Mom."

"Of course I'm right. Rule number one: Mom is always right."

"What's rule number two?"

"If Mom is wrong, see rule number one."

They laughed for a moment then grew silent again.

A Ford truck grew even with them and a German Shepherd with his black and tan coat came into view. The dog had a faded green bandanna tied around its neck. Its paws were rooted on the tire guard of the cab, its tongue was hanging out of its mouth, and its eyes were squinted from the blowing wind. The dog didn't look in his direction; he seemed perfectly happy and content where he was.

Tyler remembered how much Raven enjoyed long drives.

Finally the truck picked up speed and pulled further ahead of them.

"Mom? How's Raven doing?"

"Oh, she's fine. She's out and about," Gwen said as they turned off the boulevard into their neighborhood. "She's not her usual, perky, happy-go-lucky self, but she'll pass for Raven. I think she really misses you. She's been really bored. We've taken the time when we could to play with her so she wouldn't feel abandoned, but we're not you. It's not the same to her."

"Hope she remembers me."

"I wouldn't worry about that. You're unforgettable."

"Why didn't Dad come with you to pick me up? I was expecting both of you to be there today."

Gwen purposely answered him in a tone that made it sound as though Henry had better things to do with his time, "Oh, I don't know. He was real busy today. He had a lot of work to catch up on at the bank."

As she finished her answer, the Yukon rounded the corner and turned into their driveway.

Blue, red, green, and yellow balloons were tied to the mailbox. A huge silver, metallic banner with rainbow-painted letters stated: WELCOME HOME TYLER. Multi-colored streamers and more balloons hung from each end.

"Is this the work you were talking about that Dad had to do?"

Gwen was already smiling, "I'm afraid so."

"I get the joke, Mom. Very clever, I have to admit. You've over done it this time." He leaned over and gave her a kiss on the cheek before stepping out of the car. "Thanks. I really needed this. It really makes me feel loved."

"Anything for my baby. If we had lost you, I don't know what Henry and I would've done."

Tyler snickered as though his accident had not been as dramatic as she made it out to be, "Don't be so candid, Mom. I'm sure there were reasons why the gods saw fit to spare my life."

A thought Edward was thinking fluttered across his mind, *And I have my reasons as well.*

Tyler tried to ignore Edward's stray thoughts, but it was impossible. Edward's thoughts were like tiny, annoying gnats buzzing near your ear on a hot summer day. The constant whine was impossible to get rid of no matter how much you waved your arms. Edward's thoughts would go away for a bit but would soon quickly resurface.

Tyler walked with his arms around his mother as they strolled up the walkway. At the front door, Gwen broke her hold around him but guided him forward so Tyler would be the first to enter the house. "After you," she said.

He answered with a thank you as he entered, but his head was still focused in her direction. As Tyler turned from her he was about knocked off his feet when the eruption of voices hit him full force. Yells, cheers, and applause crescendoed throughout the house.

Startled, Tyler quickly looked around as he crossed the threshold. A couple of camera flashes stunned his eye as they captured his surprise. The house was wildly decorated with more colorful streamers and balloons. Derrick, Jay, Cass, Iris, Erica, Amber, and Savannah were standing closer to the front. Neighbors Tyler didn't even know but people that his parents had met and most likely worked with surrounded him, throwing confetti and blowing party favors that gave off irritating whistles.

There were plenty of handshakes, hugs, and slaps on the back. "Welcome home," "welcome back," "congratulations" were stated from various individuals. Even a "glad you're not dead" came from Derrick.

Tyler turned and asked as Gwen stepped inside behind him, "You did this, didn't you?"

Gwen winked and said, "Actually it was your dad's idea but we, including Savannah, planned it together. We thought it would do you some good."

Tyler glanced across the room as Henry stepped forward with two drinks in his hands; one for himself and one for Tyler. Tyler accepted.

"Thanks, Dad. I really appreciate this."

"Well, you're special, and we love you," Henry said. "We wanted you to know it in another way besides just telling you."

Savannah engulfed him with a solid embrace then gave him a quick kiss on the lips. Cat calls and whoops were expressed throughout the crowd. Not wanting to be too affectionate with him while his parents were watching, she simply whispered, "I've missed you so much, and I'm glad you're back and to prove it, the next time were together *by ourselves* I'll give you a welcome back kiss you'll never forget. Maybe more."

Tyler's response was a wink and a smile.

Tyler and Savannah were eventually split apart as other people moved in to shake his hand and to give their best wishes and welcome back presents.

As he made his way through the throng of people, Tyler heard Raven barking upstairs. He hated that Raven had to be cooped up like that but knew she would just be too excited with all the people here. Raven would just be in the way. As he neared the other side of the room greeting people, Tyler heard Raven's bark getting closer. He heard her thumping down the stairs from the back of the house.

"Great. How did she get out of your room?" Henry asked.

"Easy. I taught her how to do everything," Tyler answered and gave a short whistle encouraging Raven on.

As Raven sprinted from the kitchen into the living room, overcome with joy that her master was back, a bad feeling came over her. Raven had long since forgotten about the bad thing she had felt on that rainy night Tyler was taken from her, but all at once she felt it and remembered. That same bad presence seized her body and assaulted her senses.

Raven skidded on the carpeted floor, stopped short in front of Tyler, and immediately started backing up.

The memory of that night long ago came back to her in horrifying clarity. The same bad something she had felt then was here again.

Raven planted her feet wide and her hackles stood on end.

The same bad thing was here in this room. She quickly looked around at a few people, trying to pinpoint its source, but they didn't seem to have it. She looked up at her master again. It seemed to be coming from within him. The bad thing *was* her master. She could see it in her master's eyes. It was inside him.

Raven lowered her head, concentrated on her master, and bared her teeth. Her lips started to quiver as a deep growl rumbled from the base of her throat.

"Easy, girl. What's the matter with you? What's got you so spooked? It's just me, Tyler. C'mon, girl."

Tyler slowly advanced toward Raven with his left hand outstretched and his palm up, careful not to startle her. Raven matched each of Tyler's advancing steps with one of retreat.

"Tyler, I don't think I would do that if I were you." Savannah suggested.

Other people gave their comments of a similar value as they watched in anticipation of what would happen next. They all backed up as though Raven were a bomb that would soon detonate.

Tyler glanced around, "It'll be OK. She just hasn't seen me in a while. That's all."

Raven loved her master and didn't want to harm him in any way. She had given him sufficient warning, but if Tyler didn't stop, she would have no choice but to attack.

As Tyler turned his attention to Raven and neared her once again, her intense growl grew into a combination of angry snaps and barks.

Tyler hastily withdrew his hand. "What the hell's the matter with you? C'mon. Easy, girl. Don't be this way."

Raven backed slowly into the corner, and when her backside bumped the wall, she knew she had nowhere to go but forward. When Tyler took another step forward, Raven attacked. She lunged from the corner, her teeth bared and saliva spraying. With a quick snap, Tyler's hand disappeared in Raven's mouth and her sharp teeth sank deep into his left hand.

Numbing pain engulfed Tyler's hand as if he had just grasped the tip of a red-hot fireplace poker, and he screamed out in pain. Tyler sank to his knees as he swatted at Raven. A hollow crack resounded as Tyler's hand connected with the bridge of Raven's nose. The blow was stern. Raven whined at first, braced herself and refused to let go. Raven's growl vibrated in Tyler's hand. It was a fierce bite. Tyler felt his skin tear and felt some of his muscles and tendons rip as Raven shook her head violently from side to side.

Then something strange happened that caused their eyes to lock on each other. It was something that chilled the blood in both their bodies. Tyler felt if first and then Raven.

A force, an energy; something surged out of Tyler's mind, over his shoulder, down his arm, into his hand then finally into Raven's mouth. Tyler couldn't see the flesh of his arm moving in conjunction with the invisible force, but he could have sworn his skin was microscopically rippling from what flowed out of him. His body, particularly his arms, erupted with millions of bumpy goose flesh and every hair on his body seemed to blossom and stand on end as if he were a porcupine ready to do battle. Tyler saw Raven's dark eyes cloud over with a thin, white film. It looked as though Raven had suddenly developed cataracts in her eyes. Raven whined; her angry and scared expression grew blank, her features went slack, and the grip on Tyler's hand eased until Tyler was able to carefully slip it from her mouth. The deep gashes oozed blood, splattering his pants and puddling on the floor. Tyler didn't even look at his hand; he continued to stare into the glazed eyes of his best friend.

Grabbing his arm, Gwen pulled him from the floor and yelled, "Tyler! Don't just sit there. Go to the bathroom. You're bleeding all over the place."

Raven licked the smears of blood from her chin and muzzle but regarded Tyler with a don't-fuck-with-me stare.

Henry quickly stepped up beside Raven and grabbed her collar to take her to the back of the house, but Raven quickly switched into attack mode again.

Raven whipped her head to the side and snapped at Henry who quickly released her collar in time and jerked his hand back. Raven bounded toward the front door. By this time, everyone had been rearranged from the previous chaos and Cass happened to be standing by the door. Raven viciously advanced on him with barks and growls. Cass felt Raven was commanding him to open the door to let her out, which he did immediately. Before the door was fully open, Raven charged through it, knocking Cass down in the process. Once she was free, Raven shot off like a Greyhound after the lure bunny in a dog race. Tyler chased after her, dribbling a blood trail and calling her back, but Raven was gone.

Eventually Tyler re-entered the house and went to the kitchen to clean his mangled hand.

There were gasps of relief from people who were holding their breath.

Tyler overheard a man he didn't even know say, "She should be put down for attacking him that way. We don't need an animal like that running around loose in our neighborhood."

Tyler flashed a warning sign at him, "Try to put her down, and you will have to deal with me. Nobody threatens my dog. I don't care who it is."

"But she almost tore your hand from your body."

"Doesn't matter. She is still my dog," Tyler said coolly. "And I love her."

"That's the damnedest thing I've ever seen," Henry said in bewilderment. "Raven's never acted like that before."

"Henry, who cares about Raven right now," Gwen said. "We'll take care of her later. Don't just stand there. Be helpful. We've got to get Tyler to the hospital—" she paused then added sarcastically, "—*again.*"

"Here's a dish towel from the kitchen," Savannah said leaning over to help stop the bleeding.

"Come on, Tyler. We're going to have to get you to the doctor," Gwen said.

"What about Raven?"

"I think Raven is the least of your worries right now," Gwen said again. "She knows where home is. She'll wander back eventually."

"Would you like for me to take him for you?" Savannah asked. "I wouldn't mind."

"That's sweet of you to ask, but I think we need to be there for him."

"You could spend more time with your guests," Savannah cut in. "And the party wouldn't have to break up right away."

"I don't know, It's just that—"

"Mom, I'm a big boy," Tyler said cutting in, "I'll be fine. You and Dad stay here take care of everyone. Enjoy the party. You've spent so much time and money on it all ready. It would be a shame for that to go to waste. Have some fun for a change."

"You sure?"

"Yes, I'm sure. Don't worry about me. Savannah will take care of me. We'll call if anything of interest happens."

"I'll go ahead and get the car. I'll pull around to the front and pick you up."

"That's okay. I'll walk with you."

"No-no-no, you go ahead and say goodbye to everyone, and I'll be waiting."

Okay, that's peculiar. Tyler thought, but said. "If you insist."

"I do. I'll see you in a minute."

Savannah left. Tyler made a move toward the door and then turned to address everyone who had come, "Thank you for coming to my welcome back party. I apologize that I can't stay and enjoy it with you but," he held up his bloody dish toweled hand and continued, "Well, certain circumstances will be keeping me from that." Tyler concluded by saying, "If you have to go before I get back, I'll understand. If not, I'll see you when I return." He smiled thoughtfully then said, "Hopefully I won't be gone as long this time as I was during my last visit."

Everyone burst into laughter as Tyler exited through the front door, waving.

ങ

Savannah hurried around to the backside of the house where all the cars were parked. They had ordered everyone to park in the back of the house so there were no cars in front to alert Tyler of their surprise party. She had been one of the first guests at the house to help with the decorating so she didn't have to ask anyone to move their cars. Her VW Beetle sat at the far end of the yard away from the others. She drove around the opposite side of the house and cut back onto the driveway and pulled around and picked Tyler up.

Now with Tyler in the car, she peeled out onto the adjoining two-lane blacktop. She grimaced at his bleeding hand and said, "She really got you good, didn't she?"

"That's affirmative," he joked through clenched teeth trying to make the situation less severe than it was. "So embarrassing; I should've listened to you."

"Yeah, you should've," she agreed.

She barely paused at a stop sign and floored it again.

"Savannah?"

"What?"

"Where's the fire?"

"What do you mean?"

"You don't have to drive so fast. I'm not dying. It's just a dog bite."

"I know that."

"So, why the big hurry?"

"I just like driving fast. If I get pulled over, I have a legitimate excuse this time."

"Oh, I see, so, you're just using me."

"That's kind of a harsh thing to say to me, but it's true; I am using you."

They smiled at the brief inside joke between them.

Savannah asked, "What do you think made her attack you like that?"

Tyler was about to tell her that Raven hadn't attacked *him*. Raven had attacked the *entity* she sensed *inside him*; but Edward interfered and opted for the easy answer and placed it on the tip of Tyler's tongue.

"I don't know," he said, then, "Hurts bad, though."

"Need another cloth?" she asked as she retrieved one from the backseat.

"Thanks," he said, peeling off the bloodied rag like a second skin.

They drove in silence while Tyler tended to his hand. The blood had eased some but not enough to go without a covering. He placed the new rag around his hand and pulled it tightly to add some pressure and stop the bleeding. Small blood dots formed on the new cloth and slowly spread into widening red circles.

Savannah made her way through a number of traffic lights that all happened to be green at the time.

"Oh shit!" Tyler said slapping his un-injured hand against his forehead.

Startled she asked, "Shit what? What's the problem?"

"I just now realized that I won't be able to play football at all this season. Damn it, this sucks."

"Awwwww such a tragedy."

"It *is* a tragedy. This is my senior year and I was hoping to finish up with good ratings to figure out where I want to play in college."

"You're using football as a basis for where you go to college? Shouldn't you be trying to get into the best college based on your grades and on what kind of education they can give you instead? Isn't the education more important?"

"Yes. Yes, it is. Of course, but my grades aren't the best in the world. It will be better for me to get into the best football program, and the education will automatically be the best for me. Harvard and Yale don't have the greatest football teams, but my grades would never allow me entry into one of those Ivy League schools."

Savannah immediately shook her head. "You have your sights set too low. There is always a chance for anything to happen if you set your mind to it."

"I was planning to do that this year, but you see what happened."

"The accident?"

"Uh-huh. My plan was to focus on my studies and my football training. Nothing else. I was planning on being focused, you know. No distractions. But then I met you and that was—is—great. That is an awesome distraction. I like that distraction."

They smiled at each other.

Tyler continued, "Then the accident came. A whole three months of my life vanished and now I'm—"

Tyler was about to tell her that a teenage boy has possessed him, but again Edward immediately cut him off.

Edward scoffed inside his head, *Good try, Tyler. Why don't you try to stay focused on everything besides me.*

Tyler was just talking at random; he hadn't been able to tell her anything of that magnitude. It was just going to be an off-the-cuff statement.

"What did you say?" Savannah asked.

"Huh?"

"You were talking about the accident, you lost three months of your life, and then you were going to say something else. What?"

"I was about to mention—," Edward helped Tyler quickly form an idea, "—my hand again. This injury is going to keep me from playing football for the rest of the year."

Pulling into the emergency access driveway, she brought everything into perspective for him. "Forget about football for now. At least now you can focus more on your education."

"Yeah, I guess you're right."

Savannah had parked near the emergency wing entrance. She rushed around to help Tyler out, but he was already standing on the sidewalk re-wrapping his bloodied bandage.

As they approached the sliding hospital door, Tyler heard his name being called out and they both turned to see who it was.

"Tyler! Tyler is that you?" Dr. Suzanne Baldwin asked as she slammed the door of her silver Mercedes. She had parked nearby. "This is becoming a habit with you, isn't it? You love this hospital so much you've grown attached to it."

A flash of hate snapped his body into instantaneous recollection. The dark memory that loomed up from out of Edward's past muted any reply. He was staring blankly at her car and thought to himself, *Wow. A silver Mercedes. I'm not the least bit surprised. Top of the line too. Funny how you have everything your little heart desires. But that's going to change soon enough.*

He took in everything about Suzanne and the make and model of her car.

Noticing that Tyler didn't reply, Savannah simultaneously jabbed Tyler in the ribs with her elbow as she said, "Hey, Dr. Baldwin. Yeah, he just can't stay away."

Tyler instantly stopped his inner dialogue as he ripped his mind away from the license plate and reflexively grabbed his side.

Suzanne moved quickly up the walkway to catch up with them. "We just let you go earlier today, didn't we? I didn't think we would ever see you again; at least not until your next checkup."

Turning on the charm, Tyler replied, "Trust me; I wouldn't be here if I didn't have to be." He held up his bloody wrapped hand as she approached.

Seeing the bloody wrap she asked, "Jesus Christ, what happened to your hand?"

"My dog thought my hand would be a nice chew toy," Tyler replied.

"Unbelievable. You need to pickpocket the good luck fairy because you have none at all. C'mon, let's get you inside. I'll get someone to begin work on you immediately."

 св

When they arrived back from the hospital, there were still a few guests milling about the house chatting with one another. Most of the people who had dropped in had already eaten and then left. The ones that were still around were now just mincing over the leftover food.

"Tyler!" Gwen exclaimed in alarm as he entered by the front door. "How's your hand?"

"It's okay, Mom; not completely healed yet," he joked. But I'll live. I thought you would've known that by now from the numerous times that you've called on Savannah's cell phone."

Gwen placed her fists on her hips, gave him a go-to-hell look and said, "It's called concern."

He became serious once again. "Some ligaments were torn, but they will grow back as my hand heals. Dr. Baldwin happened to be there. She was the one who worked on me again."

Henry leaned through a doorway and shouted politely to get everyone's attention. "Would everyone migrate toward the living room, please? Savannah and my injured boy are finally back from the hospital."

Little by little, guests joined them in then living room.

Once most of the guests had filed into the room, Henry began his unexpected speech to Tyler.

"Come over here, Tyler, there is something I would like to say to you and everyone else." He paused as Tyler released Savannah's hand and approached. When Tyler stood by his side, Henry put an affectionate arm around him and said, "As you all know, Tyler here was almost taken from us a few months ago. He cheated death but is among the living with us where he belongs."

There was a small round of applause at that statement, and Henry held up his hands and waved their clapping into silence so he could continue.

"Gwen and I are very happy and thrilled that you are still with us and I wanted to take a moment and let you know how much your mother and I love you. We know we didn't have to do this, but we wanted to show how thrilled we are that you're still here. If you will turn around now and take a look out the living room window to the backyard, you will see your welcome back gift. We hope you will enjoy it and take better care of this one than you did the last one."

When Tyler turned, his breath was taken from him as if someone had slugged him right beneath the sternum with a ten-pound medicine ball.

Sitting in the middle of the backyard was a brand new fiery red Ford Cobra Mustang. It was no doubt the top of the line. Its chrome wheels and perfect paint job sparkled with showroom quality.

A silver ribbon striped down the middle of the car and a huge bow sat in the center of its hood.

"Well, say something," Gwen insisted.

"A Cobra? Are you kidding me? Do you know how long I have been wanting one of these?"

"The insurance company came through with a payment from your other car," Henry said. "It was totaled, of course. We added some with it and purchased it in time for your arrival."

"So that's why Savannah made such a big deal about pulling her car around to the front of the house to pick me up," Tyler said. "You didn't want me to see it right away."

"Right," Gwen said chiming in. "We had to think quick. We weren't anticipating Raven's behavior."

"We have our ways," Savannah said.

Breaking his gaze from the car, he embraced his father in a huge bear hug. "Thank you, Dad." He paused for a moment, letting the embrace linger then turned to his mom and repeated the action. He said, "Thanks, Mom. I love it. This is way too much."

Tyler looked out at his new ride again, but a key chain dangled in front of his line of sight. Tyler reached up and was about to grasp the keys Henry was holding there, but at the last second he snatched them back.

"Just one more thing," he said.

"What's that?"

"Can you do me a favor?"

"Sure. Anything?"

"Can you be careful this time?"

Some amused chuckles drifted throughout the remaining crowd.

"You don't have to tell me twice."

Mimicking Henry's voice, Gwen butted in and repeated his line, "No seriously, be careful this time."

Everyone laughed again at her statement.

Henry held out the keys to him again and said, "Read the key chain."

Tyler laughed aloud when he read, "I run over animals."

"The next time you see a cat or a squirrel or I don't care what it is. You have my permission to run it down and run it over. I'll take full responsibility for your actions. It's better to have you with us and alive than the alternative."

"I understand completely."

As Tyler eagerly reached for the keys, Henry hoped he wasn't giving Death another chance to take his son. Reluctantly, Henry released them into Tyler's possession.

Tyler was too enthused to stay and chat with the remaining guests. He had a new toy to play with. He wasn't planning on leaving right away, but he had to feel the metal and smell the leather. He wanted to hear the sound of the motor when he cranked the car and awoke the horses underneath the hood.

"Go for a ride?" he asked Savannah.

"Without a doubt. Since your hand is injured, can I drive?"

"Sure," he said holding the keys out to her.

She reached for them but he snatched them back just as his dad had done earlier.

"From the passenger seat. I would be insane to let you navigate from the driver's side at the speeds you take."

"Aw, c'mon, baby. I'll behave."

"Maybe. I'll let you. Try it out." he paused and thought for a moment, "In about a year or two. We'll have to see."

CHAPTER 12

LATER THAT NIGHT, after the long drive cruising in his new Mustang and after Savannah had left, Tyler found that Raven still hadn't come home.

His stitched and bandaged hand still throbbed like a son of a bitch but the Tylenol he'd taken earlier seemed to be quelling the pain.

As he lay on his bed, he took the time to ponder the day's events. It now seemed that moving to this area had jinxed him in some way. He was under the impression that he had been cursed and that everything he would ever do from now on would have definite repercussions in his life. If his bad luck continued in the direction it seemed to be headed, he would eventually be scared to do or try anything new. He would stop going places, stop pursuing his dreams, stop spending time with friends and family and finally become a loner. Tyler figured it was that way with most people; if a person failed enough times on a series of pursuits, eventually they just give up.

Tyler noticed he was unconsciously stroking the medallion that was hanging around his neck. He tilted it toward the light to take a closer look and wondered why.

I'll tell you why, his new inner voice stated.

Tyler stiffened in his seat.

That's right buddy, it's me, Edward. I'm back. I used to always stroke my good luck charm. It's a habit I couldn't break myself from doing. I did that when I was concentrating on something as you are now.

A good luck charm, my ass. Tyler thought. *What a load of crap. I should've left it in the attic where I found it.*

If you had done that you wouldn't be here today, Edward thought. *It's because of me that you still exist.*

I don't believe that. I was near death, yes, but it didn't take you to save my life, but if that's what you want to believe, then be my guest. On the other hand, if you believe that, you've got to come to the realization that it's because of me, Tyler, that you *exist.*

Touché, my friend, Edward agreed. *Nicely said.*

The thoughts of getting rid of the talisman came and went. He knew Edward wouldn't allow that since Edward controlled his mind and body. He couldn't tell anyone what was really wrong with him. Every time he tried, Edward would put another idea in his thought process or would end up changing the subject to something totally different. Before he could slip back into his thoughts, he realized he needed to unpack some more of his possessions.

Three months had come and gone, and he still wasn't fully unpacked. The first day they had arrived, he had taken the time to get most of his room arranged. It was his space, his fortress, and he had made sure it was set up right. During his stint in the hospital, his dad and mom had tried to complete his room, but there were still some boxes left to unpack. As he opened each box and set toward completing his room, his handicapped hand slowed down his progress because he kept forgetting that it was injured. It was going to take some getting used to.

Tyler finished hooking up his television, DVD player, and his stereo into a small entertainment center. He placed a *Guster* CD in the stereo as he set to work. He methodically placed football mementos from past high school games on his dresser. He hung pictures and plastered posters of his favorite rock bands, movies, and much desired bikini-clad women on his ceiling and walls. He stashed his favorite DVDs and books on the shelves his father had made.

By the time he had finished, he had completely rearranged and cleaned his room. He had even taken the time to vacuum it. He had attained four to five boxes of miscellaneous junk and memorabilia that his room couldn't hold.

"Time for another damn trip to the attic," he said as he stretched. "Then I'm going to Netflix a movie. There should be plenty of shit to choose from since I haven't watched anything in a couple of months."

You think that's bad, Edward said. *I haven't seen a movie in close to twenty years.*

Tyler shook his head. *You think I really give a shit about that, Edward? Doesn't much matter if you do or you don't.*

Well, I don't.

It'll just be a matter of time. You'll accept me soon enough.

Whatever. Just don't talk to me, Edward. I'm not in the mood. I don't like you very much.

Tyler grabbed as many of the boxes as he could manage with his impaired hand and headed toward the attic.

Edward taunted him, *Don't go away angry, Tyler. Hey, you don't mind if I come with you, do you? You can't get rid of me no matter how hard you try.*

Tyler tried to ignore his Edward thoughts.

In the attic, he found a spot where he could keep all his personal belongings together. Depending on how long they stayed here, he was sure this area would become more cluttered over the years.

Tyler was about to leave the attic when he saw the familiar old, dusty trunk sitting in the shadows. Curiosity got the better of him. He walked over to it again, slid it further into the light and opened it once more.

The first time Tyler was up here, he had just took a cursory glance over the items. He picked up one of the award again and read the name engraved in the metal name plate.

Adrian Connell? Edward thought. *Are you fucking kidding me? This has to be a joke.*

Tyler didn't say anything but was weirded out by Edward's excitement.

Her name was plaster on everything in the box.

Tyler felt his heart leap with excitement as his body was completely taken over. His hands shot inside the trunk and extracted one of the photo albums. Edward hurriedly settled on the floor under the harsh, waxy light.

Edward flipped through the pages and saw countless baby pictures.

The parents of this baby girl seemed to always have a camera shoved in her face. There were numerous pictures of birthday parties, Christmas, Easter, Halloween, Thanksgiving, and other celebrations Tyler couldn't quite tell what they were commemorating.

Edward seemed as though he couldn't look at the pictures fast enough. He thumbed through other pictures. Some had been taken with her pets and some were pictures from sporting events. Each school picture showed the way she had matured throughout life from toddler years through her late teenage years.

When the pictures neared her high school era, Tyler heard Edward's thoughts rolling around inside his head as a chant. *I can't believe it. I just can't believe it. I can't believe it. I just can't believe it.*

What? Tyler asked.

It's her.

Who?

Adrian Connell.

Yeah, I got that. What about her?

Edward thought, *I was so in love with this girl when I was in school. This is the girl that was with me on the lake when I drowned.*

I wouldn't know anything about that, Edward. Tyler thought. *I know I had bad dreams when I was in the coma but I can barely remember them now. I think you are blocking them from my mind. You've got them hidden deep inside me now, but I'm not allowed to look at them.*

That's because they are my memories, Tyler. They are all mine. That's all I have now. Everything was taken from me, and that's the only thing I have that keeps me going.

I might have a little more sympathy toward you if I knew what happened, but you just keep it to yourself.

Maybe someday I'll show you what my life was like, but not right now.

Fine. It really doesn't matter. Be a coward if you want to. I don't care.

The pictures seemed to thin out the older Adrian became.

After looking through three thick photo albums and seeing this beautiful girl grow into womanhood, he picked out an album in the bottom of the chest that stated Miscellaneous Memories. The two words were written in a bubbly, cursive script. Tyler knew this was a personal collection that Adrian had compiled.

This album seemed to capture the prime of her life, starting with high school and finishing up with graduation. These pictures showed Adrian and her friends on school field trips, her at high school football and basketball games, old boyfriends, sleepovers, cheerleading group shots, camping trips, and her acting days in local community theatre.

Toward the back of the book, Tyler felt himself becoming enraged. There were some pictures of a guy that didn't settle too well with Edward. Every time his picture came up, Tyler would get only a brief glimpse and then Edward would turn the page.

What's the matter, Edward? What's your beef with him?

Edward didn't answer.

When Edward took too long to stare at another photograph of the guy, Tyler took it from the covering and flipped it over. According to the handwriting on the back, the guy's name was Jeremy Taylor. In a different script was four words: All my Love, Always.

"Yeah, bullshit," Edward said aloud using Tyler's voice. "He never loved her. He treated her like shit when they were dating each other. I don't know what she saw in him. God, he's such an asshole."

Edward made Tyler stuff the picture back in its binder and turn the page.

On the second to last page, he found an eight-by-ten photograph whose corners were torn, cracked, and peeling at the edges. It was a perfect picture that captured the true essence of summer fun. It caught the faces of six teenagers who were staring back at him. Even though the girls wore bikinis and the guys wore shorts it wasn't taken on a beach. The teenagers were posing on a sandy volleyball court with green grass surrounding the sandy area. A group of pine trees lined the right side of the background while two small boats were attached to a pier that was jutting into the lake on the left. A partial view of a volleyball net lined the top of the picture. A girl with her arms spread wide as if trying to catch her balance was perched on the shoulders of a young man. The couple in the center was sitting back to back in the sand with their arms folded around their knees. On the right, a boy was holding another girl in the crooks of his arms. Three couples grouped together, smiling broadly in the bright sunshine, ecstatic to be relaxing in the summertime atmosphere.

Tyler removed the photo to examine it closer. Without thinking, he flipped it over.

On the back, written in a cursive script were the words Summertime Perfection—Silver Ridge Lake. Below that were listed the names of the teens in sequence from left to right. First there was Bruce Saliers holding Jessica Anderson on his shoulders. Secondly, Suzanne Baldwin and Alex Riley who were sitting back-to-back. And finally, Travis Sheridan was holding Kelly Morgan in his arms.

The picture had obviously been taken by Adrian; she wasn't one of the six in the picture.

More hatred emanated from Tyler. Tyler felt his blood pressure rising and his face starting to burn. The more Edward studied the picture the worse it became. Tyler felt that the hatred was directed toward the students but didn't know why. Edward didn't return the picture to its holder but kept it out. Tyler figured he was going to do something with it, but he didn't know what.

On the last page of the book, Tyler came across a photo of a young boy. The pale bark of an Aspen enclosed half of the background on the right side, and grass, pine needles, and pine cones covered the left. A startled, freckle-faced boy was clothed in a light orange tank top and blue shorts. His hair was unkempt with bits of pine needles sticking out like insect antennae. The boy looked surprised, even startled, as though he didn't know the picture was being taken.

"Holy fucking shit" Tyler said aloud, but it was Edward's recollection that spurned the reaction.

"What? Who is that?" Tyler asked.

Edward was quiet for a long time, then slowly whispered, "It's me." Tyler's eyes started leaking and Tyler realized that Edward was crying. "She actually saved this picture of me."

Tyler's body went ridged. It felt like a thousand hypodermic needles had pierced his body and had released ice cold water into his veins. His whole body froze in shock.

How small is this world? Tell me that. How small is it? Edward thought.

I sort of see what you mean, but could you elaborate a little more, Tyler replied in thought.

Okay. How amazing is it for me to die seventeen…eighteen years ago, and the girl that was with me on that same day, how unbelievable is it for her to keep a picture of me?

I don't know.

How amazing is it for you to come from Chicago, of all places, move into the same house Adrian Connell lived in all those years ago, and find this charm that held my soul inside it?

Wait. Hold on, Edward, Tyler thought. *If you had it on you when you drowned, how did she come to acquire it?*

I don't know.

How do you know this is her house?

Edward made Tyler grab one of the photo albums they had just viewed. He flipped through it until he found a number of outdoor pictures.

"I didn't realize it until now, but it has to be Adrian's house." Edward said aloud. "Why would this trunk of her stuff be up here hidden in a corner of this attic if it wasn't hers?"

I see your point. The outside is slightly different. They must've had some landscaping and remodeling done at some time.

It has to be, Edward thought again. *But even still, how amazing is it for you to have an accident that puts your life in jeopardy but spares you and releases me from the charm's hold at the same time and for us to finally end up here?*

"I'm glad there are two of us to think this thing through," Tyler said. "Because it's blowing my mind up."

He took the photo of Edward from the clear enclosure to examine it closer. Tyler had an odd feeling that he was staring into a mirror; although he looked nothing like the boy in the picture. Tyler shook his head and flipped this photograph over also. In the same bubbly script, Tyler read this statement: Edward McDaniel. My Guardian and My Hero. I'll never forget you.

Tyler smiled but didn't know why, then realized it was Edward who was smiling. Two tears fell from his eyes, and Tyler knew why he was crying. Edward felt honored to be thought of enough to be put in Adrian's photograph book. For one of the few times in his life, Edward felt like he was wanted, maybe even needed; who knows, maybe he could go as far as to say, he was loved, at least on some level.

Tyler didn't try to stop Edward from enjoying this moment; he knew this meant a great deal to him. The tears began to pour forth from his eyes the way they had done so many times in Edward's childhood, but this time they were tears of happiness. Tyler didn't know to what extent Adrian had cared for him and it didn't matter, Edward was just happy that he meant something to somebody. He continued to sit in the dim light of the attic, staring at the words Adrian had attached to his picture and cried in silence.

Eventually the moment passed, and Edward dried his tears on Tyler's cheeks and placed the contents back in the chest with the exception of the eight-by-ten group photograph and the picture of himself. He pushed the chest back into the shadows from where he had retrieved it, covered it again with the white sheet, pulled the string to shut off the light, and descended the stairs.

Guided by Edward, Tyler stopped off at his room and stuffed the enlarged photograph into one of his textbooks and then stuck it into his backpack. Then he placed the picture of himself in the deepest part of Tyler's wallet.

Finding that he'd done everything he really wanted to do for the moment, he released enough of Edward's consciousness to allow Tyler to do whatever he wanted to do. Edward figured that he didn't want anyone to think Tyler was acting or doing anything strange.

Naturally, Tyler went to see what his parents were up to.

Tyler found his dad watching a college football game and his mom reading a novel in the living room.

"Who's playing?" Tyler asked as he entered.

"Cardinals versus the Wolfpack in the fourth quarter. Thirty to eighteen."

"Too bad for the Wolfpack?"

"Yep. Mr. Simonson isn't going to be happy at work tomorrow. They only have less than two minutes to go."

"Wait. I thought the game started at seven o'clock tonight?" Tyler inquired.

"It did." Henry searched his watch for the correct time, "It's after nine-thirty. It's been a little sloppy tonight. The refs are making bullshit calls. I swear they never let these guys play."

"You sound shocked that it's so late," his mother probed as she looked over her reading glasses. "What've you been doing all night?"

"I was cleaning my room as best I could with my handicap," he said holding up his bitten hand. "I thought for sure it would only take me about an hour to finish it."

Tyler thought, *How long have I been looking at those pictures?*

"We thought you were in your room getting caught up on your three month backlog of homework."

"Right, like that's going to happen. I've just got two more months to go," he said sarcastically. "I think I can get that finished before I go to bed tonight." He dropped the sarcasm. "No, no, I wasn't doing homework, and could you please not refer to anything that makes me remember the car wreck."

"Is something wrong, son?"

Yes! Something is wrong! He wanted to scream. *Can't you tell what it is? I'm different. There is something definitely wrong with me!*

"No, no, I'm fine," Edward said, lying for Tyler. "Sorry. I was just wondering where my time went. I try to keep tabs on it lately since I lost a three month chunk of time in a blink of the eye."

"How's it going to feel to get back into the swing of things at school?" his father asked as a commercial came on.

"Can't wait," Tyler lied again. "It'll finally give me something constructive to do."

Gwen said, "Go on, and get out of here. Go see Savannah or call your friends over."

Tyler turned and left the room, "No that's okay, I really need to sort out my homework assignments and get a game plan together for how I'm going to finish all this material. I think I'll turn in early. Tomorrow is going to be a big day at school, and I need to be ready for it."

Tyler had no idea just *how* big tomorrow was going to be.

CHAPTER 13

THE SUN WAS hidden somewhere behind a thick mask of steel-gray clouds. The air was stifling. It hurt to breathe.

Tyler stood on a dusty patch of earth at the edge of the ghost town, wary to enter its limits. Nothing moved except a couple of wind-propelled tumbleweeds that blew through the barren streets. No sound emanated from the wasted buildings to his left and right. The only sound he did hear was the thundering hoof beats of his own heart that galloped steadily on adrenaline-fed fear.

Tyler was terrified and alone, as though Christ had already come back in the Rapture and he was the only one who had been left behind. That in itself scared Tyler to his core.

He heard a creaking from the closest bungalow to his left. The wooden door opened toward him, squeaking eerily on rusty hinges.

Framed in the doorway was a haggard woman who looked as though she had seen the last days. Dirt smudges coated her, and the thin rags she wore did little to cover her body. Her hair was tangled and matted. Dried blood was smeared on her skin. He wondered what kind of lifeless carcass lay on the hot floors inside the building she had come from. He couldn't see her hands. For some reason, she held them behind her back. Tyler could tell she used to be an attractive woman, but the life she now lived left her face and body undesirable.

Recognition struck Tyler; he knew this woman, but he couldn't remember from where.

The barbarian finally lowered her hands to her sides. That's the moment Tyler saw the glint of light reflect off a long, bloody machete blade.

Tyler instinctively stepped back when he saw her crimson hands brandish the weapon.

She stepped down the stairs and moved slowly toward him.

As before, Tyler reflexively stepped back, keeping the same amount of distance between them. They matched each other's steps; but she seemed to cover twice as much distance as he did.

Tyler was scared, but nervously tried to play it off, "W-What are you going to do with that?" he stammered.

Her thin slit of a mouth broke into a wide, black toothy grin. "What do you think I'm going to do with it?"

Tyler sounded cold, "I-I d-don't know, ah, I asked you. You tell me."

"Ah c'mon, I'll give you one guess," she crooned.

"I don't know!" he yelled.

"Well, I'm sure as hell not going to blaze a trail through that over there," she said pointing to the thorny thicket on her left. She started laughing hysterically. "Instead, *we're* going to blaze a trail through you." She paused for emphasis and trailed her tongue lightly up the sharp edge of the blade. "You know, open you up and see what's inside. We want to see what you're made of."

"The hell you will," Tyler spat.

"And this time *we'll* be doing it just for kicks."

His eyebrows furrowed in thought, "Wait a minute, why do you keep saying "we"? Who are *we*?"

"Oh, you'll see."

She advanced on him faster, raising the blade high over her head as she went.

Tyler moved away but heard the sound of rustling leaves and cracking twigs from behind him. He turned in defense but froze in horror. He stood there slack-jawed as he witnessed the impossible.

Standing everywhere behind him—on the road, on the neighboring slopes, under lifeless skeletal trees—were hundreds of hag-like savages that seemed to have materialized from thin air. They all looked exactly as the first savage except they were grasping different weapons. They hadn't been there moments before; he had just come into town from that direction. They were within a few feet from him and were shuffling toward him in a lurchy, zombiefied state. As the horde advanced, they raised their knives, spears, hatches, pitchforks, hammers, scythes, and machetes.

As though directed by a choir leader, they all chanted in unison, "We all want to open you up. We all want to see what's inside. We all want to see what you're made out of."

Tyler didn't pause to ask questions or try to calm the maniacs down. Instead, he turned and tried to run from the horde of women that were coursing upon him, but the single barbarian was blocking his way. He saw her machete rising above her head with both hands poised to deliver the deathblow.

Tyler had stopped so abruptly he thought he had frozen in his steps. As she brought the blade down, Tyler reacted. He hadn't realized he had moved but Tyler wasn't thinking now. His body movements were ahead of his brain. Adrenaline was flowing. Instinct had possessed him.

He intercepted her hands with both of his. He side stepped and brought a knee up sideways into her belly. As she doubled over trying to suck the expelled air back in, she lost half her grip on the weapon.

She was hunched to one hand and both knees but struggling to stand. He knew if she got to her feet, she would come after him again; maybe this time even kill him. He couldn't let that happen.

That's when he did the unimaginable.

In one smooth movement, he wrenched the machete violently from her remaining hand and brought it down across her neck, severing her head. It was like a knife cutting through warm butter. The head dropped, rolled about a foot from her body, and stopped face up.

A river of warm blood gushed from the still upright body, washed over his hands and painted the ground crimson. It was this warmth that finally made him realize what he had done. He found he had buried the tip of the machete into the ground from the force of the blow. It even took a little effort to pull it free.

The ghastly sight was unlike anything he had ever witnessed. Seeing the blood spew forth in heartbeat spurts caused his stomach to churn uncontrollably and his last meal—whenever that had been—shot from him in a strong wave. He tried to turn his head to avoid hitting the corpse—even though she had tried to kill him. He did have a little respect for the dead, but it was to no avail. His stomach bile and contents splattered the whole scene.

He turned from her as wave after wave of vomit continued to pour from him.

When the storm inside him subsided, he stood again only to meet the rage-filled eyes of the other hundred bitch doppelgangers. They had stopped when they saw Tyler take out their leader, but that had only fueled their anger even more.

"Tyler," a voice called out to him from behind.

Tyler turned but no one was there, then he looked down and saw the lips of the severed head moving.

"Tyler," it said leering. "We all want to open you up," she began. One by one others joined in, "We all want to see what's inside." The chant grew constantly louder. "We all want to see what you're made out of. We just want to see what you're made of."

As their chant swelled, he ran. He cut down behind the row of musty shops that were on the left side of the dirty street. He ran past a number of shacks before he slid between them into a small alleyway.

He heard advancing footsteps pounding over the hard earth.

He saw a broken opening at the side of one derelict and without hesitation ducked and belly-crawled underneath the structure. As soon as he disappeared into the gloom, the battalion of women savages came lurching by in an all out manhunt.

Tyler shut his eyes and covered his ears as he cowered in the darkness beneath the building. He heard hollow footsteps throughout the rooms above him as well as the abraded *thwack* and *cur-chunk* sounds of blades striking miscellaneous objects. He curled into the fetal position and pressed his ears harder to shut out the noise.

Eventually the chaos subsided then finally stopped. A dead silence had possessed the ghost town once more. Sensing they had given up or were searching the surrounding woods, he quietly slithered from his hiding place and crouched beside the building to remain inconspicuous.

He slowly and methodically stepped toward the back of the house, viewing his surroundings as he went. No sooner than he had turned the corner did he see the haggard woman coming straight at him in a fast-forward, frightful lurch.

This time, he had no time to react.

All he saw and heard was a menacing grin and her spine-tingling laughter. Her arms were over her head and were already arching down toward him in a blurred motion. He had just enough time to register that her hands were again clutching the bloody weapon.

A hand grabbed his shoulder, and a sharp, insistent voice called his name in two long syllables, "Ty-ler!"

Having no time to defend or counter the attack, the blade arched down between his eyes and…

…he sat bolt upright in his seat banging his knees on the underside of his desk, knocked his books to the floor, and instinctively brought his hands to his face in feeble attempt of self-defense. Finding his face in one piece, he then realized every eye in his classroom was on him. Through enclosed fingers, he saw students glaring at him in disgusted confusion. Some of the students that sat near him weren't in their seats but standing a short distance away from him.

"Tyler?" a voice asked.

Tyler was still trying to decipher dream from reality, and the voice startled him to attention.

He jerked his hands away from his face and turned toward the voice, "What!" he snapped then screamed aloud when he saw the witch from his dream.

"Get the hell away from me, you bitch!" he shouted as he scuttled away from her. "I swear to God I'll kill you!"

He found himself in the floor beside his desk. In the process of falling from his chair, he cracked his head on another student's desk. As he grabbed his head, he realized that it wasn't the hag from the dream. Instead, it was his teacher, Mrs. Sheridan. The blow to the head had finally knocked him back to reality.

Embarrassment coated his body and flushed into his face. Nothing like this had ever happened to him before.

"Tyler? Are you all right?" Mrs. Sheridan asked, ignoring his vulgarity.

"I think so," he said standing quickly, immediately apologizing for the fiasco that had just ensued. "Just embarrassed beyond belief. I'm really sorry. I didn't mean to say that. It was my dream. I just dozed off. It won't happen again."

He noticed the next few things all at once. First it was the putrid taste in his mouth, then the smell that accompanied it, and then he saw his vomit-covered desk and finally the students that were standing around him. He hadn't realized it but seeing the visual of the gore in the dream had a profound effect on him. Apparently the students near him had immediately scattered so they wouldn't be hit by the splatter of his vomit. At first, Tyler thought the looks from the other students were of dismay, but now he realized they were definitely looks of disgust.

Derrick's timing was impeccable. At the same time Tyler noticed what had happened, from the back of the room, Derrick said in a grocery store intercom voice, "Clean up on aisle four. Clean up on aisle four."

The whole class erupted into uncontrollable fits of laughter, all except for Tyler. He flashed a sarcastic look in Derrick's direction. Derrick just smiled, shrugged his shoulders and said, "Dude, that was classic. You can't fault me for giving you shit about something this crazy. That was awesome." Tyler shook his head. Embarrassment as he had never felt before rocked him where he stood.

Kelly noticed his embarrassment and asked softly, "Do you need to see the doctor?"

"I, uh, I don't really want to be here right now. I would like to be excused if that would be alright," he said, trying to figure out how to clear the books from the mess.

He reached for his book but Kelly stopped him and said, "Don't worry about this now; you can clean it up later or we'll call the janitor. Go to the nurse and get cleaned up."

"Thank you," Tyler whispered.

"You're welcome."

As he moved up the aisle, Derrick said, "Great show man; really great. You made it worth coming to class today."

He saw all the students pointing, laughing, and murmuring among themselves. All he could do was avoid eye contact and leave. Derrick was the only one capable of making light of this situation.

As he entered the hallway, he heard Mrs. Sheridan say, "All right class, the fun's over for now. Let's try to get our minds back onto the lesson. I'll try to make it as entertaining as Tyler just did."

A slight smile curved his lips. *Holy shit! How embarrassing. The whole school is going to hear about this before the day is out. I just know it.*

As he made his way to the bathroom, the nightmare filtered through his mind again.

The woman who had chased him with the machete had been Kelly Sheridan all along; he realized that now. In the dream, he didn't recognize her because of how dirty and emaciated she was and by the way she was dressed.

Reaching the bathroom, he went to a sink, turned the water on and rinsed his mouth out over and over again. He lathered his hands, arms, and face with soap to wash away the remains that were there then rinsed thoroughly. He ran his wet hands through his hair a few times, then grabbed some paper towels and dried off.

Then he set to cleaning his shirt and pants. Some splatter happened to land on his clothes but most had hit the desk, books, and floor.

After he had finished making himself presentable, he grabbed a huge stack of paper towels for the future clean up. He went back to his class but didn't enter; he just waited outside. He couldn't bear interrupting class again. He had accomplished that one too many times already.

He stood in the hallway by himself, repeatedly trying to force the incident out of his mind.

Now you know how it feels, Edward said from inside his head.

Oh God, not you again. Don't start. This game was becoming ridiculous. He wished he didn't have to talk to this…this thing, this voice inside his head. *How it feels to what?* Tyler asked.

How it feels to be embarrassed like me. You know how embarrassed you were just then?

Yeah?

Multiply that ten-fold. That was a weekly prescription with me back then. If not a daily thing.

Did you have something to do with what happened a while ago? Did you do that so I would know "how it feels to be you" when you were in school?

Oh no, God forbid. That was all and entirely you. I wouldn't wish what I went through when I was a kid on my worst enemy. Edward paused then thought. *On second thought, yes, I would. But I had nothing to do with that.*

Edward had already been seething about Kelly Sheridan and what she had done to him to warrant his hate when Tyler dozed off in class. Edward had also been with Tyler in the dream and was taking the scene in stride. When the opportunity to kill Kelly came up, revenge manifested itself and Edward was the first one up to bat. He had taken over Tyler's dream mind so quickly that Kelly's fate was sealed before Tyler actually knew what was going on. When Tyler's mind came back to his dream self and saw the headless body it was too grotesque for his dream mind and body to take, and his real mind and body reacted in the same way.

I can't believe you did that, Tyler accused.

Did what? Edward asked.

If you hadn't sliced her head off, I wouldn't have thrown up all over everybody. Now I've embarrassed the piss out of myself, and it's entirely your damn fault.

Don't blame me just because you can't hold down your lunch. How was I supposed to know you have a low tolerance for the macabre?

I don't. I've watched enough horror movies to stretch that cerebral zone. But if I remember correctly, you've only been in my body, what, close to three months now? I would've thought you would have known me a little better by now.

Most of that time your mind was snoozing. It was on a mental break. Edward explained.

I think I just had a mental break and everybody in that class was a witness to it.

As if on cue to end the mental quarrel, the bell announced the end of class and the students filed out one by one. Some of them even shot comments his way, but he just played and laughed them off the best he could.

After most of the students left, Tyler entered sheepishly, went straight to his desk—which he found had been moved to a back corner so it wouldn't be a focal point during the lesson—and started to clean up the reeking mess.

Kelly noticed him and called out, "Tyler."

Tyler winced at the sound of his name.

"Could I see you for a moment, please?"

Tyler shook his head in disgust, "Damn it," he muttered. "I was afraid of this." He turned to face his teacher.

"Oh man, not back in school a whole day and Tyler's already in trouble." Derrick said, milking the scene for all it was worth. "See you in detention hall, spew boy."

"Shut up, Derrick," Tyler said as he threw a wadded paper towel in his direction.

Derrick dodged the projectile, laughed stupidly, and ducked out the classroom.

Tyler turned his attention back to Kelly. "He only says that because I've been out for so long. It's his version of a back-to-school initiation." Tyler noticed that Mrs. Sheridan was studying him, so he dropped the small talk and became serious. "What did you want to see me about?"

"Not about that," She nodding toward his puke covered desk. "Don't worry about the clean up. We'll get the janitor to take care of that desk and floors." Kelly hesitated, unsure how she wanted to approach the subject she was about to bring up.

"Is there a problem?" Tyler asked.

"No. No problem at all. I was just wondering where you got the charm you're wearing."

Edward was instantly on edge. He wasn't ready for any questions to start up about him.

Tyler was about to open his mouth and speak then Edward took over and spoke for him.

"Why are you curious about it?" Edward asked.

Kelly was stunned over the tone of voice Tyler had asked his question. She realized her mouth was open in shock so she closed it again. Kelly pressed on, "It's just that it seems like a very rare and interesting piece, and I was just curious where you got it."

Edward said, "Believe it or not, I found it in an old chest in the back corner of our attic the day we moved into our new house here in Silver Ridge." He grabbed it, held it up, and looked at it, rubbed it a few times, then dropped it to his chest again. He looked up at Kelly and gave her a half-smile, half-smirk. "It's pretty cool, isn't it?"

Wonder if she remembers that I used to do that.

"Yeah, very cool. I just remember another friend of mine who had one just like it. I could've sworn it was the same one. He would always rub it thoughtfully the way you just did."

"A *friend* of yours?" Edward asked in shock. There was a little too much sarcasm poured into that sentence. *You were never my friend Kelly,* Edward thought. *I always wanted to be, but you were shitty to me.*

Kelly's voice brought Edward back to the moment. "Well not exactly a friend per se, but a guy that went to my school."

Yeah, that's better. Tell the truth like it really is. Don't lie.

"And who was this *friend?*"

Kelly seemed to come out of her deep thought, "What? Oh, he's not important. You wouldn't know him. He passed away years ago. That's the reason I was asking. It just reminded me of him. Just curious, that's all."

I'm not important? Edward thought. He was instantly pissed. That comment made Edward want to strike out at her right here and now. Just take her down and just keep pounding her until there was no life left in her body. Just like he wanted to do that day back in high school.

"Good memories or bad?" Edward pressed.

"Both, actually," Kelly said, without really thinking about it.

"Oh?" Edward questioned. There was surprise in his voice.

That little comment, more like a sound, was enough to make Kelly reevaluate her answer.

"On second thought, just bad. I wasn't very nice to him."

That's more like it, Kelly, Edward thought, then asked. "What did you do?"

Kelly was thinking too hard about old high school days. "Huh? Oh, nothing. It's not important now. Forget I said anything. Like I said, just curious, is all."

Not important now? Edward thought.

It was all Edward to could to contain his anger. He focused on it and buried inside himself. It was so easy to do. He was used to it. He didn't want to, but he did.

But it is, Kelly; it's very important. And I'm about to show you how important I was and still am. You just wait and see.

"That was all I really needed to ask you about. You can go now."

"You sure? You sure there wasn't anything else you needed to tell me?"

"Oh, no. That's all. Thank you for staying afterward. I'll see you tomorrow."

"Right. Yeah," Edward said and turned away, then added, "I'll see you tonight."

"Excuse me?"

"What?" Edward said, turning back to Kelly.

"What did you say?"

"I said, 'I'll see you tomorrow.'"

"Oh, sorry. It thought I heard you say something else."

"Oh, okay. Well, bye."

"Bye."

No, you heard me right, Kelly. I'll see you tonight. In just a little while.

CHAPTER 14

TYLER CURTIS, GUIDED by the spirit of Edward McDaniel, leaned forward and squinted as he peered out of the windshield of his Mustang. Rain came down in torrents as if poured out of buckets onto unprepared travelers. The headlights reflected off the downpour, making travel even more difficult. The wind howled against the windows like injured wolves trying to reach the safety and solitude that lay within. Leaves, tree limbs, and trash blew from one side of the highway to the other. Thunder clapped in the distance, followed by flashes of lightning. The constant beating of the rain, mixed with the coordinated thumping of the windshield wipers, created an effect that seemed to lull Edward into an even deeper hypnotic daze.

Edward forced Tyler's hands to turn the steering wheel off of the main highway onto a road that meandered through an expensive neighborhood. Here, the two and three story houses had BMWs, Mercedes, and other expensive automobiles in the driveways. The houses had expensive alarm systems to ward off would-be burglars.

A burst of thunder jarred the bruised sky, which brought Edward out of his trance. Deep thoughts had taken over his mind so much that he didn't realize how warm it was becoming within the car. He switched the control settings from heat to cool to off-balance the growing heat that had built up in the car.

Tyler turned on to Highland Road and continued driving until he came to the last of the dead end circles. There was a neighborhood crime watch in this area, so he parked as far out of sight as possible. He turned off the motor, windshield wipers, and lights.

Edward ran his fingers through Tyler's oily hair that fell back over his forehead into his eyes. He sat, surrounded by the security and safety of his car as he listened to the rain crash down around him.

Edward thought, recalling the word Kelly has used to describe them in their conversation at the end of class today. *Friend!* he scoffed again. *I wouldn't go that far, Kelly.*

He slipped a pair of white latex gloves over Tyler's hands. He'd bought a small box of them at the local CVS earlier in the day. He didn't know how tonight's events would play out but he didn't want to leave any trace of fingerprints behind if things went south.

Another load of thunder rumbled across the sky as Edward opened the car door and stepped out into the darkness and the tempest beyond. The rain was chilling to the bone and immediately soaked through his clothes and saturated his skin. The wind whipped at his face and the rain beat down upon his head, matting Tyler's long hair on contact. More thunder boomed as rods of forked lighting struck the ground beyond the trees.

Holy jeez, reminds me of the night Tyler released me. I wasn't expecting the bottom to fall out of the sky. I wonder if I should've waited until a better time. No. NO! Tonight is the night. It has to be done tonight.

He slowly descended through the woods, making his own path as he went. The course sloped down at a steep angle, which didn't give sturdy footing, especially since the ground was soaked. Limbs from ash and pine trees brushed and scrapped at his face.

All of a sudden, his support was taken from him, and he fell forward and tumbled down a short steep slope. His fall was stopped as abruptly as it had started, when he landed face first in a shallow creek.

"Damn it," Edward muttered. "Lot of shit to go through just to prove a point, but it will be worth it."

The left side of his face, beside his eye, and his right knee was cut and bruised by the jagged rocks that filled the creek. A stab of pain shot through his head as blood oozed out of the small wound and trickled down the side of his face.

Mud had smudged his leather jacket. He stood, shook himself, and began to wipe the sticky, wet leaves that clung to his garments.

He glanced up and saw a warm, glowing light shining through the bleak thunderstorm and the few trees that stood on the property.

This must be it.

He crossed the creek into the backyard belonging to a two-story house.

Edward moved within the blackness, a hunched shadow among shadows, from one tree to another until he leaned against an immense oak that stood near the house. He took a deep breath before continuing. The rain stung his wounds, and he wiped his face with the cuff of his jacket.

He peered out from behind the oak, *Yep, there she is. My old friend.*

Kelly Sheridan was framed in a lit window, busy cooking as she talked on her cell.

As he watched her, he thought about the way she had treated him when they were in school together. As he thought, anger began to well up within him once again.

ભ

"All right, class. Let's all settle down and get in your seats," Mrs. Bryant said, the day Edward had brought his hamster to Biology class. The few classmates that were observing and asking questions about Trevor scattered to their seats, and the spell was broken.

"Well, Edward, I see you've brought a little friend to show the class. Would you like to come up here and give us a little history about, uh, Trevor, is it?"

"Yes, ma'am," he said shyly. Edward took a deep breath, stood and walked to the front of the class. He placed the container on the table and took the rodent out. Trevor scurried about in Edward's hands as he held him out for the class to see.

"There's not really that much to tell," Edward began. "Uh, his name is Trevor. My, um, grandfather gave him to me for my, um, my birthday. I've had him for four months already." He turned to his teacher, "Mrs. Bryant, I, uh, I didn't bring him just to show the class, I wanted to, um, donate him

to this science room till the end of the year, if I could. I will still take care of him, of course. I'm not, um, not passing the responsibility of him off onto anybody else. I just thought, uh, that since we're studying mammals in science class that we could have at least one here to observe. He could be like, uh, the mascot of our science class and would add some spice to the class. Not that I think your class is boring in any way." Edward said quickly.

There were a few misplaced snickers and laughs that trailed throughout the room.

"Of course. That's very nice of you, Edward. I think we can accommodate Trevor, right class?" Mrs. Bryant asked.

The students that were paying attention to Edward agreed, except for one student sitting toward the back. Edward didn't see the look of disgust on Kelly Sheridan's face as he put Trevor back in his cage and set him on the counter.

"Now, I told you on Friday that we were going to start the dissection of our frogs today."

Most of the teens issued sighs of disapproval.

"As you can see on the counters, we have many jars and enough frogs for everyone. We probably have enough that if you wanted to dissect two you probably could. Now class, I hope everyone has strong stomachs because we just ate lunch, but let's all stick together and we will get through this. It's really not that bad once you get started. Now, I do need someone to help me pass these out. Do I have any volunteers?"

"I'd love to help," Kelly said immediately as she stood and raised her hand.

"Since you're already standing, Kelly, you might as well. Come over here to the side counter with me."

Mrs. Bryant and Kelly lined the trays on the counter and opened the jars containing the frogs. In no time, the room was permeated with the rank smell of formaldehyde. It took a few minutes, but they each placed a pale, withered frog in each tray. Mrs. Bryant took two trays to the other side of the room and started handing them out. She was teaching as she walked, so most of the students were paying attention to her. When Kelly had the opportunity, she quickly reached into Trevor's cage and grabbed the fidgety rodent and pulled him out of the cage.

Trevor squirmed to get free from her tight grip.

Kelly briefly looked around a second time to make sure the teacher and the other students hadn't seen what she was doing. She took a pair of scissors that had been placed on each tray and quickly and viciously jabbed them through Trevor's back forcing them deep into the wax that covered the bottom of the tray.

Trevor let out a small shrill cry of agony that only Kelly heard. Trevor tried in vain to free himself. He clawed weakly at the waxed bottom, squirmed briefly beneath the two sharp spires that were through his body and finally lay still. Trevor looked like a furry insect that had been badly mounted, but ready for a grade.

As a small pool of blood gathered near Trevor, Kelly sneered and whispered softly to the limp body, "This is what you get for trying to be the teacher's pet, Edward."

"Kelly?" Mrs. Bryant asked. "Is there a problem?"

"Huh?" she asked as she turned. She concealed her morbid handiwork with her body. "Oh, no, ma'am; just fixing one last one before I hand them out. Slippery suckers."

"Well, let's hurry. It's going to take the full class period for this project. We need to finish them today, if possible."

"I'm on it. I'm handing them out right now."

Mrs. Bryant turned her attention back to a student that had his hand raised.

Apparently no one had seen what Kelly had done; she grabbed the tray that contained Trevor's scissor-pinned body and another tray that was holding a bloated frog.

"Here's your frog, Gina, and here's yours, Edward. Dinner is served. Bon appetite," Kelly said in a poor French accent.

"And you're disgusting," Gina said and grimaced as though the thought of a second lunch consisting of formaldehyde frogs was enough to make her lose her first lunch.

Kelly stood in front of Edward wanting to see his reaction.

Edward gave a half laugh toward Gina and then looked down at his frog. He cocked his head like an inquisitive dog. That's funny, he thought at first. I've never seen a furry frog. It must be a brand new species. For a few seconds he didn't know what was going on, then he realized what Kelly had done.

Trevor's eyes were open and his small tongue was lolling out of his half-opened mouth. A small hint of blood had drooled out of his mouth and pooled around the scissors that protruded out of his furry back.

Edward stared at Trevor for a long moment, then a tear ran down his cheek. He finally tore his gaze from Trevor up to Kelly who was grinning malevolently down at him.

"Why the hell did you do that?" Edward yelled as he stood, knocking his chair over in the process.

Every head in the class swiveled simultaneously toward the commotion.

"What were you thinking?" Edward continued.

"Kelly? Edward? Is there a problem?"

Ignoring Mrs. Bryant's question, Kelly whispered the same phrase she had directed to Trevor, "That's what you get for trying to be the teacher's pet."

"I'm not trying to be the teacher's pet!"

Some of the students were becoming alarmed and backed away from the argument.

Edward couldn't understand why she would do something like this.

Edward wanted to do something equally bad to Kelly or maybe something even worse than she did to Trevor. Vengeful thoughts flashed across his mind. He wished he had the nerve to jump across the desk and tackle her, possibly grab the scissors in the process and plant them to the hilt in her back or chest, or even in one or both of her eye sockets as they toppled to the ground. Let her feel exactly what she did to Trevor first-hand. An eye for an eye. Isn't that what grandma always says? Edward could see her lips split, her teeth break, and her mouth explode in pain as his fist connected with each punch. Either that, or slash her pretty face with the scissors. See how she would like being looked down on and disliked for the rest of her life. Wonder how you would like being me? Could you cope with it?

Edward turned his mind back to Trevor as more tears pooled in his eyes. He blinked them out as he briefly stroked Trevor's fur. Then without even thinking, his body was in motion. He stood up as he lashed out at Kelly and grabbed her by the shirt.

The sudden attack was a shock to Kelly; she hadn't expecting it.

Edward pulled Kelly toward himself as his other hand came in from the side. Kelly threw her arm up to defend her face, but Edward's fist still connected. The punch was deflected somewhat, but it still drew blood. Edward jumped onto the desk, grabbing Gina's scissors from her tray in the process and brought them up to Kelly's face as he pulled her close.

From Kelly's point of view, suddenly the scissors were in three-dimensional clarity. She was frozen where she stood.

Words started to pour from Edward. He wasn't even thinking about what he was saying or how it sounded. He was angry and upset and spewing off at the mouth. "How would you like it, Kelly, if I stuck you with these." He pointed the scissors indicating her neckline. "I could stick these through your neck and have no problem watching you bleed out."

At that moment, Edward glanced over and saw Adrian across the room. She looked terrified as she clutched her hands to her chest in horrorified awe. Edward was instantly ashamed of his actions and was already in the process of letting Kelly go.

All of a sudden, hands were grabbing his arms and pulling him away from Kelly. He fought against them. One hand enclosed around the scissors so he wouldn't try a last ditch effort to harm her. He still had a fistful of her shirt, and he pulled her close to say one last thing.

As he whispered the last words, hate poured out along with them. "Someday when you least expect it, I'll get you. I promise you that."

Edward shoved Kelly back into the other students. He threw off the hands that had grabbed him and yelled, "Get the hell away from me!" Some of the students were slow to release him; he rounded on them also and pushed them away. "I said back the fuck off. Jesus, what's wrong with you people?"

He focused one last hateful look at Kelly and yelled as tears spilled from his eyes. "Why did you do it? Trevor never did anything to you."

"Edward! What has gotten into you?" Mrs. Bryant asked.

"Why don't you ask Kelly that question, Mrs Bryant," he said pointing to the dissecting tray. "She's the one who killed Trevor."

There were some low gasps of shock and awe as everyone saw Trevor for the first time.

"Kelly? Do you want to explain yourself?"

"What are you worrying about a stupid rat for? Who cares about Trevor? He just threatened me with those scissors."

"Yeah, only after you killed my hamster!"

"Edward, there is no need to shout. Just calm down, and we'll figure this out."

"What's there to figure out?" Kelly snapped. "Are you going to let him get away with that? He just assaulted me. He bloodied my nose."

"And you deserved it!"

Mrs. Bryant was fed up with both students and said, "Edward, you're coming with me to the principal's office."

"What about Kelly? Don't you think she deserves to go to?"

"Kelly is going to clean up the mess that she made," Mrs. Bryant said indicating the small body.

"No she's not," Edward said as he grabbed the tray that held Trevor. "I won't allow it. She's not going to touch Trevor ever again. Look what happened the last time she did. Who knows what she would do the next time."

"C'mon, Edward," she said, pointing to the door. "We're going to the office."

"And I ask again, what about Kelly?"

Mrs. Bryant held up a firm hand and said, "Don't question me. I'll take care of Kelly after I deal with you."

"In other words, you're not going to do shit about what she did to Trevor, are you?"

"Edward, don't argue with me. We're going to the office now."

"No!" Edward shouted. "I won't go unless Kelly goes! I didn't do anything. I don't deserve it. She does!"

"Edward! This is your last warning."

Still clutching the dissection pan that had Trevor staked to it, Edward yelled. "Fine! Great! Let it be my last warning! I'm not going, and you can't make me!"

Edward was afraid he might do something even worse, so he turned and kicked over another student's chair, stormed out of the classroom, and slammed the door behind him.

Edward went directly home. There was no use to stay around school; everybody treated him unfairly—even the teachers.

Once he was at home, he took one of his grandfather's old cigar boxes and lined it with some soft, red, velvet cloth he found in their cluttered basement. He also made a small miniature pillow and laid Trevor inside, making sure

Trevor's head was properly cushioned. He sat for a long time stroking Trevor's soft fur. Finally, Edward took a small piece of cloth and folded it over the small body and tucked Trevor in. He leaned in close and gave Trevor a quick kiss on his head and quickly shut the lid. Tears were already beginning to flow. He wanted and needed to get this over with. He buried Trevor in a deep hole beside an old pine tree right outside his bedroom window. Edward even made a little grave marker with an old brick and painted Trevor's name on it in block letters. Edward sat beside Trevor's grave and cried softly to himself, whispering silently for Trevor to forgive him for taking him to school that day.

ᘓ

Another loud thunder bomb exploded above him. It knocked him free from his memory. Reality rained down around him and he glanced back up toward the window into a face that was staring down directly at him.

Kelly was looking out of the window, obviously concerned about the weather; or was she trying to figure out who was in her backyard?

Lightning flashed incandescently and lit up the backyard.

The woman leaned toward the window. She stared directly at the tree that Edward was braced against.

Edward froze as the backyard was covered again in a blanket of darkness.

"Keep on cooking your food, bitch," Edward said under his breath. "It's too dark outside to see little ol' me with all the distractions of the storm. There's no one out here except the bogeyman."

He moved behind the tree again where he wouldn't be seen if lightning flashed a second time and blinked water from his eyes.

How long had he been standing here? Did she see me?

After a few moments passed, he glanced at the window again and saw Kelly had moved away from the window. She was still cooking and talking on her cell.

Tyler moved from behind the tree and sprinted to the basement door of Kelly's house.

There were two doors: a metal encasement door, which happen to be unlocked, and a locked wooden door with nine panes of glass in a wooden tic-tac-toe frame.

"This is way too easy," Edward said. Then he waited.

When another load of thunder was transported across the sky, Edward elbowed the section of window closest to the doorknob. Reaching in, Edward unlocked the door and slipped into the black warmth inside. He blindly made his way toward the stairs. Fixed on the light coming from beneath the basement door at the top of the staircase and making sure not to alert anyone of his presence, he slowly ascended the steps.

CHAPTER 15

KELLY SHERIDAN HAD a habit of taking a long, luxurious bubble bath right after work on most days. It was her little reward for doing a good job. This was just her way of giving back to herself, because she knew she deserved it.

She lay in the garden tub soaking in the bubbles for what seemed like an hour, almost falling asleep a few times. She kept draining the cooled water out and replacing it with the hottest water she could stand. To keep herself awake, she put the water jets on full blast. The bombarding water crested over her in all the right places, and after a while her body was free from tension.

Finally, the thought of homework papers, dinner, and a host of other mundane chores came back to haunt her, and she knew she couldn't stay in there forever. She knew she had to step back into reality.

She dried off and slipped into some sweatpants, a Pittsburg Steelers sweatshirt, and a pair of fuzzy socks. She truly felt warm, cozy, and finally relaxed.

The only thing missing in tonight's chain of events was a meal of Italian cuisine. She loved to cook, and that's what she did on stormy nights such as this.

Food was always better when it wasn't prepared in a half-assed manner. Her cooking always turned out first rate, and Travis, her husband, always enjoyed her masterpieces. Even though Travis was out of town this week and couldn't partake, tonight was going to be one of those nights.

As she came down the stairs to start dinner, Mosey—her cat—jumped to the corner of the couch to get her attention. He meowed softly to remind her she hadn't feed him yet.

"I haven't forgot about you, baby," she said as she lifted and cuddled him to her chest. She carried him over and set him on the bar that joined the kitchen and the living room together. She opened a can of cat food and served it along with a small scoop of dried cat food for variety. Mosey wasted no time diving into his dinner.

After satisfying Mosey, she turned on the small kitchen television to hear the latest news. She turned the volume to a low setting.

Kelly grabbed her cell phone and dialed Suzanne's number as she started to prepare dinner. As Kelly waited for Suzanne to either pick up or for the phone to drop to voice mail, Kelly pulled a skillet from its place in the cupboard and turned a burner on high. She retrieved the uncooked hamburger meat from the refrigerator and dumped it into the pan.

"This is Suzanne."

"Hey, it's me, Kel. How are you doing?"

"I am about to go insane. Can you tell me again why the hell I went into this profession?"

Kelly laughed and grabbed the cutting board from its place on the counter. "I don't know, but we can discuss it tonight over spaghetti dinner." She retrieved a green and red pepper from the fridge. "I'm cooking as we speak."

"Ohh, spaghetti. I haven't had your cooking in a long time. I get off at eight."

Kelly began to chop the peppers into small bite size pieces.

"I wish I was *getting off*. Who's the special guy? Is it someone I know?"

"Not that kind of "getting off." The leaving work, shift ending, punching a time clock kind of getting off, and I can't wait. It's been too long of a day."

"For you too, huh?"

"Yeah. I can be there shortly after eight."

"I was hoping you would say that."

Kelly took fresh tomatoes out of the crisper and began washing them in the sink.

A flare of lightning flickered as though it was attached to faulty wiring with a bad connection.

The lightning caught Kelly's attention, and she glanced up and out of the kitchen window. The lighting lit up the backyard for a few brief moments, and she saw or thought she saw a face peering up at her through the turmoil of the storm. She did a double-take as darkness fell over the yard again.

"Kelly?" Suzanne asked. "Did I lose you?"

Kelly still didn't answer.

Suzanne asked a little louder than before, "Kel? You still there?"

"Shhhh, hold on a minute," Kelly said.

She mimicked back, "Shhhh, hold on a minute for what?"

"I thought I saw something outside."

"Ohhh sccaaarrrrry. What do you mean by *something*?"

"Not something. Someone."

"No. Don't start that shit again, Kelly. You know you always get like this when Travis goes out of town. It's obvious that you're going to start imagining things because you're there by yourself and there's a huge storm outside. It's the perfect atmosphere to breed paranoia."

"I'm not paranoid. I swear I saw someone in the backyard. He was—I think it was a he—was standing behind that big oak tree out back."

"Oh, of course because mass murderers are always male…"

Even though Kelly was hearing Suzanne, she was more intent on the status of her backyard. She stared out of the window hoping to see—as well as hoping she wouldn't see—someone in the tumult. The light from the kitchen window lit a portion of the ground outside, but there was too much chaos from the storm to see anything else.

From the stove, a loud sizzling and popping brought her attention back to her uncooked meal. She moved to the stove, turned the heat down, and chopped at the meat with a spatula.

Suzanne continued with her morbid dialogue, "Have you ever heard of a female mass murderer? I'm sure they exist, but you don't hear too much about them. I guess women are smarter than the men. That must be the reason they don't get caught as often."

"Suzanne!"

"Yeah, Kel."

"You're not helping my situation."

"Sorry. I just think your imagination is going haywire, and you're seeing things that aren't there."

"Is that your diagnosis of me?"

"Sure is. You always get like this when you're by yourself."

With the meat back under control, Kelly glanced back out the window, still searching the yard below. She said, "Sorry. Guess I've cried wolf too many times."

Another mortar shell detonated in a thundering boom, allowing the explosion of lightning to seep through the split heavens.

"Nobody out there now," Kelly said—more to herself than anyone else—then turned from the window.

Hearing her mutterings, Suzanne said, "Well, what did you expect? He saw you looking at him. Do you actually think he would give you a chance to take his picture?"

Kelly filled another pan with hot water and set the water to boil. Then she began to slice and dice the onions, garlic, and tomatoes. She separated them all into piles.

Suzanne continued talking to her in a way you explain something to a child, "Kelly, I'm joking with you. Listen, don't psychoanalyze yourself or the situation too much. It's starting to play tricks on you."

"You're right. I'm a basket case." In a sarcastic, sing-songy voice, Kelly continued to ridicule herself, "I'm totally crazy, and I should be committed."

"I've always thought so," Suzanne agreed.

"Thanks for the vote of confidence. You always know how to cheer me up."

A muffled cat call came from down the hallway. It sounded like it was coming from Mosey. It sounded like he was in a cat fight or in pain. She held the phone away from her ear and called, "Mosey?"

"Kelly?"

"What?"

"Kelly, if you're trying to scare me, it's working. If you're trying to get me to knock off early, it's not. I can't leave work until my shift ends at eight. Are you hearing things now?"

"Why do you ask?"

"I can tell. You get real silent when that happens."

Kelly took a deep breath, "Again, I'm sorry. I thought I heard Mosey. It sounded like he was in pain."

"No. What happened is Mosey most likely caught that mass murderer that was lurking around your house. Oh shit, hey, the intercom is calling me. Gotta go. Just keep yourself busy with your electric shock treatment until I get there."

Kelly laughed, "You're funny. You should've chosen stand-up comedy as your career."

"You'll be all right, I promise." Suzanne said. "I'll see you soon."

"Okay. Uh, Suzanne," Kelly said before they hung up.

"Yeah, Kel."

"Thanks for always being there for me."

"Don't mention it. That's what friends are for. You would've done the same for me, wouldn't you?"

"A hundred times over. See you shortly after eight."

As she hung up the phone, she rested her head on her hand and thought again about the face she thought she had seen outside. Her body shuddered involuntarily and her skin seemed to crawl with the memory. The hair on her arms, head, and neck stood on end with chilly attention.

She rubbed and scratched the imaginary spiders from her arms and the back of her neck as she pushed the thought out of her mind and tried to focus on dinner.

"I'm am so going insane," she stated aloud.

Kelly forced herself to continue with dinner. She turned the meat on low heat, dumped the tomato sauce in, poured in all the cut vegetables, added a packet of spaghetti seasoning, stirred it all together, covered it, and let it simmer. Then she dumped the spaghetti strands into the boiling pot of water and stirred them for a few seconds.

As she turned back to stir her famous sauce, she called out again to her cat, "Moooossseey."

Noticing her cat hadn't come when she called, she looked over her shoulder into the connecting living room, only to see someone other than Mosey standing there before her.

At first sight, she was paralyzed with fear.

"What the—," were the only words she was able to get out.

CHAPTER 16

TYLER CURTIS, ALONG with the host-like spirit of Edward McDaniel, stood in the dark at the top of the stairs. He tried to ignore the uncomfortable feeling of his soaked garments gluing to his skin. They were binding and felt like a second skin he was itching to shed. He turned the doorknob gently with his unbitten hand and pushed it open enough to peer through the opening. From his vantage point, he could see the living room. Beyond the living room lay the kitchen, where Kelly worked steadily to complete her meal.

Edward had eaten lunch today, although he lost that in sixth period during the dream sequence and hadn't eaten anything else since. The aroma of Kelly's cooking filled his nostrils; his mouth began to water, and his stomach growled from the lack of sustenance.

Kelly was still jabbering on the phone. "Good God, how much did she really have to say?" Edward whispered.

Edward slowly pushed the door open further and was about to enter the carpeted hallway when something slithered between his legs. He froze for a moment then looked down. He relaxed that it was only Kelly's house cat.

"What do we have here?" Edward whispered. "Here kitty, kitty."

The dark grey furball didn't seem to mind Tyler's saturated jeans as it serpentined between his legs. Edward figured the cool moisture felt good on its fur.

"Hey there, you cute little son of a bitch," Edward said in a prayerful whisper as he stooped and scooped the cat up with his right hand. "You just scared the shit out of me, yes you did."

The cat suddenly sensed something about Tyler that it hadn't felt before. The cat hissed and lashed out toward Tyler's face. Edward jerked Tyler's head back so the claws couldn't connect.

"Oh, now don't be that way, you little shit. I'll bust that ass of yours."

The cat continued to squirm.

Edward shifted the cat into the other arm. He held the cat so its weight was distributed throughout the length of his arm with very little pressure on his bitten hand. This made it easier for Edward to pet the cat as he stood waiting in the stairwell.

He peeked again through the opening of the door as he stroked the cat's fur. The cat was tense, but his squirming had settled slightly. Kelly was still on the phone. *Who the hell is she talking to? And what are they talking about?*

As he waited for Kelly to get off the phone, he thought again of Trevor and how he looked that day so long ago, and it began to make him angry again. *What right did she have to do that to my pet?*

Edward felt the cat suddenly becoming restless again.

Edward pressed the cat's hind quarters into his ribs with his elbow to hold him tighter. He continued to sooth the cat's nerves with his right hand by petting him harder, but Edward was still lost in his thoughts.

Here's Kelly. She has a great job as a teacher. She's doing what she likes. She even has her own home and car; both of which are very luxurious. What else could a girl ask for?

The cat squirmed madly, trying to get down. It even hissed and scratched at his arms, but they were covered with long sleeves.

In comparative terms, what do I have? Nada. Zero. Ziltch. Nothing. My life has been nothing, but it is quickly turning around for the better.

The cat was feeling too much pressure from Edward's arms and hands and just wanted to be free. It made a desperate, frenzied movement and gave out a loud hissing cry.

"Shhhhhhh!" Edward said urgently as he grabbed the cat's head and jerked it upward as he leaned down to stare through the crack in the door. As he wrenched the cat's head up, he rotated his arm across his chest so his arm wouldn't bump the door open. The cat's middle was caught in the crook of his elbow and the force was too much for the cat's frail body. Two audible snaps followed the brisk movement. One was attributed to the cat's neck; the other had come from its spine.

"Mosey?" Kelly asked.

Edward saw Kelly with her cell phone away from her ear, listening for tale-tell sounds of her cat, but none came. It was clear from the puzzled look on her face that she was debating whether she had actually heard anything over the pouring rain.

Edward stood again as he pulled the limp animal from his body.

He transferred the cat's body to his right hand but picked him up this time by its tail. Edward held him up and looked him dead in the eyes.

"Shit. Sorry about that, little buddy."

Edward saw Kelly put her cell phone back to her ear a second time, say a few words and then end the call. When he saw her place the cell on the counter, he made his move. He slid the door open and moved into the hallway, leaving a trail of muddy footprints behind him.

As Kelly turned back to her cooking, she called out again, "Moooossseey."

Kelly knew Mosey wouldn't come if he was snoozing somewhere in a comfortable chair.

Kelly looked up to see if Mosey had obeyed her call and froze when she saw Tyler Curtis standing in the middle of her living room. His clothes were soaked and wrinkled. His uncombed black hair was plastered to his head. His eyes were unwavering, fixed only on her. One eye was cut, leaving a thin stream of dried blood down his face. He seemed as if he were a stone statue, and Kelly blinked to make sure she wasn't seeing things like the face behind the tree.

"What the—."

"Hello, Kelly," Edward said, interrupting her.

She didn't know what was about to ensue but did have enough sense to turn both stove burners off. She knew she couldn't manage the dinner and focus on the nearing confrontation.

He lifted the dangling cat again by the tail, "I found Mosey. He was in the basement."

Upon first sight of Mosey, Kelly knew he was dead; she didn't have to be a veterinarian to figure that out.

"What the hell did you do to Mosey?" she said angrily.

"He wouldn't sit still; he kept squirming around. Then he started making too much noise. I think I broke his back or maybe his neck. Could be both, I don't know."

"Why the hell did you do that?"

"It wasn't my fault. It was an accident. But if you think about it; there's not too much difference in what I did to Mosey and what you did to Trevor, is there?"

From the look on her face, Edward knew he had her.

"Trevor?" Kelly questioned. "Tyler, I don't understand."

"You remember my pet hamster, Trevor, don't you?"

"Yes. But that was so long ago. How did you know about Trevor?"

"Why does time play a part in this? You purposely killed my pet. I accidentally killed yours. It just happens to be a number of years later. Why are you getting so upset? Eye for an eye, tooth for tooth, pet for pet. Do unto others as you would have them do unto you. You read the Bible, don't you?"

"Sometimes. You?"

"Not in a long time. My grandmother used to quote scripture to me. I guess you could say it was ingrained in my mind."

Edward swung the cat up and released it when it was even with his shoulder. The momentum from the swing launched the cat toward the bar. Mosey landed on one of the plates Kelly had set for dinner. His body also clipped a bowl of pretzels that had been set out for munching before dinner. In a small wave, the pretzels were scattered down the length of the bar and onto the floor.

In a very convincing French accent—much the way Kelly had said it to him years ago—Edward said, "Dinner is served."

"You're crazy!"

"No, I'm Edward McDaniel." He paused, surveying the scene, then said, "You have two plates set for dinner. Who's your other guest? Your husband? I noticed your wedding ring during class today."

"That's none of your business."

"Could your dinner guest be the person you were talking to on the phone?

She glanced toward the phone in horror, then back at Tyler.

Edward didn't say anything, but knew her facial features gave her away. He would have to remember to look at her call history before he left the house tonight just to make sure who it was.

Kelly was afraid but decided not to get hysterical. She would only make a mistake because of a flustered mind. She had to think clear right now but would stand her ground if anything started to happen.

"You were behind the tree in my backyard weren't you?"

"Did you see me? Really? I was wondering about that. Was that Suzanne Baldwin on the phone?"

"Why-why do you ask?"

"Well, I heard you speak her name, invite her for dinner, that sort of thing. Was it Suzanne you were talking too?"

Not knowing what to say, Kelly stammered out a response. "It was a different Suzanne."

"You're not a very good liar," Edward whispered. "When is she dropping by?"

"She's not coming here tonight. She's too busy at the hospital."

"I thought you said it wasn't the same Suzanne."

Kelly then realized she had just let the cat out of the bag.

"If you lied about who you were talking to on the phone, most likely you lied about her not coming by here. What time is she arriving?"

"Tyler, I think you should leave."

"Leave? You're crazy," he said evenly. "I told you I'm not Tyler! I'm Edward!"

"Okay, okay, Edward. I'm sorry. Just calm down," Kelly soothed. "I don't understand. It doesn't make sense."

"It makes perfect sense. You see this?" Edward asked, as he grabbed the medallion from beneath his shirt. "You asked me about it this afternoon after school. This little medallion sucked me inside itself because I made one little wish. I barely even remember making it, but apparently I did."

"It's all science fiction."

"Science fiction? The ability to fly was classified as science fiction. Landing on the moon was impossible at one time, but by God, we did it. Anything is possible. I'm living proof of that."

"It's too much for me to take. I can't accept that."

"I'm not making this shit up. This is real. It happen and you're going to have to accept it."

Edward walked closer.

Kelly backed up to the sink.

"You want to know what it was like for Tyler? It was pure terror for the boy; much in the same way it was for me when Jeremy Taylor killed me nearly twenty years ago."

"Oh, Tyler, uh, Edward, no, that was an accident. He didn't mean to do it."

"Accident," Edward cut in. "Like in the way I killed Mosey was an accident? Don't start with all that *accident* business. Jeremy, you, and all of your other pansy-ass friends always tortured and made fun of me in school. Why did you do it? Was it fun? Did you get off on it? Did you cream your panties? Did it make you feel better? What was the real reason?" Edward barked. "Why did you kill Trevor?"

"I, I don't know why," Kelly stammered.

Tyler moved closer. "It's because you wanted to be accepted by all your peers and your friends. You know, Kelly, that's all I wanted as well."

There was a long silence between them underscored by the drumming rain.

"It's true," Kelly admitted. "We never thought about your feelings."

"Damn right, you didn't. You never thought about anyone else's feelings but your own."

Kelly gripped the knife that was in the sink and swung at Tyler in a stabbing arc.

Edward saw the movement coming and caught her arm in mid swing. He quickly twisted her arm until she dropped the knife.

She wrenched her arm from his, shoved past him, snatched up her cell phone, bounded through the living room and made a mad dash for the stairs.

The stairs were constructed in an L-shaped fashion, three stairs up, and then a right angle to the left, and then twelve steps to the hallway at the top.

Edward shouted loud enough for her to hear him, "Now why did you want to go and do something like that? What the hell did I ever do to you? I just want to talk." He followed her up the stairs.

Kelly ran into her bedroom, slammed the door, then locked it. She was looking for a hiding place and a weapon all at the same time.

"We're too old to be playing hide and seek," he said as he reached the top of the stairs. "And you thought I was childish back in high school. This is really mature, Kelly. Wonder which room could she be hiding in?" he asked to the empty hallway. He raised a foot to waist level and kicked open the closed bedroom door. The jamb buckled, the lock broke free, and the door slammed against the inside wall. "Could it be the only closed door in the hallway? Not very bright, Kelly."

Upon entering the bedroom, he looked around, but she was nowhere in sight. He quickly checked under the bed. The only other place for her to be hiding was the closet. He jerked the doors open, almost tearing them from their hinges and found Kelly crouched against the far wall with her cell phone in her hands.

Kelly stopped punching the numbers and looked up when the door swung open.

"What the hell are you doing, Kelly?" Edward asked as he moved inside and roughly escorted her out. "Who were you calling on the phone? You better pray to God you didn't call the cops."

Kelly didn't answer but went into an immediate swinging rage; she punched and kicked wildly, hoping to find a connection.

"Oh, c'mon. Don't be this way."

"Leave me alone!" Kelly shouted.

"Give it to me!" he demanded.

And she did. She charged him wildly like a wolf protecting its own turf. She grabbed hold of him, forced him across the room, slammed him up against the dresser, then bolted out the door.

"Now you've gone and done it. Now you've pissed me off!" Edward screamed. "Don't ever walk away from me!"

Enraged now, he followed her out of the room, snatching up a heavy vase from her bureau as he went.

Kelly was halfway down the hall and getting closer to the stairs.

Only wanting to stop her or slow her down, Edward drew back to hurl the vase. He felt Tyler squirming at the back of his mind. He threw the vase with every ounce of strength his new body would allow. But on his follow through, his hand didn't release the weapon as he wanted. It felt as though the vase was super glued to his palm.

Tyler had just enough time to send a brief shutdown message to the command center of his brain—a stop reflex telling himself not to release the vase, and it worked.

"I'm not going to let you do this to her!" Tyler shouted from the inside of his mind.

There was a brief inner struggle as Edward forced Tyler back into submission and gained back full control of the body again.

"You have no choice in the matter!" Edward yelled back.

Edward saw that Kelly was now at least three strides from reaching the stairs. In a desperate attempt to stop her, he cocked his arm back as far as it would go. In a blurred motion, Edward threw Tyler's arm forward again with all the fury he had kept buried inside for so many years and released the vase.

The weight of the vase wasn't as symmetrical as a football, so it couldn't be thrown in a perfect touchdown spiral, but it was thrown with precision, and it found its mark. The bottom of the vase exploded against the back of Kelly's skull. It pitched her forward and it looked as though the force of the blow lifted her slightly off her feet.

"Bullseye!" Edward shouted in devilish excitement and laughed. "I nailed you, bitch!"

Pain engulfed Kelly's head. She saw shards of porcelain whiz pass on each side of her face. The blow stunned her and crumpled her against the wall under its force. In hitting the wall, she became disoriented and didn't realize she was so close to the edge of the stairs. She tried to catch her balance, but her foot slipped from the top stair to the next one down. She grabbed at the banister post, but her fingers curled around nothing but empty air. She fell backward in a fluid movement of flailing arms.

There was a blood-curdling scream that was cut short as she disappeared into the stairwell. There was a rumble of thumps and a loud crack as Kelly tumbled twelve steps to the bottom and slammed into the banister.

Edward couldn't believe what had just happened. His mouth was open in shock. He brought his throwing hand up in front of his face in disbelief. He knew Tyler had spent years as a quarterback perfecting his throw for the football season. Tyler practiced religiously to hit the mark he was aiming for; always trying to place the football between the jersey numbers. Edward's new body tingled with excitement. All the things he couldn't do as a teen were now at his discretion. He could now, for once in his sorry life, do practically anything he wanted and finally be somebody. He felt a little like God in the flesh.

Now in the aftermath, the only sound possessing the house was the pitter-patter of rain and the exploding heartbeat in Tyler's chest and head.

Edward walked slowly to the top of the stairs, and gazed down at the lifeless marionette heap. Kelly's head, arms, and legs were contorted in unnatural ways, like a game of Twister gone horribly wrong. Her face was frozen in a look of open-mouthed wonder.

Edward stooped and pocketed the cell phone Kelly had dropped when the vase had dropped her. He laughed at the thought and turned out the lights upstairs. He moved slowly down the stairs and stood over her body. He stood for a long time drinking in the sight, then he side stepped and knelt down beside her. He bent over her and stared into her aqua-grey eyes. He leaned over and was about to whisper something in her ear when a loud exhalation of breath exploded from her mouth.

Startled, Edward stood up completely and stared down at the reanimated corpse.

"Help me," Kelly whispered in a broken wheeze.

Edward just stood there, afraid and dumbfounded.

It took the second plea from Kelly to bring him out. "Please, help me."

He stepped away from her and immediately began to pace back and forth thinking of what he should do.

Kelly was looking up at him with tortured, agonized eyes. She was in a lot of pain. He knew that look. It had been pasted on his face plenty of times as a teen.

He quickly knelt by her side again. "Help you? You want *me* to help *you*? You've got to be joking. After everything you did to me. And to Trevor."

Then an idea came to him. It hit him like a frozen water balloon to the face. He nearly leapt over the banister and moved quickly into the kitchen. He quickly opened drawers, shuffled through the contents, and slammed them again. He did this to another three drawers before finding what he needed.

He moved back to the stairwell, hiding his prize behind his back.

"Guess what, Kelly?"

Through a grimace of pain, her face asked, "What?"

Edward sat down next to her, "I have something that I think will help you out. You want to know what it is?"

Kelly's face said no and yes at the same time.

Edward pulled a pair of metal scissors from behind his back and held them up close for Kelly to see. He snicked them open and closed in front of her face a couple of times.

"No," she yelled.

"I'm afraid so. Trevor would've wanted it this way. I mean, after all, that is the way you killed him. It's only fitting that you go the same fucking way. Wouldn't you agree?"

Tears ran out the sides of Kelly's eyes. She turned away, not wanting to see what was going to come next. She remembered Trevor and how he squirmed under the scissors she killed him with.

Kelly felt Tyler's fingers feeling around the top part of her left breast. Startled, she looked back at him and with her face, asked him what he was doing.

"Sorry. I'm not trying to cop a feel. I'm just trying to find the best entry point to hit your heart. Can't very well go through the center of your chest; I would hit your sternum and wouldn't be able to go very deep."

Her face pleaded no again.

"Hey, you're the one who was asking me to help you in the first place. I'm just doing what you asked me to do. It will be better this way."

Edward continued to feel around the top left portion of her breast.

"Ah, yes, right here will be a nice entry point."

Edward, please, Tyler begged from back of his mind. *Please, don't do this. She's suffered enough. Just let it go.*

Edward ignored the pestering of Tyler's desperate thoughts and placed the tip of the metal scissors where his finger was.

All Tyler could do was watch himself murder this woman and he couldn't do a damn thing about it.

The slight poke of the scissors into her chest brought Kelly's eyes back toward his.

Kelly pleaded again with a slight shake of her head.

Edward simply smiled as he started to add pressure to the scissors handle.

Kelly cried out as the scissors disappeared into her chest.

"Sh-sh-sh-sh-sh, it's okay now. Everything is going to be fine soon. Just a few more seconds and it will all be over."

Kelly turned her head toward his, and with vehement eyes, told him just what she thought of him.

"I know you hate me, Kelly. But you just do not know how much I hate you. You could've been a friend to me if you wanted to, but instead, you chose to act differently toward me. So since that was your choice—I have no other choice but this."

Kelly's hate-filled look remained.

"Do me a favor, will you?" Edward asked. "When you get to the other side—and maybe for you it will be the right side; if you see Trevor, can you tell him 'hello' for me. I don't know how long I will be here, but tell him I hope to see him again someday."

The burning hate drained out of her eyes as tears started to flow and with that, an apologetic look took its place.

As Kelly died, a soft whisper past through her lips. "Please forgive me. I am so sorry."

Because deep with in her now-pierced heart, she knew she was wrong and had hated what she had done the moment she did it. The only thing she could do now was apologize.

"I'm sure you are sorry, Kelly. Now. Because you were confronted about it. But why couldn't you have apologized to me back when we were in school?"

Kelly didn't answer, but the apologetic look remained.

Edward looked down at the scissors he was grasping. They were now buried up to the hilt into Kelly's chest.

He leaned over and whispered the four words he was going to say to her earlier, "*Now*, justice is served."

The statement was funny to him, and his slight grin grew into a widening smile. A short chuckle soon increased into an obnoxious guffaw. He stood and jumped the last three remaining stairs to the living room floor and did a little dance and a jig to celebrate. He knew he looked stupid, but he didn't care. There was no one else around to see him. He was ecstatic. He even cut a couple of cartwheels through the house. The more he laughed, the funnier it became, and he doubled over with side-splitting laughter that drowned out the sound of the rain. During his ceremony, he stooped a couple of times and laughed directly in her face as loud and crazed as he could. He was thrilled it happened like this. He had been too far away to hear the sound of her neck breaking. That's the only thing he regretted.

Edward knew two things. Suzanne was coming here tonight after work, and Kelly's ending comment to her was, "I'll see you shortly after eight."

"This means I have a little over an hour to enjoy a spaghetti dinner."

He skipped goofily into the kitchen and turned the two stove burners on to reheat the spaghetti again. The noodles had been soaking during their "session" and were tender; they just needed some heat.

"It was so good of you to cook dinner for me tonight, Kelly. This is really special. Nothing like a little killing to build an appetite."

He hummed a little while he took a glass from the cabinet and helped himself to some Mountain Dew from the refrigerator.

When the sauce and the noodles were finally bubbling away, he turned the burners off. He took a plate from the bar that Kelly had set earlier; he chose the one that wasn't serving "Stiffening Mosey." He grabbed a spoon and dished out a large portion of noodles, then smothered them with a generous helping of sauce.

He took his plate, glass, a fork and a couple of napkins and went to the stairs where Kelly's crumpled body lay. He sat on the three steps that descended into the living room and gazed at her splayed body on the landing. He just wanted a couple of last looks to last a lifetime. No pangs of guilt washed over him, and no sorrow tugged at his heart's strings.

He ate quickly but not because he was in a hurry; he was so famished and it tasted so damn good.

He slid a finger over her forehead and brushed a strand of hair out of her eyes.

"There, that's better," he soothed.

You're sick and twisted, Tyler thought in disgust.

"Like Mosey, like Kelly," he muttered. "Kelly is probably in worse shape than Mosey though. Hey Tyler, how many bones do you think she broke on the way to the bottom of the stairs?"

No answer.

"I don't know, either." To Kelly, Edward said, "I would love to stay and chat with you more, but I hate one way conversations; besides, I have another session to attend."

He took his dirty dishes to the kitchen and deposited them in the sink and pitched the used napkins in the trash can. He ran water over the plate to wash away the last bit of sauce, washed his glass and silverware, and set it in the drainboard next to the sink.

He went to the stairs again, drawn to Kelly's body like a magnet. It was like he couldn't get enough. He stared at her one last time. Feeling satisfied with the meal as well as with what happened tonight, he slowly moved away from her body, relishing the memory.

He took her phone as a precaution.

Glancing around the room a final time, he descended the basement stairs and slipped out into the downpour of the shadowed night.

CHAPTER 17

THE PARKING COMPLEX was dark, but not nearly as dark as the perpetual blackness Tyler was submerged in whenever the spirit of Edward McDaniel took control.

Edward had found the perfect hiding place to view Suzanne's silver Mercedes. He had parked on the third level of the parking garage, underneath the overhang of the fourth floor entrance ramp. It was a perfect spot to see who came and went, yet stay hidden from suspicious eyes. The small amount of light the fluorescent bulbs shed cast a glared reflection over the Mustang's windows; anyone glancing at the car as they walked by would just assume the car was empty.

Edward glanced at the illuminated clock numbers on the dash of the car. It was getting close to that eight o'clock quitting time. Some doctors, nurses, and interns had already exited the hospital and had walked to their cars. Some passed by without giving his car a second glance.

A few automobiles rumbled overhead and descended the ramp at the far end of the parking lot.

Jittering bugs and moths continually fluttered against the overhead fluorescent fixtures, creating elongated bat-like shadows over his face.

Edward was staring at Suzanne's automobile from across the parking complex; it had been easier to find than he had expected. He knew she drove a silver Mercedes from when she had arrived at the hospital the day Raven had bitten Tyler. There were a few others of that particular model in this garage, but he was only looking for one calling card that separated hers from all the others. Her license tag. He'd committed enough of it to memory to know that this one was indeed hers.

Simple. All he had to do now was wait.

Edward didn't know what was discussed before he overheard the last of her conversation with Kelly at the top of the basement stairs. He wondered if Kelly had mentioned their conversation from the end of class, but he couldn't take a chance. Only thing he had to do now was dot his I's, cross his T's, cover his bases, and tie up all the loose ends; and Suzanne was definitely a loose end.

From the back of Tyler's mind, Tyler asked, *What are you going to do now?*

Hey Tyler, welcome back, Edward thought cheerfully. *I don't rightly know. I haven't figured that out yet.*

What, you going to kill her the way you killed Kelly?

I didn't kill Kelly. She fell down the stairs. It was an accident.

And I suppose the vase you hurled into the back of her skull didn't attribute to her fall? And the scissors you drove into the center of her chest didn't help with her death either?

Edward started to laugh, *Hey, you got me there.*

Damn right I got you. I almost stopped you too.

Yes, you did. I was surprised about that. I'm going to have to keep better tabs on you so that doesn't happen again.

Good luck. You may hold me back for a while, but I'll come out when you least expect it. I'll keep fighting you. Tyler couldn't believe he asked Edward this next question, but Tyler was doing a little plotting on his own. *How are you going to kill her?* He needed as much information as possible so he could try and stop Edward when he made his move. He didn't know if it would work, but he had to try.

I don't know how. Why, do you have any suggestions?

No! Tyler screamed.

Hey, just asking. You don't have to jump down my throat. I thought you might want to have a little fun. Since you don't; I guess I'll have to think of something on my own.

Why? Tyler thought.

Tyler, you're so naïve. Think about it. Kelly is dead. Her cat is dead.

And whose fault is that? Tyler interjected.

Ignoring him, Edward pressed on, *Most likely Kelly told Suzanne something about our conversation this afternoon. She'll be the first one to lay blame on you when she goes to Kelly's house tonight and finds them. I'm protecting you as much as myself.*

That's bullshit. You don't give a fuck about me. You're doing this because of what happened to you in school.

Now that's a false truth. I'm looking out for number one. We're both in the same body. If something happens to you, then the same thing is happening to me.

What did Suzanne do to you? Did she kill one of your pets, too?

That's not funny, Tyler.

I wasn't shooting for a comedy angle. I was just making a point.

Don't make fun of me either.

I'm not.

You didn't know how it felt. You weren't there.

Thank God for that. If I was, maybe I would've made fun of you, too. Does that mean you're going to make me commit suicide?

Keep talking and I might. Tyler? Edward asked. *Tyyllleeeerrrrr!* Edward called. *Oh c'mon, Tyler; don't be that way. Don't close up on me.*

Edward was getting impatient and fidgety. Granted, his new home inside Tyler Curtis was better than the cramped space of his grandfather's charm, but he hated sitting around in one location; he liked to keep on the move.

Where had the talisman come from? Edward asked himself. That was the billion dollar question, and he wished he had a billion dollar answer. *I'll probably never know.* That was one question that had puzzled Edward throughout his short-lived life. His grandfather had told him that the Mojo would protect him and bring good luck to his life.

"That was a bunch of bullshit," Edward muttered. *It never protected me from anything. Not from the bullies and popular kids that overpowered me in school. They always preyed on me. I just thought the charm was cool.* Edward smiled, *One thing I know for a fact is the last thing that went through Kelly Sheridan's mind when she was falling down the stairs—right before I jammed the scissors home—she remembered me. She remembered what she did to me and knew if she had treated me differently in school the incident tonight would never have happened. The only regret I have is that I wasn't able to snap her neck and spine with my own hands like I did to Mosey, but I'm okay with that. The next one will be different. If this is what this gem of a charm can give me—the chance to make things right—then I'll wear it 'til the day I die, I mean, 'til the day Tyler dies. I forgot, I'm already dead.* He chuckled about his musings.

Even though his body was restless, the thoughts of what Suzanne Baldwin did to him an eternity ago began to play again in his mind.

In everybody else's eyes, what Suzanne did to me was a whole hell of a lot worse than what Kelly did, but in my eyes they were both equally bad. Hey, Tyler! Edward snapped to get Tyler's attention. *You asked earlier what Suzanne had done to me! Well if you'll think with me for a few minutes we can stroll down memory lane together and you can experience what I felt. Maybe then you'll change your tune and start marching to the beat of a different drum. Ready?*

Edward's mind drifted.

&

It was the night of the big football game. Rivalry night, *as some people liked to call it: Silver Ridge Sidewinders going head to head against the Cypress Grove Gators. It always produced a game for the record books.*

Edward remembered planning not to go to the game that night. As it turned out, his life would've been better if he hadn't, but he knew everyone was going to be there. The possibilities of maybe making a friend, meeting a girl was limitless.

His time each night was usually spent watching movies on their limited amount of channels, and he only did that if he wasn't familiar with any of the material covered in school that day. Usually he already knew all the subject matter and occupied his time doing other things, but this Friday night, he had a wild hair and decided to do something different.

He had picked out his best slacks and shirt, which by the other students' clothing standards was slightly out of date, but he had washed and ironed them so he would look his best. He took his time showering and washing his hair. He dressed, combed his hair, brushed his teeth and added some cheap but passable cologne. He checked and double-checked himself in the mirror to make sure he looked his best, because as he always told himself, You never have a second chance to make a first impression. *He knew that, but he always felt he was trying to make that first impression with everybody at the school even though they would only see him as he was: a nothing. He could probably never earn their respect, but he nevertheless tried to constantly change their opinion.*

The game started at seven o'clock. He planned it so he wouldn't be one of the first students at the game, that's why he left his house precisely at seven. He rode his bike at a medium pace to get there shortly after the game was started. Sure, he enjoyed a great game of competition, but he wasn't a die-hard football fan who had to be there right as the ball was kicked off, and he usually left long before the fans had stormed the field. If given a choice, he could have easily sat at home and watched television rather than sit in the stands and watch a game. He figured he would just walk around and see who noticed him. Maybe he would try to strike up a conversation with someone. He was just looking for a friend to talk to and someone who might be inclined to talk to him.

The stadium had been built where the support structures were all enclosed by cinder block and brick walls. There were doors at different points at the base of the stadium, but they were always locked. The rooms under the stands were used for storage of miscellaneous athletic materials and inspection of the stadium itself. Shrubbery and tall, closely planted trees grew to a height of six to eight feet in the back of the stadium, giving the structure a nicely manicured look.

When he reached the school grounds, he peddled to the bike stands, docked and locked his bike securely, then strolled down the sidewalk toward the stadium.

The crowd was already uproarious. The sound was stifling. Chants, cheers, yells, and music rose out of the stands as each school rallied for their team.

Before he got to the front of the stadium, a hand shot out from between the trees at the back of the stadium. The hand grabbed his jacket sleeve and jerked him behind the stadium bleachers.

He was about to protest, but he was firmly pushed up against the wall and a finger was pressed to his lips indicating that whoever had him wanted him to be silent. He had been through this type of shit before; it was routine now, and he obeyed without question. He had learned the less he said, the sooner it would be over.

He had expected the owner of the hand to be some dumb jock getting his kicks off while the game was going on, but he raised his eyebrows when he saw Suzanne Baldwin standing before him.

This must be of major importance for her to grab me, *Edward thought.*

"Shhhhh, Edward. Don't say anything," *she whispered looking out through the gap between the stadium and the trees.*

"Mi kan't, ou've got mi wips piched togever."

"What?" *she asked releasing her finger from his lips.*

"I said, I can't, you've got my lips pinched together," *Edward said, licking his dry lips.*

"Oh, sorry," *she said laughing.* "You're cute." *She actually thought that was cute.*

"Don't mention it. What's wrong?"

"Can't say. Hurry, follow me," *she said as she grabbed his hand and pulled him further back into the alleyway between the hedges and the stadium wall. It was darker the further they went. He wasn't in the least bit scared with her, but he was concerned and continued to wonder why she had pulled him back here.*

"Where are we going and why are we going there?"

"In time; just come on."

Her voice seemed frantic; like something was wrong or she had to tell him something of the utmost importance. He shrugged and continued without question.

There was just enough light that spilt over the top of the stadium to vaguely see her in the dwindling shadows. As they walked, he noticed how tight her jeans looked. They almost seemed to be painted on. He raised his eyebrows and nodded his approval. He didn't comment of course, that would've been rude. Her shirt was tight also and short around the waist. Her tanned skin was smooth as caramel. He shook his head in disbelief. They hurriedly walked until he figured they were half way down the stadium wall.

"What's wrong, Suzanne? You sounded nervous. What's happened?"

She turned, smiled slyly at him, and said, "Nothing's happened—yet, but I'm wanting something to."

His forehead crinkled in confusion. "Excuse me? What the hell are you talking about?"

"You and me Edward. I want us to happen."

His head jerked back in astonishment as though she had just smacked him in the face. "Say that to me just one more time. I want to make sure I understood you."

She looked at him with seduction in her eyes. "I said, I want us to happen."

He stared at her as though trying to contemplate the impossible. "Want us to happen as in what?"

"Don't be so scrupulous," she teased. She slowly trailed a long fingernail down the side of his face then down the front of his shirt and said, "You're a smart guy. I think you know what I mean. I like a smart man. I see you in class everyday, and I just about go crazy because I can't be near you."

As her finger moved down his chest, he bent his head to follow it. "I think I know what you mean. I just want to hear you say what you mean. That way I will know for sure that I'm not imagining this."

"Whatever your first instinct was is what I want."

He nervously looked back and forth down the dim alleyways. He scratched his head as he tried to figure out the unbelievable and said, "Ah, I don't know."

With her other hand, Suzanne grabbed his chin and forced him to focus on her. "You're breaking my heart here, Edward," she said with full, pouty, red lips. "I thought you were a spur-of-the-moment type guy. Don't ask questions. Just take the bull by the horns and go with it. Take me."

"You've got to be shitting me."

Her finger had just reached the waist of his pants. Upon finding the top of his slacks, she grabbed the waist in a tight fist and pulled him to her and said, "I would never do that to you, Edward."

She rotated their bodies quickly to where her back was now against the wall. She leaned back against the wall and arched her back to make her ample breasts seem even larger in her tight-fitting top. The small buttons that closed the front of the shirt strained at the thread that held them to the fabric.

A small gold locket hung in the crevice of her cleavage; it was definitely one of the sexiest sights Edward had ever seen and he grew steadily harder with the sight. He couldn't keep his eyes off them, but he forced himself to focus on her face.

"Do you like what you see?" she asked as she trailed both hands over her breasts.

"Is that a trick question?" he said, smiling but then managed to mumble a pitiful apology.

"You haven't done anything wrong, I assure you." She slid her hands underneath her breasts, cupped them and lifted them toward him. "You have the right to stare at my breasts while you're talking to me. I don't mind." She ended her statement by pulling her shirt down even more, which left even more tanned cleavage for him to admire.

She watched him stare at her and then she grabbed his hand and said, "Come here, baby."

She was about to place his hand on her left breast, but Edward jerked it away. "No, I really don't think that's such a good idea."

"Why not Edward? Don't you like me?"

"Oh, hell yeah, I-I like you," he stammered. "One of my fantasies just came true. You."

Now it was her time to pull back in surprise. "Me? Your fantasy? Have you been having dirty thoughts about me?"

"Yeah, you."

"You bad boy. I'm flattered."

"You say that as if you're surprised. But not bad in the way you mean. It may sound stupid, but I respect you and your body. You're probably a lot of other guy's fantasy as well. I'm crazy about you; I just never thought it would happen like this.

"How did you imagine it would happen?"

Edward said nothing, afraid his explanation would come out wrong.

"It will happen if you will just let it."

"It just doesn't seem right."

"What?"

"Us. This. To be blunt, you wanting me. That doesn't make any sense."

"I don't understand," she paused when he didn't say anything. "Sometimes love doesn't make sense."

He didn't pay attention to her last phrase. He was in the process of figuring out how to explain this situation from his point of view. If he had noticed her mention of love in the last phrase, the rest of their little rendezvous may have turned out differently. He might've ended it right then and there.

"Well, when practical jokes are played on someone like they have been played on me over the years; I begin to wonder if everything is a practical joke. Even this."

"What do you mean?"

"Are you being straight with me? Is this a joke? Where is everybody else that's in on this?"

"I really don't have time to play games with you, Edward; at least not mind games. I have some other games in mind that we could venture into if you're interested. When I like something or someone, I go after whoever it is. I really can't believe that you think I would stoop to doing something like that to you. You've really got some sort of inferiority complex. You might need to talk to somebody about that."

"Well, to be frank, I don't know you. I don't know you or your true intentions."

"Sometimes words come hard for me, and I don't know how to explain some things. You ever have that problem?" she asked.

"Yeah," he said laughing. "Right now is one of those times."

"Sometimes it's easier to express my true feelings rather than put them in word form. Can I show you my true intentions right now?"

"I guess so."

She grabbed a fist full of his shirt and pulled him into her. As he neared, her grip on his shirt released and her arms encircled his neck and she gently pulled him closer.

As their heads drew together, he realized that a moment he had been waiting for his whole life was now in front of him. This was the moment. It was staring him dead in the face. Do or die. You don't get a chance like this and piss it away. This was the point of no return. Turn this opportunity down now, and it would never ever happen again.

Their lips met slowly. He put everything he had into the kiss, and at *the same time braced himself for rejection. He thought that moment came when she pulled away slightly, but then realized it was her adjusting from the initial kiss. She pulled him into her and gently but hungrily tasted his lips and mouth. His arms wrapped around her waist and he pulled her into him. He held her tight, but not in a vice-like grip. He felt her firm breasts compress against his chest and she felt his erection press the inside of her thigh.*

Through their meshed lips she said, "Touch me Edward."

"Where?"

"Anywhere. Everywhere."

Edward cupped her face and kissed her deeper. As his mouth played on hers, his hands ventured slowly down her body. Both hands stopped on each breast. They slowly examined and caressed them. He was lost in the excitement of his first-time examination of a woman. His lips moved from hers and trailed lower. Edward slowly traced kisses from one of her ears to the other. He was slow and methodical all the while his hands were examining Suzanne's full body. Her breath had grown heavier and he actually thought she was enjoying herself. No, there was no thinking about it, he knew.

"Edward," she managed in a breathy whisper.

He had started to trace kisses down the center of her chest but then immediately pulled away. He instantly thought he was doing something she didn't like.

"What?" he asked hastily. "What's wrong?"

She shook her head. "Nothing. You're perfect, but can you do something for me?"

"Sure. Anything, just ask."

"Will you rip my shirt off?"

He instantly shook his head as he hesitantly asked, "Why do you want me to do that?"

"I love a forceful man. I like it rough sometimes." She was now talking through clenched teeth. "This is one of those times. It really turns me on."

"I really don't like the sound of that. Sounds too violent. Sounds too much like—," he broke off suddenly, not wanting to say the word.

"Sounds too much like what Edward?"

He looked around, not wanting anyone to see or hear him.

She grabbed his head in her hands and turned his face too hers and asked again, "Like what?"

"Sounds too much like," he paused and dropped his voice to a whisper. "Like rape."

"I knew you were going to say that. You're the same as all the other guys. You worry too much. It's not rape if I want it that way or if I ask you to do it that way."

She leaned up and gave him quick, little, hard kisses on his mouth all the while she was urging him on. "Come on, baby. You can do it. Rip my clothes off." She grabbed his hands and made him grab her breasts again. "Dominate me. Do whatever you want with me."

It was now beginning to get a little weird for Edward, and he tried to pull away, but she held him fast.

"I don't like this. I can't do this anymore," he said.

He tried to side step her, but she followed along with him and spun him around into the wall. She shoved one hand down the front of his pants and grabbed tightly to his enlarged member. "Oh, wow, Edward. You were lying to me. I can tell you like this adventure a lot more than you're letting on."

Embarrassed by his arousal, he grabbed her arm and tried to pull it free but she held fast. It hurt him more than it did her, and he reluctantly gave up.

She pushed her hand further down and began to massage him fully. "C'mon, Edward, we both know you like it. Let me work my magic on you. Just give in a little. I guarantee I can satisfy you."

As one of Suzanne's hands worked on him down below, her other hand covered Edward's hand that she held to her breast. She slowly circled it in a clockwise motion. He tried again to pull his hands away, but she held him tight. "Don't ruin this moment, Edward, for God's sake. For my sake, please don't." She forced his hand in between the buttons of her shirt. "You like the way they feel, don't you. Squeeze me tight."

He frantically looked back and forth down both alleyways to make sure someone wasn't watching. "Don't worry, Edward, no one really knows about this place or comes back here. Anyway, everybody's focused on the game right now. I wish you would focus on me. Nobody can see us. Nobody can hear us if we get too loud, if you know what I mean. We're all alone. Make me scream."

He liked the way the phrase sounded, he definitely understood her meaning; but at the same time the phrase was strangely disturbing. It sounded too violent. This whole scenario was too much for Edward's virgin mind to take. Something wasn't right with this situation. This location wasn't right. It might be if it was a couple trying to spice up their love life in a long-lasting relationship, but she had never spoken to him since she had started at this school. Why did she want him? What if someone saw what they were doing? How would she react if confronted? For that matter, how would he react? If he gave in now, would there be another time for them to meet, or tomorrow would everything be back to the way it has always been? What kind of hoax was this?

As the questions buzzed around inside his head, his anger began to build. As a magician jerks a tablecloth, leaving the dishes where they sat, Edward did likewise. With one final desperate chance to be free of her persistent come-on, he wrenched his hands free as he turned from her.

"Let go of me, damn it!" *Edward yelled.*

Over the incessant drumming of the crowd above, a loud rip became audible in the close knit space between them. Upon hearing her blouse rip, he jerked his head back to view the damage. A huge gaping hole was in the front of her shirt. The buttons had snapped free and had shot off into the darkness. The small bra she had been wearing had a frontal closure, and the small metal clasps had broken off. Her whole chest was totally exposed.

"Now you've done it," *she said, immediately grabbing her breasts.*

He thought she was angry and immediately started apologizing. "I'm sorry, Suzanne. I didn't mean to. I was just trying to get you to stop." *He stepped toward her and tried to pull her shirt together again.*

"You've really done it now, Mister."

"What do you mean?"

"You just don't know what that did to me. Oh my God, Edward. You are such a turn-on. That's what I was talking about."

"What are you, crazy?" *he yelled.* "What the hell is going on in your head?"

"Sex, Edward, nothing but sex. Now come over here and give me some of yours."

Edward stared at her in disbelief. "Can't you take a hint? I said no."

"You're such a tease, Edward. No guy would ever turn down sex, especially from me."

Edward shook his head in protest and said, "Yeah, well let me be your first. You're too much of a woman for me. I'm out of here."

"Oh, no you don't," she said, running around in front of him. She put her hands on his chest and pushed him back. He tripped over a root from one of the trees, lost his balance, and went sprawling in the leaves. "That's just one way I like my men. On their backs. You're going to finish what you started."

"I didn't start this," he said trying to get up. "You did."

"You're just as much at fault as I am. You're as much of a consenting adult in this as I am."

"Consenting enough also to stop when it all turns to shit."

"I'll tell you what you're going to do," she said pushing him down again on his back. She straddled his waist, leaned down into his face, and said. "You're going to fuck me whether you like it or not."

"What? The hell I am."

He tried to get up, but her full weight was on top of him. She pushed him back again. She quickly fumbled with his belt, unclasped it, and jerked it from around his waist. After she unsnapped and unzipped his pants, she shifted her weight onto his stomach and ribcage. She turned around as she fought to pull his pants down. She only got them halfway down his thighs before she stopped.

"Well, it looks like one of us is ready. Now all I have to do is get out of my pants. I wish you would peel them off of me, but you keep saying you don't want me, so I guess I'll have to do it myself."

She quickly stood to slide out of her jeans then lowered herself to his body.

Edward didn't even think of getting up at that moment. He didn't even realize that her weight was lifted off of him. He had turned his head away and tears were running out of the corners of his eyes. A part of his mind had shut down. He had never really thought about it before, but he had never heard any stories of a woman raping a man. Sure, he wanted Suzanne. Who in their right mind wouldn't? She was one of the most beautiful, sexiest girls in his high school. But she had actually scared him with all the talk about ripping her clothes and making her scream. To him it seemed too fake; too staged. He didn't know if she actually wanted him, if it was just a game to her, or if he was just another virgin she could check off her fuck list.

She tilted Edward's face up, bent forward and kissed him fully, and then pulled away when he wasn't kissing her back.

"Don't cry, Edward. You'll make me feel guilty. I swear to God, you'll thank me when this is over."

She put her lips back on to his and her tongue shot slowly in and out of his mouth indicating what was to come. She bent back with one hand and inserted him slowly into her. He didn't slide easily into her at first; it took a number of tries, but once he was inside, she sat back on him, pushing him into herself to his fullest. Then just like her kiss before, she slowly gyrated on top of him.

Edward's breath was taken from him as he slid into her. He had never felt anything so amazing in his life. He felt as if he was going to immediately explode. He gritted his teeth against the sensation. He equally wanted this moment as much as he didn't want it. He put his hands up to her thighs to push her off, but she grabbed both of his hands and placed them on her breasts again. She made him squeeze them tight. He couldn't take much more of this.

Edward closed his eyes and rotated his head in ecstasy. He actually wanted this moment to last forever. He didn't know why, but for some reason he opened his eyes at that moment. He peered down the alleyway where Suzanne had guided him earlier, but something was different. He looked harder down the alleyway and saw shadows coming toward them as beams of light shot out from around them.

"Oh, shit!" Edward exclaimed. He shoved Suzanne back with all his might and sat up in the process. Suzanne went down on her butt and then her back, but she was still gripping Edward's hands. As she fell on her back in the leaves, she pulled Edward on top of her. She spread her legs wide to receive Edward's waist and he fell between them. She let go of his hands once he was on top of her and placed them on his chest to slow him down. She didn't want him to come crashing down on top of her. He tried to brace himself also. Without thinking, he tried to gain his balance by pushing off of Suzanne. One hand was still atop her breast and the other was on the ground *beside her head. Right before he was about to shift his weight to stand he heard a voice of someone behind him and he froze.*

"What the fuck are you doing to her, Edward?" the voice asked hatefully as lights encircled them from all sides.

Edward knew that voice. It was Travis Sheridan. He thought quickly. Edward? How do they know it was me? They haven't even seen my face.

In the light of the flashlight beams, he immediately knew how this looked, and he closed his eyes and shook his head against the sight he knew they had misunderstood.

Suzanne's shirt had been raggedly torn. The buttons were missing, indicating that her shirt and bra had been ripped open. Her jeans were pulled down and still wrapped around her foot. His pants were down to his knees and he was lying in between her spread legs. One hand was clutching her bare breast as he leaned over top of her. Her hands were braced against his chest as though she were trying to push him away.

Suzanne looked back to Edward and gave him a quick smile. Her face then changed into a grimace, and she began to wail. Her voice became frantic. "Get him off of me! He forced me back here and started ripping off my clothes."

That's when Edward closed his eyes and bowed his head and shook it. I was duped again.

He knelt over her, stunned. He couldn't find the words to explain. He just shook his head violently against the accusation. "That's not true. You're lying!" he yelled when he finally found his voice.

"I couldn't get him to stop. He said he would kill me if I didn't have sex with him."

He couldn't tell how many sets of hands he felt on his body, but it seemed like thirty.

The other pair of hands belonged to Alex Riley and Bruce Saliers. All three guys grabbed him roughly, stood him up, and slammed him up against the stadium wall. The back of his head smacked the bricks hard, and he fought against a blackout that was about to take over him. He shook his head to clear the coming darkness.

Suzanne turned quickly to Travis and said in a harsh low whisper, "You're late. It wasn't supposed to go this far." The two sentences weren't spoken quietly enough. Edward overheard Suzanne and looked at her and Travis in awe-struck disbelief.

Travis replied in an equally low tone. "So why did you let it get so out of hand? Did you want this?"

"Oh my God, are you kidding me?"

Travis saw Edward's face and quickly shushed her.

Suzanne turned and saw Edward staring and knew she had given herself away. She flipped the switch back and continued with playing the role of the victim. "He kept covering my mouth trying to shut me up. Whenever I did get my mouth free from his grip, I didn't think anyone could hear me because the crowd was so loud. It was awful."

"It's okay. You're safe now," Travis soothed. He hugged her close and she shuddered against him. "He can't hurt you anymore. We'll make sure of that."

"She's lying! I did no such thing! I just heard what you two said to each other."

"Shut up, Edward. I always knew you were a fucking pervert, but I never thought you would go this far."

Edward reached down to pull up his pants that were bunched around his ankles. As he bent forward to grab the waist, he saw a boot enter his line of sight and step on the pants' crotch at his feet.

"What the hell do you think you're doing?"

Edward stood again but covered himself with his hands. "I was going to pull my pants up, what did it look like?" He figured if they were going to ask smart-ass questions, they were going to get some smart-ass answers. He knew it would probably make things worse than they were, but he wasn't the one at fault here.

"Oh, we've got one with a smart mouth in the crowd. I thought that's what you were doing, but I didn't tell you to do that, did I?"

"I didn't think I needed your permission."

The blow to Edward's lower abdomen came swift and hard. Edward doubled over in the leaves and dirt.

"Stand his ass back up."

Alex and Bruce did as they were told.

"Did you say something?" Bruce asked.

"Yeah, I know. I could've sworn I heard words coming from your mouth." Alex added, joining in.

"Nothing whatsoever," Edward said. It was a sarcastic enough comment that could've earned him another blow to the stomach, but it never came.

Edward looked at Suzanne for help, but tears were actually running down her face now. How could she turn her emotions around like that in a single moment? She definitely looked like a rape victim even though she had pulled her pants up and was now clutching her shirt together.

Shit, *he thought.* I would've thought the same thing if I happened to be one of the people who had come to her aid. But I fell for it. Can't blame anyone but myself. She played me like a grand piano.

She saw him staring at her and turned from him. She leaned into Travis Sheridan's chest again and started shaking. No doubt it was more tears to sell her version of the story.

"Hey, asswipe," Travis said stepping away from Suzanne. He smacked his face to get his attention. "Quit staring at her. If we so much as see you looking at her ever again, we'll make your life a living hell."

"It already is," Edward mumbled.

"What did you say?"

"I said it wasn't me. I didn't do anything. It was that whore over there," he said as he jerked a hand free and pointing accusingly at Suzanne. *"And it was you."*

Travis grabbed Edward's hand. He squeezed it hard and forced it back down to his side.

Edward sucked air in between clenched teeth as he braced himself against the pain.

"Don't you ever accuse Suzanne of anything like that ever again." Travis brought a hand up and pointed at Edward in the face for emphasis. "Don't even go to the principal or any of the school's teachers to report this. If you do, so help me God, we won't be responsible for what happens to you. Just to prove our point even more and drive it home to you, here's a small example of what we mean. Suzanne?" he said over his shoulder without taking his eyes of Edward.

Suzanne turned back around toward them and shuffled a few feet forward. "Yeah," she said in a weak, cracking voice.

Edward rolled his eyes; she was really playing this rape victim role up well.

"If you could do anything to this piece of shit over here to get back at him for what he did to you, what would it be?"

"I don't know. I really don't want to be near him. I don't even want to look at him."

Travis turned from Edward and wrapped an arm around Suzanne's neck and pulled her closer. "Come on, Suzanne," Travis cooed. "He just had his way with you. He tried to rape you for God's sake. You've got to have some anger built up from what he did to you. I do and I wasn't even violated. It's people like this sick freak who make me want to puke. I know you want revenge, so do what you will with him."

"He needs his balls cut off, is what he needs," Alex said, trying to add drama to the situation. "He would never rape anyone ever again if that happens."

"He wouldn't do a lot more than that if that happened," Travis answered.

"Shit, I'll do it. Anybody got a knife?" Alex replied again.

Travis continued, ignoring Alex's comment, "I swear to you he won't be able to touch you now or ever again. We'll hold him. All you've got to do is release your feelings."

"She's already done that," Edward pleaded again. "Aren't you listening to me? She's the one that grabbed me and pulled me back here."

"You expect us to believe that?" Travis asked.

"Yes. I do. I would only hope."

"She may be strong, but she didn't pull you back here," Bruce said.

"I'm not even stupid enough to believe that," Alex interjected.

To shut Edward up, Suzanne stepped forward and slapped him as hard as she could. His face whipped to the side. The pain was hot and instantaneous. He wanted to put his hands to his face to gently rub his cheek, but Bruce and Alex held his hands out against the wall. He moved his jaw around to work the pain away, but the stinging remained. As he rotated his head, her backhand caught his other cheek. Bright, numbing pain flared in the other side of his face. He didn't cry out; he took the pain but bowed his head.

He could plead with them no more. They wouldn't listen. They were doing their job of protecting Suzanne. This was all a set up. That was evident from the conversation he'd heard between Suzanne and Travis. Why would they come back here right at this particular time? If it wasn't a really shitty set up to a bad joke to play on him, they would've beat the ever-living hell out of him. They wouldn't have let this assault go unpunished. They would've come down on him ten or twenty times as hard.

Suzanne put her palm on his forehead and shoved it back until the back of his head touched the wall. When he looked up, he saw the look on her face and the slight smile. That's how he knew this was all an elaborate joke played on him. She was already in the process of spitting in his face when he realized what she was doing. Luckily, Edward had good reflexes and quickly shut his eyes as she splattered a massive amount of spit on his face. He knew she wanted him to look at her, but he just leaned his head back against the wall and kept his eyes closed.

The next pain that engulfed Edward's body started between his legs. The pain was so instantaneous and unexpected that he almost threw up. Edward doubled over until his knees and forehead had touched the ground. He wanted to roll up into a tight ball, but his arms were held out from his sides, keeping him upright. He groaned in pain and cursed in anger.

Feeling like they had completed their tasks Alex and Bruce finally dropped Edward's arms. Expecting the pain to subside, Edward rolled into a tight fetal position and rocked from side to side, trying to make the pain die away. He looked like a little sow beetle that had rolled into a ball to guard itself against attack.

"What are you doing?" Suzanne asked.

"I thought we were finished here." Bruce said.

"Oh hell no. He still needs to be humiliated to the fullest degree for what he did to me."

At that moment, the crowd erupted in a simultaneous cheer.

On the field, the Gators had just tried to score a touchdown from the ten yard line. Instead of the intended touchdown, a Sidewinders linebacker had intercepted the bad throw at the two yard line.

"You hear that?" Suzanne asked.

"Yeah. Big crowd. What about it?" Bruce questioned.

"They're cheering loud out there, aren't they?"

"Yeah. So. What are you getting at?" Alex asked.

"How much do you want to bet we could shut them all up?"

"We're listening. What are we going to do?" Travis asked.

"We're not going to do anything. You, Bruce and Alex are going to take Edward out to the middle of the football field and drop him off at the fifty yard line."

"What good is that going to do?" Travis asked again.

Suzanne laughed, "Well, for one thing, he's going to be naked."

"I see where you're going with this. You're one evil bitch," Alex said smiling. "I mean that with the deepest respect for you. I love you. You know that, don't you."

"I know. It will give Edward here a lesson in humility. I bet he will think twice before he violates anyone ever again. Stand him up boys."

Her henchmen obeyed.

"You can't be serious. No, please," Edward pleaded, but Suzanne had already stooped to untie his shoes. "Don't do this please, I beg you."

"Did you quit when I pleaded with you to stop?" she asked standing again.

"You never once asked me to quit."

She continued with her lecture, "No, you didn't. I begged and begged you to quit, but you wouldn't. It's a lot different when the tables are turned on you, isn't it Edward?"

The boys commenced roughly ripping the rest of his clothes off until he was completely nude.

"What time do you want us to take him out there?"

"It doesn't really matter to me. There isn't a perfect time. Just run him out there and leave him, but you'd better run like hell or you'll get caught for doing that."

The boys hoisted Edward up. Edward squirmed in their arms like a worm on hot pavement. Travis held his shoulders, Alex had an arm around his stomach area and Bruce had his feet. He tried to call out for help but Travis's hand was clamped tightly over his mouth. They moved down the alleyway as best they could toward the opening where they had entered. Once there, they hung back in the shadows while Suzanne checked to see if anyone was nearby. She stepped out onto the sidewalk and motioned with one arm that the coast was clear.

They started jogging at first, but once they hit the sidewalk that headed

toward the field, they broke out in a run. They shot through a small group of
students near the field. The people scattered like startled pigeons in a park.
The Cypress Grove cheerleaders did likewise as the boys yelled for them to
move. Travis, Alex, and Bruce entered the field at the twenty yard line and
cut diagonally across to the middle of the fifty yard line.

At the same time the boys entered the field, the Sidewinders had just
hiked the ball at the seven yard line and shot down the field. The wide
receivers had run past the fifty yard line as the boys had reached the center of
the field.

Once there, they deposited Edward's squirming body onto the
Sidewinders emblem, split up into different directions, and exited the field as
fast as they could.

By this time, whistles had been blown for the play to stop. From the time
the boys had took to the field, the crowd's enthusiasm, the band's music and
the cheerleaders' cheers had slowly died down to silence.

No one followed the boys, though; everyone was too shocked at what
they saw.

Edward looked around as he sat up. Everyone in the stands was on their
feet, but no one was saying a word. Suzanne was right, *Edward thought.*
They shut up alright. Of course there was whispering; it swept through
the stadium like an eerie gust of wind.

He finally stood and tried to cover himself with a hand in the front
and one in the back. The football players started crowding around laughing.
People in the stands started yelling frustrated phrases like, "Hey asshole, get
off the field!", "Freak!", "Hey dingus, this ain't a nudist colony!" *and* "When
did we get a new mascot?"

The laughter started soon after the name calling. It started gradually at
first but slowly worked its way through the people, infecting the whole crowd.
Eventually, everyone was pointing, shouting names, and laughing.

He finally broke his paralysis and sprinted across the field as the crowd's
laughter droned in his ears.

Edward didn't even go back to the alleyway to see if his clothes were
there. He was sure they had doubled back and took them with them wherever
they went. Edward didn't even go back for his bike, but ducked his head and

ran blindly all the way home. He didn't stop to hide behind trees and cars for protection.

Once Edward was at his house, he didn't enter through the front door. He ducked around to the back of the house and climbed up an old pecan tree to the second story window to his room. Edward quietly entered, closed and locked the window behind him, and pulled the shades down. Not stopping to rest, he then went to the bathroom with a change of clothes and took a hot shower. He stood underneath the sprinkler head for a long time as the water cascaded over him.

On more than one occasion, Edward's grandmother came to check on him to see if he was alright. Each time, he assured her that everything was fine. He made excuses that he was tired and that he just wanted to get some sleep. Only then did his grandmother leave him alone.

With his grandmother finally satisfied, Edward finally curled into a ball underneath his sheets and tried to go to sleep. It was a long time before that happened. During the eternity before sleep over took him, Edward replayed the scene over and over in his mind. He cried many tears as he relived the embarrassing moments. Once sleep did overtake him, he slept fitfully and for a long time.

CHAPTER 18

TYLER JERKED UPRIGHT in the driver's seat when a car horn honked nearby.

On the inside of Tyler's body, Edward suddenly remembered where he was and why he was here. He had closed Tyler's eyes and curled into as much of a fetal position as he could manage. His body was reacting to the memory as it did on that distant night that now seemed like yesterday. He wasn't surprised to find tears streaming down Tyler's face.

See what I mean, Tyler? I told you it was bad. How would you feel if that happened to you?

Tyler didn't reply, but Edward could read his thoughts and he knew that Tyler felt sorry for him.

Edward had become careless in his depression and failed to keep an eye out for Suzanne. He breathed a sigh of relief when he saw her car still parked across from him.

After a long pause, Tyler began, *I agree with you. I would be angry and upset also—*

See. I told you.

—but not enough to kill somebody over it.

Then you still don't understand. You see, it gets worse. I'll show you eventually, and I know in time you'll see everything from my point of view.

Can't wait.

Edward glanced at the clock on the dash again and saw only ten minutes had passed since he had dozed off into his daymare. He was tired of waiting and began to stroke his medallion to relieve his nervous tension.

A few minutes later, Suzanne exited the hospital's double doors and made her way to her Mercedes.

Before Tyler even realized it, Edward had already opened the door and was ambling across the parking lot toward her.

Oh shit, here we go again, Tyler thought.

Edward didn't really know what he was going to say or do when he met up with her, but he continued nonetheless. He finger-combed Tyler's ratty hair into a half-decent appearance and straightened his clothes to look half-way presentable.

"Dr. Baldwin!" he called out, as she approached her car. "You got a minute?"

Startled, she quickly glanced over her shoulder but continued to her car.

Edward realized that from her point of view, all she saw was a shadow of a man coming toward her. When he got closer, he called out again, "Suzanne, I really need to talk to you. It's me, Edwa—" he quickly corrected himself. "Tyler. It's me, Tyler." He forced a little urgency into his voice. "It's a matter of life and death."

That's the literal truth, he thought. *Your life and Kelly's death.*

Upon hearing her name, Suzanne stopped. *That's odd. Why the hell did he say that?* she thought. Not understanding his presence here, she turned and prepared herself for anything. She said, "I'm sorry, Tyler. I didn't recognize you at first glance."

"That's understandable," Edward agreed. "Most of the time, anyone approaching you in a darkened parking area is probably up to no good, whether they know your name or not. You can't be too careful these days."

There was a slump in the conversation.

Suzanne asked him the only question she could think of at the moment, "How's the hand?"

Not understanding, Edward asked, "What?"

She pointed, "Your hand? How is it?"

"Oh, it's okay," he said rubbing it and holding it to his chest. "I-I'm fine. The pain is still there, but it's subsiding a little."

"That's good."

Another cold silence.

Suzanne pressed the issue, "Look Tyler, I'm sure you stopped me for a reason; could you get to the point? I really have to leave."

Tyler looked as though he was taken aback.

"I don't mean to be rude," she continued, "But it's been a long day, and all I want to do is get home." She turned away from Edward to open her car door.

"That's typical of you to lie like a dog. It's just like when we were back in high school."

She stiffened at the comment and slowly turned back around to face Tyler. "What?"

"Nothing, it's not important. It's just that, I mean, I thought you were going to Kelly's for dinner."

A defensive look crossed Suzanne's face. "I never said that."

"Oh. Well then Kelly must've told me your plans."

"No, I don't think she would've told you *our* plans. She called me shortly after six o'clock tonight." She paused, thinking. Her eyes narrowed. "What's happened to her? Is she all right?"

I wouldn't say she was all right, he thought. Instead he lied and said, "Oh no, she's fine. I mean, I guess she is."

"No. Something's wrong. You wouldn't be here if she was alright. What did you do to her?"

"Talk about jumping to conclusions. I didn't do anything to her," he said in defense.

Suzanne called his bluff, "You're lying, Tyler, and you know it." Suzanne pressed the issue, "Why didn't you just call me on the phone to ask me about her instead of coming out here to wait on me? Unless you already knew." Realization hit her like a suicide jumper to the pavement, and she knew what his true intent was. "That's why you're here, isn't it? You were waiting on me?"

A million different ideas began to form in her mind. *What happened to Kelly since our conversation? Bad things don't happen to good people like Kelly. Had there really been someone lurking outside her house tonight? Could it have been Tyler? Had he hurt, or God forbid, possibly killed Kelly?*

If so, why? That seemed like too much of a stretch, but all she wanted to do now was find out if Kelly was alive or dead.

She stuck her hand inside her purse acting as though she was trying to locate her keys.

"You're not going to tell me if anything has happened to Kelly, are you?"

He smiled again, "I like to keep people guessing. It makes the game more interesting."

"Then this conversation is over," she said and turned away.

"Not yet, it's not," Edward said as he lunged toward her to grab her arm.

As he moved toward her, Suzanne jerked her keys from her purse. She brought them up toward Tyler's face.

Edward saw the small canister attached to Suzanne's keychain as she leveled it on his eyes. He jerked his head away and closed his eyes to escape the blinding spray. He was successful in that he didn't take a direct hit in his eyes but the initial blast sprayed past the side of the head. The awkward movement caused him to loose his balance. His hands landed low to Suzanne's waist as he dropped to miss the spray. Desperate to gain his balance again, his hands clutched on anything they could grab. One hand hit the pocket of her coat, and it ripped away as Suzanne turned away back to her car door. The mist of pepper spray was strong in the air and his eyes started to stinging when he opened them to orient himself again.

The pepper spray was enough to put him on the ground screaming in pain but he lay on the concrete raking, and rubbing his enflamed eyes. His nose began to run from breathing the acrid fumes.

Suzanne quickly fumbled then found the button that unlocked her car door. She hopped in, then slammed and locked the door behind her.

Edward heard the engine roar to life and the gears slam into reverse. He realized she wasn't going to worry about where he was before backing out of her parking space. Through blurred eyes, he half-rolled and half-crawled away from her Mercedes.

It was only seconds after he moved that her car came barreling into the space he'd just occupied.

She jerked the gear shift down into drive and jammed the gas. Smoke burned out from around her spinning tires, and her Mercedes lurched forward toward the other end of the parking lot.

Through stinging and runny eyes, Edward stumbled to his car. Right as he opened the car door, he looked down to see the object he was holding. It was a picture of Suzanne. She was smiling up at him. He realized that when he grabbed her pocket and she pulled away from him, he'd ripped her security badge from her outfit. Frustrated, he pitched her badge into the Mustang. It hit the far door panel and fell between the door and the passenger's seat.

Edward got in and grabbed the half-empty bottle of water that was sitting in the console. He quickly uncapped the bottle and doused his eyes not caring where the water splashed. He wiped his eyes as quickly and as carefully as he could, then doused his eyes again with the last of the water. He dried his eyes and blinked them open. They still burned somewhat but the water had help clear most of the burning sensation.

Edward cranked the Mustang and followed Suzanne. She had a head start, but he knew he could quickly cover the distance. When he reached the bottom floor of the parking deck and exited the ramp, he looked back and forth. He needed to find out which way Suzanne had headed.

This was going to be tough. Edward had to be careful not to drive too fast or too crazy. There were more people on the road than he wanted, and a high speed chase was sure to have someone calling 911 to report it. It would just be a matter of time before the cops were in on this situation.

"I have to play it smart," he told himself.

The road to the left looped away from the hospital and then dipped to a lower grade. It was possible that she made it to that drop off point before he reached the bottom of the ramp. The road to the right was straight but rose and fell away at different elevations. There were more roads beyond those swells that it intersected. Trying to make the right decision, he saw a small streak of silver in a cascading street light on an intersecting road.

The torrential downpour that was going on when he was at Kelly's house had stopped completely. Edward couldn't tell if misty atmosphere was actually the weather or the aftermath effect of the mace mist to his eyes. He continued to blink and wipe his eyes.

Relieved, he said, "That has to be her. It's the little things in life."

He turned the wheel to the right and floored it; the car whipped into the street, tattooing black tire marks onto the pavement.

Bright headlights flared out of the darkness as Tyler—or who she thought was Tyler—came over the sloped hill behind her. Temporarily blinded, she blinked her eyes but kept them focused on the road ahead. Another car whizzed by on her left, honking his horn as he passed. Suzanne reflexively jerked her car back into her lane. In keeping tabs on Tyler, she had drifted over the double line.

She took a deep breath to calm her nerves and focused on the road ahead.

Suzanne snatched her cell phone from her purse, scrolled down until she found Kelly's cell number, and tapped the button to connect them. As the phone started to ring, she glanced in her, rearview mirror to keep tabs on her pursuer.

The car chasing her was coming up fast. She thought Tyler was going to purposely ram her, and she braced herself for an impact that never came.

The Mustang sped up to her bumper, blew its horn, touched its breaks and backed off, then the cycle began again.

"Scare tactics. He's just trying to scare me," she said aloud trying to calm herself down.

The sound startled Edward when his right pocket began to ring. Edward switched driving hands; he'd been driving with his right, but now he grabbed the steering wheel as best he could with his bitten hand. Edward pulled a cell phone out of his right pocket. He realized that it was Kelly's cell that he'd picked up from the top of the stairs.

The phone warbled again.

Edward spoke the caller's name that was printed across the screen, "Suzanne." Then it dawned on him what was happening, and he started laughing. Suzanne was trying to get in touch with Kelly. "It really doesn't get any better than this."

Suzanne saw Mountain Crest Highway coming up quickly to her

left. When Tyler's car advanced on her again, she slammed on her brakes. She knew it was dangerous and could have resulted in him rear-ending her. The car swerved to miss her, but she still expected to feel and hear the bumpers lock in a metallic kiss. She waited until the last possible second, then jerked her car off onto the connecting road.

Edward was completely caught off guard by her actions. He was in the process of figuring out the riddle of the cell phone when her car cut the hard ninety-degree turn, and he realized he had been suckered.

"Damn it!" he yelled, as he jerked the steering wheel to the right and slammed on the brakes. His hand erupted again in pain as he tried to turn the steering wheel with his wounded hand. He quickly dropped the cell phone in his lap to help steer the car with his other hand. The car fish-tailed back and forth, but he kept it under control until it finally stopped. He backed up, punched the gas again, and whipped the car onto the road Suzanne had taken.

Again, the phone rang as another two cars whizzed by on the left.

On a whim, Edward doused his headlights to give him an element of surprise of coming up behind Suzanne without her knowing it. He was almost driving blind but there was just enough light coming from the three quarter moon and the few street lamps that were spaced out over this stretch of this road.

He grabbed the phone again, slid the cell phone into connection with his thumb, faked a woman's voice, and said, "Hello. This is Kelly Sheridan's answering service. She can't come to the phone right now on account that she's lying at the bottom of her stairs with a broken neck. But you can talk to Edward McDaniel if you would like. Hold please." He changed back into his real voice, "Hello Suzanne. This is Edward. Remember me? I especially remember you."

Suzanne was stunned at the voice coming out of the phone. She pulled off to the side of the road. She knew the other driver would be coming up the road soon, but she decided to talk this through at a safe distance.

"What did you do to Kelly?" she asked, pulling to a stop.

"Hello. Whore. I think I just told you."

"I'm not a whore, asshole."

Ignoring her, he said, "Instead of reaching Kelly, you've actually dialed a direct line into your past. Are you still giving it up as easily now as you were when we were in high school?"

"What are you talking about?"

"It didn't take me a long time to figure it out…your little game, but I know what you were playing. You were quite the talk of the locker room each week before and after gym class."

"What the hell are you talking about?"

"Don't play dumb with me, slut. You know exactly what I'm talking about. Every week it seemed that one or two other guys in my class were bragging that they made it with you in some way or the other. Was that just them lying so all the guys would think they were cool, or was that the truth? I would bet Tyler's life it's the latter."

"You're a liar!" Suzanne screamed.

"Oh sure, you told each guy not to tell anyone so you wouldn't be looked upon as the slut you were and are, but let's face the facts; that was prime time news in high school. They eventually asked me if anything had happened between you and I and I *had* to tell them the truth. You remember what happened with us on rivalry night, don't you?"

Hesitantly she said, "Yes."

Another car whizzed by on the left, it's headlights briefly illuminating her car from the back windows.

Suzanne thought, *Was that Tyler's car? Doesn't look like a Mustang's tail lights but I can't be sure.*

"I know you, Travis, Alex, and Bruce told me not to tell any of the teachers, and I didn't. But I didn't think it would hurt to tell the guys in gym class. You can imagine the looks on their faces when they heard you would stoop low enough to make it with somebody like me. I was the lowest person on the totem pole. That meant anybody looking to score with a whore like you was fair game."

"Quit calling me a whore!"

Edward was relentless and pressed on, the pain from rivalry night lighting that anger inside him again. "I guess business was booming for you after that. Everyone wanted a piece of your ass after that. Everyone was better than me, so once you made me a tally mark in your little black book, it could only get better from there. You were a slut then, and you're still one today. Once a whore, always a whore. I know what kind of a game you were playing now. It was a big turn on for you, and you were keeping score.

"But how did you know about Edward?"

"Because I am Edward; I've told you that. I've come back to spend a little time with my favorite little bitch."

"I don't understand."

"If you could open your ears and shut your mouth for a few minutes, I'd be happy to explain."

He paused for a couple of moments.

Seeming to think he was waiting for an answer she said, "Okay."

"That's a good girl. Rivalry night may have been a joke on me from the beginning, but I think you just wanted another tally mark for yourself. See, I think you had a goal to make it with every senior guy that year, and I think you reached it. That was pretty sick on your part, I might add, but by doing them you also had to do me. That night at the football game you wanted to make it with me just so you could complete your mission. I was just another thrill ride in the pants for you."

"Fuck you!" she yelled. "That's not true. It was just a situation we set up to humiliate Edward. Cooked up by the boys. They asked me to do it, and I said yes. They were late, and that is why things got so out of hand. It wasn't supposed to go that far. That's all it was. Where are you?"

"Closer than you think."

When she lifted her head to check the rearview mirror again to see if anyone was approaching, dazzling beams flooded her car.

She hit the end button, terminating the call.

Tyler, Edward, or whoever the hell it was, had apparently been sitting a short distance behind her on the shoulder of the road with his lights off. *How long had he been there?* She wondered. "He's stalking me," she said in desperation.

Suzanne slammed the gas pedal down; her wheels spun again on the slick dirt, finally grabbed pavement, and then shot further down the road. The pursuing car mimicked her and followed. She was on a straightaway and kept the gas to the floor. She switched numerous times between curses and a prayer of salvation.

As a truck passed them on the left, the Mustang pursuing her swerved into the opposite lane, shot past her on the straightaway, and disappeared around the bend in the distance.

"Now that's weird," Suzanne said, letting off the gas. She was furious and began to vent her anger by talking out loud. "Edward McDaniel," she scoffed. "I had almost forgotten about that guy."

She continued thinking about it. *That story is almost twenty years old now. Why couldn't he just rest in peace? What had happened to Edward had been a terrible tragedy, but there was no possible way he could be back. Tyler was using that story as a front to get to me, and I fell for it. But how did Tyler know about what I did to Edward?*

Suzanne's speed slowly began to build again, but not because someone was chasing her. She wanted to cripple and kill the bastard that had put her life in danger. Her thoughts were like gasoline to a fire; they helped fuel her anger and she was lost in the fury.

She grabbed her cell phone again, found the number to Alex Riley's office, and punched the send button again. He was a longtime friend and head Medical Examiner where she worked as well as for the county. After three rings a recorded voice answered. "Shit, doesn't anyone answer their phones anymore?" Suzanne blurted out.

At the beep, she rambled a message into the phone, "Alex! Look, this is Suzanne! You've got to help me! Edward McDaniel is chasing me! Kelly's dead! I think Edward killed her! It may sound insane, but I think he's trying to kill me too! I'm going by to check on Kelly right now to make sure! I hope I'm wrong! I'll be there! Please, call as soon as possible! I don't know how to explain this, but there is this guy, a patient of mine that—"

She wasn't paying attention to her surroundings until a car rounded the bend she was nearing. The car's headlights were on their brightest setting, and they cascaded over her. She realized too late that the oncoming car was in her lane.

"Oh my God," she whispered into the receiver and then dropped the phone into the passenger's seat.

Tyler had been watching this progression from the back of his mind. He had been silent since it started and was biding his time. He tried to save Mrs. Sheridan earlier but wasn't successful. He had to time it right this time and not screw it up for Dr. Baldwin. She had saved his life three months ago; now it was his time to return the favor.

Edward kept the gas pedal floored. He was barreling down the two-lane highway at top speed in Suzanne's lane.

Suzanne thought, *If Edward is as persistent as he was since we left the hospital, he's not going to budge.*

She had two choices; she could either play along and collide with him head-on or swerve and hopefully stay alive. She didn't know what she was going to do, but she was definitely going to compete.

Noticing Suzanne's speed increase also, Edward said, "I can't believe she's going to play."

As their cars neared, Tyler did the same trick he had tried upstairs earlier tonight. With all his strength, soul, mind, and spirit, he forced himself from within the dark confines of his mind and willed his arms and hands to jerk the steering wheel to the right and he was successful.

Suzanne exhaled her stored breath in relief when the car veered out of her lane. She couldn't believe that she had actually been intimidating enough for him to become the chicken.

Edward had been expecting Tyler to pull another stunt like he had done earlier, but he thought he would've tried something sooner.

Counteracting Tyler's movement, he forced the car back into the path of Suzanne's on-coming car.

Startled at his indecisiveness, Suzanne pulled her car up out of the way as far as she could without leaving the road.

Tyler fought against Edward again and pulled to the right. He whipped it far enough that the driver's side headlights didn't collide.

Misjudging the width of the road, her wheels dropped off the pavement onto uneven loose earth. The wheels kicked up mud, gravel, and small rocks that scraped against the undercarriage and clinked alongside the doors of the Mercedes.

The other vehicle barreled by her on the lower slope of the curve and their driver's side mirrors disintegrated on contact. The kiss-scrape down the side of the two vehicle's side panels and the percussion of the shattering mirrors startled her and caused her to wrench the steering wheel even more to the right.

Even before the car was completely past her, she tried to swing back onto the highway, but the wheels still pulled in the opposite direction. The guard rail was coming upon her quick, and she reached for the seat belt release. She frantically grabbed at the door handle to jump free but before she could, the Mercedes shot through the guard rail, which splintered beneath the force of the car, and the metal railings gave away under the force with which it had been hit. She let out a scream of sheer terror that seemed to swell along with the whining engine when it became airborne. The front tipped down, and Suzanne saw where she was headed. She shielded her face and braced herself for the impact as the car collided with the steep, rocky hillside. The car tumbled over itself in a collage of twisted metal. Suzanne was thrown around like a child's discarded rag doll. Her body was immersed in severe pain as she felt muscles rip and bones break.

Finally, the car came to a final resting position—upside down. The body of the car was totaled; the hood was dented and buckled, the roof had caved in, and all the windows had imploded.

As though to shake remaining raindrops from the clouds as a result of the Mercedes's impact with the earth, a gentle rain began to fall.

Suzanne was disorientated, but she knew she had to get out of the automobile. Even though the car had landed on its roof, she noticed that the passenger's side window hadn't fully collapsed. She painfully maneuvered her bruised and broken body toward the opening. She pushed through the small gap with the few uninjured limbs. The acrid smell of gasoline was potent in the air, and knew she had to get free soon.

When she was halfway out of the window, she looked to the top of the hill and saw something that turned her blood to ice. Her skin prickled with goose flesh.

Standing at the top of the ridge was a figure bathed in moonlight. For all she knew, it could've been the dark Angel of Death waiting until her last breath before taking her into the afterlife. But she knew better than that. She knew it was Tyler Curtis, but she couldn't help but entertain the thought that peering out from behind those eyes was another presence—the presence of Edward McDaniel.

The smell of gasoline was becoming stronger by the second, and she realized she had paused too long. She knew there was only a limited amount of time to get free, and she struggled even harder to emerge from her metallic cocoon.

Just a few seconds shy of sliding free from the wreckage, the Mercedes spontaneously combusted when sparks cascaded from a broken electrical line into spilled gasoline near the cracked fuel tank. A mushroom cloud of fire and smoke spiraled up into the damp air and was tattered away by the rain and wind. Flames shot out around the car and burnt briefly on the sodden earth.

Suzanne Baldwin's agony was intense. A swelling cry of desperation escaped her lips. Full, pouty lips that had pleased so many men over the years were now curled into a twisted array of burnt flesh. Her eyes melted in her sockets. Her long, blond hair that she was so proud of was singed to the scalp by a fiery razor. In some places, her clothes disappeared from her body by the intense heat, but in other places were permanently attached, like iron-on patches to T-Shirts. The fire licked blisters over her skin that swelled, popped, and turned into blackened char. In seconds, her body was reduced into a repulsive denizen that lurks in nightmares.

Like an evil genie, Edward McDaniel stood laughing at the top of the hill.

Edward thought for another moment, then said, "One day long ago Suzanne, you had asked me to make you scream. That's one thing you're definitely doing now. As you requested, I have fulfilled." He stood for a long while on the hillside stroking his medallion and listening as her screams slowly died away into nothingness. He watched until the flames had burned themselves out. When everything was quiet again, he turned from the smoldering debris and stepped into the idling Mustang. As he drove away, Tyler's car was swallowed by a fog that began to slowly creep across the road.

CHAPTER 19

ALEX RILEY WAS engrossed in an old X-files re-run. The pitter patter of rain outside had helped lull him into a slight trance as he sat mummified in an afghan his mother had crocheted for him. He had been simultaneously engrossed and grossed out. It was the most unnerving episode he had remembered watching.

Suddenly, his cell phone rang.

The ringtone, combined with the scene currently playing out on his television, startled him. "Shit!" he said aloud as he jumped. He scrambled to find the remote, muted the television, and reached to answer his phone.

"That's sick," he said to the television. Into the cell phone, he said, "Alex Riley."

"Mr. Riley, this is Officer O'Malley with the Highway Department. We have a single car accident out here off of Mountain Crest Highway."

"That's not too far from the hospital, right?" Alex asked.

"That's correct. I was informed you were the medical examiner on call."

"That's right, I am."

"A medical team has just taken the body to Memorial. I'm just reporting the incident to you. I thought you might need to know about it."

"What was the status of the wreck?"

"The accident wasn't too difficult to figure out. We think the vehicle was traveling at too high of a speed for weather conditions, went through a guardrail, and dropped to the bottom of an embankment. I will warn you, the body is not in good shape. One guy already lost his dinner over it."

"Why is that?"

"She didn't make it out of the car in time. Instant crispy critter," he said, trying to be cute. "The car exploded at the bottom. The whole body was charred beyond recognition."

"If the body wasn't recognizable, how do you know it was a *she*?"

"That's where you come in. We can only speculate. We could still read the license plate, so we ran an I.D. to check. We think the car and the body belonged to a Doctor Suzanne Baldwin."

Alex stood, letting the afghan fall to the floor, "What did you say?"

"Uh, a—Suzanne Baldwin?" The officer asked in a tone as though his information he had collected might be wrong.

"Her car wouldn't happen to be a Mercedes would it? A silver one?"

"Yes," he said hesitantly. He paused as though checking his information in a notebook again. "Yes, I believe it was."

"Oh no."

"What? Did you know her? I'm sorry about the comment earlier. I didn't mean to offend you in—."

The only answer O'Malley received was a dial tone in his ear.

Alex slammed the phone shut; he didn't have time to chitchat. He threw his body into hyper-drive. He ran to his room and threw on some half-decent clothes, some shoes, and a ball cap. He grabbed his wallet, I.D., security badge, cell phone, and car keys. He left the house without turning off the television, the lights, and locking the door.

Less than thirty minutes later, Alex was in the bottom floor of the hospital. He sat at his desk across the room staring at the mound underneath the draped white sheet. The body had been in the rain for awhile and the water had bled through in most places, making the sheet opaque. The dark silhouette of Suzanne's charred remains lay beneath. He hadn't been able to approach the body, uncover it, and proceed with any form of an autopsy since he had arrived.

When Alex chose his profession, he never thought he would ever have to work on a family member, a colleague, or even a close friend.

Performing an autopsy on Suzanne Baldwin would be the most difficult task he had ever faced. He had already reached for the phone three times to turn this assignment over to someone else, but each time he had changed his mind.

"If I can't do this, then I might as well hang up my lab coat," he muttered to himself.

He glanced over and noticed that the message light on his office phone was blinking. He absently punched the button for speaker phone and dialed the number to retrieve his messages. He tapped in his security code then headed for the shrouded mound in the center of the room as the messages began to play.

"Yeah Alex, it's Barty. Where you at, man? You hibernatin' or somethin'? We haven't seen you around lately. What's up with that? Call me, bitch. Let me know what's going on with ya man."

As Barty rattled on in the background, Alex braced himself as he jerked the sheet back forcing himself to begin.

"Just wonderin' if you're still playin' B-ball dis Saturday before the big game. We need you, buddy…"

Upon seeing the grim body for the first time, he noticed it looked a little soggy. The fire had done a first rate job of burning the life out of Suzanne, but it seemed now upon first glance that the rain certainly hadn't helped matters.

"…Don't forget, it's B.Y.O.B. for the P.A.R.T.Y. but call me A.S.A.P. Tawk ta ya lata."

"Yeah, yeah Barty, I got it. I'll call you soon," he said to himself.

Don't think about it. Close your mind from it, he thought. *Pretend she is someone else. Do it quick and get it over with.*

Alex turned his back to the body to prepare his instruments when the corpse began to speak.

"Alex! Look, this is Suzanne!"

Alex whipped around at the sound of Suzanne's voice. He nearly knocked over the tray of tools as he backed away from the body.

Suzanne's voice continued, "You've got to help me! Edward McDaniel is chasing me!"

He looked closely at her mouth but it wasn't moving.

"How the—"

Then he realized the speaker phone was playing another recorded message. As he listened, he continued to stare at her as though she were actually speaking to him.

"Kelly's dead! I think Edward killed her! It may sound insane but I think he's trying to kill me too! I'm going by to check on Kelly right now to make sure! I hope I'm wrong! I'll be there! Please, call as soon as possible! I don't know how to explain this, but there is this guy, a patient of mine that—,"

Alex thought the phone had cut off, and he rushed over to his desk to replay the message.

Then he heard Suzanne say in a faint whisper, "Oh my God."

There was a sound as though the phone rattled against something.

He asked, "Suzanne, what happened?" as though she were still alive and currently talking with him on the phone. Then he realized his foolishness. *Did she drop it?*

Silence except for the sound of the car engine.

Then he heard a violent sound of scraping metal, like fingernails sliding violently across a blackboard but ten times worse. There was another crash followed by a piercing scream. The engine sounded like it went up an octave. Then there was another longer sound of torqued metal.

More miscellaneous muffled sounds.

He leaned forward, hanging on every noise. Then an explosion rumbled out of the phone. Startled, he jerked his head back from the speaker as though he had been shot. He stuck a finger in the ear that was closest to the phone and wriggled it around to soothe against the abrasive noise of the car explosion. Immediately after the detonation was heard, the phone line went dead.

He hurriedly punched in the numbers and listened to Suzanne's message again.

What the hell was she talking about? Edward McDaniel? What was she saying about Kelly? The officer was right. She was going too fast for conditions, but only because someone was chasing her.

277

He didn't know what to do. He snatched up the phone and called the Sheridans' house.

A red flag went up after the answering machine cut on.

"Fuck. Where is she?" he asked, then hung up without listening to the pre-recorded message.

Not answering could be good news or it could be bad news.

The only thing he had to do was go over to her house and check, but he didn't want to go alone. He pulled out his cell phone, retrieved Bruce Saliers's number, and punched the button to call.

He was hoping for the best with Kelly but was thankful for this little glitch in tonight's work; he could now put off performing the autopsy on Suzanne at least a few more hours.

ଔ

Bruce Saliers grumbled as he resurrected his half-buried head from his pillows in response to his ringing cell phone. He slowly turned over on his back.

His cell phone rang again.

Directing his anger at the phone, Bruce slapped the bed covers with an open palm and shouted, "I'm trying to sleep here, people!"

The phone didn't pay him any attention and continued to ring.

"All right—all right, be patient. Damn."

He wrestled to get untangled from his comforter then fumbled to grab his cell phone. Calls received this early in the morning rarely came with good news.

"Whoever this is, it better be important." His half-drunken tone didn't help sell the attitude.

"Bruce, it's me, Alex. Wake the fuck up." His voice sounded broken but it didn't alarm Bruce right away.

"Alex, you know it's close to—," he paused as he glanced over at his digital alarm clock. A one, four, and seven glowed in brilliant neon blue. "—close to two in the morning?"

"Yeah, yeah, I know it's late, or early, however you want to look at it, but listen: Suzanne is—" He couldn't contain his composure; his voice actually did break, and he muffled a sob.

Bruce knew now that something was definitely wrong. Sleep had already dissipated from his body as he pitched himself up in bed. He swung his legs over the side and sat up. "Alex, you sound upset. What's going on? What's wrong? Talk to me."

Alex took a deep breath and continued, "Suzanne's dead."

Lighting flared outside. It illuminated the room and dazzled Bruce's eyes. He squinted against the glare then darkness once again fell over the room.

Bruce could tell Alex was fighting back tears. He understood what Alex had said but instinct still made him ask "what" anyway.

Alex cleared his throat and said, "Suzanne Baldwin is dead. They just brought her body into the morgue less than twenty minutes ago."

"You're sure it's her?"

"Yes I'm sure. She's laying on the table right now. I haven't performed an autopsy on her yet. I can't seem to bring myself to do it, but a brief examination proves it's her."

"Oh my God, no. Not Suzanne. What happened?"

Alex relayed the same information Officer O'Malley had told him earlier.

"Shit. Is there anything I can do to help?"

"Bruce, I don't think this was an accident. I think somebody ran her off the road."

"Alex, I know she meant a great deal to you, but you can't start making assumptions like that."

"In this case I can. Shortly before her car went off the road, she made a call directly to me and left a message on my machine here at work."

"What did she say?"

Alex had listened to the call six times already and quoted what Suzanne had said almost word for word.

Upon hearing the name 'Edward McDaniel,' thunder boomed over head as though the name were powerful enough to control the weather.

"Edward McDaniel?" Bruce asked. "What? Are you shitting me?"

"I wish to hell I was. Look, I know I'm a practical joker most of the time, but I'm not crying wolf this time. You remember Edward, don't you?"

"Yes, I remember him," Bruce said in a whisper; almost reverently. "Jeez, I haven't thought about Edward in years."

"Yeah, neither have I."

"But how can he be back? He died when we were seniors in high school."

"I know that." Alex said. "You can even hear the beginning of her car explode before the connection is cut. The fucking message is so eerie it made my skin crawl. I'm just worried about Kelly. I called over to her house, but there's no answer. I think we need to go by there and check on her."

"You still have the message, don't you? You haven't deleted it yet, have you?"

"Of course I still have the message, Bruce; I'm not stupid. I know potential evidence when I see it, or in this case…hear it."

"Good. Okay, I'll get to Kelly's as soon as I can."

"No, don't meet me there. Just get dressed. I'm already on my way to pick you up."

"Why?"

"Why not? I'm going to pass right by your place on the way to Kelly's; besides, I don't want to go there by myself."

ᛰ

The harsh thunderstorm had settled down to a mild drizzle by the time Alex and Bruce pulled into the driveway of Travis and Kelly Sheridan's two-story, country-style home in the Medical Examiner's van. They noticed right off that some lights were burning in the downstairs area, but they couldn't tell which ones.

Alex cut the engine; they jumped out, slammed the doors, and hurried up the walk. As they approached the house, an overwhelming sense of dread came over the both of them. Maybe it was a combination of the bleak weather and the darkness, but it was as if they already knew something bad had happened to Kelly. They didn't speak of the omen they both shared but mounted the porch stairs in a silence.

At the front door, Alex grabbed the brass door knocker—which had the word "SHERIDAN" engraved across the front—and knocked three times.

No answer.

He urgently knocked a second time but a little louder.

Still no answer.

"She could be taking a shower," Alex suggested.

Bruce glanced at his watch and drummed his thumb on the face of it. "At two-thirty at night?" He shook his head. "I doubt it, besides there are no lights on upstairs and I don't think anyone would be crazy enough to take a shower in the dark."

"I guess you're right," Alex said as he knocked again and impatiently rang the doorbell. "She could be taking a bath, you know, using candles. More relaxing that way."

Bruce didn't answer, and no one answered the door.

The wind was still blowing, and a strong gale whipped under the front porch eaves and howled at them.

Alex assumed the door would be locked but tried it anyway. Finding his assumption was right, he turned and walked to the other end of the porch.

Bruce took a chance on seeing something through the long vertical windows that flanked each side of the door and glanced inside. His breath caught in his throat and he jerked his head back from the sight. He felt as though he was peering into a kaleidoscope of horror. The bottom landing of the stairs was even with the front door, and Bruce saw Kelly's twisted body three steps up on the small platform.

"Alex, get over here," Bruce whispered as he drew his sidearm.

Alex turned in time to see Bruce's gun come up and him step into a stance to kick the door in.

"Whoa, whoa, whoa, what are you doing?" Alex asked in alarm.

Bruce stopped mid-kick and lowered his leg again, "I was going to kick the door in."

"Don't do that," Alex said, then picked up a watering pitcher from the corner and turned it upside down. A key fell out into his hand. "Voila. Easy access." He walked back toward Bruce saying, "I took care of Mosey for Kelly and Travis when they were on vacation a few months ago. No need to go all Bad Boys on it."

Bruce said, "It's a good thing we came in the van. You may be transporting Kelly's body back tonight."

"What do you mean?"

"It looks as though Suzanne was right. Kelly is dead, or at least from here, she appears to be. You can see her right through there." He pointed at the vertical windows.

"You're shitting me."

"I wish to God I was," Bruce said and moved to make room of Alex.

Alex took Bruce's place, peered through the window and saw the same horrific sight as Bruce.

Alex immediately tried to push the key into the lock, but Bruce grabbed his hand. "Wait Alex, let's think about this."

"What's there to think about? There's no time. Kelly could still be alive in there. You're the one who was about to go ape shit on the door."

"I know, but now I'm just trying to think ahead. I'm just letting you know that we may get some slack about going into this crime scene."

"Well what if she's not dead? I'm not going to stand around here on the porch and debate the dos and don'ts of if we should or shouldn't enter someone's house. I can't worry about what happens later on. Kelly may still be alive. So, I'm going to do what is best for her right now."

"You're right," Bruce said. "Sorry, I'm too much in my head right now. Go ahead. Open it. Just be careful. We don't want to wreck the scene."

"Dude, I am M.E., for God's sake," Alex said. "I know how to keep a possible crime scene clean."

"Right."

As Alex slid the key home and flipped the lock, Bruce pulled a small flashlight from his back pocket and flipped it on.

When the door opened, Bruce entered first and covered all the possible hiding places an intruder might be.

The house was solemn and deathly silent. It was no warmer inside than it was out.

The floor plan was the most open than any they had seen. The living room, the kitchen, the foyer, and entrance way were all connected with no wall separating them. There were only four hefty columns supporting the upstairs. The L-shaped stairs came down right into the middle of the whole layout.

While Bruce cleared the foyer and entrance way, Alex closed the door quietly. It was possible that the intruder heard them close the van doors and were now long gone escaping out the back. They were just being careful.

Finding no one, Bruce nodded to Alex.

Alex went straight to Kelly. His profession had kicked into high gear. The only important thing now was to care for Kelly.

Alex knew she was dead before even checking her. It was a combination of two things: just the looks of her alone and also the fact that she had a pair of metal scissors protruding out of her chest. Just to be sure, Alex gave a brief check of her vital signs but found they had left her a long time ago.

His heart sank, and the realization that she was actually dead washed over him. He paused for a moment as he switched gears from doctor to medical examiner.

The first thing Bruce noticed were muddy footprints that came from the hallway to their right. They led down the hallway for a few steps then disappeared underneath a door at the beginning of the hallway. From the few times he had been in this house, he knew that door led into the basement.

Bruce gave Alex a short, curt whistle that was loud enough to gain Alex's attention. When Alex looked up, Bruce pointed to the floor with his gun and then pointed down the hallway to let him know he was going to investigate the footprints.

Alex nodded, pointed down to Kelly and whispered, "She's dead. There's nothing I can do."

Bruce nodded, bowed his head and took a quick moment of reverence for Kelly. When Bruce raised his head again, he stepped over to Alex. "I gathered as much. I noticed the scissors upon entering the house. Having a pair of fucking scissors sticking out of your chest is never a good sign. Just do what you need to do so we can call it in properly."

"Will do."

Alex began to move about Kelly's body again and said, "I'll probably go ahead and grab my camera and at least get started on that process."

Bruce nodded then focused back on the footprints again. He noticed the tracks were smeared and faded into nothing the closer they came to the kitchen but they were heavier the closer to the basement door. Bruce had a feeling that the intruder most likely broke in by a door or window downstairs. He decided to follow the footsteps down there to see if he could turn up any clues.

Downstairs, he found the basement door shut but unlocked. One of the panes of glass was broken and glass littered the floor.

Bruce said to his invisible partner, "I'll have the CSU fingerprint the door and doorknob. It may turn up something. Hopefully whoever broke in is an amateur. Maybe we'll get lucky if the person is a dumbass."

Bruce turned and slowly followed the mud tracks back upstairs. He was careful not to step anywhere near the footprints and mess them up.

We could possibly find something within the footprints.

As he walked, he studied the ceiling, walls, and floor, but nothing jumped out at him as incriminating evidence. Nothing else seemed out of order.

Nearing the top of the stairs again, Bruce saw brief flashes of light brighten the stairwell. When he came back through the living room, he heard the click of the camera, saw the flash, and knew Alex was already taking pictures of Kelly's body and the evidence around the area.

Bruce walked over and stood at the base of the stairs watching Alex move around the body taking numerous shots at different angles.

Looking away from the flash of the camera, Bruce shined his flashlight as he glanced up the stairs. The beam of his flashlight and his eyes moved over each stair. He noticed some white fragments on a number of the steps near the top. His curiosity piqued, Bruce moved between Alex and stepped over Kelly as he made his way up the stairs. He flipped the light switch as he went.

As he neared the top of the stairs, he grabbed a pen from his pocket, stooped, flipped over one of the ceramic pieces, examined it then moved it back to the approximate area he'd moved it from. At the top of the stairs, he found more littered fragments. He stooped again and inspected some bigger shards with his pen. The pieces seemed to be made of porcelain.

"Or ceramic maybe?" Bruce questioned. "Flower pot? Maybe a vase? No dirt or flowers in and around these shards. Must've just been a decorative piece."

He stepped around the debris and moved down the hallway, thoroughly checking each room as he went. Each door was open and nothing seemed amiss.

At the end of the hallway, he found the master bedroom door jab was buckled and splintered. The latch on the doorknob had been ripped free of its mooring. Bruce used his pen and put some pressure on the doorknob. It was very loose and wiggled around in the door itself. The section where the door clasp latched into the door jam was ripped through. There were splinters of wood on the floor of the room where they fell free.

Bruce smiled at how easy this was to figure out. "Yeah, maybe investigations is where I need to be. I'm going to be right at home in this field."

You don't have to be Sherlock Holmes to figure out that the intruder broke in through the basement, came up the stairs, and entered the living room area. There was probably an arguement...maybe an altercation. Kelly eventually ran up the stairs, made it to this room, and locked the door. The intruder Bad Boy-ed the door like I wanted to do downstairs. There was probably another exchange of words or an altercation in this room before she fled. The intruder probably picked up a vase to stop her—, Bruce shined the light over to the bureau near the door and saw another vase; it was sitting on the far side of the bureau. *Yep, there it is. A vase just like the one in pieces at the end of the hallway.* Bruce made his way back down the hall to the top of the stairs. *The intruder gave chase with the vase and hit her over the head with it, or maybe even threw it at her then pitched her down the stairs. Finding she wasn't dead, he found the scissors and made sure she wasn't going to walk away. Then he left the same way he entered. That had to be the story.*

Bruce looked back at Alex working on Kelly's body at the bottom of the stairs.

That was a long fall, Kelly, he thought. *You got twisted up real bad.* "I'm sorry, Kelly," he muttered to the broken figure. "I wish I could've been here for you."

Hearing Bruce's voice behind him, Alex looked around from his crouched position and said, "I'm finished with all the preliminaries if you want to go ahead and call it in. Once the proper people get here, I can finish the rest of the work I need to do in the correct manner."

"Yeah. Alright."

"You okay?" Alex asked.

"Sure. It's just going to take time."

"We'll catch whoever did this."

"Oh, I know. I guarantee we will."

Alex asked," You think we should tell Jeremy about this?"

"I was thinking more or less about Travis," Bruce said. "He and Kelly have been together since high school. This is going to crush him. But yeah, you're right. This involves Jeremy as much as it does us and Travis. I think he needs to be aware of the situation. We can call him tomorrow morning."

"He's not going to be happy about this," Alex offered.

"Not any happier than you or I."

"That's true. That's very true."

CHAPTER 20

IT WAS THE alarm clock that startled Tyler Curtis, and he cut its whine short with a frustrated slap. He jerked himself into a sitting position.

His whole body was covered in sweat; a couple of beads dropped from his forehead into his lap. He immediately felt dirty; as though he had went to bed after an intense football practice without taking a shower.

He started to remember bits and pieces of the bizarre dream he'd had last night. It was hazy, but he could have sworn it was real.

Shaking his head, he muttered to the empty room, "I've had this kind of feeling before. I really hope what I dreamed last night wasn't real." Not believing himself, he asked hesitantly, "Edward?"

He was almost thankful when no voice answered.

He looked around the room again; still no sign of Raven. He missed his dog's morning greetings.

Looking down, he noticed he was still wearing the shirt from the day before. It was wrinkled, slightly damp, and dirty. When he threw the covers back to step out of bed, fear knotted his muscles and panic coated his body.

He couldn't fathom why he was still wearing his outfit from the day before. Casual shoes, socks, jeans, and a button-up collared shirt all clung to him in a watery paste.

Why am I still wearing my leather jacket for God's sake? Tyler questioned. *Jeez, no wonder I'm sweating.*

There were smears of mud and dried leaves under the covers and at the foot of his bed.

"What the hell?"

Tyler jumped out of bed as though someone had set an electric charge to it. Terrified and wondering what this meant, he tried to remember where he was and what he did the night before, but all he could think about was the dream.

Had that really been me last night? He paused, closed his eyes, and willed himself to concentrate on what had been real and what was the dream. *Was it all in the same?* He had a deep gut feeling that it was real, and that scared him.

He looked over to his room window and saw that it was up. There were muddy footprints on the window sill and from the window sill to his bed. It looked as though he'd come right to the window, pushed it up, climbed in, and went straight to bed. From reliving Edward's previous thoughts, Tyler knew Edward had a habit of sneaking in and out by way of the tree that grew next to his second story room window. It was easy access to enter and leave if he didn't want his grandparents to know what was happening to him; especially if something tragic had happened that day at work or school. Here at the new house where Tyler had moved into three months previously, the room was on the first floor, which made it all the more convenient to enter and leave by.

He hurriedly removed all the blankets and covers from the bed. Then he stripped down into nothing and inserted his damp clothes in the center of the sheets. As he gathered the clothes together, an object fell out of his jacket pocket.

It was a cell phone; Kelly Sheridan's cell phone. His whole body shut down in frozen shock. A guilt unlike any he had ever experienced filled him up and everything from last night came back to him in horrifying clarity. *I guess it wasn't a dream after all. Oh, Jesus, Edward, why the fuck did you do it?*

Edward didn't answer.

I'll have to dispose of her cell phone as soon as I can.

Tyler placed it on his dresser with his own cell phone and keys. He quickly tied the sheets and the muddy, damp clothes into a bundle. He would have to dispose of these later today. He was glad that he hadn't come through the front door and tracked dirt from there to his room. Tyler knew his mom would have an aneurysm if that had happened or if she found out about this.

He took a long, hot shower; careful to wash all the dirt and mud from his body. Even though he wore gloves last night, he scrubbed the washcloth thoroughly around his fingernails, then he lathered and rinsed numerous times.

Tyler added some medicine to his cut eye, which wasn't as bad as it seemed in his dream. He rewrapped his bitten hand. The pain was still there, but it had dwindled to a mild throbbing. He got dressed quickly and made his way to the kitchen.

There he found the makings of a quick and simple breakfast: a bagel with cream cheese and a hard-boiled egg. While he ate, he flipped on the television, which happened to be turned to the news. As he poured a glass of Cherry Coke, the media had just switched to a news anchorwoman who was live at a crime scene.

"Two women are dead this morning here in Silver Ridge. The first is Kelly Sheridan—"

The glass he was holding slipped from his hand and shattered on the floor. He stood there, transfixed as last night's events played over again in his mind.

"—a well-known teacher at Silver Ridge High School. She was found dead in her home shortly after four forty-five a.m. this morning. Police say Kelly's death was not an accident and they are investigating possible leads."

"That is what my dream was about," he said to himself.

"The second woman, Dr. Suzanne Baldwin, was a critical patient's doctor and surgeon at Silver Ridge Memorial Hospital. Her car was found at the bottom of Mountain Crest Highway. Authorities are not yet convinced that foul play was involved, but they're not ruling it out either. Police officials are looking at these individual cases as homicides with a possibility they could be linked. Kelly Sheridan and Suzanne Baldwin had been best friends since they went to Silver Ridge High School over seventeen years ago. No one is in custody, and there are no suspects at this time. If you have any information regarding this investigation, please call the number listed at the bottom of the screen."

The number appeared.

"We will keep you informed about this investigation as it progresses. Back to you, Tom."

His appetite gone and disgusted at the news, Tyler turned off the television. He cleaned up the broken glass and the Coke and went to finish getting ready for school.

In gathering his book bag, car keys, and the two cell phones, he noticed he had two calls that he didn't remember receiving. He punched a few numbers that took him to his voicemail. He listened as he picked up the bundle of sheets and muddy clothes and left his room.

The first call was from Savannah.

"Tyler. Hey. It's me." She paused as though not knowing what to say. "Where are you? Oh well, call me when you get this. I wanted to do something tonight, and to be specific, I just wanted it to be with you. Um, okay, yeah. Well, I'll try calling you on your home number. Bye."

He clicked to save the message. Tyler liked the sound of her voice.

The second call was from his mother. "Hi honey, we're grilling out again tonight. Just wanted to know if we need to throw a steak on the grill for you, or will you be with Savannah tonight? Speaking of her, she just called here looking for you. Are you playing hard to get?" His mother laughed at her own musings. "I like her a lot. Anyway, give me a call to let me—"

He deleted the call in mid-sentence. "Yeah-yeah mom. I know you like her. I like her too. Adore her really."

As he approached his car, he noticed something was missing from its body.

He went rigid, "Where the fuck is my rear-view mirror!"

Then part of his dream came back again and he saw the closeness of two automobiles from his driver's seat. He saw the sparks cascade up as the car's sides bumped then separated. Then the rearview mirror disappeared in a small explosion of metal shrapnel. Then the other car was gone.

"That was way too close for comfort."

It was hard for him to believe he was the one in Kelly's house last night and that he was the one forcing Suzanne off the road. He knew, beyond a shadow of a doubt, that he would never ever do something like that again…

…Or would he?

If Dad finds out about this, he's really going to ream me. I have to go to a body shop today and get this fixed. I have no idea how I'm going to have this fixed with him not finding out.

He pitched the bundle of wadded clothes and bed sheets into the back seat along with his book bag.

Can't think about that now; I have to get to school.

He got in, cranked the car, and pulled out of the driveway.

On the road to school, he grabbed Kelly's cell phone and popped the battery cover off the back of the phone. He rolled his window down and checked the roadways on all sides. Finding the coast clear, Tyler chucked the battery out the window into the woods that lined the road he was traveling now. The battery cover followed shortly afterward. He didn't worry about fingerprints either; he knew these pieces would never be found since they were pitched into random places so far apart from each other. He broke the phone in half and waited a few moments before pitching one of the phone halves out. Another mile down the road, the last half of the Kelly's cell phone cleared his hand.

With the evidence out of his hands he breathed a deep sigh of relief.

Ë

The hallway at school was busy with pre-class madness. The everyday hum of conversation seemed louder and more frantic than usual.

They must be discussing the latest news, Tyler thought. *The news I was responsible for.*

No-no, you have me to thank for that, Edward reminded.

You may think you did it, but it was my hands and body that did all the work. Do you have any idea how stupid that was? Do you have any idea how much evidence we been left behind? Evidence that will point directly to me.

Tyler, don't be this way. They're not going to connect you to any of this. Quit worrying.

Well it's kind of hard for me not to worry when my life is on the line.

Jeez, I don't know why you're so upset about this. I wore gloves last night. Next time, I'll be even more careful.

There's not going to be a next time, Edward.

Edward laughed, *Okay Tyler, we'll see.*

Shut up, Edward. I don't want to talk about any of this right now.

Tyler was surprised when Edward's thoughts went away.

Tyler weaved through the throng of students and found Savannah at her locker gathering books for her first class.

"Good morning," he said.

"Good morning," she replied.

There was an abruptness to her voice. "I thought I would've heard from you last night. Didn't you get my message?"

Tyler was a little taken aback at the abrupt interrogation. "What's with the third degree?"

Savannah shot a look his direction, then said, "I'm sorry. I'm just concerned. I was sort of wanting to do something with you last night."

"I didn't get your message until late," Tyler said abashedly.

"Why didn't you call me back?"

"Just for that reason. It was late. I thought you might've been asleep. I didn't want to wake you."

"Where were you?"

"Uh, yeah. I was just—," he had nothing. Edward picked up the slack and spoke for Tyler. Edward couldn't resist the temptation. "Oh, just out and about and up to no good."

Thinking Tyler was only kidding around, she took his comment and went with it. "Uh-huh. And you didn't invite me? How dare you," she teased, then smiled. "And what did you do while you were up to no good?"

"Oh no, I can't tell you that; it's a secret."

You're pushing it, Tyler thought.

Relax, Romeo, Edward shot back. *You're the perfect boyfriend. She doesn't suspect anything. Even if she did, she's not going to link you to the murders. You couldn't do something like that. You're a good little boy.*

Savannah's voice cut into Tyler's inner dialogue, "I just wish I could've joined in the fun, but I probably wouldn't have been able to with all the homework I had to do."

"I was busy with some of that myself," Tyler lied.

"Oh, while I'm thinking of it, could I borrow your Algebra book for class today? I forgot mine at home. I have my homework from last night, thank God, I just forgot my math book. Anyway I could borrow yours?

"Sure."

He unslung his book bag from his shoulder, stooped, unzipped his backpack, retrieved his math book and handed it up to her.

"Thanks."

Tyler re-zipped his backpack and stood up right as Savannah asked, "Did you hear the news about what happened to Suzanne Baldwin and Mrs. Sheridan last night?"

Tyler stopped dead in his tracks. *You were saying, Edward?* He nervously ran his fingers through his hair and scratched the back of his head, "Um, yeah, I did. Such a tragedy, really. I liked her. She was a great teacher too."

"I was just talking to Erica about that before you showed up. I couldn't believe it." She paused and eyed him closely. "You feel okay today?"

"Huh? Oh yeah, just a little tired, that's all."

"You look a little worn out." In a secretive whisper she leaned in closer and said, "Must've been all that mischief you were up to last night."

Tyler's breathe caught in his throat. He glanced up at her but she had turned away from him to stash a book in her locker. She didn't see the admission of guilt that had crossed his face.

"You know Savannah?" Tyler said, before Edward knew what he was doing.

"Yeah?" Savannah replied.

Tyler continued, "I'm pretty sure I'm the one who—"

Edward realized Tyler was confessing. He was about to shut Tyler down in mid-sentence, but it didn't come to that because another student collided with him from behind.

"What the fuck you staring at?" A pissed off voice asked.

Tyler turned and saw it was Joshua Megilligan who had bumped into him. A few feet away stood Patrick Quinlan.

At first, Tyler thought Patrick was addressing him. Some other students had stopped in mid-stride, thinking the question was also directed at each of them. Tyler, as well as everybody else, realized differently when Joshua answered.

"Hey. Nothin', man. Cool it. I'm just tryin' to get to my locker. Damn, what's your problem?" Joshua asked.

"My problem," Patrick shot back, "Is the little punk-ass-white-boy standing in front of me. And you weren't going for your locker. You were looking at Heather's ass weren't you?"

"Well, yeah man, I mean if she's gonna come to school dressed like that." He pointed in a circular motion. "Of course I'm gonna *look* at her. There's no law saying I can't. And besides, all the other guys standing in this hallway are doing the exact same thing. She's got a body that would make a bishop kick out a stained glass window."

There was a murmur of quiet laughter from some of the nearby students who had stopped to watch the drama unfold.

Forgetting about the threat that loomed over him, Joshua turned and nodded toward her. "Good morning, Heather. You are looking, as always, undeniably and exceptionally sexy this morning." He winked at her.

Shooting a look of disgust at Joshua, Heather simply raised her fist and thumped her middle finger in his direction.

Unaffected, he said, "I love it when you talk dirty sign language to me. I was thinking babe, that maybe you and I could go—"

Patrick stopped Joshua's invitation by shoving him back against the lockers with more force than was necessary. "Hey, you piece of shit." Patrick snapped a finger in front of Joshua's face to get his attention. "Focus, focus. Right here, bitch. I'm the one you should be worried about; not her. Don't even think of hitting on my girl. You tried to grab her ass when you went by, didn't you?"

Memories from Edward's past quickly replayed in Tyler's mind as Patrick bullied Joshua. Edward had been in situations like this plenty of times; although he had never practiced the cynicism-tactics Joshua was using to try talk his way out of this bad situation. It seemed like it wasn't helping either. Sowing that type of sarcasm most of the time usually reaped split lips or swollen eyes. Edward had tried to fight back but had always fallen short or given up because he thought he wasn't strong enough.

Joshua was rubbing his head. "Well, her ass is *grab-able*, but no dude, no, honest I didn't, but now that you mention it, I wish I *had* because if I'm gonna get my ass kicked, it would've been worth it."

Joshua glanced over to catch another glimpse of Heather's short, tight jean skirt but Patrick smacked his face back in line with his.

"Don't ever let me catch you even remotely gazing in her direction again. Do we see eye to eye?"

"Not if I'm looking at Heather's ass or tits, because if I'm looking at *those*, I wouldn't be looking into your eyes." Joshua laughed at himself, thinking his comment was funny.

Patrick shook his head, "Then I'm just gonna to have to dot both of your eyes so you won't be able to see anything." He looked at the hallway of students as though the question was directed as much to them as it was to Patrick. "Right class?"

There were murmurs and more laughter from the collective student body.

Patrick held Joshua in place with one hand and slowly drew back a clenched fist with the other. He was grinning as he relished the anticipation of the beat-down that would soon follow.

Tyler and Edward both knew Joshua was about to get his ass handed to him.

Tyler knew what he needed to do, but he didn't want to get involve. *It's not my fight,* he thought.

But Tyler was already feeling Edward's overwhelming control beginning to well up inside him. He tried earnestly to resist, but the temptation to find out what it would've been like to stand up to his enemies—mainly Jeremy Taylor—back in the day was too great for Edward not to pass up.

Patrick swung—and swung hard. Before Tyler knew what Edward had planned, he found that his hand had shot out and had shoved Joshua out of the way as Patrick's fist entered the space where his face had just been.

No turning back now, Edward thought.

There was a sound like that of a yard stick slapping a desktop when Patrick's fist connected with the locker. Patrick emitted a howl of sheer misery as his wrist crumpled beneath the force of the punch.

Tripping over his skateboard that was leaning against the lockers, Joshua found himself lying on the floor staring wide-eyed at his guardian angel.

Cursing and swearing, Patrick shook the pain from his hand then cradled his arm. He whipped around to find out who had caught him by surprise.

At the sound of a slamming locker, other students turned in stunned belief and started watching the excitement. Some taunted while others encouraged the fight to go on.

"What the hell are you doing, Tyler?" Savannah asked. "Don't do this, it's not worth it."

Without looking in her direction, Tyler held up a hand to quiet her. All his attention was now focused on Patrick.

Edward said, "Aw damn man; did that hurt as much as I think it did? You knocked the *shit* out of those lockers. I think I even felt that, it sounded so bad."

Through clenched teeth Patrick said, "Oh, you're about to feel something worse, coma-boy." He took a couple of steps back to measure Tyler up against himself then asked, "Why the fuck did you do that?"

"Let's just say you remind me of someone from my past. Someone I hate more than anyone else in the world."

"What? Who?"

"Doesn't matter."

"What's happening between Joshua and me doesn't concern you in the least."

"Oh, but it does. I'm making it my business so it does concern me. You just invaded my buddy's personal space. You need to show a little more respect."

Patrick and Tyler were both standing their ground; each standing close to the lockers on either side of the hallway. They couldn't go anywhere; they were pinned in by all the other students who had crowded around straining to see.

Without any warning, Patrick charged Tyler. Edward waited until the last possible second then swung away like a matador avoiding a charging bull. As Edward moved to the side, he grabbed the back of Patrick's jacket with his good hand and gave him an added shove. Patrick slammed headlong into the lockers and slid to the ground. Embarrassed at what had just happened, he stood quickly and wheeled around to find Tyler again. He had become slightly disoriented; he rocked back and forth but maintained his balance.

Patrick was embarrassed for being made a spectacle of in front of the gaping student body and was determined to show Tyler who was boss. He charged Tyler again. Edward was caught off guard this time because there was less distance between them. As Patrick grabbed Tyler and shoved him backward, Edward grabbed Patrick's jacket collar, planted his feet, and rotated their bodies. Patrick was turned one hundred and eighty degrees, and his own momentum slammed him up into the lockers on the opposite side of the hallway. Patrick winced in pain as the protruding locker handle and combination dial dug into the small of his back. Edward released him, and Patrick dropped to the floor.

"That's two. Want to go for three?"

Patrick only answered him in grunts of pain.

"I've heard about you," Edward began. "And it's basically all bad. I really can't stand people like you. I've met your type before plenty of times. You think you own this school and that everyone in it owes you something. You think it's cool to be feared by everyone else; you and your drug dealing gang. Yeah, we know who you are; we're not stupid. You stand out like a sore thumb, and one day you're going to go too far and *you're* going to get cut off."

"Shut the fuck up, bitch," he said in an exasperated snivel. "You got nothing on me."

"So now I'm a bitch. First, I'm a coma-boy; now I'm a bitch. Is that the best you can come up with? I really feel threatened now."

Patrick came at Tyler with swinging for the fences fists.

Tyler knew a little about how to hold his own in a street fight. He had dabbled a little in martial arts over the years but had never stayed committed. He knew just enough to protect himself in minor skirmishes such as this, and Edward was tapping into that training and was using it to his advantage. For once he wasn't going to be dominated. For once he could fight back.

Patrick swung a hard left; Tyler blocked Patrick's arm with his right then punched through with the same hand. Patrick was caught off guard with the quick sucker punch and his head whipped to the side. It dazed him, and he almost went down on one knee. He shook his head to clear the dizziness and to orient himself.

Sweet. That's a neat little trick, Edward thought. *I'll have to remember that.*

Patrick didn't learn his lesson and came at Tyler again, this time with a punch from the right. Tyler blocked the punch with his left hand. He felt a twinge of pain all the way up into the wounds of his bitten and bandaged hand. He reached over with his right hand, grasped Patrick's wrist then rotated Patrick's arm and sidestepped again. Patrick cut a flip in mid-air from the rotation, and his body was thrown into the ground.

Seeing the bully dazed, confused, and staring at the tiled ceiling invigorated Edward. He was enjoying this immensely and wanted more.

Patrick rolled over and began to stand. His right hand was still cradled under his arm as he staggered to get up. His left hand was now holding his mouth. A thin, red line of blood ran from his split lip to his chin.

Patrick pulled a switchblade from his jacket pocket. He pressed the button with his uninjured hand and the blade shot out of the handle.

All the students gasped when they saw the blade. They couldn't believe Patrick was stupid enough to pull that, but wondered if Tyler could continue to fight now that the stakes were raised.

"A switchblade here in public?" Edward asked. "Are you stupid, or is that just my opinion of you? You *sure* you want to do this?"

"Oh yeah," Patrick shot back. "You scared now, aren't you?"

"No, not in the least. I am concerned for you though."

"Why you say that? I'm the one with the advantage."

"You sure about that? I can see how one, such as yourself, would believe that. I just think you need to get an appointment with your proctologist because you're going to have a hell of a hard time pulling that knife out of your ass."

Patrick waved the knife back and forth in front of his face to emphasize his point. "Don't disrespect me, bitch, and I won't disrespect you."

"Too late for promises."

Patrick was getting agitated with the small talk and was determined to show Tyler who was the dominate species.

Patrick lunged forward and swiped the knife, but Tyler countered by quickly ducking. As he came back up into a standing motion, Patrick sliced at him again in a backhanded motion. Tyler dodged his movement and jumped back out of the way. From the corner of his eye Tyler noticed Joshua's skateboard. He lifted his leg and stomped on the skateboard's fishtail. It flipped up into the space between him and Patrick. Tyler snatched it out of the air. He held it firmly with his right hand and rested the other end on the arm of his injured hand.

"You're actually going to do this, aren't you?" Edward asked.

"I'm gonna make a believer out of you one way or another."

In frustration, Patrick advanced on Tyler. He stabbed from below, trying to sink the blade into Tyler's stomach. Tyler blocked the movement with the skateboard. The blade was sharp and it sunk deep into the wood. Patrick was taken by surprise when Tyler pushed the skateboard forward toward him instead of pulling it away. Patrick lost his grip on the handle and his hand slid forward onto the blade. The blade sliced into Patrick's fingers and he immediately released it. Tyler grabbed the knife, wrenched it from the wood then pitched the skateboard aside.

"You shouldn't play with knives, dipshit." Edward said. "You just might get cut."

Patrick was furious now and charged Tyler again. Tyler saw what was coming and immediately stormed Patrick. Tyler dropped lower in his crouch and came up, driving a shoulder into Patrick's gut. Edward lifted him and then slammed him back against the lockers for a third time.

Three's a charm, Edward thought.

Edward grabbed Patrick by the throat and held him in place just as Patrick had done to Joshua.

Tyler and Patrick's eyes met. Because of Edward, Tyler's eyes were ablaze with murderous hatred. Patrick had never seen someone so pissed off and instantly regretted continuing the brawl with him. He knew what was coming next because he would've done the same thing.

Patrick saw Tyler's hand begin to slowly rise. *He's gonna do it. He's gonna stab me. He's going to fucking kill me in front of everybody.*

Tyler's mind was racing as well. *Edward's going to do it. He's going to stab Patrick right in front of everybody. I have to save him even if he is in the wrong. How can I stop him? It's not worth —*

"Tyler! Stop it!" Savannah's voice was loud and rang out in the hallway. "Both of you, just stop it!"

At the same time Edward hear Savannah's voice, he felt her hands latch onto the forearm of the hand holding the switchblade. Somehow she had worked herself into a position where she could grab him. Edward stopped and ripped his gaze away from Patrick who was frozen in fear.

Edward looked around the hallway and saw all the students staring back at him with slack-jawed expressions of awe on their faces. Edward realized what he had done and what he was going to do had Savannah not intervened. He knew it didn't look good for Tyler. Edward immediately retreated into the recesses of Tyler's mind, leaving Tyler to deal with the mess he had just created.

Patrick had been scared but now the color spread back into his face and he exhaled explosively.

A wave of relief crashed over Tyler also when he realized Savannah had probably just saved Patrick's life.

Edward knew this moment was crucial for all the witnesses that were watching, but he couldn't help but lean up and whisper in Patrick's ear, "You can thank Savannah for that one. She just saved your sorry ass." Then Edward was gone again.

"Relieved, aren't you?" Tyler asked, trying on possibilities to explain the situation. He paused, evaluating the look on Patrick's face. "Don't tell me you actually thought I was going to kill you. Man, I've got too much of a good life to waste it on ending someone else's, like yours."

Tyler leaned in close to Patrick and whispered, "We're probably going to be questioned by the principal about this fight, so just deny everything about it being a real fight. Tell them we were just messing around, and I'll do the same. Maybe we'll get out of this without getting into too much trouble."

In a low voice, Patrick said, "I would watch my back if I were you 'cause when you least expect it, your ass is mine. You should've killed me right here and now because the next time our paths cross, you might find your insides located on the outside of your body."

Edward couldn't help but jump back in as he held the switchblade up in front of Patrick's face and said, "Then you don't have a problem with me keeping your knife for awhile, do you?"

Patrick eyes narrowed, but he shook his head. "Go ahead. I have more."

Spoken as a threat and a promise, Edward continued, "Good. I'll give it back to you later."

Many thoughts of violence bubbled up in Patrick's angered frustration. Reluctant to try anything else, Patrick turned and pushed through the crowd. Heather and their gang of friends followed as well.

Joshua, not missing a beat, grabbed Tyler's arm to get his attention. "Dude, that was like, you know, so fucking awesome. You should've seen the whole damn thing from my point of view."

"I did."

"I know, but you should've seen it from my perspective. Like something out of a damn Jet Li movie. Thanks, man. You really saved my hide back there. Don't think I don't appreciate it, cause I do. It was—"

"It's no problem," Tyler said. "You're welcome."

"Yeah man, well if there's anything I can do for you, homework assignments or if you want my chocolate milk at lunch, anything at all, you just call on me. Understand? Capiche? Anything at all."

"Affirmative. That's a big ten four. I got you. Sorry about your skateboard."

"Oh don't worry about my damn skateboard. I have a fight mark on it now. It's even more thrashed now; adds personality to it. I'm gonna tell everybody about this."

"That's really not necessary."

"But it is. Every time I see my skateboard now, I'm going to think of you saving my sweet ass. That was awesome man. You are one bad ass, my friend."

Little by little, more students dispersed when they saw nothing else was going to be taking place. The horde thinned out as the students moved on to their prospective classes.

Tyler turned back to talk to Savannah. Her hands were on her hips, and she didn't look pleased.

"What in the hell was that all about?" she asked.

He glanced over his shoulder and pointed at Joshua who was picking at the stab wound in his skateboard. "I just helped Joshua out of a pickle, that's all."

"You could've killed Patrick; you know that? Were you trying to kill him? Cause it sure looked like you were about to."

"No babe, you've got it all wrong. I was in total control. I was just trying to scare him." Tyler's eyes followed in the direction Patrick Quinlan had left. "I think it worked too."

"Well you most certainly scared the shit out of me." She was sizing him up. "You looked like you lost control. Like you were possessed. You think I was impressed by your testosterone-laden show of aggression? And don't call me *babe*."

What did I do to deserve this hell? Edward thought. He helped Tyler form a sentence to get him back in the good graces with Savannah. "I wasn't trying to impress you or anybody else. I was trying to save Joshua's ass back there. I've been in his shoes plenty of times before. I just couldn't let Patrick do that to him."

She gave him a look as though he knew better and said, "You're just as bad as he is. You could've walked away. You didn't have to fight him."

"If I hadn't stepped in, he would've made mincemeat out of Josh. What was I supposed to do? Cheer the fight on and just watch Patrick rearrange his face?"

"Give it a rest, Tyler. Quit basking in your own ego."

"Well excuse me for having a heart. I would've let him get his ass kicked if I had known you were going to go ape-shit about it on me."

"You know, I can't place it, but there's something different about you."

"Different from when? You barely know me."

"Than before the accident. And just let me refresh your memory; I've known you for the last three months. When you were lying in that hospital bed, I was always there beside you getting to know you the whole time."

Tyler scratched his head, gazed at the ceiling then said, "It always comes back around to that. The accident. I'm sorry. The accident did change me. Sometimes I feel that it changed me for the worst, but I can't help that. And I know you were there, and I appreciate it. Believe me, I could not have got through that time without you."

That last statement seemed to quell her argument. She continued but at a lower tone. "I saw it during the fight just now. It was like you were another person."

He looked down at his hand and muttered to himself. "I was."

"What has gotten in to you?"

More to the point, who? he thought. "You wouldn't believe me if I told you."

"Then tell me. I'll believe. I'm all ears."

Tyler paused for a long time, but only because Edward was holding his tongue and wouldn't let him speak.

"It figures." She shook her head and said, "This is ridiculous. I need to get to class." Savannah walked off, leaving him to bask in his bewilderment. Tyler watched her go, confused as to what he did wrong.

The bell for first period rang as the last few students hurried to their classes. Finally, the last door slammed and he found he was the only one left standing in the deserted hallway.

All of a sudden, he had a feeling that he really wasn't in the mood for school today. He didn't want to be here. He needed to get the hell out of here. Now.

CHAPTER 21

BRUCE SALIERS HAD always heard the saying, "Today is the first day of the rest of your life." Little did he know that today would mark two days before the rest of his.

Bruce's mind was on the subject of death but not his own. He was deep in thought about Kelly and Suzanne's demise.

He drove as he thought.

How could this have happened to them? When did it happen? At what time? Who did it, and why did they do it?

The name Suzanne had spoken on Alex's voicemail came back to him again.

Edward McDaniel, that's who. Don't know how, but I'm going to find out. I know the reasons of why you wanted to get even with the girls. I vaguely remember the stories. What they did to you—what we all did to you. I remember what I personally did back then. Can someone hold a grudge for that many years? If so, what do you have in store for me, Edward? But how? You've been dead for years.

He shuddered at the thought.

Bruce pulled onto the shoulder of the highway and parked a good distance away from where Suzanne had crashed and burned.

Bruce gave a little stifled laugh at his unexpected thought. *Crash and burn. How original? No pun intended, but how true was that?*

This was the first time Bruce had come to the crash site. He had hopes of finding some evidence the cleanup crews might have missed. He wanted to check every inch of this stretch of road; there could still be a small piece of evidence that would point him in the right direction.

From his car he could see two faded black streaks on the road where Suzanne had applied her breaks. The streaks turned into grooves on the dirt shoulder before disappearing into nothing beyond the guardrail. The two wooden posts that held the guardrail in place had been broken into splintered stumps that were almost even with the ground. The remaining attached metal looked like two twisted metallic fingers pointing in the direction of where Suzanne's car had landed.

Bruce opened the door and left his vehicle. A few automobiles passed him on either side of the highway.

The road curved in a wide arc to the left and around a bend. The natural slope of this road drained down to the opposite side of the road.

As Bruce slowly approached the opening, he checked the high grass on the shoulder as well as the highway itself. He was methodical in his search, but the only thing he found was a couple of cans and bits of insignificant trash. The highway itself was perfectly clean, most likely washed clean from the rain last night.

Stepping to the guardrail opening, Bruce could see the disruption Suzanne's car had made. The landscape below had been changed slightly. There were deep groves where boulders had been dislodged from the hillside from the impact of her car. There were scrapes and scratches from where the wrecker truck had drug the Mercedes back up the side of the steep incline. A small diameter of scorched earth, burnt shrubs, and charred rocks lay at the bottom of the ravine.

Bruce slowly made his way down the steep embankment, securing his feet on each rock before taking another step. The rocks were spaced widely apart, and a large stride or a simple jump could get him to the next level down. Bruce was careful; he didn't want to trip, fall, and injure himself during his investigation. Coming back up was what worried Bruce. He knew he was a little out of shape and he would be out of breath by the time he reached the top.

He paused along the way and inspected some disturbed areas but didn't turn up anything useful.

Once he was at the bottom, he gave a thorough search of the crash site and the ground neighboring the shadowed circle.

"This is ridiculous," Bruce said as he pitched a rock across another gully. "There's nothing here but bits and pieces of twisted metal from the explosion. Nothing's going to turn up. I'm grasping at straws here." Bruce turned to the area where Suzanne's car had finally rested and said, "I'm trying Suzanne. I wish you could point me in the right direction." He gave a quick chuckle. "That's a silly notion, I know. Oh well, I won't give up. I want you to know that you're not going to be a statistic. Alex and I will find out who did this to you and Kelly and take care of them for you. I love you, girl."

At the top of the ravine again—after he struggled, sweated, and cussed his way to the top—Bruce stepped back up on the shoulder of the highway. A truck barreled by. The wind coming off the passing vehicle buffeted him and nearly knocked him down.

"Slow it down, asshole!" Bruce yelled in response to the truck's speed even though the hard breeze was refreshing.

He was thinking again about the message Suzanne had left on Alex's voicemail. Deciding to check the opposite side of the road on the way back to his car, he glanced both ways before crossing. As he started, his foot struck a group of small pebbles on the edge of the road that he hadn't noticed earlier.

Like a curious dog, Bruce angled his head and watched them skitter, bounce, and roll to the opposite side. He hadn't kicked them that hard, but most of them made it all the way across because of the road's slope.

All of a sudden, an idea came to Bruce. He glanced up and down the road a number of times judging and estimating distances of where her car might have been at the start of the accident. Again making sure no traffic was coming, he crossed to the other side. He searched slowly and methodically but this time with purpose. He still had no idea what he was looking for, but since it was raining that night, anything in the road most likely was washed to the other side.

Upon his initial search he came up empty handed and became frustrated. Judging the angle of the road again, he moved down a few more feet.

The grass is taller on this side for some reason, he thought. *Maybe because more rain drains off over here.*

He used his leg to sweep the weeds back, but he still came up with nothing.

He was about to give up but stopped in his tracks when he brushed back another section of wild weeds. He cocked his head again as a small glimmer of metal caught his eye. He dropped to his knees, leaned over to get a closer look then picked it up and held it toward the sunlight.

Bruce asked the invisible man next to him, "Huh. What the hell is this?" As usual, the invisible man didn't answer.

"Just a piece of metal or fiberglass." He tried to bend it but it didn't flex. "Little bit of red on it." He tried to wipe it off, but the red stayed. "Probably nothing."

He placed it upon the white-lined edge of the road.

He pulled back some more weeds and found two small bits of silver metal and four slightly larger pieces of red and a few shards of mirrored glass.

"Interesting."

He separated the different pieces of metal and glass into three different piles and kept searching.

The metal pieces didn't look weather worn or like they had been exposed to the elements. They looked fresh—almost brand new.

"Another sliver of silver metal," he said, holding it up to examine it in the sunlight again. "Could be from Suzanne's car; her Mercedes was silver. But these red metal pieces, where did they come from?"

Then the light came on in Bruce's head, and the realization hit him as hard as the image in his mind. The thought shocked him so much in fact that he stood up and stepped away from the shards of metal. It was as if they had revealed to him exactly what happened. He had an image of a red car colliding into the backend of Suzanne's car, forcing her off the road. He shouted to the top of his lungs, "Son of a bitch!" He was angry at himself that he didn't see it earlier.

He hit his knees again and frantically pulled grass, leaves, and trash away so he could get as many pieces as possible.

Little by little, the piles grew bigger.

Eventually nothing else turned up and he leaned back on his heels. He wiped a wet brow with a sweaty forearm. He hadn't realized he was tired but all of a sudden felt winded. He pulled a few evidence bags out of his pocket. He slipped the contents of each pile into their own separate bag then sealed them tightly.

Anxious to get this material to Alex for testing and deciding there was nothing else he could do here, he walked back down the road toward his car. He looked both ways before crossing over again.

Once he was in his car, he took a pen and wrote on each bag his assumption of the contents inside. He held the bag with the red painted metal pieces up in front of his eyes again.

Bruce again said to his imaginary partner, "There's a good chance some of these metal pieces are from the car that hit Suzanne, but I'm not going to get my hopes up too high. Might be nothing at all."

Bruce cranked his patrol car, checked for approaching traffic, then pulled onto the road again and headed out to get some breakfast. He had eaten something earlier that morning but this detective work was making him hungry again.

ᘓ

Tyler had never played hooky before, but there was a first time for everything. He just wanted to be away from this place more than anything else in the world.

He knew he would be reprimanded for fighting on school premises and for skipping out on classes completely. Punishment or not, that was a bridge he didn't want to cross at this particular time.

What, are they going to give me a bigger punishment now if I break two rules? Tyler wondered. *It's better to ask forgiveness than permission.*

He arrived at his car and he threw his back pack in the passenger's seat, got in, cranked the car, floored it, and sped out of the school parking lot.

Edward's mind was reeling. *What is the big fucking deal anyway? Why was Savannah so upset at Tyler for stepping up to the plate to help out somebody else who was about to get pounded? Ah, Jeez, where are we going and why are we in this hand basket?*

Everything was happening too fast. He couldn't adjust to one situation before something else occurred.

He felt alone. He desperately needed and wanted someone to talk to. *But who is that going to be?* Edward asked himself. *I wish Granddad and Grandmomma were still here. They never failed to lend a listening ear when I had a problem. Wait, maybe I can talk to them. It won't be the same thing, but I can at least go visit them at Woodland Hills. I do at least know Granddad is there. I wasn't here when Grandmomma passed. I can at least pay my respects to her, and well, both of them.*

Edward was like a kid again filled with excitement as though about to open presents that Santa Claus had left him.

Edward remembered where his grandfather was buried from when he and his grandmother had laid him to rest years ago.

Edward pulled the car into Woodland Hills Cemetery and drove down the meandering road toward the back of the lot. He parked, turned off the car, got out, and pocketed his keys.

He walked to the far end of the cemetery property where Jonas and Helen had picked out their graves years ago. Edward had always thought it weird that they bought burial plots for each other on one of their anniversaries. But they never looked at stuff like that as a negative or in a weird way. They loved each other and that was their way to make sure that even in death they would forever be together.

The area was on the far back side of the cemetery. Edward had expected this section to be overgrown and forgotten but the weeds had been pulled and the grass around the graves were neatly trimmed and edged.

The cemetery workers should be commended, Edward thought as he looked around at this area. *They have done a great job keeping up the place.*

The headstone was big enough to span both his grandparents' graves. Carved in the dark, grey granite in a block font, it simply stated: ROQUEMORE, and Edward knew he was at the right place. There were no sayings or anything of that nature, just their names: JONAS, on the right; HELEN, on the left. Below their names were their birth and death dates.

"Hi, Granddad," Edward began. "Hi, Grandmomma." He didn't

know what to say. He was quite for a moment and looked around to make sure no one could hear what he was about to say. "It's me. Edward. Your grandson. Well, not exactly me. I'm a little different now than how you used to know me." He paused, letting that sink in for them as though they were right here with him. "I know. Weird, right? I hope you like the new me. I do. I can do so many different things now than when I was in the body you knew." Edward gave a half-laugh at his comment. "Tyler really doesn't like me much, but I'm hoping in time he will grow to love me like you two did."

Edward noticed another gravestone out of the corner of his eye, and he turned his head. It was to his right a short distance from the Roquemore plot.

It was a small granite headstone, like theirs that stated: EDWARD McDANIEL. Below his name read: Beloved grandson of Jonas and Helen Roquemore. Underneath that, were Edward's birth and death dates. Seeing his burial plot filled Edward with pride, because his grandmother had taken the time to put him to rest in a place like this and beside them.

"So this is where I ended up?" he said aloud. "All these years, even from inside the charm, I've wondered. Thank you, Grandmomma and Granddad. Thank you for letting me be here with you. I love you. I love you so much."

Overwhelming happiness for how they felt about him and sorrow that they were no longer here burst from him in the form of tears. The names and the dates on the headstone blurred as he cried.

"I miss you guys so much. I can't put it into words, but I wish I could hold you and hug you both really hard right now."

Edward stood there shaking a little as he silently cried. He was afraid to speak; afraid his crying voice would sound stupid if he poured out his heart to them while he was sobbing.

He looked away and tried to compose himself. He wiped at his eyes then looked back at Helen's side of the grave.

"I'm sorry I wasn't with you during your last days, Grandmomma. I know you were getting up in years after Granddad passed away, and I so wish I could've been there to help you with—" He didn't know what to say. "With-with whatever you needed. I don't even know what happened to you. But I'm so glad someone knew to bury you here with Granddad."

Edward looked at the death date on Helen's side of the gravestone to see exactly when she had passed. Edward's forehead crinkled with confusion.

"What the fuck?" he said as he stared at the blank space of the death date.

He glanced over at his grandfather's side of the grave. There it was. A birth date and a death date.

Edward glanced back at Helen's dates again. There was a birth date, but she didn't have a death date.

What the hell? Edward thought. *Could it be possible she's still alive?*

All of a sudden, his heart was pumped with adrenaline at the possibility of seeing his grandmother again.

She's still alive? She's still alive.

Edward couldn't believe it.

Don't get your hopes up too high, Edward told himself. *She may actually be lying here. It could've been just a glitch in the Woodland Hills system and they may have forgotten to add her death date.*

"I have to go see her," he said aloud. "I have to see her for myself."

He turned and headed back to the car, then as an after thought turned back to the graves. "I'll come see you again really soon, Granddad. I promise. I've just got to go check on Grandmomma."

Edward still wasn't sure that his grandmother was still alive. Something in the back of his mind was telling him that she wasn't, but he didn't want to believe it. When he had passed on, she was in her early eighties. If she was still alive, she would be getting close to her late nineties. The chances of her still being alive were slim. Not impossible, just very doubtful.

But there is a chance, he thought.

Before getting to the home place, he decided to do some investigating of his own to make sure before he got there. He pulled out his cell phone and looked up the number for Woodland Hills Cemetery's main office. When he found the number, he pressed the button to connect him to it and waited for someone to answer.

The excitement of possibly seeing his grandmother again overwhelmed him. He pulled out of the cemetery lot and gunned it. He couldn't wait to get over to his home place and give her a huge hug. She was going to be so surprised. He had a lot to explain to her about himself, but he would figure out a way to do it eventually.

A friendly female voice picked up on the other end, "Woodland Hills Cemetery. How may I help you?"

"Hi, yes. My name is, ah—" Edward didn't know which name he wanted to use. He couldn't use Edward McDaniel, because that name was on a gravestone in their cemetery. For that matter he didn't want to draw attention to himself and use the name Tyler Curtis either. He opted to go with a name off the top of his head. "Yes, my name is Tanner Appleton," he shook his head at how dumb that sounded.

The lady on the other end took it in stride, "How may I help you today, Tanner?"

Edward continued, "I just recently got into town with my wife and we stopped by to pay our respects to some of her distant relatives."

"Yes," the lady said, letting Tanner know she understood his story so far.

Edward continued in character, "My wife's maiden name was Roquemore. We noticed when we were there that the Helen Roquemore plot on the back side of the cemetery didn't have a death date attached to it. Well, naturally my wife was surprised at that, because its been a number of years since we've been back and Helen was pretty elderly when we moved away. We had assumed she had already passed on. I'm sorry, I'm rambling."

"That's no problem. What can I help you with, sir?"

"I was wondering if you have any record of when Mrs. Helen might have passed away. I told my wife that someone just forgot to add the death date to her and Jonas's tombstone. Naturally, we hope she is still alive and we wanted to drop by and see her if we can find out where she is living now. Do you have any record of her passing?"

"Huh, let me see. And you said the name was Roquemore?"

"Yes, that's correct."

"Roquemore. Could you spell that for me?

Edward spelled the name.

"Hold on, I'm pulling it up in the computer right now. Huh, I'm not finding any record of a Helen Roquemore in the system."

"Really?" Edward asked. "That's odd."

"I do have record of a Jonas Roquemore, did you say?"

"Yes," Edward said.

He unconsciously pressed the gas a little bit harder to get to the home place quicker.

The woman continued on, barely listening to Edward's reply, "His burial was on—,"

Edward interrupted her. "Yes, his date was on the headstone at the cemetery. Why would Helen's date not be added?"

"Well sir, if there is no death date on the tombstone and no burial date in our computer system then apparently she is still alive somewhere." The woman was getting a little defensive as though Tanner was accusing Woodland Hills of some oversight in the way they do business. "We keep very strict records here at Woodla—."

Edward cut her off again, "Oh no. I wasn't blaming you or the cemetery of anything. My wife and I are just trying to find Ms. Helen before we leave town on Thursday. She was my wife's favorite aunt growing up when she was a little girl. You wouldn't happen to have a last known address for the Roquemores would you?"

"I do, but I am not allowed to give out that information."

"I'm sorry. I apologize for asking."

"That's quite alright. You understand, I'm sure."

"Yes. Just one more question, ma'am," Edward added. "And I hope you can help me out on this one."

"I don't know. You can ask and I will let you know if I can."

"If I tell you the last know address we know Ms. Helen was living at, could you just give me a yes or no to whether that is the address in your records?

"I don't see that being a problem."

Edward gave her the address of his old home place.

"Yes, sir. That's correct. That's the address we have on file here in our system."

"Perfect. Thank you so much. You have been so helpful. We will drop by soon and give Ms. Helen the surprise of her life. You have an awesome day now."

"Thank yo—"

Edward ended the call, cutting off her reply in mid sentence.

He pressed the gas just a little harder, and that is when he heard the siren.

Edward's and Tyler's immediate thought was that an ambulance was in route to pick up an injured body somewhere. He looked in his rearview mirror to see where it was in conjunction to him so he could make sure he was out of its way. Instead of the normal red and yellow light of the typical ambulance, all he saw was red and blue.

Oh, for the love of God. A cop-per top. I don't believe it. If it's not one damn thing, it's the next.

He glanced at his speedometer and saw he was well above the posted speed limit.

Edward closed his eyes and shook his head in frustration. He couldn't believe the luck he was having today. He gritted his teeth and mumbled to himself, "This just keeps getting better and better."

He eased off the gas, applied the brakes, and coasted to a stop on the side of the road. The highway patrolman did likewise and pulled in behind him.

As the officer stepped out of his car and donned his hat, Tyler went ahead and retrieved the necessary documents.

Before the officer even asked for his license and registration, Tyler held them out of his open window. "I believe this is what you need, officer."

The officer took the two items of identification, glanced at them as he said, "Looks as though you've been through this a time or two before, haven't you Mr.—?" He glanced at the card again to make sure he had the name correct. "Mr. Curtis?"

"Yes, sir. A few times. I do know the drill."

"Didn't you see my lights in your rearview mirror?

"No, sir."

"I followed you for about a mile before I turned my siren on; even then it took you a while to notice me."

"I apologize. I wasn't paying attention to anything behind…"

Bruce's mind drifted. Something about the boy's name and face was familiar to him. He tried to reason it out as the boy rattled on. The boy's words began registering with him again.

"—know that I was speeding. I have no excuse for that. It wasn't intentional. I've just already had the start on a really bad day. I know it may be wrong of me to ask, but is there any way you could give me a break?"

He was focused again on the papers in his hand. "You know, Mr. Curtis, if I were to cut some slack to everyone I pull over I would—"

Tyler looked up at him expectantly. From the back of his mind, Edward realized it was Bruce Saliers before he began speaking again.

Tyler saw Bruce's head jerked up from the licensed picture to him as Bruce realized who he was talking to.

Bruce snapped his finger and pointed at him. "Tyler Curtis," he said.

"Yeah, that's me."

"I never forget a face or name."

"And you're Bruce Saliers," Tyler said.

Bruce nodded.

Tyler continued, "You're the patrolman that saved my life when I was in that wreck on Old Cypress Highway about three months ago."

"That I am. How are you? You look much better than the last time I saw you."

"I'm better now," Tyler said. "A three month coma does wonders for the body. You should try it sometime."

"Three months? That long already? Wow, you're kidding. That's amazing, but no, I'll pass on the coma. I see your family told you a little about me."

Tyler nodded, then spoke words that Edward put in his mouth, "I know what you did to me." A thought of an incident involving guns and a lot of beer flittered through Tyler's mind. "I know a great deal about you, Bruce."

Bruce had no idea how close the past was to catching up to him.

In the back of Tyler's mind, Edward was seething. He wanted to strike out at him with vengeance. How he would love to snatch the gun from Bruce's holster and load his body with all the bullets from his full clip. Half of the clip into his chest and the other half into his face, and it would be all over. His fingers opened and closed with nervous anxiety at the thought of it. Edward's mind was wandering too far from home base. He was becoming too creative.

Now isn't the time or the place, Edward reminded himself. *It has to be in private. Much more private than here.*

"Tyler?" Bruce said, snapping his finger in front of Tyler's face.

Tyler snapped back to attention as the memory and thoughts abruptly ended.

"You still with me?"

"Oh yeah," Tyler said. "Just reliving the past."

Tyler searched his mind and picked up where he had left off. "My mom is the one who told me about you. I really appreciate what you did for me. I'll never forget it."

"No-no, I should be apologizing for not calling to find out how you were getting along. Actually, most all the credit should go to your dog. Raven, right?"

Tyler nodded.

Bruce continued, "She was blocking the road and wouldn't let me pass. She's the one who pointed you out to me. She was pretty shaken up that night."

"I bet," he said in agreement.

"But you know that whole story. I shouldn't be bringing up the past. I know you're probably trying to forget it."

"You can't forget the past," Tyler said. "It's too vivid. I'll never be able to forget what you did to me, Bruce."

"Well, you're welcome. I shouldn't do this, but under the circumstances, I'm going to let you off with a verbal warning. Fair enough?"

"Yes, sir," Tyler said. "Very fair."

"I'm glad you're better, and I'm glad I was there to help."

"Me too and listen. Seriously," Tyler paused, making it heartfelt. "Thank you."

"Don't thank me, thank that dog of yours." He handed Tyler back his license and registration papers. "Take care, and slow it down. I don't want another opportunity to save your life again."

Tyler laughed along with Bruce. "Yes, sir. I will."

Bruce was about to step away from the car when he noticed something odd. He had observed it on his approach but had forgotten about it while he and Tyler were talking. He tapped his finger on the side of the car, "What happened to your mirror, son?"

Tyler looked up from placing his license back into his wallet. He opened his mouth to answer but realized he didn't have one for this particular question.

"Were you in another wreck recently?"

Tyler thought quickly and remembered a story one of his friends back in Chicago had told him about when he had scuffed their family car.

"I-uh, no." He laughed, shrugged his shoulders and tried to downplay the incident as less than what it was. "Ha, not exactly. It's so stupid. See, I was backing my car into my girlfriend's garage to move some of her stuff into her new apartment. I didn't judge the angle right and backed into the frame of the garage instead. I scraped the side panel a little and broke the side mirror off before I even realized it. I had the music turned up at the time so I didn't hear it at first, otherwise it wouldn't have been this bad. I was so disgusted and sick when it happened. Talk about being embarrassed. I felt this small." He used his thumb and index finger to show how little he meant. "I've already looked into having it fixed."

While Tyler babbled on about whatever excuse he'd dreamed up, Bruce's mind kept flashing back to this morning's find in the weeds beside the road. *Small shards of mirrored glass and red pieces of metal. The same shade of red as this Mustang here. Could it be this easy?*

It was all Bruce could do to stand there and look calm and attentive when all he wanted to do was reach through the window and pull Tyler out by his throat. He wanted to hold him close and peer into his eyes as he watched the life drain from his body as he choked him out for what he did to Kelly and Suzanne. Bruce wanted to feel him wriggle until he hung limp in his arms.

317

But my hands are tied until I can prove it; but why would Tyler want to harm Kelly and Suzanne? It didn't make any damn sense.

Instead, Bruce said, "You've not had much luck with automobiles lately, have you?"

"No, sir."

Bruce gave a bemused chuckle and said, "You know, if you wouldn't speed and paid attention to where you were going, maybe you wouldn't keep messing up these badass Mustangs you own."

Edward and Tyler both didn't like his comment but said, "Yes, sir. I know."

"Well accidents do happen. It's a shame. This Mustang was beautiful before the accident I'm sure."

"It was, and it will be again," Tyler promised.

"Don't let it go too long. They make rearview mirrors for a reason you know. This is a driving hazard."

"I know, I know. I'm working on it."

Bruce slapped the roof of the car with the palm of his hand. "Okay, you take care and drive safe."

"Will do. You too. And hey, thank you again."

"It's not a problem. Just be careful out there."

Bruce was skeptical as he turned and headed back to his cruiser.

There's something up with that kid, he thought. *He's lying out of his ass.*

Tyler pulled back on to the highway when the coast was clear. Frustration had set in again.

"Why?" he yelled. "That's all I want to know is why?"

He punched the upholstery and the inside roof as he cursed to the top of his lungs. That helped a little, but it didn't solve anything. His so-called new life was turning into a disaster.

Yeah, accidents happen, Bruce, Edward thought sarcastically as he mocked Bruce's tone. Then he smiled with his familiar crooked grin.

Edward felt his skin crawl and realized it was caused by Tyler who had grimaced underneath.

Edward started laughing, "You're absolutely right, Bruce; accidents really do happen. And one is going to happen to you sooner than you think."

CHAPTER 22

SAVANNAH KNEW SHE shouldn't be angry with Tyler. She even told herself that as they were having the argument in the hallway. After all, all Tyler wanted to do was help Joshua out. Patrick would have annihilated him if Tyler hadn't stepped in. It was kind of heroic and amazing to watch.

But still, it just brings back bad memories of Robbie. As soon as she thought of him she immediately pushed his image out of his mind. *I can't think about him right now. I have to talk to Tyler again. He must think I'm such a bitch. I had no right to criticize him that way.*

Mr. Beaumont was talking again. Savannah tried to focus back in on what he was saying; something about how to find the "X" integer to a certain equation.

We're always finding the X to some problem, she thought as she leaned over to look at another student's text book to find out what page they were on.

After getting the page number, she flipped through Tyler's Algebra book she had borrowed to the same page number. As she did, a piece of paper flipped out from between the pages and landed on the floor beside her desk. She leaned over, picked it up, and was about to stick it back into the Algebra book when a flash of red caught her eye. She pulled it back out and stared at a picture of six guys and girls sitting and standing around a volleyball net. It was a fun pose filled with smiles and laughter that captured the essence of summer. Except this picture looked a bit more sinister with the added red. A stab of fear and panic made her suck in a startled breathe of air.

Around two of the figures head's was a circle drawn with a red sharpie marker and an added "X" crisscrossed each circle. Her first thought was that it looked as though it was a hitman's list of faces instead of names and he had already bumped two of the six characters off that were in this line up.

Savannah flipped the picture over to see if there was anything on the back. Finding a female's handwriting, she read the list and compared them to the picture.

Upon reading the name Kelly Morgan, it didn't stir up any thoughts but when she read the name Suzanne Baldwin it sparked a thought from earlier that morning when she was watching the news and eating breakfast.

Suzanne Baldwin? Can it be the same woman?

She continued to read the names in her mind. *Alex Riley, Travis Sheridan, Jessica Anderson. Wait, what? Sheridan? Kelly Morgan? Travis Sheridan? Could this be an early picture of them before they got married? Kelly Sheridan and Suzanne Baldwin. Those are the two women that died… or were killed last night.*

That stab of pain grew to full blown panic in Savannah's chest.

What the fuck is Tyler doing with this picture and why were these two women X'ed out in this picture? Did he have something to do with their deaths? Where was he last night? First he was fighting with Patrick and now this.

Her mind could barely fathom Tyler fighting, much less killing anyone in the way the news had suggested.

But I had been a witness to the fighting earlier so… She let the thought die off in her mind. *If he had killed those women, what had they done to him? Does there have to be a reason? There has to be an explanation to all of this. I have to talk with him. Now.*

Without thinking, she placed the eight-by-ten back in Tyler's Algebra book, gathered her own books and pencils, shoved them in her bookbag, and got up to leave.

Mr. Beaumont stopped mid-sentence and stared at her. As she stood to leave, he asked, "Miss Matthews, may I ask where you think you are going in the middle my integers discussion?"

"Oh, um, I can't explain right now. Just that it is an extreme emergency. You can give me demerits or send me to detention or whatever you feel is fair. Right now, I just have to leave."

Mr. Beaumont flipped the pencil he was holding up in the air and turned away in mock surrender. "Oh well, if it's an emergency then by all means. We might as well all pack up and leave class early. What do you say, class?"

Some of the class began to close their books and pack their things.

"That was a joke, class. Everybody settle down and open your books again. No one else is leaving."

Savannah was almost to the door when she heard her name again, "Oh, Miss Matthews?"

She turned, "Yes, sir."

"We'll talk later. Is that understood?"

"Yes, sir." She grimaced. "I'm really sorry but it's an emergency." Then she turned and quickly exited the classroom and headed to find Tyler.

As soon as Savannah was out of the room she grabbed her phone from her purse and typed in a message to Tyler.

SM: I need to talk with you ASAP. Can you meet me? It's really important. Where are you?

She didn't know what else to do, so she headed to the library to wait. She typed in another message to Tyler.

SM: I'll be in the library. Meet me there.

CHAPTER 23

EDWARD DIDN'T KNOW why he didn't drive straight to the old home place. With the possibility his grandmother could still being alive, it was all he could do to reign himself in. He was simultaneously nervous, excited, and a little scared at the prospects of seeing his grandmother again. He actually had no idea what he would say or do to her if she opened the door. He needed to collect his thoughts and really think about how he was going to react when they saw each other.

What would she say to me? She wouldn't even fucking know me. I'm Tyler now. It wouldn't be the same.

He found himself sitting in his car overlooking Silver Ridge Bay.

He grabbed a ball cap from the back seat and slapped it on his head. He stepped out of the Mustang and walked over to the burgundy painted picnic tables and planted himself on the tabletop. He propped his feet on the bench below and looked out over the serene water to the neighboring shorelines. He gazed toward the immense, snow-covered mountains beyond the shores in the distance. The trees that lined the base of the crags spread their broad limbs toward the sky as if they were worshipping the grand summits and were paying homage to them. In the distance, a bell clanged from an unseen buoy as it swayed back and forth on the rhythmic currents of the water.

Tyler thought within himself, *This is where my friends and I sat three months earlier.*

Edward frowned, *Yeah, this is also the place I got my ass kicked close to twenty years ago by Jeremy Taylor. God, I can't wait to pay him a visit.*

"Haven't seen him yet," Edward said aloud. "Wonder where he's hiding. I'm sure he'll turn up sooner or later. I just know it."

There were many well-built homes around the lake that had stood on these shores for nearly a hundred years. Some had been remodeled over the decades; some had been completely torn down while others were rebuilt in their place. Edward thought about the people he had known that lived in these houses when he was growing up. He wondered where they were now and what they were doing.

"What stories would be told if the walls of these houses could talk?"

But he knew those secret legends were locked up inside each house and would stay that way until they were torn down after another hundred years had passed.

He raised his arms as far as he could and stretched until he thought his bones would snap loose from the tendons that held him together. He ran his fingers through his thick hair then replaced his ball cap.

Procrastinating, that's what I'm doing. Procrastinating about seeing my grandmother. He shook his head. *This is stupid. Quit being so scared. Since I'm playing hooky, why not make the most of this time and hike the distance as I always did back then. Take a stroll down memory lane. Relive that childhood.*

Edward made Tyler hop down from the table and start his trek toward his destination. As he went, distant memories of this area were already playing at the edges of his mind.

Minutes later, he found himself following a familiar path; the path he was somewhat responsible of blazing as a way to get to the lake faster. He had hiked and biked these back trails often as a teenager. But now time had allowed the forest to almost erase a lot of them. Close to twenty autumns had come and gone and with that, the molting of all the trees in these woods. The overhanging tree limbs were thick with leaves; they folded over the trail and shaded the sun. But he knew these woods well from his teenage years, he walked them as though the paths were still there.

A variety of birds squawked as they hopped from limb to limb, and the forest floor rustled with the sounds of animals trying to find a decent mid-morning snack.

The pine trees grew denser as he continued on the trail. The barely visible path meandered through groves of maple, birch, and aspen then disappeared around a bend. He could still see the water, which helped him keep his bearings. Occasionally, he would leave the path to pitch a flat rock over the water to see how many skips it would take before gravity pulled it under. A few times he walked headlong into an invisible spider web or two, which threw him into full body convulsions. Wising up to the situation, he grabbed a stick and waved it in front of him as he went to clear the rest of the webs from the path.

The forest smelled musty like that of exhumed coffins that had been busted open and looted by grave robbers. The stench seemed to lie over the forest the way smog coated the big city of distant Chicago.

Going through these woods brought back the memory of Tyler's eccentric dream he'd had the day before school started when he had been chased by the creature in the forest. He knew it was only a dream, and he felt foolish when he looked behind him just to be sure nothing was actually stalking him.

Finally, Tyler emerged through a slight opening in the trees into bright sunshine again. He found himself standing in front of a colossal, three-story, colonial-styled house that loomed in front of him. It was set back from an old dirt road, looking as though time had completely forgotten and neglected it.

Edward frowned when he saw the condition of his childhood homestead. His heart sank with overwhelming disappointment.

Why hadn't Grandmomma hired someone to keep this place up?

Then he realized she may actually be dead.

I just wish I could see her again. I wish I could just give her a big, long hug. Hers were the best. Full of an all-encompassing love. I miss you, Grandmomma.

He had a disturbing thought. He grabbed his charm and held it up so he could look at it. He really hadn't wished with all his heart on seeing her again. It might not be the best thing to see her in her current condition if she were actually dead.

That's a wish I would never want to come true, Edward thought.

He shuddered at the hideous thought and dropped the charm back to his chest then looked again at the dilapidated house.

Thick, green, ivy-wrapped columns barely supported a sagging front porch roof. The creeping ivy continued to spread up the front wall, almost covering the attic windows as it continued over the top of the roof. It seemed to Edward that the ivy was on a quest to consume the house and was nearly there. Over the years, the paint had been badly weathered and worn; it had practically been chipped clean, leaving a dull green hue underneath. Either by strong winds or by vandalism, many of the windows were broken. Some of the vines had even slithered into those broken spaces.

The inside could be just as badly covered as the outside, Edward thought.

Many shingles on the roof were missing. Bare patches would be the blame for countless leaks during the rainy seasons. From the ground to at least six feet in height on the places the vines hadn't yet covered, graffiti marked different areas of the house in different colors. Some of the artwork was faded but a good bit of it seemed recent. The yard was overgrown with weeds. Kudzu and ivy vines had completely eaten the white picket fence and had also claimed a good portion of the front yard. Maintenance had been neglected, letting time take its toll. The house looked like it hadn't been inhabited in years.

There is no way Grandmomma would live here if she were still alive.

The only thing the vines and weeds hadn't consumed was an area of the backyard near three single dogwood trees that were planted in a triangular formation. Everything around the old house seemed lifeless except for the dogwood trees. They were in full bloom. It seemed as though it were the only color painted on this drab, vine-choked vista.

"That's so weird," he said of the trees. *It's beautiful though, no doubt about that. The only bit of beauty left around this place.*

He shrugged his shoulders and moved on toward the house.

The house had changed for the worse since he had walked its halls. Edward doubted that anyone occupied its walls, but he slowly made his way up the weeded walkway, wary of who might see him.

The front porch stairs creaked and popped noisily under the weight of his body. He wouldn't have been surprised if his body plunged through the rotted wood.

Unoiled, rusty hinges squealed in protest as Edward opened the screen door and entered the screened-in porch. Not so much a screened-in porch now; most of the screen had been ripped or torn away.

A few steps on the inside brought him to the front door. He paused then pushed it open and slipped in.

It had been nearly twenty years since Edward had set foot inside the old homestead, but to him it seemed more like a century had past. Though it was dust-covered and dingy, Edward was thrilled to be home once again and he smiled his crooked smile, relishing this long awaited homecoming.

Tyler was repulsed by the smile. The grin felt dirty—more like a sneer—on his lips.

Edward crept silently throughout the rooms downstairs, not wanting to frighten or scare any homeless tenants that may be squatting here. This was no longer his home.

The dimmed memories of his childhood flourished into vivid relived moments. Much of the furniture had been removed, but some he didn't recognize had been busted into kindling by vandalism and strewn about. *This furniture must have been from a different owner,* Edward mused.

Numerous walls had the remains of gaping holes that had been punched through either by a fist or some kind of instrument. Some holes were big enough to walk through.

The graffiti artists from the outside had made themselves at home on the inside as well. Huge murals, rude sayings, and symbols adorned the walls in most of the rooms. Some artists were overachievers; their artwork had made it all the way to the ceiling in places.

Dust danced in the diagonal slants of sunlight that flooded through the panes in the living room. Reaching the stairs, he paused and looked to the top.

Even though this stairwell was different than the one in the Sheridans' home, for a split second, he imagined Kelly Sheridan's body cascading down the stairs toward him. Through his "mind's ear"—if such a thing existed—he heard the crunch of her neck snap like strands of carrots. The crooked grin that was stretched across Tyler's face spread even wider.

As the thought faded, he precariously ascended the stairs.

He strolled down the hallway peeking into every room along the way. Nothing of value occupied the rooms; just miscellaneous crap left behind by homeless vagrants. Even his grandfather and grandmother's room was bare. Upon viewing their room, Edward, again, was left with the uncanny feeling that she hadn't survived to present day.

If my grand mother is still alive, she's probably in a nursing home somewhere. I'll have to inquire about that sometime soon.

When he entered his four-walled sanctuary, where he had spent most of his childhood and teenage years, he stopped short in the doorway. His breath stuck in his throat. He couldn't believe the sight that lay before him.

Raven was lying on an old, dirt-encrusted, yellow-stained mattress. She was facing away from him and appeared to be sound asleep.

She has to be sleeping, he thought. *With all the sounds I made coming up the hallway, I certainly would've peaked her attention and she would've come to investigate.*

A breeze gently stirred the thin, tattered curtain that still hung in one window. A bird's shrill song droned from somewhere outside.

Tyler swallowed hard and his eyes squinted in thought. *Why was Raven here of all places?*

"Raven?" Edward whispered.

Suddenly alert, Raven's head shot up and she cocked it to one side as she looked out the window. Her ears pricked as though she were trying to hear something she thought she had only imagined.

Edward spoke again. "Raven."

Unaware that someone had crept up behind her, Raven immediately jumped from her position. She landed, facing him and backed herself into a corner. She stood with her feet apart and head planted low to the ground. Her back arched and her fur ruffled. Her long teeth gleamed from behind a wicked snarl and a deep-based, steady-rhythmic growl rumbled from the pit of her stomach.

De ja vu, Tyler thought. *She can be so intimidating when she wants to be.*

Edward knelt and stuck out his unbitten hand to show he wasn't a threat to her.

Edward also released his hold on Tyler just a little bit so he could associate with his dog.

"It's okay, girl," Tyler said. "No one is going to harm you."

As soon as Raven realized who it was, she immediately relaxed. It looked as though a sudden peace came over the beast that was crouched against the corner. Her lips uncurled. The deep growl from her belly ceased, and the old Raven Tyler knew so well began to wag her tail. It thumped excitedly against the wall. Edward thought it was strong enough to add a few more holes to match the ones already there.

"That's my girl. Come on, come here, girl."

She hesitantly crept closer to him on her belly, whining the whole way. Apparently she remembered biting her master and felt she was going to get reprimanded for it.

"It's okay, I'm not going to hurt you," he soothed. "Now why couldn't you be this friendly earlier this week? Huh, girl?"

When Raven was close enough to him, Edward took her into his arms. He hugged and stroked her all over. He had never had a pet like Raven, other than Trevor, and he loved the feeling of having a best friend.

"Why didn't I get a dog like you when I was growing up," Edward said aloud to Raven. "That would've been the coolest thing ever."

Raven, excited to be back with Tyler, couldn't get enough of him and pranced around him. Tyler stroked her face, neck, and behind her ears and Raven replied with plenty of kisses under his chin and face.

Tyler and Raven were together once again and both sections of Edward were together as well. They were one now. They were complete.

Even though she was excited to be with Tyler again, she raised her head with pitiful, homesick eyes. Tyler thought Raven looked sad. She stared deep into her master's eyes. They stared a moment, both understanding what had happened and what was going on.

Her once sleek, shiny fur had been diminished into a matted, muddy pelt. A pitiful whine escaped her muzzle. She was shrunken and feeble; like a virus spirit was surviving off the dog's life force.

Then Tyler understood how true that statement was. *So that's what it was.*

Tyler remembered the rippling effect beneath his skin when Raven had bitten him earlier in the week. Edward had released a part of himself into Raven to control her. That's why she had taken off so fast and hadn't come back home. Every time Edward's spirit had been around she had gone insane trying to warn everyone else of his presence. Raven had been driven mad trying to resist the entity that was now inside her. Now with Raven so docile, Tyler knew she was just like him in that she wasn't strong enough to fight the Edward portion that was inside her.

The portion of Edward inside Tyler had come home to his roots. Likewise, Raven had also been led by her Edward portion to seek out the closest and strongest connection to Edward. That had brought her here as well.

Anger welded deep inside him, but there was nothing he could do to Edward for revenge.

From the deep recesses of his mind, Tyler thought to himself, *At least, not yet.*

Let her go, Edward, Tyler thought. It wasn't a command. It was just a simple request asked in a pleading tone. *Please let her go. She doesn't deserve this. Please, just let her live her own life free of you.*

Not on your life, Tyler. If I take my spirit portion from her do you know how insane she would become? Do you remember the night of the accident? Do you remember coming home from the hospital? She would probably attack you again. Maybe take you apart this time. No, I can't do that. She's just going to have part of me in her to keep her sane and focused so she won't give me away.

Tyler knew there was no point in arguing. He would have to just sit this one out until he could think of a way to get rid of Edward once and for all.

Edward took back control of Tyler's soul and pushed him back down inside himself again.

Edward got up and said, "C'mon, girl. There's nothing else here that

I need to see. Let's get you home. I'm going to take really good care of you."

When Tyler and Raven left Edward's old home place, they had a new kinship. Their bond was tighter than ever. They were closer—"in spirit"—now than they ever were before coming to Silver Ridge. No matter what anyone would do to them, they knew their new secret pact would never be severed.

CHAPTER 24

JEREMY TAYLOR STOOD in the basement morgue with a look of disgust already painted on his face.

The first sight of the morgue wasn't as stomach wrenching and ghastly as he had imagined it would be. He found no bloody footprints that laced the floor, no malicious pathologists running around with blood-drenched aprons and spinning saws and no miscellaneous body parts discarded on countertops and in sinks as horror movies so often misled; instead he found it clean and tidy. Instead of being dim and cramped, it was well lit and roomy. Although the morgue had an overall pleasant look, there was no mistaking that death dwelt in the bowels of this hospital. Just the idea of him being here creeped him out all the more.

The scent of antiseptic and bacterial cleaner was strong, and a smaller but definitely noticeable smell of human remains that couldn't be washed away hung lightly in the cool air.

Lining one wall, steel doors enclosed temporary coffins. No doubt more bodies were stashed inside waiting for their meeting with the medical examiner's scalpel.

Two covered bodies lay beneath white sheets in the middle of the room.

Jeremy Taylor stood with Alex Riley and Bruce Saliers.

Alex approached the two forms and said, "All I can say is brace yourself. This isn't a pretty sight."

Not giving them time to prepare, he grabbed a corner of each white sheet and whipped them back in one graceful arc. He had done this so many times in the past and now he had it down to a practiced science.

Jeremy and Bruce gaped both in amazement and horror upon witnessing these grotesque denizens. Even though Bruce had seen many different faces of death from his tour on the police force, the shock of this sight sickened him. He turned, doubled over, and gave the floor his breakfast. Jeremy simply winced at Bruce's reaction and turned back to the two forms on the table.

"Lightweight," Jeremy said.

Alex laughed, "Hey whoa, take it easy there, pal," he said to Bruce as he patted him on the back. "You okay? Don't worry about that. I'll clean that up in a bit."

"Shit, Alex, why didn't you warn us," Bruce wheezed, as he spat to clean his mouth.

"You had a chance to preview the bodies before Jeremy arrived. You said, oh, no-no-no, I'll wait for Jeremy. And I told you to prepare yourselves. I said it would be rough."

Two bodies lay sprawled out on cold, steel gurneys in abnormal arrangements. Both women had been completely stripped of all their clothes. The only thing they did wear were identification tags attached to their toes.

On the right, Kelly Sheridan's neck was twisted in a severe angle. Jeremy's eyes lifted when he saw the scissors sticking out of the center of her chest.

Jeremy said nothing. He just continued to observe the corpses.

The burnt woman's features on the left had been charred into oblivion as the highway patrolman had stated earlier. Her face was withered into a hideous evil Mardi Gras mask. Her eyes were empty dark sockets. Her once smooth skin was grafted into thin layers of tracing paper. The acrid smell of burnt flesh and hair wafted off of the blackened form.

"Talk about being over cooked; that's an understatement," Jeremy said.

Alex said, "Shut up, Jeremy. There's no reason for the disrespectful comments."

Jeremy simply lifted his eyebrows at Alex.

Alex continued, "Don't say anything remotely negative about anyone who is on the slabs in my morgue, especially about Suzanne. Keep your snide remarks to yourself."

Jeremy was holding his arms up to ward Alex off. "Jesus, who pissed in your cornflakes this morning, Alex?" Jeremy asked.

"He's still upset about Suzanne," Bruce said, still trying to calm the tension between them. "He's been in love with her since before high school and throughout college. He wanted more of a relationship, but they never hit it off on a romantic note. They remained only close friends, and he's a little torn up about her death right now."

"Close to twenty years and you're still pining away about her. Jesus, build a bridge and get over her."

"Shut up, Jeremy."

"Just fucking around, that's all. I didn't mean to offend. Just trying to keep a lighthearted mood about this or I'll lose my breakfast as Bruce did and puke it all over your nice, shiny floor. I thought you morgue people cracked jokes like that to make this job easier to handle?"

"I take my job very seriously," Alex said.

Bruce jumped in, still trying to play referee between the two. "Yeah yeah, just go easy on this subject for Alex's sake."

"Sorry. I take it back, and I'm sorry." He looked again at the bodies, then asked, "Are you going to tell me what this is about?"

Without looking at Suzanne, Alex swept his arm down the length of her body as a hostess of a game show might do. "This is Suzanne Baldwin if you hadn't recognized her already."

Both Jeremy and Bruce nodded to let Alex know they were already with him on the subject.

"Yes we see, but why did you bring us down here to view her?" Jeremy asked.

"Bruce and I have been talking, and we thought you should know what's happening that's all."

"And what would that be?"

"We both suspect Kelly and Susanne were murdered."

Jeremy was skeptical from the looks on their faces. He glanced back and forth between Bruce and Alex. He turned his head toward the bodies. He figured it was possible but didn't believe it was actually true.

Jeremy mulled the idea over in his head for a few moments then said, "Okay. What makes you so sure?"

"Bruce, you want to do the honors?" Alex asked.

"Sure. I'll take the baton and run with it."

Bruce told Jeremy everything, starting with Alex's call that morning. He told him about how they went to Kelly's house, found the body, and about all the evidence they had collected and what they believed happened.

Jeremy said impatiently, "Thrill kill by an intruder? You actually believe that?" He paused then asked, "Does Travis know about her yet?"

They both shook their heads. Bruce was the one who spoke. "We wanted to talk with you first before we did anything. Travis is out of the country on a news assignment."

Alex added, "I don't know when he will be back, but I do have a number to reach him."

Jeremy asked, "What about Suzanne? What happened to her?"

"She was run off the road."

"She could've just lost control of the car and run off the road. It *was* raining last night, wasn't it? You don't know for sure she was forced off the road."

"Yeah, we do," Alex said proudly.

As he walked to his desk, he said, "I received a message from Suzanne seconds before she died. I know that sounds hokey but it actually was just seconds before. I think when you hear it, you'll agree with Bruce and myself that it's for real."

He hit the button for the speaker phone again, dialed the number, and retrieved the message.

Jeremy stood in rapt attention as Suzanne's frantic words sluiced over the line. They sounded hollowed out in this broad room. They all looked away from Suzanne's wrinkled body; it felt too much as though she were pleading from beyond the grave.

When her voice stopped in mid-sentence, Jeremy leaned forward as

Alex and Bruce had done, expecting and hoping to hear the rest of her broken sentence. Instead Jeremy heard three whispered words.

"Oh my God."

They sounded so eerie down here he could've sworn, just as Alex had, the corpse behind him had actually spoken to them. Upon hearing these words, Jeremy felt as though his ears had been kissed by an invisible wraith. Chills spread over his arms; they multiplied as they scurried down the length of his back and up across his scalp. He involuntarily shivered.

Then the final explosion cut the line to a dead silence.

"And that's all she wrote," Alex said, then punched the button and silenced the speaker line. "I think we're witnesses to her murder."

Jeremy stood in shock. "Edward McDaniel? Why the fuck was she babbling about Edward for?"

"It's pretty apparent that she was warning us that Edward is after us," Alex said.

There was a slight pause as Jeremy and Bruce turned and stared hard at Alex. Alex took turns glancing back and forth between the two.

Suddenly Jeremy burst out laughing. "And that's one hundred percent stupid, Alex. Edward McDaniel is not coming back. He's not after us. The boy is dead."

"We were pretty awful to him growing up," Bruce said, more or less to himself.

"Well, somebody is after us," Alex said raising his voice.

"It seems that way, doesn't it?" Jeremy said. "But it's not Edward McDaniel."

Alex chimed in, "*Seems?* What are you talking about? *Seems?* You heard the recording, didn't you?"

Jeremy said, "Yes, I did. But it's absurd. Shit like this only happens in the movies. Edward's not coming back."

Alex said, "You can do what you want. She's warning us and I'm not going to take the warning lightly."

"Edward back from the dead?" Jeremy asked. "You've got to be shitting me."

Bruce said, "It doesn't have to be a sci-fi version like Alex is talking about. It could be something totally different."

"Like what?" Jeremy said.

Alex began to think hard to come up with a decent idea, "Like… like a…like a distant family member not believing that his drowning was accidental."

"After close to twenty years? Come on now. Why would someone wait that long if it were true?"

"You heard what she said about a patient of hers, didn't you?" Alex said.

"Yes. So."

"Maybe he or she knows the history or something about the incident and is trying to set the record straight."

"That's ridiculous," Jeremy said. "If that's so, why doesn't whoever is doing this just come after me. I'm the one who accidentally caused his death."

"We all were shitty to him at one point or another before that. Maybe that's why he's using all your friends to get to you. That means we all are involved."

Jeremy said, "I think we're getting carried away with this subject. There has to be a logical explanation about this."

"Logical," Alex spat.

"Well it's got to be something, Mr. Spock. Suzanne and Kelly didn't just die; whether it was Edward or someone using that history, somebody killed them. Think about it, two girls who are our best friends both end up dead. On the same night, mind you. What are the chances, right? How weird is that?"

"What are you so quiet about, Bruce?" Jeremy asked.

"Huh?"

Bruce had been in deep thought about Suzanne's warning from beyond the grave. This was actually his fourth time hearing the message. The first time he'd heard it, nothing major jumped out at him from her words. It had just been alarming to him. On the second and third times hearing about "a patient of hers" it began to ring more true. After hearing it a fourth time, there was a major gut feeling about one patient in particular that could be linked to Suzanne and the rest of them.

Tyler Curtis, he thought. Tyler could also be linked to me. I was the one who had saved his life three months earlier. Suzanne had said someone was chasing her. I just gave him a warning about his speeding this morning. *Is it possible that Tyler is the culprit?*

The speed at which Tyler was traveling was a point to be considered, but the main thing that was bugging Bruce it was his missing driver's side rearview mirror and scratches down the side of his Mustang. His mind kept drifting back over the different sounds on the recording. It was disturbing, but he couldn't figure out how Tyler's missing mirror could be tied to Suzanne's death.

Guess I'll just have to do some detective work on my own and try to work this puzzle out.

Jeremy repeated his question. "Why did you get so quiet all of a sudden? Don't tell me you're going along with this guy's scenario."

"Oh nothing. I wouldn't say I agree, but I have been wondering about the same thing," Bruce said.

"Well gentlemen, we can wonder all day about this if we want to, but I really can't waste any more time on this subject. My day is already booked up with personal shit to attend to. I don't know what's going on and frankly, I don't really care. It may not seem like I am but, yes, I am broken up over Kelly and Suzanne's deaths." Jeremy turned to Bruce as he changed the subject at hand. "I will tell you what I want though."

"What's that?" Bruce asked.

"I want you to get me an explanation." Jeremy glanced over at Alex, even though the comment was still directed to Bruce. "A more believable one than what Alex is thinking. An explanation that doesn't revolve around Edward at all. This matter needs to be taken care of and seeing that you have connections on the police force; you're the best candidate for the job. I'm sure they will cooperate with you as you do your own investigating. Can you handle that?"

"Hell yes I can do that."

"And Alex," Jeremy said waiting for his attention. Alex glanced his way. "You might want to stop watching those X-files and Supernatural shows on the television. It'll warp your mind."

Alex sneered at Jeremy.

Jeremy continued, "When are you going to call Travis?"

Bruce and Alex shot a glance at each other then shrugged. The gaze drifted to the floor.

After a moment, Bruce angled his head back up in Jeremy's direction and said, "We were both hoping you would do the honors."

"Me? Why me?"

"You were slightly closer to him than we were when we were in school. It would be better coming from you than one of us."

"There's no honor to have to tell a friend that his wife is dead."

"Somebody has to do it," Alex said.

"Okay, fuck it. Just give me the number; let's get this over with."

Alex pointed to the number on the legal pad on his desk.

Jeremy dialed the number and waited through several long rings. He half-expected to hear a recorded voice telling him to leave a message at the sound of the beep, but he heard, "Hello, Silver Ridge Journal. Travis Sheridan speaking."

"Hey, Travis. Jeremy Taylor here. It's been a while, buddy. How you been doing?"

"Jeremy? Holy shit, man. Doing real good. Oh my God. Jesus, forget about me; how have *you* been?"

"Me personally, not too bad but—"

"But? But what?"

"But…well, I don't know."

"Why, what's wrong?"

Jeremy paused, trying to put the information in the best way possible.

"Jeremy?"

"Ah, yeah, Travis?"

"Am I on speaker phone?"

"Yeah."

"Why is that? Who's there with you?"

"Bruce and Alex."

They voiced their greeting over Jeremy's shoulder.

"Hey guys, where've you been? Having a party without me, huh? I've been missing you guys. We need to get together, you know, drink some beers and play some poker; do some sort of shit together."

"Yeah, we're going to have to do that, Travis."

"Boy, you fuckers sound really glum. What's going on? To what do I owe this honor?"

As Jeremy said before, he said again, "Travis, it isn't really an honor this time. I'm afraid I have some bad news to tell you."

"Why, I mean, what is it?"

Jeremy paused again, trying to formulate the best way to convey his thoughts.

Travis made it easier on all of them by saying, "It's Kelly, isn't it?"

"I'm afraid so, buddy," Jeremy said.

"What's wrong with her?"

"She's—ah, oh Jesus, I'm so sorry to have to tell you man, but Travis, Kelly is dead."

℞

Halfway around the world, Travis Sheridan hung his head and dropped the phone when he heard the news.

For a split second, Travis thought the guys might be playing a trick on him, but that thought didn't last. They always had good ideas for practical jokes; some bordering more toward the evil side of pranks. They had gone through with some of those ideas and wished later that they hadn't. They weren't as close these days as they were during high school. He knew they wouldn't play a trick on him this morbid. Something like this was beyond them.

As Travis watched the phone fall from his hands, he felt his life was falling away from him as well. When it clattered to the hardwood floor, the backing cracked and skittered off to one side. He lived his life completely and utterly for Kelly and she had done the same for him. Since high school, they were inseparable as so many people had said over the years, and now it was all over.

Jeremy, Bruce, and Alex exchanged glances when they heard the phone drop. It sounded the same as when Suzanne dropped her phone on the recorded message, and they held their breath, hoping the connection wouldn't be cut at this point in the conversation.

In the background, they heard Travis whisper to himself, "Oh God" as Suzanne had done during her recorded message.

As Travis stooped to pick the phone back up, he heard Jeremy calling his name over the line.

"I'm here," Travis said in a weak voice. "Sorry. I just dropped the phone."

Jeremy wondered. *What would his life be like now without Kelly?*

"What happened?" Travis asked.

"I would rather tell you in person when you get in."

"You know I can't wait until I get home to find out about Kelly; I would go crazy. How did she die?"

Prolonging the inevitable, Jeremy said, "I assume you will be coming back right away."

"I'm already packing," he said dropping a suitcase on the bed. "How did she die?"

"It's really not a subject to discuss over the phone."

"Jeremy. Quit fucking around," Travis demanded. "Tell me how she died, and you tell me right now."

Jeremy knew he had pushed the matter too far. Travis was agitated; his voice edgy.

Travis continued, "I don't care how bad it hurts. Just tell me."

"Okay Travis, calm down. Give me a second; it's not a pleasant subject for me to discuss."

"Just tell me."

As Jeremy started to explain, Travis was already emptying drawers and stuffing everything in tight. He would be leaving immediately after this phone call, story or no story. He would drop the article and have another journalist finish it up.

When Jeremy began, he didn't spare any details. Alex and Bruce joined in and told what information they knew to give Travis the most detailed story of his wife's outcome. Jeremy told Travis that it couldn't have been an accident, but that they think she was killed by an intruder. They told him they didn't know who did it but they were working to find a suspect. Then, Jeremy told how they found Kelly's body lying at the bottom of the stairs with a broken neck. They didn't tell Travis about the scissors protruding from her chest. Somehow it seemed to graphic for telephone conversation. They could tell him that information when he arrived.

The last comment—the one about Kelly falling down the stairs and breaking her neck—was the final blow in this conversation. It stopped Travis in his tracks, and he lowered himself to the bed. He was aiming for the mattress but missed it completely and continued to slide all the way to the floor. His other hand moved to his forehead, and he started sobbing into his hands.

Jeremy didn't tell Travis about Suzanne's car accident and death. He didn't tell him of their suspicions that the same person that killed Kelly most likely had their sight on them as well. There was no use putting more information on him than he could take.

It is going to take a lot more time to get over this. Jeremy thought.

"You still with us, Travis?" Jeremy asked.

"Yeah," he whispered as he composed himself. He wiped the tear streams away and cleared his throat. "Just give me a second. This is a lot to take in."

"Take your time; we're in no hurry."

"Where are you going to be later tonight?" Travis asked.

"I'll be out and about all day till pretty late, then at the house. You can call me when you arrive."

"All right, let's do it that way. I'll be leaving the hotel within the hour. I don't know when the next flight out will be, but I'll be heading that way when I hang up. I could be there by late tonight or early tomorrow morning.

"That's fine. I'll be waiting for you. Call when you get in."

"All right."

"Hey, Travis."

"Yeah."

"We're going to take care of this asshole for you."

"Oh no, you won't." Travis said. "Whoever did this is mine. I'm taking him out. The son of a bitch is going to pay. Don't do anything until I get into town. I will take care of whoever is responsible for my wife's death. Do I make myself clear?"

Everyone simultaneously agreed and Jeremy said, "If that's what you want, buddy; that's what you'll get. Bruce is doing some investigating; nothing concrete yet," Jeremy lied. "But we'll try to figure out who did this before you blow into town."

"Well, just make sure that's all you do."

Shortly after that, Travis hung up with his three distant friends.

He sat on the bed for a few minutes collecting his thoughts then realized he needed to be on the move. There would be plenty of time to brood on the plane. He packed completely then left for the airport.

It's going to be a long flight home, he thought. *Home. There was no home anymore now that Kelly was gone.*

CHAPTER 25

IT WAS MID-AFTERNOON when Tyler was awakened by the doorbell.

Raven's head jerked up. She jumped down off the couch and padded over to the door to see who it was.

Tyler shook the last of his sleepiness out of his head, grabbed his cell phone, and glanced at it as he shuffled into the foyer.

Raven started her typical half-whine, half-bark of excitement when she saw it was Savannah. All she wanted to do was get to her to show her some affection.

"Hey," Tyler offered squinting against the mid-day sun.

"Why have you been ignoring me?" Savannah asked.

Not knowing how to answer, Tyler squeezed out from between the door and the door jamb and shut the door behind himself leaving Raven to her whining.

"I haven't been ignoring you."

"This makes twice that you've done it. Last night and now earlier today. I am assuming you received my texts."

"Yes. I got them."

"So why haven't you answered me back?"

"I haven't had a chance."

"What have you been doing all day? You certainly haven't been at school. Did you play hooky?"

"Yeah. So. Looks like you did too since it's only around one thirty."

"What, did you just wake up from a nap?"

"As a matter of fact I did. I found Raven. She finally came back, but she looked awful. I took her to the groomer's earlier to get cleaned up."

"That took up your whole day? You have had plenty of time to answer me back with a courtesy text or a phone call. It doesn't take that long. That brings me back to the question I asked earlier. Why have you been ignoring me?"

"Maybe I didn't call or text because I had a feeling I would get this accusatory attitude you have going here. It's not your best trait."

"Well a lot of your bad traits are beginning to come out in you."

"Wow, you don't waste any time do you?" Tyler shot back.

"No, I don't. Not when it comes to this."

Tyler blew out a curt breath of frustrated air. "Look, I'm sorry I beat Patrick up. It's obvious you're still pissed about it and that we don't see eye to eye on this scenario so why don't we just drop it and move on."

"No-no, it goes way beyond that, Tyler. Especially when murder is involved."

"Murder? What the hell are you talking about?"

"Don't play dumb with me. You know exactly what I'm talking about."

"What? Tell me cause right now I'm clueless."

"Then what the hell is this?"

She lifted the piece of paper she'd been holding and snapped it in front of Tyler's face for him to see. It was the photograph of six teenagers.

The memory of what Edward had done late that night after getting home from dealing with Kelly and Suzanne immediately came back to Tyler. His body broke out into a wave of icy fear. Tyler knew of the picture from when Edward had snagged it from the trunk. He realized now that the textbook he must have stuffed it in was his Algebra book.

"What the hell *is* this?" Tyler asked, remaining poker-faced.

Tyler hesitantly took the picture from her grasp and that's when he heard, in the back of his mind, Edward cursing himself for what he'd done. It was a mistake that was now biting both of them in the ass.

Savannah continued. "Suzanne Baldwin. Kelly Sheridan. Our teacher. Your doctor. Their names are on the back. You want to tell me why you have this picture with their heads crossed out in red marker hiding in you Algebra book?"

Tyler spoke naturally before Edward had a chance to put words in his mouth. Tyler decided to go with honesty. He looked up at her and said, "This isn't mine. Where did you find this?"

"I just told you. In your Algebra book."

"Well, I didn't put it there. You think I had something to do with their deaths?"

"The thought has crossed my mind."

"And you actually believe it? Without asking me about it first?"

"I am asking you about it right now."

"No you're not. You're not asking me shit. You're straight up accusing me. I didn't have anything to do with these ladies' deaths. Would you listen to yourself? You're actually accusing me of murder. It's me. Tyler."

"I don't know you, Tyler. I really don't know anything about you. You're new here. I have no idea what your background is. We've just gone out a few times, had some lunches, and dinners together. But that doesn't tell me who you really are. That is not enough time to actually know someone."

"Look, anyone could've harmed those ladies. Anyone. But yet you sound like you are already convinced it was me."

"Because the evidence is right here in front of me."

"What? A photograph with red X's over two people's faces?"

"The same two women that have been murdered. Haven't you been watching the news? How can I think differently?"

"Be objective, for God's sake." He didn't know what else to say. "This isn't mine." He held the picture up in front of her, pointed it at her accusingly, and said, "You say you got this from *my* Algebra book? How do I know someone else didn't put it in there? How do *I* know *you* didn't put it there yourself? You had my Algebra book last. Why did you put this picture there?"

"Don't do that. Don't turn this around on me. That's a cheap shot."

"Sucks, doesn't it. Now you see how I feel."

"What exactly were you doing last night that you couldn't text me back?"

"Oh, Jesus Christ. I'm not going to answer anymore of your questions."

"Why not?"

"Because it's obvious you've got it in for me for some reason. You've already made up your mind. It seems there is nothing I could say to change your mind."

Savannah couldn't argue with his logic. She had come on strong; too strong in fact. Her mind was too locked into her accusations.

"This conversation is just too weird for me. I really can't believe you accused me of doing something like that. It really hurts."

"If you were in my shoes, Tyler, what would you think?"

"Nothing of murder, that's for damn sure. But you think what you want. I can't stop you. Go ahead and turn me in if that's what you want to believe, but I'm not going to talk about this subject anymore with you. I've said my peace."

And with that, Tyler turned on his heals and squeezed back through the door, grabbing Raven as he went.

Savannah was about to say something else, but the door slammed behind Tyler a little harder than normal; then she heard the deadbolt lock into place.

It didn't matter how much she knocked on the door, she knew Tyler wouldn't answer. His mind was made up. Too bad hers wasn't.

She turned and walked back down the stairs and over to her car. She got in, cranked the car, put it in drive, and floored it. All she needed now to help get her out of this gradually depressing mood was speed—and a lot of it. She floored the gas pedal as she left Tyler's neighborhood.

CHAPTER 26

AT THE END of class as the students left for after-school programs or to their prospective homes, Patrick Quinlan ambled down the hallway in a trance. He had carried out most of the day in his current dazed state. He was still shocked that he had lost a fight to the new kid in school.

What a fucking shitheel. What right did he have jumping into my business? I could've taken that little punk kid; I know I could have. I should find that Josh Megilligan dickhead and kick his ass on principle alone. I was assuming too much; assuming I would win. In losing the fight, I lost what respect I had in this school. Now I'm gonna have to start all over again.

With that thought drifting through his mind, he simply pushed a student he was passing into the lockers and kept walking. He didn't even look back.

Caught off guard, the kid said, "Hey, watch it. Oh damn. What the—"

Patrick smiled. *Sounded like that hurt. He should watch where I'm going.*

He shuffled up to his locker and spun its combination dial with his left hand.

His right hand was still throbbing from his misfortunate contact with the locker this morning. He thought his wrist was either broken or sprained; probably the latter because he could still flex his fingers with a minimal amount of pain. His bottom lip had swelled slightly from the sucker punch Tyler had thrown.

Even I have to admit; that was a good move. Didn't even see it coming.

He licked his split lip and it left him wincing from the pain.

The wound on his bottom lip had become chapped from the numerous times he had subconsciously licked the sore throughout the day. Each time the pain stung, it reminded him of the humiliation he had suffered. This in turn made his anger toward Tyler Curtis rise, and he began to seethe even more.

Where is he? I haven't seen that son of a bitch since this morning. Yeah, he'd better be hiding 'cause the next time I see him, I'm going to knock his fucking head off.

When Patrick opened his locker, a white piece of folded notebook paper fell to the floor. It landed face up and he saw his name—PATRICK QUINLAN—written in block letters. He stared at it for a moment then looked up and down the hallway to see if anyone was watching him. There were only a few students left in the corridors but they seemed oblivious to his presence. Even the kid he had shoved into the lockers had cleared out.

He picked up the piece of paper and opened it. The handwriting looked like a child's scrawl and was almost unreadable. Patrick had to sound out some the words as he read the message to himself.

Silver Ridge Lake.
Pier 13.
Midnight tonight.
Come alone.
If I see anyone else besides you…
You won't see me and I'll know you can't be trusted.
Bring the stuff to make a deal.
I'll have enough money.
You know what I'm talking about.
Don't disappoint me.

T.C.

He felt as though he were reading a ransom note from a child abductor or a message from a stalker.

He smiled. "Very mysterious, Mr. Curtis, but not very smart. I can't believe you initialed the note. That tells me who you are and *that's* the equivalent of signing your death certificate."

He glanced up and down the hall again to see if anyone was watching, but he saw no prying eyes.

Patrick had a gut feeling that he should ignore the note. He felt as though it was a portentous message foreshadowing some future catastrophe.

As soon as he got the feeling, he immediately sloughed it off.

He re-read the note again and nodded his head in agreement.

Okay. I'll play by your rules, but don't expect me to be Mr. Nice Guy about it. I'll meet you tonight and we'll see what goes down...or should I say who goes down.

He shoved the note into the back pocket of his jeans and stared at the books he needed for tonight's homework assignments. He gave the homework idea a second thought then slammed his locker and headed home empty handed.

No time for homework today, bitches, he thought. *I have to get ready for tonight's meeting.*

☃

After midnight, a three-quarter moon shimmered off the burnished surface of Silver Ridge Lake. The nearby tree boughs stirred lightly from the cool breezes that swept over the western ridges. Crickets took turns chirping in the high grass and toads droned their never-ending mating calls. An owl asked "who" Patrick was from a neighboring tree. The water lapped continuously at the pier posts and shoreline.

Patrick paced back and forth on the pier. He mouthed a cigarette from its box and lit the end. He took a deep drag.

"Where the fuck is he?" he asked aloud as he nervously rechecked his wristwatch. The watch itself had no built-in light but there was enough moonlight to glare off the placement of the hands when he held his wrist at the correct angle. "Twenty-two after midnight? What the fuck. This is ridiculous."

Patrick had arrived at eleven fifty-two, so he knew he hadn't been late. He doubted Tyler had already been here and left.

Why would he leave before the appointed time? This is all a hoax; I can feel it. I should've known not to trust that little bitch. I swear when he gets here, I'm gonna rip him a new asshole. Guaranteed. No questions asked.

No sooner had he thought those words that headlights blinked through the trees and a car slowly pulled down the narrow path into the parking area.

"Who-who-who-who-who?" the owl hooted again as though curious about who was approaching.

Patrick's heart skipped a few beats as the car approached, and his thought process started running wild.

Yeah, who *is right,* Patrick thought after hearing the owl. *It better not be a fucking cop, that's for damn sure. I would be in deep shit if it is. All this could've been a setup. Didn't think about that. What if Tyler made this appointment but had planned all along to never show up and called the cops instead? I shouldn't have brought the drugs with me. That was really stupid.*

"This better be you, Tyler, that's all I've got to say."

The car stopped near his battered truck. Patrick breathed a sigh of relief when he saw Tyler in the glare of the car's dome light. Tyler emerged from the car and slammed the door then proceeded down the grassy slope onto the pier. Tyler was a lighter shadow among the deeper backdrop of darkness.

When Tyler was in ear-shot, Patrick said, "Where the fuck have you been?" He took another long drag on his cigarette and thumped it out into the water.

"Making sure you kept your end of the deal by not bringing any surprise guests to our little meeting."

"You're late, damnit."

"Hey, take it easy, buddy boy. Don't get your penis in a knot. This rendezvous starts when I'm ready. I made this appointment. You'll play by my rules."

"Let's just get this shit over with. How much money did you bring? And how much do you want?"

"Actually, I didn't bring any money. There's been a huge change of plans. I'm not going to be buying any drugs tonight and neither will anyone else. This meeting was never really about that. I just wanted to talk, and the prospect of a deal was the only way I knew I could get you down here. That or another opportunity to kick my ass. Or both."

Instantly on the defensive, Patrick said, "Look pal, I don't know what you're up to but I didn't come all the way out here for nothing. One thing I know for sure is that you don't like me, and I sure as fuck don't like you. You told me to bring the stuff and we would make a deal. Let's cut the bullshit."

"Patrick, my god, you're so edgy. Loosen up. Enjoy the atmosphere."

The owl hooted again.

Restless, Patrick glanced around at the landscape and said, "What's so great about it? It's fucking spooky out here."

"To you maybe, but this is nothing. I've lived in darkness much deeper than this—much scarier than this—for most of my life now. Guess you could say I'm unaffected by it."

"The fuck's that supposed to mean?"

"That's not important, but you seem like you're close to being scared shitless. I don't know why. There are just as many evils that walk about during the day as there are at night."

"So."

"You probably read a lot of horror stories and watch a lot of horror movies, right?"

"That's none of your damn business."

"I think you do. You seem like the kind of guy that gets off on shit like that."

"Is this conversation going anywhere?"

Edward laughed. "No. Not really, I'm just trying to spook you. I think it's working."

"You're weird, Curtis, really fucking weird. You're acting different tonight than you do in school. It's almost like you're another person."

"You know, my girlfriend said the exact same thing," Edward said laughing. "And you're right. I am someone else; someone totally different from Tyler. It's like night and day between us guys."

351

"Are you going to make a purchase or not? Because if you're not, I'm out of here."

"I'm really not interested in anything you have to sell, Patrick. But—"

"Then what's the point of this meeting?"

Edward took one of his hands from his pocket and held it up to quiet him. "You interrupted me. That's rude. I was going to tell you the two things I *am* interested in."

"Yeah, and what's that?"

Edward held up his index finger and said, "Number one: is seeing that you never sell any type of drugs around here ever again. And number two: is seeing that you never beat up any of your weaker classmates ever again. That's what I'm interested in." Edward's last comment was sarcastic and laced with undertones of pure hatred.

"Fuck you and your interests!"

Patrick tried to push past Edward but Edward placed a gloved hand on Patrick's chest and shoved him back against the handrail.

"You don't have any manners, do you? You can't just leave in the middle of my thought process. What's wrong with you?"

"I don't know what you've got planned for tonight but I'm going to make damn sure it's not going to happen."

Edward heard the familiar sound of a switchblade being extracted from its handle. He glanced down and saw a switchblade in Patrick's right hand. In Patrick's left hand, he gripped a handgun. Edward couldn't tell what make it was, but that really didn't matter. A gun is a gun and can kill if in the wrong hands.

"I see you've brought some more toys with you tonight," Edward said.

"Surprised?"

"Not at all. Can I play too?" Edward asked.

"You didn't think I would come out here in the middle of the night unprepared, did you? I'm not as stupid as you credited me to be."

Edward didn't say a word. He was too intrigued at how the past had come back to him in an instant. The night around Edward suddenly transformed into the warmth of a hot summer day. The memory from nearly twenty years ago came flooding back along with the cool breezes, birds singing, conversation with a gorgeous girl, and punches to his face and stomach and the memory of humiliation. He thought for a second how fate brings everything around into a full circle.

Patrick raised the gun until its cycloptic eye stared Edward down then Patrick started taunting him. "What's the matter, Tyler? Now that I have a gun dead in your face, you're not the talkative type that you were earlier tonight. Why is that?"

Edward cocked his head to the side. The gun was still at point-blank range, but Edward could see Patrick now. No, not Patrick. Patrick's face had changed, and now he saw Jeremy Taylor standing before him holding the gun. He still looked the same as he did on this pier close to twenty years ago.

"Jeremy," Edward breathed in awe. "There you are."

The owl hooted again.

Mimicking the owl, Patrick asked, "Who?"

"I've been waiting a long time to meet up with you again."

Patrick gave a quick look behind himself to see if anyone was there then raised his voice, "What the hell are you talking about?"

For a few seconds, Tyler tried to control the anger that was consuming him. The embers that were burning white hot in Edward's memory flared into an even more intense hatred.

Patrick's answer came in a blur of motion. Edward threw his hand up and knocked the gun away from his face and ducked away from where the gun's muzzle was. When the gun was deflected, it discharged as Patrick anxiously jerked the trigger.

With a flurry of wings, some nearby birds squawked away into the night.

As the gun realigned itself with Tyler's face again, Edward ducked under Patrick's arm and faced away from Patrick. He grabbed Patrick's wrist with both hands and jerked down hard. Patrick's arm caught on Edward's shoulder and cracked at the elbow joint. It folded backward and down in a forty-five degree angle.

Patrick let out a squeal of abject misery as his elbow joint splintered and his tendons snapped. His cry was actually louder than the gun blast had been.

Worrying more about his arm than anything else, Patrick released his gun and the switchblade from his hands. They clattered to the pier decking. Tyler kicked the gun out of the way, and it slid down the dock toward the cars. Then Edward moved to face Patrick once again. Without pausing, he punched Patrick in the center of his chest as hard as he could. The force of the punch knocked Patrick back toward the end of the quay. He shuffle-stepped as he tried to regain his balance and catch his breath all at the same time. The handrail caught Patrick in the middle of the back. It splinter under his weight but didn't break through. As Patrick tried to regain his balance, Edward rushed over, bent down, grabbed Patrick's pant legs then jerked them up and pulled them toward himself. Patrick was jerked up horizontally to the pier and hovered in mid air for a second before he landed squarely on his back. His head thumped the wooden slats, and unconsciousness threatened to take him under.

Patrick immediately felt a few rough slaps to his face, which caused his mind to clear. He heard Tyler say, "C'mon, Jeremy, stay with me."

Jeremy? Why does he keep calling me Jeremy? Doesn't he know my real name?

"I have to admit; you're one of the smarter dealers. You didn't get hooked on the stuff like a lot of the others dealers do, did you? You know what acid, marijuana, ecstasy and all that other shit you sell can do to a person, don't you? You've probably seen most of the effects from it, but you've never taken any of it yourself, have you? You sell this crap to other students, even smaller kids in school, knowing they'll get hooked on it and ruin their lives. But that never stopped you, did it?"

Patrick heard the familiar sound of metal on metal. He slowly turned his head in its direction and saw his extended switchblade. It was his knife Tyler had kept this morning after their fight was over.

"No. Please. Don't."

"Don't beg. Begging is for cowards. Begging won't do you any good now, Jeremy."

"Jeremy? My name isn't Jeremy!" Patrick yelled. "Why do you keep calling me that?"

"Time for you to own up to what you did to me."

"Me? If anyone did anything, it's *you*. You won the fight today. What more do you want me to say? Or do? You want me to say I'm sorry? Okay then here goes; I'm sorry." Noticing no change in Tyler's demeanor, he asked more urgently. "Tell me what you want!"

Still seeing the personification of Jeremy before him, Edward said, "You can't give me what I want. I want back the past eighteen years of my life that you took from me so I can live them to their fullest. I want to be alive again—*as me*—in my own body, but that's purely impossible. You took my life, and the only alternative is for me to take yours. Only then will we be able to call it even." Edward held it up in front of Patrick's startled eyes so he could see it up close and personal. "You remember this knife?" he asked.

Patrick looked from the knife to Tyler and then back to the blade again; then he nodded.

Edward continued, "You remember me telling you I was going to give it to you later?"

Patrick was still cradling his mangled arm. He was breathing hard and he swallowed as though something he was eating didn't taste quite right. Patrick nodded, then in a raspy voice he managed to say, "Yeah, I remember."

"Well, I always make good on my promises. I'm going to finish what *you* started. This morning Savannah stopped me and it's a good thing he did. But tonight's an entirely different story. Savannah won't be able to succeed this time."

Patrick wore a bemused look on his face again. "Why do you keep referring to yourself as someone else? You are Tyler."

"That's a big negative there. I'm Edward. Edward McDaniel. Guess I forgot to introduce myself."

Edward slowly brought his clenched fist—that was still wielding Patrick's switchblade—higher into the moonlit sky.

Patrick's eyes followed the knife and saw the moonlight caress the edge of the serrated blade as it poised above him.

"Wait. What are you doing?"

"Doing what I wanted to do this morning in the hallway before Savannah stopped me."

But Edward no longer had time for chit-chat. His fist fell in a blinding flash and the blade entered Patrick's chest, cutting off his scream.

Tyler lost it and screamed inside himself. It was so insane, inhuman, and filled with fear and hate of what Edward had made him do. The cry rolled from Tyler's mouth, out over the calm water, and echoed back once it hit the distant ridges.

Only when Tyler was finally out of breath did he stifle his cry and breathed in again. Tears had burst from Tyler's eyes as the guilt of killing someone washed over him.

For a few seconds, everything was deathly silent except the water slapping against the pier posts. No animal or insect moved or made a sound. Then, one by one, the crickets started playing their treble fiddles and the toads began blowing their bass notes and the night's orchestra was once again in full song.

Tyler finally opened his eyes. He saw his gloved death grip on the switchblade that was now protruding from the center of Patrick's chest. Tyler forced himself to let go of the handle. He stood as though in a daze and backed up until he felt the handrail in his lower back.

In a flooding instant, Edward washed through Tyler and took hold of him again. Tyler knew Edward was pissed, but neither said anything.

Edward moved to Patrick in a rush. He checked all of Patrick's pockets quickly and thoroughly. In his jacket pocket, he found the stash of drugs. He left them there.

Whoever finds Patrick might think this is a drug deal that went bad. I can only hope, Edward thought.

In a continued search of Patrick's pants pockets, Edward found the note he'd scrawled and stuck in Patrick's locker earlier that day. Edward took it out and shoved it deep into his back pocket.

Thank God for small favors, Edward thought again. *I'll have to dispose of that later.*

Finding nothing else, he gripped the sides of Patrick's jacket, jerked him to his feet, pulled him closer and stared into his face. Jeremy's face had disappeared; now all he saw was Patrick again.

Just wanting to be rid of him, Edward spun Patrick's limp body around in a counter-clockwise direction to gain some momentum; then pitched him toward the end of the pier that was only a few steps away. Patrick's dead weight slammed through the already weakened banister, fell off the edge and splashed into his watery grave.

The body surfaced face down. It drifted about ten feet from the pier then stopped.

What did that accomplish? Tyler finally asked from within.

It accomplished a lot.

Like what?

Consider this a lesson plan, Tyler.

What?

Edward had been anticipating Tyler to try and stop him tonight the way he had with Kelly and Suzanne last night and then Patrick earlier this morning. But tonight, he'd been ready. Each time Tyler tried something, Edward was right there to counter his movement. Even though he was able to sustain Tyler tonight, there was one thing that shook him to his core.

The scream. Yes, the scream, Edward thought.

It was just another way Tyler had broken his possession. It didn't matter how hard Edward tried, he couldn't quite hold Tyler back. Maybe it was because he didn't have his full spirit with him. A part of himself was in Raven and keeping him docile. Whatever the reason, it was going to become harder and harder to control Tyler if he continued this quest for Jeremy.

I'm going to give you a piece of advice, Tyler.

What's that?

You really like that Savannah chick, don't you?

Yeah. Why?

If you interfere one more time with anything I try to do, I'll kill her, and I won't think twice about it.

You wouldn't dare.

You saw what I did to Patrick just now, didn't you?

See? Uh yeah. I was right here, wasn't I? I feel like I just killed Patrick myself.

Uh-huh. Remember that. He's a floating corpse now. How would you deal with it if you felt as though you just killed Savannah? I have no problem with dreaming up how I would do away with her. Do we understand each other?

Tyler wasn't going to answer.

I asked you a question. Do-we-understand-each-other?

Yes, we do.

Good, now let's get the hell out of here.

Edward checked to make sure there was no other evidence lying around that might incriminate him. There was probably something he had overlooked because everything had happened so fast. He double checked in his mind if there was anything he could think of that could link Patrick's death to him. The only thing he could think of was today's fight in school.

When his body is found, questions will be raised. The only thing they have to go by is word of mouth. There are no fingerprints to link me with his death. I was smart enough to wipe the blade clean earlier today and to wear gloves tonight. And there was nobody around to witness this murder.

"I was," Tyler said.

Right. You won't turn yourself in; you're not that stupid. Just remember what will happen to Savannah if you try anything out of the ordinary.

Tyler didn't answer.

Feeling everything was as perfect as he could make it, Edward strolled toward his car. On his way, he picked up the revolver and the other switchblade that was dropped when Patrick's arm was broken. Giving no thought to the switchblade, Edward flung it as hard as he could out into the lake without giving it a second thought.

Looking at the gun, he thought, *Huh, who knows, I might need this later on down the road.*

He placed the gun in his jacket pocket then whistled the rest of the way to his car.

The last thing Edward heard as he stepped into his Mustang was the owl asking his redundant question over and over and over again. Apparently, the owl was the only witness to tonight's madness and had stayed to watch the scene unfold in its entirety.

PART THREE: BLOODLINE

Subconscious choices are made by whispers of coercion.

-Excerpt from *Macabre Dreams* by Wofford Lee Jones

CHAPTER 27

IT WAS A crisp morning when Bruce Saliers drove his unmarked police car off of Berkley Avenue onto Stockheed Highway. The sun flared off the back windows of the few cars that already possessed the highway, temporarily blinding him. Bruce put on a pair of mirrored sunglasses to subdue the glare.

Bruce whistled then said, "It's going to be a hot one today, people."

Bruce was headed into police headquarters. He was currently driving over Half Mile Bridge that crossed a smaller portion of Silver Ridge Lake; it connected the city of Silver Ridge to the other out lying communities and the neighborhood where he lived.

As he reached the other side of the bridge, a flash of blue caught his peripheral. He realized it was a blue truck and continued to follow it as it appeared and disappeared behind the flanks of trees between him and the truck. It was sitting in the small parking area under some low hanging spruce limbs. Bruce probably would have missed it if the sunbeams hadn't flared off of the side panels of the parked vehicle.

"It's nine o'clock in the morning parents; do you know where your kids are?" he asked aloud.

His immediate thought was that maybe two students had skipped class and had come out here to hang out or make out.

"Doing a little fooling around before third period is underway, huh?" he said chuckling to himself.

He pulled into the parking area and drove as slowly and as cautiously as possible. Even though he thought it might be two students having sex, he could be mistaken. Every situation heeded caution.

He remembered other occasions when he had caught teenagers on the weekends. The blush of embarrassment on the girls' faces as they hurried to cover themselves. The expression of shock on the boys' faces when they realized their secret hideout had been discovered. It was always the classic look of guilt after they were caught with their hands in the proverbial cookie jar.

"Crazy kids," he muttered to himself. "Don't they know better? If you want sex so bad, just get a room at the nearest Motel 6. It would definitely be more comfortable."

Bruce opened his door and stepped out as he surveyed the tree line to see if anyone was lurking nearby. He knew the chances of that were slim, but looks in any situation could be deceiving.

"You never know when you could be walking into a drug deal, a rape situation, or even a murder," he whispered to himself.

But he heard no scream or other tell-tale signs of mischief. It was pretty quiet except for the passing of cars on the nearby highway. For all he knew, someone could be down by the lakeside fishing. Bruce unbuckled the clasp that held his gun in his holster in case the circumstances proved needful for fire power.

Disappointed, he found the Ford empty.

"Damn," he muttered. "Even though the truck is unoccupied, that's no sign for me to let down my guard."

He searched around the truck for any clue that would tell the location of the owner. He decided that the answer would reveal itself nearer to the lake, so he ventured toward the pier area.

Bits of trash that had been left by irresponsible users of the picnic area and teenagers that hung out here late at night blew across the grass.

He walked toward the dock as he thought about the situation. There were a couple of small fishing boats in the distance, but the mystery truck would've needed a hauler to pull a boat here.

Bruce walked to the end of the pier. He was trying to figure out where the owner would have gone if he weren't here to fish.

That's when Bruce noticed part of the banister's handrail was missing.

"That's not good," he said, examining the broken areas closer. "Someone could fall in. Maybe even drown."

He turned around on the dock to survey the area at a different perspective.

This section of the park was closed off from the other properties. There were three roofed picnic sheds and various other picnic tables underneath the shade of the trees. The children's recreational areas were built to the side at the top of a grassy slope.

As he walked back down the quay toward his patrol car, he spotted an object that he had missed when walking down the pier the first time. The object was partially exposed, floating underneath the dock. As he looked closer, he saw an arm and realized...

"No, no, no. Shit, another body. Fuck. Leave it to me to find the prize of the day."

The body floated face down in the water. The body's arms were splayed out to the side of the body and the legs were slightly submerged underwater.

Even as he noticed the body, he was already leaning down through the balustrade and grabbing a handful of the figure's clothing with his left hand.

All his sense of caution left him, and helping the figure was his only focus. He cursed aloud as he pulled the limp body out from under the pier.

He scooped a hand up under the right shoulder to secure the body, and then quickly slid his left hand under the boy's left shoulder. Bruce rotated his body so he was kneeling over and pulled the limp body up on the wooden decking.

The boy's head flopped back and banged on the pier.

"Oh shit. Sorry, man."

When Bruce leaned back to survey the body, he noticed the knife protruding from the center of his chest. There was a faded red stream of blood coming from the knife wound.

The boy's face and complexion were ashen, but his lips were a dark purple. The teen's eyes were open, gazing through him. Bruce shuddered.

Even though Bruce knew the boy was dead, he continued feeling the figure's wrists and neck for possible vital signs.

Finally realizing it was hopeless, Bruce called dispatch by way of his shoulder radio mic. He reported his findings and asked that someone be sent to pick up the body.

Bruce thought of the night three months ago when he had found the body of Tyler Curtis. He had saved that boy's life. He now felt helpless that he couldn't do anything for this one.

ဆ

Bruce Saliers sat in his patrol car under the shade of an ancient pine tree and surveyed the empty sight from a distance.

Even though it was a sunny day, the sunshine didn't offer any warmth to him or the scene that stretched out before him. This area seemed like it had morphed into a dead-of-winter-landscape view minus the snow. It looked and felt cold, bleak, and lifeless.

The forensic guys had already come, walked the scene, gathered what little evidence they could find, and were now gone again. Yellow police banners that marked the crime scene fluttered in the mid-morning breeze. The roped-off area seemed hollow and drab as though the remnants of the dead boy still lingered even after the body had been carried away.

As he stared, previous thoughts began to sift through his mind.

Bruce didn't know which situation was worse; finding a body such as Tyler Curtis that had a miracle-chance of surviving or finding this other body that hadn't been identified yet, but had been dead—by his estimation—for close to twelve hours. Both situations had been devastating and had a severe effect on his mind.

Bruce shuddered as the scene from this morning briefly flashed through his mind again.

There was nothing else he could do here. Bruce looked away from the lake scene and cranked his car. He pulled out of the parking lot onto the highway and headed toward the high school.

From the moment he had found the dead boy's body until the EMS unit had driven away with it, this day had already been taxing. He found that he was mentally and physically drained. From the viewing of the crime scene to the non-stop questions the EMS and a few mid-morning joggers had asked, Bruce had been distracted from his previous suspicions.

One main thought that had been gnawing at the back of his mind wasn't even about the dead boy he'd just found. This so-called "hunch" was that he knew Tyler Curtis was lying when he asked him about his missing rearview mirror. Something wasn't right with the information he had told him. Naturally, Bruce had questions about the situation, and even though he had no proof, Bruce knew Tyler had lied through his perfectly aligned teeth.

"It seems odd that Tyler would lie since I'm the one who found him after his car accident," Bruce said to himself. "Everyone around town swears that I saved his life. He knows I'm the one who rescued him. You would think he would have a little more trust in someone who had done that for him. But would that be enough for him *not* to lie to me?" Bruce shook his head, answering his own question, "No. He lied to me because he's hiding something. I'd bet my life on it."

Bruce continued to drive in a thoughtful haze. He wondered about the phone call Suzanne had made to Alex shortly before she lost control of her car. After he had listened to the information on the tape repetitively, he had come up with his working conclusion.

His brow wrinkled in amusement as he shook his head. "Backing into the garage door?" Even though it sounded absurd, that was the story Tyler was sticking with, at least for the moment. Bruce thought, *How could a person back into a garage and get so close to it that they clip off the rearview mirror and scuff the doors like that? With a Mustang like Tyler has? You would really have to* not *be paying attention for that to happen. For that matter, how could a person in a high speed car chase get so close that he emerges from the incident missing only the side mirror and their car receiving a couple of bad scratches down the length of the car but no other major damage?* "High speed car chase," Bruce said, laughing. "Sounds so absurd." He pressed his lips together in confirmation, "No, his story was too far-fetched. Mr. Curtis is trying to cover something up."

Tyler told a good lie, there was no doubt about that, but Bruce's first impression of his story was that it had been too well thought out. It was as though he was covering up something bigger, and he had already figured a story out in case someone asked.

This day was turning out to be one of the worst days Bruce had ever had on the force. Silver Ridge was an area that had a low crime rate. Sure, it had its share of crime and more each year since it was growing into a metropolis, but Silver Ridge was low on crime compared to other areas of the United States.

Bruce could do any number of things right now to get to the bottom of this matter. He could bring Tyler in for questioning. And depending on where he was at the time, that would most likely result in a scene. He would then take him to the station and interrogate him to figure out if he had anything to do with the three recent deaths. But if his hunches were wrong, he could get into some serious trouble from his allegations. No, Bruce figured he would play this out and get some more evidence to support his hunches before he accused anyone of anything.

When he pulled into the school parking lot, he surveyed the grounds for Tyler's car. Classes seemed to still be in session, but he could see a few students milling about.

He drove up and down between the rows of cars until he finally spotted Tyler's red Mustang sitting toward the end of the parking lot. It was the only car here missing a driver's side rearview mirror with racing stripe scratches. Bruce even noticed that the scratches had silver highlights. Could be the same color of Suzanne's Mercedes.

He pulled to a stop behind an old, dented Jeep with mud-caked tires and turned the engine off. As Bruce stepped out, he nonchalantly looked around to see if anyone had a curious eye trained on him.

"Good. No one's around." Bruce said to himself. "Let's get this shit over as soon as possible. I don't want to have to explain myself to anybody. All I need is a few pieces of metal from the housing that held the mirror in place so I can compare it to the ones found at Suzanne Baldwin's wreck site. If they matched, it would be positive—or at the very least a very good chance—Tyler Curtis is a murderer."

What about a search warrant, hot shot? Bruce though to himself as he stepped our of his car. *Aren't you forgetting about that?*

Even though he asked himself those questions, he knew he should get one just to cover his ass and all the bases; to do things by the book. He shook his head, not really wanting to think about that right now.

The evidence is going to be right there in plain site, he thought again to himself. *But then again, I am really not the main investigation officer. I don't really have a right to be here. I'm just doing this on my own, on the side, for Suzanne. Shit, it's too much of a gray area to really decide. I have to go with my gut instinct right now. There's not enough time. Tyler's going to get his car fixed any day now. I have to get what I can now and quick before it's gone for good; just to be safe. Then I'm getting the hell out of here. If I get in trouble for no search warrant, I'll face that music if it ever starts playing.*

Bruce remembered how a man was convicted for a hit and run incident. The man had been driving under the influence of alcohol and had hit a jogger. The jogger died shortly after he had been hit, but the police were able to track down the drunken driver because the jogger had been hit so solidly that part of the man's license plate number had been imprinted into his skin. The police ran a search on the partial number and came up with a few possibilities. They checked out all the plate numbers, narrowed them down, and apprehended the guy the same day.

Bruce thought, *It's funny how the little, seemingly insignificant things in a crime are the ones that end up telling on the person.*

Bruce knelt between a Volkswagon Beetle and the Mustang to observe what was left of the mirror's housing. He pressed and prodded the metal, but there weren't any loose pieces he could pry away. There never was a simple way of doing anything anymore.

After he hurriedly broke two pieces off, he fished inside his shirt pocket for a plastic evidence bag and stuffed the pieces inside. Retrieving the other bag of pieces found at the wreck site, he held them up beside each other.

A broad smile spread across his face as he stood and said, "I've got you by the balls now, Mr. Curtis. This is all the evidence I need to convict you. Now all I have to do is get these metal fragments examined by a professional and see where that road leads. Enter Alex Riley," Bruce said, chuckling to himself. He continued with his thoughts. *Alex can tell me if they truly match. Of course, having Alex test this evidence may make it admissible in court, but that is just a chance I'll have to take.*

"Who are you, and what are you doing?" a voice asked from behind him.

Bruce's body when rigid. His smile faded quicker than it had been pasted on his face. "Shit," Bruce whispered. As he turned, expecting to face Tyler, Bruce said to himself, "This day just keeps getting better and better."

Two boys stood by the bumper of the Jeep with their arms folded over their chests waiting patiently for an answer.

Bruce hadn't heard them approach; he had been too engrossed in collecting the evidence. Bruce's mouth was open in surprise; realizing he didn't have an answer, he quickly closed it again. He folded the ends of the bags around themselves and shoved them into his pocket as he cleared his throat. Bruce chose to take the easy way out and smiled. "For a minute there, I thought you were Tyler himself. What's your name?"

"I asked you first," Derrick said standing his ground.

"That doesn't matter," Bruce said taking a few steps closer to the two boys. "I'll ask again, who are you?"

Derrick didn't reply. He was going to stand his ground.

Not wanting to cause any trouble, Cass blurted, "I'm Cass. He's Derrick."

Derrick gave Cass a backhanded slap on the arm, "Don't volunteer information to him you dick; he's a cop." To Bruce he asked, "We caught you red-handed, didn't we officer?"

We've got ourselves a smart-ass here, Bruce thought. Ignoring his comment, Bruce said, "I wouldn't say that, Derrick."

"Cass told you who we were, now it's your turn. Who are you?"

"Bruce Saliers."

Derrick gave him a curt nod, silently acknowledging him.

Bruce thumbed a hand motion toward the Mustang, "Is this Tyler Curtis's car?"

"It depends."

"On what?"

"On who wants to know, and why they want to know it."

Bruce took a deep, irritated breath.

Derrick smiled slightly and thought, *Like an ant under a magnifying glass on a sunny day.* He knew he was getting under Bruce's skin.

Bruce wasn't going to put up with any of Derrick's pansy-ass bullshit.

"The *who* is me, and the *why* is none of your business. Just answer my questions, and there won't be any trouble."

Not wanting to push the law too far, Derrick said, "Yeah. It's Tyler's car, but something tells me you've already determined that."

"You know Tyler?"

Cautiously nodding his head, Derrick said, "Yeah. I guess you can say that. We've talked to him. We're not best friends or anything like that, but he's an acquaintance of ours. He was in the hospital for awhile, so we haven't been able to get to know him that well."

Ignoring the last of his sarcastic statement, Bruce said, "I know. He was in a car wreck. I was the one who found him the night of his accident."

Derrick raised his eyebrows and nodded in agreement.

Bruce asked, "Has Tyler Curtis acted out of character at any time since he was released from the hospital?"

"If we knew of something, what you're wanting us to do is rat out our friend?"

"Just a minute ago you were calling him an acquaintance. All of a sudden he's a friend? Which is it, Derrick?"

"Look, I don't know what you're getting at with Tyler. He certainly hasn't been acting strange. Is that what you're looking for? Even if he was, I probably wouldn't tell you. Something isn't right with you and this situation. What were you doing to Tyler's car, anyway?"

"Nothing you need to concern yourself with and nothing that I have to explain to you. This is an official police investigation. I can't go into any more detail about it at this time."

"Can't or won't?" Derrick asked.

"Both. That's all you need to know."

"Of course, I figured as much. Do you have some sort of paperwork disclosing you to be able to search his car? I would be more than happy to give it to Tyler for you."

Bruce ignored his comment but said, "His missing rearview mirror was what concerned me."

Pressing the issue, Derrick said, "You know, you could be indicted for that," Derrick said.

Bruce laughed at the thought of being indicted for something so trivial. He shook his head at Derrick then swept his hand back toward Tyler's car. "I'm not going to be indicted over this."

Derrick gave him a sneer and said, "You don't have a search warrant? Haven't you ever heard of the Exclusionary Rule?"

Cass's mouth dropped open and he turned to look at Derrick because of the nerve of him challenging this cop.

Bruce didn't like Derrick's comeback line. He flexed his jaw muscles, then stepped forward and said, "You threatening me, son?"

Derrick didn't flinch; he just calmly stood his ground. He had really pushed Bruce's buttons that time.

Bruce stepped forward again to emphasize his point. "I'll put it to you plain and simple. You don't want to tangle with me. The fewer waves there are, the better the boat ride. Understand what I'm saying?"

Derrick and Cass didn't reply.

Bruce continued, "If you feel like I am violating Tyler's Fourth Amendment rights and you want to do your civic duty and report me, that is your right. Feel free to do so." To emphasize his point even more, he pointed at his badge that was stuck to his chest and tapped it lightly with his index finger. "I don't need paperwork. This is all the disclosure I need, and I don't have to answer to you or anybody else unless they are a higher power than me."

"We'll see what Tyler has to say about that when he gets here."

Bruce countered, "It wouldn't matter; besides I've wasted enough time here already talking with you. I've got what I came for." He stepped between them, bumping them out of the way in the process and calmly walked back to his car without giving them another look.

Bruce was about to step into his car when Derrick called after him, "We're going to report this."

Bruce stood with one arm on the roof of the car and the other perched on the open car door, thinking for a moment. Then he quickly leaned inside for a moment, stood, and then shut the door again. He started back toward the boys with a small piece of paper with him.

"Good. You do that, Derrick. Report me," Bruce said as he held his personal business card up in front of Derrick's face. "When you report me to whoever you're going to tell, make sure you spell my name right so they get in touch with the right person. You can even give them my card if you wish; I have no problem with that. But if you want to do the wise thing, keep my card and contact me if you happen to think of anything about Tyler that might be a little off kilter."

As soon as Derrick had grasped the business card from Bruce, he turned without saying another word.

Back at the car, Bruce turned and winked at Derrick. Smiling at them one last time, he eased into his car and slammed the door. He drove slowly out of the school parking lot, turned the corner, and was gone.

Cass waited until the police cruiser was out of sight before he lit into Derrick. "What in the hell is wrong with you? What the fuck were you thinking? Just exactly where was your head? Was it up your ass, because that was a really asinine thing to do. Don't you know you can go to jail for mouthing off to an officer like that?"

"Ease up, Cass. You're just as bad as my mom. You saw how guilty he was when I asked him what he was doing. We caught him red-handed doing something that he had no business doing. He was violating Tyler's rights as a human being. He wouldn't do anything to us 'cause we had him by the balls. Not that I really want to have him by the balls."

"I just think you're stupid for doing that. Mouthing off to a cop? You know how retarded that was?"

"Get off it, Cass. I did what I thought had to be done. These cops that think they own the world. They hide behind their badges to protect themselves when they break the law. That pisses me off."

"Okay," Cass said holding up his hands in defense. "Forget I said anything." He paused then said, "That was pretty cool, though. I have to hand it to you, that was pretty awesome."

They laughed about if for a moment then were solemn as they thought about why a cop was interested in Tyler's car.

Cass asked, "Where did you learn all that lingo you were throwing at the cop?"

Derrick laughed and said, "I watch a lot of court TV."

"You really gonna report him?" Cass asked.

"I don't know. Gonna wait and see what Tyler wants to do. If he does, then yeah; probably."

They waited around for Tyler to keep the cop from possibly circling around to gather more evidence from the Mustang. Finally, they saw Tyler approaching and leaned against their cars waiting for him.

Tyler noticed the smug look on Cass and Derrick's faces as he neared. Their squinted, suspicious eyes had a trace of confusion.

"What's the look for?" Tyler asked.

"I don't know, buddy; you tell me." Derrick said putting the ball back in his court.

"Tell you what?" Tyler chuckled as he braced himself for some practical joke. "What are you talking about?"

"How about, why?" Cass suggested.

"Why what?"

"Why would a cop be snooping around your car? More to the point, what did you do to warrant a cop to snoop around your car?"

Edward immediately took over. He'd been expecting some questions to be asked but not this soon. He played dumb to their questions. "Cop? What cop?"

"Yeah, dumbass, a cop," Derrick confirmed. "We found him snooping around your car about ten minutes ago. He even left us his business card. Wasn't that nice of him? He wanted us to call him in case we notice you doing anything that was *off kilter*. His words, not mine." Derrick held the card up in front of Tyler's face so he could read it. "That name ring a bell?"

Reading the name, Tyler said, "Bruce Saliers. Yeah, that was the guy that—"

"—rescued you the night of your accident," Derrick said, interrupting. "Yeah, yeah. He made damn sure we both knew that. He thought we might be a little more lenient to his breaking the law if we knew he saved your life. Like that would somehow make what he was doing *un-illegal*."

"Did you ask him what he was doing and why he was doing it?"

"Yeah,"

"What did he say?"

"Nothing concrete," Cass interjected. He motioned to Tyler's car.

"Although he was messing around with what is left of your missing side view mirror. While we are on the subject, why is it missing? It totally ruins the new look of your Mustang."

Inside, Edward was getting upset and that was making Tyler nervous.

"But I explained all that to him yesterday when he pulled me over for speeding," Tyler said.

"You got a speeding ticket?" Cass said. "Dude!"

"No, he just gave me a verbal warning, but he was asking me some heavy questions about why my rearview mirror is missing." Tyler paused for a moment then said, "Sorry. I'm just upset, that's all. I was pissed yesterday morning when I left school and I wasn't paying attention to the speed limit." His anger was directed toward himself for being careless. "What exactly did he want?"

Derrick and Cass took turns telling what happened as they remembered it.

"He wouldn't give us a straight answer when we asked him," Cass said. "He kept babbling on and on about how it was an *official police investigation*."

"Investigation?"

"Again, his words, not mine."

Tyler shook his head. "I don't know. I have no idea what this guy is up to. It's enough to make anyone nervous."

"If it's about the cop," Derrick said. "I wouldn't worry about him, he can't do anything. He didn't even have a search warrant to search your car. Any evidence attained that way can't be entered in court."

Cass bursted out laughing, "What are you saying? What is this? Court? Evidence? Listen to yourself, Derrick, you sound like Tyler's committed murder or something."

A sudden silence fell over the three of them. They paused and looked at Tyler as they imagined the unimaginable.

Tyler jerked his head back in astonishment that they were even entertaining the idea. "What?"

"You didn't, *did* you?" Derrick asked.

"Do what?"

"Murder someone?"

Only because they really deserved it, Edward thought.

"Oh, for crying out loud; no; of course not. Don't be ridiculous. That's absurd." Tyler looked at both of them as they stared back. "Oh, come on, you don't actually believe this Bruce character do you? He's obviously got his wires crossed or his screws loose."

They continued to quietly stare at him.

He held his hands up as if to surrender, "This is getting stale. Screw this and fuck you. I don't need this in my life right now."

He walked to his car, threw his book sack in the passenger's seat then turned back and approached them again. "You know something? I haven't been here that long, I mean as far as *really being here.* I finally wake up from a coma and three months of my life are gone." He slapped his hands together. "BAM! Just like that. Just fucking gone. My relationship with Savannah is three months behind because of that accident. Three months that I haven't been able to learn about her and get to know her likes and dislikes. I haven't been able to really hang out with you guys. I don't know about you, but that's a hard thing for me to accept and get over." He placed his hands on Cass and Derrick's shoulders, "I'm not gay, you guys, so don't take this the wrong way. I really like you guys. I already consider you my best friends. I've also missed three months being with you guys as well. I haven't got to hang out with you and drink some beers, go to the movies or hang out; you know, just doing the regular everyday guy stuff. I haven't been able to be involved with any of the fucking football games for Christ's sake. I've really missed that. I hope you were just joking about that earlier comment because I can't believe you're even entertaining the idea that I would have anything to do with someone else's death. Murder?" he asked again chuckling at the thought. "That's a fucked up idea. I'm out of here."

He turned and headed back toward his car again.

"Tyler. Don't go," Cass said stepping toward him.

Tyler stopped in his tracks with his back to them. Inside Tyler, Edward grinned. Tyler's skin curved into a wry smile.

That was way too easy, Edward thought.

When he turned back to them he wore had a serious but hurt look on his face.

Edward was having fun switching the infinitely different faces to manipulate his friends. *If they only knew*, Edward thought.

"You're right, that was a crazy notion," Derrick said. "I didn't mean anything by it."

Cass agreed, "Yeah, man. That was pretty stupid."

Derrick followed suit. "Yeah, me too.

"You guys are crazy, you know that?" Edward said. "Are we going to get something to eat or what?"

"Why not? I could eat," Cass said. "Pizza? Can we do pizza?"

"I don't see why not."

"You're feeling better all of a sudden," Derrick said.

"This is what I'm talking about. This is what I've been wanting to do. I'm not going to worry about all that until there is something to worry about."

"That's the spirit," Derrick said. "Where are we eating; Tyler's buying."

"Oh hell no, I'm not. You should be buying mine as an apology for what you guys just accused me of."

"Damn, I said I was sorry. What more do you want?"

"I want you to buy my food, bitch."

"Okay, okay, I guess I deserve that," Derrick said giving in, "I'll get yours this time, but you can't pull that guilt gun on me next time."

"Oh no, next time it will be Cass's turn to buy my dinner."

Cass said, "Talk about using and abusing your friends."

They all laughed as they got in their prospective cars and exited the school grounds.

As they drove away, Edward's smile slowly drained away from his face and his thoughts returned to Bruce.

You shouldn't stick your nose in where it doesn't belong, Bruce. Didn't anyone ever teach you that? Well, you're about to get a one-on-one personal lesson. And you're going to find out first hand that if you stick your nose where it doesn't belong, sooner or later it's bound to get cut off.

CHAPTER 28

AFTER A FEW slices of pizza with the boys, Tyler had come straight home. Tyler had just stepped out of his parked car and slammed the door when he heard two quick beeps from Savannah's car horn. He threw a hand up and gave a non-committal wave then locked his car. Seeing Savannah, Edward was immediately on edge.

Savannah pulled behind him and jumped out of her VW Beetle.

Edward decided to let Tyler have as much of himself as he could get away with in case Savannah started asking more questions. Edward didn't want to answer any of the questions if he could help it. He didn't want to inadvertently cause Tyler to look guilty.

"What did I do this time?" Tyler began.

"I don't know. You tell me," Savannah replied.

"Again, and for the last time, I haven't done anything. Is that the way it's going to be between us? Always thinking I did something or accusing me of something I didn't do."

"I hope not but I wanted to ask you about it this time rather than what I did last time. I went about everything the wrong way, and I'm sorry."

Tyler ignored her apology and said, "I'm afraid to ask but here goes. What did you want to ask me?"

She paused, not knowing how to word her question, then said, "Did you have anything to do with Patrick Quinlan's stabbing?"

"Stabbing?" Tyler said, playing dumb to her accusation. "No. What? Patrick's dead too?"

Savannah just stood there saying nothing, staring deep into his eyes trying to read his face.

Tyler opened out his hands palm up, shrugged his shoulders, and gave her a look as though he had no idea what she was talking about.

"You mean you didn't know?"

"No," he lied. "Why should I?"

"Because Patrick was killed in pretty much the same way you seemed like you wanted to end your fight at the school yesterday."

"What are you talking about? Why are you asking me anything about him in the first place?"

"Because you had a fight with him yesterday. During the fight it sure looked like you wanted to stab the shit out of him. You should've seen your face."

"Yeah, I hate bullies. I was pissed. I was in a fight. What does this have to do with me?"

"Patrick was found floating facedown in Silver Ridge Lake earlier this morning with a switchblade protruding from the center of his chest."

"Doesn't mean I had anything to do with it."

"Yeah, it kinda does." Savannah continued to stare at him. She was studying him too intently, and that unnerved both Edward and Tyler.

"For the love of God I didn't. Jesus, what is it with you lately?" He paused and looked at her and then realized something. "You still think I had something to do with Kelly and Suzanne's death's, don't you?"

Savannah didn't know what to say; neither did Tyler. They were at a stalemate. Finally Savannah broke eye contact and stepped away from him.

Tyler shrugged, "Serves him right, you know. You live in that kind of lifestyle, you die in that lifestyle. It's his own fault, you know?"

"Why would you say something like that?"

"Because it's the truth. Just being honest."

"You seem very happy about it."

"I wouldn't call it happy. He wasn't exactly the best person on the planet, you and I both know that. I wasn't his biggest fan. He's a drug dealer. It was bound to happen to him sooner or later. Guess he learned his lesson a little too late."

"Don't say things like that."

"Why not? It's the truth."

"You sound like you don't give a shit that he's dead."

"I don't really have an opinion about it. I'm—," he paused to think of the right word. "I'm indifferent." Tyler noticed again how Savannah was looking at him. "What difference does it make anyway? I've already told you the truth, but I can tell you don't believe me. You've already convicted me. Again. Your mind is already made up."

"You kept his switchblade, didn't you?"

No, I gave it back to him, Edward thought. *Up to the hilt I gave it back to him.*

Tyler ignored Edward as best he could. "Yes, I did. I kept it."

"Why?"

"We were having a fight. I didn't think it was the best thing for him to be walking around with it. I didn't want him to sneak up behind me and shank me later on that day in school."

"Then what is he still doing with it?"

"Really? Do you really think that was the only switchblade he had? A person living that lifestyle; he probably has a dozen or more of those things lying around."

"You have a point there. Where is the one you took?"

"Gone."

"Where?"

"Does it matter?"

"To me it does."

"I threw it away."

"Where?"

"Do I need a lawyer present?"

"You tell me. Do you?"

"No. Just wondering why the game of twenty questions all of a sudden."

"This isn't a game."

"Jesus," Tyler said. He was getting pissed again. "Yesterday, after our little disagreement and the fight with Patrick, I went down to Silver Ridge Lake to think. That's where I always go when I want to think.

While I was there, I realized I still had it in my pocket. I threw the knife as far as I could out into the bay. Who knows where it is now. A little later on I left."

"That's the same place Patrick was killed."

"Oh, Jesus Christ!" Tyler said as he threw his hands up in the air. He turned away from her. "That doesn't mean we were out there at the same time. Nobody was down at the lake when I was there. This is unbelievable. I can't win for losing." He took a few steps away from her, because he wanted to punch something. He didn't want Savannah to be on the receiving end of this frustration. "You know, if you are so sure that I did these terrible things why haven't you already turned me in to the police?"

"I don't know," Savannah said.

Tyler pressed on. "For that matter, if I'm so guilty, why haven't the cops come and arrested me?"

Those thoughts and many others had already crossed Savannah's mind a time or two.

"I don't know," Savannah said.

"You do know. I want you to tell me."

"I don't know."

Tyler answered the question for her, "It's because you're the only one accusing me of these crimes. It's because deep down in your heart, you know me just enough to know I couldn't do anything like that. That I would *never* do anything like that."

She looked at him knowing he was right but wasn't going to admit it to him right now. Not yet. She needed to be one hundred percent sure, but she didn't know how to get to that one hundred percent.

Tyler turned away from her again. "You know, this is bullshit. You're really starting to piss me off. Hunt me down when you've made up your mind about me. Once you've figured it out, you will either find me and apologize for accusing me of this shit and we will go on with our relationship as if nothing happened or you'll report me to the cops and they will do whatever the fuck they have to do; then I'll know what choice you've made. Until then, I'm not going to keep claiming my innocence to you because I'm wasting my time and my breath."

Tyler let the sentence hang in the air. He turned and left her standing there with her mouth open in shock and a sinking feeling in her heart. He jogged up the few stairs to his front porch, entered his house, and slammed the door just as he had done before.

Savannah felt that she had betrayed him—again. And that is what hurt the worst. She bowed her head as a void deep in her heart opened. She walked back to her car and got in. The tears began to fall as she drove away.

CHAPTER 29

THE AMETHYST DARKNESS was tranquil, but the restlessness inside Tyler wasn't anything like the night. Edward, for so many years, had been everything but calm.

Edward and Tyler, as one, were standing on the sidewalk in front of a house that sat at 37 Plateau Edge Avenue; the residence of Bruce Saliers. A brown paper bag was now sitting at Edward's feet.

Edward was gnawing on one of Tyler's fingernails as he concentrated. He was comparing the numbers on the mailbox and double checking them with the ones on the business card Bruce had given Derrick earlier that afternoon.

You're getting slack, Bruce, Edward thought. *It's pretty stupid for you to have personal identification listed on your business card; especially a home residence.*

Edward wanted to make sure no one was home. He stood stock still; listening. Nobody was out walking their dog or for a late night jog. This neighborhood was quiet.

Good. No lights on inside; just as I expected. Just one car in the driveway. He's probably in his cruiser and this it his everyday car.

Edward's nervous tension had been worming its way through Tyler ever since he'd found out Bruce Saliers had been "collecting evidence" as he'd so eloquently put it. He was so nervous, in fact, that Edward had caused Tyler to bite all his fingernails down to the quick. Tyler never had a habit of biting his nails. Since this afternoon, Tyler had been consumed with Edward's rage and could barely contain himself during dinner.

I can't believe the nerve. Who the hell does he think he is? He shook his head in disgust. *There's one thing about it though; Bruce is one smart cookie. He certainly was putting two and two together.*

Edward had wanted and needed to get away from school and figure out what he was going to do with Bruce. But he couldn't be too hasty; he had to pacify everyone so they wouldn't become suspicious of his impending actions. So Edward had waited as patiently as he could.

Edward already knew what tonight's outcome would be. Bruce's fate was inevitable and would be the same as the others—he hoped. He even knew how it would happen or at least how he wanted it to happen. He kept fantasizing and experiencing Bruce's death over and over in his mind. There was a sense of power that went along with the fantasy the more he dwelled on it. He definitely had to stop Bruce from getting any closer, and there was only one way to do that.

Earlier, when Edward first arrived in the neighborhood, he had parked further down the road around the corner on another intersecting street. He parked the driver's side toward the curb. He didn't want Bruce to accidentally notice his Mustang with the driver's side scratches as he arrived home if he came from that direction. Edward figured it was concealed enough and wouldn't be noticed.

When Edward got out of his car, he grabbed the brown paper sack from the passenger's seat, shut and locked the door, then pocketed his keys. He had stopped by the nearest CVS store while en route to Bruce's place and had picked up the housewarming gift for him. If Bruce was a smart man, he would know why Edward would be giving this item to him. But it had happened a long time ago, so he didn't know how Bruce's recollection would be.

When headlights slashed over the ridge to his left, Edward's heart sank. He barely had enough time to stoop, grab the sack, and duck out of sight behind some nearby shrubbery and garbage cans. Knowing Edward's intent, Tyler thought it was two-faced of him to pray, but Edward prayed nonetheless, hoping it wasn't Bruce arriving home before he was prepared for him. Luckily, the automobile continued around a corner until it was out of sight. Edward's tension abated somewhat.

Before Edward left his hiding place for the front door, he slid on a pair of thin gloves so fingerprints wouldn't be left behind.

Can't be too careful these days, Edward thought. *And I also don't want to hear if from Tyler anymore about possibly leaving evidence behind.*

He was more prepared for tonight than when he visited the Sheridans' home. He kept forgetting that he was an entity in a tangible body and whatever he did would leave all sorts of evidence that would point the police directly to Tyler.

Once he was at the front door, he found it locked.

Shit; of course. Just as I assumed.

He quickly made his way around to the back of the house. He moved between the darker shadows of the night letting them do all the work and conceal him from prying eyes.

Finding the back door locked also, he pulled a roll of duck tape from the bag. He quickly tore long strips and applied them to a pane of glass that was nearest the doorknob. He rubbed each strip firmly to make sure the glass was stuck securely to the tape web. He didn't want to leave a mess like he did at the Sheridan house. Finally, he gave a quick punch to the window; just enough force to break it. The tape sagged slightly. Edward peeled it back, leaving a hole large enough to slip his hand through and unlock the door.

"Just like magic," he muttered.

The whole process had taken less than two minutes.

Once Edward was inside, he peeled the taped section from the door and put it the broken glass into the bag he had with him. Edward took a little more time to tear off numerous strips and re-tape the hole. He made sure to put multiple pieces over the broken window section in case investigators examined this area later on. Edward was hoping to make it look like maybe Bruce had forgotten his keys and had to break back into his own house and just hadn't gotten around to fixing it.

By this time, Edward's eyes were getting use to the darkness, and he maneuvered through the house with more ease. He made his way to the living room where he found a comfortable sofa, love seat, recliner, nice entertainment center, widescreen television, a fireplace, and a small bar area.

From the bag again, Edward pulled the housewarming gift and set it in the middle of the coffee table. He hadn't wrapped it—there was really no need to—but he added a green Christmas bow to the top so it would grab Bruce's attention.

Edward placed the bag that held the duct tape and the broken glass under the couch. He didn't want to hold anything in his hands later on. He didn't know how this scenario would play out and he needed his hands free in case anything got out of hand. He would retrieve it later on when he left.

With a little time on his hands, he checked out the entire house. He went from room to room opening closets, finding hiding spaces, checking distances. He was getting a basic lay of the land because he didn't know what would happen later on.

With everything being completed in the house, he set down in the center of the couch and waited for Bruce to arrive.

As Edward did with the last victims, he drifted back to another time and another place. He remembered back to the unforgivable thing Bruce Saliers had done to him, and he let the familiar hatred creep back in and possess him once again.

ෆ

The forest was ablaze and brimming with fall color. The trees were stitched together in a tapestry of reds, oranges, yellows, and browns. The colors blurred together as they passed by in Edward's periphery.

Edward rode his bike down a narrow dirt trail that he had cleared the previous summer. He had blazed the path as a shortcut to and from school and also to other parts of the town. His grandmother was constantly sending him out on short trips for odds and ends she'd forgotten when she had been to the store earlier in the day.

He ducked under a few low-hanging tree limbs and pumped the pedals faster to gain speed for the steep incline that was ahead. Sometimes he was able to make it to the top without stopping, but other times he had to get off and walk his bike the rest of the way to the top. Today he had a good start and was determined to ride it out. He would then be able to coast down the backside of the trail. He forced himself the last few feet and smiled when he crested the hill. Anticipating the feeling of his stomach disconnecting itself from his body, he let himself go.

After he had built up speed when he was closer to the bottom of the incline, he heard a voice shout.

"Now!"

Edward had been looking to the right at something in the woods. He looked forward expecting to see someone standing in the middle of the trail. Instead, he saw a rope levitating horizontally above the ground between the next two trees up ahead. There was only a split second between the time he saw it and the time the rope whipped across his chest. He didn't have any time to react. If the rope had been any higher it would've either crushed his windpipe or taken his head clean off.

Edward had been so startled by the whole ordeal that he didn't have time to prepare for a proper landing. The rope was pulled taunt, and it lifted him off his bicycle and dumped him to the ground. It was only about a three to four foot drop, but the way he landed on his back drove the breath out of him. He was already confused but became dazed as his head struck the ground. He immediately began to see constellations in the daylight. He struggled for his breath and fought the blackness that was starting to seep in at the corners of his vision.

He heard rustling leaves and footsteps all around him.

Three teenagers walked up from all sides of his vision and loomed over him. Each boy was dressed in camouflage fatigues and carried shotguns or rifles. Edward knew these boys from school. Dread covered his body, and his stomach seemed to fall even lower into his bowels.

"What the fuck do you think you're doing, Edward?" the first voice asked.

Edward knew the voice belonged to Bruce Saliers before he looked his direction. Edward groaned as he tried to breath but said nothing in response to the initial question. He coughed and tried to get to his feet.

Bruce stuck the barrel of his shotgun in the middle of Edward's chest and pushed him back to the ground, "Oh, no you don't. You just stay right there where we can talk to you."

"Yeah, you little retard." Alex Riley chimed in.

In a bad British accent, Jeremy Taylor said, "Nice of you to drop in so unexpectedly."

"You want to explain yourself, Edward?" Bruce asked. "Where are you going in such a hurry?"

Edward tried to reason with them, "Look guys, I was just riding down my trails."

"That's not what we asked you, numb nuts. You were blatantly speeding."

"There's no speed limits on these trails."

"There are when I'm around," Bruce shot back.

Wanting to be in on the fun, Alex added, "Yeah, we saw your little punk ass ride by a little while ago. We decided to have a little chat with you if you came back this way."

"I-I have to get-get this medication to-to my grandmother. I just went to-to the pharmacy," he confessed.

Well, maybe if you slow down you'd get there a littler faster, "Bruce added, trying to be funny.

"Medication?" Jeremy asked.

"You mean drugs," Bruce said pulling the pharmacy bag from Edward's jeans pocket. "You know, Edward, it's against the law to peddle drugs around Silver Ridge."

"I'm not peddling any drugs. It's a prescription that I am allowed to pick up for her." Edward shook his head and pleaded. "I'm on the list at the pharmacy. I'm cleared to pick up any of her meds."

"Well then, that makes it alright then don't it?" Bruce shot back. "We'll just hold on to them for the time being."

Bruce shoved them into one off the side pockets of his camouflage pants.

"What-what are you guys do-doing down here anyway?" Edward asked.

"That's none of your damned business!" Alex remarked.

"We're not doo-dooing down here," Bruce said in a goofy cartoonish voice. "If we need to shit we'll go drop a load in a public bathroom."

All the boys laughed aloud. Edward was still confused. He didn't realize they were making fun of his out-of-breath stuttering.

Coming back to the subject, Jeremy said, "We can tell Edward what we're doing; he can keep a secret. Can't you? He's not going to tell anyone about this; isn't that right, Edward?"

"Tell anyone about what?"

Bruce chimed in, "About us down here drinking beer and hunting. Just

*wasting time, getting drunk and shooting some squirrels and birds. We saw
a buck and we were gonna bag and tag him but he was too far away. Come
to think of it, I don't remember you getting our permission to ride your bike
through our woods."*

*Edward spoke before he thought, "I-I don't need your-your permission.
This is my grandfather's land."*

*"I know I just didn't hear you talk back to me," Bruce said. "If you didn't
notice, I'm the one who's got a shotgun pointed at the center of your chest."*

*Edward pressed on, "It's private property down here. Nobody's supposed
to be hunting on his land. Didn't you see the signs?"*

"Sure; we saw the signs. We just don't believe everything we read."

*The other two boys could barely contain themselves; their chuckles
erupted into a bray of laughter.*

"Can you prove it's your grandfather's land?"

Edward didn't say anything.

*"That's what I thought. You're not gonna tell on us, are you buddy?"
Bruce asked.*

*Edward thought about it briefly, then saw the guns again and that made
up his mind, "No, I'm not going to say anything."*

*"I don't know, you guys," Jeremy began. "I think he paused a little too
long to decide. That means there is a possibility he would tell."*

Edward repeated emphatically, "I promise. I'm not going to say anything,"

"Was that a believable enough answer to you guys?" Bruce asked.

"Sounded kind of weak to me," Jeremy said.

*"Yeah, I think he said that just so you'd let him go. Didn't sound too
convincing in my opinion," Alex retorted.*

*"He probably wouldn't get an Academy Award for that performance,"
Jeremy said, again.*

*Bruce leaned close to Edward and ruffled his hair, "You're going to have
to do a little bit better than that, Edward. Make us believe you."*

*Bruce's words sounded slurred from the booze he had already put away.
The smell of warm, stale beer wafted from his mouth, and Edward turned
his head away from the stench.*

*"I'm not going to tell my grandfather!" Edward shouted. "I don't care if
you shoot up the woods. I don't care if you shoot each other. Just let me go!"*

"Oh hell no, you shouldn't have said that," Alex warned.

Bruce laughed out loud for a few seconds and then became silent and deadly serious. As if on cue, he automatically changed the subject. "Hey guys, have you ever seen what happens when a bullet goes through an unopened beer can?"

Alex and Jeremy shook their heads.

"It basically disintegrates on contact," Bruce continued. *"It turns into aluminum confetti."*

"Whoa, really?" Alex asked.

Still confused, Jeremy asked, "What's that got to do with Edward?"

Seeming to change subjects again, Bruce asked to the others, "You want to have some real fun?"

Alex laughed, "You mean more fun than we're having now?"

"Oh yeah. Loads more," Bruce confirmed.

"What kind of fun are you talking about?" Jeremy asked beginning to see where Bruce was going with this line of questioning.

"The kind of fun where Edward here holds our targets for us."

Bruce removed the shotgun, leaned over, grabbed a handful of Edward's sweatshirt, and yanked him into a standing position.

"What-what do-do you mean?" Edward stammered.

"Trust me Edward; you're going to love this."

Bruce pulled three beers from his backpack then stuck two in Edward's jean pockets and continued to hold one.

"Wait here, you guys. I'll be back in a few seconds. I need to talk to Edward alone. You know, guy talk."

Still bewildered, they reluctantly obeyed.

He swung a muscular arm around Edward's neck and guided him to a gnarled oak tree about thirty or forty paces away. He casually shook the third beer with his other hand as he continued to talk in a soothing but slurred alcoholic speech, "Listen carefully to me Edward and you won't get hurt."

"What are you going to do to me?" Edward asked, as he started to cry. *The whimpers were noticeable in his voice.*

"You like games, don't you Edward?"

"Yeah, I guess."

"I thought so. We're going to play a little game with you." Bruce was

being game-show-host nice. "Now, if you do what I say, you'll be the winner. If you don't, you'll be the…what?"

Edward hesitated, then, "Most-most likely the lo-loser."

"That-that's right. You'll be the lo-loser. Now all you have to do is stand in front of this tree, hold this beer can, and don't move. Remember, if you move even the slightest bit, it'll all be over for you. Got it?"

"I think."

"No. You got it?" Bruce confirmed.

Edward sniffled and wiped his nose with the back of his hand, "What da ya mean it'll be over?" Even though he asked, Edward knew the outcome.

"You'll see once the game starts. Now turn around and put your back against the tree."

Edward obeyed.

"That's it, there you go. Are you comfortable?"

Edward nodded.

Bruce stopped shaking the beer and shoved it into Edward's nervous hand, "Here, hold this. Good, that's real good. Now, put the beer can on top of your head."

"What?"

His voice became stern, "Which word didn't you understand? He repeated the words slowly and precisely, "Put the fucking beer can on top of your fucking head."

"Why?"

"BECAUSE IT'S ALL PART OF THE GAME!" Bruce shouted, "Don't talk back; don't ask questions; JUST DO IT! Now don't let me have to tell you again."

With trembling hands, Edward feebly placed the beer can on top of his head. As he did so, he added, "You said I was supposed to hold it."

"You're right; I did say that, didn't I? But I didn't say how you were going to hold it. Now remember what I told you, not even the slightest movement."

Tears started to stream out of Edward's eyes, "I wanna go home."

"You can. We'll let you go home to your grandma-ma soon enough. We just want to make absolutely sure this is just between us and that you're not going to be a little tattle-tale."

"I've already told you, I'm not going to say anything. What do I have to do to convince you of that?"

Without saying a word, Bruce sneered, turned on his heels, and walked away.

Tears blurred Edward's vision, stung his eyes, and ran down his cheeks. One tear traced a clean line on the dirty side of Edward's face. He tried his best to control the sobs that racked his body.

When he met back with the others, Bruce said, "Watch this."

"You're not going to do what I think you're going to do, are you?" Alex asked.

"You can't be serious." Jeremy stated.

"Trust me, I'm a professional."

He took a shooter's stance with his legs shoulder width apart and both hands holding the pistol firmly in front of him. Bruce took a couple of seconds to take aim and then squeezed the trigger.

Through his obscured vision, Edward saw a small puff of smoke emanate from the muzzle of the pistol. In a split second, he heard the bullet's whine cutting the air over his head. He heard the bullet pierce the can and burrow deep inside the tree. He felt the can rupture as it released its contents from the growing pressure. The can exploded into a cloud of beer foam and sprayed in every direction. Most of the beer rained down onto Edward's face and shoulders, but his eyes were already closed. Edward had been holding his breath but gave a small cry of shock when he heard the can explode. His knees buckled, and he went down on all fours as he continued to breathe in explosive pants.

"Holy shit," Alex said in amazement. "That was an awesome shot. Let me try it."

"Hell no, you've missed everything you've shot at this morning. You would probably kill the poor bastard. I'm not taking a chance on that."

"Do another one, Bruce," Jeremy encouraged.

"Keep your shirt on, I will." Bruce shouted to get his attention, "Edward! Take one of the other beers out of your pocket and set it on your shoulder!"

"Why?"

Bruce whipped his arm up in anger and fired another shot barely taking aim.

The bullet whizzed overhead again and bit out a chunk of the tree above Edward's head.

Edward screamed as he covered his head with his hands and dropped to the ground for protection. But it was a delayed reaction; the bullet had already struck the tree.

Dislodged pieces of bark sprinkled down into Edward's beer-matted hair.

"JUST DO IT, EDWARD!" Bruce screamed. "DON'T MAKE ME COME BACK DOWN THERE!"

"All right, all right, I'm doing it. I'M DOING IT!"

Edward hurriedly extracted the can from his pocket and placed it on his right shoulder.

Bruce shouted again, "Now stand still! I don't want to take off your fucking ear!"

Edward turned his head away from the powerful spray that he knew would come. He heard the shot; the egg-cracking sound of a bullet ripping the beer can into shreds and the beer foam that once again drenched him. Edward screamed as aluminum shrapnel from the exploding can bit into his ear and neck. Beer stung the freshly cut gashes. Blood oozed from the open wounds and mixed with the hot, stale beer. His muscles relaxed as his bladder and bowels simultaneously released. The center of his crotch grew dark and he felt a warm, wet sensation trickled down his left leg. He looked down at his pants in unbelief and continued to hang his head in shame.

"Holy shit, you guys," Alex said disbelieving, "He's pissing himself. You can see it from here."

Jeremy doubled over and Alex dropped to his knees laughing.

"Bruce, you probably scared the shit out of him too."

"That's the idea boys; that's the idea. I don't want him to go telling anyone on us."

Edward heard them laughing over their snide comments like a pack of wild hyenas.

"EDWARD! You've got one more can to go, little buddy! Put it on your other shoulder!"

Edward wanted to run as far away from these demons as he could. He knew if he tried to bolt from the scene, they could easily chase him down without any problem. He didn't want to know what other evils they would do when they did catch him. He decided to get this over with. Maybe Bruce was telling the truth and they would leave him alone after this last can.

He slowly pulled it out of his pocket and with an unsteady hand balanced it on his left shoulder. Almost before Edward had removed his hand away from the balanced can, a third shot was fired and a third bullet ripped the can into confetti. Another beer mist exploded and rained down into Edward's tear filled eyes. The beer burned and blurred his vision even more. Edward's knees unlocked, his legs became jelly, and he slid slowly to the ground. His body was sticky and reeked of sweat, body waste, and beer. He heard footsteps approaching once again and curled up into a tight ball on the ground, covering his head with his hands for protection. He was expecting a pounding from all three boys but it never came.

Through his splayed fingers he saw Alex and Jeremy demolishing his bicycle. They took their hunting knifes and slashed the tires from the rims. They somehow unscrewed the bolts that held the rims to the bicycle and removed them. They threw both rims and the chain as far as they could in different directions. Alex ended the procedure by picking up the frame of the bicycle and slamming it into a tree until the body was dented and crumpled beyond repair.

As they destroyed his bicycle, Bruce knelt beside Edward. He patted Edward's face to get him to focus in his direction. Edward turned in his direction. Bruce said, "If you tell on us Edward, we'll bring you back down here in these woods again. You think you're scared now. If you tell on us, next time I'll miss the can on purpose." For emphasis, Bruce placed the barrel of the pistol in the center of Edward's forehead and for emphasis yelled, "BANG!" as loud as he could.

Edward recoiled as though a bullet had actually been discharged from the pistol's barrel.

"Understand what I'm saying?"

Edward nodded weakly and curled up into a tighter fetal position with his hand and arms protecting his head.

"Good boy. We'll see you at school on Monday, if not before."

Bruce stood and paused.

Edward heard the crinkle of a paper bag above his head. He opened his eyes in time to see the pharmacy bag with his grandmother's medication drop in front of his face.

"Give our regards to your grandmother. Hope she gets to feeling better real soon."

Edward's hand shot out and snatched the medication and pulled it back in to his chest and hugged it close.

Bruce left Edward sobbing like an abandoned baby that was lost and alone.

The boys' laughter echoed throughout the woods and finally faded away, but inside Edward's head it lingered and played over and over and over. After a long time, Edward cried himself to sleep.

CHAPTER 30

EDWARD AND TYLER together came out of their shared thoughts to the sound of keys jingle-jangling in the front door lock. Edward kicked Tyler's body into high gear and they vaulted the coffee table and moved out of the living room.

Bruce came through the door just as Edward turned the corner into the kitchen.

Edward prayed that Bruce hadn't seen or heard any tale-tell movement or sound. Part of the living room wall was missing so you could see into the kitchen from the living room and vice versa. Edward peered over the kitchen counters into the living room.

Bruce hung his hat and coat on the rack inside the small foyer. He started unbuttoning his uniform shirt and pulled it from his pants as he made his way down the connecting hallway to his bedroom.

Edward tiptoed to the kitchen door and watched him moving away down the hall. Edward knew he couldn't stay here. It was only a matter of time before Bruce would come back into the kitchen. He quietly but efficiently moved down the hallway toward Bruce's bedroom.

The door to the laundry room was partially closed, but Edward slid through without a sound.

From his earlier inspection of the house, he knew what each room was and what it held, and this laundry room barely held a washer and dryer. He hoped Bruce wouldn't come in here after he undressed because the only place to hide was behind the door.

In the bedroom, Bruce began to whistle while he changed.

Edward smiled when he heard the sound; if Bruce kept it up, he could easily judge where Bruce was at all times.

Bruce unbuckled his gun holster and placed it on his nightstand where he always kept it. It was always within reach in case he heard suspicious noises in the middle of the night, but that had never happened. He changed into sweatpants, a tee shirt, and socks. Bruce felt unbelievable weary from today's tasks, and all he wanted to do now was just relax in front of the television with some dinner and a couple of beers.

Standing behind the laundry room door, Edward held his ear to the crack and listened harder. When he heard the whistling grow slightly louder, Edward figured he was coming back down the hallway. Thinking Bruce would pass by and continue to the kitchen or living room, he was surprised to see the laundry room door swing open toward him.

No, no. Not now, Edward thought. He held his breath. *Don't come in here. Please don't open that door any farther.*

The light came on.

Suddenly blinded, Edward quickly closed his eyes as the bright light pierced his eyes. He blinked them open and squinted as his hands turned into fists. He brought them up near his chest ready to strike if Bruce entered.

Come in here and you'll wish you hadn't, that's all I can say.

He saw Bruce's clutched hand drop the clothes he had been wearing in the pile of clothes that were still waiting to be washed. Edward prayed that he wouldn't start a load of clothes now.

After the clothes were dropped, the light was extinguished and the door was shut.

A bright outline of everything in the laundry room was imprinted on his vision. With a soft burst of air, Edward released the breath he had been holding.

That was just too damn close.

The whistling was very faint now, and Edward figured Bruce was in the living room or even the kitchen. He needed to get to Bruce's bedroom for the next thing he needed for tonight's occasion. If Bruce saw the gift on the coffee table before he could get the item from the bedroom, Bruce would start searching the house.

The whistling became slightly louder when Edward opened the door. Judging from the sound, he had a hunch Bruce was in the kitchen. He quietly moved into Bruce's bedroom.

There it is; that's what I need.

He walked to the nightstand and unholstered Bruce's standard issue. The gun felt surprisingly heavy in his hand. Caught up in the gun's rapture, he trailed his fingers over its barrel. He ejected the clip from the butt of the gun to check to see if it was loaded.

"Good. Full clip," Edward said to himself.

Forcing himself not to get too caught up in the moment, he quickly dismantled the gun and pocketed all the pieces. Then he carefully retraced his steps back down the hallway.

Once he was at the kitchen entrance, Edward slowly peered around the corner. Bruce was still preparing dinner in the kitchen. When Bruce's back was to him, he moved across the doorway entrance back into the living room again. Edward noticed that his present still hadn't been noticed.

That's good, that's real good.

Edward liked the layout of this house. It was so open. Anyone coming down the stairs could see into the living room and the kitchen.

It's such an advantage for me. I like it when things go my way.

With Bruce's back to him, Edward casually walked past the kitchen window and moved up into the darkness of the stairwell. He had a perfect seat to watch the next bizarre chain of events, and he waited anxiously for Bruce to come into the living room.

While he waited for Bruce, Edward heard mail being opened, the release of air as he popped the top on a cold one, a plate and silverware being taken from the cabinet and drawer, and the whirring of the microwave.

Probably one of those TV dinners that takes forever to heat up.

Eventually, Bruce came into the living room and set his steaming plate of food and his beer on the coffee table.

Edward smiled.

This is it. Showtime. This is where the shit either hits the fan or misses it completely.

Bruce leaned over and switched on the end table lamp.

When Bruce turned back around; he reached for the remote control but stopped a few inches shy of picking it up. He noticed something he hadn't seen when he had entered his home. He looked closer in astonishment.

"What the hell is this?" Bruce said aloud.

Edward smiled.

Sitting on the coffee table was a six-pack of Budweiser beer garnished with a bright green Christmas bow.

From the stairwell, Edward shook his head; he could see the wheels spinning in Bruce's head. Confusion had definitely set in.

"Where did this come from?"

On edge, Bruce looked around the room, suspicious. He squinted up into the darkened stairwell. Edward figured the light didn't illuminate as far up as he was sitting. Bruce's gaze lingered for a few moments then moved on.

More questions spun through Bruce's mind. He scratched the back of his head as if it would coax any hint to the forefront of his mind.

Edward could tell there was an obvious concern about the gift.

Bruce moved to the other side of the couch and flipped the other lamp on. He continued to stand and stare at the beer.

If it was a present, why isn't there a name on it?

Finally, he hesitantly picked up the six-pack to examine it closer.

"Hello, Bruce," Edward said from out of the darkened stairwell. "I see you found my present."

Bruce jerked as if shocked by a bolt of electricity. He dropped the six-pack as though he had been caught stealing the crowned jewels of England and squinted back into the gloom. Earlier he hadn't noticed, but now he saw a vague outline of a person perched on the stairs; the figure's arms were resting on its knees. The added light from the second lamp was just enough to illuminate the figure's silhouette.

His voice was apprehensive but stern. "Wh-who's there? Wh-what do you want?"

"You should know who is here," Edward said as he stood and strolled slowly down the remaining stairs. "From what I've heard around school, you seem to have me all figured out. Apparently you have all the answers to all the questions. You've been all over town today gathering up a lot of intel about me."

"Tyler Curtis? Is that you?"

At the landing, Edward held out his arms like a magician who had just finished an amazing magic trick. "In the flesh; or at least part of me is." He laughed. "I guess you could say I'm here in body but someone else is here with us in spirit."

"What's that suppose to mean?"

"Nothing. Don't worry about it."

Bruce's voice became strict, "H-how did you get in here? What do you want?"

"I don't have the time to explain all my secrets to you," he said dryly. "They are the least of your concern." Edward guided the conversation back in his direction as he asked, "So is it true? What is it that you think I've done?"

"I don't know what you're talking about."

"So you're saying my two best friends are liars?"

"Who?"

"Cass and Derrick. They said you had a little conversation with them today in the school parking lot."

"No, that's not true. They didn't say anyth—," he stopped in mid-sentence, realizing he had just confessed to Tyler's accusation.

"Didn't say what?" Edward asked.

Bruce didn't answer.

Edward continued, "So the truth comes out. What evidence did you gather on me and where is it?"

As Tyler moved into the living room, Bruce slowly inched his way down to the end of the couch to keep a safe distance between himself and Tyler. Bruce looked down the hallway toward the bedroom.

Reading Bruce's thoughts, Edward started laughing, "Could I make it in time?"

Bruce jerked his head back toward Tyler. "What?"

"That's what you're thinking, right? That's what you're asking yourself right now, isn't it? Could I make it in time?"

Bruce was scared, and the nervousness showed through in his voice. "Ma-make what?"

Edward called his bluff, shaking his head at the idea. "I'm afraid it wouldn't really do you any good."

The same question he had just asked was still etched on his face.

"I'm not stupid, Bruce. You're thinking about running down the hallway to get your gun off the nightstand where you placed it earlier when you came in."

Bruce looked shocked that Tyler knew exactly what he was thinking. He quickly drudged up the tough guy persona and said, "So what if I did, who's going to stop me? You?"

"Yeah, most likely me since I'm the one who has your gun." Edward pulled a handful of bullets from his left pocket and dropped them on the floor. They bounced in different directions. "See, there's your bullets. Oh, and here is the clip that they go in." Edward dropped it on the floor also. "Oh, and this part here that the bullets come out of won't stay hooked to the gun itself. I don't think it's working properly. And if that's not staying attached to the gun itself then there is no use in having the base part with this trigger thingy, right?"

Bruce looked on at this fiasco in astonishment.

Edward held out his hands again to his side. "Tada. Look familiar? I took it from your holster a few minutes ago, so why don't you just slide back to the middle of the couch and try to relax, okay?"

Bruce reluctantly obeyed. "Okay, just don't do anything foolish."

"I *can't* promise you I *won't* do anything crazy."

Bruce tried to look unaffected by Tyler's comment, but the fear showed through.

"Back to my original question: what exactly did you gather on me today, and where is it?"

"I didn't find anything."

"Don't make me out to be the dumb one. Asking my friends about me behind my back. Inquiring about my missing rearview mirror. I'm not stupid, Bruce."

Bruce said nothing.

Edward charged Bruce. He put his hand behind his back and jerked out Patrick Quinlan's gun from the crook of his back. With the pistol stuck straight out in front of him, Edward asked again, "What evidence did you collect on me, and where the fuck is it?"

Startled, Bruce pulled his legs up to his chest and folded his arms over his head for protection. He spilled his guts before he realized he had spoken, "Alex has it. I took it all to Alex for him to analyze."

"Alex?"

"Yeah."

"Alex Riley?"

"Yeah."

"A little more detail, please."

Bruce confessed about everything he had done during his long day. He told Tyler about the cell phone message Alex received, about their venture to the Sheridans' house, about finding Patrick Quinlan's body, and how he had dropped the evidence off with Alex right before he came home.

Edward let out a sigh of relief, "Well, this just keeps getting better and better. I guess I'll have to go talk to Alex and Travis next. And Jeremy…I'll save that asshole for last."

"Travis isn't in town yet. He will probably be getting in soon. He's in Europe covering a story."

"Well then I will talk to Alex first. I'm sure Travis and I will cross paths sooner or later."

Bruce looked as though he'd just betrayed his best friend, and in a way, he had.

Changing the subject, Edward asked, "Did you like the present I left for you?"

Bruce stuttered, "What present?" He motioned to the cans of Budweiser and asked, "These?"

"That's right, dumbass." He motioned with the gun. "Go ahead. You're a beer man, drink up."

"No thanks, I don't care for any."

Edward tucked Patrick's gun into his pants, moved to the coffee table, snatched a beer from the plastic holder, and chucked it at Bruce. It landed on Bruce's belly with a slight thud. Edward followed that movement by drawing down on Bruce as he shouted, "It's not an offer, it's a request. I SAID DRINK THE FUCKING BEER RIGHT NOW!"

"Okay, okay. I'll do it. I'll do it. Ease up."

Bruce popped the top of the can and took a swig.

Edward wasn't amused, "C'mon Bruce, don't be bashful! Don't hold back! Chug that bitch like you mean it, and don't stop until you've drained it dry!"

Bruce unwillingly obeyed.

When he finished, Edward commanded, "Again."

"What?"

"Are you a fucking lightbulb?" He mimiced Bruce, "What? What? Quit saying, *what*. I said, AGAIN! Drink another one."

Bruce pleaded to Edward, "What is it that you want from me?"

"I want you to quit asking questions, and drink that fucking beer."

"But I don't want any more!"

He mimicked Bruce in a small child's voice, "But I don't want any more." He continued, "Well, this gun fucking says that you do."

"You're going to kill me anyway."

"You don't know that. You don't know me, and I don't appreciate the accusation. You have no idea what my intentions are so quit trying to manipulate me. Just drink your beer and shut up. That's all I'm asking you to do. And be just a little more appreciative about it, too. Jeez, you make it sound like drinking beer is torture for you."

Bruce was angry. He snatched up another beer, popped the top, threw his head back and guzzled the contents of the can without stopping. When he was finished, he crushed the can and pitched it against the wall. It clattered and dropped to the carpet.

"There. Are you happy now? You want me to go again?"

Bruce repeated his action without Tyler's answer. He grabbed another can from the six-pack, popped the top, and guzzled the contents without spilling a drop. Once he was finished, he grabbed the top of the can and smashed it against his forehead. The can instantly flattened. He tossed it toward Tyler. It landed on Tyler's shoe and bounced to the side.

"Is that what you wanted? Does that make you happy?"

Edward smiled and nodded in approval. "There you go. Well done. Now you're getting into the school spirit. That's the Bruce I remember from high school."

Bruce's face went flat. "High school? What are you talking about?"

"You'll know soon enough. Hey, that's three down."

"You want me to drink another one?"

"Yes."

"What good is that going to accomplish?"

"It accomplishes a lot. I'm trying to bring back your memory here, pal. Does it remind you of anything, Bruce?"

"I don't—I don't follow you. Should it?"

A frustrating itch had started in the crown of Tyler's head. Edward used the barrel of the pistol to suppress it. "See that's the problem all of you have had."

"What problem? All of who?"

"Owning up to your own mistakes, *friend*. Taking responsibility for your own actions. That's the problem both Kelly Sheridan and Suzanne Baldwin had."

In his mind, Bruce saw their cold, lifeless bodies lying out on the morgue table, naked and exposed. He thought, *How long would it be before I join them on my own personal morgue slab?*

Edward continued on his rant, "That's the problem Patrick Quinlan had." Edward saw Bruce's mind working again as it had when he found the present of beers.

"Patrick Quinlan? What about him?" Bruce asked.

"I dropped that asshole last night like a used condom."

"You're responsible for Patrick as well? You killed him? Just like that?"

"Just for kicks. Didn't think twice about it. What of it?" Edward saw the shocked look on his face. "Hey, I did you a favor. He was dealing drugs to the teens in school. I'd bet money that I did more to him in one day than the cops did all of last school year."

"Why?"

"For two reasons. The first reason is because he sells drugs. That is reason enough in itself. Reason number two is because he reminded me of Jeremy Taylor. Well, all you fuckers from high school all rolled into one, really, but mainly Jeremy. Patrick was about to beat up someone smaller than him, just like you and Jeremy, Travis, and Alex did to me and I couldn't let that happen." He paused for a long moment. "How did it feel to find Patrick's body today? I bet you wish you'd gone into a different profession, huh?"

"How did you do it?"

"If you found the body you should know. I drove his switchblade knife of his into his chest as hard as I could. I'm amazed that I didn't get carried away and do more harm to him than I did."

"No, Tyler, listen." Bruce was pleading. "I don't have a clue about what you're talking about."

"Quit calling me Tyler, my name's Edward."

Bruce cocked his head, "No, you're Tyler. I saw your license the day of the wreck and when I gave you the warning about speeding."

Edward took a deep breath in frustration, "Let me make one thing perfectly clear. Tyler isn't here. Tyler doesn't exist anymore. I am Edward McDaniel from now on, okay? Do you think you can handle that?"

Bruce was thinking hard. He didn't understand Tyler's ranting but nodded in agreement as though he did.

"Don't tell me you've forgotten me also? Boy, you really *were* drunk that day."

"No Edward, I remember you, if that is really you inside there. How could I forget the number one mistake I did in life. What I did, I mean, what *we* did to you was unforgiveable. And I understand your anger. I do. I am just hoping you can try to forgive me."

"You say you understand but you really don't. Those days were nightmares for me."

"The guys and I never talked about it after that day in the woods. After you died, we sort of drifted apart."

There was a long pause between them, neither one knowing what the other should say.

Edward broke the silence. "All I ever wanted you guys to do was to admit you were wrong and apologize to me. It was that simple. You made my life pure hell. Do you remember what the last thing you said to me that day was?"

Bruce just nodded his head. "I said if you ever told anyone that we would bring you back down in the woods again and miss the can on purpose."

"You know, through the rest of the summer, I didn't tell a soul."

"I know. And I'm sorry, Edward."

"You just didn't give a shit. You and your high society friends, thinking you're better than everyone else, preying on the weak. I hate all of you."

"Please, Edward, don't." Bruce was begging for his life. His words were coming out in jagged gasps. "I'm sorry."

"It's too late for redemption, Bruce, you know that."

Bruce didn't answer; he just held his clasped hands out in front of him in a beggar's plea.

"Do me a favor," Edward said.

"Anything."

"Grab one of those remaining cans of beers and balance it on top of your head."

Bruce looked up as fear coursed through him. He knew what was to come.

Edward coaxed him again, "C'mon Bruce, you've wasted around seventeen years of my time, don't waste any more of it. Put it up there, big guy."

Bruce obeyed, but with a slow uncertainty. With pleading in his eyes, he stared at Tyler with a longing to be anywhere but in his living room.

Tyler stood in a shooter's stance with his feet shoulder width apart; it was the same stance Bruce had used on that awful autumn day a millennia ago. His arms were locked at a center point where his hands firmly held the pistol. The sorrow in Bruce's eyes met the unspeakable hatred in Edward's. Bruce humbly closed his eyes; he couldn't look at Edward as he played his game; besides, he didn't want to get sprayed with contents once the bullet ripped into the can.

Edward stared down the sights of the gun. The barrel was aimed at the center of the small oval in the lower case letter "e" that was in the middle of the can's name brand.

Bruce was petrified with fear and tense with the expectation of a gun blast that was soon to come.

Edward whispered, "Bruce."

Bruce's eyes fluttered open at the sound of his name, careful not to knock the can from his head. Bruce and Edward's eyes locked together for a moment and Bruce looked ahead expectantly for mercy.

Instead of finding mercy, Bruce saw the gun drop the short distance from the target on his head to his face. He looked up the barrel into a face that was partially hidden behind his gun and saw one unsquinted eye gleaming with menacing hatred. He caught a glimpse of a crooked smile grinning out from behind clenched hands.

Edward pulled the trigger. The gun blast was deafening in the confined space. The gun recoiled wildly in his hands, but he didn't resist its movement.

For Bruce, everything dissolved into blackness. The bullet penetrated Bruce's head above his right eye. The back of his head exploded against the high couch cushion and wall in a wash of crimson. The fragments of skull, brain, skin, and blood smacked against the white wall and couch in a sickening wet spatter. The force with which the contents hit the wall caused them to glance off and become briefly airborne before falling in a small crimson rain over Bruce's body. The blood shower dotted Bruce's sweatpants, T-shirt, and socks.

Edward's broad grin remained as he lowered the gun slowly to his side. He stood for a long time with open, excited eyes, immersed in the catastrophe of the scene.

Bruce's forehead was caved in slightly from the force of the bullet. Even though his head was sagging to the side, it looked as though it was surrounded in a scarlet halo.

Bruce didn't stir; there were no more synaptic currents running through his head to cause his nerves to twitch. He had been dead before the bullet exited the backside of his head.

After retrieving a dishcloth from the kitchen, Edward wiped Patrick's gun clean and gently placed it in Bruce's left hand. He had made a judgment from looking at the holster earlier that Bruce was left-handed. It was a fifty-fifty chance that he would be wrong but it seemed like a logical assumption. Edward then held Bruce's arm and gun up to the bullet hole and then released it to let it land wherever it fell. He arranged Bruce's other arm so that it looked as though they had fallen naturally after the deed had been done. The beer can that had been balanced on his head had simply fallen forward and rolled down his chest. It now rested on the floor between his feet.

Edward took the can, wiped the blood splatter off of it with the dish towel, and popped the lid. He made a motion toward Bruce in the form of a toast, and poured a long swallow into his mouth. He was careful not to touch his lips to the rim. He didn't want anyone tracing him to the scene. He poured some beer onto Bruce's chest and arms so it would appear he was drunk when he wasted himself.

Edward strategically placed the beer cans on and around the coffee table so it would give the illusion that Bruce had been deep in a drunken stupor. He was careful not to disturb any blood splatter that may have landed on the can itself.

He gathered all the dropped pieces of Bruce's gun, wiped them clean as he reassembled it again, then returned it back to its place in the holster on Bruce's nightstand.

He grabbed the paper bag he had stuffed under the couch and double-checked that the section of duct-taped glass was still inside with the roll of duct tape. Finding that it was, he added the dish towel he'd cleaned the gun and the cans with, then he rolled the small bag up and tucked it up under his arm.

You can't be too careful these days, now can you?

Most people, when committing suicide, eat a bullet rather than just holding the gun out level with their head, unless it is held to their temple.

Edward didn't know if this would be chalked up as a suicide but still hoped this would pass as one instead of looking like a murder scene. Cops were smart these days; they could find the smallest piece of evidence.

Rethinking and retracing the steps he'd made tonight, Edward finally made his way to the back door again. He closed it and made sure it was locked tight even though one of the window panes was missing. He took just enough time to slap some pieces of tape over the window opening to make it look like Bruce had just made a quick fix on the pane until he could actually do a better job.

As Edward came around to the front of Bruce's house, he looked back one last time. A soft afterglow from the lamps still radiated through the windows into the nighttime blackness.

Edward took a deep breath and admired the scenic vista. There is such a soothing and peaceful feeling. The lighting was so tranquil, such a soft contrast between the inside radiance and the outside shadows.

Makes the night look less threatening. Edward thought. *Too bad the inside isn't as serene. It kind of ruins the mood if you know what's going on on the inside of the house; at least it will for the person who finds Bruce.*

He smiled at the thought as he turned toward his car.

He stopped along the way to discard the brown paper bag into the side of an open garbage container. Along with the duct tape and the duck taped glass shards, he also pitched the gloves he was wearing. The garbage collectors would be by as the sun came up and those materials would be lost forever in the landfill of the city's grim. He didn't want to keep any evidence that would even remotely link him to tonight's escapade.

Edward started whistling the tune that Bruce had whistled while he made his microwave dinner.

I feel clean, he observed. *Now, that's a funny thought. Clean of the pent up anger that I've been harboring for so long.*

As he slid into his drivers seat, he felt completely justified in what he had done. He felt as if another chapter in his new life had closed. Tomorrow would be a fresh new page and he was going to write his life into what he had always wanted.

As he pulled slowly into the road and out of the neighborhood, he thought to himself, *I make a great judge, jury, and executioner.*

He thought of the ones he had dealt with already and smiled. Then he thought of the ones who would eventually come to terms with their past actions and his smile broadened even more.

CHAPTER 31

"DAMN, SON, YOU look like shit," Jeremy Taylor said as Travis Sheridan ambled into Jeremy's study.

Travis was dressed in worn jeans, a wrinkled blue T-shirt underneath an untucked, unbuttoned oxford shirt, tennis shoes, and a faded Georgia Tech ball cap. He hadn't showered or shaved since he had received Jeremy's phone call. All in all, he looked like death warmed over.

A quick, wry smile escaped Travis's somber face, "Thanks, Jeremy.

"How was your trip?"

"The worst. Things always seem like they go the slowest when you are in the biggest hurry."

"I know how that is. Believe me, I know."

There was another slight awkward pause.

Jeremy continued, "It's been a long time, hasn't it?"

"Yes, it has."

"The only time I see you anymore," Jeremy said, taking his seat in his reclining desk chair, "Is when your picture is next to an article that you've written for the *Journal*. You're in there quite a bit. You're a busy man these days."

"Not so much lately, but I try to stay up on current events."

"Sure."

There was a small silence before Travis thought of something to say. "It's pretty sad, though."

"What's that?"

"That everyone hasn't kept in touch."

"I know."

"Since graduation, seems like everyone has grown up and moved on. Went their separate ways."

"True."

"No one takes the time to get together to remember the good old days. To me, that's sad."

Jeremy didn't know what to say about that so he didn't comment; instead, he changed the subject.

"So, how've you been, besides the obvious and latest news?"

"I was doing great until your call."

"I know. I know, and for that, I'm sorry. It's one of the hardest things I've had to do. I know it was hell having Kelly's passing on your mind during your flight back."

"I really don't want to talk about it, if you don't mind."

"I understand, but for what it's worth, I'm sorry for you. When I say that, I don't mean pity. I mean that I'm genuinely sorry it happened, and it pains me to see you hurting like this."

"Thanks. I appreciate that."

"You're welcome," Jeremy said. He motioned to a leather bound chair on the opposite side of his desk. "Have a seat."

"No, thanks. I'd rather stand."

"Suit yourself."

"I've been sitting for most of my trip back through two flights. I'm too keyed up."

"Rough trip back, huh?"

"Yeah, the worst."

Jeremy noticed Travis's demeanor. He looked nervous; anxious. Travis was wringing his hands now as he slowly paced back and forth.

"Travis?" Jeremy asked trying to gain his attention again.

Two audible snap from Jeremy's fingers directed his attention back to the conversation at hand.

"Yes. What? Oh sorry," Travis said. "My mind drifted. I was just thinking about the shitty trip. I'm running on fumes. What did you say?"

"I asked if you wanted something to drink."

"No, I'm fine."

"Oh come on. Let me play the host."

"No, really, I'm fine."

"You mean to tell me that we haven't seen each other in God knows how many years and you're not going to have a drink with me?"

"Look, I'm not really here for a social visit."

Jeremy approached another small table on the far side of the room and said, "I understand that." He slipped the glass top from the crystal Bourbon container and poured himself half a glass of its contents. Then he turned back toward Travis. "But it's been a long trip for you, I'm sure; I just thought you would like something to calm you down a bit. Soothe your nerves."

Surrendering, he dropped heavily into the chair near Jeremy's desk and dropped his head to his hands.

"Okay, since you put it that way, I'll have a beer. Nothing too stout. I want to keep my head clear."

"That's what I like to hear."

"You hungry?"

"Um. Yeah, sure; I could eat."

Jeremy picked up his phone and punched a button. After a few short moments, a barely audible voice came over the line. "Yes, Mr. Taylor."

"Miles, could you bring a sandwich and a beer for Mr. Sheridan please."

The only reply Travis could hear was a slight, "But of course, Mr. Taylor."

"Alright, tell me everything, and I mean everything you know about what happened to Kelly."

Jeremy paused. "It's not a fun story to tell."

"It's not a fun story to listen to either."

"Fair enough."

Jeremy stood motionless near his chair staring down at the light, brown liquid in his glass. He was trying to come up with the right words to use.

To Travis, he seemed like he was trying to figure out how to soften the blow but couldn't figure out how.

"Jeremy!"

Jeremy's head snapped up in Travis's direction.

"I'm not getting any younger."

"Right. Sorry."

Jeremy took a long whiff of his drink then downed half of its contents. He grimaced and shook it off, then spit out the words without any hesitation. He told Travis everything he knew about the incident.

When Jeremy finished, Travis said, "I want to see her."

"I don't think that would be a good idea."

"I don't fucking care what you think!"

"Travis! You're not listening to me."

"And you're not listening to *me*! She's my wife! If I want to see her then I have every right in the world to see her!"

"Yes, you do. But Travis don't you want to remember her the way she was?" He paused to let his words sink in. "Trust me; you don't want to see Kelly in her present condition."

"Yes, but you don't understand; I have to see her! It's the only way I can let her go! I have to see her with my own eyes! It's the only way that my mind will know. I can tell myself that all day long but my mind won't grasp it unless it has a visual to accompany it."

"Alright, Travis, alright. Settle down for a few seconds. We'll let you see the body if that is what you really want. We'll do that as soon as possible, but there's something else."

"What's that?"

He paused for a long moment, almost too long, and then went on. "When I viewed your wife's body, I viewed Suzanne Baldwin's body also."

"Suzanne Baldwin?"

"Yeah."

"What?"

"Yeah, um, she's dead as well."

"What the hell happened to Suzanne?"

"Suzanne had an even worse fate than Kelly."

"What's the story with her?"

Jeremy told Travis what happened; or what had supposedly happened.

"Why didn't you tell me this earlier?"

"We thought it would be best. We knew the trip was long, and we didn't want you worrying about anymore than you had to. We didn't know how much information to give you over the phone, so we just stuck to giving you all we could about Kelly's passing."

"You mean Kelly's murder."

"Yes, we just thought it would be best."

There was a slight lull in conversation. Neither man knew where to go from there.

As if on cue to the silence, a silver tray containing a Coors Light materialized at Travis's side.

"Your drink, sir."

When he heard the voice, Travis almost jumped out of his skin as well as his seat. Miles had entered with the silent efficiency of a ninja.

"I apologize for the interruption and for startling you."

"No. God. That's quite alright. I'm still a bit shaky from the trip and the news."

Travis took his drink and muttered a thank you.

"Your dinner is being prepared. It will be ready shortly."

"Thank you."

"It's not a problem," Miles said as he retreated from the room.

As soon as the door closed, Travis said, "Who do you think the killer is?"

"A guy by the name of Tyler Curtis."

"Who's he?"

"Are you serious? You don't remember? I thought you would remember since you're the news man. Tyler Curtis. That's the boy that Bruce Saliers saved about three months ago. Remember that? You did a couple of cover stories on him, didn't you?"

"Oh yeah, I remember now. I interviewed Bruce about that a time or two for the paper."

Jeremy continued, "Bruce rescued him. Suzanne was his doctor. Kelly taught him in school. That's another reason why Bruce thinks it was Tyler. Their paths crossed way too many times for us not to consider him. Seems like our lives would've been better off if Bruce had just left him there to die when he found him the night of his accident."

"You don't mean that."

"No, not really, but it seems like things have went downhill ever since he rescued that kid. I don't know what it is. But there is something wrong about all of this."

They were silent for a moment, then Jeremy went to his desk phone.

"Listen to this." Jeremy punched a button for the speaker phone. Then he punched in a number. There was a voice who asked for an extension. Jeremy pushed that number. "Alex forwarded me this message that Suzanne had left shortly before she died. I think you will find it interesting just as we did."

Suzanne's voice came through the speaker.

"Alex! Look, this is Suzanne! You've got to help me! Edward McDaniel is chasing me!"

At the sound of Suzanne's voice, Travis slowly sat up in his chair as the message played through. When he heard Edward's name, he stood and listened to the remainder of the message in a tense standing position.

When the message was finished, Jeremy said, "See what I mean?"

"That's just too weird, plain and simple. What's this business about Edward McDaniel? I thought he died back when we were teens."

"Yeah, I thought he did too.

Travis said, "I remembered I and some of the others had to drag you away from him that day at the docks. You were really pissed off that day."

"This business about Edward is like a bad rash. You can't get rid of it no matter how hard you scratch it. You know how hard I've tried to cover up that part of my life?"

Travis did a double take to Jeremy.

"What do you mean?"

"Meaning, it has been a sore spot in my life ever since that boating accident."

"Oh, thought you were meaning something else. Using the words 'cover up' admits guilt."

Jeremy was about to explain further, but they were interrupted by a brisk knock at the door and they both turned as Miles reentered again. This time he was carrying a tray of food.

"I'm sorry to interrupt your meeting again, but you had requested dinner for Mr. Sheridan."

Travis crossed to intercept it and shut the door in Miles's face with a curt "thank you". He placed the tray on Jeremy's desk and started eating.

The phone on his desk rang.

Jeremy leaned forward to look at the caller ID, then he picked up the phone. "Hey, Alex, talk to me." There was a slight pause. "Yeah, he's here. He got in a little while ago." Another pause. "I'm telling him everything right now. He's coping as best he can with the news. Have you come up with anything?" Jeremy was quiet for a long time as he listened to what Alex had to say.

Travis slowly circled the room as he ate.

Jeremy watched Travis and winced as bits of bacon, lettuce, and crumbs dropped to the floor.

As Travis moved, he stopped briefly at the tables and bookshelves to pick up and inspect items from each. He rolled them over in his hand then replaced each in its proper place and moved on.

When he came to the opposite side of the room, he noticed something that sent a chill down his spine.

Sitting on a shelf near the top of the bookcase was a dark, wooden display rack. This particular stand had been built especially for displaying a winning homerun baseball bat used in a championship game. Perched on the four-pronged frame, looking strangely out of place, was a light-colored wooden baseball bat. The odd thing about seeing it in Jeremy's house was that Jeremy had never played baseball for school, church, work, or anything. Travis had seen this bat before; remembered it from years earlier. Even more bizarre were the initials that had been gingerly and expertly carved into its wood grain. A capital 'E' followed by a capital 'M.'

Travis trailed his fingers over the initials and whispered, "Edward McDaniel. What the hell is this doing here?"

He examined the middle of the bat. There was no fracture or break line. It was complete. Travis was confused.

We broke this bat. We fucking broke it into. Why—

The phone was placed in its cradle a little harder than usual. The sound made Travis jump and jarred his thoughts. He angled himself toward Jeremy. He continued to stare at it as memories raced through his head.

414

"Good news. That was Alex," Jeremy said, trying to pull Travis's mind from the brainstorming he was obviously brewing over.

"What news is that?"

"Remember when I told you Bruce had collected some different samples he had found at the crash site?"

Travis nodded.

"It seems that one metal matches up with Suzanne's car and the other matches with the metal taken from Tyler Curtis's car."

"There's no doubt. It's the same metal."

"No question. It's a perfect match. It seems Mr. Curtis is doing some extracurricular activities after hours."

"So it's confirmed. Tyler Curtis is the one who killed my wife?"

"No, but wouldn't you agree that the two are too closely related that he should be questioned about it?"

"Without a doubt."

"Alex was headed over to Bruce's house to let him know as well. He said he tried to call him earlier but Bruce wasn't picking up. Bruce is probably asleep. Alex just pulled into his driveway when we hung up to tell him the news."

Travis changed the subject on Jeremy. "What are you doing with Edward McDaniel's baseball bat?"

Without hesitation, Jeremy said, "What makes you think it's his?"

"Your initials and the ones on this bat don't match."

"That's a good observation; a good reason."

"I remember breaking Edward's bat a long time ago. Word in school back then was that his grandfather had made it for him."

"I remember that day too. This isn't the same bat. Apparently, his grandfather made him another one."

"So, why do you have it?"

"Let's just say I used it to take care of some business a long time ago and that is all I am going to say about the matter."

Travis slid his hand down the broader surface of the bat. As he did so, he slowly rotated it with his other hand. The opposite side of the bat was tainted with a light maroon color, barely visible but was definitely there.

"You say you took care of some business with it?"

"That's right."

"I thought Edward drowned?"

For the first time, Jeremy raised his voice. "Hey, I didn't touch Edward with that bat so don't go assuming anything about me! It's nothing you need to worry yourself with! That was over and done with a long time ago. Just forget about the bat."

"Ask me no secrets, and I'll tell you no lies. Is that what you're saying?"

Jeremy took a deep breath to calm himself, "Yes."

"Okay. Understood."

"I'm glad we see eye to eye with that subject."

"Would you like for me to talk with Mr. Curtis?"

"If you wish, but that is strictly up to you. Feel free to use that bat to help persuade him to talk. Give him an attitude adjustment with it for all I care."

"I'll see if I can turn over some answers."

"Don't just get answers; solve some problems."

"If it comes down to it, I might."

"I didn't really think you had it in you, Travis."

"I don't, but sometimes some people can be pushed a little too far. And with Kelly being dead now, Mr. Curtis pushed a little too hard. I'm just going to push back a little harder."

"Now that is the Travis Sheridan I love and adore."

The phone rang again. Jeremy looked at the caller I.D. again. "It's Alex." Jeremy picked up the receiver. "Talk to me."

Travis could tell by the look on Jeremy's face that Alex had nothing but bad news. That seemed to be the norm around here.

When the call was finished, Jeremy slammed the phone back into its cradle. He picked up the half-filled glass of bourbon and pitched it against the far wall. The glass shattered.

"SON OF A BITCH!"

"What-what? What did Alex say?"

Jeremy took a few moments to calm himself before answering. "Alex just called to tell us that Bruce committed suicide earlier tonight."

CHAPTER 32

"HEY, MOM," TYLER said calling back into the house as he left for school. "Can you let Raven out before you go to work?"

Travis Sheridan barely heard Tyler's statement from his hiding place. Travis didn't hear Tyler's mom answer but assumed she had consented.

"Okay, thanks. I'll see you tonight. Love you."

Good, Travis thought. *God knows that dog would've surely pitched a bitch fit if Tyler had let him out now. No doubt he would have found me here.*

Travis rolled his eyes as he rolled the last two words over in his mind. *Love you. Yeah, love you is right. You can still do that and say that because she's still alive. I can't even say that to my wife anymore because she's dead now. That's entirely your fault.*

Travis was waiting behind a huge oak tree that was standing near Tyler's Mustang. Earlier that morning, he had parked his car a couple of blocks down the street and had walked to Tyler's house and was waiting for him now.

His grip tightened around the baseball bat he was holding. He brought it up in front of his face and softly bounced it against his forehead. He was trying to psych himself up to go through with this.

This was the crossover moment in time. If he acted now, he would be committing himself to these actions from here on out. On the other hand, he could not do anything, stay hidden and hope he wouldn't be seen, leave this situation alone, deal with his hurt and pain another way and go on with life.

Deal with my hurt and pain, he thought. *Isn't that what I'm doing?*

Feeling himself nod his head yes seemed to finally make his mind up.

"This is the only way to deal with it," Travis whispered to himself.

Again he looked at the bat and shook his head. *I should've brought a different weapon—one with more punch—one that's more threatening. Why did I even bother with this? Guess it will be good enough to get my point across.*

Tyler's car was parked in the driveway but with the front end faced away from the house. He had parked it this way so the driver's side door—with the missing rearview mirror—couldn't be seen by his mom or dad.

On approaching his car, Tyler stepped off the pavement onto the grass and circled around to the driver's side. He pulled his keys from his pocket and unlocked his car door with the button on his keychain.

When Travis heard the rattle of keys and the bleep of the car alarm, he peered around the tree and saw Tyler standing next to his car.

That's when Travis made his move. He came out quickly and moved around the back of the Mustang with purpose.

"I've got a bone to pick with you," Travis said as he started to swing.

Tyler was in the process of opening his car door when he heard the statement. As he turned to the speaker, from his periphery he saw a baseball bat coming around right in line with his head.

Instinct took over. Tyler's upper body flinched back to avoid being hit. His feet tried to move along with his body but the bare patch of dirt and gravel that was on the surface of the ground was too slick, which caused his feet to shoot out from under him. The result of the movement made him drop in place to the ground. It was just enough to get him out of harm's way.

The bat cut the air above Tyler's head with a whoosh and continued arching across until it connected with the back side window. It exploded on contact; the back seat collected all the fragments.

"Shit," Travis exclaimed. *Why did I say anything?*

"What the hell do you think you're doing?" Tyler asked as he uncovered his head with his arms. He stood from a clump on the ground. "That's my fucking car, man."

Travis said nothing; he swung the bat back over his shoulder getting ready to strike again and he stepped toward Tyler again.

As Tyler continued to counter away, Edward saw and recognized an older version of Travis Sheridan.

Why the hell is he here? Guess he finally found out about Kelly.

Travis was still slowly advancing toward Tyler.

"Travis," Edward said. "What do you want?"

His spoken name was enough to stop Travis dead in his tracks.

"How did you know my name?"

"I've known you for a long time now, Travis."

Frustrated, Travis took another full swing into the side panel of the car door. The swing was nowhere near Tyler but he stepped further away. It was only natural since he was dealing with a mentally unstable individual. The swing to the Mustang resulted in a nasty dent with chipped paint.

"Dude, ease up! You're ruining the paint job!"

"You think I give a fuck about your car. Who the hell are you and why did you kill my wife?"

"You should know. You're the one who sought me out, remember. But I think I know why you're here."

"Why is that, smart guy?"

"This so-called bone you have to pick with me most likely has to do with me killing your wife a few nights ago. She took a nasty tumble down the stairs."

Travis was stunned that Tyler admitted to it so easily. He was about to interject, but Edward held up a hand to stop him, then continued.

"I know it's tragic and that you may be upset."

"Tragic?" Travis asked. "You don't have the first clue about how tragic it is for me."

Ignoring his comment, Edward changed the subject. "I really wasn't expecting to hear from you so soon, but I'm really glad you stopped by."

Travis laughed, "Glad I stopped by?"

"Well of course. It'll save me the trouble of hunting you down later. I was eventually coming to see you, you know. You are actually the next one on my list."

Travis wasn't feeling that great right now; he was starting to feel like this whole ordeal was a mistake. Actually, the way Tyler spoke those words so calmly scared him to death. There was a slight amusement on his face; an amusement Travis didn't like.

"I guess Alex was right." Travis said under his breath.

"Right about what?"

"Silly, really," Travis said. He was about to explain but realized who he was talking to; his demeanor suddenly changed. "Nothing. It's none of your business."

Frustration continued to plague Travis. This meeting wasn't going as he had planned. To soothe his irritation, he did the only thing he knew to do. Create havoc. He whipped the bat back over his shoulder again, glanced toward the front windshield then back to Tyler. He gave a quick wink and a smile as if to say, "It's all over now, pal." He raised his arms even farther and began a harsh, sideways, downward swing to demolish the front windshield.

For a moment he had focused all his attention on the car and had blocked everything and everyone else out.

Travis never had time to connect with the window.

Edward saw Travis's intentions and let Tyler's natural instinct take over. He knew Tyler wouldn't let anything happen to his car if he could help it. Tyler charged Travis like a linebacker to a quarterback. Tyler caught Travis in the stomach with his shoulder then grabbed both sides of his upper thighs.

As both bodies collided, Tyler lifted Travis as high as he could before planting him into the grass.

The initial tackle wasn't hard enough to drive the air out of Travis; it startled him more than anything. The air was driven out of him when he felt the ground in his spine on the secondary slam. He felt a jarring pain as his head bounced off the blacktop. Pain flared out from the impact point and surrounded his head.

When Travis hit the pavement, the bat rolled from his hands. Tyler rolled from the top of Travis for fear he would latch on to him and a ground and pound scuffle would ensue. As Tyler stood, he grabbed the bat; he knew there would be no more damage to his car as long as it was in his possession.

As he stepped back, he asked, "Why are you here? Who sent you?"

Travis was still grasping for daylight as well as gasping for air. He shook his head trying to clear his clouded mind. Travis finally rolled over and onto his hands and knees, grunted, and slowly stood. He wavered as both hands went to the back of his head and rubbed gently to quell the throbbing.

Things had taken a terrible spin out of control from what he had planned.

"Who sent you?" Edward asked again as he shoved the thick end of the baseball bat into Travis's stomach. His voice was even more threatening.

"No one," he said in a defeated voice. "I came alone."

"I don't believe you."

Upon saying that, the garage door began to slowly open. Both heads turned in the direction of the noise.

"Dad!" Tyler exclaimed. He then turned back to Travis and pointed the bat at him. "Get behind the car and stay there until my father leaves."

"No. No, I don't think so; not today, pal."

A single stream of fury surged through Tyler's body.

Without warning of a backswing, Edward swung the bat forward into Travis. The first blow nailed Travis right below the rib cage. Tyler's left hand couldn't grip the bat as firmly as he wanted with it being injured. But it was a hard enough swing to take the breath from Travis again, and he doubled over. Travis clutched his stomach to soothe the aching. Edward immediately cocked the bat over his head and brought it down over the back of Travis's head. Travis crumpled to the ground and lay still.

"Whoa, no doubt about it, that's going to leave a nasty bump. Should've done what I said, chump."

Edward hoped he hadn't killed Travis. It would have been unfair to him if he had. He had already made plans for the two of them to spend some quality time together. The problem was getting Travis to the location he had already picked out.

The garage door finally clicked open. Tyler heard his father's car start up and knew he only had seconds before his dad left.

Wasting no time, Edward was already moving. He grabbed the car keys from the ground where he had dropped them during the initial attack. He quickly reached the back of the car and popped the trunk. Before the lid was completely raised, he had already scooped Travis's body up and more or less pitched him into the trunk. He took no special care in doing this. Edward stooped again, grabbed the bat, and threw it inside then he slammed the lid.

Edward glanced toward the house again to make sure no one was looking out the windows and had seen what he had done. He saw his dad's car backing out of the garage. He looked down at his book bag lying near the wheel well. As his eyes shifted that direction, they fell on the back side window that had been busted out.

"Holy shit! Can't let my dad see that. I would never hear the end of it. What excuse would I use?"

He moved toward his back pack and kicked as many stray glass shards underneath his Mustang as he did so. He scooped his backpack up and placed it up into the side window and pretended to look for something in it as his dad pulled next to him.

"You're still here?" Henry asked Tyler from over the roof of his car.

Tyler looked up and said, "Oh, hey, Dad. Yep, still here. Just about to leave though."

"I thought you were already long gone."

"I thought I was too. Just making sure I've had everything before I go."

Puzzled, his dad looked at him with concern. He didn't need to say anything.

"You go on," Tyler continued. "No need for both of us to be late."

"That's true."

Tyler looked guilty, as though he were hiding something.

"You alright, son?"

"Yeah, why?"

"Just curious. Looks and feels like something fishy is going on, that's all."

Tyler laughed, "No, don't be silly. Everything's fine, Dad. You worry too much."

"Yeah, I guess I do. Have a good day, son."

"You too, Dad."

With that, his dad pulled away and left him standing there next to his Mustang. Edward waited until he turned left at the end of the driveway and disappeared down the road.

Edward quickly unlocked his car door, threw his book bag in the far seat, jumped in, cranked the car, and pulled to the end of the driveway. He looked right; that was the only way to get to Silver Ridge High. Then he looked left, smiled, and pressed the accelerator. He wasn't going to school again today, but he was going to take Travis to school. He was going to play the teacher, and he had an important lesson. Edward had a strange suspicion that before the day was over, he would get his point across.

As Edward drove, he also took a ride down memory lane. The memories he had were seldom pleasant. He just wanted to remember one last time why he hated Travis Sheridan so much and why he couldn't forgive him.

CHAPTER 33

WHHAAACCCCKKKKK!

The old, familiar sound of a softball hitting the sweet spot of a bat echoed out of Edward's memory again. Edward always loved that sound and the solid feel of the bat when it connected perfectly with the ball.

The only job Edward ever had was at T.J.'s Golf 'N Games Amusement Park from the time the facility had opened. He had worked every station from the go-carts to Putt-Putt and from the water rides to serving food in their restaurant. He was always trusted to do his work without constant supervision and could always be counted on to fill in if someone couldn't make it to work that day. He had worked his way up through the employment chain until he had become assistant manager.

Along with his assistant manager position, there were a certain number of personal benefits that he collected on from time to time. One of those benefits was time spent in the batting cages for free.

Edward always enjoyed hitting softballs and baseballs but he never practiced in front of the customers. Observing eyes always made him nervous. He always waited until the park was closed.

When Edward was alone and if he'd had a particularly stressful day at school, he pretended that every pitched ball was the face and head of one of his classmates at school. Edward knew it was a morbid game, but it always made him feel in control. The students that treated him the worst always took first priority, but he would envision whacking their heads to the opposite side of the fence enclosure time after time after time.

One night, Jonas Roquemore had come to Edward with a wrapped present. Edward knew right off it was a baseball bat from its simple wrapped shape, and he ripped the paper off with excitement.

Surprisingly enough, the bat wasn't one of those mass-produced, cheaply manufactured, expensive, aluminum bats that you find in any sports store as Edward had expected. It wasn't even a store-bought wooden bat either. It was wooden, but what made this one so special was that it was crafted from the highest quality of wood his grandfather could find and carved with his grandfather's own arthritic hands.

He remembered the feel of the bat after he ripped it free from its wrapping; cool and natural. It was the smoothest, most perfect bat he had ever held in his hands.

"Thaddeus tells me that you're quite a slugger down at the batting cages," his grandfather said.

Still inspecting the bat, Edward replied, "Really? He lets me stay after while he counts the night's money and straightens up, but I never knew he watched me."

"Oh yeah, he's watched you on a number of occasions. Says you could knock it a lot farther if those damn fences weren't in the way."

Edward laughed, "You got to have those fences. I wouldn't hit as many if I had to chase after them when I was finished."

Jonas smiled, then said, "I suppose not. He say's you're pretty good, so I thought you should have your own bat instead of using those worn out bats down there at T.J.'s." His grandfather started to hint, "What I was getting at is maybe you should try out for a league; might build a little confidence. Might even be fun for you. Believe it or not, you might even make some friends."

Edward knew it would make Jonas happy to see him play for a team but he had no desire to. He loved the game of baseball, but he didn't even think he could get up the courage to play for a team. His imaginations were pretty vivid when he was by himself in the batting cage, and that was good enough for him.

A couple of days later, Edward returned to work and had taken his new baseball bat with him. He intended on taking some of his pent up aggression out at the batting cages. He was long overdue for his personal session.

When everyone was gone and after all his cleanup assignments were complete, Edward took his bat and some tokens from the token dispenser and headed for the batting cages.

When he walked outside, a cool breeze pebbled his arms and legs with goose bumps. Then the chill bumps disappeared as a slightly warmer breeze warmed him.

"Beach weather," Edward said as he turned his face into the breeze and breathed deeply. "No real fragrance, just a pure, clean smell."

The smell of the night breeze and the feeling of his chilled skin brought back to mind one of those perfect moments in time.

Funny how one memory will bring up a chain reaction of memories, *Edward thought.*

Edward had certain "perfect" moments in his life that stood out in his mind. Every so often, they would come to mind and he would experience them over and over as if he were actually there for the first time.

One summer, Edward and his grandparents had taken vacation for about a week at Edisto Beach. Near twilight, about an hour before the sun took its nightly dip in the ocean, Edward had taken a lounge chair down to the ocean's edge and set it within five feet of the incoming surf. He sat there as the cool-but-at-the-same-time-warm breeze blew in off the ocean.

He had also brought a novel with him. He tried to concentrate and read, but there were too many distractions. Eventually, he stopped trying to read, and drank in all of his surroundings.

He watched the sunset slowly extinguish itself in the Atlantic as the wind stirred the palm trees and blew across his body. A few boats drifted on wavering currents in the distance. He listened to the seagulls cry out unceasingly. He sat there marveling at the panoramic vista that lay in his line of sight.

It wasn't busy at this time of night; in fact, it was almost deserted. Occasionally, a man or a woman would walk or jog by. Edward figured they were meditating in their own thoughts and marveling at the night scape as he was. Every now and then, a pair of lovers would stroll by, arms around each other and holding their sandals in their hands.

"Perfect is the only word to describe it. Wish I could be back there again. I wish I could have another one of those perfect moments in time."

Edward never bothered with the batting cage helmets. He had been out here many times without supervision and never worn them before. Besides, Jonas had told him that Thaddeus watches him occasionally, and he had never reprimanded him for not wearing them. Furthermore, the helmets got on his nerves; they were uncomfortable and didn't fit on his head properly.

He fished one of the tokens from his pocket and slipped it into the slot to start the softball machine. The machine started to churn to life. He tapped the plate and swung the bat over his shoulder in anticipation. The machine soon spit a softball toward Edward in a perfectly pitched arc.

Edward swung hard and missed completely. It had been a while since he'd been down here, and he knew he was a bit rusty.

The machine spat again. Edward swung hard again. Again, Edward missed completely.

"No problem, no problem. Shake it off. Shake it off. You'll get the next one," he said psyching himself up. He was his own cheerleading squad.

The machine spit another softball. Edward swung. The ball ricocheted off the side of the bat into the ceiling of the cage and fell beside him.

"Getting closer; you better watch it," he said, directing his comments toward the pitching machine. "I'm going to smack your ass like the bitch you are," he promised.

Finally he got in a groove and smashed a few of the pitched balls against the opposite fence. Right as he was warmed up, the machine stopped and Edward fed it another token. The machine soon began shooting perfectly thrown pitches, which he knocked against the far fence.

Before the next set of softballs was through being pitched, Edward heard a familiar voice behind him. He recognized the voice.

"That's the sorriest damn batting average I think I have ever seen in my life."

The comment was made right as the pitch was nearing the plate. Distracted by the voice, Edward knew he wouldn't be able to hit it but swung at it anyway, a little harder than usual. He missed it completely and knew he looked ridiculous as he spun around to catch his balance.

There were a few chuckles of laughter as Edward turned toward the voice.

"What do you want, Travis?" Edward said without looking around. He knew who was behind him.

"I don't want anything," Travis said. "But I think you need me to show you how to hit that fucking softball."

The other two boys, Alex Riley and Bruce Saliers, started laughing to encourage Travis on.

It's always three of the four. They're always together. You never see them separated, *Edward thought*.

Another softball whizzed by Edward's shoulder and smacked the fence where Travis stood.

Startled by how close it had come to him, Edward moved further away from the pitching line.

"*Like that one right there. Watch it, Edward. Pay attention. You're supposed to hit the ball. That's the way the game is played, not the other way around.*"

"*I think I can manage, Travis.*"

Alex said, "*If you think you can do it better, Travis, why not get in there and show him how it's done?*"

"*I don't mind if I do.*"

"*I don't think you can, Travis,*" Bruce said. "*I think Edward has a much better batting average than you.*"

"*We'll see about that.*"

Edward didn't want them around but knew they were going to make a party of it like they always do. Travis's unhinging and entering of the batting cage confirmed that.

"*Alex, hit me with a token. Let me show this pansy how it's done.*"

Travis held out his hand for Edward's bat. Edward was hesitant to give it to him at first but eventually turned it over to him.

After Alex buried the token in the machine, the first pitch was struck firmly on the sweet spot of the bat. It was one of those perfect hits that Edward enjoyed smacking every now and then. It wasn't slammed to the far side of the cage but was hit solid right back toward the pitching machine.

"*Now if that was a real pitcher,*" Travis said pointing with the broad end of the bat. "*He would be picking himself up off the mound with one hand and holding his nuts with the other. That's the way it's done right there. You have to know how to place your hits. See, this next one is going over in right field.*"

And it did. Travis smashed it to the far corner of the batting cage. If he had hit that ball in a real game, it would've dropped close to the fence, if not over it.

"Are you noticing the placement of my body, Edward?"

"Yeah, I see it."

After each swing, he took his time getting in position for the next few pitches. He hit the rest of the set of softballs with ease, never missing any of them.

After the last pitch, Travis turned to Edward, "You have to be able to change your body angle at the last possible second to put it where you want it. Did you see how I changed my feet up after the pitch was thrown?"

"Yeah," *Edward lied.*

"I don't think you did. You're not in the best position to view this batting lesson. Hey guys, show him a better angle so he can see what I really mean.

"No guys, really, I can see fine."

Alex and Bruce entered the batting cage and grabbed Edward anyway and shoved him directly in the line of pitched softballs.

Edward realized what they were going to do. He tried to jerk his arms free from their grasp, but they held him firmly in place.

"Quit squirming, you little turd, this is for your own good."

Travis walked over and inserted another token for another round of balls. As the machine started up again, Travis stepped back to the batting area to get ready for the first pitch. When it came, Edward froze because he just knew Travis was going to purposely miss so it would hit him. At the last possible second, Travis whipped the bat through and knocked the ball to the left side of the batting cage.

Travis glanced around and said, "That made you a little nervous, didn't it?"

"Yeah. Maybe a little."

Did you see the way my feet were positioned?

With a sigh of relief, Edward said, "Uh-huh."

"No you didn't. You were too busy thinking I was going to miss the ball."

Travis noticed Edward's eyes getting bigger with terror. He turned again, took aim on the already pitched softball, and swung again. The ball spun out into the center of the cage.

"You don't have to worry about that. I never miss; that is, unless I want to."

Travis swung too low on the next ball that was pitched and Edward knew for sure that Travis missed on purpose. He really didn't have time to dwell on the thought, because the softball hit the front of his right leg. Pain flared in his thigh, and it brought him to his knees.

Indicating toward Edward's leg, Travis said, "Hey Edward, meet Charlie. He's a horse."

Alex and Bruce laughed as though a dirty joke had been told.

Edward sucked air in through his clenched teeth.

Travis said, "Stand him back up, guys. We're just getting started."

About the time they picked Edward back up, another ball had already been pitched. Edward saw it coming and anticipated Travis's purposeful miss again. He pushed off to the side with his injured leg. The ball snagging his shirt as it sailed by and then smacked the chain-link fence with a metallic ripple.

"That was a close one, Edward. Quick moves for a gimp. Alex. Bruce. Can't you guys hold that little shrimp boy steady?"

Edward had told himself after the last time that he wasn't going to be bullied ever again. So as they stood him up for the next pitch, he jerked his arms free and lunged toward Travis. Travis wasn't ready for an all out assault but threw his hands up to guard his upper body. Hoping and anticipating this move, Edward dropped low and punched through where Travis had left himself open. Edward's fist connected with Travis's groin area and he started to drop like a sack of rocks. As Travis was falling, Edward veered to the side, stood and pushed Travis into the pitching zone as another ball was shot out of the pitching machine. The ball caught Travis high in the middle of the back. He cried out in agony as he continued in his fall toward the pavement.

"Son of a bitch!" he yelled.

Travis rolled on the ground in agony clutching his family jewels and simultaneously grabbing for his back.

"Doesn't feel very good, does it, Travis? If any of you guys ever touch me again I swear to God I'll kill you."

"Don't make promises you can't follow through with, Edward," *Travis said.*

Alex and Bruce came up behind him and grasped him firmly.

"Hold on to that little prick bastard and don't let him go!" Travis yelled.

"Sorry, Travis," Alex said.

"Yeah, man. Sorry. He just got away from us."

By this time the machine had run its limit of ten softballs from the last paid token.

"We're just going to make sure that he doesn't," Travis said.

Travis stepped out of the batting cage and walked over to an advertisement banner that was tied onto the fence with four thin strands of Nylon rope. Each strand was tied to a different corner of the banner. Travis pulled a pocket knife from his jeans and sliced the bottom two lengths off, leaving the banner to flutter in the beach breeze. Travis closed and pocketed his knife as he entered the fence enclosure once more. He tossed one of the strands to Alex and the other to Bruce.

"Tie him up to the fence and make sure he doesn't get loose."

While Bruce and Alex obeyed, Travis picked up the bat Edward's grandfather had made and examined it as Edward had done when he first received it.

"Nice bat, Edward. Where did you get it?" Travis asked.

"None of your business."

"I asked you a question, Edward," Travis began again. "Where-did-you-get-this-bat?"

"And I gave you an answer; none-of-your-business."

The blow came swift, fast, and out of nowhere. It was a half-swing, but the bat caught him high in the sternum. The air was driven from his lungs and he slumped forward.

"What did you say again? I didn't quite catch it. I sometimes listen to my music really loud in my car and my ears aren't what they used to be. You were saying."

Edward was quiet for a few moments, trying to catch his breath.

Travis grabbed a handful of Edward's hair and pulled his head up to where they were facing each other.

"I can't hear you."

Reluctantly, Edward said, "My grandfather made it for me, you asshole."

"Your grandfather, huh? Well you tell your grandfather that his carpentry sucks because it can't hold up to the conditions of this sport."

Confused, Edward asked through struggling gasps of air, "Why? What do you mean?"

"Well just look." Travis walked to one of the side enclosures, wedged the bat against the fence and the pavement, grabbed onto the fence, and jumped high in the air.

Edward watched in horror as Travis dropped all his weight onto the center of the bat. There was a loud, audible snap as the bat broke and folded into two pieces as though it were nothing more than kindling.

"See what I mean?"

"Fuck you," Edward yelled. He lunged at Travis, but he was pulled back against the fence because his wrists were tied. "Why did you do that? Why are you doing this to me?"

"I don't know, Edward. Does there really have to be a reason?"

"Yes!" Edward shouted.

"I never really thought about it like that. Alex, Bruce; do you have any ideas on the subject?"

They muttered as though they didn't know what Travis was getting at.

"They don't know either, Edward. Guess you're shit out of luck on finding a reason. But if I had to come up with a reason off the top of my head it was probably because you punched me in the nuts and then pushed me into the firing line.

"You started this way before that happened. I did that because I was trying to protect myself from you."

"Don't try to turn this around on us like we're the ones at fault."

Edward didn't understand what he was getting at. He couldn't believe that they were turning this situation around on him. Edward figured the best thing to do was to just be quite and eventually this incident would be over. It was just like all the other times.

"Just leave me alone."

"Oh c'mon, Edward, don't be that way. We just want to play a game. We're going to play a really whacked out version of dodgeball. There are only three things that are different. One, the balls are smaller. Two, the ball is

harder, and three, you only have a minimal amount of room to maneuver. You like those odds? Do you think you can handle that?"

"Fuck you," Edward said again.

"Ohh, big words from such a small guy, and by the way, that's fuck you, sir." Travis dropped his last token in the slot.

Edward ripped his gaze from Travis to the churning pitching machine again and braced himself yet again for the oncoming barrage of red-stitched white missiles.

The first ball came fast, but Edward was able to maneuver his body so it hit the fence instead of him.

"Good job, Edward. That's the way to do it."

He did the same for the second and third balls.

"Hey man, you keep this up and we'll give you another round with that whore Suzanne Baldwin. We know you have some unfinished business with that slut."

Those sentences distracted Edward, and he glanced over toward Travis, who was grinning.

"Don't look at me. Focus, Edward," Travis said as he pointed toward the pitching machine.

The machine had already spit the fourth ball, and he wasn't ready for it. He anticipated his move too quickly and lost his balance. He fell back into the line of fire and the ball stuck him hard in the lower stomach. Even though it hit him low, his breath was taken from him.

"Hey guys, pay up. You both said he would be able to go a whole round without getting hit with a softball. Now both of you shitheads owe me money."

"But you distracted him," Bruce whined.

"Doesn't matter. We never said we couldn't distract him. You both are orphans and I just showed you who your daddy is."

All Edward wanted to do was double over and curl into a ball but his arms were tied securely in place.

He looked up when he heard the metallic spitting sound of the pitching machine again. Edward threw himself out of the way but forgot his arms were tied. The reaction of his tied hands stopped him in his tracks and pulled him back to where he had just been standing. He had dropped closer to the *ground and the ball nailed him in the center of his left pectoral muscle. It felt like his arm immediately went numb. Tiny needles of pain stabbed in and out of his shoulder with every heartbeat.*

"Don't just stand there, guys. Help the man up. He's injured."

Alex and Bruce quickly stood him up on his feet just as the sixth ball was pitched. He had moved slightly to the right when standing and the softball hit him in the lower part of the left leg. It caught him right above the knee. The pain was excruciating. Edward yelled aloud and dropped back down to the ground. If the ball had struck him any lower on his leg, it might have shattered his kneecap.

Edward watched as the seventh ball came toward him at bone-breaking speed. At the last possible moment, he threw himself out of the way, and it was timed perfectly. The ball just grazed his side and smacked the fence behind him.

Edward let out a sigh of relief but knew he had a few more to go out of this batch. The next unavoidable softball caught him high on the right side of the stomach. It was already hard to breathe and now the latest ball had nixed that. His air was coming to him through ragged breaths. His legs gave out and he slumped even lower. He felt like giving up. He couldn't do anything. He was tied up and useless.

The next ball struck him in the center of his chest. His wrists were still bound but he fell forward as though knocked unconscious. He felt paralyzed. He couldn't move his legs. His stomach and legs ached. His arms and wrists hurt from straining against the ropes that held him in the line of fire.

Edward heard the sound as though someone blew a dart through a blowgun. It was all he could do to raise his head. Time seemed to have slowed down as the softball arced toward him. He tried in vain to throw himself out of the way, but his body wouldn't budge. He was too tired and drained from the other blows his body had already received. He couldn't move; he was paralyzed. All he could do was brace himself for the incoming impact. For a second, he thought it was going to sail over him, but it dropped lower at the last second. It was the last thing Edward saw.

An intense pain engulfed his head as the softball glanced off the left side of his forehead. The softball hit him with enough force to push him back parallel to the ground. His body fell back against the fence and slumped to the ground.

Along with the pain came an all encompassing darkness.

The last thing he heard before he drifted away into Never-Never Land was Travis Sheridan saying, "He better be glad the fast pitch baseball machine was out of order."

As usual, the boys just laughed as they walked away.

Edward thought, I'm just glad you didn't check my pockets for any tokens. I had close to three dollars worth. I have no doubt they would have used—

Before he could finish his thought, unconsciousness infected him like a quick-spreading disease, and as always, he surrendered to it.

CHAPTER 34

A LOUD, METALLIC slap echoed in Travis Sheridan's ears and he slowly opened his eyes. What he saw was out of focus, but he knew it was his arm that was stretched out beside him. Tiny, sharp pin pricks simultaneously pierced his arm when he tried to move, and he winced at the pain. Not only was his arm asleep, but it wouldn't budge either; something was restricting it. When he opened his eyes again, he saw double vision. Two right arms swam in different directions for a moment then settled back into focus.

Travis furrowed his brow and cocked his head in confusion. A metal ring was clamped around his wrist. The other ring was attached to what looked like a four-foot-length of chain that was pulled tight and attached to the mesh of the nearby chain-link fence.

"Handcuffs?" he asked himself as he jerked against the restraint. It rattled against the fence and the car he was propped up against. Pin pricks needled his arm, again and he cringed against the sting. He flexed his fingers as the blood began to circulate through his arm again.

He whipped his head around in the opposite direction and saw that his other arm was in somewhat of a same scenario only slightly lower. Another pair of handcuffs gripped his wrist and was attached through the handle of whatever car he was leaning against.

"A car handle? What the fuck? Why the hell is my arm—" he began but was stopped in mid-sentence as another loud, metal slap popped in his other ear.

Travis felt as though he had been hit by the unidentified flying object. Startled, he jerked his head back and screamed in alarm. "Ooh! Holy Jeez! Shit!"

He heard the sound before he acknowledged the white blur that flew in front of his face. The white blur bounced off the car and disappeared from eyesight; most likely because he had closed his eyes from being startled by the sound.

When he opened his eyes again, he noticed a small impact crater where the white blur had just been. The faded, slightly rusted paint had chipped and fallen away to the ground.

"Good morning, Travis," a distant voice said cheerfully. "We thought you were dead."

Travis didn't answer. He was still bemused about everything that was happening and was trying to figure out a way to escape from his confines.

"Didn't you hear me?"

Travis finally jerked his head toward the voice and saw a blurry figure. "What?"

It felt as though someone was screwing around with the focus of his vision. The figure was so out of focus that he was seeing double again. As though an invisible hand was trying to bring everything into a central focal point, the two turned into one, then back into two. Travis shook his head vigorously, blinked his eyes, then stared at the figure again. The two figures finally slid together into one person.

It was that guy, Tyler Curtis, whom he had approached earlier this morning. He shook his head as he remembered the incident that took place. *Why was I so stupid to try that?*

Tyler stood on a mound of dirt about forty feet away and was in the process of leaning over. He dipped his hand into a nearby box then reappeared with what looked like a pale grapefruit and stood again. Tyler's other hand gripped the inside of a baseball glove. Then it all came back to Travis in horrifying clarity; he knew what was happening.

Another memory flowed through his mind—the one where he was on the opposite side looking back at a teenage boy who was pulling against yellow banner ropes just as he was doing now.

That's no grapefruit at all; it was a baseball; no-no, more like a softball.

He's aiming near me or at me; no doubt the next one is going to land somewhere on me.

"I said," Edward began as he wound up to pitch the next ball. As he released it he repeated himself, "Good morning!"

From Travis's mental haziness it seemed as though the figure's body shuddered for a moment. Travis realized another softball had just been pitched.

The ball came directly toward Travis, but he had nowhere to go. He was locked down. He closed his eyes, leaned his body as far left as he could, and waited for the impact. At the last second, the softball curved away into the metal of the car with another hard, metallic smack.

The abrasive sound tingled in his ears again and echoed across the overgrown car lot.

Travis shouted as though he had just been branded, "Stop it! What the hell's the matter with you?"

"That, my friend, is what we call a curveball," Edward said. He changed his pitch to a whiney, sarcastic voice, "Better be glad I'm not using *baseballs*." He dropped back to his regular voice again. "Those, I'm sure, would leave permanent tattoos."

Travis looked again at both of his out stretched arms and jerked against the restraining metal.

"Oh-no-no, I wouldn't do that if I were you," Edward said, preparing to throw another pitch.

Travis stopped and focused his attention back on Tyler.

Reading Travis's face, Edward continued to explain, "You might cause your whole world to come crashing down around you."

Still bewildered at his comments, Travis hesitantly asked, "What?"

Edward pointed above Travis, "Above you, stupid."

Travis looked up as he was told. Above him he saw five other crushed cars that were stacked on top of each other.

At first glance the looming tower of cars startled Travis and he let out a small gasp of air. He shot quick looks around and finally noticed his surroundings. They were in a junkyard that was filled with old, wrecked cars and trucks that were overgrown with tall weeds and choking ivy. Travis didn't know which dominated the scene more, the lush vegetation or the forgotten automobiles. Most of the cars were rusted through; their doors and mirrors barely hanging on by corroded hinges or loose wiring. Others sat discarded with their hoods up and windows smashed. Severe body damage had mangled most of the automobiles' bodies; others had nothing more than a few dings, dents, and scratches, but all were forgotten. Bits of trash and old signs littered the lot as far as the eye could see.

There didn't seem to be any type of special sorting system in the lot. As long as they were not in the way of the main road, that seemed to be all that mattered.

He jerked against his restraints. The cars above him swayed slightly. From his point of view, they looked as though they were Jericho's walls that were on the verge of tumbling down.

He slowly stopped, rotated his arms, and placed his palms against the rusty finish as though that would be enough to steady them from toppling over.

Travis's surroundings were distracting and he was focused on everything except the person who was conducting this meeting.

Edward didn't like that.

Travis didn't notice Edward grab another softball from the box at his feet. He didn't see Edward wind up and pitch a hard fastball either. That realization came only after the ball connected with his top portion of his left leg about six inches above the knee. It was a rich pain and it started throbbing immediately.

Travis let out a howl of sheer misery. He didn't know why they called them softballs because that one hurt like a son of a bitch. Travis had thick legs from the days he did workout so there was a lot of muscle to cushion the blow. It felt like a severe muscle ache that was still with you two days after an intense workout.

Travis yelled, "I stopped. I quit!"

"Meet Charlie, he's a horse." Edward said indignantly. "Does that phrase bring back any memories for you?"

It did, definitely; but Travis didn't understand how Tyler could possibly know about that. Travis played it safe and continued to rant and rave with painful commands. "Stop it! Just stop it! Please!" Travis shouted.

"Huh, funny. I can remember saying those exact words myself."
Edward said. "You remember me saying that?"

"Of course not. I barely know you."

"Huh, pity," Edward said. "Well, it doesn't matter; just give it some
time and I *know* it will all come back to you."

"What do you want with me, Tyler?"

"Oh, so we're on first name basis now. I could ask you the same
question, *Travis*."

There was a brief silence between them. During that time, Travis
shook his arms vigorously against their confinement. "What the hell are
you doing?" Travis screamed. "What the fuck do you want with me?"

"I'll tell you what we're going to do. We're going to play a little
game, you and I, and how we're going to play is, I'm going to ask you a
question, and you're going to answer it."

Travis started to protest, but Edward held his hand up and stopped
him before he got a word out.

"If at any time I feel you're trying to pull a fast one on me or if I
feel that you're lying in any way, I won't hesitate to…" Edward's voice
dropped off; he leaned down, dipped his hand in the box of softballs,
extracted another one, and righted himself again. He held it up for Travis
to see. He repeated himself for emphasis, "I won't hesitate to hit you
with one of these again. I pegged you one time and I can do it again. You
can be assured of that."

"Who are you?" Travis finally said gasping between deep breaths.

"I think you know the hard answer to that."

"What do you want?"

"What makes you think I want anything?" Edward said. "Listen, you
came after me first."

"Quit beating around the fucking bush and tell me what you want!"
Travis yelled.

"Answers. Just some answers, Travis."

"What kind of answers?"

"Answers to my questions."

"I'll be damned before I'll play along with this charade. Let me go!"

Without thinking twice, Edward pitched another over-handed fastball.

Travis saw the movement and braced himself for the impact again. He lowered his head just in case it was going to be a head shot; he figured the skull portion of his head could take a blow better than his facial features. He had flexed all the muscles in his body on the account that the ball would make contact this time.

The softball caught Travis low in the right side of his stomach. Even though his abs were flexed, the softball was like a penitent fist and it packed a lot of punch. It didn't drive the breath out of him as he expected, but it would've dropped him to his knees if his arms weren't restrained. Travis doubled over and hung from the car by his handcuffed wrists for a few seconds before he was able to gain his balance again.

"I told you I wouldn't miss. Now, what were you saying to me?"

"Cut it out!" Travis screamed. "That hurts!"

In any other setting, that phrase might sound childish, even silly coming from a grown man, but here, in this isolated place, it was uttered with 100 percent pure rage.

Amusing, Edward thought as he smiled at Travis's choice of words.

"Yeah, no shit it hurts. That's one thing we both agree on. It hurts like hell when it happened to me years ago at T.J.'s, and I'm here to make damn sure it hurts like hell for you."

"Help! Somebody help me!" Travis screamed, realizing he wasn't going to get out of this situation alive. He was frantic and looked around in all directions at once for anyone who might be nearby.

Edward glanced behind himself to see if Travis had seen somebody he hadn't. No one was in the vicinity. They were alone in the wasteland of cars that time forgot.

"Somebody help me!" he continued shrieking as he jerked against his shackles. He turned his head to look through the wire mesh behind him hoping to see anyone. "Help! Somebody! This guy is trying to—"

Travis had been too busy looking in different directions that he didn't see Edward stoop again, grab two more softballs, wind up, and release them one right after the other. After he released the second softball, he charged toward Travis. If the softballs wouldn't shut him up, he definitely would.

Edward was hoping both softballs would land on Travis's body, but he had thrown them with such haste that he doubted either would find a target. The first ball shattered the side window above Travis's head. Glass shrapnel rained down into Travis's hair and clothes. Travis didn't have any time to react to it before the other one found a spot high on the right side of his chest. The second one seemed to get his point across.

Lightning erupted throughout Travis's shoulder area. The pain was intense.

Travis instinctively moved his arm to caress and massage the now throbbing pain away, but he couldn't move his hands to his shoulder.

Travis let out a stream of obscenities as he sucked air between his clenched teeth. When his verbal outburst abated, he asked, "What the hell's your prob—"

Travis wasn't able to finish; Edward had already reached him. He slammed into Travis as he let out some more curses as his body was sandwiched between the car and Tyler's body. Edward grabbed Travis's face and forced him to look him dead in the eyes. "My problem is you. QUIT YELLING! You're about to wake the neighbors!"

Travis yelled back defiantly, "THAT'S WHAT I'M TRYING TO DO, YOU FUCK!" He strained against the cuffs as he tried to lash out at Tyler.

No sooner were the words out of his mouth that an open-handed smack stunned him into silence.

"Oh, I'm sorry; I forgot. There isn't anyone around that can hear you. We're out here in the middle of nowhere. We're in a forgotten car lot on the north side of the city. There's no one around for miles. But I suggest that you shut up because it's getting on my fucking nerves. I won't tell you again. Quit screaming or I'll give you something to scream about."

It sounded rudimentary, Edward thought, but it was successful in stopping Travis's tantrum. Travis lowered his head, pouted, and tried not to let the pain get the best of him.

As Travis thought about what was said, Edward turned and headed back to the mound where he had been standing.

By the time Edward got there, Tyler's words had sunk in. Travis asked, "What do you want to know?"

"First of all, who sent you?"

"Nobody," Travis said almost immediately.

"Oh, you have a habit of attacking people on your own in their front yard for no reason?"

"Yes. I mean, no."

"Ah-oh, somebody is indecisive," Edward said. He had just picked up his baseball glove but on second thought dropped it again. As it landed in the patch of dirt near his feet, Edward picked up the baseball bat that was leaning against a nearby dilapidated truck. Edward continued speaking as he slowly walked toward the manacled Travis. "Better make up your mind quick before you lose a battle with my ugly stick. Over the years, I've become a real heavy hitter."

Travis hadn't noticed the baseball bat earlier. From his vantage point, he couldn't see it behind the demolished truck.

"Wait; now hold on for just a second," Travis pleaded.

"Where—in the world—did you get—this bat?"

"What do you mean?"

He held it up in front of his face as he continued to approach. "This bat? You had it with you when you met me earlier today. Where did *you* get it?"

There was a long pause; too long in fact.

Travis blurted, "I don't know. I didn't get it anywhere. It's just one I had."

"No, sir. This isn't one you "just had," this bat is a rare find. So rare, in fact, that it's the only one in existence. You remember, oh seventeen, eighteen years ago when you and your asshole buddies came down to the batting cages at T.J.'s where I worked? You remember tying me up, sort of the way you are now, turning on the pitching machine and watching it strike me out? You remember taking the bat I was using, my bat, wedging it between the fence and the ground and purposely breaking it?" Edward stepped into Travis. "You remember that?"

Travis did remember but opted to play dumb, "No. What are you talking abo—"

From out of nowhere a pain ripped through Travis's stomach and he doubled over as far as his manacles would allow.

Frustration getting the best of Edward, he had jerked the bat back and had swung into Travis with as much force as he could gather.

The bat had connected solidly. Travis's breath was completely knocked out of him and he struggled to gather it again in raspy gasps of air.

Edward took a quick moment to shake out his left hand. He had gripped the bat too tightly and swung it too quickly, not registering the pain in his left hand until after he'd hit Travis.

As the pain had subsided, Edward immediately slid the barrel of the bat up Travis's torso until it rested under his chin. Edward then lifted him up and shoved him back against the car until they were at eye level.

"Remember the rules I explained earlier?"

"Yes," Travis wheezed.

"I told you earlier not to lie to me. Remember?"

"Yes."

"Good. Now that you really understand, do you remember the episode I just explained?"

Resigning to the truth, Travis confessed, "Yes."

"I knew you did. What you didn't know is that my grandfather slaved for days to make that bat for me. He spent hours sanding down the wood and polishing it for me until it was perfect."

"What are you talking about?"

No answer.

There was a span of time when neither of them said anything; they just stared hollowly at each other. To Travis it seemed that Tyler's body had just shut down. There was no emotion whatsoever.

Figuring he'd better say something, Travis said, "I'm sorry about your bat. I didn't know your grandfather had made it for you."

Edward said, "It wouldn't have mattered if you did. You couldn't have cared less about me or anything about me."

"Now wait just a minute, you've got it all wr—"

Edward cut him off when he held the baseball bat directly up in front of Travis's face. He didn't want there to be any mistake in Travis's next answer.

"You see these two letters?"

There was an engraved 'E' and an 'M' surrounded by a carved oval toward the tip of the bat.

"Yeah, so?"

Edward tapped him in the head with the bat.

"Stop, damnit," Travis exclaimed. "What was that for?"

Edward held a finger up to emphasize his next statement, "Cut the sarcasm." He rotated his hand to where his finger was pointing at the bat. "They aren't just letters. They're my initials. You know what the 'E' and the 'M' stand for, don't you?"

"No," Travis lied again.

Edward was quick; he sidestepped away from Travis and swung the baseball bat again. Another hard, breathtaking blow was delivered a little lower in the midsection of his stomach. There was a crunch and crack of breaking bones when the bat struck home. Travis sucked in a deep breath of air between clenched teeth and doubled over again from the pain.

"Don't lie to me, Travis," Edward said, shaking his bitten left hand again. "Or the next one is going to be aimed at your kneecap, understand?"

Responding only in a whisper, Travis said, "Of course. Yes."

"You know what these initials stand for, don't you. I know you do."

Dumbfounded, Travis looked at Tyler.

"I'll get the truth out of you even if I have to beat it out of you."

"Come on. Wait. Now hold on—"

"Sorry, but I don't have any more time to waste. It's getting late."

"The initials stand for Edward McDaniel! Is that what you wanted to know?"

"Yes, very good. That's correct. See, I knew you knew. When my grandfather made that first bat that you purposely broke, the last thing he did was personalize it for me. It was something of value to me. After you broke the first one, he slaved away to make me another one; this one. He did the same thing with it; he engraved my initials on it."

"That can't possibly be your bat."

"And why not?"

"Because you're Tyler Curtis."

"I can see how you would think that but I'm sorry, you're sadly mistaken. I am Edward McDaniel." He grabbed three of Travis's fingers and gave him a limp handshake. "I'm so pleased to meet you. Alright, I'll come clean. I am Tyler Curtis but I'm also Edward McDaniel. I've taken up my permanent new residence in Tyler Curtis's body. Why is it so hard for you people to realize that?"

"So it is true."

"What's true?"

Travis was silent.

Edward lowered the bat and tapped Travis's kneecap three times, "Tell me or you'll wish you had."

There was a heavy sigh. "Alright. Okay. It's Alex; you remember him I'm sure?"

"Yes," Edward said shooting back his own bullet of sarcasm. "*Definitely.*"

"We didn't believe what he was saying."

"Who's *we*. And what did *he* say?"

"It really wasn't anything in particular."

Travis saw Tyler's arms rotate the bat back in another batter's stance. Then he saw Tyler's eyes drop to the level of his kneecaps.

Urgently he said, "No, really. That's the truth," he said as he moved his legs as far out of the bat's reach as possible without losing his balance. He moved to hold his hands out in front of him, but they wouldn't budge. His hands automatically opened palm up in a stopping gesture. "For the love of God, would you just listen? It's just second-hand information. I don't even know if it's true. Jeremy told me that when he, Bruce, and Alex met in the morgue, he said that Alex mentioned that he believed you had somehow passed back over or had come back. It was the only explanation they could come up with as to why Edward McDaniel is back haunting us. Bruce and Jeremy thought he was talking nonsense. Alex always watched too much of that science fiction shit anyway. They, I mean, we…we've always thought he was a little off in his head."

"Where did they get the idea that I was back in the first place?"

Edward asked. "Someone had to tell them or give them the idea that I was back in town."

"They have a recording from Suzanne on the night right before her car went off the road and blew up. She called Alex's work number in the morgue and told him that you were chasing her and that she thought you had harmed or killed Kelly."

"Oh, so that's how everything got out of hand," Edward mused. To Travis he said, "Are you convinced now?"

"What do you think?"

"Where did you get this bat?"

"I got it from Jeremy Taylor, alright." Travis confessed. "I have no idea where he got it from and that's the God's honest truth. I was with Jeremy in his office. I saw it sitting on one of the highest shelves on a display holder as though it were a winning trophy. He gave it to me to use on you after I left his house this morning. That's all I know."

"Did you have a chance to look at this bat closely before you came after me?"

"No," he said sarcastically. "Why would I want to do that?"

"Because it already has dried blood on the back of the bat."

"What?"

The bat entered Travis's view again. He had no choice but to look at the bat; it was directly in his line of sight.

Edward rotated the bat. The initials moved around to its back side and were replaced with a long, faint, splotch of maroon. Upon closer examination, Travis saw some smaller splotches that could in fact be blood along the shaft of the bat.

"Any idea whose blood that might be?"

"No, I don't, but then again, you don't even know if it *is* blood?"

"If I were a betting man, I would make a very high wager that it is."

"Well, I don't know whose it is. Don't really care either. Jeremy's the man you need to talk to, not me."

"Oh I will. Believe me, I will. Very soon."

"What's going to happen to me? Are you going to let me go now? I've told you all that I know."

"What is this talk about letting you go? I can't let you go. I don't trust you enough to let you go. You would go immediately to the cops. I know it."

"No. Please. I wouldn't. You've got to believe me. I swear on everything that is holy. And on everything that isn't. If you've never believed in anyone, believe in me. I swear I will never talk to anyone about this. Ever. I promise; I'll take this secret to my grave. You've got to trust me on this one."

"I'm sorry, but you're just talking up the impossible."

"You mean to tell me you're just going to kill me right out here like this?"

"Is there another way you would like to go?" Edward flashed a huge grin. "I'm open to suggestions."

"I just want to go! That's all I want!"

"Go?" Edward asked in dismay. "Go? After all the shit I had to go through to make our little meeting happen? There will be no going."

"If you're going to kill me then kill me. Quit being a bitch about it. Get it over with."

"I'm taking my time with you, Travis. Just like you and the others did in days past."

"We'll see how you like it when I don't talk back to you. You'll get nothing more out of me."

Edward's angered heat engulfed Tyler's body, fully possessing him with hatred.

Tyler knew Edward was about to do something crazy. He'd known it ever since he had thrown Travis in the Mustang's trunk back at his house. Ever since then, Tyler had tried over and over to squirm free from Edward's submission. It was like he was throwing himself at grinding wheel and was being worn down, but he kept trying.

"Oh you'll talk," Edward said, flipping the bat from one hand to the other. "You'll say plenty more before it's over. Just like it was with your wife."

"Yeah, I know all about that, Tyler!" Travis shouted. "You've made your point. You killed my wife too! I get it."

"And your cat Mosey; let's not forget about her."

"You killed Mosey?"

"Yes, sir. Broke her neck and back. Kelly had almost the same injuries as Mosey after she took that crazy tumble down the stairs."

"You smug son-of-a-bitch. I'll—"

"And here is just a small sample of what that was like for them."

Tyler felt and saw his arms fly up and over his head as though he were a lumberjack about to chop a piece of wood. It happened so quickly Tyler was powerless to stop them. Both of his fists clenched the handle of the bat even tighter. Edward brought the bat down in the vicinity of Travis's head.

Travis saw Tyler's quick arm movements and saw what was coming. He threw his body to the right as far as the manacles would allow. It was just enough.

The bat whizzed by Travis's left ear with a whoosh. The downstroke was a crushing blow. Travis felt his left collar bone splinter as the bat connected with his shoulder area.

Travis's body immediately erupted in a white-hot agony. He almost passed out. Travis's scream was deafening to both he and Edward; it was louder and longer than any he had released today.

Edward grabbed Travis underneath his jawbone and slammed him back up against the car. Travis's head bounced off the metal of the car's roof and was accompanied with an immediate dull ache. "I said shut up! Don't you ever talk to me about what I've done, understand? You have no right. But you're right; you are absolutely right. I did kill her and I enjoyed every minute of it. I had my reasons for doing it too. Do you know what happened? Did they tell you what I did to her?"

Travis nodded.

Edward continued, "Of course, you and Kelly had a perfect relationship. Did she tell you what she did to me…to Trevor?"

Travis answered by nodding again.

"I thought so. If you knew that then you'll know why I did the same to her. It all goes back to that eye for an eye material that my grandmother always preached to me. But that situation has nothing to do with you so why don't you for once just think about what you did. I want you to focus on that."

Anger seized Edward again. He backed up two steps, swung the bat over his shoulder then came at Travis with everything he had.

Travis was expecting another blow to his upper body, but the bat came down in a diagonal sweep. His eyes followed the arcing bat in a paralyzed horror and saw it connect to the top of his kneecap. The pain was instantaneous and excruciating. His left kneecap shattered and his leg folded back on itself. He instantly looked away as he witnessed it crack backwards and yelled to the top of his lungs. His normal curses erupted at first but soon turned into pleas of mercy and requests of forgiveness.

It felt as though the middle of his leg had exploded. When he looked down at it again, he half-expected to see the bottom portion unattached and discarded like one of the old cars. In his mind, he prayed to God that his other leg wouldn't be next. There was no way he could stand and put pressure on both at the same time.

As though talking to a child, Edward said, "Now you listen to me and listen good. Just to set the record straight, Tyler didn't harm a hair on your wife's sexy little head; but I, Edward McDaniel, did. I want to make that perfectly clear. He gets no credit for this."

Through clenched teeth and stinging tears, Travis managed to say, "Look, I'm sorry. Is there any possible way we can forget everything that has happened? I mean now and from years ago. I was stupid back then. I didn't know what I was doing. I came on my own to have it out with you but only because you killed Kelly. Can't we just forget the whole thing? You've paid me back for what I did to you by killing Kelly."

"No, no. Correction; I paid Kelly's debt off in full for the incident that happened between us in Biology class. You've just begun to pay for yours. I would love to be able to say yes to your request, but you see, I don't have the ability to forget, therefore I will never be able to forgive."

The brief memory of Travis's sins flickered in Edward's thoughts again then faded. When he came back to reality, he found his arms tingling with anticipation.

From out of the distant past, his grandfather's advice rang true in his mind: *Keep your eye on the ball, Edward.* Although there was no ball for him to hit, he kept his eye on the target. Travis's head was a bigger target than he was used to.

Travis leaned further back into the automobile silently praying Edward would stop. Edward didn't; he swung the bat again and with everything he had.

Travis couldn't move because his body was already numb with pain. He couldn't even close his eyes.

Two engraved initials was the last thing Travis saw before the bat crushed his face into an unrecognizable mask.

CHAPTER 35

AFTER EDWARD HAD taken care of Travis Sheridan, he had a hard time bringing his anger under control. His mind kept spinning, reliving the moment that had just happened as well as what Travis had done to him as a teen. Although justice had been served and Edward was thrilled with the results, his anger seemed to swell rather than diminish.

As he relived the memories of his teenage years, his mind latched on to the image of Adrian Connell. That is what seemed to bring him down off his angered high. Adrian Connell, the one girl from his high school that made him feel normal and accepted. The more Edward thought about her the more relaxed he became.

Edward caught himself rubbing his talisman again.

Old habits die hard, he thought.

As he rubbed the charm, his mind drifted back to the moment when Tyler had found it in Adrian's old trunk that sat askew in the back of the attic.

Edward decided to look her up and see where she was and what she was doing since he had drowned so many years ago.

Tyler's already missed the first few classes at school today when he helped me deal with Travis, Edward thought. *So what difference would it make if he missed the rest of the day. His parents are already at work so it would be easy to drive back by the house, slip inside, go up to the attic, and leave with the trunk.*

So that is exactly what Edward made Tyler do.

Tyler was now parked at the curb of a quaint two-story house with

Adrian's chest in the trunk. He looked at the address he had scrawled on the piece of paper and double checked it with the address painted on the mailbox.

A sign planted near the mailbox stated:

ADRIAN CONNELL
Professional Photographer

The word "compact" was the first thought to cross Edward's mind when he glanced at the house. It wasn't extravagant by any means. It was modest and looked comfortable.

The second thing Edward noticed was how immaculate the yard looked. The lawn was freshly mowed; the flower beds weeded and the hedges neatly trimmed. Everything had been tended to on the outside and Edward assumed the inside was in the same condition. It could have easily been photographed for one of the covers for Lawn and Garden Magazine.

"Adrian was always a neat freak in school," Edward said to himself as he continued to survey the area. *More like a perfectionist really,* he thought. *A perfectionist. Yeah, that's the word that best described her. Makes me wonder why she left her hope chest behind.*

Edward had been ecstatic during the drive from Silver Ridge. He had acted like a high school teenager who was going out on a first date. He was singing along to the songs played on the radio. If he had still been in his old body, the songs would've been sadly sung off key. Now in his new body with a new voice, he sounded unbelievable; at least he did to himself. The vibrato had a steady pitch and rhythm. He thought if he had the right connections, he would easily be in the running as one of those singers for one of those girl-crazed boy bands. Not that he was interested in doing so, but he had the looks, the voice and the talent, but that was the furthest thing from his mind right now.

He was on the equivalent of a PCP high minus the actual drugs. He needed to force himself to calm down or take a Valium and let the effects of the drugs do it for him. He couldn't help it. It had been more than seventeen years since he had seen Adrian.

Wow, I wonder what she looks like now. Wonder if she's married? Wonder if she has kids? Wonder if she is still as friendly as she was with me the day I talked with her on the pier? Wonder if she even remembers me?

Even though his life had been snuffed out early on, he still remembered that moment together—*their* moment—like it was yesterday.

He sat in the car and debated whether or not he should proceed with this task. Eventually, he forced himself into motion. If he chickened out now, he would damn himself all the way back home for being a coward. If he had to listen to himself bitch and complain all the way back to Silver Ridge it would be enough to drive him insane. He would be a basket case by the time he arrived home and then what would he have accomplished? "Not a damn thing," he told himself. "I've come this far, I might as well go through with it."

What if she doesn't like me now, Edward thought as he looked into the rearview mirror. "Damn, I keep forgetting," he said in frustration as he angled the mirror toward his face. "Look at what you've turned into. You've shed that pitiful cocoon of Edward and emerged into this amazing butterfly of Tyler." He paused to take an extra look in the mirror and said, "You handsome devil. What's not to like?"

Without anymore hesitation, he flipped the lever that unlocked the trunk as he got out. He retrieved the wooden chest from the back and slammed the lid. He took the chest with him to the front door, set it down, and knocked briskly with his knuckles. As he waited, he smoothed out a few wrinkles on his shirt and set his hair in the reflection of the windowpane. He waited; then he knocked a second time. Finally, he heard the click of the door lock.

As soon as she opened the door wide enough to frame herself in the open space, Edward's heart pounded a nervous arpeggio that traveled through his ribs and down his spine. He was stunned and raised his eyebrows in surprise. It was Adrian Connell, all right; she hadn't changed much over the years. Just as he had expected, she was still arrestingly beautiful as she had been on the pier so long ago. Only now, the soft babyish features of her youth had become more defined. She looked distinguished.

"Sorry it took me so long to answer the door," she said with a short laugh. "I was in the dark room developing some pictures." Becoming inquisitive, her thin eyebrows furrowed as she looked at him more directly. "Can I help you with something?"

Inside, Tyler also knew it was Adrian the minute he saw her. He knew her from Edward's memories.

Yep, no wonder Edward had a crush on her back in high school. No wonder he wanted to see her so badly. But did he think there was even a chance now? What did he expect to gain through this? She's almost twice his age; in her mid-thirties, for God's sake. She would never go for a teenager even if she wasn't married; or would she? The age difference was too great between them. But why the sudden urgency to see her now?

Tyler had no idea what Edward had in mind for Adrian, if anything. Even if Edward did, Tyler was powerless to do anything about it. But Tyler didn't think Edward wanted to harm Adrian in any way. It was just in the way Edward admired her, so Tyler was a bit more relaxed on the inside. That explained the state of well being Edward was in on the trip over.

Realizing he had probably stared too long at her and that she was about to speak again, Edward stammered out a response as he removed his sunglasses. "Yes, ah. Hi, my name is, ah, Tyler Curtis, and I—"

As his sunglasses came off, her facial expressions immediately changed. "I'm sorry; I'm not interested in anything you have to sell. Thank you. Goodbye." She stated it quickly and directly.

"—uh, no ma'am, wait, please liste—," was the last thing Tyler was able to get out before the door was shut in his face.

ဢ

As soon as the door was closed, Adrian leaned against it. She felt like she was about to pass out but then realized she wasn't breathing. When she forced herself to take a soothing breath, the air came in ragged breaths. A sense of fear seized her body, and tears immediately burst from her eyes and ran the length of her face. Embarrassed, she hurriedly wiped the tears, but they were quickly replaced as more tears streamed from her eyes. Her breathing became more labored. She was beginning to hyperventilate. She was simultaneously afraid and overjoyed.

She turned again to look out of the peep hole at the boy on her stoop. *It's him,* she thought. *How did he find me?*

The boy had a confused look on his face as though thinking: *Okay, where is the hidden camera. What TV show am I on?* He definitely hadn't been expecting her reaction.

Her vision blurred again with more tears. She blinked and wiped absently at her face.

"Pull yourself together, Adrian," she demanded of herself. Then she whispered, "He doesn't know."

He didn't look like he was going to budge. He looked as though he was coming up with some other way to get her back to the door.

I have to put a stop to this, she said. She took a few deep breaths to gain her composure.

Another knock sounded on the front door.

She quickly wiped the remaining tears away from her eyes. Feeling presentable, she opened the door again.

ଔ

Tyler stood at the door, dumbfounded.

"What the hell was that all about?" he asked to his reflection in the glass. Tyler scratched his head, contemplating her reaction. He couldn't tell what kind of look her face had changed into. It looked as though she was shocked or guilty to see him, maybe a little recognition, but no, that was a crazy notion; they had never laid eyes on each other before.

He shook his head in confusion and knocked on the door again, "Ah, Miss. Connell? Miss Adrian Connell? I really need to speak with you. I'm not here to sell you anything. I have something I believe is yours. I don't mean to bother or inconvenience you in any way."

The front door abruptly opened again.

"Listen," she said. "I don't have time to discuss anything with you." She wouldn't meet his eyes. She looked everywhere but his face as though trying to avoid eye contact. "I am very busy in my studio right now, so if you will excuse me." She was about to shut the door again but did a double take when she saw the wooden chest near his feet.

Tyler could tell she recognized it right off.

"Oh my God!" she exclaimed as she threw the door open and walked out on to the porch. She had forgotten about Tyler completely. "Where did you find it? I've been wondering where this has been all these years." She knelt down in front of it and ran her hands across its lid.

"I found it in our attic."

"Your attic?"

"Yeah, way back in the corner of our attic. My parents and I moved in a few months ago. I noticed most of the pictures in the photo albums were of you in and around that house. I assume you lived there for a while during your youth. Is that correct?"

"Yes. Many, many years ago." Her voice trailed off, then she smiled and glanced up at him but then quickly diverted her eyes away. "That's where I grew up."

"I figured as much," he said smiling.

"How did you find me?"

"I won't bore you with the details, but it wasn't that hard. I just did a little bit of detective work. I hope you don't think I've been snooping into your private life. I figured this was an important part of your life and that you would probably want to hang on to it. I'm sure you have plenty of memories tied up in there."

"Yes. It's my whole childhood."

"Would you like for me to help you move it inside?"

She paused, weighing her options carefully. He almost thought she was going to decline but then reluctantly agreed, "Yes please, that's very considerate of you."

"It's really not a problem. It's the least I could do."

When Tyler leaned over and picked up the chest, his medallion slid out from beneath his shirt. It clinked noisily on the wooden top as he stood. The sound caught Adrian's attention and she recognized the piece of jewelry at once. As he moved past her, careful not to scrape the corners against the doorjamb; he noticed the astonished, open-mouthed, wide-eyed look on Adrian's face. Only after Edward was through the door—when his back was to her—did he smile. Just the look on her face told him she hadn't forgotten about him because she had recognized the medallion itself.

Adrian didn't say anything as he passed through the doorway. It had been a long time since she had seen that amulet and she couldn't believe that it was around his neck right now.

Tyler set his wooden burden in front of a plush recliner so she could sit and look through its contents from the comfort of the chair. When he turned around, Adrian was standing directly in front of him. Being that close startled him and he did an embarrassing backward stutter step. Her piercing dark eyes were focused intently on him. She seemed to be searching for something.

ভ

Adrian stared directly into Tyler's face. Her eyes jittered nervously as she studied him and took in every facial feature. Being this close to him she wanted to embrace him, to pull him close, to breath him in and hold on to him for an eternally long time. She felt if she didn't then she would lose him forever. After all, it had been close to sixteen years since she had last held him. Her heart swooned with an unconditional, undying love for him.

"Miss Connell?" the boy said. He sounded shocked, almost offended; then she realized why.

No sooner had she thought of embracing him before her thoughts turned into actions. She had unconsciously moved forward and had grasped him tightly. One arm had looped around his neck and the other arm came up under his opposite arm and around to the middle of his back. Her open hands latched on to his shoulder and back and she pulled him into her. Her head lodged perfectly within the nape of his neck.

"Miss Connell? Are you okay?"

She didn't answer, afraid anything she said might inadvertently end this moment.

She hadn't yet felt his arms return the embrace, but she didn't care. It didn't matter at this point in time. All she knew was that she was near and close to him now and that was all she cared about.

She knew he had to be confused and she knew she would have to explain her actions and feelings toward him, but she didn't know how, or if, he was going to accept them.

Eventually, she felt his arms slowly encircle her and pull her into a tight, comforting embrace.

That's the moment she lost it, and feelings long buried erupted from deep within her body and soul. Along with those sequestered feelings, heart-wrenching sobs and tears came pouring out of her.

He said nothing, and she hoped he wouldn't; she wouldn't know how to explain herself if he had. He just held her ever closer.

She kept holding on as though her life depended on it. She wanted to stay and relish the moment she had with him, but she also had to get away. Her inner body heat had skyrocketed and she now felt as if she were going to faint. She ripped herself from him as she pushed him away. She almost broke into a run as she made her way to the kitchen. She looked back briefly as she made her escape.

He was left standing with his arms thrown wide. The same confused look that he had on the porch was now again painted on his face.

"I'm sorry," she said meekly as she excused herself to the kitchen.

"No-no, don't apologize. It's alright," he said pausing, then, "Are you okay?"

She didn't answer. She didn't know how. She just needed to escape if only for a few minutes to compose herself.

ॐ

Edward didn't say anything more but just watched her disappear into the kitchen. He wouldn't know what to say even if he tried. Once she was out of the room, he swiped at his shoulder. His hand came away wet from her tears. He shook his head as he rubbed his fingers against his palm to wipe away the residue.

That's the oddest reaction I have ever received. Wonder why she was crying? Must be going through something and just needed some comforting.

He didn't know what to do. He took two steps toward the kitchen, thinking it may be a good idea to follow her to see if she was okay but then thought better of it. He didn't want to impose on her any more than he already had. He was a stranger to her, but on one level he felt connected to her in some strange way.

Must be the Edward connection, Tyler thought from deep within himself. Even though he thought that, he didn't know how because Adrian was only seeing Tyler for the first time.

The whole situation was confusing. He shook his head then looked back at the wooden hope chest.

"Why did I even bring you all the way out here?" Edward said. "Huh? Can you tell me that? No, of course not; you're just a damn box."

He began to walk around the room. He paused long enough to look out the living room bay window. He saw the front lawn, his car, and the neighbor's house and lawn which looked equally immaculate as Adrian's. There was a car in its driveway.

Neighbors must be home.

There was now a dark van with tinted windows parked on the road that hadn't been there when he drove up.

That's odd; must've just arrived. Huh. Nothing spectacular about this neighborhood, Edward thought as he turned back into the room. *Except for its cleanliness. Nice but bordering on boring.*

Edward began to pace around the room. As he did so, he grabbed a small ceramic elephant from the coffee table and flipped it into the air and caught it. He pitched it back and forth like a baseball as he walked.

When he passed the living room bookshelf, a photograph caught his eye. He took a quick second look. There, peering out from behind the other frames, was a picture of a teenager. The photograph made his blood run cold.

The teenager was clothed in a football uniform of navy and yellow. He was hoisted in the air and surrounded by his teammates. He was holding his helmet in one hand and the championship trophy in the other. Everybody around him was cheering over an obvious football victory.

Allowing Tyler to express himself freely because there was no threat of a bodily takeover, Edward allowed Tyler to snatch the picture from the shelf to get a closer look.

Tyler peered down into the eyes of the picture. *His* eyes. Tyler was staring at a picture of himself. What he was seeing was impossible.

What are the fucking chances of that? Edward and Tyler both thought together.

If Edward had seen this picture anywhere else, he would've thought nothing about it. But here in this house and here in this body, holding it in this frame seemed more like the picture of Tyler was taken purposely.

Tyler said to himself, "What the hell is she doing with a picture of me in with her other family photos? How long ago had that been? Two? Three years now? That was my freshman year, my first year playing ball."

Tyler thought back. That year had been so amazing to him. It was the first year he had established in his own mind who he really was. He had found popularity with everyone in school. He had been new to that school his freshman year but had helped bring the underdog team to their first championship. They achieved the same goal again during his sophomore year. Then because of his dad's job, he and his family had to pull up roots and move again to another town to begin his junior year. And earlier this year, they had moved, yet again, to Silver Ridge for his senior year.

Still stunned and amazed, Tyler trailed his finger over the picture in the frame.

෯

To Adrian, it seemed she couldn't get out of the living room fast enough. She knew she looked—or at least felt—stupid as she hurried to the kitchen.

Why am I acting this way? Can you solve that *mystery, Adrian?*

As soon as she was around the corner of the kitchen out of Tyler's sight, Adrian immediately fell to her knees and silently cried. She clutched her hands to her chest and rocked slowly back and forth as tears streamed her face. She hadn't cried like this in years. It felt good; a release she needed. She was unbelievably happy and overjoyed.

She didn't know how long she had been on her knees, but she didn't care. Only after the tears subsided did she feel level-headed enough to stand.

She snatched off a few paper towels and wiped her face clean and dabbed at the corners of her eyes. She rubbed her face again with open palms.

She grabbed a glass from the cupboard and retrieved the filtered water container from the refrigerator and poured herself half a glass. She downed the water in two swallows but it didn't seem to help. She needed something stiffer; something much stronger. She flung open the cabinet door and pulled the brandy from the top shelf. She poured herself a half a glass and downed it quickly. She grimaced at the bite of the liquor. She poured another and began to sip it slower as she looked out the kitchen window into the backyard.

She thought back over the years of the time she'd had with him. Distant memories that were still as vivid as the day the memories had been made.

I love him, she thought. *I love him more than anything in this world. I know this much is true. I have to tell him, no matter how he feels about it. Or me. I know I have to tell him the truth.* She prayed silently to herself. *Please God, give me the right words to say to him.*

Making up her mind, she downed the remaining brandy. She turned without thinking twice about the situation and moved from the kitchen back to the living room to tell Tyler what he'd needed to hear for years. Upon entering the living room, she stopped short.

She saw Tyler standing in a three quarter turn away from her near her book shelf. He was focused intently on a picture frame in his hands. And she knew exactly which one it was. It was the football picture. He was going to ask a million and one questions, and she knew he was going to want some answers. She braced herself for the barrage of questions that was to come.

◌

"You were so proud after you threw that winning touchdown pass." Adrian said from the kitchen doorway.

The voice startled Tyler so much he almost dropped the frame. He didn't know how long Adrian had been standing there. He didn't trust himself to speak in his current and confused state of mind.

Adrian continued, "Don't get me wrong, I don't mean to say you were full of yourself. You were very noble. It was a beautiful moment in your life. It was an amazing play and an unbelievable game. You knew you were awesome and so did everybody else, but you didn't show it in your actions. That made me very proud."

"I-I don't understand. What the hell do you mean, that made *you* proud." Edward was allowing Tyler to put his emotions into words. "Why do you have a picture of me from when I was a freshman here in your house?"

There was a long moment of silence that was filled with a growing tension.

Tyler's emotions were coming through and he raised his voice, "Are you going to explain yourself or is silence the best you can do?"

"Follow me," Adrian said, looking up. She turned and went back into the kitchen.

Tyler quickly followed in behind her. From the kitchen, they moved into a short little hallway then further into her den near the back of the house. This room was smaller and much cozier than the living room, but it was the pictures on the wall that captured Tyler's attention.

Above the fire place was a much larger version of the freshman football winning pose he continued to hold in his hand. He stood in awe for a moment then started to move slowly around the room.

There was another picture him—this one a black and white—hunched over a basketball, sweat dripping from his face, as he prepared to shoot a free throw.

Another picture caught him coming out of a building with a backpack slung over his shoulder. He was looking in the direction of the camera as though someone had just called his name. There was only a twinge of a started smile.

Another picture showed him and his sophomore high school sweetheart, Julie Brekken. The shot caught them in mid laughter. It was picturesque; one that you would find on a picture-perfect Hallmark card or even in a fine art museum. He thought back to that day and remembered the park where they had taken an afternoon walk, but there was no memory of a photographer at all that day.

Holy shit. She's really good to always stay hidden so well.

Some pictures were big; others were smaller pictures and laid out in a collage form of him with friends, past girlfriends, even a few with his current parents. But the main focus in all the pictures was always Tyler.

There were two remaining pictures. These two were more present day and up to date. One was of Tyler and Raven. Tyler was down on the balls of his feet even with Raven's height. Adrian had caught them just as Raven had stuck her tongue out and licked Tyler's chin. The other picture was of Tyler and Savannah. Tyler was leaning back against a boulder and Savannah was lying back with her head on his chest. Both of those pictures were taken when they were at the lake the day of his accident.

Did she know about my accident?

"I know what you must be thinking. I assure you I'm not a stalker."

"No, on the contrary, I wasn't thinking that at all," Tyler said. "I don't feel threatened by you at all by seeing these."

That's not entirely true, Tyler thought. *But maybe it is because of the memories Edward has of you that I don't feel threatened by you.*

"This is amazing work. It is a bit odd, though. Seeing different pictures of myself taken by someone I have never even met. Goes back my original question."

"Which was? I've forgotten."

"Why *do* you have pictures of me from all different time periods of my life in your house?"

As she always did when she was embarrassed, she glanced down at her hands, unable to speak. She didn't know how to begin.

Was it possible he really didn't know? I guess so.

"Oh. I see. I understand now," she said, realizing the seriousness of the situation. Disappointment had tainted her voice, "Your parents never told you about me, did they?"

"My parents? I have no idea what you're talking about. Why would they?"

"No. I can see now they didn't."

"Didn't what? You're doing a real good job keeping me in suspense."

"I don't really know how to tell you."

Tyler just stared at her as if to say, well, I can wait here all day until you do.

"I've thought of what I would say if this day ever came, but words seem to fail me now." In a hushed voice, Adrian asked, "Tyler. Your parents never told you that you were adopted, did they?"

The phrase rocked Tyler where he stood. He didn't know how to react to the word. It scared him at first. His surprised emotions surfaced and he quickly looked back up from the picture in his hands. He gave her a look as if she were utterly insane. Her words were jolting. He wondered if he had heard her right and for a moment repeated the words in his mind. His mouth was open in amazement, but he closed it and swallowed hard.

"Adopted," he said, testing the word.

"Yes, that's right."

He asked again, "Adopted?" He shook his head in disbelief. "No. Why? Should they?"

"I thought they would've done that by now, but it's evident they didn't."

"You want to explain yourself in a little more detail?"

"In short, *you* are adopted and *I* am your real birth mother."

Tyler started to laugh. "Jeez, that is short. You're kidding, right?"

"No. I'm afraid not."

"I don't believe you," Tyler said without hesitation. "Is that the reason you acted so weird on the porch earlier? You recognized me as your *son* and you thought I was here to talk about that?"

"Yes. In a way. I instantly became nervous when I saw you. Your face didn't register with me until you removed your sunglasses."

"That's not good enough. What's the real story. Why is my picture here?"

"That is the truth. I'm your birth mother."

Edward's demeanor changed and anger flashed, "Well, it's a bunch of bullshit is what it is, lady! I have a mother and I have a father!"

"That's right. Henry and Gwen Curtis are your parents. They adopted you when you were four months old. I should know; I was there. I'm the one who handed you over to them. I took care of you for the first four months of your life."

Adrian had heard stories about people finding out years later their parents weren't their real blood kin. News like this had caused some families to separate. She could tell he wasn't taking this very well and she needed to calm him down.

With all her bottled up motherly love, Adrian softly said, "Tyler, listen to me. Give me a chance to explain. I think I can shed some light on the situation."

She walked toward Tyler and opened the bottom drawer of the coffee table and pulled out three thick photo albums. "Come over here. Sit down and look at these. I've always been told that a picture is worth a thousand words. Maybe these will be able to explain some of the confusion of it all."

Tyler still stood firmly by the bookshelf, still rocked by the news.

Adrian patted the sofa for him to sit beside her and said, "Seeing is believing."

Edward finally unhinged Tyler's feet from the floor and tentatively approached the couch but didn't sit.

"I don't understand why your parents never told you about me. They promised me they would. They promised me years ago they would bring you up in the understanding you were adopted. I guess over the years, they changed their mind."

With a tinge of anger that wasn't directed at her he said, "They've never said a word to me about it. Or you."

"I guess they wanted you to believe you were their child."

"Hold on a minute. I never said I believed you."

"Of course, I never assumed you did." She paused for a moment, then, "I'm sure they love you and didn't want you to get hurt."

"If they loved me, and if this is true, then they should have told me." Tyler shot back. "That is, if it's true."

"I don't think it's that. I really believe they didn't want their child to have to grow up dealing with any of the confusion."

Even though she spoke the words, she became angry toward his parents for keeping the real truth from him. It was a betrayal on her as well. If he hadn't found out this way, he probably would've lived his life and died without ever knowing he was deeply loved by someone else.

She continued, "Come over here and just look at these to start. They will answer many of your questions, I assure you."

Reluctantly, Tyler sat down and slid the album from her lap to his.

When he flipped open the book, the first picture staring back at him was a baby boy that was just old enough to sit up by himself; he was laughing at the photographer. The little baby had black hair just as Tyler did. The bold calligraphy script underneath the picture stated the baby's name: GABRIEL QUINN CONNELL.

Feeling stupid for asking, already knowing the answer, Tyler asked, "Is that me?"

"That's you, all right."

"Why Gabriel?"

"I have no idea. It wasn't pre-planned. The name just popped into my mind the moment the nurse handed you to me. No other name came to mind; just Gabriel. It sounded powerful, meek, noble, and distinguished all at the same time. It seemed perfect for you, so I made the decision right then and there."

Tyler smiled as he ran a finger over the baby picture he'd never seen of himself, "Cool. I like it."

"It suited you. Still does."

Tyler turned the page a little more deliberately than he intended.

Adrian noticed the attitude change and immediately said, "I know your name is Tyler. It's what you grew up with. I will try to get used to that name, but you have to understand that when I think of you, I always think of you as Gabriel. You'll have to give me some time as well to get used to this whole situation. That is, if you allow that to happen."

Tyler just nodded in agreement as he scanned the next few pages. He saw a number of hospital pictures of an infant right after birth. The small baby had a small crocheted hat and was wrapped in a warm blanket. Other pictures showed him in the nursery at the hospital, him in his crib at home, lying on a couch and playing on the floor of a bedroom. Page after page, Tyler saw pictures of the first four months of his life; pictures he'd never seen before. There were a number of pictures by himself but many were of him and Adrian. And he could sense Adrian's love for him in each picture.

Adrian pretended to look at the photos in the album but what she was really doing was watching him out of the corner of her eye. She was silent, letting him come to terms with the truth before him instead of her forcing her will on him.

Tyler thought again of his parents and their features. He'd never thought about it before but he now saw them in a different light.

He remembered his mom and dad's hair color. His mom's was strawberry blond with that natural reddish tint to it and his dad's hair was dark red. Then there was the factor of their fair skin color and freckles. Tyler himself had dark, evenly tanned skin without freckles.

Tyler never noticed the differences between him and his parents; he was never given a reason to. He always took them at face value. But now, he couldn't see anything but those differences.

I'm sure that two people with that type skin and hair color could have someone like me. It isn't impossible, but I'm not sure.

Tyler glanced over at Adrian again who was looking at him with expectant eyes.

He did favor her a little; a lot actually. He did have black curly hair much like hers and she did have darker skin like him.

"It's a lot to take in," Tyler started. "I'm not saying I believe you're my mother but…," He became concerned. "Wait, if you're my mother who the hell is my real father? You haven't said anything about who my father is."

Before Adrian could remark, Edward knew the answer. He knew it from deep within his soul. Call it intuition, call it a gut feeling or a sixth sense; he knew before she could speak. It hit him dead in the face like an uppercut knockout punch.

"I was hoping you wouldn't ask me that, but I knew the question would come at some point during this conversation. It takes me a while to even get used to talking about him."

Without looking up, he gently commanded, "Tell me about my father. I have to know. I've noticed that he's not in any of these pictures. I guess he left you. I guess he didn't want to have anything to do with me."

"No," she said emphatically. "It's not like that at all. The truth of the matter is that I'm the one who left him. To tell you the truth, I don't believe he even knows you exist. I didn't tell too many people—only the people I trusted—so I doubt word ever got to him about you."

"Really? Why did you leave him?"

"Oh, there's a very good reason, but first let me start from the beginning." Adrian cleared her throat then said, "During my senior year, I dated off and on with different guys in my class. Our small group of friends was close-knit, so they didn't take to the less popular students that I started to go out with. That eventually became a problem for my friends, so I would break up with the guy because I felt like I needed friends more than male companionship. I figured that was the best thing for me at that time, until I started dating this guy named Jeremy Taylor."

When Edward heard the name, a violent shudder rippled throughout his body, *I knew it. I fucking knew it.* Tyler's eyes closed in disgust and he slowly shook his head. *Why did it have to be him?*

Edward turned Tyler's head away to compose himself.

Adrian noticed his body movement and asked, "You okay?"

"Oh—yeah. Sorry; I, uh, I—I just had a cold chill," he lied. "Go ahead with your story."

As soon as the shudder passed through him, an intense heat immediately followed. His heart rate sky rocketed. His hands were turning white in the grip of the album.

Adrian continued, "I figured I could kill two birds with one stone if I dated him since he was liked by the others in our group. I honestly liked him at first and it was good for a while. I guess you could say I even loved him." Adrian paused working up the nerve to go further. The next few words came out from between clenched teeth. "Then his true colors came out. He became possessive and abusive, especially when he got drunk. It finally got so bad I couldn't take it anymore, so I broke up with him. He apologized and made promises, and we soon started dating again. That cycle continued for a good portion of my senior year until I finally broke up with him for good." She bowed her head and fidgeted with her hands. "Over time, slaps and punches can kill the love someone can have for another. It killed it pretty quick with us. But there was a specific event that severed our ties to each other for good. I couldn't handle it, so I got out. I just up and left town without telling anybody. My parents were the only ones who knew, and they understood and supported my decision."

"You're saying this guy, Jeremy Taylor, is my father?"

She looked at him inquisitively, "You sound as if you know him."

Oh I know him alright, Edward thought. *I've known Jeremy Taylor a very long time now.*

"No," Edward lied. "Just getting the facts clear in my mind." He paused then went on. "You said something about an event that made you and Jeremy cut ties. What happened? What was the event?"

She stood and crossed the room. She felt like she had to get away, but that would be running again. She wanted desperately to tell him, but she didn't know how.

Edward was half expecting her to tell him a story of the circumstances surrounding the drowning death of a young teenager in the middle of Silver Ridge Lake.

"I would rather not say if that's okay with you."

He wanted to hear her say it. He pressed her further. Standing as he dropped the photo album to the coffee table, he said, "No. It's not okay. I think you owe me the whole story since it's been kept from me all these years." Tyler's voice now carried an edge to it. "If what you're telling me is true; don't you think I need to know the whole story?" Tyler paused. "What happened back then that caused you to cut ties with my dad?" The words, "my dad" didn't feel right when he said them. He tried again. "With Jeremy."

Adrian didn't answer.

"What happened that caused you to abandon me completely?"

Adrian closed her eyes and started shaking her head.

"Were you embarrassed by me? Is that it?"

"No. Jeremy raped me!" she yelled, as she turned to face him. Tears were again running the length of her face. Embarrassed by what she had said, she turned away from him again and stared out of the nearest window. Her body shook as the new tears poured forth as the pain returned.

Edward and Tyler stood there, stunned. Edward hadn't been expecting that reaction and that truth from Adrian. The statement rattled him. He slowly sank back to the couch. That thought hadn't even crossed Edward's or Tyler's mind. They were too busy thinking how they could even the score with Jeremy. It was the first time their thoughts were on the same track.

"There, I said it. Is that what you wanted to hear?" Realizing she had spoken too soon, she immediately looked down at her hands, unable to turn back and look Tyler in the eyes. She was ashamed and embarrassed.

"I didn't want to tell you because I didn't want you to feel you were abandoned because you were the result of—" She was about to say, "a rape" but quickly though of a substitute phrase, "Of something so horrible."

But now it had been brought to Tyler's attention and he couldn't help but think about it. It seemed unbelievable to him; to think that he was conceived in hate rather than in love. He was created in violence and domination rather than in passion and a desire of two beings wanting to create something beautiful. It was almost more than he could handle.

Edward was suddenly engulfed in rage. He felt the embers that had been smoldering for so long flare up into an intense heat inside him. His thoughts were alive with feelings of revenge. Not only would he kill Jeremy for causing his death, but would also kill him for the torture and emotional distress he had caused Adrian all these years.

Edward had to remind himself that he had to react as Tyler would. It was probably one of the hardest things for him to do, but he forced himself to speak in a calm soothing voice. "I am so sorry, Miss. Connell."

"Your father raped me," she said continuing in a whisper. This conversation had drudged up painful feelings she had tried to forget. "I wouldn't consent to having sex with him one night because he was drunk but he—" She muffled a pitiful sob, then said, "But he—he—forced himself on me anyway. It was on a night when he was deep under the spell of the bottle. So drunk he barely even remembers raping me. He tried to start something but I stopped him. We would fight and then he would apologize for being an asshole, but all the time he would still be tipping back the bottle. Then at one point he snapped; he just—," she stopped, broken by the twisted memories, "—it was unbearable. I should've seen it coming, but sometimes love is extremely blind. But after that moment, I could see rather clearly. I don't know why I didn't see it sooner. In the aftermath of the incident, I told myself that was the last blow he was ever going to give me. It was just one blow too late. Even if I hadn't become pregnant with you, I would've left him anyway. I couldn't live in the same area with him anymore. I felt that if I ever saw him again that—," she knew the words she wanted to use but was unsure what Tyler would think of her if she said them.

"That you would what?" Edward said, prodding her to the words he knew she wanted to say and probably needed to say.

"—that I felt. That I would kill him."

"So why didn't you? He deserves it."

"Yes, I know he deserves it and he still does. Ten times over. Stuff like that is easier said than done."

"No, actually it's easier to do than you think."

"What?" she asked in alarm.

Edward realized he'd voiced his thought and had to backtrack out of this conversation.

"Ah, nothing, I was just trying to make a point. It was a bad use of words on my part."

"Oh, okay. I don't think I have the guts or would ever have the willpower to do something like that."

"Is that why you gave me up for adoption?"

"What?" Adrian asked. She was confused with his question.

"I can see why you would, and I can't blame you. I mean, you must have been ashamed of me since I was the result of something so traumatic. I wouldn't want to keep me either if I reminded you of being—"

"No honey, please, put that out of your head. Do not think that for a second. There wasn't anything wrong with you then. There's isn't anything wrong with you now. You were perfect. You still are. I was on my own and I could hardly provide for myself, let alone for you. My parents didn't have the money to support or help me and I didn't want them to. It was a situation I got myself into and it was something I had to see through to the end even if it was on my own. I kept you as long as I could. I never, ever, wanted to give you up. It broke my heart the day I did and I still regret it even now to this day."

She started to cry again. Tyler could feel the emotions and sensed the anguish she was going through. It was hell for her just to tell him these feelings.

"After I was raped, I didn't have it in me to date anyone. I wasn't fit mentally or emotionally to see anybody. I just got lost in my photography. That's the reason I have all these pictures of you here in this room." She swept her hand in the direction of the pictures of Tyler. "You were and have always been the center of my life. Every time I had an opportunity to see you—even if it was through the lens of the camera—was a perfect day for me. I captured as many moments of you as I could because that is all I have. I just wanted to be part of your life. I didn't think it would be right for me to barge back into your life after I had given you up. I just prayed for a moment to present itself like it did today."

Tyler still said nothing. It was all he could do to sit and listen.

She quickly wiped her face and said, "I feel like I am talking myself in circles. I just—I just had to give you up so you would have a better life. You've got to understand that. Please, I beg of you, don't hold a grudge against me for what I had to do. I would give anything if I could've kept you. Please believe me when I tell you this."

Tyler said nothing; neither did Adrian. She didn't know what else to say.

Finally she added, "Other than my parents you are the first person I have told that story too. Except— " She paused thoughtfully for a moment, smiled, then added, "There was another boy in school who I was going to tell but I never could get up the nerve to come out and just say it. It was too fresh in my mind and extremely hard to talk about."

Edward immediately knew what she was talking about. *That had to have been the secret she was going to tell me the day of the accident,* he thought.

Another memory flitted across his mind; the thought of a younger Adrian standing up in a boat and stripping down to her two piece bathing suit. Edward was caught up so much in her beauty that he totally missed the hint of her running her hands down the slope of her lower abdomen.

Edward's mind reeled, *You were conveying to me that day that you were pregnant. How did I not see it? Why didn't I pick up on it?*

He remembered the troubled expression on her face and the tears that filled and fell from her eyes. For that brief moment she had relived the rape all over again.

You did tell me, Edward thought. *I was just too stupid to read the signals.*

She looked at him expectantly and said, "Talk to me. What are you thinking?"

Tyler admitted, "I feel betrayed. From both sides actually. My parents have lied to me my entire life. Do you know what that does to trust? How am I ever going to be able to trust them again? I'm not saying I completely believe you. I mean your story is way out there; even though it's a crazy notion, it is very convincing. I don't know you from anyone else. How do I know *you're* not lying to me?"

"That's just it, you don't. But deep in your heart I believe on some level you know."

Tyler was silent.

"You know, I try to do a good deed by bringing your old hope chest you forgot in my attic, and I find out that you're my mother." He gave a short laugh of disbelief, "Or you say you're my mother. The irony of this whole situation is stifling. I don't know what to think anymore."

"You're just going to have to trust me. In the meantime, while you're wondering whether to believe me or not, look at some more pictures. Maybe the truth is in the pictures."

"It's going to take a long time for me to accept this, even if it is the truth."

"I understand. That makes perfect sense. I'm not asking anything of you, Tyler, except that you look at it from a different point of view. Maybe a different set of eyes?"

I already am, Edward thought.

He thought again of what happened to her so long ago and what she must have gone through. The hideous word appeared in his mind again.

Rape.

His mind's eye conjured up unspeakable visions of the act and he shook his head at the images.

"I'm sorry. I just need some time to put this in perspective."

"I understand. Take as long as you like."

"While you are looking at those, I am going to brief through the contents of my hope chest. It's been so long I think I've forgotten half the stuff that I stored in there."

"I'll get it from the other room for you."

"Thank you."

When Tyler arrived back in the den and set the chest down, Adrian knelt in front of her long lost container of mementos.

"Miss Connell?" Edward asked. "There is also another reason why I am here. There are some other questions I would like to ask you, if that's all right?"

"I suppose, but only if you promise to call me Adrian."

He nodded an unsure nod. "Sure, I promise. Adrian."

She smiled. "What are your questions about? You sound so serious."

"I wouldn't consider them to be serious. They would more or less be classified as questions to solve my curiosity." He pulled a photograph from his pocket and handed it over to her. "This picture was also in your hope chest, but I was hanging on to it because my questions are centered around it."

He watched as she took the picture and looked it over.

Edward continued, "I hope you don't mind, but I looked through a good bit of the material here to try and figure out whose stuff this was."

She shook her head absently, obviously lost in the memories of the pictures.

"Aww, Edward. I had almost forgotten about this picture."

What the hell. Go ahead. Ask her, Edward thought. *You know you want to see if she remembers you.*

"First of all, I was wondering who Edward McDaniel is? I assume you know or knew him because his name is written on the back of that picture. I also noticed that you noticed my medallion when I brought the hope chest inside earlier."

"*Your* medallion?" she asked in alarm.

"Yeah, my medallion," he said then realized the meaning of his words. He could've slapped himself. He was speaking as though he were Edward. He had to remember that he was still Tyler. At least for now. Choosing his words wisely, he said, "No-no, I mean *your* medallion. The one I found in your trunk. I was just wearing it for a little while until I got the chest back to you. I'm sorry. It was very rude of me to assume I could wear it without asking you first."

"It's okay, but it was a special gift from a friend. I would like it back at some point."

Edward started to take it off to give it back to her, but her words stopped him, "No. Tyler. It's all right. You can wear it. But only for the time being."

He hesitated then said, "Thanks." He collected his thoughts then continued. "Edward has one just like it—or he's wearing this same one in that snapshot." Tyler pointed to the photograph in her hand. "If it is the same one he's wearing in that picture there, I was wondering how it came to be in your possession."

Reluctantly, Adrian stood from her kneeling position in front of the chest and moved to where she was seated on the couch beside Tyler. She hesitantly reached for Edward's medallion to examine it closer. When she made contact with it, she didn't lurch from a shock of energies emanating from within the stone piece, but the contact did throw her mind back in time as a memory resurfaced.

∞

Adrian pulled into a tire-worn dirt driveway and coasted to where the road dead-ended. She breathed deeply as she sat behind the wheel, trying to muster enough courage to go through with her decision.

As she stepped from her car, she gazed up at the immense house.

"Someone hasn't been doing their fair share of the chores around here," she said as she carefully made her way through the overgrown walkway to the screened in porch. Opening the screen door, Adrian moved through the porch area to the main entrance and knocked on the front door.

Eventually, she heard the sound of slow shuffling feet through musty glass panes as though someone were carrying a heavy burden. Then an old woman's voice crooned. "Who's there?"

Adrian stated with a raised inflection, "It's Adrian Connell. I'm trying to find a Mrs. Roquemore?"

The door opened a crack, and a single cataract-filled eye peered through at her.

"Are you Helen Roquemore?"

"I may be, child. Who wants to know? What do you want?"

"Are you the grandmother of a boy named Edward McDaniel?"

Upon hearing the name, she got defensive. "I am." She paused, then said, "I was."

"I'm so sorry to bother you like this, um, my name is Adrian Connell and I was—"

Upon hearing Adrian's name, Helen opened the door wider. Adrian stood quietly taking in the old woman's obese and haggard appearance. Folds of skin hung loosely on her body. The woman had solid white, stringy hair that zigzagged away and down from her scalp. Her face was wrinkled and her eyes were milky blue. The woman didn't seem blind, but her eyes stared straight ahead, unblinking at her.

The old woman was dressed in a gray dress with a white apron over the top of it.

Helen asked, "You were what, dear?"

Shaking herself from her temporary shock, she said, "I wanted to come apologize and tell you how sorry I am about what happened to your grandson Edward."

"It's been more than a couple of days since his passing, dearie. More like a few weeks now. Don't you think it's a little late for that?"

Adrian understood the old woman's animosity but said, "I don't like to say it, but I think I have a pretty good excuse for not coming sooner."

Amused, the woman said, "And what would that be, dearie?"

"I had been in the hospital for most of that time re-cooperating myself. I was with Edward the day he died. I almost died myself. I just wanted to come and pay my respects and say I'm sorry for what happened to him."

The old woman launched her body toward Adrian. Adrian wasn't expecting the sudden movement and didn't have time to respond. The old woman threw her arms around Adrian and hugged her tightly. Realizing what the old woman was doing, she slipped her trapped arms from her sides and returned the embrace as best she could.

The old woman smelled of urine, cedar chests, and mothballs. Her hair felt oily as it pressed against one side of Adrian's face. Adrian grimaced but didn't pull away. She flushed at the feeling of the old woman's slimy face and sweaty body embracing her own. Adrian desperately wanted to pull away but was compelled to stay. Comfort was what the old woman wanted and needed right now, and she hugged the woman tightly in return.

"*Thank you for being a friend to my little Edward,*" *she sobbed.* "*He didn't have many, but he often, so many times, talked about you.*"

Adrian felt something wet drop onto her shoulder and realized the old woman was crying. Caught up in the emotion, Adrian cried also. Adrian held the shaking woman until she was finally finished but she let Helen be the first to pull away. The embrace might have been the only sympathy she had received. She had lost her grandson, and that had to be devastating for her.

Finally, Helen released her tight squeeze and shuffled backward. As she did so, she pulled a wadded handkerchief from her apron pocket and dried her eyes and wiped her runny nose. She couldn't speak, but fluttered her arms in a motion for Adrian to have a seat on one of the porch chairs.

"*Nobody told you about me being in the hospital?*"

Helen shook her head no.

"*I think that's a pretty important part of the story, don't you?*"

Helen nodded her head in agreement.

"*You heard what happened, didn't you? You pretty much know the whole story.*"

"*Oh, Lord yes. The police were nice 'bout it from the beginning and they always kept me informed about the situation. They took care of the funeral plans an' everything. But I'm not totally convinced it was an accident. I believe that Jeremy Taylor had a lot to do with it, and I'm not going to rest until something's done about him. I still feel like he could've done something.*"

Adrian didn't know what to say. It seemed like a touchy subject for Helen. "*Yes, ma'am. I understand. You should do what you feel is best.*" *She paused for a moment, not knowing how to continue. Then she said,* "*It was probably difficult reading about it in the paper each morning and hearing about it on the television each night, wasn't it?*"

"*We never had a television and lately don't get the paper no more. Letters that small seem to just blur together for me. Oh I can see, mind you.*" *Changing the subject and patting Adrian's arm, she added,* "*And I see that you're a beautiful young woman.*"

Blushing, Adrian said, "*Well, thank you, ma'am.*"

Helen continued, "*But my eyes aren't so good anymore. Diabetes is taking its toll on them.*"

"*I'm sorry to hear that.*"

"Thank you for your concern. I 'preciate you comin' all the way out here and sayin' whacha did about my grandbaby. That really means a lot. At the funeral, no one showed up but a few family members. A few teachers did but none of the students from school even graced the scene. Now that's sad, ain't it?

"Very sad," Adrian agreed.

"So far, you're the only one of his classmates that showed up. That says a lot about your character."

Curious about her earlier comment, Adrian asked, "When you said he often talked about me, what did you mean?"

"Ah yes," Helen said laughing. "You were the sparkle in my little Edward's eye. Most days he would complain 'bout how most kid would pick on him in school. Some days were worse than others, you see."

Adrian nodded her head, understanding what she was meaning.

"I can't remember everything he said about you. I couldn't take the time to tell you everything he said even if I did remember, but it could be the simplest things as just a quick hello or you acknowledging him in the hallway. It just made him feel important and liked. He never had anything bad to say about you. Yes indeedie. Edward always thought the world of you."

"Wow. I didn't know I made such an impression on him," Adrian said, more to herself than to Helen.

Even though Adrian hadn't planned on staying long, they sat there for a while talking together as the wind blew through the screened in porch.

When it came time for Adrian to leave, they stood and embraced once again.

"Thank you for coming to see me. You're company has been wonderful. No wonder Edward liked you so much."

"You're welcome. I'll come again if that's all right with you."

"That would be lovely, dear. I would very much like and appreciate that."

As Adrian stepped to leave the porch, Helen said, "Wait just a minute, dearie; I've got something I need to give to you."

Adrian didn't have time to protest, because Helen had already turned and was shuffling back through the open doorway. Adrian moved to the door and shouted toward the back rooms, "Ms. Roquemore?"

Adrian heard the sound of wooden drawers opening and closing. Helen was obviously looking for something. Adrian sat down again to wait.

Helen came back through the kitchen talking to herself in a sing-songy voice, "Oh, I found it, I found it; I knew it was back there in one of those boxes."

As she stepped back out on the porch, Adrian said, "Ms. Roquemore, you don't have to give me anything. I don't deserve anything at all."

"Now you hush up, dearie, it's not really from me. It's a present from Edward."

Helen handed Adrian a small red, folded bandana.

Confused, Adrian unfolded the gift. A shiny talisman attached to a leather strap sparkled in her hand.

"I don't know if you want to wear it or not. You don't have to, dearie. My husband Jonas gave it to Edward about a week before his passing. It was something Edward really treasured. It was probably one of the most important things in his life. He wore it all the time."

"I know. I've seen it before. He constantly rubbed it whenever he was deep in thought, whenever he was reading, studying, or taking a test. He was always seen clutching it in his fist."

"Sad thing 'bout it, though. When they pulled his body from the lake, he still had it clutched in his hand. Since you were so nice to him, I want you to have it. I'm sure he would want it that way."

"I can't take something this important from you. It's a keepsake. It should remain here with you. You should hang on to it to remember Edward by."

"Nope. My mind's made up, and I feel it's the right thing to do."

"Okay, if that's what you want."

"It's what Edward would want."

"Well, thank you. I will accept it and I appreciate it."

ᛉ

A tear fell from Adrian's cheek as she dropped the medallion back to Tyler's chest. Embarrassed, she quickly wiped the wet stream away and said, "I actually went back one other time to see Helen after that initial visit even though by that time I had already moved away from Silver Ridge. That second time I went to see her, she wasn't at home.

I discreetly asked about her around town, but no one seemed to know what happened to her. It was as if she just disappeared. I finally chalked it up that she was really lonely and maybe went to visit or live with other family out of state." She paused and stifled a whimper and wiped away more tears. "I have always wondered where she is and what she's doing now and if she is still alive. I really miss her. She was a nice lady."

Edward wept for her on the inside. He wished he knew where she was as well. He couldn't think of what other family lived away from Silver Ridge or where she might go to.

Adrian changed the subject, "As far as the charm goes, I never wore it. Not because I didn't want to but because I didn't feel right wearing it." She briefly touched the amulet again. "I just stashed it away in my hope chest and eventually forgot about it."

Pity, Edward thought. *Maybe if you had, you would've felt the power of the charm. Maybe I might have been released sooner. Wonder what it would've been like to possess Adrian's body. Would it be different than possessing Tyler's? Yes, I'm sure it would've been much different.*

Edward couldn't resist asking, "You wrote Edward's name on the back of the picture along with the words, *My Hero.* What did you mean when you wrote that?" After seventeen years, Edward wanted to hear her side of the story.

She told Tyler about the incident at the pier; how Edward had tried to stand up to Jeremy on her behalf and the beatdown that followed because of it.

"Even though he couldn't physically stand up to Jeremy, at least he tried. And on some level, he did. It was more than anyone else had done. He took a beating for me. And looking back, Edward probably saved my life. I have often wondered what would've happened to me if I had been made to get into his truck that day at the lake. It was his action; his heart was there and that's what impressed me. I knew he wanted to help. I felt like he would've done anything to protect me."

"I would have," Edward agreed in a bare whisper.

"What?" Adrian asked.

Caught unaware, Edward said, "Nothing. I was just curious as to what really happened on the day Edward died and exactly what happened in the days that followed. When was this picture taken?"

Sadness painted her face and she gathered her thoughts before she spoke, "The same day everything went to hell. I surprised Edward when I took this photo. I'd just woken him up. He was half asleep."

"If you don't mind my asking, how did Edward die?"

"Oh, that's a long story," she paused. "But if you have the time?"

"I've come all this way; I'm interested. I wouldn't have asked if I didn't want to know."

Adrian started from the beginning and told the whole story in vivid detail. She had kept this story deep in her heart for so long. She made sure not to leave anything out. She spoke in a hushed and reverent manner as a speaker who is giving a eulogy. When she had finished, they sat in silence for a long while.

"Damn, that's tragic. And nobody was able to rescue him?"

"No," she said simply, but the statement seemed to have an underlying hesitancy to it as though there were more to the statement.

Edward said, "That's too bad." He paused but continued looking at Adrian's face the whole time he talked as if urging her to reveal more of the story. "I'm sure Edward would've loved to have grown up and done something useful with his life, but it seemed to have been taken from him way before he had a chance to really live. Seems like Edward died so much sooner than he should've. I only wish someone was there who could've saved him."

"Yeah. To be honest with you, I don't know."

"Don't know what?"

"I really don't know if there was anyone there to save him."

He prodded, "Oh? What do you mean?"

She paused. Edward was on pins and needles and wanted to just reach down her throat and pull the statement from her mouth, but he sat as patiently as he could. He realized his leg was moving up and down in a nervous jitter as he sat on the couch. He forced it to stop and sat there waiting for Adrian to begin talking again.

"Yeah, that's where it begins a blank new page in my mind. Everything from me being knocked unconscious by the boat's hull until I woke up in the hospital is totally erased. There were only the three of us out there at that time of day from what I remember. It was late in the afternoon. I couldn't help Edward because I was unconscious at the time. When I woke up in the hospital, I heard second-hand stories that Jeremy had tried to rescue Edward but was unsuccessful. Jeremy was an excellent swimmer, but he said the lake was just too deep. He said it was all he could do to save me. Jeremy said he flipped one of the boats and fought to get me into it then tried several times to retrieve Edward. He then rushed me to shore, found a phone, and called the ambulance and police. He told them that Edward hadn't resurfaced and they immediately got a search team together. They got a boat rigged with equipment to drag the bottom of the lake. Some local men with scuba diving equipment volunteered to help as well. They rushed to the area where our boats had flipped. The diver's eventually located Edward directly under the wreck site. After all was said and done, they said Edward's foot was intertwined around the rope that was connected to the boat anchor. They said that it had pulled him straight to the bottom and that he didn't have any chance of surviving."

"What did they do to Jeremy?"

"I don't know. Nothing. When I woke up in the hospital, I asked about Edward, and found out he was dead and that the case had been closed under the heading of accidental drowning. I thought that was peculiar because of the circumstances. Jeremy may have been playing a practical joke, but he didn't have to come so close to our boat. It was just too dangerous."

"Tell me about it."

"For the longest time, I wanted to believe Jeremy had tried to save Edward, but I had my doubts. Then around my second or third night in the hospital, I caught Jeremy off guard when I questioned him about it. I was talking to him about something else completely different then when he wasn't expecting it, I threw in some questions about Edward. I remember there was a split second that his facial expressions gave away a different answer than what he was saying. It was then that I knew he had lied to everybody—to the police, to Edward's family, and to me. It was as though he didn't care. I felt so guilty for persuading Edward to go with me out on the lake."

"There was little persuading to do. Edward wanted to go with you."

"How do you know?"

"Oh, believe me. I know. Edward's closer than you think. Me being a guy and imagining you some years younger; I mean, Ms. Connell, you are beautiful now but back then I'm sure you were stunning as well. It wouldn't have taken much to get me, I mean, Edward, to go with you. So don't beat yourself up about that. It's not your fault, I assure you."

She flushed and looked down at her hands. That statement sounded weird coming from her son, but she knew it was only a innocent compliment.

"If you had suspicions about Jeremy, why didn't you do or say something about it?"

"You don't think I tried? I had plans to, believe me I did. When Jeremy heard that I was inquiring about the facts surrounding the drowning, he threatened me. He never said anything specific like he would kill me, but he had already raped me and it looked like he killed Edward McDaniel because of his jealousy. As I've already said before, Jeremy said it was an accident. But it was murder. I don't have any real proof; I just more or less have a gut feeling about it. He hated Edward. You think it was easy for me to just walk away and say nothing? It was probably the second hardest thing I ever had to do in my life."

"What do you think Edward McDaniel would do if he were here today and heard what you just said?"

She thought about that statement for a long moment, and then said, "I would hope he would understand the situation I was in and not be angry at me because I didn't press the issue further. I was and still am afraid of Jeremy Taylor."

"I'm not talking about you. I'm mainly talking about Jeremy and what he did."

"Oh, well, Edward would probably kill Jeremy plain and simple and I wouldn't blame him if he did." She gave a half-bemused, half-serious laugh thinking. "Oh, I wish I could have a front row seat if that ever happened."

"Really?" Edward spoke the words his grandmother had often shared with him when he wished misfortune on his persecutors, "Be careful what you wish for, it could very well become a reality."

CHAPTER 36

A FEW MINUTES after Tyler had left the neighborhood—when it was apparent he wasn't going to return—two figures emerged from a dark van with tinted windows. Both men were wearing dark suits and sunglasses. Both men looked both ways before they crossed the street. Then they moved across the road, walked up the walkway, and mounted the stairs to Adrian Connell's house.

☙

Adrian jumped when she heard the doorbell ring again. Instead of being alarmed, she was excited that Tyler may have come back. She smiled as she hung another picture up to dry then left the dark room to answer the door.

"I guess you changed your mind after all," she said opening the door.

The question caught the men in black suits off guard. The thin man said, "Ah, no ma'am. No change of mind from us."

"Oh, I'm sorry," she said as an embarrassed laugh escaped her. "I—I thought you were someone else." She brushed her bangs out of her face to see the men more clearly.

"Miss Adrian Connell, is it?"

She nodded, "Yes, that's correct."

"I'm Detective Osborne. This is Detective Miles."

They already had their credentials out and flashed them in her direction.

"How do I know those are real?" Adrian asked before the guy named Osborne could continue.

"You don't. You'll just have to take our word for it," Osborne said. "We need to ask you some questions about Tyler Curtis and your involvement with him. Could we come in and talk?"

She had an ominous feeling about these men. Intuition was telling her these men weren't the real deal and not quite right.

"No, you can't," she said and pulled the long-sleeved shirt she was wearing a little closer to her body.

"We will only take a few moments of your time."

"What does this have to deal with? Why do you need to know about Tyler Curtis?"

"Don't be alarmed, Miss Connell. I can assure you, he is in no trouble. No trouble at all. He's being looked at as a potential sus—um, a witness, in a crime we're investigating."

"Whatever it is, it has to be pretty serious for you to come asking questions, but unfortunately for you I have no comment."

She moved to close the door, but Osborne's hand flashed out to stop it.

"Miss Connell, let's be reasonable."

"I am. I don't have anything to add to your investigation. Now if you'll let go of my door."

She moved to close the door again, but Osborne was relentless. He pushed against it then wedged himself between the door and the door jamb.

"Let go of my door!" Adrian demanded as she continued to press the door into him.

"Are you going to cooperate with us?"

"No."

"Then we'll just have to take you downtown and talk about this like civilized people."

She stared directly into his eyes and said, "I'm not a fool. I can see straight through your masquerade. You are not the police."

Realizing she was losing this battle, she let go of the door and retreated into the living room. The first thing her eyes fell upon was the fireplace poker. *Good enough for me*, she thought as she snatched it up. She turned to meet Osborne just as he entered the room.

Osborne's eyebrows lifted. "So, it's going to be like that, is it?"

"Apparently. You're really not cops are you?"

Osborne and Miles, who was a few steps behind him, didn't answer. Their silence was the same as answering her question.

"That's what I thought. Who the hell are you then?"

Osborne who was stooped in a "ready for anything pose" rose to his full six foot, two inch height. He flashed his hands out in front of him, palms toward Adrian as though he were a magician about to perform a magic trick. One hand disappeared into the breast pocket of his jacket. When it reappeared, it held a small black device.

He smirked at Adrian as if to say, "Bet you didn't see that coming." He pressed the button on the front of it. A small blue electrical charge became visible at the end of the taser.

Osborne was smiling, humored by her fear. "Miss Connell. It's either the easy way or the hard way. I think you know which is which. You can either come peacefully of your own accord or you can come by force. The choice is yours."

"Which isn't really a choice at all now is it?" She brandished the fireplace poker out in front of her.

"Okay. Don't say I didn't warn you. These things don't feel very good when you get kissed by them."

"Bring it on, shithead."

Osborne smiled at the thought of her challenge. "I thought you would never ask."

Osborne slowly approached, but Adrian stood her ground. As Osborne neared closer, he stooped in a crouch again as if getting ready to spring. He gave Adrian a few reflex tests. Each time he drew near her, the electrical device pulsed in his hand.

At first, Adrian reacted to his movements to protect herself then she realized he was only toying with her and sizing her up. Adrian began to do the same thing.

"Oh, so you're going to play it that way?" she asked.

Osborne was enjoying taunting her. "Oh yeah. Playing it the only way I know how, sweetheart."

Adrian moved into a fighting stance. She stood before him with one bent leg behind her while the other leg was straight back behind her for support. Her body was straight; her hands were curled around the handle of the poker, which she held at a forty five degree angle in front of her body. She looked like a female Samurai warrior standing her ground and ready for attack from any direction.

Osborne was growing bored of her little charade and tired of pussy-footing around. He wanted to bag this bitch and be on his way. He kept trying to scare her with the stun gun.

Adrian remained implacable.

At last, when his hand shot too close to her, she swiveled her body away from him as she brought the poker down quick and hard on his wrist. As the poker made contact, Osborne cried out and dropped the stun gun. Adrian had already turned her body toward him again and was swinging the poker like a baseball bat. It connected solidly with the side of Osborne's neck and head. He was already in the process of stumbling back when Adrian hit him again in the side of the head for good measure. Osborne crumpled to the ground and didn't move.

Adrian looked around on the floor for the stun gun but couldn't locate it. She wanted to shock the shit out of this asshole but apparently it had been kicked somewhere out of reach during the scuffle.

When she realized he was down for the count and out of commission, she turned back toward on the doorway where Miles was standing.

She threw the fireplace poker back up in front of her face aiming it at Miles. Anger was hot on her face.

Miles said nothing but slowly moved into the room toward her. As he neared, she swung the poker like a bat, aiming for Mile's head. He read her movement and intercepted the blow by catching the poker in mid air as it descended on his head. With his other hand, he grabbed a handful of the long-sleeved shirt she was wearing. He leaned down as he pulled her toward him.

Adrian could almost taste the rank smell of coffee and peanuts on his breath as he exhaled on her.

Adrian let go of the poker and swiveled away from Miles as she shed her long-sleeved shirt. Miles was left standing there, dumbfounded. He looked under his arm in the direction she had escaped. He threw the shirt down and pitched the poker behind him.

Adrian entered her dark room and locked the door.

Seconds later, Adrian heard the door knob rattle, then the sound of a foot kicking against the door.

On the second kick, the molding splintered and the lock buckled and released.

Adrian ran forward from the back of the dark room, snatching up a pair of scissors in the process, and slammed her body against the door to keep it closed.

Miles pushed the door open enough to get one of his hands through.

Without hesitating, Adrian stabbed the scissors through the back of his hand. The scissors slid through easier than she had expected.

Miles let out a string of anguish-coated curse words as he tried to pull his skewered hand back through the narrow opening. He made several feeble attempts, but each time the scissors kept getting blocked between the door and the door jam. He finally realized the only way he could get his hand back was to rotate it forty five degrees. He quickly did so and pulled his hand back through. He pulled the scissors free and cradled it protectively as he leaned his full body weight against the dark room door. Miles was instantly angered that he had been injured so easily. He grabbed the door and gave it a hard shouldered shove. The door connected with Adrian's forehead.

Damn, that was unexpected, she thought as her vision blurred.

She stumbled back, grabbing anything she could to keep her balance. Her vision began to clear and she heard the door slam completely open. The big man who was pursuing her filled her frame of vision. She tried to move back farther but her legs wouldn't budge. The last thing she saw was the big man charging down on her and his fist connecting with the side of her face. She dropped to the floor and into a darkness far deeper than the room they were in.

Miles smiled as he brought his fists up in front of his face. "Who needs stun guns when you have these babies?" He winced as he tried to make a fist with his injured hand.

No one commented; no one had heard Miles speak. The only other people in this house were all out cold.

Realizing no one had heard him speak, a frown replaced the smile Miles was wearing.

CHAPTER 37

WHEN TYLER FINALLY arrived home, the shock of the day's news had not subsided; if anything, it had intensified. His thoughts had grown into a dark storm of raging emotions that continued to churn inside him. Even though his anger was heightened, he didn't burst into the house in an outrage but rather entered cautiously through the front door.

From the living room, Tyler heard the familiar sound of silverware clinking together. He peered around the corner of the doorway and found his parents in the dining room eating dinner.

He could see they were enjoying steaks that had been cooked on the grill, baked potatoes, and tossed salads as they sipped on glasses of Chardonnay. To see them savoring this meal when the truth about him had been buried for years was enough to turn his stomach.

He felt betrayed on so many levels.

They have kept a part of my heritage hidden away from me my whole life, he thought. *How do they live with themselves?*

Unable to control his anger, he moved without thinking. He was going to have it out with them right here, right now.

"Hello, *Dad,*" he began in a sarcastic tone. "Hello, *Mom.*" His demeanor wasn't at all pleasant.

Henry apparently hadn't caught Tyler's cynical tone. Surprised, he said, "Hello, Son."

Gwen, on the other hand, sensed something was up. "Tyler. What's going—"

Ignoring her, not giving her time to finish, Tyler plowed ahead, "I suppose you still want me to call you by those names? *Dad* and *Mom?*" The disdain was dripping from him.

"Of course, dear," Gwen gave a nervous laugh. "What are you talking about?"

Not understanding Tyler's comment but standing because he sensed some sort of tension, Henry wiped his mouth with a napkin then dropped it on the table beside his plate. He rested his hands on his hips. "What's on your mind, Tyler? You want to try and explain yourself?"

"*Me? You* want *me* to explain *myself* to *you?*"

Still not understanding, Henry and Gwen exchanged glances.

Tyler continued, "Well, *Dad*, if you must know, I'll tell you. But can I see you both in the living room?" Even though it was a question; it came out more as a command.

They continued staring at each other, waiting for a punch line to the joke.

Tyler had started toward the family room, but when he heard no movement from them, he paused and turned back.

"Tyler, we're eating right now," Gwen said. "Can't this wait until after dinner?"

"Better yet, why don't you join us. There's plenty," Henry said. "We can talk while we eat."

"No, *Gwen*. No, *Henry*," he said curtly. "No, it can't wait. No, I'm not hungry. I don't want to eat. I need to talk to you and we're going to do it in the living room. Right now!" he said in a demanding shout. "We're not going to discuss this over dinner. It is much more important than dinner; I can guarantee you that."

Tyler turned and exited the room, leaving Henry and Gwen blinking in confusion. They stared questionably at each other. Reluctantly, they left their steaks and quickly followed Tyler.

When they entered the living room, they found Tyler with his back toward them, his hands resting on his hips and his head bowed. He was obviously troubled about something. He wouldn't have acted with this kind of attitude unless he had something extremely important on his mind.

Henry came into the room with purpose, ahead of Gwen; he was going get to the bottom of this situation. It didn't matter what was on Tyler's mind; he wasn't going to be treated with disrespect. Tyler had never spoken to them like that, but it was going to be the last time.

"What's the meaning of this?" Henry asked as he put a hand on Tyler's shoulder to turn him around to face him. "Son, you want to tell me what the problem is?"

Tyler turned quickly and slapped his hand away.

"Son?" he asked then laughed in Henry's face. "Good one, Dad, I bet you really like using that word? How does it make you feel when you use that word, 'son'?"

Henry looked as though Tyler had actually slapped his face instead of his hand. He was unsure of how to proceed. "Well, as a matter of fact, yes. I guess. That's who you are to me. It seems that *you* have forgotten you are still our son and we are still your parents; you're not going to disrespect us like that."

He scoffed at the use of the word "parents." "*My parents?* Are you sure about that, Henry?" He looked back and forth between them. "Did you just think I would never find out?"

The question stunned them into silence.

"What's this all about, Tyler?" Gwen chimed in forcefully.

Tyler didn't say anything. He continued to look back and forth at his fake parents. He was grinding his teeth. His jaws flexed slowly in a steady rhythm. Anger was evident in his features, but now tears puddled in his eyes.

"What have we done?" Gwen asked

"You lied to me. That's what you did."

"Lied?" Henry asked.

"Yes, lied."

"That's a major accusation you're making."

"It's not an accusation. It's the truth."

Tyler slowly shook his head in disbelief. He couldn't believe they hadn't figured it out yet. Or were they just continuing with the lie. He took a deep breath, stared both of them in the eyes, and asked in a broken tone, "Why didn't you ever tell me I was adopted?"

The question posed was like an actual slap in the face. They weren't expecting that question but had always wondered how they would answer if it were ever asked. They knew the truth would eventually come out, but they weren't expecting to have to answer questions about it today.

Tyler looked between the two to see either a look of guilt or innocence. The look of guilt won, hands down.

Henry started to protest, "Where did you get an idea like that, Tyler?"

"Henry. No." Gwen said, shaking her head. "It doesn't matter where or how he found out. The reality of the situation is that he knows now. We both knew this day would come. Well, it's finally here, and we can't deny it anymore. And we can't deny telling Tyler either."

Hurt and embarrassed, Henry scratched the back of his head. "Yeah. I know. You're right." He sat on the love seat, bowed his head, and said nothing more. He suddenly looked exhausted, as though a great weight had been lifted from his shoulders.

"So it *is* true? I *am* adopted. You're *not* my real parents."

Gwen nodded her head, embarrassed to even voice her reply. She followed Henry's example, sat beside him, and hung her head in shame as well. They both waited for their chastisement. They knew they had wronged Tyler by keeping something this meaningful from him, and now they wished they hadn't.

Tyler sat down on the couch, believing yet not believing. His body was numb from the shocking news. Everything felt like a dream; a dream that was all too real.

Gwen started in a gentle voice. "Yes. It's true, Son. Everything you just said is true. We only wish that we could've had the nerve to tell you that truth. Believe me, we were planning to tell you at the right time, but—"

"That's the problem, *Mom*," Tyler interjected. "There never *is* a right time to tell someone something like this. You should've been straight with me from the beginning. You've had seventeen years to tell me the truth, but everything you told me up to now has been nothing but lies. You can't imagine the way I feel right now."

Trying to console him, Gwen said, "Honey, yes, we—"

"No, Mom, don't even say it, because you don't. You will never know how I feel."

Henry asked sarcastically, "So now that you've found out we're not your biological parents, are you going to stop calling us Mom and Dad?"

"I don't know, Henry. I just might do that."

The words cut deep, but he didn't let it affect him. He needed to get through to Tyler someway and explain their side of the story.

"Cold turkey. Just like that? As if we never existed?"

Tyler shrugged.

Henry continued, "You think that's the answer to this problem; to just turn us away, to turn your back on us after all that we've done for you." Henry's voice wasn't threatening. It remained fatherly but firm. "Have you ever thought of where you might be today if we *hadn't* adopted you?"

"No I haven't, Dad. The thought had never crossed my mind because up until today I thought you were my real parents. I didn't have to wonder about that. That's not what concerns me right now. That's not the point of this conversation. Don't try to turn this around to your advantage and make me look like the bad guy. You're wrong and you're trying to smooth things over as though they didn't happen and that is grossly unfair to me. So stop it."

"I'm not trying to turn things around. But do me a favor; think about that for a moment. I'm not saying that we were right by not telling you the truth from the start."

"You're absolutely right, Dad. You're wrong for not telling me about my past."

"Okay. I'll give you that," he said, nodding his head. He paused to collect his thoughts. "Alright, I'll level with you. I admit it. Yes, we lied to you. We're sorry for holding that information from you and not telling you all the facts. Your mom and I talked about this many times before. We discussed how and when we should tell you, but the truth of the matter is—as you've already said—there never was a good time. Eventually, we stopped talking about it, or talked about it less frequently, and just hoped you would never find out."

"Hoped I would never find out?"

"I'm sorry. That was a bad choice of words."

"Damn right is was."

"I guess we just waited too long," Gwen added weakly.

"Basically, you gave up," Tyler said relentless. "Gave up and buried the truth." Tyler was heartbroken and his emotions were seeping through. His voice wavered on the verge of tears. "Did it ever occur to you that it might be of major importance to me?"

Henry didn't know what to say. Refusing to lose this battle, he continued by changing the subject, "To be completely honest. Yes, it occurred to us many times as you grew up. By then, I feel we thought it was too late. You were up in years."

Tears bubbled in Tyler's eyes and then ran the length of his face.

Henry began again, "There's one thing about it though. One thing you can't deny."

"Yeah. What's that?"

He focused all his attention toward Tyler. "Even though you were adopted, we have always loved you as though you were our biological son and we always will."

Tyler couldn't speak and shook his head.

His body was flooded with emotion as numerous questions filled his mind. He finally nodded as more tears shimmered in his eyes; he bowed his head. Even though he was crying, he managed to ask his question without his voice breaking. "Why *did* you adopt me? What's the real reason?"

Tyler's parents exchanged glances in grave fascination.

It was Gwen who spoke. "It was a part of the lie."

Tyler shook his head and a hint of mock laughter escaped his lips. "I should've known it. One lie right after another. When do they stop?"

"Right now, Tyler. It stops right here and now. Please, for just this moment, listen. We're trying to make up for what we've done."

"Only because you got caught. We probably wouldn't even be having this conversation if I hadn't brought the subject up."

"Probably not," Henry said.

Tyler looked intensely at Henry; it was cold and unwavering. Henry met his gaze but was the first to look away.

Gwen just wanted to get through this conversation. Emotions were hampering the confession. Tears began to fall from her eyes. Gwen continued, "We had told you that I couldn't have any more children because of complications with you. Actually, the truth of the matter is that we couldn't have any children of our own because our first child died when I was in labor."

That was a sideswipe blow that Tyler didn't see coming. "Unbelievable," he said as he expelled a breath of air he'd been holding.

Gwen trudged forward, "Complications during that delivery prevented me from ever becoming pregnant again. We wanted a child so bad and when we found out we couldn't, we were devastated. Then we realized the world hadn't ended for us and we began thinking of adoption. We thought long and hard before we made the decision. We just wanted a child, plain and simple. That's why we adopted you."

"So, in other words, if your first born, oh, I don't know, let's just call him Jack. If *Jack* had been born healthy, you wouldn't have even given adoption a second thought, would you? I wouldn't even be here if that had happened now, would I?"

"Now Tyler, we have no idea what we would've done."

"Well, I will answer it for you. You would not have thought twice about it because *Jack* would've been the one you wanted. It is as simple as that. I know that's what would've happened. And you do too."

"Maybe," Henry said. "We've never even thought about that. Why are you dissecting the situation so meticulously?"

The question set Tyler off. "I have every right! This is my life we're talking about! A life I don't even know anymore. A life I never really knew!" He paused, then in a defeated voice, he said, "I'm just trying to understand, that's all."

"Well, look at it from our point of view. Do you think you can do that for a moment?"

"That's all I've been doing for the past seventeen years. What if I don't want to see it from your point of view at all anymore? Why can't I take a few moments and dwell on this news the way I want to? What the hell do you expect me to do anyway? Just roll over and pretend I don't have a different mother or father? Why don't *you* take your head out of your perfect little world you created, turn the tables and look at it from my point of view."

"Tyler," Gwen said in a soothing voice. "We don't know if we would have adopted you if our other child had been born healthy. You can look at our unique situation in a number of different ways and it still comes down to one idea."

"Unique? And what is so unique about our situation?" Tyler questioned.

"It's that we're together right now. This is the way our lives turned out. That we both love you beyond belief, and nothing, no matter how big or small the situation or obstacle, can ever tear us apart."

"Nothing huh?" Tyler asked.

"Nothing," she confirmed shaking her head.

He looked in Henry's direction to make sure he felt the same.

"It is true, Son. Nothing."

"So I guess if I were to tell you that I was the offspring and the end result of a rape—" he shrugged his shoulder as though this question were no big deal, "—that wouldn't change your opinion about me in any way, would it?"

"What?" they both said in unison.

"Yes. Rape," he said emphatically.

"Where did you get that information?" Gwen asked.

"Yeah and who told you you were adopted?" Henry asked. "How did you find out about it?"

Setting his jaw and bracing himself to his parent's reaction, he said, "I heard it from the woman who was raped. I heard it from my mother. My *other* mother. Who do you think told me? I accidentally met her today. You can imagine my surprise. "

Henry and Gwen felt like they had been sucker-punched. Their reaction was a genuine look of shock and amazement.

"My *real* mother," Tyler repeated. "Do you remember a woman named Adrian Connell?"

The name had not been forgotten. They remembered the mother, but they hadn't heard or spoken her name in close to fifteen years.

"I see the name rings a familiar bell with you."

"Yes." Gwen said as Henry bobbed his head in agreement.

"My mom—Adrian Connell—became pregnant because she was raped and then, TA-DA! BOOM! Here's Tyler! I was a major oops baby! A big mistake! She didn't tell you that piece of detailed information at the adoption hearing, did she?"

"No. She never mentioned it."

Tyler continued, "You see how it feels to be lied to, huh?"

And they did. Both of them were beginning to see the first hints of anger rise in their bodies.

"I didn't think she would mention it. I mean, why would she? She was trying to get rid of me. Tell somebody that; they would think twice about adopting a kid from an outcome like that. They might think they were getting stuck with a psychopath kid or a sociopathic child."

"She told us that he left her."

"Yeah, he left her alright; right after he rode her hard and hung her up wet."

"Tyler!" His mom's voice was nearly a shout in the living room. "That's rude."

"No, *Mom*, it's the truth. He beat the living shit out of her, had his way with her, and left her high and dry."

"That's a shame," Henry said.

"Yeah, it is, Dad. A damn shame. That drunken son of a bitch should be shot in his fucking nuts for what he did to her."

"Tyler!" Gwen warned again.

"Well, its true, isn't it?" He paused, shook his head then changed the subject. "Are you having second thoughts about adopting me now; because, you know, that's my history."

He waited for an answer but they had been stunned into silence by the news. The thought that Tyler was a product born from such a savage incident was as shocking for them as it was for Tyler.

He stood to leave. "I thought that news would change your opinion about me."

Not registering what Tyler had said, Henry and Gwen stared at Tyler in anticipation. Finally realizing he was leaving, Gwen said, "No, Tyler, Wait. Where are you going?"

"I have to get out of here. I need some time to myself; to think about everything. You should have done a little more research about me. You might have found you didn't want me after all. But that's beside the point; what you should've done is told me the truth from the very beginning."

Those last thirteen words made the guilt rise inside them again.

"I know," Gwen said. "We should've and we wanted to, believe me, we did; but we were unsure how you would react."

"Well now you know."

"Yes, we do now. That's what we were afraid of."

"If I had grown up knowing this, I would've never acted this way. I would've known I was adopted and would know that you had been honest with me from the beginning. It would've been engrained in me early on. But now, I don't know if I can ever trust you again."

A long, awkward silence poured into the room. They all stared at the floor.

"You've hurt me," he continued.

Henry was the one who spoke first, breaking the quiet hush that had fallen, "Tyler, can I tell you something?"

"Sure, I guess. As long as it's the truth."

The words stung Henry and he bobbed his head in submission then calmly continued. "We don't know how you feel right now, but we know we're the cause of your pain. We betrayed you and all we can do is ask for your forgiveness so we can start over again. We don't expect you to do that right away. We know you're upset and that you need time for your wounds to heal. It will give us time to earn your trust back, if that is at all possible. We know you need some time to adjust to this news you've just learned. I just ask that you don't dwell on it too long. Don't bottle your anger up and close us out. I don't know what else to say except that we're sorry, we love you and hope, in time, you can forgive us."

Gwen nodded her head, expressing her sorrow as well.

"I have one other question before you go," Henry said.

"What's that?"

"How did you find her? Your mother?"

Tyler smirked a little as he remembered. "It was an accident, really."

"Oh,"

"Yeah. Remember that old chest I found in the attic?"

"Yes."

"It was actually Adrian's. I figured that out from all the medals and trophies and pictures that were in it. Apparently she lived in this house when she was younger and in high school years ago. That chest had been forgotten when they moved and was presumed lost after I was born." Tyler switched gears. "She's a photographer. I don't know if you knew that about her or not."

"No. We didn't talk to her much after all the adoption papers were signed and everything was taken care of. We thought it would be best for everyone."

"You mean it was better for you, but not me. You didn't even think of how that would affect me."

Gwen nodded, "Yes, that's it exactly."

"Did you think I would leave you one day and love my real mother more? How could you think that? I may have had questions about where I came from, but I would've never left you."

They smiled and nodded, curious as to what Tyler was going to say next.

Gwen said, "We were so excited when we brought you home. We value you above everything else."

Tyler nodded then changed the subject back to the original conversation. "She had a bunch of pictures of me, you know, her being a photographer and all. Most of the ones I saw were recent high school photos. I guess she wanted to see me grow up in some way. She spent a lot of time and energy to find out where I was living just to observe me. Some people might find that creepy, but not me. I felt it more as a desperate love or a longing of something important to her that she had to give up. I call that love if nothing else, especially since it was agreed upon that she have no contact with me whatsoever. She'll probably keep observing me still and I hope she does. I hope that won't be a problem with you. I certainly don't mind it in the least."

They shrugged as if to say, *She's been doing it for close to seventeen years with no major incident; what's the use in stopping her now?"*

"I'm going to go now," he said. "I think I've said pretty much all

I wanted to say, at least for now. I'm sure when I leave, there will be a million other questions and comments that crop up. I guess you can go back and eat your dinner now. Hope it's not too cold. Sorry to be an inconvenience to you."

As he left he heard his mom say, "Tyler, wait. Please, don't go." Then he heard his father say, "Let him go for now. He needs some time alone. He has some things to work out in his mind. Let's go eat." He could picture his father placing an arm around her to guide her back into the kitchen. He knew he was going to have to coax her to finish her dinner, although, he knew for both of them their appetite had vanished.

Only when Tyler was outside leaning against the closed front door, did he breathe a sigh of relief. His hands were still trembling. He had actually been nervous about this meeting but didn't know that until just now. He didn't know where to go now or what to do. No, he knew exactly where he needed to be. It was the place that had always been a solace for him when he needed to be alone. Come to think of it, in some ways, he had been alone his whole life.

CHAPTER 38

TYLER AND EDWARD, together in one body, sat on the edge of the dock listening to the water lap at the legs of the pier below. The lake hadn't changed much from when Edward used to sit here years ago, except that the water seemed higher than it used to be. It was also colder than he remembered, and his bare feet were slightly numb.

The lights lining the dock flickered for a moment then came on, lighting certain areas of the pier.

The two opposing forces—the souls of Tyler and Edward—were still fighting; a war of wills was continuing to rage within the confines of Tyler's body.

Tyler was perplexed and didn't know how to cope with the news he had learned today. He thought about the information he received time and time again. It was all so unbelievable but at the same time believable.

Tyler and Edward realized that their lives were connected in some strange way. The medallion was just another tool used by the hands of fate that allowed their paths to cross.

If Tyler hadn't found the charm, the misfortune of the amulet would have rested on the shoulders of some other teenager or adult. The nightmare his life had been spun into would be causing turmoil in somebody else's life. The end result would be the same. If somebody else had released Edward they would've been forced by Edward to take the same actions Tyler had been forced to take. The same people that had died at his hands would still be dead today by the hands of another.

I wish someone else had found the amulet. One good thing though, Tyler thought. *Without Edward, I might never have found my birth mother. But on second thought, I would've still found the hope chest that was in the attic; that would've put me on the path to finding her, so I still would've met Adrian. Shit, the possibilities are endless, and my head is beginning to hurt thinking about all this.*

"What the hell did I do to deserve this?" he muttered to the water. "It's not fair."

"What's not fair?" Savannah asked as she silently strolled down the pier behind him.

Startled, Tyler turned. "What? Oh. Hey. You scared me." Realizing who it was he turned back and looked out at the darkened horizon. As Savannah sat beside him, he asked, "What do *you* want?"

"Okay. I deserve that." Savannah said.

Tyler said nothing. He just continued to stare out into the middle distance.

They were quiet; an awkwardness growing between them.

"Well?" he said.

"Well, what?"

"What do you want?"

Savannah glanced out at the horizon then took a moment getting up the nerve to say what she came here to say. "To be honest, I came out here to apologize to you."

Tyler glanced over at her. When she turned to look at him, he returned his gaze back out to the lake.

"You were right," she continued. "Deep down I know you even though I barely know you."

"Oh."

"Wasn't what you were expecting to hear was it?"

"Actually no."

"I don't really know why I came at you like I did, but I honestly don't believe you killed those people. Jesus, sounds so wrong even saying it out loud."

"I'm kind of shocked you're even apologizing at all," Tyler said.

"Why do you say that?"

"Because you seemed pretty sure I was guilty."

"I've since changed my mind about you. I've given it a lot of thought."

"Why? What caused that?"

"I don't know, but I just have this feeling about you. I'm going with my gut instinct on this. I've never been wrong when trusting it so I'm trusting that I'm making the right decision."

"You are. But it sounds like there is still a little doubt in that last sentence."

"Doesn't mean I don't have questions, because there are a lot of empty blanks left to fill."

"Well, I hope one day all your questions will be answered so everything will be clear in your mind."

"Yeah. Maybe. I just don't believe it was you and I don't want to miss anymore time without you. So I came here to apologize, hoping we can start over. Is there any way you can forgive me?"

Tyler smiled and grabbed her hand, "The thing is, I've already forgiven you. That happened the day of the argument. I know I was mad about your accusations, but it doesn't mean that I was going to hold a grudge. I was just waiting for you to make up your mind about me so we can pick up where we left off."

"So that's it?"

"What's what?

"That was kind of easy."

"What more do you want?"

"I was expecting us to have this huge fight and worried about us not even working out at all."

"You worry too much. Just hearing you say it and knowing you believe it is apology enough for me. I've missed you just as much but I really couldn't do anything about us with you feeling the way you did about me. I had to hope you would change your mind about me."

"I did. I really did."

"I believe you, and I'm glad."

They leaned against each other. They were quiet for a time.

Savannah broke the silence and asked, "What's got you down?"

"What do you mean?"

"Earlier when I came up behind you I heard you say, 'What the hell did I do to deserve this' and 'It's not fair.' What's not fair?"

"Oh nothing," he said in disgust. "Just something that's going on between my parents and me."

"I figured it had something to do with your parents. I mean, that's what your dad told me."

"Did they call you and ask you to check on me?"

"No. No, as it turned out, I called them to find out where you've secretly been hiding yourself. Your dad told me you guys had an argument. He said he didn't know where you were, so I made a guess. You told me one time that you like to come down here to think so I decided to try here first."

"Did my parents happen to mention what the fight was about?"

"No, we really didn't talk long. He didn't seem in the mood to talk."

"It figures. They didn't have the balls to tell me for all those years; why would they tell you."

"Whatever happened between you and your parents is no business of mine, but I'm here to listen if you need a sounding board."

"Where do I start?" Tyler asked more or less to himself.

"Wherever you want," Savannah said.

Tyler continued, "You sure you want to hear this?"

"I can't think of anything else I'd rather do than to listen to your problems and maybe help you figure them out."

Hearing her say that, he knew she cared for him. A new trust was beginning to form between them when he began his story.

He started from the beginning with finding the wooden hope chest in the attic and the quest to locate Adrian Connell. He told about his recent conversation with Adrian and he described in exhaustive detail how Jeremy Taylor was involved with the drowning of Edward McDaniel and the rape of Adrian Connell. Then he finally informed her that he was the result of the rape and that Adrian Connell was his birth mother and that his parents had never told him he was adopted.

"Oh my God. You have got to be shitting me," Suzanne said.

"No. I shit you not. It's the truth." He paused, then added. "How do you like me now?"

"You think something like that is going to change my feelings about you. That is unfortunate for you, but it is like the most interesting story I've ever heard. I'm disappointed about the news of course because I know it must be hard for you to take. Your parents lying like that. Sorry you had to find out about it like that but maybe it's good that you did. At least now you know more about who you really are."

"Yeah. That is pretty much the whole argument I had with my parents. I feel like I am a different person now that I know my—" he paused as though the next word was hard for him to say, "—heritage."

"That's what you and your parents were fighting about?"

"Yeah. I can't believe I cussed them out. I was really bad to them."

"They hurt you; you hurt them. You guys are even."

"No way, we're not even close to being even. You can't imagine how I feel right now."

"I know, I know. I was kidding about that. They can't blame you for being upset. They're the ones that kept the secret from you, not the other way around."

Tyler whispered in a broken voice. "I know." He paused, "You mind if we not talk about this anymore. It's not that I don't want to share any of this with you. Just tired of thinking about it."

"Of course. And I wasn't trying to pry. I'm just here to talk about it if you need to."

"I know. I appreciate it."

They were quiet for a while longer, letting the news settle in their minds. When Tyler finally glanced back over to Savannah, he found her face was closer to him than he expected. Her eyes were half closed from the wind that blew off the lake.

Tyler gave her a startled double-take, paused, then slowly leaned into her and met her slightly parted lips head on. The kiss was soft and gentle even tentative at first. They pulled away, hesitated slightly, then met again more firmly and with more purpose. The second kiss was full, smooth and slightly wet. It slowly began to build as their tongues finally met and started dancing over each other.

They kissed for a long while wanting nothing more than to just enjoy the heat of this passionate moment.

His lips eventually dropped down below her jaw line and skittered over the nape of her neck. She smiled as chills erupted over her body.

"Oh Tyler, you shouldn't have done that. That area drives me crazy."

"You mean…this area?" he asked innocently. Barely touching her neck again with his lips, he kissed slowly up her neck again.

Unable to bear the torture of his gentleness, she pushed him away playfully then grabbed the back of his neck and pulled him back to her and right into a open-mouthed kiss. Her tongue went deep into his mouth; it probed urgently and licked hard over his tongue.

She pulled away from him and took a long, deep breath as though she had been suffocating.

"Yeah, that area. It gets me every time."

"I'll have to remember that."

They came together again with a less intense kiss but it was just as passionate as all the others. That was all it took.

Soon four hands were nervously fumbling with belts, buttons, zippers and clasps that held them back from pleasure that was soon to come. The barriers of clothing were quickly stripped away and their hands were soon roaming slowly with urgent but tentative caresses. They were lost in the nervous exploration of new bodily territory.

Inside Tyler's body, Edward's new hands finally felt three dimensional curves that his mind had always wished and dreamed to feel. He had wished for this day for years; now it was here, and it was unlike anything he had ever experienced before. His lips and tongue soon followed where his hands had roamed moments before.

Tyler ran his hands down from Savannah's face then over her breasts. In smooth steady strokes, he gave them loving attention they needed and that she wanted. He moved further down her exotic body to her sloped stomach and sensually kissed around her navel. Before he could go any lower, he felt her hands on his head pushing him down between her legs, wanting and needing him to go lower.

He consented without hesitation. He wanted to please her and he could tell by the sounds she was making that he was. She reached out for anything to grasp and hold on to. She found nothing but her own breast and the top of his head. She gripped as much of Tyler's hair as possible and held on as he sent her into violent shudders of ecstasy.

"Oh-my-God-oh-my-God-oh-my-God-oh-my-God-oh-my-God," she chanted urgently as though it were a prayerful mantra. When the last of her orgasms had rolled through her, she pushed his head away.

Tyler moved in beside her, pressing his body as close to her as possible. He wrapped his arms around her, pulled her close to him, and held on to her tightly.

Savannah finally rolled over where she was now facing him and she kissed him softly.

Their eyes met. Tyler saw tears in hers. He immediately became alarmed.

"No, Savannah; wait. What is it? What did I do? Are you—,"

A finger came to his lips silencing whatever he was going to say next. "Don't be alarmed. Nothing's wrong. Everything is perfect. Tears of happiness, remember?"

"Oh. Okay. As long as you're okay with everything."

"Yes. It was perfect. I loved every minute of it. It couldn't have been better."

Before he could reply, she rolled on top of him and straddled him.

Tyler half expected her to begin moving on top of him but she quickly leaned down into his face. She started with another sensuous kiss. She whispered, "I've wanted to do this to you ever since I saw you in class the first day you arrived. I've waited a long time for this moment. I hope you're ready for me."

"Believe me. I'm more than ready."

Grabbing his hard on between his legs, she said, "Oh yes. Yes you are."

They snickered together at the cheesy innuendo.

Tyler lay back and began to relax as she began a slow decent from his neck to his chest. She continued down his lower abdomen until she came to his pleasure center between his legs and started him on a trip he would never forget.

Tyler's and Edward's mind were simultaneously reeling; especially

Edward's. He had never experienced this before in his life. It was unimaginable and he wanted it to go on forever.

She made the trip lengthy for Tyler; lots of teasing and toying with him. When she felt he couldn't take the teasing any longer she focused all her full attention on the most sensitive area with long, smooth, quick strokes until he erupted with pleasure.

Tyler was panting hard, trying to catch his breath when she slid in beside him just as he had done to her. She was lying halfway on top of him; one leg over his waist, her arm thrown over his abdomen and her head on his chest. She could feel his heart beating wildly beneath her ear as though it were a trapped bird fluttering to escape.

She smiled as she listened to it thump out an excited beat beneath her ear. She hoped Tyler was just as happy and satisfied as she.

After they rested, they went skinny dipping. Diving into the water they found it chillier than they expected. They were hot but the refreshing water cooled them to their core.

With their heads being the only thing breaking the surface of the water, they continued to run their hands over each other's slick bodies. The exploration of each other's wet curves was addictive and they couldn't get enough of each other. They hugged each other tightly and Savannah wrapped her legs around Tyler's waist. Tyler slid into her. Savannah's breath caught in her throat then she let out a small squeal of excitement. "Oh God, Tyler."

"Are you okay?"

"Oh God, yes. Never better. That was the best feeling ever; a little surprising but really nice. I'm perfect now. Hold me tight."

"I will. I always will. I'll never let you go."

And with that, he wrapped his arms around her and pulled her to him and held her close.

They stayed like that for the longest without any movement. Just being complete as one body was enough and they slowly water danced as they kissed.

When the water became too cold for them to endure any longer, they found their bodies huddled together again on the pier. They hugged tightly as their naked bodies slowly warmed. Before long, they were touching, feeling and kissing each other all over again.

Savannah leaned back as Tyler moved on top of her body. Her legs parted again giving him permission to penetrate her.

"I'm ready for you this time," she said smiling.

Amused, Tyler replied, "I am too."

They both laughed then he slowly slid inside her making sure he didn't hurt her in any way. She responded by wrapping her arms and legs around him, pulling him closer forcing him inside her as far as he could go. He lovingly stroked her face and swiped a few wet strands of hair from of her eyes. Within seconds, they were slowly rocking back and forth; their sleek, wet bodies moving together to the steady tempo of the lake water slapping against the piers below.

After they made love, they lay there in each others arms.

A cool breeze blew off the lake and drifted over their bodies. The air chilled them and pimpled their skin with gooseflesh. They were completely exposed but unembarrassed. They lay there clutching each other tightly in the moonlight.

Tyler turned and looked intently into her eyes and whispered, "Hey, Savannah, guess what?"

She stared back just as intently and took a chance on saying it first, "I love you too, Tyler."

His head jerked back in slight shock as he grinned, "How did you know?"

She smiled in return, "I just do. I can tell. I can feel it."

"Well, I do. Do you believe me?"

"Yes, but I have always known."

"Well, believe it because it's true. I do."

They stayed there for a long time late into the night because time was the last thing on their minds.

PART FOUR: TWIN MINDS

Greater love hath no man than this,
that a man lay down his life for his friends.

St. John 15:13

CHAPTER 39

AFTER A LONG kiss goodnight following their rendezvous at the dock, Tyler was wide awake. He was in his Mustang nearing his house, but he didn't want to go home and he didn't feel like going to bed.

Tyler knew if he pulled into his driveway, he would be stuck. The purring of his car engine would be enough to alert Raven of his arrival. If his parents were already asleep, Raven would start barking until Tyler made it inside and petted her to calm her down.

She's such a diva, he thought smiling. *I love that damn dog.*

He pulled his car to the curb a few houses from where he lived and downshifted to first, applied the parking brake, and killed the engine.

Edward's mind was racing. He was so amped up from the feeling of losing his virginity to Savannah that he couldn't calm down. Technically, his virginity was lost with Suzanne Baldwin on rivalry night but he never really considered that as the day he lost it. The only thing he tried to do about that night was forget it had ever happened. That memory connected with what the other guys did to him shortly after that made his mind swell with anger. That thought lead him to relive what he'd done to Travis Sheridan. Then he backtracked to what he'd done to Bruce Saliers. Then his thoughts moved to Alexander Riley

Alex Riley, Edward thought. *I haven't done anything to you yet. I should pay you a visit. How can I get to you, Alex? You're always at that damn hospital. If only there was a way to get in to see you. Even if I get to you, how am I going to get back at you for the pain—the literal pain—you put me through. What you did to me, Alex, is worse than what Jeremy did.*

He gave that last sentence a second thought, then said, "Almost worst."

Edward's thoughts drifted to Kelly Sheridan—Kelly Morgan, as he knew her—Edward relived her final moments on earth again.

He felt the strength of his throw as the vase left his hand and spun toward Kelly's head. He saw the vase connect with a shattering blow, then he saw her fall into the stairwell. He felt the scissors puncture her skin. Then he felt her body release from this earth when the scissors couldn't go in any farther.

His mind jumped ahead to his approach on Suzanne Baldwin in the parking garage. He saw her turn away. He remembered lunging at her then abruptly turning away from the canister of pepper spray. He remembered the burning fumes irritating his eyes and grasping at Suzanne's outfit and ripping away her security badge. The frustration swelled in him again and he saw himself pitching the badge away in anger.

He thought again of the security badge in his hand and the anger he felt as he pitched it away.

The security badge.

Edward slowly turned his head from the windshield to the passenger's seat. *Could it be? Was it still there?*

Edward quickly leaned across the seat and felt between it and the door panel. He couldn't find it.

Where the fuck was it?

Edward stepped out of the car and jogged around to the other side and opened the passenger door. He didn't see it at first glance but he felt under the seat and there it was.

He pulled the security badge out and stared again at Suzanne's smiling face.

Edward thoughtfully tapped the badge against his hand.

A plan started forming in his head.

This is it, Edward thought. *Thank you, Suzanne. I knew there was a reason I liked you most of all.*

Edward cranked the Mustang and punched the gas pedal. The car surged back into the road, making a U-turn and he headed back the way he had come.

Alex was next on Edward's hit list, Tyler thought.

Yeah, Edward replied. *And I'm going to make damn sure Alex gets hit.*

Edward was once again in complete control, but under his own skin Tyler was fighting to regain control of himself.

Before Tyler knew it, they were again slowly cruising through the Silver Ridge Memorial Hospital parking lot.

Edward was looking for Alex's car just as he had done when searching for Suzanne Baldwin's Mercedes.

Edward's eyes eventually fell on Alex's Corvette. He said, "Hello, Alex. Working late again tonight I see."

A brand new, bright red Corvette in immaculate condition was parked in a secluded spot at the far end of the east wing of the parking lot. It was parked diagonally, occupying two parking spaces.

Edward let out a breath of disgust as he shook his head. One of Edward's pet peeves was people taking up more than one parking space.

Edward noticed the license tag. It stated Alex's last name in capital letters: R-I-L-E-Y.

It's about time Riley bought a new car, Edward said thinking back. *That piece of shit truck he drove in high school should've never been allowed on the road. The truck,* Edward mused. His mind was being pulled back in time but he didn't want to relive that memory; not just yet; it was too painful in a number of different ways.

Upset, Edward pulled out of the parking lot and parked across the street in the shadows underneath the low-hanging limbs of a spruce tree. From his vantage point, he could still see the Corvette. In Edward's mind, the Corvette magically morphed into the truck Alex used to drive during his high school days. He hated that truck. It was the same abomination that almost took his life.

He couldn't shake it. The memory was forcing its way out of the repression of his mind. It was time to relive the past. Still eying the vehicle, he leaned his head back on the headrest and finally let his mind replay one of the harsher memories from his childhood. This was the one memory that caused more pain—psychologically and physically—than any of the other memories combined.

In Edward's mind's eye he saw himself on his bike, his *second* bike, once again.

CHAPTER 40

IT HAD BEEN a little over a month since the incident with guns, bullets, and the boys in the woods. Edward had mainly stayed around the house, not venturing far from home except to go to school, to work or to run an occasional errand for his grandparents. As soon as school was out or when he was finished with his work, he came back home as quickly as he could by the most direct route unless his grandparents picked him up.

He never told anyone about what had happened deep in the woods. He believed, to a certain extent, what the boys had said they would do to him if he did. His grandparents didn't even know his bicycle had been demolished and discarded. His grandmother had shown concern over the cuts he'd received from the exploding beer cans, but he had simply told her some branches he hadn't seen had caught him in the face as he was riding through the woods. She eyed him suspiciously but eventually accepted his measly excuse, and Edward was secretly grateful.

But that was over, done with, and behind him. He was riding his brand new mountain bike down a ten-mile stretch of road that people had dubbed Desolation Highway because it seemed to have been forgotten over time.

The road itself was very bumpy, but his new ride was very smooth. The suspension system was unbelievable on the uneven asphalt. He couldn't wait to take it on a trail ride through the woods; something he'd decided to wait on since the last excursion went to hell in a hurry.

Tall grass had sprouted up through the cracked pavement because it had been unattended for years. The recent redirection of a newer, wider, main highway had taken traffic on a more straight path into the city.

Ever since the new highway had been built, the area around the old highway had slowly become a seedier place. Litter began to pile up along its ten-mile stretch. Occasionally, there were some people who volunteered to clean up the length of meandering road, but within days the area was always back the way it had been. Almost every time he traveled this route, he found a plethora of discarded beer bottles and cans, porno magazines, panties that had been tossed aside and used condoms. Graffiti stretched from one end of the highway to the other depicting lewd symbols and drawings in all shapes and sizes.

Edward trekked along at a pretty steady clip, his arms held out to his sides. He was listening to music on his walkman, an impulse purchase he added when he bought his bike. He was coasting down a small slope in the road when all of a sudden a bad sensation of impending danger overcame him.

Spidey sense, *he thought and inwardly laughed.*

He quickly reached for the handle bars with one hand as his other hand pulled the headphones from his hears. The music he was listening to faded from the headset only to be replaced by the sound of approaching heavy metal music. The music seemed to confirm his feeling.

Thinking it was just a passing car, he nonchalantly glanced over his right shoulder; he immediately wished to God he hadn't.

He screamed at the sight advancing on him and he turned and pedaled faster to escape.

What he saw was a row of sharp teeth gleaming in the sunlight. The mangled, metal fangs were each attached inside an open maw that was bigger than he had ever seen. It was bigger than life and was quickly bearing down on him.

As he turned to pedal away from the metal beast that was gaining on him, he realized who and what it was.

Alex, *Edward thought.* What the hell is he doing out here?

Alex wasn't an artist by any means, but he had welded small pieces of jagged metal to the front of his truck grill to give the effect of an open creature's mouth. Along with the added steel grin were two evil-looking red eyes painted on two metal plates that had been welded above the mouth. On any other truck it would've looked strangely stupid, but on this monstrosity it somehow seemed to fit its character.

A blast from the truck's horn sounded right behind him; nearly in his ears. The sound immediately put his nerves on edge.

Obnoxious, is what it is, *Edward thought.* That goes for his artwork too.

He had seen Alex's truck at school, even the welded teeth, but that had always been from a distance. Now seeing them up close and personal, he realized the effect worked.

Alex's Dodge looked as though it had already seen its last days. It was a petrified shit gray; in the other areas where the paint was peeling, white showed through. Mud was caked along the truck's bottom panels and around the wheel wells. Across the windshield was the phrase: DON'T DODGE IT...RAM IT!

The phrase made Edward pedal faster to get away from the highway monster but Alex kept weaving back and forth behind him, blowing his horn. He knew Alex wanted him to turn around and look, but Edward focused his attention on the road ahead.

The metal land shark mimicked Edward's actions and matched his speed. Alex also kept the horn sounding to abrade Edward's nerves.

When Edward could no longer take it, he gave a half turn and shouted, "Get away from me!"

That's when he saw the other two boys in the truck with him. They were all pointing and laughing at him.

"Cut it out!" he screamed, then as an after thought added, "You assholes!"

Their response was another blast from the horn.

Edward's ears were already ringing from the numerous blasts.

"Leave me alone!"

Yet another response from the horn; this one seemed to go on forever.

Without thinking, he gripped the hand breaks tightly and abruptly slowed. As soon as he did, he knew it was a bad idea; he immediately expected the truck to slam into the back of him. He just wanted them to leave him alone.

Is it that hard for them to do? *Edward thought.*

Edward closed his eyes and waited for the truck to strike his back tire and body. There was a loud squeal of tires as the truck's breaks suddenly locked up. It veered sharply around Edward who was nearly stopped near the highway's shoulder.

He heard the growling motor drop into a bass purr as it pulled up on his left side.

A hand closed around the base of his neck, and Edward's heart dropped to the pit of his stomach.

"I love your new bike. When did you get it?" A voice asked.

It was Travis Sheridan.

Edward didn't answer.

"Where have you been, Edward?"

Another voice yelled from inside the truck, "We've been missing you."

That was Bruce Saliers.

"Leave me alone!" Edward shouted again.

"Oh, don't be that way. We've been worried about you."

"Bullshit," Edward mumbled beneath his breath. "Leave me alone!" he shouted a third time as though repetition would cause them to stop.

In response to Edward's outrage there was a sound of a spitball being shot out of a straw. The wad caught Edward right below the temple on the left side of his face.

Confusion lined Edward's features and he glanced inside the truck to find out who had shot it at him. He saw Bruce wiping his mouth as he leaned back into the middle of the bucket seats with a huge grin on his face.

There were three howls of laughter from the inside of the road beast.

Edward moved his right hand from the handle bars and wiped the left side of his face. He grimaced as he pulled his hand away and sticky, wet strands of mucus clung to his middle three fingers.

Tobacco juice. Oh God; that's just plain nasty.

He moved his hand toward the shoulder of the road and shook it vigorously. Some of the tobacco juice dropped off his fingers, but there was still some excess that he needed to get rid of.

He wiped the remaining tobacco juice on the shirt sleeve of his left shoulder. Edward's heart sank again when he felt skin instead of fabric.

Too late now, *he thought and continued to wipe the excess from his fingers on the back of Travis's hand.*

He heard the laughter suddenly die off in a chain reaction, first from Travis, then Bruce, then Alex as they saw what had just happened. Edward too turned to see Travis's reaction. It wasn't good. Travis pulled his left hand back through the window after switching his grip on Edward to his right hand. For a moment, Travis's focus was split between Edward and the back of his own hand. He stared in shock at the mucus, seeming at first not to believe, but realization finally set in.

On Edward's third glance through the open window, he sensed it was time to get the hell out of dodge or at least away from this Dodge. Travis had been so in shock that his right hand had eased up on the back of Edward's neck instead of clamping down harder as expected.

Edward jammed his foot on the pedal and simultaneously jerked his head away from Travis's grasp. As he pulled ahead of the truck, he heard Travis say, "Gun it, Alex. That son of a bitch isn't getting away with this."

He got as far as a bike's length in front of the truck before he heard the highway demon growl and advance on him again.

Edward glanced back just in time to see Travis pitch himself halfway out the window. Travis went for the back of his neck again. Edward tried to duck away from his grasp and thought he had succeeded but felt four fingers hook around the collar of the loose tee-shirt he was wearing.

"Oh, no you don't. Get back over here you little shit," Travis commanded.

Edward could do nothing but obey; the front of the neckline dug into the base of his throat as it was gripped tightly and yanked back.

The hand held him firmly in place. From his periphery, he could see Travis lean a little farther out the window. Travis's other hand, the one with the tobacco remains, came up in front of his nose.

"What the fuck were you thinking?"

"That's just it, I wasn't thinking. I didn't mean too. Honest. It was just a reaction."

"Well, are you thinking now?"

Edward nodded.

"I can't hear you."

"Yes! Yes, I'm thinking now!"

"What do you think we should do with this shit that's on my hand?"

Edward thought for just a second and opened his mouth to give him a smart-ass answer. When he turned to speak, Travis jammed the back side of his hand into Edward's mouth.

"How about we do that?"

Travis rotated his hand in all directions to make sure all the mucus came off.

Travis's hand scraped against Edward's teeth and the insides of his lips. Edward hadn't ever tasted tobacco. By this time the remainder of tobacco juice wasn't much, but it was enough to send Edward into sputtering gasps of air as he tried to rid himself of the rank taste.

Laughter erupted from inside the truck again. For a couple of moments they had their fun, but it was short lived because a car horn sounded behind them.

Everybody froze except for Edward. He was still trying to get rid of the taste in his mouth, but he was smiling now; at least he was on the inside.

Edward was relieved that someone had come along to stop this madness. Realizing the grip on his shirt hadn't loosened, he glanced inside the window again. He saw Alex with his arm out the window waving them around to pass.

He heard the sound of the other car accelerate; after a few seconds, it came into view through the driver's side open window and had slowed to an even crawl with Alex's truck.

"Let's wave to the nice people," Bruce said, holding up and shaking an open palm.

"Yeah, let's wave," Alex agreed and did likewise. "Nothing but the best of friends here."

More to himself than to anyone else, Edward pleaded, "No. Please stop. Don't pass."

"Shut up, Edward," Travis said through gritted teeth and waved as the others were doing. "Be a nice little boy and wave at the nice couple too."

"No," Edward said.

The collar around his neck became tighter.

"I said wave at the people in the car or, I swear to God, you'll wish you had."

For a split second, he thought about giving them the middle finger as a way to make them stop, but as he raised his hand, he felt it moving back and forth in a gesture of friendliness.

Edward figured from the couple's point of view it must've looked like three guys had pulled up beside a friend who was just out riding his bike on a nice warm day. They must've thought he was holding on to the side of the truck as they moved along at a slow pace.

All four boys noticed the driver and saw he was in his college years. He was the good-looking type, the ladies man type; and boy did he have the lady. Upon seeing her, the driver was forgotten and their attention became focused on her. When she noticed them wave in her direction she smiled and turned in her seat to face them.

"Holy smokes, guys. Check out the rack on her," Alex said.

Her tanned body seemed to make the white skirt and equally matching tube top—both articles of clothing that bordered on the mini side—glow a fluorescent white. The outfit didn't leave too much to the imagination. She had an athletic body, no doubt about that. They could tell by her lean, muscular arms and flattened stomach.

She brought a hand up to her pouting lips, kissed it, blew it their way and then winked. They were already speechless and each of their mouths was wide open.

The woman started at the top of her head and ran her fingers slowly through her brown hair then proceeded to slide her hands over her well-shaped body. When she got to her breasts her thumbs hooked into the sides of her tube top and slowly slid it down. When her nipples were peeking over the top of the fabric she jerked the garment all the way down to her waist. She gave them all a wry smile, more like a sneer—but it was sexy, and immediately ran her hands back up the length of her body. As she cupped her breasts again with both hands, they noticed that she had also extended both her middle fingers. When the message was relayed, she pulled her top back up and turned back in her seat again as the car pulled away.

In no time the couple—now laughing—had disappeared around the bend in the far distance and with it, Edward's hope of escaping what Alex, Bruce, and Travis had in store for him.

"What a fucking tease," Alex said. "Can you believe that shit? Huh, if she were my girl, she wouldn't be showing and shaking it around like that."

"That's the problem with you." Travis said. "You'll never own anything that nice."

"No tan lines, did you notice that?" Bruce said.

Again Travis said, "Well I was looking right at them. How could you not miss something like that?"

From a wishful-thinking daydream Alex said, "Wish I could get a hold of her for a couple of hours."

"Yeah right. A couple of hours, more like a couple of seconds," Bruce said.

Everybody started laughing at the comment.

When they realized Edward was laughing along with them, they abruptly stopped. When Edward realized he was the only one still laughing, he turned and stared into the interior of the truck. Three heads swiveled from the horizon line and stared at him. The looks on their faces weren't pleasant; he braced himself for what they might do next.

"And what the fuck were you laughing at?"

"Nothing. I, um, I just—"

"Shut up, you little faggot," Travis said, "How would you know?" Changing the subject, he directed the question to the other boys, "Well that was fun. What in the world do you want to do next?"

Edward turned and saw Bruce move past Travis as he leaned a good distance out the passenger's side window. Bruce was close enough to kiss Edward.

Bruce sucked in a mouthful of air and spit another tobacco stream before Edward had a chance to react. Edward clamped his mouth shut as the mucus hit the inside of his throat.

"Ah-ha-ha. Bullseye, bitch. That'll shut you up," Bruce yelled.

Swallowing some of the acrid juice, Edward gagged and spit some of the wad from his mouth.

The boys all laughed again and cheered aloud as Edward spluttered against the bile.

"Ah shit, Bruce. I can't believe you did that," Travis said between laughs.

"I needed to spit. Can't help it if he got in my way."

Alex said, "That was fucking disgusting. I loved it. Do it again."

Edward knew he couldn't let that happen. The only thing he could think of was something his mother had always told him. Something from the Bible;

it was always something from the Bible. She had said in the past, "When someone does something to you, like hit you, turn the other cheek and offer that to them as well."

Fuck that, *he thought.* I want the pain to stop not continue. I don't want to do anything that would continue it. If I want more pain, I'll run out in front of a moving truck.

It sounded stupid even to him, but that was the only thing he could think of at the moment. Edward didn't have time to really think if there was any future irony to that thought.

Another saying his grandmother always quoted was, "Do unto others as you would have them do unto you."

That's more like it, Edward thought. They wouldn't have spit on me unless they wanted to be spit on themselves. I'm not going to wait around and find out if Bruce would actually repeat his actions.

While the boys had been grab-assing and high five-ing in the truck, Edward kept moving his tongue around in his mouth working up saliva to spit the last bit of the tobacco out. When he had a big enough wad and when Travis was looking in his direction, he turned and leaned toward Travis and launched the spit wad directly at Travis. He then threw Travis's arm from his shoulder and pedaled away from the truck as fast as he could.

As he pulled ahead for the second time, he heard Travis say, "Oh shit! My eye! That creepy little bastard spit in my eye. Oh fuck, it burns."

Edward hadn't been aiming for Travis's eye, but what the hell, you get lucky sometimes. He couldn't suppress the smile that crept in at the corners of his mouth.

Edward heard the roar of the engine as Alex gunned it again. Edward wasn't going to let these guys pull up beside him again, so he quickly moved further into the middle of the lane they were in.

The horn blew again in frustration. Edward tried to ignore them and pedaled faster.

Edward kept glancing behind him to see where the truck was and to judge its movements. When the truck started to move around him into the opposite lane, Edward followed suit. Each time the truck slowed, it swerved back into the other lane and tried to go around. Edward guided his bike back in front of them and continued to ward them off. Each time Edward cut them off, Alex blew the horn and revved the engine.

Edward kept telling himself, "I can do this. I can keep this up. I can't let them catch me. If they do, it would be another mouthful of tobacco or something worse."

Something hit Edward between the shoulder blades. It didn't hurt, but it startled him. It bounced off and clattered to the ground behind him. He turned just in time to see an empty beer can skitter off into the weeds at the side of the road. He turned back to the road ahead and saw another one pass in front of his eyes. Another one bounced off the spokes of his front tire.

Great, *Edward thought.* Not only do I have to dodge this truck but now I have to dodge this shit they're throwing at me.

He glanced around in time to veer away from another lobbed beer can.

What happens when they start throwing more solid objects? What do I do then?

He tried psyching himself up for anything.

Cross that bridge when you get to it. Just keep doing what you're doing.

Travis was hanging half way out the window, sitting on the window portion of the door, pitching objects that Bruce was handing him.

Even over the racing engine and the blaring horn, Edward heard someone give an Indian war cry from inside the truck, cheering Travis on.

Edward's heart flared with relief when Travis asked, "What do you mean we're out?"

Edward didn't hear Bruce or Alex's response because he was in front of the truck, but he did hear Travis's next phrases because he was still hanging out the window.

"Well find something, damn it. We've got to hit him with something. Use your truck, for God's sake. I don't give a fuck."

Again Edward didn't hear the responses from inside the truck.

Surely they aren't going to take that chance, *Edward thought.*

The revved engine was response enough; his heart sank again for the third time in a row.

They're actually going to hit me with the truck.

He couldn't believe their nerve and whipped his head around and stared in horror as the metal beast lunged at him as an extra kick of gasoline surged through its system.

As the truck closed in on its prey, he saw the boys through the truck's dirt-smeared windows. They looked like demon trolls with a truck load of banished souls headed for a deep dimension of hell.

Travis was bouncing up and down in the passenger's seat like a hyperactive chimpanzee on crystal meth. Bruce was thrumming the dashboard as though he were the drummer in the heavy metal band that was still blaring out of the speakers. Either that or he was just excited to see Alex take the dare that would normally be turned down. Alex seemed to be leaning forward in his seat as far as he could.

Above the three heads, across the top of the truck Edward read again:
DON'T DODGE IT…RAM IT!

That statement seemed to put everything in perspective.

How's that for irony? *Edward thought.* They're taking this shit literally.

Edward forced himself to pedal faster but his legs were already burning from the chase. If anything, he was slowing down but he pumped the pedals nonetheless.

Edward glanced around more frequently to check the truck's position to his. Each time, the truck's bumper had inched closer. The already open mouth of gleaming, steel teeth looked as though it was ready to snap the bicycle in half.

Edward tried to veer away again, but each time, the truck followed, gaining momentum.

Alex started gunning the truck then immediately applied the brakes. The gunning-breaking action caused a rocky-horse movement. The see-saw movement became bigger each time Alex jammed the gas then slammed on the brakes.

Edward cried out when the front bumper grazed the back of his bicycle tire. Edward forced his legs to churn faster. He pulled away from the truck, but it immediately gained on him and was back nipping at his tires again.

Alex saw he was moving in too close to Edward and moved to hit the break, but his foot landed the gas instead. The truck surged forward.

"Shit!" Alex exclaimed and slammed on the breaks.

The front of the truck was already in an upward sweep from the amount of gas being pushed through its system. When the break was applied so tightly, it caused the front end to lower drastically.

Edward heard the engine swell and looked around in time to see the front bumper drop down on his back tire. From Edward's point of view, it looked as though the highway demon had just devoured the back of his bicycle.

That was the last thing he remembered seeing before his world spun into blurry shapes and intense pain.

When the truck came down, crushing the back tire, the abrupt stopping movement jerked Edward from his bicycle seat onto the hood of the truck. The added force of acceleration slammed into Edward's back and forced him further onto the truck's hood. That's when Edward felt and heard something give within his pelvis. It felt as though thousands of rubber bands simultaneously snapped in two. Bones shifted and tendons ripped from somewhere deep in his body beneath his waist. The pain sensors throughout his body lit up his waist and back with agonizing torture.

The three boys stared in stunned amazement as the bicycle disappeared underneath the truck.

Not thinking, only reacting, Alex was already in the process of slamming both feet down onto the break pedal to correct his misjudgment; so hard, in fact, that he was practically standing on the pedal, his butt half-way out of the seat.

The truck fishtailed back and forth two times as it drastically slowed and Alex fought to keep it under control. When the truck was nearly stopped, Edward was thrown from its hood like a rag doll a little girl no longer wants to play with.

All Edward saw was bright sky then pavement.

The three boys stared helplessly as Edward's body seemed to be jerked from the hood and flung down the road. He flipped-flopped two more times then came to rest face down in the road a few feet in front of the idling truck.

Edward lay in the road with his left cheek warming from the hot pavement, gazing back at the passenger side wheel of the truck that had almost claimed his life. Edward knew if Alex hadn't slammed on the brakes when he had; the truck would've certainly snuffed him out. He tried to turn over, but his body wouldn't respond; at least it wouldn't from the waist down. His body was numb.

Am I paralyzed?

Breaking their paralysis, the three boys scrambled out of the truck and came up on different sides of Edward's twisted body.

Upon first sight of Edward's mangled body, everyone except Alex turned away. He seemed to be in a frozen shock. Squatting beside Edward with his head in his hands, Bruce immediately started chanting, "Oh Lord! Oh shit! What have we done? Oh Lord! Oh shit! What have we done?" Travis was pacing out a triangular path and he ran his fingers through his hair.

"Great. Way to go, Einstein," Travis accused as he backhanded Alex's shoulder. "I don't believe it. That was just brilliant."

"Don't blame me; you're the one who suggested I use the truck," Alex shot back.

"I didn't expect you to take me so fucking literal about it."

The mantra Bruce was chanting was unnerving them. "Shut up, Bruce!" Travis screamed. "Just! Shut! Up!"

"Yeah," Alex agreed. "You're tap dancing on my last fuckin' nerve."

"Me shut up?"

"Yeah. You."

"Why don't the both of you shut up," Bruce suggested. "Forget about who the blame falls on. If anything, it's all of us. The question now is what are we gonna do?"

Pointing, Travis suggested, "Alex, turn him over."

Hurriedly shaking his head, he said, "I'm not gonna turn him over. You're not supposed to move someone when you don't know their injuries. You could make whatever's wrong with them even worse."

"And who told you that, Mr. Medical?" Travis asked, frustration tainting his voice.

"It's basic CPR, stupid ass," Alex said shaking his head. "It's something everyone should know."

"Well I think we should at least see if he's still alive," Bruce offered.

"And how do we do that?" Travis asked.

"See if he's breathing." Alex offered. "Put your finger in front of his nose if you can. If you feel air, he's alive." Alex's CPR instruction was coming back to him. Alex then added, "Hey, or touch the side of his neck to see if there's a pulse."

Noticing Bruce's hesitation, Travis said, "Fuck it, I'll do it. Move."

Edward, listening to the whole conversation, was saying softly, "No, no, no. Don't turn me over. Please don't turn me over." He was speaking the words, but they were only coming out in a whisper.

Travis pushed Bruce out of the way and moved in beside Edward. He grabbed the shoulder furthest from him and quickly rolled Edward over. The top portion of Edward's body turned easily but his lower waist was left behind to catch up. The injuries received from being slammed onto the hood of the truck ignited as the body was unevenly torqued.

The earlier numbness in Edward's body was instantly awakened and revived with new pain. A short helpless whimper escalated into a crescendo of agony.

Edward lay on the warm pavement, arms held up in a feeble attempt to grasp anything but found nothing. His face was stretched into a rictus of unbelievable pain. Tears flowed uncontrollably from the sides of his eyes.

"Oh shit," Travis said. He realized what he had done and wished he had listened to Alex.

"No, no, no, don't move me," Edward pleaded. "I beg of you, please, don't fucking move me."

"You idiot, I told you."

"What do we do now?"

"We get the fuck out of here, that's what," Travis urged

"We can't just leave him here," Bruce said.

Alex said, "Well we sure as hell can't help him."

"Why not? I thought you knew CPR."

"I do but that's for someone who might've drowned and is maybe unconscious. The guy's been hit by a truck. Does he look unconscious to you? No man, this is way beyond lifeguard certification CPR training."

"We'll call somebody who knows what the hell they're doing."

"Someone should stay here with him," Bruce suggested

"Stay here with him? Don't be stupid. If you stay here they'll know it was us who hit him," Alex said. "You can go to jail for something like this. I'm not going to do time for something that was a fucking accident."

"You think he's going to sit by and let us get away with it?" Travis said. "He'll tell!"

"He's not going to tell," Alex said shaking his head.

"How do you know?"

"I know," Alex confirmed. "He hasn't told on us for what we did to him down in the woods a few weeks ago." To Edward, he said, "You're not going to tell on us, are you, McDaniel?" He nudged Edward in the shoulder with his foot to urge an answer. "You're not going to tell. Are you?"

All Edward could do was quickly shake his head. Alex didn't know if it was an answer or if it were spasms causing his head to shake like that.

"What was that? I couldn't hear what you said."

With all the vehemence Edward could summon, he screamed, "GET ME A FUCKING DOCTOR!"

For a few seconds, the boys stood stock still and open mouthed, stunned at the aggression with which Edward spoke. They all three felt the hate Edward had for them and knew if he was able to stand and fight, this session here on Desolation Highway wouldn't be over until he or the three of them were dead.

He screamed again, "I'M DYING HERE!"

The boys still stood there with dumbfound looks on their faces.

"I won't say anything to anyone. Just call somebody please," Edward begged. "It's the least you could do."

Bruce was the first to move. "He's right. Let's go."

He grabbed Travis and pulled him in the direction of the truck. Noticing Alex wasn't moving, he stepped near him and grabbed his shirt with one hand and slapped him back to reality with the other.

"Come on. We can't do anything for him now. Let's call somebody," then as an after thought added, "Then we'll go see if we can find that big-tittied bitch and see if she will flash us her boobs again."

The other boys started laughing in spite of the situation.

"I guess you're right."

"Damn straight, I'm right. Let's roll."

Edward heard the shuffle steps as the boys slowly retreated to their truck. They didn't seem to be in a big hurry to leave. He wondered if they were actually going to call anyone when they did leave.

Helpless and alone, Edward lay in a cocoon of suffering. The point where his legs joined his upper body seemed engulfed in flames. He wanted to relieve the pain somehow. He felt if he could curl his legs up into his chest, wrap his arms around his knees and pull himself into a tight ball it would be the simplest way to alleviate the pain. It seemed to always work before. When he tried to move his legs, nothing worked.

Am I paralyzed? *Edward wondered again.*

Finally the doors opened and slammed shut and the engine roared to life again. The boys backed up and then peeled away in a flurry of squealing tires and a gust of wind. The grit of dirt kicked up by the spinning tires peppered his face. Edward even smelled the stench of burnt tires as they raced away, leaving him there to wallow in his agony. Two long, black tire treads rotated around Edward's head and stretched down the road.

Before the rumble of Alex's truck engine died away, Edward surrendered into a dark unconsciousness.

CHAPTER 41

EDWARD DIDN'T KNOW he was crying until his sobs jarred him out of his nightmarish memory. His shoulders were shaking uncontrollably. His chest was heavy with anxiety. He wasn't surprised in the least to find tears tracing lines down his cheeks.

He had relived every detail and every stitch of pain.

"Oh Jesus, Jesus, Jesus," he mumbled to himself. He self-consciously wiped his face with the back of his hand. He shook his head roughly to rid his mind of the mental images. "That was some of the worst pain I have ever felt." He took some deep breaths to calm himself. "But that was only physical. The psychological and mental anguish of what they did to me hurt far worse and lasted much longer."

He closed his eyes; his brow furrowed as he tried to remember more. He wanted the hate to come back—wanted it to consume him. He wanted to be justified with what he was about to do.

He looked up at Alex's Corvette again. *Time to make restitution for somebody's actions.*

He stopped the waves of memory that were crashing against the inside of his mind. He cleared his tears again then opened his car door.

I didn't come all this way just to relive the past. I have a job to do and I'm going to do it, then I'm going on to live the rest of my life as Tyler Curtis.

He popped the Mustang's trunk. He took out two containers and headed toward Alex's pride and joy.

When he reached the car, he stooped beside the passenger's side rear tire. He unscrewed the containers and poured the contents over the whole car, saturating it from top to bottom and front to back. He stepped back and smiled as he pulled another piece of cloth and a lighter from his other pocket.

"Sianara, Alex," he said as he lit the cloth strand. He talked as though Alex were standing right there in front of him. "I only wish I was destroying that shitty truck of yours as well. But beggars can't be choosers, can they? You destroyed my favorite possessions in school. You remember? Both my bikes. One in the woods; the other on Desolation Highway. So now, I'm destroying your trophy. An eye for an eye; isn't that what the Bible says? I think that makes us even. Well, *almost*. It's a long way before we are completely even."

That said, he flung the burning cloth onto the top of the car, grabbed the gas cans and ran.

The rag touched down on the car's surface and the fumes ignited; the car was instantly engulfed in flames. Edward felt the intense heat wash over him as he moved toward his own car.

Edward was only halfway across the street when he turned to see the Corvette erupt in a huge fireball.

Upon detonation, the Corvette was forced into the air, turned a complete circle and landed back on four blown tires. The force of the explosion blew both the doors and hood off, and the exploding windows scattered glass in every direction. The once beautiful paint job was cracked and charred from the intense heat. The leather upholstery bubbled and melted. A masterpiece of precision and perfection was reduced to a pile of wreckage within seconds.

"Damn, he must've had a full tank of gas in that damn thing." He laughed, "Holy shit that was better than the fourth of July." He stood in rapture for a few brief moments to watch the remainder of it burn. Not wanting to be found at the scene of the crime, he gathered up the empty gas containers, ran to his car, and fled the scene.

☙

The sound of thunder detonated in the sky above Silver Ridge Hospital; at least that's what Alex Riley thought. He looked up from the cadaver he'd been working on for the past fifteen minutes and stared in confusion at the tiled ceiling for a few seconds.

"I didn't know rain was in the forecast for tonight. Did you, Bruce?" He looked back down at the body that was lying on the morgue table then began to work again. "Huh. Strange."

Bruce Saliers lay naked on the autopsy table. Bruce's body had been picked up earlier that morning, but Alex hadn't had time to process it until now. Truth be told, he hadn't gotten up the courage since they had been best buddies back in high school. Bruce's apparent suicide had actually scared him.

First it was Kelly Sheridan, then Suzanne Baldwin, then the mysterious guy, Patrick Quinlan. I don't know what is up with that guy. And now Bruce Saliers has turned up with a bullet in his head. No doubt about it, the way he had committed suicide was weird. I have never seen or heard of anyone holding the gun away from their face and pulling the trigger. There is too much of a chance for the bullet to go rogue and not hit its mark. Most people just place it against their head or up under their chin to make sure they're going to check out when they end it. I have no idea where Travis is. He has to be back in town by now. It was going to be either Travis, Jeremy, or me. It's no coincidence that everyone is dropping dead like flies around me. I tried to warn them. I don't know why they didn't listen.

Forgetting about the oncoming thunderstorm, he continued working until the phone on his desk rang a few minutes later. Irritated, he refused to answer. He would let the voicemail take a message and would answer the call later.

Shortly after the phone stopped ringing, the intercom came alive. "Alex Riley, please call the security desk for an important message. Alex Riley, please call the security desk for an important message."

"I heard you the first time," he said as he pitched a pair of tweezers in the pan to the right of the autopsy table. "Great. What the hell could this be about?" He peeled off his latex gloves and pitched them in the wastebasket as he made his way to his desk.

Alex pushed the speaker phone button then punched in the number to the security office.

"Diggs Belfrey. Security."

"Yeah, this is Alex Riley. I had a message to call you."

"Yes sir, Mr. Riley, I'm sorry to be the one to tell you this, but I've got a bit of bad news."

"What's up?"

The security guard didn't answer right away.

"Hello?

"—Yes sir, I'm here."

"I have a cadaver drying out across the room. Make it snappy. What do you need?"

"Sir, we need you to come up here to where you parked your car."

"Why? What's wrong? Is it gone? Did someone steal my car?"

"No. Uh—no. Your car is still here; it's just uh—, he sucked air between his clenched teeth not knowing how to explain, "ah—the condition that it's in is what I think will concern you."

"Condition? What the hell happened to it?"

"Well, ah—it uh, it blew up, sir."

"Excuse me."

"I don't know how it happened, but your car has exploded. It's uh—totally demolished."

"Is this some kind of fucking joke?"

"I'm sorry. I wish it was, but no, I'm afraid it isn't. A fire truck is in route right now to put out the last of the flames."

"He's coming for me. I know it. Whoever's doing this is coming for me."

"Excuse me?"

"Uh, nothing. I was talking to myself. I'll be right there."

He pushed the speaker phone button again to end the call. He picked up a paper weight, spun around, and hurled it against the wall in anger. It dented one of the lockers across the room where the bodies were housed. Still fuming, he left the morgue without taking time to put Bruce back in a locker.

ೞ

Edward made his way around to the opposite side of the hospital. The emergency care wing was always open and that seemed like the easiest access to get inside.

He parked his car near the entrance; no need to park in an out of the way place.

Now that Alex's car is out of commission, he won't be going anywhere; maybe now we could meet up and have a little chat.

Edward tried not to bring attention to himself when he entered but acted as though he had a purpose here.

Come to think of it, I do have a purpose. I know exactly what I'm doing here.

Three months ago, when Tyler came out of his coma, before the doctors could sign his release form, he had to go through a good deal of physical conditioning. The coma had definitely taken its toll on him. But during that time, he had walked around the hospital a number of times and was familiar with the hospital layout.

He made his way directly to the morgue downstairs. He figured the stairs would be the easiest access. He didn't want to answer any questions from curious elevator passengers.

As he neared the door that led downstairs to the autopsy room, the door itself swung open toward him.

Oh shit, somebody's coming, Edward thought and stopped dead in his tracks. He turned quickly to the bulletin board to his left and pretended to read one of the articles posted there. He even threw his hand up and pointed to the words as he pretended to read.

Alex slammed the door behind him and passed behind Edward, mumbling as he went. "I can't believe my fucking car is totaled. I'm going to kill that son of a bitch."

It was all Edward could do to stifle the laugh that was building inside him. He only wished that Alex could have been there when his Corvette actually went up in flames.

Edward peered over his shoulder. After Alex turned the corner, Edward checked the hallway in the other direction. The coast was clear, and he made his move.

He moved again with purpose toward the door to the stairwell, opened it, then slipped inside.

He moved quickly down the dimly lit stairs into the bowels of the hospital. At the bottom where the lighting was surprisingly better, he moved down a short, wide hallway to the main door that opened into the morgue.

He peered through one of the nine by nine windows built into the door and saw that the room was empty save for the body that was still on the morgue table. He could tell from where he stood who it was. It hadn't been that long since he'd left that body with a hole in his head.

Edward held Suzanne's security badge up in front of his face. If this didn't work, he would have to wait and have this meeting with Alex at a different time. He took a deep breath—moment of truth and all that. He quickly swiped the slot near the morgue door. A small, green light on the panel blinked on and Edward heard a small click within the door. He pushed on the morgue door and breathed a quick sigh of relief as he entered.

Edward shook his head as he approached the body. He made a tsk-tsk sound with his tongue. "Bruce, Bruce, Bruce. I don't know why he's doing an autopsy on you. It's obvious what happened to you. Alex should've just asked me; I would tell him what really happened to you."

Through his own eyes, Tyler stared down in horror and unbelief at what lay before him. Bruce's face was surprisingly normal—save for the bullet hole in his forehead. What was hard to look at was the way his head lay on the autopsy table. Since so much of the back of his head and brain was missing because of the exit wound, Bruce's head tilted back and lay flat on the table's surface.

Tyler wished he could take it all back, but he couldn't divert his eyes from the carnage. He stood there, unable to grasp what he was looking at. He remembered turning away in his mind when he couldn't repossess himself the night Bruce was killed. Now looking down and seeing the results of what Edward had done, Tyler's head began to shake uncontrollably. He could hear his heartbeat in his ears. His body was warm to the point of high fever. Finally having enough, Tyler willed himself to close himself off from the gore and forced his mind to think on other things. Edward, on the other hand, continued to look on with fascination.

Tyler could hear Edward thinking. His thoughts were a message to him. *You don't like this do you, Tyler? Well, get used to it, cause there's more to come. It doesn't matter if you don't look now. I've stored all the vivid memories up in your mind—I mean, my mind—for your viewing pleasure if you're ever interested. Eventually, you'll cease to exist.*

Edward moved briskly to the lockers that were built into the wall. He opened one and found a body covered in a sheet. He opened the one next to it and found another body. He didn't check to see who they were; he was only trying to find an empty space. On the third try, he found an empty locker. He pulled the steel sliding tray table completely out then crossed back to Bruce's body.

Edward scooped his hands under Bruce's neck and knees then picked him up. Because rigor mortis had set in, the body didn't give. It didn't fold at the waist nor did it give in the neck or the knees. It was like carrying an armful of stiff two-by-fours.

Tyler felt the texture of Bruce's skin when Edward picked him up. It was cold to the touch. Rubbery. He felt very dead. It was sickening, and bile rose in the back of his throat. Tyler managed to swallow it back down, but it still left an acrid taste in his mouth.

That's nasty, he thought.

It sure is, Edward mused then asked, *Don't you just love it?*

Tyler didn't comment; he was still trying to keep his stomach contents from coming back up.

Carrying Bruce's body across the room, Edward placed him on the steel tray, slid the tray back inside the opening then closed and latched the door.

"Good; that's done. Now, I'll just take Bruce's place and wait on Alex to return."

He looked in a number of different drawers and cabinets before he found the sheets that they cover the bodies. He snagged one and moved back to the table. He quickly jumped upon the table, whipped it open, and carefully covered himself with it as he lay back into the space Bruce had just occupied moments before.

All he had was time now.

Lying on the steel morgue slab under the white sheet, he let his mind drift back again to the events following the wreck—the jumbled bits and pieces that he remembered.

CHAPTER 42

EDWARD REMEMBERED HE didn't awaken the second time to the sound of sirens or the bustle of excited voices. The thing that brought him back to consciousness was the small pin prick of a needle sinking into his arm.

I.V., he guessed.

As he became more aware, the silence surged into a crescendo of hurried movement, roaring in his ears.

Numerous faces came in and out of his line of sight. Sometimes they were accompanied by beams of lights shined into his eyes, temporarily blinding him. Numerous hands carefully moved over his body, probing and prodding. Blurred shapes moved in and out of the red, yellow, and blue lights of the ambulance and police cruisers.

A technician put a hand on his chest and eased him back down after a failed attempt to sit up.

"Steady now. Easy. Lie back. Be still. You've been hurt really bad."

Edward eased back down; not because of the stranger's urgings but because a flare of pain burned up the length of his spine.

"Don't try to move," the technician continued. "Let us take care of you. Talk to me; what's your name?"

"Edward," he whispered.

"Nice to meet you, Edward, my name's Seth. I just want you to know you're going to be okay. Just relax for me and we'll get you all fixed up."

Edward nodded as best he could.

Seth began to ask more questions like, "What's today's date? How old are

you? What's your favorite color? How many fingers am I holding up?" and
"When is your birthday?"

Edward answered them all then managed to ask, "Do you have any
harder questions? Those are a bit too easy."

Seth laughed, then laid a reassuring hand on his shoulder and said,
"Not at the moment, Edward; maybe later. You're doing great." After a few
moments, Seth spoke again. "Okay Edward, I want you to brace yourself.
This may hurt a little, but we need to move you to a backboard so we can
move you to the stretcher so we can get you to the hospital."

Edward nodded in agreement.

"Now we're going to rotate you evenly just enough to get the board under
you. Are you ready?"

The pain was immense, his screams filled the sky. It was as bad as being
hit by Alex's truck a second time and in the same place. Thinking he had
given up for the last time and dropped over into the afterlife, he unwillingly
surrendered again to unconsciousness.

∞

In the afterlife, he was on his new mountain bike and traveling down
Desolation Highway again. But where the highway in the waking world
had slopes and turns, this dream highway continued in a straight route to a
pinpoint on an endless horizon.

The firmament in the distance and above him was a churning mass of
black bile. An unseen cortege of rainmakers continuously thundered their
drums; it seemed to be the reason for the agitated gloom. Dim flashes of
lightning managed to escape the malignant darkness and briefly lit up small
areas of the skyline.

Tall telephone poles flanked both sides of the road and held jagged
barbed wire instead of normal telephone conduit. The razor wire was lashed
so close together—even overlapping in places—that it looked more like an
impenetrable wall than anything else. There was no escape. All he could do
was move forward as fast as he could.

And he was. His legs burned and his body ached because he had been
trying to escape a gigantic, mechanical beast that had been pursuing him
for hours. In his mind, he knew it was Alex's truck, but when he turned to

look behind him, all he saw a hideous monstrosity bearing down on him. It looked like a thrasher machine that some clandestine alien race used to harvest humans like crops from their fields; a harvesting machine whose inner workings were lubricated with blood—from the thousands slain before him—instead of oil. He could hear the symphony of whirling blades, rotating saws, and pinchers that quickly opened and shut in anticipation of a kill.

Edward pedaled faster as the human harvesting machine closed in.

He felt a claw-like gripping device seize his right shoulder and vigorously shake him.

Startled, Edward shouted, "No. Let go of me!" as he tried to sit up in bed. He barely had the words out of his mouth before a branding iron of intense pain seared his lower back, preventing him to move further. Tears burned in his eyes again.

The hand flinched back and released him, then hesitantly touched him again.

"Edward!" a voice said. "Edward, wake up!"

Edward opened his eyes a second time to find a beautiful angel in white hovering over him. He noticed a tag pinned to her outfit that stated her name: ANGEL. Even though she was in white and her name was Angel, she had no wings.

"Guess the machine got me after all," Edward whispered to himself. "I guess I did die."

"Die?" Angel asked. "What are you talking about?"

"The harvesting machine. It was, ah, chasing me, uh, but I-I didn't get away. Tried to; but it got me."

"No, darling," she said as she laughed under her breath. "It didn't get you. You were dreaming. It must've been pretty real from the sound of it. We've really been worried about you. Glad to see you're finally awake."

"Awake?" Edward asked.

Noticing the look on his face, she said, "Oh, don't look so glum. You're not dead."

"Right. Sorry. It's just that I thought I died and was in heaven, because I woke up and saw you there." He looked away shyly, knowing that it must've sounded like a load of bullshit. Edward continued humbly, "I thought you were an angel."

She would've thought that phrase coming from a different guy at another time and place was the cheesiest one liner ever attempted. But she saw the innocence on Edward's face and heard the honesty in his voice.

She smiled, "Well that's probably the sweetest thing anyone has ever said to me. You and I are going to get along just fine. I can tell. You're going to be one of my favorites. I'm no angel, but thank you for the compliment. You were close to being dead, but you're one of the lucky ones."

"I don't feel so lucky."

Angel realized how silly her statement must've sounded, but she said nothing to correct it.

After a few moments, Edward said, "Where, exactly, am I?"

"Silver Ridge Memorial. Don't worry. You're going to be fine now. Rest up. I've given you something to dull the pain. It will make you sleepy, but don't drift too far away; you're due for x-rays pretty soon. Sweet dreams for the time being."

As Angel left the room, his eyes became heavy. He was still overly exhausted from the hit-and-run. He drifted slowly off into dreams, but they weren't the least bit sweet. The harvesting machine was starting to close in on him again.

⌇

For two long, agonizing days, he remembered lying in a broken heap of suffering. Edward often wondered when and if they were ever going to do anything to help mend him. He asked his nurses numerous times about the plan for his recovery. He always received the same answer. "We're waiting on the results of your x-rays."

He wanted to scream at them and say, "Well do it a little faster! I'm dying here!"

In fact, more times than not, Edward thought they were purposely not doing anything to help him get better because they secretly knew he wasn't going to make it—that he was somehow "not mendable." If I'm not going to make it, why go to any trouble at all. Shoot something in my veins and take me out of this misery.

Then when he'd given up all hope, a doctor came to his bedside late on the second day. He was an elderly black man—possibly a couple months shy of reaching retirement—with a head of salt and pepper hair.

"Hello, Edward. My name is Doctor White."

"Hi," Edward said. He was still miffed from being forgotten about for the past two days.

"I hear you're a little banged up?"

"Ha. That has to be the understatement of the year, Doc," Edward said.

Amused, the doctor smiled and nodded at how outrageous his words must've sounded.

"I'm sorry, silly me. You're right. You're a little more than banged up, but I want to try and fix that. I've been studying your x-rays and we've found that your pelvis has been severely fractured in four different places."

Edward's heart dropped.

The doctor went on, "That's not the part that concerns me. Those areas will heal in time. The part of the pelvis that we're concerned about is the bone in front that holds your pelvis together. It's broken completely in two."

Thinking his heart couldn't fall any further, it did. It seemed like it dropped out of his body, through the bed, and spilled out on to the hospital floor.

"I want to change that for you. It's not impossible to fix you, but it is a very difficult procedure. If what I do works, then you'll eventually get better and possibly walk again."

Immediately he asked, "How long are we talking?"

"It's hard to say. You are young and I believe you will bounce back quicker than if this happened to an elderly person."

Edward wasn't expecting such a vague timeline, but it was better than nothing.

Doctor White went into more detail explaining the difficult procedure of the surgery. He tried to make the explanation easy enough for Edward to understand, but his extensive medical knowledge of the body caused him to drift back out of layman's terms. He finished up by asking the crucial question. "What do you say, Edward?"

"Since my current situation isn't working for me, I believe I'm going to have to take you up on your offer."

"Good." The kind doctor stood and told him a few more details regarding

the surgery. "I suggest you get to bed early tonight. We begin early tomorrow morning. So get your rest. I'll see you in surgery."

***

The next day when Edward awoke, the sun was already filtering through his hospital window.

He felt groggy and exhausted, as though he hadn't slept well and felt as though he had been run over again by another runaway truck.

Window? That's funny, *he thought.* I have a window now? They must've moved me during the night. Wonder when they're going to come get me for surgery?

He noticed he was sitting up in bed at a forty five degree angle. The sheets looked funny also. It looked like there was a pup tent down around his waist area; more like a miniature circus tent had been erected during the night. And this had nothing to do with morning wood, either.

He grabbed the covers and lifted them.

Jutting out from his pelvis were four thin, metal shafts about six to nine inches in length. There were bandages surrounding the protruding metal but he could feel they were connected deep inside him.

He was about to buzz the nurses' station for assistance when he heard a voice near the door.

"Good morning, Edward. I see you're already awake."

It was Angel again.

"Morning. What the hell is this?"

"Didn't you know? You've already had your surgery. Man, you must've really been out of it. But you came through it with flying colors. I hear everything went as planned."

"Yeah. Okay, but what is all this?" he asked again.

Puzzled, the nurse asked, "Didn't Doctor White explain the procedure?"

"Yes, but I really didn't pay too much attention to it. I was a little distracted. I was in a lot of pain, remember?"

"Of course. Should I get him for you?"

"Of course. Yes. Please."

The nurse retreated and while she was gone, Edward studied his new attachments more closely. He felt the metal shafts that extended from his pelvis. He tried to wiggled them but they didn't budge; they were grounded firmly inside himself. He flicked the end of the metal bar. It didn't really move, but the vibrations from the thump extended down the bar into the muscle. It tickled.

The four bars that extended out of his body were all connected by a flat crosstie bar. It was like a mini shelf that crossed in front of him although it wasn't big enough to put anything on it.

"Mr. McDaniel, how do you like being part robot?"

It was Doctor White's feeble attempt at humor. At another time it might've even been funny.

I hope you're a better surgeon than you are a comedian, *Edward thought.* "What the hell did you do to me?" *he asked.*

"I fixed you. Remember, we talked about this."

"You did something, but I don't know if you fixed me."

Doctor White laughed, "I know you're confused, but I assure you you're going to be fine."

"Why did it take two days to decide to have the surgery?"

"We had to special order your hardware from a company that specializes in these types of injuries. Sure, we get the occasional hip breaks from the elderly, and granted we've seen injuries like yours but yours was different in a number of ways. We didn't have materials just lying around for your type of injury because it happens so seldomly."

"What did you do to me?"

Doctor White began the long arduous speech of what he did and how he mended Edward's body.

"So it is possible. I will walk again."

"Oh, heaven's yes. By all means. I don't know how long it will take but eventually. Sure. We just have to make sure your pelvis will be able to support the weight of your upper body. Just don't get impatient at this point in the game. You need to rest up because when you do start the exercises, you're going to be in major pain."

☙

And it was painful, Edward thought, mentally reliving the agony he went through in his therapy. *I'm talking boot camp from hell painful. I did the work and I did become strong again. I showed all of those doctors and nurses that I wasn't a pussy. Some thought I would never walk again. At first, I thought I wouldn't either, but I showed everybody I could do it. The pain was intense, but I did all the work; all the exercises. I stretched and flexed and braced myself against the pain. I bottled up the tears when anyone was around and cried to myself when I was alone. I let every thing flow out of me when I was alone. And soon, minute by minute, hour by hour, and day by day, I slowly became strong again. It was a slow, tedious process but I was well sooner than they expected. I got better as fast as I could because I had a score to settle.*

"That's funny." Alex said, confusion tainting his voice.

Edward's inner monologue died in his mind and he froze where he lay underneath the white sheet.

It's Alex. He's back.

Edward finally remembered where he was. He had been so lost in the memories from the wreck he hadn't paid attention. He had almost drifted off to sleep.

Alex continued, "I don't remember putting a sheet on Bruce's body? Or did I? Hmmmm."

Edward could hear latex gloves being stretched on and snapped at the wrist.

"Oh well, let's put you to bed for tonight, Bruce. It's been a hell of a day. We'll finish up tomorrow if that's OK with you," Alex said, then jerked the white sheet off of the cadaver.

For a couple of seconds, time stood still for both Alex and Edward. At first, Alex's mind couldn't grasp what he was looking at. He remembered leaving Bruce's body on the table before he went to check on his car. At first glance, he still saw Bruce in his mind because logic assumed Bruce would still be lying here. But realization slowly set in as Bruce changed to someone else…someone with a face…someone with a grinning face— or was that a leer?

"What's up, buddy? You look like you've seen a ghost," Edward taunted.

Before the words registered, Edward's right hand shot up and clutched Alex around his throat.

"Hey! Wait! Oh fuck! Hey! Let go!" he managed to say through pinched vocal chords. Alex's bladder released, and a warm sensation began to trickle down his legs. He brought his hands up to defend himself and break the hold on his throat. He lost his balance as his feet became entangled in the sheet he'd pulled from Edward's body. He stumbled backwards and fell to the floor.

From the floor, Alex scooted away from the intruder but managed to ask, "How did you get in here? This place is supposed to be secure."

"Don't worry about it. I have my ways. Where is it?" Edward asked.

"Where is what?" he said, gathering himself from the floor.

"Whatever Bruce gave you to analyze."

Alex laughed, "What, the metal pieces? Over there on my desk, why?"

"I'll be taking those with me when we leave."

"Leave? You think you're just going to waltz out of here with evidence in an investigation."

"Yes, and no one, not even you, is going to stop me."

"We'll see about that. I'm calling security," he said and turned toward his desk phone.

"Oh no you're not."

"Yeah, try and stop me."

Those particular words set Edward off.

He went after Alex, grabbed him by the back of his lab coat and slung him back—almost throwing him—onto the gurney. From his near horizontal position, Alex slapped, hit and threw wild punches to get away. When Edward let go of him, he rolled—half jumped—to the opposite side of the gurney. He lost his footing again and threw his hands out to catch his balance on anything. One of his hands found the edge of the surgical utensil tray but instead of steadying him, it gave away, flipped up, and he spilled onto the floor again. The dislodged tray fell over on top of him and the utensils cascaded down on top and around him in a metal rain. He stood quickly and spun around to face his attacker.

"Who are you?" Alex shouted. "What do you want?"

"Oh how many times have I heard that question?" Edward said. He didn't wait for an answer but pressed on. "I think you know who I am. If you don't know by now, you're stupid. Think back."

"Edward? Edward McDaniel? Is that you?"

"Ding, ding, ding! We have winner. You *do* remember me, don't you? That makes me feel good that I made such a memorable impression on you."

"You! You stay away from me, you."

Edward pointed to the circular wet spot at Alex's groin. "Do you have any idea that you pissed yourself? Pretty embarrassing isn't it? A grown man pissing his pants. You know, most people would laugh at something like that. I remember you and your buddies laughed at me when I peed myself in the woods a long time ago."

"What?"

"I know, I know; you probably don't remember. I mean, after all, you *were* drunk. I can't fault you for getting drunk, can I? But try to think back. It's the day you guys had a little drunken target practice with me. Oh I almost forgot *you* also totaled my bicycle. Remember that? I do. It wasn't the only time that happened either."

Realization hit him full force. "You! My car! You're the one who totaled my car!"

Edward gave a quick Tiger Woods fist pump. "Yes, baby! Now we're getting somewhere."

"Why did you do that?"

"Eye for an eye and all that shit. You shit on me—I shit on you. See how it works? I loved my bikes. You destroyed my bikes. You loved your Corvette. I demolished your Corvette. Fair and square. It's that simple."

"You mean to tell me because I destroyed your bike, you blew up my Corvette?"

"Bikes," Edward corrected. "There were two of them." He let it sink in then went on, "And yes, I'm the one to blame. I blew the fuck out of that little piece of perfection. You should've seen it. It was beautiful. Better than any fireworks show I've ever seen. My grandmother always told me to turn the other check when bad things happened to me. And I did—for awhile. I've turned the other cheek so many times I felt like that red-headed step child everyone keeps talking about. I'm doing things differently now. I'm turning over a new leaf and you know what?" He tilted his head to one side as one corner of his mouth upturned in a lopsided sneer. "I don't feel so bad about my bikes now."

"You son of a bitch!" Alex stooped; grabbed a bloodied scalpel from the mixture of spilled utensils and stood again as he held it out in front of him. "I'm gonna kill you! I can just stash your body here in one of the lockers. Make a false autopsy report. I'll doctor it so it reads that you were brought in as a stabbing victim…some shit like that. Then make you disappear."

"Strong words coming from a guy who just pissed his panties. But it's funny you should say that, because that's what I was thinking about doing to you—make you disappear." He leaned over the gurney and said, "You think you can take me out, big shot? You think you're that good? Come on, let's tango." Edward held up his chin, leaving his throat exposed. "Give it your best shot. But I warn you, you better make it good. It'll be the last chance you get; then it'll be my turn."

Alex lunged forward with a flick of his wrist. When he did, Edward jerked back as the blade sliced under his chin. Edward grabbed a halogen lamp above their heads, brought it down, and swung it into the side of Alex's head. Alex managed to stand again although he was dazed from the hit. For a moment, Edward thought he hadn't hit him hard enough so as an added precaution, he swung the lamp again into Alex's already stunned face.

"Bullseye! Right between the windows."

The scalpel slid from his hand and clatter on the floor.

That's right, Alex. Edward thought in a mock-authoritative tone. *Put the scalpel down and step away from the gurney.*

As if hearing Edward thoughts, Alex took a step away but then crumpled to the floor beside the gurney and lay still.

Edward almost wanted to laugh. "You finished, Alex?" He waited. "That's what I thought. Glad we finally see things from my perspective. We'll talk again very soon. We have such a long night ahead of us."

CHAPTER 43

ALEX RILEY AWOKE to the sound of what he thought was a ringing in his ears. As he became more aware, he recognized the sound as that of chirping crickets.

Could be cicadas, he thought groggily. *Some kind of damn insect.*

He was lying face down, his cheek pressed hard against the surface of the ground. The smell of dirt was heavy in his nostrils. His whole head was throbbing.

When he opened his eyes, all he could see was darkness. He couldn't remember how he'd gotten here—wherever "here" was. *Was I in a wreck?*

As his eyes adjusted to the moonlit-blackness, he was able to make out the object directly in front of his face. It was the first object that caused a warning sensation to rise up inside him.

Tire tread. A wheel? That's weird.

He groaned and rolled away from the tire and rested the back of his head against the ground. In the vast expanse of darkness above him, a host of stars twinkled in the night sky.

Where am I, he wondered.

He tried to move his hands to his sides to help himself sit up, but they were tied in front of him at the wrist.

He lifted his head off the ground and looked down his chest at his bound hands. Trepidation started to seep into his veins.

Something's not right here. Wait! Now don't panic, he urged himself. *Everything is going to be all right.*

He rolled over to his side, caught himself with his elbow and pushed himself into a sitting position.

The wind picked up and blew by him. He shivered slightly from the chill of the breeze. Above the abundant smell of dirt, a scent of juniper filled his nostrils.

He brought his bound hands up to his face and squinted his eyes.

"Rope?" he muttered. "What the fuck? Why?"

He was instantly scared. He looked around and saw a dirt road stretching away from him in the darkness to his left. Overgrown grassy fields were in front and behind him. When he turned to his right, he came face to face with the front bumper of some kind of car. In the front grille he saw the silver emblem of a galloping horse. *Mustang*, he thought. *Has to be.*

All was quiet, except for the crickets. Then an owl hooted in the far distance. It was answered by another bird that was closer to him.

He tried to stand but was woozy from his throbbing head and had to sit down again. After his mind settled, he got to his knees, braced himself with the hood of the Mustang and pushed himself the rest of the way up. As he stood, he felt something tighten around his waist. He looked down and notice another rope tied tightly around his midsection. He grabbed the rope and pulled it taught. He saw that the other end disappeared somewhere beneath the Mustang.

He jerked against his restraints. Something wasn't adding up; although it was being spelled out for him—D.E.E.P. S.H.I.T.—and he was standing waist high in it. He didn't need any psychic flashes to know where this was heading.

Then he remembered the scene in the morgue earlier tonight.

"Edward," he muttered to himself.

He now remembered why his head hurt and why he was here. Now finding the rope, he knew exactly how the rest of this night was going to play out.

He looked into the windshield but the inside was darker than the night sky. There didn't seem to be anyone there, but he couldn't be sure. He peered around in panicked alarm but no one else could be seen. The trees that lined the dirt road were too small in circumference to hide an adult. There was one big tree in the distance. He could barely make out its outline; a darker shadow in the murky light. He doubted Edward would stand behind something that far away from the action. The only thing big enough to hide someone was the car itself.

This has to be where Edward, I mean Tyler—whoever the fuck he is—is hiding.

He reached down again for the rope tied around his waist and began to tug at the knot that held him. He saw that Edward had also looped the rope through all his belt loops. He couldn't just slide the ropes down off his waist and legs as he'd hoped because the knot had been tied tight around his waist. He couldn't just slid his pants down off his hips. The knot was definitely going to have to be untied. Before he even started to untie the knot the front headlights flared on. Alex looked up and froze in their glare with a deer-in-the-headlights look on his face.

In the backwash of light, he could see a figure sitting in the driver's seat.

Of course, it was the same guy that was in the morgue earlier today. As before, he muttered to himself again, "Tyler Curtis." He remembered the guy hitting him with the light fixture. *That was a cheap shot if I've ever seen one.* A part of his brain was saying, "Tyler Curtis," but another part of him was saying, "Edward McDaniel." He was pulled between reality and…and what? His mind couldn't come up with a word to describe what he knew was impossible.

Not knowing what to do, Alex stepped back from the Mustang. As he moved away from the car he yelled, "What do you want from me? Why are you doing this to me?"

No answer came from within the car. The figure just sat there.

Alex kept retreating with his tied hands above his head so the person would know he wasn't trying to escape. He yelled again, "C'mon, you gotta tell me something! At least give me something to go on!"

By the time he reached the end of his rope, there was still no answer.

"You're an asshole, you know that?" Alex yelled. "Huh? Can you hear me in there, you deaf fuck?"

☙

One pair of eyes saw the same thing for two different entities.

Tyler had not yet gotten used to being a prisoner of his own body. He stared blankly out the windows of his body. He was being held captive so far back in his own mind that it seemed he had to strain to see what was going on outside himself as well as the confines of the car. He shook his head in disgust.

Edward, on the other hand, relished watching the hunched bound figure squirm to get free. He noticed his head shaking back and forth and realized that Tyler was looking on also. *You don't approve?*

Ignoring the question Tyler simply asked in thought, *How many more?*

How many more what?

Don't be stupid. How many more people are you going to kill before you stop?

Edward shrugged his shoulders, *I don't know. I'm not keeping track.*

Yes you are. You've been holding this grudge against them for close to twenty years. You've off-ed a few and you don't know how many is left? Don't tell me you're not keeping tabs.

After this one, it should only be Jeremy Taylor, but I don't know how many will get in my way before I take care of him. Patrick Quinlan wasn't one of the originals. I wasn't counting him at first.

Yeah, and you didn't need to take him out either.

He reminded me of the way Jeremy Taylor treated me back in school. He was just the equivalent of a bad memory that I took care of. I guess you could call it therapy for me.

I'm tired, Edward. I want to stop.

No, absolutely not. We don't stop until Jeremy Taylor is in a body bag.

Well let this guy go, and we'll go straight for Jeremy. We'll go tonight. You don't have to do this, you know.

Yes I do. Did you not see what Alex did to me? You were paying attention to the memory when I took a stroll down memory lane, weren't you?

Yes I did, but that was a long time ago. Can't you just forgive and forget?

No I can't. I don't want to forget. I want to remember. Remembering is what makes me who I am. I want to remember what I'm going to do to Alex for the rest of your life.

The rest of my life?

Yeah, why not. I've got a second chance at a whole new life once this bullshit is over. I'll, for once in my life, be able to move on. Move on to bigger and better things. I'll have a chance to do all those things I've never been able to do since they killed me.

And what about me?

What about you?

You just expect me to roll over and allow you to take over my body?

Yeah, I do. You have so far. You'll get used to me. He could feel negative waves wash over himself. Tyler was fuming. *What are you going to do about it? You can't do anything to me or about me. I'm more powerful than you. Since I'm the new pilot of this body, you might as well sit back and enjoy the ride.*

Tyler became quiet for a long while. Deep in Tyler's subconscious, further back in his mind than Edward had dared to reach; Tyler realized something. It was something he already knew, but he'd been so busy trying to figure out how to take back over his own body that he hadn't really stopped to reason it out. That something was as clear now to him as that summer day Edward died. He took a mental note of what his own left hand was doing. It was slowly and methodically stroking the talisman that was hanging around his neck.

Everything revolves around the medallion, Tyler thought. *He's so—so protective of the charm. Must be what grounds him here in this afterlife. I have to destroy it. But how?* he asked himself. *Edward isn't going to just let me take it off and smack it with a hammer.*

This realization set his mind in motion and he secretly started planning what he had to do.

ଔ

Alex was determined to elicit a response from the driver. He stooped quickly to pick up a hefty stick that had been lying near the car's driver's side tire. Because of his tied wrists, he pitched it at the car with an awkward double-handed throw. The branch arced over and clattered on the hood then slid off the passenger's side.

The natives are getting restless, Tyler thought.

"Fuck," Edward said aloud. "What the hell is his problem?"

His problem is that he's tied to a fucking car. Can't you see he's a little frustrated at his situation? If it's bothering you so much, do something about it. You have some killing to do, shouldn't you get to it?

I'm pacing myself. You can't rush this perfection.

Right. Yeah, tell me, what's so perfect about this situation.

Edward didn't answer.

Well, you take your time with that.

"What the fuck is your problem?" Alex yelled. "Why am I here? What are you planning on doing with me?"

No answer.

The driver didn't do anything but sit there. This pissed Alex off even more.

"Fuck you!" he said as he held up both fists with their middle fingers extended. In frustration, he stooped and picked up another object to throw; a descent sized rock this time. He pitched it with both hands and it struck the center of the hood. Alex's face went slack with disappointment when it didn't shatter the windshield as he'd wished. It was hard to get any velocity with the way his hands were tied.

"Damn it," Edward yelled and jammed the horn in frustration. He pressed it down again, held it firm, then released it.

Startled, Alex took two shuffle steps back in alarm.

A voice from within the car asked, "How's your head?"

Alex was so surprised he had finally received a response, he was struck dumb for a few seconds. Before he could answer, another statement was directed toward him.

"You bumped it pretty badly back at the morgue," Edward said again.

He squinted in the glare of the headlights as he strained to see the driver. "Yeah, thanks for that, buddy. Really appreciate it. Speaking of the morgue, how'd you get me out of there without raising any eyebrows?"

The car door opened and Tyler stepped out. He rested one of his arms on the open car door and the other on the roof of the car.

"You don't need to worry about how I got you here. I think I did exceptionally well. You just worry about why you are here."

"So now that you've got me here, what are you going to do to me?"

"Seems pretty obvious, doesn't it?"

He paused for a moment, not answering.

"What do you want from me?"

"I think you know, Alex."

"Yeah, I know. I know what you're trying to do. You're trying to scare me into giving you an apology. Well, it's not going to work."

"Then we have nothing more to discuss, but before tonight is over, you'll beg for me to accept your apology." That said, Edward ducked back into his car.

The ignition turned over and the engine roared to life. Alex knew he'd said and done a little too much. He'd just pushed too many of this guy's buttons.

He feverishly tried again to loosen the knot.

As if on cue at seeing Alex pulling at the knot, the car bucked forward. Alex just knew the car was going to slam into his knee caps, but he couldn't move. In his mind, Alex saw his legs buckling backward and folding in on themselves as the weight of his upper body forced his legs to bend the wrong way.

The Mustang stopped on a dime, inches from his legs. Alex let out a pitiful squeal as a breath of held air as relief poured out of his body.

He slapped the hood of the car with both hands. "Why are you doing this?"

The engine revved. It jerked forward an inch then slowly moved forward again. The front bumper touched the top part of Alex's shins and knees, urging him backward.

"Cut it out!" Alex yelled. "You've had your fun!"

The car pulled forward even more, touching his legs again.

Alex kicked the car then obligingly stepped back.

The Mustang kept advancing, and Alex continued to counter its movement.

Alex dropped his hands and feverishly began to undo the knot around his waist.

Edward gunned the gas and immediately braked. The bumper nudged Alex across his shins, causing him to pitch forward against the Mustang and slide to the ground.

Alex took a moment to rub some of the pain away then stood and slammed his fists against the hood of the car. "Alright! I get it!" he yelled. "You don't want me to untie the knot! Understood!"

The car seemed to growl at him as Edward revved the engine, emphasizing he would hit him again, even harder, if he tried another escape.

Alex stood there for a moment unsure of what to do. He realized he was holding each of his breathes longer than he should and that was making him tired. He took some deep breaths to try and expel some of the anxiety and calm his nerves. He thought of whiskey. *How good would it be to have a small glass right now?*

"So this is it, huh? This is all we're going to do tonight. Me, just stand here and you, just sit there. You think this is going to solve anything?"

There was no response from the other party. This was a one-way conversation.

"Who are you? What do you want? I've done nothing to you, you little shit. I'm not going to let you sit there and bully me! You got nothing to say to me?" He paused to let his words sink in. "If you got nothing to say then I'm out of here! I'm leaving! You can hit me with your car if you want but I'm leaving!"

Alex grabbed the knot that was tied around his waist again and tried to undo it.

By the time he grabbed the knot, Edward jammed the gas pedal to the floor. The car shot forward.

Alex looked up as soon as he grabbed the rope around his waist and saw the car advancing on him.

"Oh shit!" he yelled as he turned and ran away from the advancing Mustang.

He looked back after a few steps and saw that the Mustang was eating up the distance between them. It looked as though the rope was a thick piece of spaghetti and the car was sucking it up until it would finally eat him.

When the car was close enough to pull him under, Alex reacted. He jumped as high as he could to avoid contact. When he did, he rotated his body in mid air.

Edward slammed on his breaks when he saw Alex had become airborne.

Alex came down flat footed, feet near the windshield wipers, facing Tyler.

"Ha, how do you like that?" he said as he stomped on the hood of the car for emphasis.

After another three stomps on the hood, Alex tried to put his foot through the windshield. "Hey, you hear me in there? I'm talking to you shithead," he yelled as he lifted his foot again for a harder blow. "—Do you hear me?"

Before his foot could make contact with the windshield, Edward had already put the car in reverse and punched the gas.

Because of the reverse movement, Alex lost his balance. He fell backward and landed squarely on the hood of the car and tumbled to the ground in an awkward landing. He landed on his left arm, which sent a flare of pain throughout the left side of his body.

Alex saw the car still retreating and saw that the rope was becoming longer. In sudden horror, he realized he was still attached to his end of the rope. He quickly stood and ran after the retreating Mustang. He wasn't quite to his feet when the rope snapped taut between the distances. The force of it jerked him forward, almost throwing him to the ground. A sharp spasm of pain seared his lower back.

Like before with the thought of his knees bending in opposite directions, another thought entered his mind. It was the thought of being jerked forward so hard that his back would break in two at the waist—his upper body folding backward on to his lower body severing his spine and snapping his spinal nerves.

The car was in motion again. He tried to make his feet move in time with the speed of the car but they wouldn't cooperate. They were moving much too slowly. Finally, when he couldn't keep up at all, he was pulled to the ground and drug over its uneven surface.

Alex rolled back and forth along the ground using his hands for leverage. The ground was rough and rocky; it abraded his skin, even through his clothes. He started coughing and sneezing as dirt was kicked into his face. The car kept changing directions as it backed away. The movement spun Alex over and over and over until the car came to a stop.

He looked up and in a dizzying kaleidoscope effect saw the car was coming directly at him. He had just enough energy to stand and throw himself out of its way.

Alex didn't even have time to stand again before the rope jerked tight again, pulling him in the opposite direction. This time the rope was coming from the back end of the car.

The ground felt like a cheese grater on his skin. He could feel pieces of skin curl away underneath his clothes. His body was aching all over. He couldn't take much more of this.

The car finally stopped and Alex looked up in time to see the dust cloud that had been kicked up by their excursion drift off in the night breeze.

Alex coughed again then wheezed slightly. He sat up and stared into headlights.

Edward had turned the car around to face Alex. He watched as Edward switched the car's high beams on. It looked like the car had blinked at him.

"What the hell is he doing now?" Alex asked.

Alex held his tied hands up across his face to shield his eyes from the glare. He heard the engine swell even though it remained stationary. He could barely make out the dirt plums kicked up in the background by the Mustang's wheels.

Alex wasted no time scrambling away from it in a full speed run trying to outrun death. His body was charged with adrenaline.

Alex had expected to feel the bumper slam into his back and legs.

Instead reality hit him square in the stomach, and it felt like it had ripped him in half. The blow forced his legs to kick out in front of him and his upper body to fall forward. Alex felt like a dog that had run the length of his chain, causing it to snap back.

Alex stood, brushed himself off, and turned to the car. He was about to send another string of curses Edward's way but noticed the car was slowly moving away from him. Alex took off running toward the car.

The car quickly began to pick up speed; Alex could barely keep up with it.

Alex was running full force toward the car when Edward braked.

Alex turned to the side at the last second, causing his right hip to slam into the front of the car. The momentum slowed him somewhat, but he continued to roll over the hood and halfway up the windshield before sliding off the passenger side of the car.

He rolled over, coughed hard to catch his breath that had been knocked out of him, sat up, and tried to stand; the Charley horse kept him grounded. He softly beat and rubbed his throbbing leg, but it didn't seem to quell the pain.

From his periphery, he saw the car moving again; he rolled and crawled out of the way to give it room.

He sat on the ground and continued to doctor his leg. The car moved away, pulling the rope until it was tight again.

Alex knew it still wasn't over. Edward was still having his fun.

The engine revved. He wished he could continue sitting here, but the game of cat and mouse was starting over again. He slowly stood, favoring his injured leg.

Alex knew he couldn't survive if he didn't get out of this ball and chain relationship. Edward was going to drag the life out of him. He was sure of that now. He knew he couldn't hold out until the car ran out of gas.

The car's engine revved again; louder and longer this time.

Alex looked up and held up his bound wrist. One of his balled fists held an extended index fingers extended as if to say hold on for a few minutes.

"Jesus Christ, just give me a second," he muttered. "Damn."

The car jerked forward and stopped. It seemed to be a warning for Alex.

"I'm hurting here. Just give me some time. I beg of you."

The engine roared and was poised to spring forward again.

Alex lowered his head. "This is the moment," he whispered told himself. "You either take this moment to try and escape or spend the last hours—if you're that lucky—of your life getting your skin slowly peeled off by this terrain. There is always a chance."

The engine's roar had died down and was now at a steady growl.

In one swift movement, his hands found his waistline. He found the button of his pants and unbuttoned the waistline as the fingers of his right hand jerked the zipper down. His feet were already in motion. Each foot turned and found the heel of the opposite foot and was already in the process of sliding each shoe off.

Alex's pants were already to his knees when Edward realized what was happening. The

Mustang surged forward.

An "Oh shit," escaped Alex's lips.

One leg was totally free of its fabric but the sudden forward acceleration of the car unnerved Alex, causing the other foot to become bound up in the fabric of the other pant leg. In the struggle to get free, he lost his balance and fell backward. He quickly sat up and wrestled briefly with his pants to get free. As the car quickly approached, he abandoned the idea of escaping and jumped out of the way, but not before the car clipped him as it passed by.

The pain was excruciating. His knee all the way down to his foot was throbbing immensely. He forced his mind not to think about the pain.

Edward must've swerved toward me when I dove out of the way, Alex thought. *At least I'm free now.*

As that thought passed through his mind, his whole body was jerked in the opposite direction. His pants were ripped off and he was left sitting in his underwear in the middle of a field. At last he was free of the rope.

A wave of relief washed over him. He started laughing hysterically. Before he could relish the release that flooded his body, a wave of terror crashed in and took its place.

The brake lights blinked on and the car stopped dead in its tracks. There was a momentary pause before the car backed up and whipped around, the headlights pin pointing him where he sat.

The car didn't hesitate but came after him again.

You don't get this close to freedom and piss it away by sitting here being scared, he told himself. *RUN!*

Alex listened to his own advice. He scrambled to his feet, turned on his heels, and ran with all the strength he could find within his body.

The car was on his heels in no time.

Alex's legs were getting weak, especially since one of his leg had been clipped by the Mustang moments before. His strength was running out. He didn't have the muscle to jump out of the way. He turned to try and fall on the hood, but he wasn't able to get his legs high enough before the front parts of the car's grille caught him high on the thighs. The car pushed his legs out behind him, and he fell on the hood of the car. Instant pain swelled throughout the top part of his legs. It felt as though his legs had been jerked free from each of their sockets. In his mind's eye for the briefest of moments he saw his legs punched free of their moorings and drop underneath the wheels of the car. He could just imagine all the blood that went along with the mental image. If, by some miracle, they were still attached to him, he knew he wouldn't be able to stand for a while even if the car stopped at this moment. The new charley horses were too painful to warrant any movement.

Once Alex was attached to the hood of the car, its speed increased dramatically. Alex tried to see inside the Mustang, but it was too dark. It was as though the car itself was driving and was out to get him. He peered over his shoulder to see where they were headed. Only thing that was ahead of them was that big oak tree he'd noticed earlier. He did a double take.

Surely he's not going to ruin his car by ramming it into a tree.

He gripped the hood tighter, rotated his body to the side, pulled his bruised legs up as close as he could to his upper body, and braced himself for the impact.

Edward slammed on the breaks only inches from the old tree and Alex's body was launched from the hood of the car. He was jerked so hard that it felt as though his fingers were left behind still clutching the car's hood. Alex slammed into the tree trunk then fell to the ground in a mangled heap.

He instantly felt a dizzying pain and saw starbursts. For a brief moment, darkness folded in from all sides, blocking out the numerous lights; then as quickly as the darkness had come, it dissipated and he was left viewing constellations again.

Groaning, he sank to the ground because his injured legs couldn't hold the weight of his upper body. He wanted to sleep. He needed sleep. He was exhausted just from the pain. It had zapped all of his energy. He wanted to wrap himself in a warm blanket, curl up and sleep for a very long time. He closed his eyes to do just that when the engine sounded again.

The car was creeping now. It was slowly inching itself toward him. It was already too close, but he couldn't move. He was powerless to do anything.

He slapped the front grille of the car with his bound hands with each choked word that came from his dry, crack-lipped mouth. "What-do-you-want-from-me? What-did-I-ever-do-to-you?" But even as he asked, he knew. He had always known, and part of him knew that one day what they did to Edward would come back and bite them in the ass. And his day had finally come.

The car moved even closer. Alex rubbed his legs again. They felt numb from the beating he'd received earlier. He used the car hood for leverage and he pushed himself up, bracing his back against the tree trunk. He swung his body to the left to get his legs and feet out from under the car. He was about to pitch himself to the side and out of harm's way of the advancing car but before he could the Mustang's bumper moved the rest of the way in and wedged his hips against the tree.

Then Alex heard the faint click of a car door open. He looked over in time to see a dark figure rising from out of the driver's side. There was enough light from within the Mustang to illuminate the body of Tyler Curtis.

"Looks like you're stuck. You need a hand?" Edward asked.

Alex lowered his head in defeat and nodded. "Yes. Yes, I do. Whatever I've done, I apologize and take full responsibility for it. I'm sorry."

"Whatever you've done?" Edward asked in surprise. "Whatever you've done? You do remember, don't you?"

Alex nodded.

"Then you know this has to be done, right?"

Alex shook his head, "It doesn't have to be, Edward."

Edward blew a disgusted breath of air out of his mouth. He said nothing but turned and guided Tyler's body back to the driver's side and slid in behind the wheel.

Alex heard the voice of the engine rise in pitch again.

Alex felt a little more pressure on his hips. He looked down, wondering where the pressure had come from then he realized what Edward was doing.

Panic set in from all sides. He tried to wrench himself from the growing pressure. His tied hands convulsed first against the tree and then against the hood of the Mustang as he continued to try and find an escape. He tried pushing against the car and pulling on the grille to unwedge himself, but the pressure just intensified.

Alex knew he couldn't take any more pressure on his hips; he was sure his hips would shatter. "Wait!" Alex exclaimed, but he was saying it more to himself.

His mind fell on the broken memory again; the memory he'd tried to forget but couldn't. He saw Edward's agonized visage as he lay sprawled out on the blacktop of Desolation Highway with a shattered pelvis beckoning for someone's help.

In a domino effect of memory slices, one thought fragment bumped against another until the whole memory spiraled down, clicked into place, and became one solid picture event in his mind.

Even as the thoughts dropped sideways in his mind, the Mustang revved then moved closer. Everything from his lower waist to halfway up his chest began to get tighter. He felt like an anaconda had wrapped itself around him and was squeezing the life out of him.

A small, startled cry escaped his mouth. *Oh God, please God. No.* Pain flared in the same spot. Air involuntarily whooshed out of his open mouth. A scream accompanied it. The squeeze kept coming. It wouldn't let up. Edward was actually going to crush the life out of him.

As Alex remembered accidentally jamming the gas pedal instead of the brakes and slammed into the back of Edward, something deep with in his own waist snapped. For a split second, a rush of cool fluid seemed to burst in his middle but it quickly turned into liquid napalm and ignited his core.

His screams became louder. His lungs hurt from breathing in the dust-filled air. His throat hurt from his strained vocal chords.

The memory burned hotter and clearer as the car pushed in for a tighter hug.

Tears upon tears poured from his eyes in uncontrollable streams. Snot ran just as freely.

With one last forward movement, the car lurched forward and with an audible crunch, Alex's waist disintegrated and folded in on itself.

With a howl at the moon any wolf would be envious of, Alex reared back and let go with a cry that was filled with agony. Both hands thrummed uncontrollably on the car hood as though he were tapping out of a wrestling match. His legs involuntarily kicked and bucked against the tree roots and the undercarriage of the car. The excess leg movement caused the injured areas around his broken pelvis to flare up in intense pain. The motion made his screams swell rather than diminish.

The Mustang slowly backed away. Alex rolled away from the tree and fell on his back, staring up at the stars once again. The movement torqued his lower body much in the same way Edward's body had be wrenched when Travis flipped him over on Desolation Highway. Thinking the pain couldn't be worse than it already was, Alex's pain flared up again and seemed to multiply across his whole body.

Curse after curse poured from his mouth in violent streams. Screams melded with inventive combinations of profanity, but it did nothing to soothe the pain that was swelling throughout his body.

Even through his yells and curses, Alex heard footsteps approaching. He looked up out of tear-filled eyes.

Tyler came into view again as he bent at the waist and lowered himself toward him. His voice was husky now. "You remember now, don't you?"

Alex nodded as a measly, "Yes," escaped his lips. "I always have." Injuries aside, he didn't want to live any more after recounting that memory. "How could I have done such a thing?"

"I have asked myself that very same question, Alex."

"I just want to die."

"Good. That makes two of us. I want you to die too."

"I'm sorry," Alex said in a hoarse whisper.

"Don't start. I've heard it all numerous times before."

"I deserve everything you've done to me; everything and more."

That statement shocked Edward. "You're going for broke on this one, aren't you?"

"I have nothing else to live for now. I've got to make amends while I can."

"It's way too late for that."

Alex reached up and grabbed Tyler's shirt and pulled him slightly closer. "Do me a favor and do it quickly. End it for me. Please. You were planning on killing me anyway. Can you speed up the process for me? Please. I can't go on like this." The last few words died out in a whisper. He barely had the energy to talk.

"No," Edward said. "I can't speed up the process. I won't speed it up."

Alex angled his head to see Edward better. He was about to protest when Edward continued.

"What I will do is stay here and watch the life drain out of you, cause I, for the longest, have wanted nothing more than to see you dead."

Alex knew there was no use in arguing or pleading with Edward in any way. He had made up his mind. All Alex could do now was just stare up at his executioner that was gazing back at him with amusement painted on his face.

For the longest time, Alex and Edward just stared at each other saying nothing. Alex was unable to because of a lack of energy and Edward simply refused. Edward just simply wanted to sit and watch him die.

Then after an agonizing eternity, the light in Alex's eyes finally faded to a vacant glazed look as death took control of his body. Edward saw the exact moment of the exchange when life vacated and death possessed him. As Alex's facial features slowly went slack and his body relaxed the slight smile Edward wore on his face turned into a satisfied grin.

Alex's unblinking eyes were wide with wonder, perhaps because for a few brief seconds his real eyes saw the brilliance of the afterlife. It looked as though he was staring into the night sky straining to watch his soul travel to a far, distant realm in another galaxy.

Judging from the look on Alex's face and the devastation of his unmoving body he knew Alex was gone.

Edward finally stood and observed Alex for another short moment then, smiling, walked back to his Mustang and slowly drove away.

CHAPTER 44

IT WAS LATE when Tyler pulled into his own driveway. He turned the ignition off and stepped out of the car.

The night was still chilly and his body tingled as a breeze swept across his face and brushed through his hair. He thought about Savannah and their perfect moment by the lake. The memory made him smile.

As he made his way up the walkway, he thought, *So beautiful. So damn sexy.* "I love her," he stated to himself. He stopped for a moment in mid-step, thinking about those three words. They had said it in so many words down by the lake. He smiled again and said, "I do love her."

Tyler climbed the few steps to the front door and opened it to find Raven patiently waiting for him. She sat on her haunches, looking quizzically at Tyler as he entered.

"Hey, girl," he whispered, stooping to scratch her behind the ears. "You need to go out, don't you?"

Raven whined in response and licked his face.

"Alright. C'mon, let's go."

Tyler gave her a playful slap on her rump as she bolted out the still-opened door. Raven disappeared into the darkness beyond.

Tyler followed quickly and quietly shut the door. He couldn't risk waking his parents. The thought of having a discussion with them that would inevitably turn into an argument was just something he couldn't deal with right now.

As Tyler moved to sit down on the front porch stairs, the cell phone in his pants pocket began to vibrate. His heart gave a little two-step shuffle in hopes that it might be Savannah calling just to say, well, just to say anything. He hurriedly whipped out his phone and checked the number before answering. It was her. He punched the button to answer.

"Hey, Savannah. I was just thinking about you."

"I was just thinking about you as well," a male voice stated.

It took Tyler's mind a couple of seconds to catch up with what he was hearing, because he was expecting Savannah's voice to come through the line.

Tyler was immediately on edge.

The voice was curt and oily. The man continued, "Good evening, Mr. Curtis."

"Who is this?"

"My name is Fenton Osborne."

"Why are you calling me on Savannah's cell phone? Is she with you?"

"Yes. She's right here."

"Is she alright?"

"Yes. She's safe and sound," Fenton said, then added, "for the moment. I bet you feel like you're on cloud nine for being able to tap that, aren't you?"

"What are you talking about?"

"Don't play dumb with me, son. I saw you two down by the lake tonight having sex on the pier. Your girlfriend is very beautiful. I wouldn't mind having a little taste of my own."

Fury rose deep inside Tyler and his pulse quickened immediately, "You touch one hair on her head and you'll find your insides on the outside. I'll cut your fucking head off and sew it back up inside your abdomen where your insides once were. Are we clear?"

The man chuckled to himself, "That's adorable, standing up to me for your little girlfriend." He cleared his throat then continued, "Listen, I'm calling on behalf of Jeremy Taylor. He would like to meet with you at your earliest convenience."

Tyler felt Edward come to the forefront of his mind and body at the mention of Jeremy Taylor's name. Tyler's entire body went rigid as Edward took control.

"Excuse me? Jeremy Taylor?" Edward asked.

Osborne gave a quick, courteous laugh, "Yes, I'm sure you've heard of him."

"Let me speak to Savannah."

"No. You will have to take us at our word that she is well and unharmed. You, on the other hand, are wasting valuable time making these trivial threats and demands. If you would like to get Savannah back in one piece, meet us at 1423 Aberdeen Lane. We would like to see you in the next thirty minutes, but we are generous people and will give you a full hour to arrive. Do not attempt to involve anyone else. Do not call the police. Come alone, Mr. Curtis. Do you understand?"

"Yeah, yeah. I got it," Edward said.

"Excellent. When you reach the address, drive around to the back of the house. Miles will be waiting to escort you inside. You have one hour Mr. Curtis, after that I don't know what will become of Adrian and Savannah. I suggest you get started. Your time starts now. Goodbye Mr. Cur—"

Adrian? They have Adrian too?

Edward was already moving toward his car when he killed the call. He didn't take the time to put Raven back inside but called to her instead. Raven came immediately. Edward opened the car door to allow Raven to slip inside. By the time Edward closed the door and started the car, Raven was perched on the passenger's seat, staring out in anticipation to the late-night drive.

Edward didn't worry about being quiet now. He was on a mission and gunned it as he backed out of the driveway. The wheels only gave a quick squeal as he headed out of the neighborhood.

"1423 Aberdeen Lane, 1423 Aberdeen Lane. Where the hell is 1423 Aberdeen Lane?"

Tyler's new car was equipped with a GPS and he typed in the address.

Edward reached over and gave Raven a scratch behind the ears. "Looks like the time has come to face Jeremy once and for all; you think you're up for that?"

Raven barked in agreement.

"That's my girl. Me too."

附

Edward continued to follow the directions to the address Fenton had given him and soon pulled up in front of a huge, black, wrought iron gate.

After he pressed the button, a monotone voice came over the intercom speaker. "State you name, please."

"Tyler Curtis. Who else are you expecting at this time of night?"

"You're eighteen minutes early, Mr. Curtis. I'm impressed. Well done."

"I'm glad I have your approval. Now open the fucking gate."

"Pull up the driveway and around to the back. Miles will be waiting."

The heavy gate slowly swung open and Edward proceeded as instructed.

As he came up over the rise in the driveway, a huge mansion loomed out of the darkness. Lawn lights lit the mansion from its base as a means of showing off its impressive architecture. There were many windows but very few lights were on inside. The mansion had a foreboding presence that was unsettling.

He regretted not taking the time to get some sort of a weapon before he left. Then again, he assumed Jeremy's "bodyguards" would search him as soon as he arrived.

He drove to the back of the mansion as instructed and turned off his car. When he stepped out, Edward hesitated momentarily.

A stout man stood motionless like a statue on the back deck at the top of the stairs. He had stone features and was dressed in a tan suit and starched white shirt. His placid features shifted into a smirk when he saw Tyler get out of the car, but it faded when Raven stepped out on the pavement and stood at Tyler's side.

A growl began to rumble deep in Raven's throat when she saw the man.

Edward put a hand on Raven's head to calm her nerves.

"I know, I know; I don't like him either, girl."

Raven stopped growling and whined softly.

"That must be Miles. C'mon, girl. Let's go."

Edward, followed closely by Raven, moved cautiously up the stairs.

As Edward approached, Miles said, "I thought you were instructed to come alone."

Edward took on a sarcastic tone. "Yeah, well I didn't have time to put my dog back up if I was going to get here at the appointed time; besides, she likes to ride in the car late at night. I didn't think it would be a problem."

"I'm sorry, but you shouldn't have brought the dog with you."

"Yeah, you just said that. The guy who called never said I couldn't bring her either. He just said not to call the cops and not to involve anybody else. I don't know about you, but to me that means, 'people.' He never said anything about animals. If he didn't want me to bring animals, he should've been clearer in his instructions."

Miles didn't like to be zinged.

"I'm afraid your dog will have to stay outside in your car."

"No," Edward said defiantly. "I'm afraid I can't do that. Wherever I go; she goes. Now just get on your little walkie-talkie thingy there and okay it with the big man inside."

Miles wore a communication device that traveled from underneath his suit up into his ear. He let out an annoyed breath of air as he turned slightly and whispered something into the mic at the end of his sleeve.

Edward noticed that the hand with the mic was wrapped tightly with a thick bandage.

While he was waiting on a reply, Edward nodded toward Miles's hand and asked, "Did you get bit by your dog as well?"

Miles simply said, "Not a dog, but definitely a bitch."

Some sort of reply came through Miles's ear piece. He listened. After a moment, Miles said, "He's not thrilled about it, but Jeremy says the dog will be fine."

"Good. I'm glad we both see eye to eye."

Miles grabbed Tyler by his shirt, turned him around and pushed him up against the wall.

"What the—"

"Spread 'em."

Raven growled again.

"You've got to be kidding me. Are you serious?" Edward reluctantly did as he was told.

Edward wanted to make another comment to the man that this was the way he got his rocks off—by feeling little boys up—but he didn't think Miles would appreciate the value of his comment.

After Miles finished his thorough search and confiscated Tyler's car keys, his wallet, and three small evidence bags of mirror and metal shards that he'd taken from the morgue when he'd visited Alex, Miles grabbed Tyler's collar and shoved him roughly toward the back door.

"Hey, watch it, shithead."

Miles ignored Edward's comment and Raven's growl, grabbed the door and swung it open. He stood to the side giving Tyler and Raven room to pass. Miles jerked his head toward the opened door.

Edward hesitated, weighing his options. He stood stock-still, refusing to budge and stared Miles down with hate-filled eyes.

Miles's patience was growing thin from Tyler's unheeding. "Look, we can either do this one of two ways. Either you can go inside willingly or I can fucking carry you. Make a choice."

Giving him a sneer, Edward walked slowly inside the doorway but he didn't break eye contact until he was well past the threshold.

"Just keep moving," the man ordered. "Don't be difficult and control that bastard of yours or I'll do it for you."

"For your information, she happens to be a bitch. Why does everyone keep thinking otherwise?"

Upon entering the mansion, Edward was hit with the clean smell of furniture polish and the scent of antique wood. The massive foyer's hardwood floors were polished to a rich shine.

Taking the lead, Miles replied, "Stay close, Mr. Curtis, and don't touch anything, especially the sculptures and the paintings. They are very expensive."

The inside was just as vast as Edward had imagined. The crown molding, the stairs, and the window castings were of expert craftsmanship. Intricate designs in dark wood gave the house somewhat of a gothic look.

The lighting had been turned down to a dull ambiance this late at night, but Edward could imagine what the house would look like when the lights were turned to their highest setting.

A banister split the wide staircase and sloped up approximately ten to twelve steps before branching off into two different staircases that led to rooms on the right and left sides of the house.

As they walked, Edward noticed the cathedral ceilings that allowed for a vast array of ornate artwork to adorn the walls. The collection of artwork, which was illuminated by track lighting, gave Edward the feeling he were strolling thought a fine art gallery.

Some paintings were abstract, created with bright, rich colors. Long tendrils of paint seemed to be flung onto some of the canvases with harsh whips of the wrist or applied with angry brush strokes; other paintings were much more intricate and obviously took more care to create. All colors were blended to create a dazzling display for the eye to behold.

There were a host of paintings geared toward wildlife nature scenes, such as a buffalo staring out at his herd in the distance, a lone wolf caught howling at the moon, or an inverted whale tale shimmering in dusk's twilight.

A re-occurring theme was of the old west with the hard lifestyle the cowboys and Indians had lived. Life on the plains seemed to be captured perfectly.

A vast amount of paintings were imaginative works of muscular swordsmen rescuing half-clothed, big-breasted women from huge, scaly monstrosities. Still others showed tough, battle-clad, ax-wielding women on winged horseback fighting immense fire breathing dragons. All the fantasy artwork seemed to be clipped straight from a distant time period then painted on a tapestry capturing the essence of that era.

There were a few paintings in Jeremy's collection that pushed the limit to the extreme. A nightmarish collection showed men and women being savagely beaten, raped, and tortured—even mutilated—by mysterious figures dressed in dark cloaks. The only feature you could see on the robed forms was glowing, contemptuous, green eyes peering from beneath their hoods. Some paintings suggested demonic possession; while others were outright Satanic, featuring demons tormenting people in Hell's inferno.

It didn't take long for Edward to look away as though just admiring it as art were enough to condemn him to the tortured depths of Hell.

Edward thought it odd that Jeremy could paint pure, radical evil to the simplistic innocents of a flowered still life. All were of almost picture perfect clarity all the way down to a simple glass of wine looking as though it could be lifted from the canvas and its contents sipped.

Not only were there paintings, but there were also sculptures that had been placed on tables throughout the rooms. The ones that were too big to complement the furniture sat in the corners of the room waiting their turn to be purchased.

Miles was already standing at the end of the corridor. Edward hadn't realized he had lagged behind; he was so caught up in the rapture of the spectacle of Jeremy's artwork. He knew it was Jeremy's work because each painting was signed with his name.

They finally came to a large open room toward the far back side of the mansion. Miles opened the door and ushered Tyler in followed closely by Raven. As Edward and Raven passed, Raven yelped in pain. Edward quickly turned back and saw what had happened. Miles had stuck his stun gun into Raven's side and had pulled the trigger. Raven lay sprawled on the floor, her feet kicking uncontrollably.

Instantly pissed, Edward turned on Miles and went directly for him. "You son of a bitch. Why the fuck did you do that?"

Miles stood just in time to brace himself for Tyler's attack. Not giving Tyler time to react, Miles dropped low and lunged forward in a quick fencing type move and stabbed Tyler directly in the stomach with his stun gun and pulled the trigger again.

Electrical shock surged throughout Tyler's body and he dropped to the floor in a jittering pile of misfiring nerve endings.

Replying to Tyler's earlier question, Miles said, "Because Mr. Taylor asked me to, that's why. And I always do what Mr. Taylor requests. You should have left your dog in the car as I suggested."

Seeing that Raven and Tyler were down for the count, he turned and closed the doors behind him.

☙

Edward felt something grab his tingling foot, raise his leg, and drag him across the floor. His head bounced off two carpeted stairs as he was pulled into a lower level of the room.

Edward saw the room pan by as he was dragged along. He saw two pairs of legs as he passed by. The legs were bound with rope. He strained his eyes and saw Adrian and Savannah sitting on a couch, rope bound around their wrists and duct tape covering their mouths. They stared down at him as he passed by. Fear was painted on their faces. It was evident they had been crying.

He felt two arms slide under his armpits and hoist him up and seat him in a chair. When the hands released him, his body slid from the chair and dropped back to the floor again.

"Leave him there for now," a voice said. "Give him some time to come around."

Edward didn't know how long he had lain there before the tingling finally started to dissipate.

He heard soft piano music playing in the background.

He noticed the sweet smell of cigar smoke tickling his nose.

From his upside down point of view, Edward saw a stream of it drifting up from an ashtray that had been placed on a table near one of the three easels in this room. The smoke merged with the already hovering cloud near the ceiling like an ethereal spirit.

He turned his head to get a better view of what he was looking at. From below the center easel Edward saw two legs from the knees down. He knew they were the legs of the man he hated most in this world. He had waited years for their paths to cross again, and now the time had finally come. Their lives had come full circle. Edward panicked, causing movement that alerted Miles he was coming around again.

Miles cleared his throat to attract Jeremy's attention.

Jeremy's head shot out from behind the easel. "Ah, there he is." He placed his painting supplies on the small table and moved toward Tyler. He held his hands up to stop Miles who was coming to help. "That's alright, Miles. I will take it from here." Jeremy stooped and helped

Tyler to the seat that he had been placed in earlier. "There you go. Are you comfortable?"

Still disoriented but able to answer, Edward said, "Yeah. Sure."

"Good, good. Can I get you anything? Brandy? Coke? Water? Beer? We have anything."

"No. I'm fine."

"Alright. I just want you to be comfortable. I always take care of my guests."

"By shocking them into submission? Real hospitable."

Jeremy laughed, "You're a funny guy, Mr. Curtis. Tyler Curtis, the man of the hour. There's the guy who has this whole town turned inside out. Everyone's looking for you."

"I seriously doubt *everyone* is looking for me."

Jeremy laughed then returned to his easel and picked up his brush and paints and began dabbing his brush on his canvas again.

Jeremy wasn't dressed as Edward had expected such as a nice suit and tie; maybe double breasted with nice shoes to match. Instead, he was barefooted and wore a pair of worn jeans with numerous holes—especially around the knees—and a ratty old tee shirt underneath a long sleeve green flannel shirt; all of which were paint encrusted.

As if reading Tyler's mind, Jeremy said from behind the easel, "I apologize for not dressing up more for the occasion, but I have clients that insist on deadlines."

"No problem. I didn't think you would go to any trouble on my account anyway."

Jeremy's head shot out from behind the canvas again, "You're absolutely right. I wouldn't."

In contempt, Edward whispered, "Asshole."

There were two other easels in the room; one on either side of Jeremy. Each one had a different sized canvas perched on it. From his viewpoint, Edward couldn't tell if they were blank canvasses or ones that already had artwork painted on them because they were turned to face away from him.

"What's with the canvases?"

Jeremy's head jerked out from behind his easel again. "Oh, you'll see. In time."

"Why did you call me here?" Edward asked.

"Boy, you don't waste any time do you?"

"Answer the question." He paused for a moment, then added, "Where's Savannah? Where's Adrian?"

Answering with only a small sweep of his brush, Jeremy indicated off in a direction behind Tyler.

Edward was so focused on Jeremy that he hadn't remembered until now about the phone call from Fenton and the women.

Edward turned and saw them sitting on the couch behind him, bound and gagged.

Edward's heart leapt in his chest and he rushed to them and pulled the tape from their mouths. Edward hugged Adrian then kissed Savannah.

"Hello, Tyler," Adrian said, then worked her jaw a few times. Tyler knelt in front of her. She gave him a pitiful smile. "I'm so sorry."

"No don't be sorry, it's my fault. I'm the one who should be sorry."

He looked at Savannah and their eyes locked. He could see the look of flooded relief that had come across her face. Tyler was equally happy to see that they hadn't injured her as far has he could tell.

Savannah asked in a panicked tone, "Tyler, what's going on?"

"I have some ideas but not exactly sure. You okay?" he asked.

"I'm fine. Just scared. What the hell are we doing here, Tyler? Who are these guys?"

"It's a long story, but I'm sure everything will be explained in time. Guess you could say all those questions you had about me will soon be answered." Edward looked back and forth between them and said, "I'm going to get you both out of here. I promise."

Instinct immediately made Edward reach for her ropes to untie them.

"Tyler, no," Adrian said. "It's not worth it."

"Tyler, look out!" Savannah yelled.

Edward was in the process of turning to see what Savannah was yelling about when something hard struck him in the back of the head. He blacked out, went limp, and slid to the floor near their bound feet.

CHAPTER 45

EDWARD WAS INSTANTLY awake when water was doused in his face. He coughed and sputtered as he leaned over. When he sat up and opened his eyes again, he found he was the center of attention; all eyes were on him.

He groaned and reached around to the base of his skull, and slowly massaged the dull ache away.

In the time he was out, they had moved Adrian and Savannah from the couch to chairs that had been placed on either side of him. Adrian was on his left; Savannah on his right. Both were still bound with rope but duct tape hadn't been replaced over their mouths. All three of them were in the center of the room in front of Jeremy's main easel.

Edward looked over to Adrian and gave her a weak smile.

"You okay?" Adrian asked.

"Yeah. You?"

"I've been better."

Edward turned to Savannah and allowed Tyler's thoughts to be voiced.

"Did they hurt you?"

"No. Why are we here?"

"You wouldn't believe me if I told you."

Edward took control over Tyler again and turned his head toward Jeremy. "Let them go," he demanded. "They've done nothing wrong. It's me you want."

"And it's you I got."

"How did you find me?" Adrian asked.

"Wasn't even looking for you, honey," Jeremy said. "I simply had my men follow Tyler to find out what he was up to. He's the one who led me to you. My men called me and said he was with a photographer—Adrian Connell. You can imagine my surprise. I figured if he was talking to you; something strange was going on. I just had to see and hear for myself what that might be. That's why you're here."

As Edward sat there listening, he conspicuously surveyed the room. It was a combination library and study. Behind him were two couches, one on either side of the room. A man—Edward could only assume was Fenton Osborne—was sitting in one of them reading a magazine.

Edward noticed that Miles was guarding the double door entrance/ exit to the office. The humanoid robot eyed him conspicuously as he waited for his next command.

In front of him—behind Jeremy and the three easels—was an alcove that contained Jeremy's desk. Behind the desk—framing it—was a massive glass window that overlooked the now-blackened backyard. Most of the walls were adorned with tall bookshelves that reached from ceiling to floor. An assortment of leather bound books and best sellers lined each shelf.

Jeremy placed his paint and brushes on the table again, picked up his cigar and ashtray and stepped up the two steps behind him and leaned against his huge desk. He placed the ashtray on his desk and took a big puff from his cigar as he sized Tyler up.

Edward noticed Jeremy hadn't changed much over the years. He was still the tall, lean, imposing man of his teenage years. He could tell Jeremy still worked out on a regular basis. His hair was still long as it had been in school. It always gave him a rugged look.

Cutting right to the chase, Jeremy said, "Tyler Curtis. I don't know who the hell you think you are but I'm certainly going to find out."

"Meaning?"

Jeremy either didn't have an answer or was just choosing not to answer Tyler's sarcasm.

Edward made a point. "Oh you'll find out all right, I can assure you of that. Just like all the others."

"And just what do you mean by *all the others?*" Jeremy asked.

"All your high school friends. Do I need to list them for you? I don't think I do. You know what's going on. You just don't want to believe. If I were you, I wouldn't waste your time trying to find out who Tyler is. I would be more concerned about who is on the inside of Tyler. That's what really counts."

"And who's on the inside of you, Tyler? Edward McDaniel?" Jeremy sneered then laughed aloud. "I told Alex Riley where he could shove that sci-fi bullshit when he started spouting off about it."

Edward glanced over at Adrian and then to Savannah who already had confused looks etched on their faces. Edward nodded and smiled to each as if to confirm what Jeremy had just said was the truth. Edward had a feeling Adrian couldn't believe this. But he knew Adrian must've been thinking that if this *was* true, then everything she said when she met Tyler for the first time she had also said it to Edward although she hadn't known it then.

Edward smiled and nodded in answer to her disbelieving look. Not knowing what to say or do he turned back to Jeremy.

Noticing Tyler was unwavering, Jeremy stopped mid-inhale on his cigar. He placed it in the ashtray again and walked to where Tyler was seated. He bent down close and puffed a mouthful of smoke in Tyler's face.

Edward didn't cough but sat there unblinking.

Jeremy peered deep into Tyler's eyes for a moment then asked sarcastically. "Edward? Edward, are you in there?"

Edward continued to stare. He was studying Jeremy as much as Jeremy was studying him.

Jeremy waved a hand in front of Tyler's face, still unbelieving. Raising his voice, he said, "Edward? Jesus, this sounds so silly to be talking like this. You know, Tyler; I don't believe for a second that Edward McDaniel is inside you. That's just a bunch of bullshit."

Savannah felt like she was a spectator at a tennis tournament. She had no clue as to what was going on, but she looked in the direction of each spoken volley. She hoped it would eventually make sense, but she wasn't about to say anything to stop this conversation, so she stayed quiet and looked on in wonder and confusion. She also sat in fear saying nothing because she didn't want anymore duct tape pasted across her mouth.

"Why do you say that?" Edward asked.

"You're really going to go there with this, huh?" Jeremy asked.

"You'll just have to trust me on this."

"Okay, I'll bite. But do me a favor. Prove to me that Edward is inside you. Can you prove it?"

"Sure."

"How so?"

"By asking you one question."

"And what's that?"

Edward smiled, then said, "How's your nose, buddy boy? Did it finally heal okay after I broke it that day on the pier?"

The amused smiled was wiped clean from Jeremy's face. "Oh, you smug son of a bitch." He started to smile again, "You're good. You're really good. You've done your homework, that's for sure." Jeremy looked over and appraised Adrian. "Is that what you two talked about when you met?"

Adrian said nothing. She just looked away.

Jeremy leaned down into Tyler's face again. "If you're really and truly in there and you can see and hear me, there are some things I need to tell you."

"I'm listening." Edward said.

"Good." Jeremy paused, then, "You know, Edward; I owe a lot to you. More than you realize. If it hadn't been for you, I don't know where I would be today. It's because of you that I am what I am and that I have what I have. It's all because of you." Jeremy looked directly at Tyler and said, "Sounds so silly to be telling you this, Tyler, but what the hell. I'll play along with your little charade. If you really think Edward is inside you, I'll indulge you for a few minutes."

Edward and Adrian exchanged looks, unsure of where Jeremy was going with this story.

Jeremy continued, "I guess I should start by showing you the very first painting I ever completed. I painted it the night after your death, Edward. Now this piece isn't my best work, so don't judge me by it. But by painting this, it caused me to see that I was pretty good and that is what caused me to continue on with my artwork." He flung out his arms to bring attention to his mansion. "And the rest is history."

Jeremy went to the easel on the left side of the room and stood directly in front of it. He flipped the painting over, stared at it for a few moments, then moved aside. Jeremy immediately looked at Tyler just to observe his reaction. If Edward was truly inside Tyler, this painting would unnerve him.

The painting wasn't as good as the other masterpieces that hung on the walls of his mansion. It was painted close to twenty years ago.

The painting was from a fish's point of view. The point of view was from behind a figure that seemed to be hovering underwater. A rope was attached to the figure's ankle which was connected to an anchor that was resting on the lake's floor. Even though the figure was facing away from the viewer, Edward knew it was himself. The painting was all wrong because it was too vivid. There was way too much color. It wasn't at all like the dismal murkiness that Edward remembered.

The unnerving part of this painting was the second figure that accompanied Edward at the bottom of the lake. The second figure was the main focus of this piece. Edward instantly knew it was Jeremy. The Jeremy figure was dressed the same way he had been the day of the confrontation on the pier. The Jeremy figure was also hovering, but no rope was attached to his foot. It looked as though he was just there watching and waiting for the Edward figure to die.

Remembering the shadowy face of death when he was drowning, Edward whispered, "It was you."

Not hearing Tyler or just ignoring his comment altogether, Jeremy said, "I call this piece, *Unsavable*, because that is exactly what you were."

"It was you under the water; all along it was you. I always thought it was something else, but I see now that it was you. You let me die?"

"Now let's not become narrow minded or split hairs here. How did you come up with that scenario?" Jeremy said, puffing on his cigar again. He didn't think Tyler would have an answer.

Edward said, "Because a search party found me hours after the accident. But if this painting is correct then you let me die. If you dove under the water looking for me the day of the accident and found me, you could've untied my foot and helped me back to the surface."

"How did you know that? Who are you?"

Not answering Jeremy, but continuing on his tirade, Edward yelled, "I SAW YOU! I WAS ALONE! I WAS FRIGHTENED!" He began crying as that feeling of abandonment flooded back over him. "You could've saved me, but you just left me there to die. You killed me!"

"You've got a wild imagination, Edward, if that is really you inside there. If that's what you want to believe, then I can't stop you."

Edward hung his head; his body shook as he silently cried for a long moment. Everyone else in the room stared at him, not knowing what to say.

Savannah had no idea what they were talking about. She looked on, amazed at the conversation that was unfolding. *Why was Tyler acting like another person?* She *had* noticed small changes with Tyler after his accident. She had so many question running through in her mind.

Jeremy was about to speak again, but Edward beat him to the punch.

"So you killed me. It seems you have no remorse about it. I will deal with that aspect later on, but there is one question I would like to ask."

"Shoot."

"Why did you send Travis Sheridan after me?"

Edward already knew the answer from when they were in the junkyard. He was just curious as to how Jeremy would answer.

"I have no idea what you are talking about."

"You sent him after me with *my* baseball bat."

"Hey, if you're really Edward, you would know Travis is a hothead and goes off whenever he feels like it. I didn't send him after you. He's the one who had it out for you. He simply wanted revenge for what you did to Kelly. I couldn't stop him."

"But you gave him my baseball bat on purpose, didn't you?"

"Yours? Where did you get an idea like that?"

"Because my initials are carved into it."

"Your initials."

"Yeah. E. M. Edward McDaniel."

"Oh yes, that's right; you still think you're Edward. I keep forgetting."

He paused, shaking his head, unable to figure Tyler out. "You are so delusional. Where are you getting your information?"

"I'm not getting it from anywhere. I lived and experienced all of it firsthand. See, I think you gave him my bat as a way to draw me out and come to you. It was just a precaution in case Alex might be right about me coming back to pay all of you a visit. It would've worked too, but you sped up the process by taking something that is more important to me than my baseball bat." He looked over to Adrian for emphasis. He smiled at her sheepishly.

Adrian's brow crinkled in confusion.

Edward then turned to Savannah. He said nothing but winked at her. She smiled and looked at her bound hands in her lap.

Jeremy asked, "Where is Travis? Did he meet up with you?"

Looking directly at Jeremy, Edward said, "You could say our homecoming was a *hit*. My baseball bat even has a few more blood stains on it to prove it. Travis spilled his guts about everything before I scrambled his brains. The bat's in the trunk of my car if you don't believe me."

"Oh really?" Jeremy picked up Tyler's keys that were now on his desk and bounced them thoughtfully in the palm of his hand.

Miles must've put them there when I was out from the stun gun, Edward thought.

"Osborne."

"Yes, Mr. Taylor."

He pitched the keys across the room to Osborne who was sitting on one of the couches leafing through a magazine. Osborne snagged them out of the air.

Jeremy continued, "Would you go to Tyler's car and retrieve the baseball bat Tyler—or Edward—says is in there?"

"But of course, sir."

"Make sure you don't touch the bat itself. It's evidence now."

"Certainly, Mr. Taylor," Osborne said, then turned and left the room. As he left, Edward noticed a bandage taped to the side of Osborne's head.

Adrian or Savannah must've fought back when they came for them, Edward thought. *Good for you girls. Good for you.*

587

Edward turned his attention back to Jeremy and asked, "Why were there dried blood stains on my baseball bat?"

"What? Previous bloodstains?"

"Don't play dumb with me. I'm not stupid."

"Why are you asking me that? You said yourself there is dried blood splatter on the bat. How do I know it wasn't placed there by you?"

"Because it was already on there when I took it from Travis. Which means, if you had it before him, you did something to add the stains. Travis even told me he got it from you."

To himself, Jeremy said, "That son of a bitch could never keep a secret."

"Who else did you kill, besides me?" Edward pressed.

Jeremy gave an amusing smile. He glanced at the other painting sheepishly. "That's a loaded question, Edward. Are you sure you want to know where the blood stains came from? Are you sure you can handle it?"

Edward swallowed hard. He was scared of what lie Jeremy might tell, or better yet, what truth he might unfold. Mentally preparing himself for the worst, Edward said, "Yes. I asked you, didn't I?"

"Okay. But don't ever say I didn't warn you. You're not going to like this answer; I can assure you of that. The truth will involve a little showing rather than telling," he said, walking to the second canvas. Before he flipped the painting, he turned and added, "I'm not one to brag, but to answer the question means that I will have to reveal my second finished painting. It's a bit on the darker side. It's still one of my earlier works so again, please don't judge me too harshly."

He paused for dramatic effect.

Edward looked ahead expectantly.

Jeremy quickly turned the painting, stepped back, and looked at Edward's face to see his reaction again.

Edward thought he had prepared himself for Jeremy's answer, but the painting itself was like a penitent fist that drove the air out of him.

"You see, Edward, after your death, your grandmother, Helen Roquemore, had a hard time keeping her big mouth shut about the whole situation. She kept going to the police and to the newspapers with these crazy accusations telling them I was responsible for your death. I was getting a lot of heat from everyone, so I went to reason with her."

Jeremy kept talking. His words faded slightly as they fell on Edward's ears. Instead of hearing Jeremy tell his story, the words formed into pictures and the pictures became a flurry of movement. They moved faster and faster until it was like he was viewing this history lesson as a movie in his mind.

❣

Jeremy Taylor walked quickly up the front porch stairs. He passed through the porch screen door to the inner front door. He heard a labored moaning and crying coming from the inside. He knocked briskly. The crying stopped suddenly. A tortured shuffle-step became audible as slippered feet slowly made their way toward the door.

The door swung inward and the face of Helen Roquemore peered through the opening. Her face suddenly became afraid and angry at the same time.

"YOU! How dare you come here after what you did."

"Mrs. Roquemore. Please don't be afraid. I just need to talk with you."

"Go away!" she shouted. "I don't want to talk to ya. Thay's nothing you could say or do to make things better." She began to close the door again.

Jeremy's hand shot out and stopped it before the latch could click. "Mrs. Roquemore, I just want to help."

She jerked the door open again, "Help! Don't you think you've helped enough already!"

"I didn't do anything," he said, trying to reason with her.

"You killed my boy! You know it and I know it. Everybody in this whole damn town knows it. They're just too chicken shit to do anything 'bout it. And you're just too chicken shit to admit you did it."

Anger swelled in Jeremy's chest and head. He punched the door with the back of his fist. The hit was harder than he intended. The door slipped from Helen's grasp and opened wider.

Startled, Helen immediately backed up.

"You. It's true. You did kill 'im. It's all there in your anger; written all over your face."

"Now wait. Just calm do—"

"No! You get outta here, you hear me?" she said, cutting him off. "Get the hell outta my house. I'm calling the police."

"NO! Don't! Please!"

But Helen had already stepped forward again and slammed the door in his face.

"Helen!" he called after her from outside the door. "Please, don't do this."

Barely thinking, he turned the doorknob and entered.

Jeremy saw Helen was already through the kitchen and into the living room. Jeremy immediately followed her and was on her heels in seconds. He saw her move toward the phone.

In a fit of panic and rage, he shoved her. Hard.

She became off balanced with the forward surge of movement and with her weight became top heavy. Her feet couldn't catch up in time to balance herself. She toppled headlong into the table.

The flimsy table couldn't hold the added weight. The legs splintered like kindling and dropped her to the floor.

She grunted as her bulk landed. She rolled onto her back and tried to right herself.

Jeremy was already there standing above her, breathing deeply. He was standing too close to her for her to get up enough movement to stand.

"Move back!" she ordered.

"No. Not till we talk."

"Help me up," she pleaded. She was looking around for a weapon; anything to make Jeremy back up and give her room to stand.

"Why don't you just stay down there and think about all the lies you've been telling."

Helen's eyes fell on Edward's bat. The second one Jonas had made for him. Jonas had spent hours whittling and sanding to make it the perfect bat for his grandson.

With a new sense of power overtaking her, she lashed out and snatched the bat's handle. As she grabbed it, she swung it into Jeremy's legs.

From her immense weight and having no leverage from being on the ground, the swing and hit weren't enough to shatter bone or his knee cap. But it was enough to be painful though.

Jeremy howled when the bat connected on the backside of his knee. It made his leg buckle, causing him to crumple backward to the ground.

Embarrassed and madder than hell, Jeremy rolled over and stood as quickly as he had fallen. He stepped back then stooped to rub his throbbing knee.

Helen used this time to maneuver herself into a standing position. She immediately assumed a batter's stance and was about to swing away home in self defense, but Jeremy had stood too quickly.

He saw her motion in his periphery and stepped back out of the way.

"You get the hell outta my house you son of a bitch!"

"Put the bat down," he ordered.

"If you don't leave right now, I'm going to put this bat into the side of your head."

"Now you're threatening me."

"Yes I am. And if you know what's good for ya—"

"I don't like being threatened."

Helen was on the verge of tears, "And I don't like havin' a missing grandson."

"What happened to Edward was tragic, but I assure you I had nothing to do with it."

Her defenses weakened for a moment as self doubt entered her mind. Her arms dropped slightly, as did the bat.

It was just enough. Jeremy lunged at her, going straight for the bat.

Helen saw his advancement and tried to get her defenses up again, but it was too late. She tried to swing, but Jeremy's hands had already locked on hers, stifling her mobility.

There was no struggle to keep the bat; Jeremy was too powerful for her. As he wrenched the bat with one hand, he shoved her in the chest with the other. She hit the wall and crumpled to the floor again.

"You lied to me," she wailed.

"I certainly did. But you believed me, and that is what everyone else is going to believe once I silence your voice."

"Silence?"

"Yeah, after you're gone, everybody will forget about you. And Edward.

Everybody will once and for all finally be able to accept that Edward's death was an accident."

"But it wasn't an accident, was it?"

"No. Far from it. The initial boating accident was. Yes, I take full responsibility for that. But his drowning wasn't so much of an accident."

"Meaning you didn't want to save him."

"Correct. I was under the water with him." He gave a small bemused laugh. "I watched him die."

"You're the Devil."

Helen tried to get up. Jeremy stuck the fat end of the bat into the big woman's cleavage and stopped her.

"Stop it!" she yelled pushing the bat away.

"Stay down," he ordered.

With vehement eyes, she shot him a look and said, "Own up to what you done and turn yourself in."

"It will be a cold fucking day in Hell before I let anyone know what I have done and what I'm going to do. You can bet your fat ass on that one, baby."

She tried once more to stand up.

"Don't get up, Helen! I'm warning you!"

"What are you going to do 'bout it?"

"I can make damn sure you never get up again. I've killed before, I can kill again. Don't test me on this subject."

Knowing she wasn't going to get out of this situation alive, Helen stood.

The blow to the side of her head came before she was fully standing. Darkness clouded her vision as she dropped back to the ground again. She tried to stand again, pushing up off the floor with her hands, but the second blow to the back of the head came immediately. Her arms gave out and she dropped to the floor, groaning.

Jeremy went into an uncontrollable rage. Blow after blow rained down upon her. When he noticed there was no movement or sound coming from Helen's body, Jeremy finally stopped and dropped the end of the bat to his side and leaned on it for balance.

CHAPTER 46

"YOU FUCKING ASSHOLE!" Adrian yelled. "You killed Helen? All this time I thought she went somewhere and lived out the rest of her life with friends or family in another state, but you killed her too?"

"I did what I had to do," Jeremy said.

"You are, without a doubt, the biggest piece of shit I have ever known. You're nothing but a murderer."

"That may be true, and I'm sorry you feel that way. I can't change your mind. What do you think Tyler, I mean, Edward?" The sarcasm was oozing off of Jeremy.

Edward said nothing. Waterfalls of tears were pouring down Tyler's face and dropping off his chin. He was numb from what he had just heard and the painting he was now viewing.

Cutting the canvas in two diagonal halves was the painted rendition of the bat Jonas had constructed for Edward. The bat even had the "E.M." initials his grandfather had carved in its side. The end of bat was streaked with blood. On the left side of the canvas was a hint of Jeremy's jean pant leg and a dark, mud-encrusted work boot. There were splatters of red paint indicating blood on her shirt, his pants, and on the wall of the painting. In the background, more to the right side of the canvas, Helen Roquemore lay still and lifeless; her eyes staring vacantly ahead. Her face was bloody with trails and smears of blood that had come from the massive head wounds Jeremy had dealt to the back and side of her head. It was the exact picture Edward saw in his mind's eye as Jeremy came to the conclusion of his story.

Edward hadn't noticed until now, but during his storytelling, Jeremy had moved to the alcove and was standing behind his desk. He'd also turned off the piano music that had been playing earlier.

Raven began to stir. She whined, sneezed twice, shook her head and slowly sat up. She looked around the room, trying to decipher where she was and why she was here.

Raven was also in the library office along with everyone else. After she'd been stunned into immobility, Miles had picked her up, carried her to a section behind one of the couches, and placed her on the floor so she would be out of the way to what would be happening during the rest of the night.

"So that's why you kept my bat? So you could have a little memento, a little reminder of what you did? Did that make you feel like a man?"

Jeremy only smiled in response to Tyler's questions.

"Why did you do it?" Edward asked. "Why the fuck did you do it?"

Not giving Jeremy time to answer, Edward charged Jeremy. Jeremy had expected a reaction of this magnitude and adjusted quickly. As Edward came for him, Jeremy's hand shot smoothly and confidently into the desk drawer he was now standing behind. He jerked out the gun that was placed there and brought it up into the center of Edward's face, stopping him short of reaching him.

"There's no need to get ugly about this *Edward*, but I'm afraid that's my business and my business only. Now sit down."

Edward stood his ground, weighing his option.

"Are you really that stupid, Tyler? I said sit down. Trust me, you do not want to tangle with me. You did that once before and you see where that got you, don't you?"

Unwavering, Edward continued staring holes through Jeremy. Edward heard the door opening behind him. Osborne must be back with his newly found bloody treasure.

"Osborne," Jeremy said, not giving him time to enter the room before giving more commands.

"Yes, Mr. Taylor."

"Take your gun and blow his dog's head off. My time is too valuable and I will not waste it with these little charades. If he won't do what I want then—"

"No, Jeremy, please," Adrian pleaded. "Not his dog. You can't do that to him."

"Shut up, Adrian. I can do anything I damn well choose. I've been doing it for years and I'm not about to stop now."

With only the hesitation of leaning the retrieved bat against the wall, Osborne stepped toward Raven as he withdrew his gun from beneath his jacket and pointed it at the dog's head.

Raven began to growl and tried to stand, but she was still weak from the electrified effects of the stun gun. She tried to stand again but sank back down to the ground. She barked in protest at the man's advancement on her.

Inside, Tyler realized Jeremy and Osborne weren't bluffing. In a split moment, and in a fit of desperation, Tyler made the motion to move to Raven. Edward allowed Tyler to take back over his body. "Raven. Shhhh!"

Raven whined again and gave a half bark as if to question why she was being shushed.

"Wait. Please don't," Tyler said as he moved away from Jeremy toward Osborne.

Osborne immediately swung his gun toward Tyler to stop him in his tracks. Tyler held his hands up to show he wasn't a threat but continued moving toward Raven. "Please don't kill my dog," he pleaded. He stepped into the small space between Osborne and Raven. Raven backed herself up into a sitting position to make room for Tyler. Tyler knelt so he was between the two, using his body as a shield to protect Raven. Osborne kept his gun trained on Tyler the whole time and now had it pointed directly at Tyler's forehead. Raven's head ducked under Tyler's arm and began to growl at Osborne again. Tyler put his hand on Raven's snout and pushed her back behind him again.

Savannah continued to look on in stunned silence. This whole scenario was so unbelievable.

Tyler continued, "That's all I ask. Please don't kill my dog."

Osborne looked out from behind his gun site and said, "I don't believe it. You would actually take a bullet for that mutt. You can get another one at the pound for free."

"Maybe," Tyler said, "But this dog is irreplaceable. There isn't another one like her."

"Mr. Taylor?" Osborne asked, waiting for his next orders.

Tyler chimed in again, "I'll take my seat. Just don't harm Raven."

Osborne looked at Jeremy for a confirmation. Jeremy shook his head, "Fine. Just remember the next time, there will be no hesitation."

As Osborne holstered his weapon, Jeremy said, "I think we've found our bargaining chip. Osborne, go get some rope for Mr. Curtis. I don't want him running around again."

"Gladly, Mr. Taylor."

Raven barked at Osborne as left the room.

"You better shut that dog up or I'll shoot her myself."

"Raven! Quiet! Lay down!"

Raven obeyed but she was on guard, looking for any behavior that didn't look quite right.

"Good girl."

As Tyler moved to the chair in the center of the room and sat down again, Edward pulled the switch on Tyler and took over his body again. Inside his mind, he whispered to Tyler, *I allowed you to do that. I figured you could work something out with that showdown better than me. Never thought you would sacrifice yourself for your damn dog. That was stupid, but it worked. But don't think for a second that you are more powerful than me because of what just happened. I am in constant control. Remember that.*

Edward looked up at Jeremy again, "Where did you bury her?"

"Who?"

It took Edward a moment but he finally said, "My grandmother. I assume you covered your tracks. Got rid of her body in some way."

"Don't worry about your grandmother. I made sure she had a proper burial."

"Where?" Edward asked emphatically, his voice cracking a little with heartache again.

"I thought about weighing her body down with stones and burying her in Silver Ridge Lake but thought better of it. Too much had already gone down with your death there. I didn't want anything else to hint back to that. I mean really, two bodies found in Silver Ridge Lake. No thank you. No, that would be way too suspicious. Besides, she was a big woman and to get her fat ass all the way down to the boat and row it all the way out there… I would've had to purposely capsize it to get her body to the bottom of the lake. That was way too much work; too much trouble that I didn't want to deal with. I simplified things and buried her in the backyard of her house right in the middle of three dogwood trees."

Three dogwood trees? Edward thought. His mind spun backwards in time. He remembered when he went to his old house and found Raven upstairs in his old room. Once he stepped onto the property, he noticed how everything else around the house was so overgrown but looked drab and lifeless. The only thing that looked alive were the three dogwood trees in full bloom. He remembered thinking how vibrant the dogwood's looked. He also remembered how everything had seemed to grow in the outer vicinity from the three trees.

"Grandmomma." Edward whispered to himself. "The vibrancy of the trees. Was that your way of crying out from beyond the grave to let someone, anyone, know you were buried there. I'm so sorry I didn't realize it was you."

No wonder there was no death date on her headstone, Edward thought. *She was never buried there. I guess most people just assumed that the loving grandparents and their beloved grandson were all buried together in the far back corner of Woodland Hills Cemetery. No wonder Adrian couldn't figure out where she was. She had disappeared. Disappeared into a secret grave of Jeremy's choosing.*

Adrian's voice broke the brief silence. "You buried her in the same place?"

Simultaneously, Jeremy, Edward, and Savannah turned in her direction.

Edward said, "Come again?"

"Her body. Jeremy buried Helen in the exact same location *she* had buried Edward's body. In her backyard?"

"What?" Edward asked, still not believing what he was hearing.

"Yeah. In the triangle space between three dogwood trees?"

"That's what I said, didn't I?" Jeremy said and laughed at the irony of the situation; if that irony was the truth. "You have got to be joking."

"It's no joke, Jeremy. She took me and showed me herself when I went to pay my respects to Edward." She turned to Tyler and continued with her story. "It was after I got out of the hospital. I finally worked up the nerve to go and face her. That was the day she gave me Edward's medallion. I had just thanked her for the gift when she said…

ȣ

"Don't thank me. Thank Edward." Helen said. "You can, you know?"

"No, I don't. How?" Adrian asked.

"You can tell 'em at his grave. I can show you where he's buried. Would you like to do that?"

"Sure, I guess I could."

"It's right this way. Follow me."

"What do you mean?"

Helen flapped her hands as she waddled down the front porch stairs as a jester for Adrian to quit pestering her with detailed questions.

They moved around the house to the backyard.

Adrian was amazed at the difference between the maintenance of the front yard and the back yard. The back yard had been neatly cut. The hedges were trimmed. It was groomed perfectly. There were flowers of all color, shape, size, and type. It was obvious this was where Helen spent most of her time.

"Right over here," she said as she led Adrian over a stony foot path.

They stopped near a grove of dogwood trees that were in full bloom.

"He's right over there," Helen whispered in reverence as she pointed to the space between the three trees.

There wasn't a main headstone of granite with carved words to mark Edward's final resting place. There was only a decent sized, smooth, rounded stone sitting in the midst of the trees. To anyone else who came across this area, it would have just looked like a decorative rock that was placed here to make this outdoor area's Fung Shui complete.

"You can do that?"Adrian asked.

"Do what, dear?"

"I didn't think you could just bury people anywhere."

"I okayed it with the city. I also used some of my own money to have him laid to rest here. They didn't put up too big of a fuss about it. I just wanted my Edward near me so I could take care and watch over him.

"That's very sweet of you. This has to be the most beautiful gravesite I have ever seen.

Helen beamed with pride at Adrian's compliment, "It is beautiful isn't it?"

"Gorgeous. Edward would love it. He would be proud. He's definitely at peace now."

"Yes. Yes, he is."

☙

"We sat there at his grave for a long time just reminiscing about Edward." Adrian said. "She really loved you, Edward. She told me so many stories about you and what you had done for her and Jonas before your passing. She truly missed you. She was very heartbroken. She loved you tremendously."

Edward sat there stunned at her story, unable to speak. He had never really spent too much time wondering about his body and its final resting place. He just assumed and figured it was buried in the plot near his grandparents since it had his birth and death dates.

She wanted me near her so she could watch over me and take care of me. Probably because she couldn't do anything when I was being picked on in school. Edward also mused, *Grandmomma must've had the dates added to my headstone as a precaution so no one would wonder about me like I did about hers.* Edward also thought, *Once I started confronting my old classmates, time got away from me. Maybe it is a good thing I didn't do any other searches for grandmomma. I wouldn't have found any other information about her since Jeremy was the only one who knew her demise.*

It was a bittersweet moment for Edward. He was happy Helen cared so much for him to bury him near her. And after hearing the news, he was also happy that they were buried together. But he was also sad that his body—their bodies—lay buried in an unmarked grave and not with Jonas as he had wanted.

Edward bowed his head and smiled at what Adrian had said. He was satisfied knowing that question that had been nagging him was now answered.

"Well there's one thing about it," Jeremy said, interrupting Edward's thoughts. "Edward and his grandmother were always close. Can't get any closer than that, now can you? Buried in the same damn grave."

"Shut up, Jeremy," Adrian said. "I wish on everything holy and unholy that I had never met you. Why I ever went out with you I'll never know. God, I fucking hate you."

Abruptly changing the subject, Edward said, "You know, Jeremy, there is so much more you don't even know about. More back history you can't even imagine. It all stems from that day at the lake, even before that, actually. And it's all right here staring you dead in the face."

Jeremy had no clue what Tyler was talking about. "Well then why don't you enlighten me on that subject."

Shocked, Adrian turned toward Tyler, "No, please don't."

Without glancing her way, he said, "I have to."

Intrigued, Savannah turned her head to hear more.

"I beg of you, Edward. Don't. Please, I don't want him to know."

"Adrian. Shut up," Jeremy commanded. "Know what?"

"He'll never let us leave here if I don't tell him."

"He'll never let us leave here if you do," Adrian shot back.

Edward shrugged his shoulders. "So what's it going to hurt? Don't you want to see the look on his face when I tell him. Or if you want, you can tell him."

Pointing his gun at Adrian, Jeremy said, "You. Quit talking. I'm asking the questions." He came out from around the desk and stepped down the two stairs toward them. "Tell me what? What are you talking about?"

Edward looked Jeremy square in the eyes, smiling as he said, "She told me *you* raped her."

Adrian shouted, "Tyler, I said no!"

"I had to."

The blood drained from Jeremy's face and he turned ashen. Anger became evident in his features. He slowly turned on Adrian and yelled,

"You lying whore!" Seething with instant rage, he backhanded her across the face.

Adrian tried to move out of the way, but the blow hit its mark. In trying to avoid the blow, she fell out of her chair and collapsed to the floor.

Edward stood and came at Jeremy. Sensing his movement, Jeremy turned and hit Edward in another backhanded motion. The force of the blow sent him sprawling. Edward toppled backward over the chair he was sitting in and crashed to the floor.

Before he could stand, the brawny hands of Miles grabbed him roughly and planted him back in his chair again.

"Aren't you going to sit Adrian up in her chair?" Edward asked.

"No. She can stay there for the time being. On her back. The position she's used to being in."

"Can you at least see if she's all right?"

"I'm not worried about her at the moment."

"Don't worry about me. I'll be fine," Adrian said as she rolled over and leaned against her fallen chair.

"By your reaction, I guess Adrian was telling the truth. I think it's been eating away at you every day since."

"That's a lie."

"No it's not, Jeremy, and you know it. Who're you kidding? Yourself?" Edward changed the subject on him. "Tell me this; you never saw her after that accident at the lake, did you?"

"A few times in the hospital, but not many after that, no."

"She wasn't in town very long after that, right? You have any idea why?"

"No, I don't. Care to enlighten me?"

"Because she was pregnant with your baby."

The news from Tyler rocked Jeremy where he stood. He stood there frozen for a moment or two internalizing the news as quickly as possible trying to figure out if Tyler was yanking his chain or if somehow this was actual truth being spoken.

True or not, the news pissed Jeremy off and all of a sudden his body was moving. He moved quickly to Tyler.

The punch to Tyler's face was instantaneous and came out of nowhere. After the punch was thrown, Jeremy grabbed Tyler's shirt and jerked him out of his chair until they were staring each other directly in the eyes. Jeremy shouted in his face as bits of spit arched from his mouth. "YOU'RE A LIAR! You're nothing but a god damn liar!"

Pain burned the side of Edward's face, and tears welled up in his eyes. He tried to exercise the soreness out of his cheek by rotating and flexing his jaw muscles. Sarcastically, he asked, "May I have another, please?"

Disgusted with Tyler, Jeremy shoved him down and back into his chair and slowly moved away. The chair almost tipped backward, but Edward was able to save himself this time.

Edward turned to the sound of a door opening again. Osborne was back carrying the ropes with which to bind him.

Knowing there was very little time, Edward said in a panic, "You like doing that, don't you? Gives you a sense of power, doesn't it? You used to do that to Adrian. I even remember that day at the lake. You did it to Adrian back then and you did it to me."

Jeremy didn't reach his office desk but stopped in mid-stride and turned back around toward Tyler. "What the hell did you just say?"

"I said you did that to Adrian. And you did it to me."

Jeremy shook his head as he tried to comprehend, "You? You're nothing but a damn teenager, Tyler. You weren't even around back then."

"Oh, I was there. I'm still closer than you think in both senses of the phrase."

Edward didn't understand why Osborne started to tie his feet first, but as Osborne stooped, his jacket billowed open and Edward saw his chance. When Osborne was ordered to shoot Raven he had removed his gun. In his haste to go get the ropes, he had replaced it back in his holster but never took the time to snap it into its holster.

Edward turned to Savannah and whispered, "Do you trust me?"

"I don't know now. I guess."

Jeremy's interest peaked, "Closer than you think? What do you mean?"

"You had raped Adrian a few weeks before. That day at the lake was going to be her last. Her and her family were leaving, but she only wanted one last day with her friends. She never told anybody what you did to her or what she was planning on doing because she was too embarrassed by the situation. But she told me. Not in so many words. But she confided in me enough to hint at what happened."

Edward turned to Savannah again, "Do me a favor. Close your eyes. You don't want to see what is about to happen."

"What are you going to do?"

"Just close your eyes."

"What's wrong with you, Tyler?" Jeremy said. "Are you crazy? There's no way she could tell you, you weren't even born yet?"

"But I was born about eight months later."

Edward let that sentence hang in the air for a long moment. Everybody stopped what they were doing to take in the simple shocking phrase. Edward relished the look on Jeremy's face. Even Osborne stopped wrapping Tyler's feet. He looked up at Tyler, then he glanced around to see Jeremy's reaction. That's when Edward struck.

In one smooth stroke, Edward's hand shot down inside Osborne's jacket and snatched the gun from its holster. Stunned by the sudden movement, Osborne turned back, stood, and stepped back in self defense. This movement gave Edward more room to maneuver and he used it to his advantage. He immediately rotated the barrel so it caught Osborne firmly under the chin. Edward didn't hesitate and pulled the trigger two times in quick succession; one to deliver the killing blow and another one for good measure.

The bullets ripped through and removed Osborne's skull from the top of his head. Sickening blobs of blood and brain matter spattered the ceiling. As Osborne was falling backward, a mist of brain and blood rain cascaded around them. Edward closed his eyes as the particles fell on and around him as well. Osborne was dead even before the bullets had exited the top his head.

Savannah and Adrian both screamed and turned away from the execution. Adrian rolled away to the two steps and crawled up them to the far wall. Savannah did the same but dove out of her chair and moved up the two stairs on her side of the room to a space between the bookshelves. It was equally hard for both because of their bound hands and legs.

I guess she didn't close her eyes after all, Edward thought.

Edward immediately turned toward Miles and pulled the trigger three times in quick succession. Three blood carnations bloomed on Miles's chest; one even looked like it budded out of his breast pocket. Miles looked down quizzically as though he had never seen that type of flower before, at least not on himself. He rocked back and forth in his shoes before he finally fell backward against the doors and slumped to the floor. Blood smears from the exit wounds painted three diagonal stripes down the doors.

Raven was standing now and was barking again.

Edward shouted at her. "Raven! Hush!" She stopped and lowered her head. She sensed it was someone else.

Whipping his aim back around, Edward found that Jeremy already had his gun trained on him again. He had never actually put it down.

"Well wasn't that just fucking amusing," Jeremy said. "You leveled them pretty quickly."

"Put the gun down." Edward said evenly.

Jeremy swung the gun over and aimed it at Adrian huddled against the wall. "No. You put *your* gun down."

With their guns trained on each other, Edward stepped in front of Adrian to accept her bullet if Jeremy decided to fire. He continued the conversation where he left off, "That's right. Tyler wasn't even born yet, but she was pregnant with him the day you killed me." With a blood-spattered face and through a mischievous grin, Edward said, "I'm speaking on Tyler's behalf now and he would like me to say, "Hi, Dad. It's a small world, isn't it?"

Jeremy's mouth went punk dry. He didn't know how to process this information. His voice was constricted in his throat; he couldn't speak. He needed a drink of whiskey really bad.

"That's right, Daddy," Edward said sarcastically. "Whether you want to believe it or not, you have a son and that child is me. I mean, Tyler here. Or Gabriel, if you want to go with the name Adrian gave to him when he was born."

Jeremy's mouth was ajar and his mind tried to link the information together. He tried to speak, but no words were there for him to voice.

"This is great, isn't it; the whole family together at last." With his gun, Edward motioned to each person for emphasis, "Mom, Dad, and me; just one big happy family." Edward's smile faded in mock-concern. "Aren't you going to say anything, Dad? Something like, 'You look great kid.' or, 'I'm proud of you, Son.' or maybe even a, 'I am so glad to finally meet you.'"

Jeremy grew paler with each word. "It can't be. That's impossible."

"Nothing's impossible, Jeremy. I'm living proof of that."

"You're not my son," he said defiantly.

"Dad, you hurt me when you say things like that. Don't be like this; you disappoint me," he said in a sarcastic tone.

The dad reference was grating on Jeremy's nerves. In sudden anger, he yelled, "And you're not Edward! I killed that little shit close to twenty years ago!"

Edward was getting angry now. "So you admit it?"

"Yes, I admit it. I told Travis that I hated that son of a bitch. I didn't care if the little shit lived or died. Whether *you* lived or died. Once Adrian was inside the boat, I made one last dive. When I found you, I just watched you struggle until my air was about to give out. Then I shot to the surface. I immediately started the motor and left. Serves you right. You got what you deserved. I was glad you drowned."

"You should've waited a little longer down there. You might've seen something amazing."

"Like what?"

"You never really got rid of me. You killed my body, but you never killed my spirit."

"How is that possible?"

Edward grabbed hold of the leather strand with one hand and pulled the medallion from underneath his shirt.

"Because of this. Remember this?"

Jeremy slowly nodded, "Barely, but yes. I remember."

"It's all because of this little charm. Don't ask me how it works, because I don't know. But the day of the accident, I made a wish with every fiber of my being. I don't even remember what I said or how I worded it. I just had faith and believed. Just think about it. It's truly amazing."

Jeremy nodded in agreement. The way everything had happened was astounding.

"Is your arm getting tired?" Edward asked. "Mine is. Can we take a break from this John Woo macho bullshit?"

Tentatively and simultaneously, they lowered their guns.

As the guns lowered, recognition caught Edward's eye and remembrance flashed in his mind. Something about the gun Jeremy was holding was familiar. Edward recognized it even at this distance. Edward didn't know what triggered the recognition, but he knew it instantly.

"Where did you get that?"

"What?"

"That gun?"

Jeremy was truly baffled. "From my desk drawer. You saw me pull it from there. Why? What does it matter to you where I got it?"

"No, I mean, where did you get *that* particular gun. That's *my* gun."

"No it's not."

"Yes it is. I mean, it was my grandfather's. I stole it from his bureau the day he passed away. Where did you get it?"

"To be quite honest, after your body was recovered and everybody had taken off from the lake, I went back down there to sort of be by myself. I walked around to think things out and clear my head. I needed to figure out what to do. And guess what I found? Your backpack. It's a good thing I did because of what I found inside. All these years, I've always wondered—why were you carrying this gun inside your backpack?"

There was a dead silence as Jeremy waited.

Adrian broke the silence. "You're the one who found my camera? You told me someone had found it and turned it in anonymously. You lied to me."

"No, I didn't lie to you. I said *anonymously* which means they didn't want to be known. That was me."

"You lied to me."

"Wouldn't be the first time, babe. Just covering my tracks like I always do. I asked you a question, Tyler; I mean, Edward, or whoever the fuck you are. Why were you carrying this gun inside your backpack?"

Edward glanced over at Adrian.

Jeremy continued, "I don't think Adrian knows the answer to my question, so you're not going to get any help from her."

"Go ahead, Edward. Tell him," Adrian said. "Whatever the reason was, tell him. It's okay."

Edward turned back to Jeremy and stared him dead in the eyes. "I was planning on shooting everyone at the lake that day." He quickly glanced back to Adrian and corrected himself. "Everyone, that is, except you. The only reason I didn't is because I didn't want to do it in front of you. I cared too much for you to make you a witness to some mass shooting and I didn't want you to think badly of me. I actually turned the gun on myself thinking I would off myself, but I didn't even have the courage to do that. Anyway, that is the only reason they were alive until recently; it's all because of you."

"Awww, that's touching," Jeremy said breaking in. "That is so beautiful. Edward was in love."

"I wouldn't call it that," Edward snapped. "I just cared and respected her a hell of a lot more than you ever did. If you want to call it love, then yes, I guess I'm guilty even though it wasn't reciprocated in the same way."

Edward paused to gather his thoughts. He never actually thought this was going to be a night where he was the one confessing.

Edward continued, "She wasn't hitting on me that day. And I wasn't hitting on her. She needed someone to spill her guts to and not feel like she was being judged. I was willing to just be there for her, if nothing else. But yet you let me die because I was just talking with your girlfriend. That's sad, Jeremy. That's really sad. No wonder you're all alone today."

Jeremy shrugged, "Yeah, well, shit happens."

"It's unforgivable is what it is," Edward said as he raised his gun again. "I've waited close to twenty years for this moment. And I'm going to relish every minute of this. Hey, Adrian?" Edward turned to her. "Remember what you said when we met recently. About if Edward ever met up with Jeremy again. Remember what you said?"

"Yeah. I said, 'I wish I could have a front row seat if that ever happened.'"

"What?" Jeremy asked.

Edward replied, "Fate has a funny way of making our wishes coming true, doesn't it?"

"Yes, it does," Adrian said, but it came out more or less to herself.

A voice inside Edward's head resounded from the depths of his mind. "That's enough, Edward."

Ignoring Tyler's voice, he turned back to Jeremy and continued, "I've thought of so many ways to get revenge on you. I just can't believe it's me inside your unknown son that's going to be the one pulling the trigger." Edward was ecstatic and laughed aloud. "Me. Edward McDaniel. I'm the one true person that hates you more than anyone else in the world. And Tyler Curtis, wonder how he feels about his real-life dad?"

Jeremy cocked the hammer back on Edward's grandfather's gun and said, "I don't have a son."

Raven's ears pricked at the sound of the hammer being cocked. She didn't like that sound or the look on the man's face who was holding the thing that made the click. She tilted her head toward Jeremy in keen observation.

Jeremy lowered the gun slightly, directing it at Tyler's heart. "There's no proof that you are mine. So if you don't exist to me, you don't exist at all."

Reading Jeremy's intentions perfectly, Raven charged.

The gun bucked in Jeremy's hand and the sound of the discharge exploded in the room. Tyler didn't have time to even close his eyes. If he had, he would've never seen Raven jump in front of his body, taking the bullet that would've surely ended Tyler's life.

Everything happened so fast and startled everyone. Because of the shock of the situation, Edward was thrown off enough for Tyler to repossess his body.

"RAVEN!" Tyler screamed.

Forgetting about Jeremy and his gun, Tyler ran to where Raven had landed. He was already sobbing as he fell on the floor beside her. Raven was trying to stand; one of her legs was pawing the air. She began to whine. Tyler took her into his arms and held her close. Raven licked Tyler's cheek and mulled.

"NO!" Tyler screamed.

Edward saw red, turned and brought the gun up and leveled it on Jeremy. It was like looking in a mirror. Jeremy was already doing the exact same thing. They were back in a stand-off again.

They stood there, transfixed staring at each other. Tyler wanted to kill Jeremy just as much as Edward.

"You can't do it can you, Tyler?" Jeremy stated. "Or Edward? Or whoever the fuck you are."

"No, I can do it. You bet your ass I can do it."

"Then do it. What are you waiting on?" He held his arms apart as though offering himself to Edward.

Tyler's voice rose up from the back of his own mind. It was more authoritative, *I can't let you do this, Edward. It's gone on long enough.*

What are you talking about, Tyler? He just shot Raven. You're not going to let him get away with that, are you?

He was shooting you, not Raven. Raven saved my life.

No, he was shooting you.

Because you are in me. That's the major problem with this situation. You're in me. Get the hell out of my body, Edward.

Laughing, Edward directed his next few comments to Jeremy. "You see Tyler here?" He pointed the gun at himself. "Tyler was adopted but had never been told that little tidbit of information until he met Adrian. Tyler's parents just went along pretending it was alright to lie to their son. In my opinion, I think that's betrayal of the worst kind. That's almost as unforgivable as what you did to me, and now it's time to own up to your mistake."

"I've already owned up to it, Edward. I admit it. Confessed to it. I have nothing to hide."

"What? Are you just going to sit there and let me blow your head off? Are you not going to fight at all for your piece-of-shit life? You're going to make it that easy for me?"

The gun was aimed straight for the center of Jeremy's face.

All of a sudden, the gun began lowering below its target line.

From Jeremy's point of view, he saw Tyler's brow crease in confusion.

Edward didn't understand what was happening and he started to panic. He was losing control of his right arm.

Jeremy was afraid of being shot anywhere on his body and wasn't ready to die. He took a quick step out of the gun's path.

Finally understanding what was happening, Edward concentrated his mind and strength and countered Tyler's move. He re-trained the gun back on Jeremy.

Edward started to laugh out loud, "I don't believe it, this is something I never thought I would see or experience."

Noticing the gun was aimed on him again, Jeremy held his hands up in defense. "What?" he asked quickly.

"Tyler is trying to take back over his body. I think he might be trying to save your pitiful excuse of a life. That's very heroic, but what I thought he knew by now is that I'm stronger than him. I have been ever since I killed everybody else that treated me like shit."

Again, Jeremy moved out of the vicinity of where the gun was aimed. Eventually the gun swung back into the line of sight. Then before Jeremy could move away again, the gun was forced away from his face again.

Jeremy didn't know what to do, so he just stooped behind his desk as Tyler fought with the force within himself.

The fingers around the trigger and handle were frozen in a death grip. Edward tried to force Tyler's finger to pull the trigger, but he couldn't tighten or loosen it.

Jeremy closed his eyes and turned his head away from the expected boom. He thought that within the battle for his life, Tyler would fire off a few blind shots.

Jeremy cautiously peered above the desk. He was truly baffled by Tyler's peculiar reactions. Tyler's head was twitching as he fought back whatever raging insanity was awaking inside.

Tyler's voice boomed out in the room. "EDWARD! This whole charade is over and done with! LET IT GO!"

A different voice, Edward's voice, yelled back, answering Tyler's, "I CAN'T! I'VE COME TOO FAR TO LET IT GO!"

Edward swung his other arm over to give support to the one holding the gun. He pulled the gun back in line with Jeremy's face.

Jeremy ducked back down farther behind the desk again.

"STAND THE FUCK UP JEREMY! TAKE IT LIKE A MAN!" Edward exclaimed.

Jeremy shouted from behind the desk, "You're insane!"

"I'm not insane."

"Yes you are," Jeremy replied.

Tyler agreed and said, "He's right, Edward, you are. Revenge on Jeremy is the only thing that is driving you now."

"Shut up, Tyler," Edward hissed. "Stay out of this."

"No, I've been a part of this since you made me your little slave. I can't and I won't stand by and watch you kill another person...especially my biological father."

"Even after everything he's done?"

"This is all about you and your feelings. What *they've* done to you. How *you've* been wronged. I'm sick of hearing about it. I don't care what he's done. I don't even care about you anymore. I never have. I just want my life back. I'm not going to let you drag me through this hell anymore."

"What are you going to do to stop me?"

"I'm not going to *tell* you. I'm going to *show* you."

There was a moment before anything happened; then Tyler's eyelids slowly began to close. Edward wasn't sleepy in the least; his whole body was on an adrenaline-pumped high.

"What the hell?" Edward muttered.

Tyler softly whispered, "You can't shoot what you can't see."

Edward strained to keep his eyelids open. He tilted his head back for a better angle from which to see his target, but all he could see was darkness. He jerked his free hand toward his face and tried and pry one of the eyelids open long enough to see and get a shot off, but Tyler had rotated the gun away. Blinded, Edward wheeled in circles swinging in frustration and hitting nothing.

That's it, Tyler thought. *I have been going about this all wrong. Of course, Edward was always more powerful than me because I was trying to take back over my whole body. That was too much for me to do. But I can deal it out in smaller doses…just like throwing the vase at Kelly Sheridan. I stopped him long enough to almost save her. If I had continued with the smaller maneuvers maybe there would've been a different outcome already. I can definitely control the mere movement of my arm or the flutter of an eyelid or two.*

Edward screamed inside Tyler's head as the battle of good and evil raged within his worn out body. Edward's hatred for Jeremy was so fierce and vehement that if he had the power to will spontaneous combustion he would have made every cell and particle in Jeremy's body explode and splatter his gore from the ceiling to the floor and into every corner of this room.

Then without warning, Edward stopped and in a calm, pleading voice asked, "Just do this one last thing for me, Tyler, and that's all I'll ask. Please, pull the trigger one time. One time for me and it will all be over."

"NO!" Tyler shouted. "I WON'T! I can't do this anymore! IT'S OVER, EDWARD!"

Jeremy slowly stood from behind his desk with his mouth open again. He couldn't believe what he was witnessing. Tyler's face contorted into a grimacing mask when it spoke. Then the face muscles grew slack when the next sentences were spoken. Each time Tyler or Edward spoke, a new facial expression would dominate his features. Something was definitely trying to get out of his body or worse: stay inside. He was watching a truly classic case of colliding split personalities.

Tyler's face transposed into an evil grimace. "You were always a coward," Edward snapped. "I have to do everything for you. You never had balls until I came along. Where would you be if it weren't for me? Huh?" There was a pause. "ANSWER ME, DAMMIT!" Rage had filled and tinted his face red. "Where would you be?"

Tyler's face relaxed and he said humbly, "I would be in a hell of a lot better situation than I am now that's for sure. And furthermore, I wish I had never found Adrian's charm that had you inside it. You've ruined my life and you should burn in hell for it. Matter-of-fact, I hope and wish you would!"

"So you feel that way," Edward snapped again. "Okay. Alright. If you don't have the backbone to do it then I'll get somebody who will."

In that instance and without thinking, Edward's spirit uncoiled like a serpent from around the base of Tyler's brain. His connection to the major sensory areas unraveled and released. The puppeteer strings on Tyler's mind and body were severed, and Tyler slowly dropped to the floor as though exhausted. Thinking only about revenge, Edward discarded his temporary flesh and blood cocoon. In doing so, he left Tyler with all his common sense and knowledge that he had learned over the years.

As Edward tore himself loose, Tyler grimaced in pain and his body and face contorted as the specter emerged. An agonizing yell accompanied the transformation then grew silent again as he writhed on the floor.

Jeremy didn't know how it was possible, but he was able to see the metamorphosis. He actually saw the spirit form of Edward McDaniel pull itself from Tyler's body. Whether it was the power of the charm or something else, he watched in utter horror, as Edward shed the husk of Tyler's body.

Edward sneered at Tyler who lay in a discarded, exhausted heap. Jeremy heard Edward say with a sneer, "Excess baggage."

Standing beside Tyler, Edward looked over at Jeremy who was still cowering behind the desk but staring back at him in wide-eyed disbelief.

Jeremy saw the spirit of Edward. He looked like the same innocent little boy that he beat up on the pier close to twenty years ago. He stood there barefooted in his blue shorts and light orange tank top with his hair all askew. The only thing with this Edward was that Jeremy could see through him.

Edward smirked first, grinned with his lopsided smile, then said, "Bet you never thought you would see me again, right Jeremy?"

The smile was evil, and it sent chills skittering underneath Jeremy's flesh. It felt like tiny bugs crawling over his body and he involuntarily scratched to get rid of them.

Tyler rolled over on his side, facing up. He saw the wraith of Edward looking around the room. Tyler knew what he was looking for. Edward was seeking a new host.

Edward looked at Jeremy again. The thought of slipping through

Jeremy's openings and pores to take control of him made him laugh. He chuckled to himself; how much fun it would be to make Jeremy stick my grandfather's gun to the side of his head or shove it deep into his mouth and make him pull the trigger. Better yet, he could make Jeremy hold it out in front of his face; that way when he pulled the trigger he could see the bullet a split second before it tore the back of his skull away. No, he didn't want to make Jeremy commit suicide. He wanted to kill Jeremy himself. He wanted to watch it happen and feel the satisfaction of a job well done.

He looked down at Osborne and saw the sad remains of his body. Edward shook his head in disgust. Blood and brains had spilled out onto the floor. There was no use possessing the dead, they were useless to him.

Edward looked over at Miles who looked like a fat Hawaiian Cabbage Patch doll. He didn't even give him a second thought but turned and looked in Adrian's direction instead.

Adrian sat unmoving against the wall staring at Edward. He considered her for a long moment then thought better of it. That wouldn't work; not the best match up. It might be therapeutic for Adrian if he did use her body, but Jeremy might be able to overpower her too easily. He had done it before when he had raped her. If he did possess her, she would be able to get the revenge for the rape he'd committed against her, but right now that was too much of a gambling chance. If she had played it right, she could've gotten even years ago.

Hell, I would've even been glad to assist her with that back then if I had known. Edward thought. *I would've killed for her. All she had to do was ask.*

Edward glanced over at Savannah's horrified face. She looked as thought she'd just seen a ghost. Edward was considering her as a host when Raven whined again and tried to sit up.

The ghost of Edward turned toward Raven then back at Jeremy with a crooked grin on his face.

"Oh, this is just too perfect," Edward said.

Jeremy couldn't see Raven because the couch was in his line of sight, but he knew what Edward was looking at. He now understood what Edward was about to do.

Edward disappeared behind the couch and descended on Raven with an intense killing compulsion. He slammed into the dog's body. Edward surged through Raven's ears, nose, mouth and penetrated through every pore, possessing her body completely. Edward joined the rest of his spirit that he had transferred into Raven to keep her loyal the day Tyler came home from the hospital. As he joined up once again with his other portion he took control of Raven's mind as he had done with Tyler's.

For a long moment, Raven lay motionless except for her shallow breathing. Then Raven suddenly jerked into a standing position. She shook her head wildly from side to side, trying to shake the insane fever that had seized her body. Then as if giving up under the pursuing force, she stopped and stood still. Her ears were pricked in attention and trained on every sound in the room.

When Raven looked up, she locked eyes with Tyler who was still lying on his side across the room. Tyler stared in shock as he took a double take on his dog. He could've sworn Raven had just grinned at him. But it wasn't the typical amused, quizzical Raven grin. This one was sinister. Pure evil.

That's the moment that Raven changed in front of Tyler. He witnessed the change and saw that she was no longer man's best friend. She had been transformed into a demon hound from the pit of Hell. Her sleek glossy coat was now erect and ruffled. The muscles in her body quivered, and she tensed with the anticipation of a kill. Her feet were spread wide as she crouched in expectation for the attack; her head was set low to the ground. A low, deep-throated growl rumbled inside her body. Raven's lips curled back in a wicked snarl, exposing her razor sharp, white teeth. Long, clear strands of saliva dripped to the floor.

Raven staggered forward on unsteady feet. Tyler thought she was coming after him, but Raven turned without giving him a second glance. As she came around the far end of the couch to the center of the room, her head lurched to the side. Like two yellow, sulfurous embers of coal fire, her eyes blazed with a burning hatred that were now trained on Jeremy.

Jeremy slowly backed up from behind the desk nonchalantly,

gripping the pistol as he went. He held the gun on the back of his leg so it couldn't be seen.

"No!" Jeremy whispered through gritted teeth. "Easy, doggy. Let's not do anything rash, alright. It's ok." Jeremy spoke in a hushed tone, trying to find the right words and pitch combination to calm the beast down. "Tyler. Do something for God's sake, control your dog. Tyler! Son? Tyler?"

"Don't call me, *son*." Tyler said. "You have no right."

He was back to his old self. It felt good to speak his mind without anyone else trying to do it for him.

Tyler calmly sat up, trying not to startle Raven. He knew there wasn't anything he could do at this point. Edward couldn't be talked down no matter how hard he tried. Edward was going to go through with this until he had his justice. But he couldn't just sit there and let him kill Jeremy, he had to do something.

He noticed he was still gripping the gun in his right hand. He held the gun up and aimed it at Raven. The thought came and went. *No, I can't shoot my dog. I won't shoot my dog.*

Savannah realized it first. She saw what he was contemplating. She caught Tyler's attention by slowly shifting her body between the bookshelves.

Tyler turned to her, braking the daze he seemed to be in. He mouthed the word, *What?*

Pointing to an area high on her chest with her bound hands, she mouthed the words, *The charm.*

His brow furrowed and his shoulders shrugged, telling her he didn't know what she was talking about.

Savannah tried again. With hand motions and mouthing the words more emphatically she whispered, "The charm. Around your neck. Destroy it. Shoot it or something."

Then he realized what his left hand was doing. He looked down and saw that he was subconsciously stroking that medallion hanging around his neck. That damn habit he had started ever since he got the charm.

The charm. That's when it hit him. *That's what is holding Edward's spirit in this realm.* He never had a chance to destroy it when Edward was inside him because of his control, but now he could. He gradually slid it from around his neck.

Trying to scare Raven, Jeremy yelled, "STAY AWAY FROM ME YOU SON OF A BITCH!" Terror had engulfed his voice.

Without warning, Raven sprang from her coiled roost and charged Jeremy.

Tyler and Jeremy both froze.

Lightning-quick Raven bounded across the floor. She hurdled Osborne's body and surged forward. Raven mounted the desk, sprang from its surface and soared through the air like a mountain lion attacking its prey.

Jeremy barely had time to raise his gun and get a shot off. Amazingly, he quickly jerked the trigger two times. The shots weren't calibrated but aimed in the general vicinity of the charging demon. Both bullets tore separate wounds into Raven's body because of the short distance she had put between them. Jeremy merely had to point and shoot.

Raven shuddered under the force of the blows but didn't cry out. Like an arrow from Robin Hood's bow, Raven wasn't diverted from her target; she was on a mission of pure hatred.

Jeremy's eyes widened as the hellhound leapt up and streaked across the desk: mouth open, saliva dripping from exposed teeth, eyes blazing with revulsion. Jeremy saw the open maw of sharp teeth before they dropped below his line of sight and clamped deep around his throat.

"NOOOOOOO—"

In that instance, Jeremy's subconscious pulled a forgotten memory—seeming to come out of nowhere—to the forefront of his mind. He was on a pier kneeling in front of a young boy who simply promised him, "One day, I am going to fucking kill you in the worst possible way."

Jeremy's memory and scream was cut short as Raven hit Jeremy square in the chest. The force of the attack caused him to slam backward against the huge window that framed his desk. The window cracked from the weight of Jeremy's upper body but didn't shatter and fall. He threw himself away from the window, landing awkwardly out to the side of the desk. If Jeremy said anything, it was lost in the snarls and the fury of the attack. Jeremy left this world twitching in spasms of agony.

"Edward!" Tyler yelled, trying to get Raven's attention.

Edward was so in tune and focused with getting his revenge on Jeremy that the mention of his name was unnoticed.

Tyler yelled again, "EDWARD!"

Raven—her jaws still clamped around Jeremy's throat—whipped her head up, pulling Jeremy along with her. Tyler stared in disbelief. Jeremy's throat—still locked in Raven's jaws—was barely attached to his torso. Raven had nearly decapitated Jeremy at the neck.

"EDWARD! THAT'S ENOUGH!"

Reluctantly, Raven unclamped her death bite from around Jeremy's neck. Jeremy's upper body dropped back into a puddle of blood with a sickening splat.

Raven looked over at Tyler. The fur on her body shook involuntarily as muscle spasms twitched beneath her coat. She licked her muzzle to clean the last few drops of sprayed blood away.

"IT'S OVER!"

A twinge of dread stabbed Tyler's body when Raven mechanically shook her head in disagreement. She seemed to be saying, "Oh no, we've just begun." Then Raven glanced back down at Jeremy's body and began to sniff his corpse.

A halo of crimson had encircled Jeremy's head and was slowly continuing to spread from his open, exposed throat. One of Jeremy's arms was splayed out to the side, the gun inches from his curled grasp.

Tyler realized what Raven was about to do and yelled at her to stop.

Sinking her muzzle down into the still gushing wound, Raven clamped her jaws around Jeremy's spinal column one last time. As she raised her head, Jeremy's body sat up in a forty-five degree sitting position. Raven stared directly at Tyler to prove her point. Then biting down as hard as she could, Raven bit through Jeremy's spinal column, causing his body to drop back into the still widening blood circle. Jeremy's head dropped and rolled a few feet from his body, facing toward Tyler.

"EDWARD!" Tyler yelled again.

Raven was sniffing the body but raised her head and focused on Tyler. Drops of blood flipped from the end of her tongue as she licked her chops.

Tyler held the medallion up in front of his face.

Raven turned more toward Tyler and angled her head with interest.

Then Tyler raised the gun still clutched in his other hand and held it flush with the medallion's surface.

Raven lowered her head again and her eyes narrowed into menacing slits as if to convey Edward's inner dialogue. *Don't you fucking dare.*

"How fast are you, Edward? You think you have enough time to stop me before I blow this piece-of-shit charm to kingdom come?"

Raven took another step, but Edward shifted her feet to counter balance her weight. Blood was dripping out of one bullet wound in her chest like a leaky faucet; it poured out like expensive Merlot from the other.

Jeremy's bullets must've severed an artery, Tyler thought.

Tyler was nervous, shaky; he couldn't hold the gun or the amulet steady. The charm kept sliding down the side of the gun's barrel but he quickly readjusted.

Still holding the talisman by its leather chord, Tyler moved the pistol to the floor long enough to push himself back with his hand until he was leaning against one of the many bookshelves in the room.

Raven made another awkward advancement toward Tyler.

Using the shelving for leverage, Tyler stopped her in her tracks by placing the gun's muzzle against its surface again.

All of a sudden, Raven's demeanor changed and the fierceness went out of her eyes. She was herself again. She whined and turned in two circles and almost lay down but then just as quickly, her demeanor changed again. Her body was immediately charged with hate-filled adrenaline. Her hackles rose again, she lowered her head to get ready to charge Edward.

"She's fighting it, the way I fought it." *Come on girl, you can do it. Fight,* he thought.

Raven took a tentative step toward Tyler as though to test her balance and to stop Tyler from destroying the charm.

"Don't tempt me, Edward; I'll do it. I swear to God I will."

Raven's demeanor changed again and she took a step back. She shook her head violently from side to side, trying to shake the madness from her senses. She whined again.

Tyler had an idea. He started wrapping the leather strap around the barrel so it would hang over the gun sight in line with the bullet's chamber; that way if he had to shoot the gun the bullet would be sure to hit its target.

Better to be safe than sorry, he thought.

Edward knew it wouldn't be long before Raven was useless to him. She was losing a lot of blood, and he could feel her getting weaker by the second.

Edward thought, *If this is it for me and I'm going to die for good this time, I'm going to take one last person with me. Tyler shouldn't have betrayed me like that. All he had to do was pull the fucking trigger one last time.*

With all the remaining strength Edward could harvest, he forced Raven into attack mode again. He charged without reservation, focusing in on one last target.

This is going to be too easy, Edward thought.

Tyler was in the process of wrapping the straps around the barrel of the gun when Raven launched herself, and there was no time to finish.

"Tyler!" Savannah screamed.

Tyler looked up and saw Raven in mid-charge.

For a creature that was quickly wasting away, Raven closed the distance quicker than expected and with a fury of snarls.

Tyler witnessed the exact same evil Jeremy saw in the few seconds of his life—a diabolical Wendigo; half-animal, half-spirit—that was thirsty for more blood and another soul.

Tyler clenched the medallion's straps, steadied the barrel against the surface again, and calmly squeezed the trigger.

The gun's discharge was deafening even in the expanse of the library. The bullet hit its mark. With all the oddness that had happened since his accident, Tyler half-expected a huge energy release, a power surge, or a bright discharge of light to explode out of the charm, but nothing happened. The medallion didn't explode into an oblivion of fine dust either, but it did shatter into individual pieces that spun away into different areas of the room.

Raven descended on Tyler in a rage of gnashing teeth and hate-filled eyes. Tyler had just enough time to throw his arms up in defense to help brace against the oncoming collision.

Tyler couldn't look away either and saw the effect of the destructed talisman.

Edward's hold over Raven was abruptly severed. It seemed like invisible strands had reached into Raven's body, attached themselves to Edward's soul, and ripped him from Raven's body as Raven continued on her downward attacking arc toward Tyler.

Raven slammed hard into Tyler's chest. The death bite didn't come, but the impact knocked him back hard against the shelving. His head slammed violently against the bookshelf. Raven dropped like a stone by Tyler's side with a loud thud. She lay still and quietly with her head in his lap.

Edward's spirit was left hovering in mid air. Tyler could see right through Edward like he was a holographic computer image. Edward's hands were outstretched beseeching Tyler not to pull the trigger; but his plea was too late and in vain.

The deepest silence Tyler had ever experienced finally settled over the room.

There was no bright light that shown down through the ceiling to help guide Edward's soul into the afterlife. Tyler doubted he would be going in that direction anyway. For that matter, the floor didn't crack apart and crumble causing him to be sucked beneath the carpeted surface.

Edward looked down at Tyler who was still leaning against the bookshelf.

If looks could kill, Tyler thought, *I would already be dead a thousand times over.*

Edward asked, "Why the fuck did you do that?"

Tyler looked up and saw Edward's spirit. He didn't answer, but the silence was broken by what Tyler thought was the sound of wind blowing under the front porch eaves. It wasn't loud like the cry of a lone wolf howling at the moon; it was more like the rustle of wind gently blowing fallen leaves over a rustic landscape.

Tyler noticed it first. His ears pricked and he turned in the direction he thought the sound might be coming from.

Adrian and Savannah finally noticed it and began searching the room for the source.

Still staring in contempt, Edward noticed Tyler's curiosity and became aware of the noise. "What's that?" he asked nervously.

"Shhhhh!" Tyler said. "I don't know," but he couldn't help but let his mind wonder. Even though the talisman was in pieces on the floor, Tyler half-expected something else to happen. He had the feeling this was only the beginning and that something bigger was approaching or being summoned.

Everyone looked around the room to see if they could find out where the breeze and the source of the sound were coming from.

"What did you do?" Edward asked.

As if to answer Edward's question, the wind gradually grew into a low moan. Puzzled, they searched the room again and soon realized the sounds were not one and the same. Each was coming from a different origin.

"Oh. My. God," Savannah said in a hushed whisper.

Tyler finally saw the source of the moaning and wished to be a thousand miles away.

Edward saw Tyler stiffen at the sight behind him. He turned to see what Tyler was looking at and then wished to God he hadn't.

CHAPTER 47

EDWARD INSTANTLY BECAME a petrified mass as he saw what emerged from thin air.

Savannah and Adrian both screamed as a lurching figure came out of an invisible gateway. The half-crawling, jittering specter moved as though not all of its marionette strings were attached. Its legs and arms were twisted and broken, bent in places where joints should've been. Its head was wrenched abnormally to one side, peering at everything in a sideways tilt. A gleam of light reflected off the piece of silver that protruded from the figure's chest.

No. No, not the scissors, Edward thought. *It can't be her.*

Its eyes were a brilliant aqua-gray. At the time of her death, Edward had leaned over and peered deeply into a pair of eyes of exactly that same color. Now, Kelly Sheridan was staring back at Edward with the same electrified intensity.

Burning hatred, Tyler thought.

Tyler felt as though he were gazing into the mythological serpent-haired visage of Medusa.

The hunched figure whispered his name in a long mournful dirge. "Eeeeeedwwwwaaarrd."

She began groping for him.

"GET THE HELL AWAY FROM ME!" he yelled as he slowly backed away.

Shortly after Kelly had birthed herself into this realm, her husband's soul appeared behind her. Travis Sheridan walked abnormally with a hobble-shuffle step. He only had one good leg. The other leg, barely usable—almost limp around the kneecap—was only used to shift himself forward and to help him keep his balance. The shoulder area where the baseball bat had broken his collar bone was useless. That arm just hung limply and farther down on the left side of his body, causing him to lurch even more. The worst part about Travis was his face. He was hideously bruised and discolored. The top left side of his head was caved in tremendously from one of the blows the baseball bat had dealt him. His left eye, his nose, and top part of his mouth had almost disappeared by folding in on itself. The only part of his face that seemed normal was his right eye but it was enflamed by a red, starburst hemorrhage. The eye jittered back and forth nervously as though he was having a hard time focusing on what he was staring at; Edward being the current target of choice.

Still starring in contempt, Travis murmured with only the lower part of his mouth, "Eeeedwwwaard. Did you think—you could get—rid—of me—that easily?"

Edward said nothing. He was too scared to speak.

Savannah and Adrian exchanged glances then looked at Tyler. Tyler was staring in rapt attention unsure of what to do—so he did nothing.

Kelly stumbled on wavering legs. Travis stooped, grabbed his wife's arm, and helped support her.

Still together even in death, Tyler thought.

Another voice groaned undecipherable words from beyond the grave, but Tyler thought it too was calling Edward's name. Accompanying the words, appeared a leering face hovering a foot off the ground. A thin veneer of burnt and blistered skin tightly covered the face. If this face could've been mass-produced, it would've been the best Halloween mask to date; all the teens would be buying it for years to come. The face, combined with the accompanying figure sliding from the beyond was a terrifying sight. The further Suzanne Baldwin slid into this realm, the worse her body looked. A claw-fingered hand reached out and seized a handful of carpet and slowly pulled herself into this world.

Tyler couldn't fathom how Suzanne was managing movement. All her muscles seemed to be charred into immobility. The skin overlaying her muscles was burnt into paper-thin parchment. In some places, the intense fire had burnt completely through, leaving holes where blackened bone showed through.

No wonder we couldn't understand what she was saying, Tyler thought. *Her tongue was completely burnt away in the fire.*

Tyler stared in awe as the spectacle unfolded before him. Each soul was coming from the same space, but they were emerging out of nothing. Basically out of thin air. He could still see the far wall and the furniture that occupied that side of the room. Each half of Suzanne's body was caught on different sides of the portal; like the magician's trick of sawing a woman in half gone hideously wrong but without all the blood and gore.

Before Suzanne's scorched body finished emerging, Bruce Saliers staggered over from the land of the dead. He was pallid with a bullet hole above his right eye. A line of blood had drained from the wound in his forehead, dropped to his cheek, and had spread into a small dark stain on his shirt. It looked as though he had been crying bloody tears from his right eye.

When Bruce turned around and reached back through the portal to help another soul to this side, Tyler saw that the entire back of Bruce's head was completely gone. The only thing that remained was a dark, concave cavity where most of his brain had been. The last remains of his brain wiggled as he moved and threatened to fall out. Sick to his stomach, Tyler turned his head away from the ghastly sight.

With the help of Bruce's guiding hand, Alex Riley came through next—a lumbering zombie with outstretched, flailing arms shuffling awkwardly on crippled legs and torn ligaments. His pelvis had been shattered as Edward's had on that long ago summer day. He was a pitiful sight; trying to stand by himself then falling back to the floor only to be pulled up again and practically carried by Bruce.

Adrian and Savannah tried to look away but were compelled to look on.

All the emerging apparitions were focused on Edward. As the medallion had been the source of their fear in the past days, now they were the source of Edward's.

Shortly after Alex appeared another figure materialized. His eyes were bloodshot and encircled by a dark brown hue. The teenager's skin was a pale shade of blue. Protruding from the center of his chest was the switchblade Edward had planted up to the hilt. Patrick Quinlan rubbed his hands together as though he were plotting the world's fate; no doubt making plans for Edward.

Two more figures emerged simultaneously. Osborne, with the top of his skull missing, and Miles, with his blood corsages still in full bloom on his chest stopped and stood at attention just inside the boundaries of the invisible gateway. They merely stood there waiting patiently, saying nothing.

Jeremy Taylor was the last animated soul to emerge from the portal. Even though Raven had bitten cleanly through his neck earlier, somehow Jeremy's head was sitting atop his shoulders, threatening to fold over onto the bloody bib covering his shirt.

Simultaneously, the zombie-like corpses surrounded Edward in a half-moon circle and slowly began to edge, creep, slither, and crawl toward him.

"We're all coming for you," one of them taunted.

"NOOOOOOO!" Edward screamed. "Please. Don't!"

"Did you quit when each of us begged you to stop?" another one stated.

"No," he admitted. "But-but you didn't either when I was pleading with you. I'm sorry!"

"Oh no, it's way too late for forgiveness, Edward. Isn't that what you told us?"

Another one rasped, "There's no redemption for you."

Trapped like a caged animal, Edward was finally backed into one of the cornered walls. His feet continued to push against the carpeted floor. That's when Tyler noticed he wasn't floating above the ground any longer. From the time the horrors had appeared and inched toward him, Edward's body had actually become a solid state. He had transformed into the boy he had been twenty years ago before he had died.

Edward slid to the floor and rolled himself in a small tight ball as he had on so many occasions when he was alive.

Bruce walked faster than the others. He was impatient and wasted no time reaching Edward.

Edward fought back, swinging his arms wildly as Bruce leaned down to get him.

Bruce waited for the right moment then caught Edward's arms in mid-swing. He jerked Edward into a standing position then flung him around into the awaiting arms of all the others. Sixty eager fingers grasped hold of his body and clenched into twelve fists to make sure he couldn't escape.

Edward's head darted back and forth, trying to look at each of his attackers simultaneously.

Seeing that Edward was captured, Osborne and Miles turned and disappeared back through the invisible portal almost as quickly as they had appeared. Half-dragging, half-carrying Edward's screaming body-soul, Alex, Bruce, Travis, Kelly, Suzanne, and Patrick slowly turned back and retreated into the something-nothing.

Edward turned toward Tyler and pleaded for his help with imploring arms, but Tyler had been exposed to the effects of the afterlife far too long already. He wanted nothing else to do with the hereafter for at least sixty-five or seventy more years. He only shook his head and sat motionless where he was.

In a blind panic, Edward turned to see where they were taking him as they carried him toward the invisible portal and into the unknown. Edward screamed in horror as though he might have caught a glimpse of what awaited him on the other side. When he turned back toward Tyler, his face had changed into utter dread.

"PLLEEEAAAASSSSSEEEEEE!" Edward wailed at the top of his lungs.

Chilled to their cores, the hair on the necks and scalps of Tyler, Adrian, and Savannah stood on end. They only sat there in frozen terror at what they were witnessing.

Tyler imagined Edward had been able to see thought the portal and had just gazed into the bare-boned face of Death or even Satan himself. His body shuddered.

Edward fought as hard as he could, but it was to no avail. Too many hands had latched on to him. There was no escape this time.

As they locked eyes one last time, Tyler saw tears streaming down Edward's face. But the tears didn't work on Tyler. He didn't feel the least bit sorry for Edward. Tyler had no pity for him now. Edward had made his bed, and now he was going to have to lie in it for all eternity.

Inevitably, Edward's soul slowly vanished completely along with the others as they disappeared through the gateway. After they were gone, the door to that unknown world closed and finally cut off the howls of torment. Tyler was thankful for that the most; too much of a glimpse into the afterlife could drive a sane person mad.

The wind still circulated quietly throughout the room but was slowly dissipating.

In one last desperate attempt to free himself, Edward lunged back onto this side of the universe. He landed hard on his stomach, reached out as far as he could and clutched the carpet as though his life—his soul—depended on in. He looked the same way Suzanne looked when she came slithering through earlier. Edward had been able to thrust three-quarters of his body out. The invisible portal looked as though it had amputated his legs at mid-thigh. He had almost succeeded in his escape but Tyler knew unseen hands had grasped his ankles and were holding fast to them.

Edward slowly began to slide away from Tyler as he was pulled back through into the other realm. Little by little his torso disappeared. First it was his waist and then his chest and finally his head, all swallowed by a huge, invisible mouth.

Edward continued to grab for anything that would give him leverage to fight back but the only thing within reach was the carpet.

Finally, a forearm was all that was left of Edward; it looked machete severed. The fingers frantically searched for a handhold but the carpet was too short.

With a final blood-curling scream, Edward's hand was jerked free from its grasp on the few strands of carpet clutched in his fingertips and was gone.

Silence slowly dominated the room again.

Tyler's body had been rigid throughout the whole battle, and he relaxed as he slumped against the bookshelf, exhausted. The pounding in his head continued to throb. His body was exhausted from the draining release of Edward's spirit.

He looked down at Raven's bloody body lying in his arms. She looked awful. Blood was everywhere. Her breathing was ragged, forced, and seemed to grow shallower with each breath. He began to stroke her sticky pelt. Soft, ceaseless whimpers escaped her muzzle and her legs involuntarily twitched.

When Tyler stroked behind her ears, Raven tried to rise but her legs buckled from her agony. She collapsed from her loss of blood and the weight of the misery. Her body slumped on the floor beside Tyler and her head dropped onto his lap again.

In a choked whisper, Tyler promised, "It's gonna be all right, girl. You're gonna be all right."

Savannah and Adrian sat nearby, silently crying as they looked on.

Raven strained to peer into Tyler's eyes; it was forced and painful but she looked nonetheless.

Raven blurred as Tyler's eyes welled with tears and dropped down his cheeks and onto her fur.

"Everything is going to be fine, girl. I'm right here. I've got you. I won't let you go."

She mewled softly and nudged Tyler gently with a wet nose then she whined and licked his face.

Raven and Tyler peered into each other's eyes one last time. The sparkle in Raven's eyes began to fade as the last bit of life drained from her body. She slowly placed her head back on Tyler's lap and with a long, pitiful breath, Raven surrendered.

"Don't leave me, girl," Tyler begged. He shook her gently, trying to wake her up again. "Please, don't leave me. I need you. I need you. Come back. Please, please come back."

As tears streamed down his face, Tyler held Raven tightly in his arms and continued to rock her gently, refusing to let her go.

Finally drained of all energy himself, he slumped back against the bookshelf and closed his eyes.

CHAPTER 48

WITH A THROATY gasp and a sudden jerk, Tyler awoke. His body lifted slightly as though he had been hit with a shock from defibrillator paddles.

"Oh thank God. You're back. You're okay." Savannah said with relief. She was gripping his face with her hands and gently slapping his face with the other, trying to revive him.

Adrian was on the other side of him patting one of his hands urgently to wake him up.

"How long was I out?" Tyler asked.

"Not very long," Savannah said. "What in God's name did we just witness?"

Tyler shook his head slowly in disbelief at what had happened.

"It was the death forms of all Edward McDaniel's victims. That's what Edward did to them. I think the power of the charm turned on Edward at the very end. It's a friend of no one and completely evil."

Adrian looked around the room and asked, "What are we going to do?"

"I have no idea, but we'll figure it out. Just give me a moment."

Tyler found his other hand was clamped tightly around fistfuls of Raven's thick fur. It was tacky from her drying blood. As he slowly loosened his grip, panic struck him as the recent events flooded back into his mind again.

Tyler looked around the room. "It looks like a war zone in here."

"Tell me about it." Savannah replied.

Most of the blood that had been shed was strewn in trails and patches across the floor and walls. A single diameter of blood splatter dotted the ceiling above Osborne's body.

Dead ahead of him, Tyler saw Jeremy—his father—lying partially behind his desk one hand reaching out beseechingly for help. Blood had run down the lower portion of the wall where it was splattered by arterial spray. His detached head lay two to three feet from his body; his horrified orbs glaring at Tyler. Tyler felt nothing but disgust for him and looked away from the accusing stare.

Savannah and Adrian eyed Tyler quietly, wondering what he was going to do.

Tyler tried to move, but his body ached. The pain was somewhat exhilarating. It was the kind of pain one experiences the day or two after an intense workout. To a certain extent, Tyler had been working out extremely hard for the past few days doing things he had never done before. He would've never found himself in this situation under his own conscience, but it was Edward McDaniel who had made him do it.

"I finally have my life back," he whispered to himself.

Tyler tenderly moved Raven's head off his lap and set it on the bloody carpet beside him. He forced himself to stand and stretch. He looked around the room and tried to figure out what he needed to do next to take care of this situation.

Osborne was still lying in the center of the room. Tyler was thankful that the top of his head was facing away from his line of sight. He had seen enough bloodshed for one lifetime.

When he turned, he saw Miles sitting up against the office doors but still very much dead. Three bullet holes pock-marked the door where they had exited his body. From the three exit wounds, three blood trails had followed him down the surface of the door.

Out of the corner of his eye, he saw a small glimmer. He walked to it, leaned over and picked it up. On closer examination, he found it to be part of the broken medallion.

"What is it?" Adrian asked.

"Piece of that damn charm. Help me find the others."

"Got one," Savannah said, already bending down to pick a piece up.

"Me too. Right here," Adrian said.

He saw the other individual pieces glittering on the floor and went to each and collected them. One piece was still attached to the leather strand that was wrapped around Osborne's gun. Tyler found it where he had dropped it after blowing it to bits and catching Raven when she had attacked.

He counted the pieces.

Seven. Huh, unlucky number seven.

They double checked the room in another sweeping motion but didn't see any more reflections of light. Assuming they had all the pieces, Tyler went to Jeremy's desk and searched for something to hold them in. In the bottom drawer, Tyler found a small leather pouch with a draw string. Discarding the pieces in the pouch, he tied it up and shoved it in his pocket.

"What are you going to do with it?" Savannah asked.

"I'm going to bury it some place where no one will ever find it. I don't know where yet, but I'll figure it out."

Looking at Raven again, Tyler hurried to the window and jerked one of the light blue curtains from the curtain rod.

"What are you doing now?" Adrian asked.

Tyler didn't answer but spread the curtain on the floor beside Raven. He gently picked her up and placed her into the center of it. As new tears lined his face, he draped each end over Raven's limp body. He tied her body securely with the cords from the curtains.

Picking Raven up, Tyler moved to the main library doors. Careful not to disturb Miles, Tyler opened the door Miles wasn't leaning against and made his way toward the garage. Not knowing what to do, Adrain and Savannah had followed.

When they entered the garage, they found four expensive automobiles. They were washed, waxed, and gleaming. All of the cars were the top of the line models. There was a red Mercedes, a midnight blue BMW, a white Jaguar, and a black Porsche. After briefly admiring the cars, he went outside through a small side door; his Mustang was parked a few feet away.

Out of habit, he reached for his keys but didn't find them in his pocket.

"Fuck, Tyler said, as he placed Raven on the ground beside his car.

"What?" Adrian asked.

"My keys. They're still in the house. Miles took them when I arrived. Stay here, I'll be right back."

Tyler quickly retraced his steps to the library. He searched all around then finally found his keys in Osborne's pocket from when he went to retrieve Edward's baseball bat. He also grabbed his wallet and the evidence bags of car metal and mirror fragments from Jeremy's desk as well as Jeremy's silver-plated Zippo lighter.

As Tyler made his way back through the garage again, he saw a few yard tools hanging on a rack. He noticed a shovel and knew he would need one to bury Raven. He stepped over to the rack and took the shovel then continued to his car.

Outside again, he took his keys, opened the trunk, and laid Raven's slowly stiffening corpse in the back. He added the shovel he'd picked up from the garage then slammed the lid.

Tyler moved back toward the house but stopped when Savannah grabbed his arm and pulled him back toward her. "Tyler, talk to us. Don't close us out. We're in this as much as you are. What are you thinking? What can we do to help?"

"She's right, Tyler," Adrian said. "We can help if you will let us."

Tyler seemed to come out of his dazed state. "I really don't know. I'm going about this only by instinct; doing what I think is necessary as I think of it."

Tyler looked down at the ground and put his hands on his hips as he thought of the next thing that they could do. He saw that his pants, shirt, and hands were covered with dried blood.

"Well first things first for me. I have to get cleaned up."

"You are covered pretty badly," Adrian said. "It might be a good idea if you do."

"It is a long drive to Adrian's house and just in case I get stopped, I can't be seen like this. It's a long shot that anything would happen; it's just a precaution. Can you give me just enough time to take care of this? Then we will figure out what we need to do."

Adrian nodded, "Okay, but be quick. I don't really like standing around with dead people nearby. It just isn't normal."

"Just give me ten or fifteen minutes. I'll be thinking of what we should do. Be back in a few."

He started walking back to the house, then stopped and peered all around him. He had the weird feeling that somebody was watching him. He had no idea who it might be. He finally passed it off as nervousness, but he remained aware, as he began walking again.

He then paused once more as he glanced down the driveway. He remembered about the huge gate at the end of the driveway.

"What is it?" Savannah asked.

"The gate at the end of the drive is probably closed and locked."

"What do we do?"

"Hold on."

Tyler rushed back to the garage. Savannah and Adrian followed.

He checked the cars to find a remote for the gate at the end of the driveway. Finding a two-buttoned remote in the BMW, he gave it to Savannah. "I'm just assuming here but put this in your pocket and don't lose it. It's has two buttons. I think one is for the garage and one if for the gate at the end. We'll need it later. I'm going to get cleaned up."

She took it and pocketed it.

Tyler went immediately to Jeremy's bathroom. When he looked in the mirror, a blood-splattered hobgoblin peered back. He almost cried out in alarm.

"Holy shit, that's more blood than I expected."

A simple clean up wouldn't do, he had to do a complete overhaul. He didn't feel very comfortable taking a full shower with dead people in the house, but after seeing the extent of blood on his face and small bits of brain matter in his hair, he changed his mind. He shivered with disgust; something about being here gave him a morbid feeling. He felt filthy to his very core. He hopped in and showered and scrubbed himself as hard and as fast as he could. He was becoming more anxious each minute he was in the mansion. The longer he stayed here, the greater the chance someone else would come by.

After a quick shower, he dried off and he checked the pockets of his old clothes to make sure he wouldn't be throwing anything of value away. He shoved the leather pouch with the medallion pieces, his billfold, his keys, the evidence bags of car shards, and the silver Zippo into the pockets of the new pants he had grabbed from Jeremy's dresser. Tyler stuffed all his bloodied clothes, his shoes, the wash rag, and towel inside a duffel bag he'd found in Jeremy's closet.

He raided more of Jeremy's bureau drawers and closet and found a gray sweatshirt, some socks, and a pair of slightly oversized Nike's. He didn't bother to dry his hair but slipped on a baseball cap instead.

When he came back downstairs, he found Adrian peering out the blinds of the living room as if she were on a stakeout with the FBI. She looked nervous.

"What took you so long?" Savannah asked. "Did you take a shower?"

"Had to. I was filthy. Don't worry. I made sure I didn't leave any evidence behind for anyone to find."

"What? Are you a pro at this now?"

"Let's just say I've had a lot of practice during the time Edward was inside me."

The phrase shocked both Adrian and Savannah.

"Well, I did. Look, I'm not proud of what Edward made me do. I've been sick to my stomach with guilt inside ever since he took over and made me do those things. It's going to be something I'll have to live with for the rest of my life. You two can either stand by me or not. I'm not going to stop you if you feel like you need to turn me in. But I didn't kill those people. Edward made me kill them. Anyway, we can talk about all of this later. We don't have time to discuss it here. Now you can either help me do what I think needs to be done, or you can go wait by the car until I finish."

"What are you going to do?" Adrian asked.

"If you're going to wait by the car, it doesn't matter. I can only tell you if you're in one hundred percent."

"I'm with you, Tyler," Adrian said. "I've been with you to a certain extent since you've been born. Tell me what you want me to do and I'll do it. No questions asked."

"Savannah?" Tyler asked. "How about you? What's the story?"

"I don't know."

"I need an answer right now."

She glanced at Adrian to get a read from her. Adrian gave her a half smile then shrugged her shoulders.

"Okay, I'm in. I don't feel comfortable about this, but I know what I saw in there. I don't want to have to explain all this to anyone. No one would believe us anyway. Tell me what to do."

Tyler handed Savannah the duffle bag and the keys from his pocket. "Take this to the car and put it in the back with Raven. When I bury Raven, I'll bury this evidence with her. After you do that, come back in here and get a few dishtowels from the kitchen and wipe down anything and everything—from the door you came in to anything you touched in the library."

She grabbed the duffle bag and keys as she shook her head, psyching herself up. "Give me that. I'll be back in a few."

"Just make sure you don't lose the keys. We will be leaving real fast when we do so be ready."

"Of course."

Savannah left and Tyler turned his attention to Adrian.

"Let's get this over with. Follow me."

They made their way back into the garage where Jeremy's prized cars were parked.

"Jeremy always had a fetish about hot cars, huh?" Tyler asked.

"He didn't have the best ride back when we dated, but I guess he liked hot cars about the same as any guy his age would."

"Somehow I think Jeremy was into a lot more than he let on. You don't just have two or more 'security guards' hanging around just for artwork. An alarm system could take care of securing the house."

"That's true. I hadn't thought about it like that."

Tyler started rummaging through the tools on the worktable on one side of the garage. He chose a hammer and a pair of pliers then began to look around for one more item. In one corner of the garage, Tyler finally saw what he was looking for and made his way toward it.

"What are we looking for?"

"Gasoline," Tyler said, holding up a full five-gallon, metal can. "There's two more here too. There's enough here to kick-start an arsonist's wet dream."

Adrian grew quiet.

"Sorry," Tyler said, thinking she didn't like his lewd comment.

Adrian ignored his apology.

"You're not going to do what I think you're going to do. Are you?"

"Yes. Gonna burn this place to the ground."

"Why?"

"It's just another way to cover our tracks. If we get rid of as much evidence as we possibly can, the fire, smoke, and the heat will hopefully take care of anything that we might've missed. I can't promise this will work, but I have to be sure that this doesn't come back on us."

"Holy shit. I can't believe we're going to do it." Excitement was growing in her voice.

"You don't have to help if you don't think you can go through with it."

"Oh no, I wasn't saying that because I'm not committed. I am; believe me I am. This will actually be great therapy for me. This is something I have secretly wanted to do to Jeremy ever since, well, you know, since high school. Destroy his world the way he destroyed mine."

"Well then. Let let the healing process begin," Tyler said as he held out one of the gas cans and offered it to her.

Adrian took it without hesitation, turned, and was about to head back toward the library where all the chaos ensued. They stopped in their tracks when the side door slammed. Savannah had just come back from putting the duffle bag into the car. Adrian and Tyler both looked like they had just been caught doing something they shouldn't have been doing.

"What?" Savannah asked.

"You scared us," Adrian said.

"Sorry. I'm just coming back in to wipe down the library like Tyler told me to do. What are you going to do with those?"

Adrian and Tyler held them up, trying to figure out how to explain it.

"Nevermind," Savannah countered. "I don't want to know. I don't need to know. I just have to get dishrags."

They made their way back through the house. Savannah branched off to find the kitchen as Adrian and Tyler headed back to the library. At the door, Adrian turned and said, "I've got this room. You take the rooms upstairs and start up there. I'll handle this area down here. That is, if you don't mind."

"No. I don't mind in the least." Tyler paused then asked, "You sure?"

"Positive."

Savannah came around the corner with two dishtowels. They exchanged glances again. Again, they didn't know what to say.

"Okay, you guys are weirding me out. What are you doing?"

"Adrian needs to do this room," Tyler said taking the dishtowels from Savannah and handed then to Adrian. "Wipe everything down."

"I know," Adrian said.

"If she's going to do that, what do I do?" Savannah asked.

"I don't know, but I need to do this," Adrian replied.

"Go ahead, Adrian," Tyler said. "I have something else for her to do."

"Okay. Thanks."

As soon as Tyler left the library, Adrian set to work wiping down every piece of furniture that she could remember they could have possibly touch.

Adrian then grabbed the container and started on one side of the room, shaking the gasoline over the bookshelves and artwork that hung between the shelving. She worked herself into a steady rhythm and in a counterclockwise circle. Once she wound her way back to the main doors to the library, she shook a bit more of the gasoline over Miles's body and then began to back up dousing back and forth through the center of the room. Adrian took a few more moments over Osborne's body making sure he was drenched as well. Again, she moved back toward the three easels. She looked at the painting of Helen Roquemore, bloody and beaten, lying dead on the floor of her house.

"I wish I had known you better. Maybe I would've done something then. Since I wasn't brave for myself back then, maybe I would've been brave for you. I'm sorry."

Then with a flick of her arms, she doused the painting. She moved over to the other painting of Jeremy looking on as Edward drowned beneath Silver Ridge Lake.

"I wish I had've known about you too. Maybe this is my moment to help you out. It's not much, but it sure feels good to me."

With another flurry of her arms, she brought the gasoline can up and doused it too. She moved on, heading toward Jeremy's divided body.

"And now we come to you. I've waited a long time to do something to you. I've said so many things out loud over the years about you. So many hateful things. I've often wondered what I would say to you if we ever saw each other again. Now, nothing really comes to mind because I've said it all out loud over the years. I'm just glad I was able to witness your death. That was so *satisfying*, I guess it the best word to describe it for me. I'm glad it happened like it did, and I'm glad you're gone. Goodbye, Jeremy. And good riddance."

She lifted her gas can and dumped the remaining contents over his body and head until he was completely soaked.

While Adrian was attending to the library, Tyler told Savannah what he needed her to do. When she left, he then took his gas can upstairs as Adrian suggested began to douse the furniture and all the curtains in each room. The rooms wouldn't be drenched but it was enough to initiate a strong blaze. In sweeping motions, he poured a stream of gasoline from each room into the hallway and joined each stream with a line down the hallway and to the bottom of the stairs. He took the other can of gasoline and did the same to the rooms downstairs as he did to the ones upstairs.

In the living room, Tyler pulled the grille away from the front of the fireplace. He was relieved to find, just as he'd suspected, that the fireplace was equipped with gas logs. He pulled the pliers from his pocket and set to work. Not able to find any connection to unscrew and release the gas, he simply severed the thin metal line in two with the pliers. A small hiss of exposed gas escaped.

After he snapped the living room gas line, he made his way back to the library. Adrian was just coming out as he rounded a corner.

"Everything is ready in here now."

"Okay good. Did you wipe everything down before you doused it?"

"Uh-huh. Anywhere there was a wood surface that I could think of. The chairs we sat in. Jeremy's body is going to join his soul in hell."

"Damn, Mom. That's harsh."

Adrian was taken aback. She smiled, "You called me, *mom*."

"I know. Just trying it on for size to see if I like it."

Adrian was all smiles.

Savannah came around the corner looking for them. She was carrying a Molotov cocktail in her hands. Just a rudimentary Mason jar with gasoline and a red rag coming out of the top of the lid.

"There you are," Savannah said placing the jar into Tyler's open hands. "One Molotov cocktail as ordered. How much do we have left to go in here?"

"Just this. Here you go," Tyler said handing the present off to Adrian.

"For me."

"Sure. Happy Birthday."

"Isn't this a bit excessive? I mean, couldn't we just light a match and touch it to a gasoline trail?"

"Oh sure, but this is part of my three-fold elaborate plan. Number one, if the police find the evidence of this house being burned down by one of these..." Tyler pointed to the jar for emphasis. "It could lead them on a trail thinking maybe professionals did this or some type of drug dealers got pissed at him. Who knows? I doubt very seriously they will be thinking that ordinary people like us did this. Number two, I think you will feel better. You know, like you are actually getting back at Jeremy. Like what you said, destroying his life like he destroyed yours. And number three, this way is way more fun."

"Alright. You've convinced me. I'll do it."

In the garage again, they placed the empty gas cans where Tyler had found them earlier and Savannah wiped them clean. Tyler fished in his pocked for the Zippo.

"You ready?" Tyler asked.

"Yeah. This day has been a long time coming," Adrian replied taking a stance in the garage doorway.

"Make sure you know where you're aiming," Tyler said. "We don't want this to flare up here in the garage because you didn't even get it inside the door."

"I got it, I got it. I've been watching you play football for a number of years now. I've picked up a few things by watching you."

"Then you should be a pro. Alright. When I say, *now*, you throw it immediately. Understand?"

"Sure. Got it."

Everyone took a deep breath and watched as Tyler lit the end of the cloth with the lighter. The flame leapt toward to the rim of the jar.

"Now!"

Adrian took two side steps forward to gain momentum and hurled the Molotov cocktail with all her might. The fire bomb sailed through the short foyer hallway. They had already turned away and were exiting the garage door but they heard the distinct sound of shattering glass and the whoosh of accelerant as the Mason jar touched down in the gasoline trail.

The jar exploded as it struck the floor and sent flames cascading across the floor. The floor erupted in a blaze and ignited the gasoline-etched paths. The burning trails serpentined throughout the house in a lightning-quick domino effect.

A flaming serpent slithered into the gasoline trail, crawled over Osborne, Miles, and Jeremy's gasoline soaked bodies. They were quickly consumed by the pyre and charred into ash.

The flames scrambled over furniture, scaled the stairs, snaked down the hallway, and branched out into separate streams of fire. The fire licked its way into each room, devouring everything in its wake, unable to satisfy its hungry appetite.

A cyclone of fiery demons surged into the living room and it detonated in a fireball of extreme heat as it found the broken gas line. The force of the explosion blew up and out from its confined space, spreading through the house with destructive intensity. The roof above the living room was blown loose and fell in on itself.

Outside, Tyler slipped into the driver's seat of the Mustang as the living room erupted. He quickly started the car as Savannah slipped into the back; Adrian took the front seat.

The Mustang squealed down the driveway. Savannah grabbed the remote from her pocket and hit the button on the remote and the gate doors swung inward. Tyler had to put on breaks so he wouldn't hit the gates as they slowly swung open. Judging the width of the opening barrier, he floored it and fish-tailed out of the driveway. He didn't look back to view the mansion erupt, although he was tempted to do so.

Tyler glanced over to Adrain and then to his rearview mirror to see Savannah. Both women were turned in their seats, observing the destruction before it disappeared behind the slope in the driveway.

Walls disintegrated and the ground outside were littered with glass as the windows all over the house exploded. All throughout the mansion, antiques, beautiful furniture, and expensive tapestries were demolished and turned to flaming debris. What took Jeremy Taylor years to build was reduced to smoldering rubble within minutes.

By the time Tyler reached the end of the street, fire had completely engulfed the house. Dark smoke billowed out of the windows and roof and ascended into the warm night air. Tyler turned right at the end of the street and vanished into his new life.

CHAPTER 49

IN THE DARKEST of night while the rest of the world slept, Tyler drove as fast as he dared without drawing attention to himself. He didn't want to be pulled over for any reason. He wouldn't know how to explain the two slightly bloody women he carried with him. Even though they cleaned themselves up a little during the cover-up, they all had traces of the recent ordeal on them. There was also the bullet-riddled corpse of a Labrador, a shovel, and a duffle bag of bloody clothes in the car as well. Not exactly the normal things you would expect to find in the trunk of a car.

Tyler lightened up on the accelerator.

Mile after darkened mile, Tyler drove. They traveled in silence, each one in their own little world, trying to wrap their mind around what they had witnessed tonight.

Tyler continued to check all his mirrors to see if anyone was secretly following them. He had no idea if Jeremy had other men working for him. He doubted it. Surely they would've come to Jeremy's aid if they had seen or heard anything out of the ordinary during the ordeal tonight.

Tyler tried to relax, but he was too tense. He would only be able to truly calm down after Adrian and Savannah were safely back home, Raven and the bloody clothes buried, and the charm pieces disposed of.

He glanced in the rear-view mirror again and saw that Savannah wasn't looking out the window but had drifted off to sleep. Adrian had also fallen asleep. He hoped it was fitful for both women and wondered if anything had changed between him and Savannah; for the better or the worse.

I wonder if she will still like me as much as I think she did after all this is all over? Only time will tell.

A few miles from Adrian's house, Adrian started to come around. At first she just rolled her head sluggishly from side to side and groaned. Suddenly remembering what had taken place, she quickly sat up, arms out in front of her. She was ready to fight.

Tyler placed a hand on her shoulder and said, "Easy. Calm down. You're all right now. You're safe."

Her startled reaction and Tyler's response caused Savannah to wake as well. "Where are we?"

"We're near Adrian's house."

"Oh, Tyler. Thank God it's you," Adrian said, grabbing his hand. She breathed in ragged breaths as she sat back in her seat.

"Yeah it's me," he assured her. "Me and only me."

She looked deep into his eyes to check for herself before Tyler had to look back at the road ahead.

"Yes. It is you."

"You've been asleep for a long time. But rest, we're almost there."

She lay back, pressing her hands to her head trying to relieve the pain of the instant headache she received from sitting up so fast.

"I'm so sorry you were dragged into all that tonight," he said.

"It's not your fault. I'm just glad it's over now."

Tyler didn't know what else to say, so he said nothing. A long silence filled the car and they rode in solitude the rest of the way home. All three were thinking of the hows and the whys of that evening.

At last, they finally pulled into her narrow driveway. He turned off the engine and dosed the headlights. He jumped out and ran around to Adrian's side to help her and Savannah into the house.

As they neared the porch, she felt her front and back pockets then said, "I don't have my keys."

"Where are they?" Tyler asked, instantly on edge.

"I think they're in the house."

"In Jeremy's house? How did we miss that?"

Tyler's mind began to race. *Where are her keys? Will anyone find them after the fire? Can they be traced back to Adrian?*

"No. I mean, I think they're inside *my* house. They didn't give me time to gather anything. That guy Miles knocked me out cold. Next thing I know, I'm waking up on the floor of their van."

"Oh thank God," Tyler said. Relief was evident in his voice.

"Sorry. Didn't mean to scare you."

"Scare me. You just gave me heart failure. In my mind, I was just seeing someone sifting through the remains of the fire and finding your keys. The smallest thing could link back to you. To us."

Knowing it wouldn't open but trying it anyway, Tyler turned the doorknob. Surprisingly, the door swung open.

"It's not locked."

"What?"

"Yeah. It's open. See."

Adrian was glad but was instantly pissed, "Those assholes. Just leave the door wide open, fellas! That way anyone can come in and help themselves to anything I own!"

Tyler grinned and shook his head as he pushed the door further open and allowed her to pass.

She rushed in and looked around the room to see if anything was amiss in the house. Taking a quick mental inventory and finding that everything seemed to be in place, she finally evaluated herself. "I look horrible and I feel nasty."

"Rest here for a few minutes. I'll go get everything ready so you can take a hot shower. I know you don't want to sleep all night in those bloody clothes."

"You don't think this darkened, dried blood look brings out the color of my eyes and accentuates my hair?" Adrian asked.

Tyler gave her a quick curtesy laugh. "Uh, definitely not."

"No, seriously; the sooner I get out of these things the sooner I can forget."

"You'll never be able to forget," he reminded her. "I know I won't."

"I can at least hope, can't I."

"For all the good it will do." Tyler changed the subject. "I think it would be best if I take your clothes with me. I have to get rid of all the evidence linking us to Jeremy."

"You mean, you're not going to stay here with me tonight."

Without thinking about it, he said, "No, I can't. I've got to get home or my mom will kill me."

Adrian laughed first, followed by Savannah. Tyler joined in with them after realizing what he'd said. The laughter made Adrian's face ache again from where she had been hit and she held a hand to her cheek to rub the pain into submission.

When the moment was over, Tyler said, "This is going to be a strange new life for me. I don't know how I'm going to get used to having two mothers."

"If I can be included in your life, that would be enough for me."

Tyler nodded, "I wouldn't have it any other way." Changing the subject, Tyler said, "Go ahead and take a shower. You'll feel so much better."

"You won't leave before I get out, will you?"

"No, of course not. What kind of son do you take me for?"

"Just checking."

"We do have to get back soon, but we can stay for a little while longer."

"Good, I'll be quick."

While she showered, Tyler and Savannah plundered in the kitchen until they found all the ingredients and utensils for making hot chocolate. By the time they had gathered everything and boiled the milk, Adrian had finished and entered back into the kitchen.

"Feel better?" Tyler asked.

"Yes, thanks."

Her hair was damp and she was carrying all the garments she was wearing earlier. She grabbed a plastic grocery bag from under one of the counters and placed the contents inside.

"You want me to get rid of those for you?" Savannah asked.

Adrian stared down at the clothes. "If you don't mind."

"Not in the least. I'll just set them by the front door so we don't forget them when we leave. You sit," she said, taking the clothes, then added, "Have some hot chocolate."

Adrian washed her hands and sat at the bar in front of Tyler.

"You look relaxed," Tyler said.

"I'm very relaxed now."

"I made myself at home. Hope you don't mind," Tyler said, pouring a cup of hot chocolate and setting it down in front of her.

"I'm glad you did."

"I figured you would need something like this."

She took a couple of sips. "It's just right. Hot enough to soothe but not enough to burn the tongue. Perfect. Delicious."

"It better be. I did slave most of the night away to fix it for you."

She smiled and drank some more.

"You want to lie down? We have to leave soon."

"I know. *Your mom.*" There was a joking sarcasm in her voice.

Remembering what he'd said earlier they smiled then made their way to her bedroom.

He held her cup of hot chocolate as she climbed in bed and settled back on the pillows, she asked, "You remember what it said on the back of the picture I took of Edward?"

"Sure. It said, *My Hero,*" Tyler said returning her cup for a few more sips.

"I should start calling you my hero. You saved my life tonight."

Tyler didn't know what to say. He placed his cup on the night stand.

"Edward was only coming for Jeremy. No one else mattered to him. Not Savannah. Not you. Well, maybe you. Edward really cared for you. You may not believe it now, but he did. It was really Edward that came calling. I just tagged along for the ride. I mean, I really didn't have a say in the matter."

Adrian said, "You know what I mean." She placed her cup on the night stand as well and settled back against her pillows again.

"Yeah, I do. You can call me 'your hero' if you want, but I think I would prefer your 'son' better."

Adrian lunged forward and bear hugged him. Surprised by her

abrupt reaction, Tyler was slow in returning the hug but slipped his arms around her and hugged her just as tightly.

"You don't know how long I waited to be accepted by you. I never thought I would get a chance to explain my side of the story."

"It all happened by chance, you know. If I had never moved here to your home town and your old house, I would've never found your hope chest. But since I did, the rest, as they say, is history." Tyler paused, then said. "We could probably talk about this all night long, but you need to go to sleep, and I need to get Savannah home. If her parents come home to an empty house, they will send out a search party for her. It won't look so good if she has been out with me all night. You know parents."

Adrian didn't want him to go. She was greedy and wanted to keep him all to herself but she knew she couldn't. He had another life waiting for him. She knew she was going to have to share him. She was just glad he was in her life now, if only for a little.

"Stay with me till I fall asleep."

"Sure. Love to. But no talking. Sleep."

"Okay."

He switched off the bedside lamp and the darkness filled in around them.

Tyler sat and Adrian lay there in silence as the room grew quiet around them. Tyler reached out and grabbed his mother's hand. She grabbed it and held it tight. She was eager for the loving touch of her son. It had been seventeen years since she had held his hand.

In less than fifteen minutes her grip on his hand loosened. She had drifted off into dreamland quicker than expected. When he felt like he could stay no longer he slowly slid his hand from hers and quietly eased himself from the side of her bed.

He gingerly felt on her night stand for the two cups of hot chocolate. Before he turned and left the room, he paused at the side of her bed and whispered, "I love you, mom."

Tyler waited but knew Adrian was too far gone into sleep to reply to his words.

With a cup in each hand he slipped quietly from her room.

He turned out each light as he made his way back through the house.

In the kitchen, he found Savannah quietly cleaning up everything they had dirtied.

"She okay?" Savannah asked.

"Out like a light. She's going to sleep well tonight."

Savannah was placing the last of the dishes she had cleaned in the tray by the sink. She took the two cups from Tyler, quickly washed them and added them with the other dishes.

"Thanks for doing that," Tyler said.

"It's not a problem. Really." Savannah glanced toward the bedroom. "You know, I really like her."

"I like her too. And just so you know, she likes you."

"Really?"

"Yeah."

"When did she tell you that?"

"Earlier tonight; back at the mansion."

Savannah smiled as she quickly wiped the counters. She hung the rag in place then turned out the lights.

They made their way to the front door. Tyler grabbed the bag of clothes he had promised to dispose of and then turned one last time to survey the room. He took a moment to think if he was forgetting anything. Thinking of nothing, he made sure her front door was locked this time then softly closed it behind them.

CHAPTER 50

BEFORE THEY WERE even out of Adrian's driveway, Tyler turned to Savannah and asked, "What do you think of me now?" He braced himself for the worst.

"What do you mean?" she asked.

"About me. And what I've done."

"I really haven't given it any thought."

"Seriously?" Tyler asked. "You haven't been the least bit scared of me or about what I might do to you seeing as how I've killed seven people in the past couple of days?"

She cocked her head to one side and gave him a questioning look. "What *are* you going to do to me?"

"Nothing."

She shrugged her shoulders, "Then no, I'm not scared about what you might do to me. Why would I?" Savannah saw the dumbfounded look on his face. She pressed him. "Why do *you* say *you've* killed those people?"

"Because I did."

"I thought you said earlier tonight, and I was under the impression, that Edward killed all those people not you."

"Edward did, but it was like I killed them too. I was there. It was me as much as it was him. I did those actions. I held the gun and pulled the trigger. I stabbed Kelly with those scissors and Patrick with his switchblade. I swung that baseball bat. I crushed Alex's pelvis with my car. I ran Suzanne off the road. I—"

"Tyler!" She raised her voice slightly to stop his ramblings. "Calm down. But *you; you,* Tyler, didn't really kill them, did you?"

"No. Not technically. I was fighting against Edward every step of the way and as best I could the whole time."

"Then why the discussion about it? Listen, everything I questioned you about doesn't matter anymore. You don't need to explain anything to me. I know you were telling me as much of the truth as you could during those times I questioned you. I understand everything now. "

"I don't know, I just thought that—"

"I know what I saw tonight. I am a witness to the whole psychotic thing. I saw the inner struggle between you and Edward. Had I not, I might be thinking differently toward you."

Savannah turned to look at him. Tyler's eyes were glued to the road ahead. His mind was half-there, half-somewhere else.

Savannah raised her voice again to get his attention, "Tyler!"

He turned briefly and made eye contact for a few seconds then he turned back to the road again.

Seeing that she had his attention, she continued, "I saw it, and I saw what you did. You wanted to spare Jeremy's life even though Edward should've been able to end him right then and there because of what Jeremy did to Edward and to Edward's grandmother. And what he did to Adrian. Man, that was really bad. That was unforgivable. And what he was going to do to us."

"So are you saying I shouldn't have fought Edward so hard; to give him a chance to have his revenge?"

"No, I'm not saying that at all, and I don't want to get into any of the "what ifs" and "why didn't Is. What happened, happened and there is no use living in the past now to try to figure out if you should've or could've done something different. Quit second guessing yourself. Life is too short to live in the past. We're here now. Let's just move on and close this weird, eerie chapter in our lives. That's what I'm planning on doing."

"I guess I was just worried about us, and if you still wanted to see me after this was over. I was even wondering if you had any plans to turn me into the police for killing all those people."

Savannah gave him a short, amused laugh. "Tyler, would you listen to yourself? Turn you into the police? What am I going to say to them?" She held her right hand up to her face as though she were talking on a phone. She changed her voice and said. "Um, excuse me, officer, yes, um, I would like to report a crime. Actually, I would like to report six crimes. Hold on just a minute." She turned to Tyler and asked, "How many people did you kill, hon?"

"Seven," Tyler said.

Savannah continued in her chosen character's voice. "Excuse me, officer, make that seven. Yes, seven. My bad. See, my boyfriend has this medallion charm thing and it had a little kid-spirit inside it. Well, to make a long story short, the kid-spirit escaped from the charm and it possessed him and forced him to kill those seven people. I know, crazy right? Well now I just want to go on the record to say he is not guilty, at all, for any of these seven murders." She paused and acted like she was listening to the imaginary officer on the other end of her finger phone, "Uh, what's that? Uh-huh, no, I know he's innocent because I saw the whole, crazy incident."

"You're having a lot of fun with this aren't you?"

She changed back to her regular voice again. "Yeah. Kinda. But do you see how bizarre it would sound? They would throw you and I both in the looney bin for years to come."

"True. You do have a point."

"This scenario is unexplainable to anyone but Adrian and us. It's best to just forget about it. I say we just keep our heads down and ride this one out and hope it blows over. I do not want to go to any institution or jail over this."

"Neither do I."

"Good. Then let's just try to forget this ever happened."

"Easier said than done. This memory will be with us the rest of our lives."

"I know, but we have to at least try to put it behind us."

They drove in silence for a while. Savannah glanced over to study him. She saw a smile playing at the corner of his mouth. Finally, she saw the grin creep across his face.

"What? What are you smiling about?" she asked.

"Did you just call me *your boyfriend?*"

Savannah laughed out loud, "Oops. Did I say that?"

"I heard it."

She shrugged her shoulders and gave him a sheepish nod. "Didn't mean to assume anything."

"What *did* you mean?"

"I don't know. It just sorta slipped out."

"Accidentally on purpose?" he asked.

"No. Just…accidentally."

"So tell me this. Why me? Why are you so crazy about me?"

"Is it that obvious?"

"It's definitely a different feeling than any other girl I've dated. I hope you get the same vibe from me."

"Probably not exactly the same, but then again you've had a second mind to deal with lately. You've been a little preoccupied. But it's been enough to where I still want to be in a relationship with you." She was quiet for a long moment.

"But?"

The spoken word brought her out of her inner thoughts. She gave a quick laugh. "No "but", I was just thinking of how to explain the question you asked to you."

"I'm all ears."

"A couple of years ago I got involved with this guy, Robbie Steadmond, who was perfect on the surface but after a while a different, darker character started to come out. It was just little things at first that were sort of forgotten or brushed off but then he started doing more shady things."

"Like what for instance?"

"Well." She paused to think of one. "One time we were out in his car and this squirrel darted out in the road in front of him." She paused getting a little choked up about the memory. "You know how squirrels are?"

"Sure, I guess."

"They're cute but they're stupid. They get nervous when they jump out in the road and don't know which way to go when a car is bearing down on them."

"Yeah, they usually make the wrong decision and jump right in front of the car wheels instead of jumping to safety."

"Exactly. Well on this particular day that squirrel jumped out in front of Robbie's car, and like always the little guy got skittish but he made the right decision and bounded to the middle of the opposite lane. He was totally safe. He was out of harms way but Robbie jerked his car onto the other side of the road and aimed his wheel so that he would purposely hit the squirrel. It was so blatant."

"My guess is he probably drilled him, huh?"

"Yeah. It was a bulls eye. The little guy didn't know what hit him."

"What did you do?"

"I cussed him out. I punched him and slapped him. I made him take me home right then and there."

"Bet Robbie didn't like that."

"No. None of it. I think that was the first breaking point between us."

"The first?"

"Yeah. He pursued me a lot after that. Apologized for his actions. Sent me presents, flowers; bullshit like that. And, me being a dummy, I finally gave in. He was great for a while but then the real Robbie set back in a little at a time. He beat me up pretty badly later on in our rekindled relationship. That's what ended us. It was the first time he had actually hit me and it was his last too. I'm not one of those girls who get abused and stay in the relationship just because they need somebody. I have too much pride for myself to stay in a shitty relationship like that."

"So, you dated this asshole and you learned you didn't want a guy like him but what is it about me that strikes a chord with you?"

"Well, it was after dating asshole that I did a lot of soul searching. I really thought of what I wanted in a guy and sort of did a daily wishing or positive thinking on the matter. There's a saying, "You become what you think about". I don't know if it holds true for finding that perfect guy but you can imagine my surprise when I saw you sitting in English class. When we exchanged looks that first day you came to school there was definitely a strong energy. I knew something was going to happen between us even if I had to initiate it."

"And you did."

"I did, didn't I? See, I've been here in Silver Ridge practically my whole life and I've dated only a handful of guys. The two main reasons I don't often date is, one: because of Robbie and my trust issues he caused me to have. And two: I don't really date guys around here until were good friends and I know them really well. But that becomes difficult if it doesn't work out. It then becomes an awkward friendship. And friendships never really last after a breakup. There is always something weird between whoever it may have been. I got tired of loosing my friends because I date them for a little while. I didn't want to wait until we became good friends for something to happen. I just decided not to be afraid and just went with it.

"But you had a problem with me when the murders started happening, right?"

"Yeah, I started thinking what happened with Robbie was happening all over again with you, only worse. But after our argument when I really thought about it, the feeling of a duplicate Robbie relationship left me and was replaced by another feeling.

"You were afraid you were going to loose me?"

"Yeah, it came to me the night shortly before we made love on the pier. I just got this feeling that I had to believe. That's when I let everything go and began to trust with all my heart. Trust that everything would work out between us."

"I'm glad you did. It was one of the best nights of my life."

They rode in silence for a little while longer.

"So?" Savannah said breaking the quiet again.

Tyler glanced over at her not knowing what she was meaning, "So. What?"

"I told you some of my feeling about you. What do you think? About us?"

"I don't know. I think I'll have to check with my *real* girlfriend to see if it's okay if I can take you out every now and then."

Savannah slapped his arm. "Hey now!"

Tyler laughed, "I'm kidding, I'm kidding." He reached over and took her hand in his, "Seriously, all I can tell you right now is that I don't know if you'll be able to handle the real Tyler. Now that I am back as my regular self. Things will definitely be different than they were before. I think you will like the new me and I for once am going to enjoy getting to know you and having you all to myself."

Another short silence fell over the car again.

Tyler glanced over at Savannah. The huge smile that was on her face had faded. She was staring off at the road ahead as though mesmerized by the broken line dividing the lanes. "What's on your mind now?"

"I was just thinking about my parents," Savannah said. "You know, wondering if I would ever see them again."

"I know, scary time," Tyler suggested.

"Terrifying. So what do you think Jeremy was going to do with us?"

"I believe he was going to kill us without giving it a second thought."

"That's what I was thinking."

"I think he was just confused about everything and wanted to know the reason behind all that I was doing. He just couldn't wrap his mind around Edward really being back."

"Would *you*? Well, yes, of course you could; you were living with him inside your head. It's was a lot to take in. I didn't even want to believe it at first."

"One thing about it though," Tyler said. "Edward got his revenge just like he wanted."

"That he did. Jeremy got it in the worst way too."

"Just like Edward promised." Tyler squeezed her hand. "How did they get you?"

"Who? Osborne and Miles?"

Tyler nodded.

"I was duped. It's stupid and embarrassing for me. After you left that night, I was sitting in the living room trying to find something decent to watch on TV. I heard the doorbell ring and I thought you had come back for whatever reason. Maybe to make out some more, I don't know."

They shared a smile.

"I just opened the door without looking to see who it was. And that guy Miles was standing there holding his cell phone out in front of him. He introduced himself and asked if he could borrow my cell phone because his cell phone battery had died. He said something was wrong with his van and that it had stalled in the road or something. He was just a distraction because Osborne had apparently picked the locks and snuck in the back door and came up behind me. Next thing I know, I was waking upon the floor of their van. But I'm smarter than that now," Savannah said. "It'll never happen again, because I'm signing up for self-defense classes next week."

"Good idea."

Changing the subject, Savannah said. "That's gotta be weird, huh? To find out when you're seventeen that you have another mother."

"Extremely weird. I'm not quite used to it yet."

There was another lull in the conversation, then Savannah said, "I don't know how all that possession stuff work."

"It's just possession," Tyler said. "You really have no control over anything you want to do or say. You feel helpless. I only had enough strength to close my eyes so Edward couldn't see his target or stop my finger from pulling the trigger. Small things like that. And I think I was only able to do that because part of Edward had already been transferred into Raven's body."

Savannah obviously didn't understand so Tyler told her everything that had happened from the time he had been bitten and the partial transfer of Edward's soul until Edward rejoined that smaller portion of himself when he fully possessed Raven for the attack on Jeremy.

"Tyler concluded by saying, "That's my take on it anyway. Whether that was truly the case, I really don't know."

"Wow. Really? That's so strange."

"It's kinda funny, or odd, or I don't know what you would call it when you think about it," Tyler began.

Not knowing where he was going with his statement, Savannah asked, "What are you getting at?"

"We're both so concerned about what the other was or is thinking about them."

"Yeah. Sorry about all that."

"No, don't apologize. I think that's great. I'm just glad you had the same thoughts about me. All night I was worried about what you might be thinking of me but you were doing the same thing as I was."

"Is that why you were so quiet?"

"I wasn't aware that I was quiet."

"Focused then. You were extremely focused."

"You're right about that. Focused. There was a lot to cover up. It's just that when I was inside myself, I was constantly thinking of you. I just kept thinking how I didn't want to loose you or drive you away."

"So you do care about me," Savannah said.

"Yeah, of course I do. You thought I didn't?" Tyler asked.

"I know now that you really didn't have the means to express yourself with Edward manning your feelings and body. Although I must say that night on the pier. You showed me a lot of yourself that night."

"I could say the same about you."

Savannah smiled. "I don't mean about how physical we were that night. You truly showed me your inner feelings that night, even though you were still somewhat quiet about them. I felt them through your touch."

"Good, I'm glad you at least sensed that part of me coming through."

"This is going to be creepy for me because I'm scared of the answer but I just have to ask one question."

"Sure. What's that?"

"That night when we made love on the pier," She paused trying to figure out the best way to phrase her question.

"Yeah,"

"Was it you or Edward making love to me? I hope to God it was you."

"Believe it or not it was me. Just me. That is one thing that Edward allowed me to do is make love to you. He experienced it through me but for that moment in time it was me and only me and it was a beautiful."

"Yes it was."

"I think Edward was too scared he would fuck up our relationship if it turned out to be, I don't know, unfulfilling for you."

She gave a short burst of laughter. "Pun intended?" she asked.

Tyler laughed at his choice of words. "No-no, I didn't mean it like that. I meant that he was inexperienced, almost a virgin. And didn't want it to be a bad experience for you."

"Oh, so you're experienced? How many women have you been with?"

"Let's see now," Tyler made a quick jester with his index finger as though he were doing imaginary arithmetic on an invisible pad in front of him. "Carry the four."

"Hey!" Savannah exclaimed as she backhanded Tyler's bicep. "Gross."

Tyler joined in with her and they laughed together.

Savannah held her hands up in mock surrender. "On second thought, I don't need to know. I don't *want* to know." She paused, eyed him suspiciously then complimented him by saying, "You do know your way around a woman's body though; I'll have to give you that."

"Thank you. You're pretty great yourself. We need to do that again sometime soon. That was—,"

"Amazing," Savannah said, finishing his sentence for him.

"Yeah. Really amazing."

"I'm game anytime you are."

"Not tonight though, right?"

"No. Definitely not tonight. But sometime soon."

"Sometime soon it is."

Savannah yawned and curled both arms around Tyler's bicep and laid her head on his shoulder. Before long, she was sound asleep. Tyler smiled to himself, marveling at how lucky he was being in a relationship with such a perfect girlfriend.

CHAPTER 51

AS THE FIRST few rays of the morning sunlight lit up the horizon, Tyler pulled into the parking area near Silver Ridge Lake. Although exhausted from the confrontation the night before and the long, arduous drive to and from Adrian's house and getting Savannah home, he still had some unfinished business.

He still had to bury Raven and wanted to do it by himself before anyone asked where she was. Eventually, they would miss her and Tyler would tell them she ran off again the way she did after he arrived home from the hospital.

You know dogs. They've got a mind of their own.

During the drive to and from Adrian's house, he had wondered where he would bury Raven. It couldn't be any ordinary place. It had to be special. It didn't take Tyler long before he finally decided on the perfect place.

On the day Edward's spirit guided Tyler to Edward's childhood home, Tyler had passed across a tranquil area that overlooked the bay. The secluded spot was set back from the water's edge nearer to the treeline. There was a small incline to a grassy slope where five rounded boulders jutted out of the ground. The area was back dropped by three flourishing pines. The day Tyler had stumbled across the spot he had stopped and stared at the picturesque landscape for a long time. Tyler thought of how perfect the view was as though it could have easily been a shot for an Ansel Adams landscape photograph. That was the perfect spot to bury Raven.

Tyler parked his car near the trail that led down to the lake. He was surprised that no one was here, but then again he had come early so as not to look suspicious carrying a shovel, an old duffle bag and a cloth-wrapped package that was the size of a small child. He didn't want to have to explain anything to anybody.

He placed the plastic grocery bag with Adrian's clothes in the duffle bag that held his bloody clothes. He slung it over his shoulder as he carefully retrieved the shovel and Raven's body from the trunk. He slammed the trunk lid and set off.

From the picnic area, Tyler made his way onto a trail through dense underbrush. Along the way, he fought tree limbs that scraped and clawed at his face and arms. He climbed over rocks, slipped, and fell as he fought to keep his balance with the burden he was carrying. Raven's body became almost more than he could bear, and on three occasions, he had to stop and let his arms rest from the dead weight of his dog. Eventually, he picked Raven up again and pressed on through the warming sun, through the silken filigree of spider webs, and the burning in his arms until finally he broke through the forest and into the modest clearing near the water's edge.

Tyler set Raven's body on the grass and leaned against one of the tallest boulders to take another short rest before he started the hardest part of this journey. He wanted to get finished as soon as possible and leave Raven to rest in peace.

After his rest was over, Tyler grabbed the shovel and stabbed it into the ground. The soil was soft and rich. Shovelful after shovelful was pitched to the side, and after a while, the pit became wider and deeper. Because of the soft earth, Tyler finished sooner than anticipated.

With the hole dug, Tyler did something he wouldn't have expected of himself. Instead of going ahead and burying Raven, Tyler unwrapped her body a second time. He uncovered the bloodied blue curtain just enough to remove Raven's collar. Tyler gave one last soft stroke to Raven's head. She seemed to be at peace in an opened-eyed sleep. In times past, Tyler had seen Raven slightly kicking and whimpering as she played in whatever dreamland dogs go to when they sleep. Her facial features were slack except for a small hint of a grin that played at the corner of her mouth. Tyler imagined Raven in a dream chasing phantom rabbits and squirrels across a plush green meadow.

He covered Raven's head again but didn't tie her back up. Even though

Raven was dead, Tyler couldn't bring himself to let her body be constricted after she was covered with dirt. He made a pillow out of the duffle bag and placed it under Raven's head. He wanted to take every precaution to make Raven comfortable as possible.

Tyler shook his head thinking, *I know it's stupid but I still can't break the habit.*

Ever since Tyler was a child, he had always had the feeling that inanimate objects such as toys and stuffed animals had feelings too. On numerous occasions, if an action figure had been twisted into an uncomfortable position he would take and extra moment to rotate the arms and legs into a natural position and would leave it that way until he played with them again. If he found a stuffed animal lying upside down or under something heavier than it, he would make sure they were sitting upright and in a comfortable position before he left the room. Tyler had enough of an imagination to believe that when he was out of the room, toys would always come alive and play until he came back.

Last, but not least, he fished in his pocket for the pouch the broken talisman was in. Holding it above the grave, he thoughtfully bounced it up and down on the palm of his hand. This was the key that had caused everything. He had planned to bury it with Raven, but on second thought, now decided against it.

No, I can't do that to her. I won't dishonor Raven's body or her grave with something that is this cursed.

He placed it in his pocket again, unsure of what to do with it but positive he would dispose of it soon. The sooner he could get rid of it the better.

With Raven's body in the grave, he started to slowly cover her. Little by little, the bloodied curtain disappeared under the layer of dirt. This was the breaking point for Tyler; his heart broke again and he sobbed like a baby. Tears flooded his eyes and traced dual paths down his dirty cheeks. He shoveled faster. He wanted and needed to be away from this place. Eventually, the earth was replaced and Tyler softly patted the mound with the flat side of the shovel. After he finished, he collapsed to the ground, sobbing over the loss of his best friend.

Tyler searched for two fairly stout tree limbs under the trees in the forest. Finding them, he drove one into the ground with the flat end of the shovel. Making sure it was sturdy; he took the other and made a horizontal crosstie, securing it tightly in place with the curtain cords. Tyler slid Raven's collar over the vertical limb and let it slid down to the intersection of the limbs.

Tyler doubted anyone stumbling across this grave would call and tell him they found his dog. Tyler hoped they would think, as he did, that it was a good place to bury a favorite pet. Tyler wanted anyone that found this grave to know how special Raven was to him. The inscription on the back of the dog tag couldn't have stated it any better.

It read: RAVEN, THE BEST DOG IN THE UNIVERSE.

After the burial, Tyler dried his tears and sat on one of the boulders for a long while gazing out over the tranquil water. Tyler noticed the water looked as calm as his spirit inside, now with Edward gone, he felt whole again.

There was still one piece of the puzzle left for Tyler to put in place before this nightmare would be completely gone forever.

In one sense, Tyler was thankful for this good luck charm. If he'd never found it, he doubted he would be alive today. Lately, he was wishing he had died that night. If he had, he would never have the memory of hearing Edward's victim's screams or seeing the pain emblazoned on their faces. They were a part of him now. He would see them constantly and knew they would have a profound effect on his life from this point on. Tyler doubted that these images would fade and disappear completely from his mind forever.

What Edward's grandmother's told him whispered again through Tyler's mind. *Be careful what you wish for; it could very well become a reality.*

"Helen," Tyler began. "That is a wish I could definitely live with."

He pushed himself from the boulder he was sitting on and went to Raven's grave again. He paused by the small mound, not knowing what to say. Finally he whispered, "Goodbye, girl. I love you and I will never forget you."

He picked up the shovel and slung it over his shoulder and made his way back the way he'd come. He continued to cry as he left Raven's grave and the small secluded spot by Silver Ridge Lake.

CHAPTER 52

WHEN TYLER ARRIVED back at the docks, his body was weary from the hike and the load he had buried. He leaned the shovel against the railing and walked the length of the pier. As he walked, he trailed his fingers along the banister as his mind drifted back years earlier to the time when Edward had walked a dock similar to this one.

Over time, harsh weather of the seasons had ruined each pier, so new ones had to be built.

The earlier pier had been narrow, only big enough for two people to walk together. Now the pier had more than doubled in length and in width. Benches had been built into the deck's railing along with evenly spaced lampposts to light the way. The end of the deck opened into a twenty-four foot square landing.

There had been a drastic overhaul, not only with the pier but to the whole area; it was now a park site and was regularly maintained.

Tyler leaned on the pier and gazed out over the bay as a breeze gusted his face. He smiled and closed his eyes.

As he stood with his face to the wind, he remembered a day identical to this years ago. He remembered the anger that had churned inside Edward as he watched his classmates play volleyball—the ones who had caused so much turmoil in his life. He recalled Edward's hate and how it faded to nothing when Adrian came around. He relived the fight with Jeremy and the humiliation Edward had suffered as the other teens looked on. He reminisced about Edward being with Adrian later that day on the lake and how perfect that moment had been for him. Then the tragedy of the boat accident flashed across his mind. He stared in dread as Adrian's head was struck by the bow of Jeremy's boat. He saw the look of malice, as well as surprise, on Jeremy's face right before the boats collided and Edward fell backwards into the water. Tyler saw the view of the two boats slowly growing smaller and then the more terrifying feeling as death wrapped its dark, watery cloak around him and carried him into the deeper depths of the lake.

Tyler opened his eyes. In that brief remembrance of conjured memories, he knew exactly what to do with the talisman.

He stepped off the dock into a row boat tied to the end of the pier. He untied it, and began rowing toward deeper waters. His body was so sore from the events of the night before and from recent burial of Raven. Nevertheless, he pressed on with sure, strong strokes.

When Tyler felt he was in about the same location Edward had drowned, he finally stopped rowing.

He felt like he was being watched. He looked around guiltily, as though what he was about to do was wrong. He surveyed the distant shores and could still see the pier in the far distance. He scanned the surrounding water and saw there were other boats on the lake, but the people on them weren't close enough to make out what he was doing.

No wonder Edward had been nervous that day with Adrian, Tyler thought, judging the distance from the dock and how dismal, deep and intimidating the water seemed to be.

He dug into his pocket for the leather pouch with the medallion pieces. He found it as well as the plastic bags with the automobile pieces. This was as good a place as any to get rid of the evidence. He opened both plastic bags and dumped all the fragments into his hand. They twinkled briefly in the sunlight. With a quick flick of his wrist he chucked them over the side of the boat. Not wanting to litter, he kept the bags so he could pitch them in a receptacle when he arrived back to the docks.

Finally, he took the leather pouch that held the charm pieces and held it up in front of his face by its leather straps.

Tyler shook his head at the sack, "You've lost your hold on me now." He swung his arm over the side of the boat and with absolute disgust said, "I hope to God I never see you again."

He opened his fist and dropped the small pouch into its watery grave.

The pouch entered its wet tomb with a dull, hollow splash. Instead of dropping straight toward the bottom, it more or less glided into the murky depths. The length of the tied leather strands offset the weight of the broken amulet. Tyler watched as it spiraled around and down, around and down, around and down until the murkiness of Silver Ridge Lake swallowed it forever.

As it traveled deeper, the watery currents would sweep it in different directions until it finally rested somewhere on the muddy bottom. As time went by, the shifting currents would pile dirt, leaves and trash on top of it until it was a permanent part of the sediment.

Tyler had no idea if what Jay said during his ghost story around the campfire about Wisherman's Abyss was true or not, but from what he had seen since his accident he wouldn't doubt that part of it could be. Either way, he hoped he and the charm never crossed paths again and that it landed in the deepest and darkest part of Wisherman's Abyss.

Tyler continued to stare into the inky blackness of the lake. He knew this was the best place for it. "I'm the only one who knows it's down there," he said in a hushed voice. "I only wish I could bury all the memories I still have with it down there as well, but I guess I'll have to live with them for the rest of my life." Falling silent, he thought, *We all have our crosses to bear. I guess this one is mine.*

Tyler stayed out on Silver Ridge Lake for a long time just thinking of what had happened since his accident.

"I can't dwell on this forever. I have to move on with my life. All I have to do is forget. It will probably be the hardest thing I will ever do. All I can do is try."

Picking up the oars, he slowly paddled back toward the dock.

As he rowed, he thought of Savannah. He thought of where she was and what she was doing right now.

He smiled.

Thinking of Savannah was the beginning of his healing process.

CHAPTER 53

IT WAS MID-MORNING by the time Tyler returned home. When he opened the front door, it hurt not to see Raven padding toward him, tail wagging and the sound of her toenails clickety-clacking on the hardwood floor. He stood in the doorway for a moment, waiting, half-hoping last night was just a weird dream, half-expecting Raven's head to poke around the corner to look at him. Seeing no Raven, he pushed the thoughts from his mind and quickly closed the door. It would take a long time to get used to never seeing her again.

Tyler expected to find his mom and dad in the living room or kitchen but they were nowhere to be found.

Must still be in bed, he mused. *Or maybe they're out somewhere.*

Although last night's events were strenuous on his body, he didn't feel tired at this specific moment.

I guess I got my second wind, he thought. *I'll sleep later.*

He busied himself in the kitchen making coffee. As the coffee maker puttered to life, he grabbed a packet of oatmeal from the cupboard, added some milk, and nuked it for about thirty seconds.

By the time he'd finished wolfing down the oatmeal, the coffee was ready. He had just finished adding cream and sugar when he heard his dad shuffling down the stairs.

Tyler slid onto one of the bar stools as his father entered the kitchen.

"Morning," Tyler said.

"Morning, Son." Henry caught himself. He gave a cover-up cough. "I mean, morning, Tyler."

"Didn't know you were here," Tyler said. "Thought you guys might've gone out early."

"No, not today. Your mom and I slept in."

"She still in bed?"

"Yeah." Henry paused. "She was up late last night worrying about you."

Tyler thought his dad was wondering whether he should add that last comment.

"I'm alright."

"That's good. But she didn't know that."

You're going to start that? Tyler thought. *After all the lies, you're going to hit me with that attitude?*

Tyler looked down at his coffee and shook his head.

This is so awkward. Then thinking better of the situation, told himself to just let it go.

Henry began again, "She said she couldn't sleep. I think it was early morning when she finally drifted off."

"I'm sure the sleep did her some good."

"Yeah."

"Could you wake her for me?"

"I think it's probably best to let her sleep. At least for now."

Tyler didn't let up, "Dad, it's important. I need to talk with you guys."

Upon hearing the word "dad," Henry brightened. He nodded and said, "I'll see if I can coax here down here." He headed for the stairs.

"Thanks."

Henry wasn't gone very long before he and Gwen were back downstairs in the kitchen. They both looked at him expectantly, wondering which way this conversation would go.

Tyler sipped some of his coffee. As he set his cup down, he looked at the coffee cup ring on the counter. He guided the cup back to the ring and set it down again on top of it.

"I don't know which way to go with what I need to say," Tyler began. "And I don't know how you are going to take it. But I will tell you the truth and what I feel is right. I don't feel like I need to apologize. I feel one hundred percent wronged and feel like it's you two that need to apologize to me."

Tyler paused, giving them a chance to respond. He was met with silence, so he pressed on.

"I understand why you did it. You know, I get it. You made a choice, thinking it would protect me. And maybe it did in your eyes. I feel like part of my heritage has been kept from me. Like maybe you didn't like my other mom and dad. It's like you don't like that part of me and you wanted to keep it from me."

"Honey. No," Gwen soothed.

"I know. I didn't say that's what it was. I'm saying, it just seems like it. I know now that it was just your way of dealing with adopting me. You wanted me to forever think that I was your kid. I get it."

"We really didn't know them long enough to know whether we would like them or not. At least your birth mom."

"I know."

"We never met your birth dad."

Tyler almost blurted out that he met his dad tonight, but said, "Me either. I'm still hurt about the whole situation. It will take some time for me to get over this and trust you again, but I'm going to try, starting now. I don't want to hold a grudge. I've seen first hand what happens when people hold grudges. I want no part of that."

Confused, Henry and Gwen exchanged glances again.

Gwen was about to say something, but Tyler continued again before she could speak.

"I love you guys. You got to know that and believe me when I say that."

"We know," Gwen said.

"I don't know what I was thinking when I even hinted at the idea that I was going to jump ship on this family. I was crazy to say that. I guess all I need to know is if you still want me as a son, because I still want and need you two as my parents."

"Of course," Henry said.

"Honey. Yes we do. We've always wanted you. We *chose* you. We love you more than you will ever know."

Everyone was quiet, no one knowing exactly what to say.

Gwen noticed the look on Tyler's face, "Tyler, what is it? It seems like you want to say something else."

Tyler glanced up at her then back down to his coffee.

"I do have something I want you both to consider. More or less you, Mom, but you too, Dad."

"Name it," Henry said.

"What? What is it?" Gwen pressed.

"Since I have met my other mother, I want her in my life, too."

That remark took something out of Gwen. Deflated, her eyes shifted to the floor.

"I don't want you to think that she will be replacing you, Mom. Or you either, Dad. It's just that I have met her and I like her. She's told me some things about my childhood that I didn't know, and I would like to know more."

Tyler noticed that Gwen's demeanor had changed toward him.

"Mom," Tyler said getting her attention.

Gwen looked up.

He held out his hand toward her, "Come here."

Gwen obeyed, grabbing his hand with hers. Henry followed in behind Gwen and put two comforting hands on her shoulders.

"Please don't be disappointed in me for asking this. Even though Adrian is my birth mother, it doesn't change the fact that I consider *you* my real mom—and I always will. "

Gwen looked up into Tyler's eyes.

Tyler smiled at her. "Nothing could change that."

"If it will make you happy, Tyler, I can do that for you," Gwen said.

"It will. I don't know why; this is just something I need. No one, I don't care who it is, could ever take the place of you. I want you to know that. I love you both more than words can express."

Without realizing it, Tyler had already stood and moved in, embracing them both.

"We love you too, Son," Henry said.

"I love you both so very much."

They stood in a group hug for a long time, knowing they were a family again.

EPILOGUE: AFTERMATH

EPILOGUE

THE SUN WAS hotter than two hells as it spiraled over Silver Ridge Lake and made its way toward the end of another long day. The wind was stifling as it blew off the lake and through the surrounding trees.

Tyler Curtis sat under the humid shade of an Aspen. He was staring off in the distance, transfixed on nothing in particular.

He was holding the Zippo he'd lifted from Jeremy's desk. He flipped the lid, stuck the flint, and closed the lid repeatedly. Tyler had picked up a new habit since the ordeal at the mansion.

He was deep in thought and had been for the better part of the afternoon. He couldn't get rid of the images. In the memories Edward had left with him, Tyler knew this was the same Aspen Edward had sat under nearly twenty years ago when he watched his now dead classmates play volleyball.

He came out of his funk, shook himself, and wiped away his tears.

"It all started and ended here," Tyler said to himself. "Everything has come full circle."

He glanced over at the aged gray etchings in the Aspen's trunk and saw the arborglyph of four letters—E M + A C—encircled by a heart.

He loved her even though he knew she couldn't love him back, at least not in the same way he was hoping.

He traced around the heart and letters with his finger as more tears began to fall.

Tyler was contemplating everything that had happened in the past few days and grieved for the men and women he had murdered. Edward was gone now, but Tyler was left with the grisly memories and the guilt of that carnage. He would've given anything if he could change history and bring them back. But history had been made and would remain that way forever. It was something he would have to live with for the rest of his life.

One of the worse feelings Tyler felt was that he had been helpless to get the small section of Edward out of Raven and she had lived her last days in fear and being controlled. He knew what he himself had went through and could only imagine the madness Raven went through as well from the time she had bit Tyler to that last moment when she died on his lap. He hated that Edward had taken Raven's last days and that she might not have been happy during her last moments or that her life wasn't complete before she past on. Then he thought again of her sacrifice for him. That's when he really began to cry.

He sat under the tree for a long time, letting the heartache wash out of him.

"Is there a particular reason you've been avoiding me lately?" Savannah's voice came out of the blue and from behind him.

Startled and embarrassed, Tyler quickly sat up, wiped his eyes and tried to compose himself. "No. No, of course not. Why do you ask?"

Tyler shoved the lighter into his pocket.

Savannah sat down beside him. "It just seems like you are." She was silent for a moment as she studied him. "I dropped by your house a little while ago looking for you. Your mom said you would be down here. The mom named Gwen."

Tyler smiled at her comment, "I know who you were talking about."

Tyler diverted his face away from her as he continued to compose himself. Savannah knew he had been crying but pretended not to notice his tears.

He must still be really broken up about what he did, she thought. *I can't blame him. I wish there was something I could do.*

"It's been a couple of days since, um," her voice trailed off. "Since, you know, that night at Jeremy's. It just feels like you've been avoiding me."

"I know," Tyler replied. "I'm sorry. I'm not avoiding you though."

"You haven't called me since then or returned my text messages. This past week is a lot different than the conversation we had in the car on the way back from the mansion. I'm beginning to think you don't want to be around me anymore and I can't help but wonder what the hell I did."

"You haven't done anything. You are perfect. There's nothing wrong with you…or *us*." He looked over at her to see her reaction.

Savannah didn't turn to look at him but continued to gaze off in the middle distance. He could see she was smiling at his comment.

He turned back to the lake and watched as three birds plunged toward the lake. "I've just been sitting here trying to sort out everything that happened."

"Here? You've been sitting here for the past three days?"

"Obviously not."

Savannah suddenly changed the subject on him. She gave a quick squeal of excitement. "I can't wait any longer. I just can't."

"What?"

She turned to face him straight on. "I hope you don't mind, but I took the liberty and did something for you. Well, got you something, actually."

"You did? Why? What is it?"

"Yes, I did. And it's because I like you. And when I like somebody as much as I like you, I do things without putting too much thought into it. I mean, I did think about it. A lot. But it was impulsive. That's it. Yeah, that's what I meant. And I can't tell you what it is. I gotta show you."

"Savannah. Calm down. Take a breath."

"Sorry. I'm just excited. That's what I am."

"Well, clue me in so I can join in on the excitement with you. What is it?"

"Can't tell you. You have to wait until I go get it."

"You didn't have to get me anything."

"I know I didn't have to. But I did."

"Well. Are you going to get it?"

She quickly leaned into him and kissed him hard on the lips. Tyler was about to pull her closer to expound on the kiss, but she pulled away and stood. She smiled and winked as she left. She turned back one last time. "I hope you like it."

"With the way you're carrying on, I'm sure I will."

She turned and dashed off. "I'll be right back," she said calling back over her shoulder.

"Don't be long."

She turned and pointed at him. "Don't *you* go anywhere. You're hard enough to find as it is."

Tyler laughed and pointed back, "I'll be right here. I promise. Now go."

Tyler turned back and looked out over the lake again.

Weird, Tyler thought. *What the hell is she up to?*

There were a number of boats on the lake today. A couple of jet skis skimming across the water. A few people were water skiing. He saw a boat out in the vicinity of where he'd been a few days ago. He became transfixed on it as he zoned out again.

Startled by something wet touching his elbow, Tyler jerked his arm away. He turned quickly only to be confronted by a small, yellow Labrador puppy with a thin blue collar around his neck.

"What the— What is hell is this?"

"Looks like a puppy to me," Savannah said, laughing.

"Uh, yeah, I can see that."

Tyler was hit with a strange sense of de ja vu and felt as though he had been catapulted back in time to the day his parents had given him Raven when she was a puppy.

Straining at the leash, the puppy peered up into Tyler's face with bright blue eyes. The dog sniffed the air around Tyler and whined softly.

"Is this for me?" he asked, already knowing the answer. He was touched by Savannah's gesture of affection to him. He sat frozen as the tears began to pour down his face from immediate happiness.

"Tyler, are you alright?" Savannah asked. "If it's too soon, I can take him back. I'm not bound to the deal."

He held up his hand, shaking it back and forth to try and let her know it had nothing to do with the dog. When he was able to speak he said, "I believe I understand now what you couldn't explain the first night we kissed. Happy tears, remember?"

Savannah nodded.

"Believe me when I say, this is the perfect gift."

"Good. Good, that's great. It's a boy. He's not a mix. He's a full-blooded Lab. I have his official papers in the car."

Tyler smiled as he held his hand under the young dog's nose. The dog sniffed a few times and then began to feverishly lick Tyler's palm.

"I have no words. He's simply amazing," Tyler said.

"I know you were heartbroken when Raven died. She was your heart and soul; your whole world, and I loved watching the way you two were with each other. I didn't know if it's too soon for you after losing Raven, but I just thought he might be a really awesome gift for you."

A pang of mixed guilt and sorrow hit Tyler in the chest as he relived the final moments with Raven before she passed on.

Tyler said the only thing he could think of. "Yeah, it's been really tough for me the last few days. I miss Raven a whole hell of a lot."

"Raven was the coolest dog ever. I know how much you loved her. I know this little pup won't replace her. I just wanted to do something for you, and this is the only thing I could come up with. I couldn't pass up the opportunity."

"No, this is great. He's the best. He's perfect."

Savannah watched as Tyler got to know the little dog. He picked him up, held him high in the air, brought him down, and hovered him in front of his face. The little dog flipped his tongue out and licked the end of Tyler's nose. Tyler started laughing and placed the pup on the ground again and scratched him around the ears.

"So. You have any idea what you're going to name him?"

"Yeah," Tyler said. He all of sudden seemed to be talking from a far off place. Without hesitation, Tyler said, "Gabriel."

Savannah nodded in agreement, "Wow. Okay. That was really quick. You sure you don't want to think about it?"

"Nope. Solid choice. His name is Gabriel."

Savannah tried the name out for herself. "Gabriel. Huh. Any reason why?"

"That's the name Adrian gave me when I was born. It's my original birth name."

"Oh. OH! Yeah, well then, Gabriel it is. That's just...perfect."

Savannah sat down beside him again.

Tyler turned to her. "Thank you," he said.

"Sure. You're welcome."

He wrapped his arm around her and pulled her close. He hugged her tight and gave her a long kiss. "This is truly the best gift anyone has ever given to me."

"I just want you to be happy, Tyler, that's all."

The tears came again from out of nowhere. He smiled and said, "I am. I definitely am. I'm sorry I've been so distracted lately. I've just been trying to cope with the guilt of everything. I don't know what to do." His words broke in his throat.

Savannah put her arms around him, kissed the side of his head, and whispered into his ear. "You know you don't have to do this alone. I'm here for you and always will be. I did go through this too, you know. Not in the exact same way as you, but I did experience it to a certain extent."

"I know. I just—"

"Don't shut me out, Tyler," Savannah said cutting him off. "Please don't shut me out. I need you. And I know you need me."

"I know, and I do. I guess I feel like I have to deal with it in my own way first before I can deal with it with someone else. But you're right. I can't do it alone."

"Then we'll do it together."

Tyler nodded then reached into his pocket and pulled out the eight by ten of Edward's classmates. He handed it to Savannah and asked, "You remember this picture, don't you?

Savannah looked down at it and said, "Yeah. What's so special about this picture?"

"What do you see?"

She gave the photo a quick once over, "It um, it looks like six kids goofing off around a lake. There's a volleyball court and sand. It looks as though they just finished playing a game. Maybe. Really bad poses. Why, Tyler? What's this about?"

"What else do you see? Take your time. Really look at it. Look deeper into the picture. Focus strictly on the background."

She shrugged her shoulders, "There are a lot of trees. Most of them are in the far distance, I see part of the lake, the pier," she paused and bent closer to the picture to make sure her eyes weren't fooling her. "It looks like someone sitting underneath one of the trees in the background. Is that right?"

"Bingo. You see him too, huh."

"Who?"

"Edward McDaniel."

"Edward McDa—. You mean the person sitting beneath the tree is Edward—Edward? The Edward that was inside you?"

"Yeah."

"How do you know?"

"From the memories Edward left me when he left my body." He tapped the side of his head. "All his memories are up here with mine. I have the memory of watching them as Adrian took that picture. It is as though I were there that day too."

"Is that weird? Living with someone else's memories?"

"Yeah. It's a little mind-boggling. It's so hard to explain."

"I get it. At least, I think I do."

Tyler pressed on about the picture. "If you invert this picture in your mind and pretend you are over there." He pointed in the direction of where the volleyball sandlot used to be. "Look at this tree in conjunction to the lake." He patted the Aspen beside him. "Wouldn't you agree that this is the same tree as the one in the picture?"

"I guess. Maybe."

He pointed to the pier in the picture, "Look, this pier is in the same place as that one out there. Bear in mind that one out there has been replaced since this picture has been taken."

"And you think this is the same area that's in the picture."

"I know it is. Remember, I have all of Edward's memories right here." He tapped his temple again. "You want to hear something really spooky?"

"No. Not really."

He pointed to the photograph again, "We are sitting in the exact same spot Edward McDaniel sat when Adrian Connell took this picture of them. And this picture." He gave Savannah the headshot of a sleepy Edward. Tyler nodded, "What do you see in that picture?"

She laughed as she answered, "A sleepy kid that just woke up. There are some letters scratched into the tree's bark surrounded with a heart."

"Can you read the letters out loud to me please?"

"E M plus A C?" She looked up, perplexed, "Yeah, so."

"E M are the initials of Edward McDaniel, the boy in the picture. And A C are the initials of Adrian Connell. My birth mother. See." He leaned back far enough so she could peer around him.

When she looked, she saw the same letters that were in the photograph scratched into the pale bark of the Aspen. The letters weren't as fresh and pristine as they were in the picture, but they were readable.

"Wow, that's amazing," Savannah said, continuing to study the pictures.

Gabriel was busy pulling on one of Tyler's shoe laces.

They turned to survey the view of the lake again and sat in silence for a long time, enjoying each other's company. She laid her head on his shoulder. Tyler smiled at the gesture. Everything was going to be alright.

The sun was still high in the sky but was beginning its slow descent in the western sky. The wind was cooler now as it whipped across the lake. From one side of the lake to the other, miniature whitecaps glided across the water's surface. The effect of the shimmering surface reminded Tyler of the surface of the medallion and how it had glimmered upon first sight.

In comparative terms, Tyler realized that as a fish is attracted to alluring bait, he had been enticed by the amulet's shiny surface.

A shudder rippled through his body as he thought of the charm again and the events that had transpired because of it. The movement of his body caused Savannah to stir.

"You okay?" she asked.

Tyler stroked Gabriel's head.

"Yeah, a black cat just walked over my grave, that's all."

Savannah didn't understand his comment. "What's that mean?"

"It's something my mom always says when she gets a cold chill."

"Which mom are we talking about? Your real or adopted?"

Tyler laughed, "My adoptive mother. Gwen."

"You said you got rid of your medallion. Where did you bury it?"

"Why?" he asked and eyed her suspiciously.

"Good Lord, Tyler, I don't want to go dig it up and wear it for God's sake. Not after what I witnessed a few nights ago. I'm just curious what you did with it, that's all."

He studied her for another long moment then slowly smiled to let her know he was just giving her a hard time. He turned back toward the lake and pointed to the boats tied at the end of the dock, "The day I buried Raven, I took one of those boats and rowed out to the middle of the lake." He pointed higher in the direction of another boat that was out in the middle of the lake. "You see that red and white boat with the green flag way out there on the horizon?"

She paused as she followed his finger and squinted as she saw the boat he was talking about. "Yeah."

"Well out there about where that boat is, that's where I buried the charm. I buried it out there in the deepest, darkest part of the lake I could find. I hope to hell I never see it again."

"You speak for both of us when you say that."

He looked over at her. She was studying his face.

"What?" he asked.

"You seem so different. It's good to have you back. The *real* you I mean. Don't ever leave me like that again."

"Don't worry, I won't. I can promise you that."

Tyler leaned into Savannah and wrapped one arm around her lower waist and pulled her closer. Their lips met and they kissed for a long time.

When they pulled away from each other, she said with a smile, "It's been a long time since we've done that."

With a small sigh and a nod of his head, he said, "Yeah, I know. Way too long." Giving her a mischievous grin he said, "Let's make up for lost time."

She smiled and nodded in agreement then they kissed for an eternity.

CB

Charlie DeMarco was bored. She sat on the deck of her grandfather's boat in one of the boat chairs hunched over with her elbows perched on her knees and her chin resting on her fists. She stared blankly at the fishing lines waiting for something, anything to bite. She was trying to catch a few more fish before it got too late. The boat gently rocked to the rhythm of the lake. They had caught some fish earlier in the day, but nothing was biting now.

"This is the pits. It's so *boring* up here," Charlie said to no one in particular.

Charlie pulled her ponytail that was hanging out of the back of her ball cap around to her mouth and began to chew on the end of it. It was a bad habit her mother constantly corrected her on.

Charlie wished she was below deck watching her grandfather gut the fish that had already been caught. That was gross but a hell of a lot more fun and interesting to watch than sitting up here waiting for the dumb fish to bite, but she had been told to stay and watch the rods.

She had rummaged around in all the boat's compartments for objects to occupy her time with. She had found a pocket knife and a piece of wood; she had whittled it and some of her time away. Abandoning that task, she had played around with the bait until that became dull and boring. Finally, on the top shelf of one of the boat's compartments she had found her grandfather's high-powered binoculars.

Charlie pretended she was a Navy Commander and started to give orders to imaginary officers. She hadn't been running surveillance on the surrounding shorelines for hostile enemies very long before she saw a couple kissing beneath a tree. This intrigued her, and she waited and hoped things would get a bit steamier.

After a while they just continued to sit there talking.

"Boring," she said in a sing-songy voice.

Charlie began to look for other enemy forces elsewhere, but she kept a tab on the couple just to make sure.

They could be spies, she thought.

One time when she double checked the couple's actions, Charlie's skin prickled when she saw the black-haired guy point directly at her. She quickly lowered the binoculars and ducked out of sight below the ship's bow. She knew she was too far from shore for them to see her, but you never knew what kind of special devices spies carried with them these days.

Charlie raised the binoculars again just as the couple started to kiss again.

"Jeez, get a room you two and get it over with," Charlie said, as she leaned further over the side of the boat.

"Charlie Ann," her grandfather, Horace, said as he climbed out of the cabin below.

Charlie jumped when she heard his voice.

"Yeah."

"You'd better put those peeping tom eye glasses away and keep your mind on those reels."

"I am, Grandpa. But nothing's biting right now."

"Uh-huh,"

"Two people are making out on the shore. They are much more interesting. They are currently tongue wrestling as I speak. I can't tell whose winning. Looks like a tie so far."

"That's interesting hun, but we didn't come all the way out here to watch that. You want a Coke?"

"Sure," Charlie said over her shoulder.

She set the binoculars on the seat beside her. She picked up her rod and began to reel it in to re-bait her hook.

As Horace descended into the boat for the drinks, he heard Charlie Ann say, "Grandpa, I think I got a snag. My line is caught on something."

Horace paused on the steps and called over his shoulder, "Well, it's not the end of the world. Just re-weight, re-hook, and re-bait your line like I showed you."

"Yeah. Yeah, I know. I'm just saying."

As Charlie wrestled to free her line, Horace continued down the stairs. Charlie struggled, jerked, pulled, and fought with her line until it came free with a soft twang. She continued to reel it in until the end was out of the water.

"That's just great. I caught a dumbass tree limb. That's just what I needed. It will be great for dinner. I just cannot wait to eat it. That bark will be delicious."

She hurriedly unhooked the limb and was about to pitch it back over the side when she noticed something else hanging from one of the mud-covered branches. Entangled in the limbs was a leather strand, and fastened to it was a small leather pouch. It was barely identifiable because it was covered and dripping with muck and small strands of green algae.

Charlie eyed it suspiciously. It looked like some kind of giant spider egg sack.

"Cool," she said, drawing the word out.

Charlie hesitated at first then grabbed it and jerked it free. She pitched the muddy tree limb back over the side of the boat. Charlie unraveled the leather bindings as she knelt. She poured the contents out onto the deck of the ship.

Seven reflective and iridescent pieces glittered in the sunshine.

Stunned by the initial brilliance, Charlie pulled away from its contents.

"What the hell is this? Aww man, I wish it wasn't broken."

Intrigued with the items, she kicked her legs out behind her and lowered herself to the boat's deck to get as close to the items as she could.

She fiddled and nudged the pieces around for a few moments. One by one, the fragments fell into place. They seemed to fit together and form in a small, round jewelry piece.

She was about to get up and go inside the cabin to find some glue to piece it together when she noticed something odd.

She blinked her eyes and jerked her head to the side, confused as to what she was seeing.

Readjusting her view, she saw the impossible. She couldn't believe her eyes.

One of the rock pieces she had just placed near another one was now a whole piece instead of the initial two. She could still see a hairline fracture dividing the piece as though it were still two separate pieces.

Charlie curiously picked up the new single piece to study it better.

She tried to bend it to the point that it would break apart again at the hairline fracture but nothing happened. It was one solid piece.

"Weird," Charlie said, drawing the word out as long as the last one.

Curious, Charlie picked up another separate piece and added it to the new bigger section. With unblinking eyes, she saw the two pieces become one. As though magnetized, the two pieces joined together as soon as they touched.

Startled, Charlie quickly flung it away to the boat's deck.

It sat there where she had pitched it. It lay unmoving.

Again, curiosity got the best of her and she tentatively picked up another piece and studied it closely. Finally getting up the courage again, she picked up the bigger piece and joined them together. The same thing happened. Charlie pulled it in closer and grinned.

Grabbing the last sparkling shard, the one attached to the leather strap, she held it close to the main piece, and as it did before, with a quick magnetic jerk, it left her fingers and attached itself to the main piece. The round, smooth rock was complete.

"Awesome," she whispered to herself.

Admiring her handiwork, she stood and walked to the side of the ship.

Charlie flipped it over in her hand.

Sunlight glinted off its radiant surface. A shimmering kaleidoscopic of colors fell across her face and dazzled her eyes. The reflections reminded her of the inside of an Abalone shell she had once found on a beach.

Without hesitating, she flipped the leather loop over her head and let it hang around her neck. As she did so, a soothing peace unlike anything she had ever felt in her life coated her body.

Charlie closed her eyes, embraced the feeling, and smiled.

ACKNOWLEDGEMENTS

I would like to acknowledge the following individuals who have helped me with the technical aspects of this story.

Their knowledgeable contributions have enhanced this story in so many ways, and I can't thank you enough.

Weylin Brown, an RN Clinical Coordinator at Greenville Hospital Systems in Greenville, South Carolina.

Kelly Crooks, editor for Soul Dreams.

Damonza.com, the book cover and formatting specialists that helped me create the awesome cover design and for helping me with the amazing layout on the inside of the book itself.

Max Dodson, a friend who knows and loves his Mustangs and softball.

William Gary, a former police officer of twenty years with the Spartanburg County Sheriff's office in Spartanburg, South Carolina.

Bill Kennedy, a former police officer with the Mauldin Police Department in Mauldin, South Carolina. He is now a real estate agent with Keller Williams Realty in Greenville, South Carolina.

Ann Lukens, a practicing paramedic in Murphy, North Carolina.

Jake Mycko, a writer, actor, and producer in Greenville, South Carolina

Warren Mowry, a prosecutor/deputy solicitor at 8th Circuit Solicitor's Office in Laurens, South Carolina.

Chris 'Doc' Murphy, a psychologist who works with Veterans at the Hunter Holmes McGuire VA Medical Center in Richmond, Virginia. He has previously deployed to Iraq with the US Army.

Silas James Rowland, a writer, actor, director, and filmmaker in Greenville, South Carolina.

Kim Valenti, a nurse practitioner at Spartanburg Regional Medical Center in Spartanburg, South Carolina.

Jeff VanDyke, an engineer at Jacobs Engineering in Greenville, South Carolina.

Shane Willimon, a former security guard for Greenville Memorial Hospital in Greenville, South Carolina.

℣

There have been a number of friends and family who have read Soul Dreams or selected chapters, sections, and portions of my novel early on. These individuals gave me the encouragement to continue writing. Apologies to anyone I may have left off the list.

Deborah Arledge, Lee Bagwell, Chris Cashon, Allison Chandler, Brian Coker, Laurie Griffith Cox, Krystal Donald, Dean Ferreira, Kimberlee Ferreira, Matt Fisher, Amanda Fryar, Sonya Gilmer, Evan Harris, Stephanie Hopkins, Emily Hyder, Landon Hyder, Larry Hyder, LaShannon Hyder, Clay Keller, Kelley King, Wallace Krebs, Paula Mosley, Bill Neel, Casey Neel, Melanie Nordwall, Elizabeth Pandolfi,

Emile Pandolfi, Judy Pandolfi, Kristen Pandolfi, Nick Pasternak, Beth Pistolis, Dave Puleo, Morgan Rose Rand, Marilyn Rhodes, Dia Robinson, Trish Shields, Jill Spires, Jill Swanson, Linda Tapp, Cheryl Taylor, Jason Underwood, Don Watson, Lauren Paige Wilson, and Jan Williams.